Horror
by lamplight

Horror

by lamplight

CHANCELLOR
PRESS

First published in Great Britain in 1993
by Chancellor Press an imprint of
Reed Consumer Books Limited
Michelin House, 81 Fulham Road, London SW3 6RB
and Auckland, Melbourne, Singapore and Toronto

ISBN 1 85152 315 4

A CIP catalogue record for this book is available at the British Library

Printed in Great Britain by William Clowes Ltd, Beccles.

Contents

Acknowledgements

The publishers wish to thank the following for permission to reprint previously printed material. Every effort has been made to locate persons having any rights in the stories appearing in this book. Any omissions will be corrected in future reprints upon written notification to the publishers.

'The Golem', from *Selected Stories* by Y. L. Peretz, edited by Irving How and Eliezer Greenberg. Copyright © 1974 by Schocken Books Inc. Reprinted by permission of Schocken Books, published by Pantheon Books, a division of Random House, Inc.

A. P. Watt Ltd and The Literary Executors of the Estate of H. G. Wells for 'The Red Room' from *H. G. Wells: The Complete Stories*. First published in *The Idler* in 1896.

A. P. Watt Ltd and Sheila Reeves for 'Ancient Sorceries' by Algernon Blackwood.

The author for 'A Place of No Return', first published in *Fantasy 8*. Copyright © 1981 by Hugh B. Cave.

'Yours Truly, Jack the Ripper' reprinted by permission of the author and the author's agents, Scott Meredith Literary Agency, Inc., 845 Third Avenue, New York, New York 10022.

The estate of Angela Carter, Random Century Ltd and Rogers, Coleridge & White Ltd for 'Peter and the Wolf', from *Black Venus*. Copyright © 1985 by Angela Carter, published in 1985 by Chatto & Windus and the Hogarth Press.

Little, Brown, UK and Alfred A. Knopf, Inc., for an extract from chapter one of *Interview with the Vampire*. Copyright © 1976 by Anne O'Brien Rice. First published in Great Britain in 1976 by Raven Books in association with Macdonald and Jane's Publishers Ltd.

ACKNOWLEDGMENTS

The publishers wish to thank the following for permission to [illegible] copyright material. [illegible] the publishers.

[illegible]

A. P. Watt Ltd. and the Literary Executors of the Estate of [illegible] for The Red Badge [illegible] [illegible]

A. P. Watt Ltd. and [illegible] for [illegible] [illegible]

The author for [illegible] [illegible]

[illegible] and the publishers [illegible] permission of the author and [illegible]

[illegible]

[illegible]

Wandering Willie's Tale

SIR WALTER SCOTT

Ye maun have heard of Sir Robert Redgauntlet of that Ilk, who lived in these parts before the dear years. The country will lang mind him; and our fathers used to draw breath thick if ever they heard him named. He was out wi' the Hielandmen in Montrose's time; and again he was in the hills wi' Glencairn in the saxteen hundred and fifty-twa; and sae when King Charles the Second came in, wha was in sic favour as the Laird of Redgauntlet? He was knighted at Lonon court, wi' the king's ain sword; and being a redhot prelatist, he came down here, rampauging like a lion, with commissions of lieutenancy (and of lunacy, for what I ken) to put down a' the Whigs and Covenanters in the country. Wild wark they made of it; for the Whigs were as dour as the Cavaliers were fierce, and it was which should first tire the other. Redgauntlet was ay for the strong hand; and his name is kend as wide in the country as Claverhouse's or Tam Dalyell's. Glen, nor dargle, nor mountain, nor cave, could hide the puir hill-folk when Redgauntlet was out with bugle and bloodhound after them, as if they had been sae mony deer. And troth when they fand them, they didna mak muckle mair ceremony than a Hielandman wi' a roebuck – it was just, 'Will ye tak the test?' – if not, 'Make ready – present – fire!' – and there lay the recusant.

Far and wide was Sir Robert hated and feared. Men thought he had a direct compact with Satan – that he was proof against steel – and that bullets happed aff his buff-coat like hailstanes from a hearth – that he had a mear that would turn a hare on the side of Carrifra-gawns – and muckle to the same purpose, of whilk mair anon. The best blessing they wared on him was, 'Deil scowp wi' Redgauntlet!' He wasna a bad master to his ain folk, though, and was weel aneugh liked by his tenants; and as for the lackies and troopers that raid out wi' him to the persecutions, as the Whigs caa'd those killing times, they wad hae drunken themsells blind to his health at ony time.

Now you are to ken that my gudesire lived on Redgauntlet's grund – they ca' the place Primrose Knowe. We had lived on the grund, and under the Redgauntlets, since the riding days, and lang before. It was a pleasant bit; and I think the air is callerer and fresher there than onywhere else in the country.

It's a' deserted now; and I sat on the broken door-cheek three days since, and was glad I couldna see the plight the place was in; but that's a' wide o' the mark. There dwelt my gudesire, Steenie Steenson, a rambling, rattling chiel' he had been in his young days, and could play weel on the pipes; he was famous at 'Hoopers and Girders' – a' Cumberland couldna touch him at 'Jockie Lattin' – and he had the finest finger for the back-lilt between Berwick and Carlisle. The like o' Steenie wasna the sort that they made Whigs o'. And so he became a Tory, as they ca' it, which we now ca' Jacobites, just out of a kind of needcessity, that he might belang to some side or other. He had nae ill will to the Whig bodies, and liked little to see the blude rin, though, being obliged to follow Sir Robert in hunting and hoisting, watching and warding, he saw muckle mischief, and maybe did some, that he couldna avoid.

Now Steenie was a kind of favourite with his master, and kend a' the folks about the castle, and was often sent for to play the pipes, when they were at their merriment. Auld Dougal MacCallum, the butler, that had followed Sir Robert through gude and ill, thick and thin, pool and stream, was specially fond of the pipes, and ay gae my gudesire his gude word wi' the laird; for Dougal could turn his master round his finger.

Weel, round came the Revolution, and it had like to have broken the hearts baith of Dougal and his master. But the change was not a'thegether sae great as they feared, and other folk thought for. The Whigs made an unco crawing what they wad do with their auld enemies, and in special wi' Sir Robert Redgauntlet. But there were ower mony great folks dipped in the same doings, to mak a spick and span new warld. So Parliament passed it a' ower easy; and Sir Robert, bating that he was held to hunting foxes instead of Covenanters, remained just the man he was. His revel was as loud, and his hall as weel lighted, as ever it had been, though maybe he lacked the fines of the nonconformists, that used to come to stock his larder and cellar; for it is certain he began to be keener about the rents than his tenants used to find him before, and they behoved to be prompt to the rent-day or else the laird wasna pleased. And he was sic an awesome body, that naebody cared to anger him; for the oaths he swore, and the rage that he used to get into, and the looks that he put on, made men sometimes think him a devil incarnate.

Weel, my gudesire was nae manager – no that he was a very great misguider – but he hadna the saving gift, and he got twa terms' rent in arrear. He got the first brash at Whitsunday put ower wi' fair word and piping; but when Martinmas came, there was a summons from the grund-officer to come wi' the rent on a day preceese, or else Steenie behoved to flit. Sair wark he had to get the siller; but he was weel-freended, and at last he got the haill scraped thegether – a thousand merks – the maist of it was from a neighbour they ca'd Laurie Lapraik – a sly tod. Laurie had walth o' gear – could hunt wi' the hound and rin wi' the hare – and be Whig or Tory, saunt or sinner, as the wind stood. He was a professor in this Revolution warld, but he liked an orra sough of this warld, and a tune on the pipes weel aneugh at a bytime; and abune a', he thought he had gude security for the siller he lent my gudesire ower the stocking at Primrose Knowe.

Away trots my gudesire to Redgauntlet Castle wi' a heavy purse and a light heart, glad to be out of the laird's danger. Weel, the first thing he learned at the castle was, that Sir Robert had fretted himsell into a fit of the gout, because he did not appear before twelve o'clock. It wasna a'thegether for sake of the money, Dougal thought; but because he didna like to part wi' my gudesire aff the grund. Dougal was glad to see Steenie, and brought him into the great oak parlour, and there sat the laird his leesome lane, excepting that he had beside him a great, ill-favoured jackanape, that was a special pet of his; a cankered beast it was, and mony an ill-natured trick it played – ill to please it was, and easily angered – ran about the haill castle, chattering and yowling, and pinching, and biting folk, specially before ill weather, or disturbances in the state. Sir Robert caa'd it Major Weir, after the warlock that was burnt;[1] and few folk liked either the name or the conditions of the creature – they thought there was something in it by ordinar – and my gudesire was not just easy in mind when the door shut on him, and he saw himself in the room wi' naebody but the laird, Dougal MacCallum, and the major, a thing that hadna chanced to him before.

Sir Robert sat, or, I should say, lay, in a great armed chair, wi' his grand velvet gown, and his feet on a cradle; for he had baith gout and gravel, and his face looked as gash and ghastly as Satan's. Major Weir sat opposite to him, in a red laced coat, and the laird's wig on his head; and ay as Sir Robert girned wi' pain, the jackanape girned too, like a sheep's-head between a pair of tangs – an ill-faur'd, fearsome couple they were. The laird's buff-coat was hung on a pin behind him, and his broadsword and his pistols within reach; for he keepit up the auld fashion of having the weapons ready, and a horse saddled day and night, just as he used to do when he' was able to loup on horseback, and away after ony of the hill-folk he could get speerings of. Some said it was for fear of the Whigs taking vengeance, but I judge it was just his auld custom – he wasna gien to fear onything. The rental-book, wi' its black cover and brass clasps, was lying beside him; and a book of sculduddry sangs was put betwixt the leaves, to keep it open at the place where it bore evidence against the Goodman of Primrose Knowe, as behind the hand with his mails and duties. Sir Robert gave my gudesire a look, as if he would have withered his heart in his bosom. Ye maun ken he had a way of bending his brows, that men saw the visible mark of a horseshoe in his forehead, deep dinted, as if it had been stamped there.

'Are ye come light-handed, ye son of a toom whistle?' said Sir Robert. 'Zounds! if you are— '

My gudesire, with as gude a countenance as he could put on, made a leg and

[1]A celebrated wizard, executed at Edinburgh for sorcery and other crimes.

placed the bag of money on the table wi' a dash, like a man that does something clever. The laird drew it to him hastily – 'Is it all here, Steenie, man?'

'Your honour will find it right,' said my gudesire.

'Here, Dougal,' said the laird, 'gie Steenie a tass of brandy downstairs, till I count the siller and write the receipt.'

But they werena weel out of the room, when Sir Robert gied a yelloch that garr'd the castle rock, Back ran Dougal – in flew the livery-men – ye'll on yell gied the laird, ilk ane mair awfu' than the ither. My gudesire knew not whether to stand or flee, but he ventured back into the parlour, where a' was gaun hirdy-girdie – naebody to say 'come in,' or 'gae out.' Terribly the laird roared for cauld water to his feet, and wine to cool his throat; and Hell, hell, hell, and its flames, was ay the word in his mouth. They brought him water, and when they plunged his swollen feet into the tub, he cried out it was burning; and folk say that it *did* bubble and sparkle like a seething cauldron. He flung the cup at Dougal's head, and said he had given him blood instead of burgundy; and, sure aneugh, the lass washed clotted blood aff the carpet the neist day. The jackanape they caa'd Major Weir, it jibbered and cried as if it was mocking its master; my gudesire's head was like to turn – he forgot baith siller and receipt, and downstairs he banged; but as he ran, the shrieks came faint and fainter; there was a deep-drawn shivering groan, and word gaed though the castle that the laird was dead.

Weel, away came my gudesire, wi' his finger in his mouth, and his best hope was that Dougal had seen the money-bag, and heard the laird speak of writing the receipt. The young laird, now Sir John, came from Edinburgh, to see things put to rights. Sir John and his father never gree'd weel. Sir John had been bred an advocate, and afterwards sat in the last Scots Parliament and voted for the Union, having gotten, it was thought, a rug of the compensations – if his father could have come out of his grave, he would have brained him for it on his awn hearthstane. Some thought it was easier counting with the auld rough knight than the fair-spoken young ane – but mair of that anon.

Dougal MacCullum, poor body, neither grat nor grained, but gaed about the house looking like a corpse, but directing, as was his duty, a' the order of the grand funeral. Now, Dougal looked ay waur and waur when night was coming, and was ay the last to gang to his bed, whilk was in a little round just opposite the chamber of dais, whilk his master occupied while he was living, and where he now lay in state, as they caa'd it, weel-a-day! The night before the funeral, Dougal could keep his awn counsel nae langer; he came doun with his proud spirit, and fairly asked auld Hutcheon to sit in his room with him for an hour. When they were in the round, Dougal took ae tass of brandy to himsell, and gave another to Hutcheon, and wished him all health and lang life, and said that, for himsell, he wasna lang for this world; for that, every night since Sir Robert's death, his silver call had sounded from the state chamber, just as it used to do at nights in his lifetime, to call Dougal to help to turn him in his bed. Dougal said that being alone with the dead on that floor of the tower (for naebody cared to wake Sir Robert Redgauntlet like another corpse) he had never daured to answer the call, but that now his conscience checked him for neglecting his duty; for 'though death breaks service,' said MacCallum, 'it shall never break my service to Sir Robert; and I will answer his next whistle, so be you will stand by me, Hutcheon.'

Hutcheon had nae will to the wark, but he had stood by Dougal in battle and broil, and he wad not fail him at this pinch; so down the carles sat ower a stoup of brandy, and Hutcheon, who was something of a clerk, would have read a chapter of Bible; but Dougal would hear naething but a blaud of Davie Lindsay, whilk was the waur preparation.

When midnight came, and the house was quiet as the grave, sure enough the silver whistle sounded as sharp and shrill as if Sir Robert was blowing it, and up got the twa auld serving-men, and tottered into the room where the dead man lay. Hutcheon saw aneugh at the first glance; for there were torches in the room, which showed him the foul fiend, in his ain shape, sitting on the laird's coffin! Ower he cowped as if he had been dead. He could not tell how lang he lay in a trance at the door, but when he gathered himself, he cried on his neighbour, and getting nae answer, raised the house, when Dougal was found lying dead within twa steps of the bed where his master's coffin was placed. As for the whistle, it was gaen anes and ay; but mony a time was it heard at the top of the house on the bartizan, and amang the auld chimneys and turrets where the howlets have their nests. Sir John hushed the matter up, and the funeral passed over without mair bogle-wark.

But when a' was ower, and the laird was beginning to settle his affairs, every tenant was called up for his arrears, and my gudesire for the full sum that stood against him in the rental-book. Weel, away he trots to the castle, to tell his story, and there is he introduced to Sir John, sitting in his father's chair, in deep mourning, with weepers and hanging cravat, and a small walking rapier by his side, instead of the auld broadsword that had a hundredweight of steel about it, what with blade, chape, and basket-hilt. I have heard their communing so often tauld ower, that I almost think I was there mysell, though I couldna be born at the time. (In fact, Alan, my companion, mimicked, with a good deal of humour, the flattering, conciliating tone of the tenant's address, and the hypocritical melancholy of the laird's reply. His grandfather, he said, had, while he spoke, his eye fixed on the rental-book, as if it were a mastiff-dog that he was afraid would spring up and bite him.)

'I wuss ye joy, sir, of the head seat, and the white loaf, and the braid lairdship. Your father was a kind man to friends and followers; muckle grace to you, Sir John, to fill his shoon – his boots, I suld say, for he seldom wore shoon, unless it were muils when he had the gout.'

'Aye, Steenie,' quoth the laird, sighing deeply, and putting his napkin to his een, 'his was a sudden call, and he will be missed in the country; no time to set his house in order – weel prepared Godward, no doubt, which is the root of the matter – but left us behind a tangled hesp to wind, Steenie. – Hem! hem! We maun go to business, Steenie; much to do, and little time to do it in.'

Here he opened the fatal volume. I have heard of a thing they call Doomsday Book – I am clear it has been a rental of back-ganging tenants.

'Stephen,' said Sir John, still in the same, saft, sleekit tone of voice – 'Stephen Steenson, ye are down here for a year's rent behind the hand – due at last term.'

Stephen. 'Please your honour, Sir John, I paid it to your father.'

Sir John. 'Ye took a receipt, then, doubtless, Stephen; and can produce it?'

Stephen. 'Indeed I hadna time, an it like your honour; for nae sooner had I set doun the siller, and just as his honour, Sir Robert, that's gaen, drew it till him to count it, and write out the receipt, he was ta'en wi' the pains that removed him.'

'That was unlucky,' said Sir John, after a pause. 'But ye maybe paid it in the presence of somebody. I want but a *talis qualis* evidence, Stephen. I would go ower strictly to work with no poor man.'

Stephen. 'Troth, Sir John, there was naebody in the room but Dougal MacCallum the butler. But, as your honour kens, he has e'en followed his auld master.'

'Very unlucky again, Stephen,' said Sir John, without altering his voice a single note. 'The man to whom ye paid the money is dead – and the man who witnessed the payment is dead too – and the siller, which should have been to the fore, is neither seen nor heard tell of in the repositories. How am I to believe a' this?'

Stephen. 'I dinna ken, your honour; but there is a bit memorandum note of the very coins; for, God help me! I had to borrow out of twenty purses; and I am sure that ilka man there set down will take his grit oath for what purpose I borrowed the money.'

Sir John. 'I have little doubt ye *borrowed* the money, Steenie. It is the *payment* to my father that I want to have some proof of.'

Stephen. 'The siller maun be about the house, Sir John. And since your honour never got it, and his honour that was canna have taen it wi' him, maybe some of the family may have seen it.'

Sir John. 'We will examine the servants, Stephen; that is but reasonable.'

But lackey and lass, and page and groom, all denied stoutly that they had ever seen such a bag of money as my gudesire described. What was waur, he had unluckily not mentioned to any living soul of them his purpose of paying his rent. Ae quean had noticed something under his arm, but she took it for the pipes.

Sir John Redgauntlet ordered the servants out of the room, and then said to my gudesire, 'Now, Steenie, ye see ye have fair play; and, as I have little doubt ye ken better where to find the siller than ony other body, I beg in fair terms, and for your own sake, that you will end this fasherie; for, Stephen, ye maun pay or flit.'

'The Lord forgie your opinion,' said Stephen, driven almost to his wits' end – 'I am an honest man.'

'So am I, Stephen,' said his honour; 'and so are all the folks in the house, I hope. But if there be a knave amongst us, it must be he that tells the story he cannot prove.' He paused, and then added, mair sternly, 'If I understand your trick, sir, you want to take advantage of some malicious reports concerning things in this family, and particularly respecting my father's sudden death, thereby to cheat me out of the money, and perhaps take away my character, by insinuating that I have received the rent I am demanding. Where do you suppose this money to be? I insist upon knowing.'

My gudesire saw everything look so muckle against him, that he grew nearly desperate – however, he shifted from one foot to another, looked to every corner of the room, and made no answer.

'Speak out, sirrah,' said the laird, assuming a look of his father's, a very particular ane, which he had when he was angry – it seemed as if the wrinkles of his frown made that selfsame fearful shape of a horse's shoe in the middle of his brow; – 'Speak out, sir! I *will* know your thoughts; – do you suppose that I have this money?'

'Far be it frae me to say so,' said Stephen.

'Do you charge any of my people with having taken it?'

'I wad be laith to charge them that may be innocent,' said my gudesire; 'and if there be any one that is guilty, I have nae proof.'

'Somewhere the money must be, if there is a word of truth in your story,' said Sir John; 'I ask where you think it is – and demand a correct answer?'

'In hell, if you *will* have my thoughts of it,' said my gudesire, driven to extremity, 'in hell! with your father, his jackanape, and his silver whistle.'

Down the stairs he ran (for the parlour was nae place for him after such a word) and he heard the laird swearing blood and wounds behind him, as fast as ever did Sir Robert, and roaring for the bailie and the baron-officer.

Away rode my gudesire to his chief creditor (him they ca'd Laurie Lapraik) to try if he could make onything out of him; but when he tauld his story, he got but the worst word in his wame – thief, beggar, and dyvour, were the saftest terms; and to the boot of these hard terms, Laurie brought up the auld story of his dipping his hand in the blood of God's saunts, just as if a tenant could have helped riding with the laird, and that a laird like Sir Robert Redgauntlet. My gudesire was, by this time, far beyond the bounds of patience, and, while he and Laurie were at deil speed the liars, he was wanchancie aneugh to abuse Lapraik's doctrine as weel as the man, ond said things that garr'd folks' flesh grue that heard them; – he wasna just himself, and he had lived wi' a wild set in his day.

At last they parted, and my gudesire was to ride hame through the wood of Pitmurkie that is a' fou of black firs, as they say. – I ken the wood, but the firs may be black or white for what I can tell. – At the entry of the wood there is a wild common, and on the edge of the common, a little lonely change-house, that was keepit then by an ostler-wife, they suld hae caa'd her Tibbie Faw, and there puir Steenie cried for a mutchkin of brandy, for he had had no refreshment the haill day. Tibbie was earnest wi' him to take a bite of meat, but he couldna think o't, nor would he take his foot out of the stirrup, and took off the brandy wholely at twa draughts, and named a toast at each: – the first was the memory of Sir Robert Redgauntlet, and might he never lie quiet in his grave till he had righted his poor bond-tenant; and the second was a health to Man's Enemy, if he would but get him back the pock of siller or tell him what came o't, for he saw the haill world was like to regard him as a thief and a cheat, and he took that waur than even the ruin of his house and hauld.

On he rode, little caring where. It was a dark night turned, and the trees made it yet darker, and he let the beast take its ain road through the wood; when all of a sudden, from tired and tired and wearied that it was before, the nag began to spring and flee, and stend, that my gudesire could hardly keep the saddle. Upon the whilk, a horseman, suddenly riding up beside him, said, 'That's a mettle beast of yours, freend; will you sell him?' So saying, he touched the horse's neck with his riding-wand, and it fell into its auld heigh-ho of a stumbling trot. 'But his spunk's soon out of him, I think,' continued the stranger, 'and that is like mony a man's courage, that thinks he wad do great things till he come to the proof.'

My gudesire scarce listened to this, but spurred his horse, with 'Gude e'en to you, freend.'

But it's like the stranger was ane that doesna lightly yield his point; for, ride as Steenie liked, he was ay beside him at the selfsame pace. At last my gudesire, Steenie Steenson, grew half angry, and to say the truth, half feared.

'What is it that ye want with me, freend?' he said. 'If ye be a robber, I have nae money; if ye be a leal man, wanting company, I have nae heart to mirth or speaking; and if ye want to ken the road, I scarce ken it mysell.'

'If you will tell me your grief,' said the stranger, 'I am one that, though I have been sair miscaa'd in the world, am the only hand for helping my freends.'

So my gudesire to ease his ain heart, mair than from any hope of help, told him the story from beginning to end.

'It's a hard pinch,' said the stranger; 'but I think I can help you.'

'If you could lend the money, sir, and take a lang day – I ken nae other help on earth,' said my gudesire.

'But there may be some under the earth,' said the stranger. 'Come, I'll be frank wi' you; I could lend you the money on bond, but you would maybe scruple my terms. Now, I can tell you, that your auld laird is disturbed in his grave by your curses, and the wailing of your family, and if ye daur venture to go to see him, he will give you the receipt.'

My gudesire's hair stood on end at this proposal, but he thought his companion might be some humoursome chield that was trying to frighten him, and might end with lending him the money. Besides, he was bauld wi' brandy, and desperate wi' distress; and he said he had courage to go to the gate of hell, and a step farther, for that receipt. The stranger laughed.

Weel, they rode on through the thickest of the wood, when, all of a sudden, the horse stopped at the door of a great house; and, but that he knew the place was ten miles off, my father would have thought he was at Redgauntlet Castle. They rode into the outer courtyard; through the muckle faulding yetts and aneath the auld' portcullis; and the whole front of the house was lighted, and there were pipes and fiddles, and as much dancing and deray within as used to be at Sir Robert's house, at Pace and Yule, and such high seasons. They lap off, and my gudesire, as seemed to him, fastened his horse to the very ring he had tied him to that morning, when he gaed to wait on the young Sir John.

'God!' said my gudesire, 'if Sir Robert's death be but a dream!'

He knocked at the ha' door just as he was wont, and his auld acquaintance, Dougal MacCallum – just after his wont, too, – came to open the door, and said, 'Piper Steenie, are ye there, lad? Sir Robert has been crying for you.'

My gudesire was like a man in a dream – he looked for the stranger, but he was gane for the time. At last he just tried to say, 'Ha! Dougal Driveower, are ye living? I thought ye had been dead.'

'Never fash yoursell wi' me,' said Dougal, 'but look to yoursell; and see ye tak naething frae onybody here, neither meat, drink, or siller, except just the receipt that is your ain.'

So saying, he led the way out through halls and trances, that were weel kend to my gudesire, and into the auld oak parlour; and there was as much singing of profane sangs, and birling of red wine, and speaking blasphemy and sculduddry, as had over been in Redgauntlet Castle when it was at the blithest.

But, Lord take us in keeping, what a set of ghastly revellers they were that sat around that table! My gudesire kend mony that had long before gane to their place, for often had he piped to the most part in the hall of Redgauntlet. There was the fierce Middleton, and the dissolute Rothes, and the crafty Lauderdale; and Dalyell, with his bald head and a beard to his girdle; and Earlshall, with Cameron's blude on his hand; and wild Bonshaw, that tied blessed Mr Cargill's limbs till the blude sprung; and Dunbarton Douglas, the twice-turned traitor baith to country and king. There was the Bluidy Advocate MacKenyie, who, for his worldly wit and wisdom had been to the rest as a god. And there was Claverhouse, as beautiful as when he lived, with his long, dark, curled locks streaming down over his laced buff-coat, and his left hand always on his right spuleblade, to hide the wound that the silver bullet had made. He sat apart from them all, and looked at them with a melancholy, haughty countenance; while the rest hallooed, and sang, and laughed, that the room rang. But their smiles were fearfully contorted from time to time; and their laugh passed into such wild sounds as made my gudesire's very nails grow blue, and chilled the marrow in his banes.

They that waited at the table were just the wicked serving-men and troopers, that had done their work and cruel bidding on earth. There was the Lang Lad of the Nethertown, that helped to take Argyle; and the bishop's summoner, that they called the Deil's Rattle-bag; and the wicked guardsmen in their laced coats; and the savage Highland Amorites, that shed blood like water; and many a proud serving-man, haughty of heart and bloody of hand, cringing to the rich, and making them wickeder than they would be; grinding the poor to powder, when the rich had broken them to fragments. And mony, mony mair were coming and ganging, a' as busy in their vocation as if they had been alive.

Sir Robert Redgauntlet, in the midst of a' this fearful riot, cried, wi' a voice like thunder, on Steenie Piper to come to the board-head where he was sitting; his legs stretched out before him, and swathed up with flannel, with his holster pistols aside him, while the great broadsword rested against his chair, just as my gudesire had seen him the last time upon earth – the very cushion for the jackanape was close to him, but the creature itself was not there – it wasna its hour, it's likely; for he heard them say as he came forward, 'Is not the major come yet?' And another answered, 'The jackanape will be here betimes the morn.' And when my gudesire came forward, Sir Robert, or his ghaist, or the deevil in his likeness, said, 'Weel, piper, hae ye settled wi' my son for the year's rent?'

With much ado my father gat breath to say that Sir John would not settle without his honour's receipt.

'Ye shall hae that for a tune of the pipes, Steenie,' said the appearance of Sir Robert – 'Play us up "Weel hoddled, Luckie."'

Now this was a tune my gudesire learned frae a' warlock, that heard it when they were worshipping Satan at their meetings, and my gudesire had sometimes played it at the ranting suppers in Redgauntlet Castle, but never very willingly; and now he grew cauld at the very name of it, and said, for excuse, he hadna his pipes wi' him.

'MacCallum, ye limb of Beelzebub,' said the fearfu' Sir Robert, 'bring Steenie the pipes that I am' keeping for him!'

MacCallum brought a pair of pipes might have served the piper of Donald of the Isles. But he gave my gudesire a nudge as he offered them; and looking secretly and closely, Steenie saw that the chanter was of steel, and heated to a white heat; so he had fair warning not to trust his fingers with it. So he excused himself again, and said he was faint and frightened, and had not wind aneugh to fill the bag.

'Then ye maun eat and drink, Steenie,' said the figure; 'for we do little else here; and it's ill speaking between a fou man and a fasting.'

Now these were the very words that the bloody Earl of Douglas said to keep the king's messenger in hand while he cut the head off MacLellan of Bombie, at the Threave Castle, and that put Steenie mair and mair on his guard. So he spoke up like a man, and said be came neither to eat, or drink, or make minstrelsy; but simply for his ain – to ken what was come o' the money he had paid, and to get a discharge for it; and he was so stout-hearted by this time that he charged Sir Robert for conscience-sake (he had no power to say the holy name) and as he hoped for peace and rest, to spread no snares for him, but just to give him his ain.

The appearance gnashed its teeth and laughed, but it took from a large pocket-book the receipt, and handed it to Steenie. 'There is your receipt, ye pitiful cur; and for the money, my dog-whelp of a son may go look for it in the Cat's Cradle.'

My gudesire uttered mony thanks, and was about to retire when Sir Robert roared aloud, 'Stop, though, thou sack-doudling son of a whore. I am not done with thee. HERE we do nothing for nothing; and you must return on this day twelvemonth, to pay your master the homage that you owe me for my protection.'

My father's tongue was loosed of a'suddenty, and he said aloud, 'I refer mysell to God's pleasure, and not to yours.'

He had no sooner uttered the word than all was dark around him; and he sank on the earth with such a sudden shock, that he lost both breath and sense.

How lang Steenie lay there, be could not tell; but when he came to himsell, he was lying in the auld kirkyard of Redgauntlet parochine just at the door of the family aisle, and the scutcheon of the auld knight, Sir Robert, hanging over his head. There was a deep morning fog on grass and gravestane around him, and his horse was feeding quietly beside the minister's twa cows. Steenie would have thought the whole was a dream, but had the receipt in his hand, fairly written and signed by the auld laird; only the last letters of his name were a little disorderly, written like one seized with sudden pain.

Sorely troubled in his mind, he left that dreary place, rode through the mist to Redgauntlet Castle, and with much ado he got speech of the laird.

'Well, you dyvour bankrupt,' was the first word, 'have you brought me my rent?'

'No,' inswered my gudesire, 'I have not; but I have brought your honour Sir Robert's receipt for it.'

'How, sirrah? Sir Robert's receipt! You told me he had not given you one.'

'Will your honour please to see if that bit line is right?'

Sir John looked at every line, and at every letter, with much attention; and at last, at the date, which my gudesire had not observed, – *'From my appointed place,'* he read, *'this twenty-fifth of November.'* – 'What! – That is yesterday! – Villain, thou must have gone to hell for this!'

'I got it from your honour's father – whether he be in heaven or hell, I know not,' said Steenie.

'I will delate you for a warlock to the Privy Council!' said Sir John. 'I will send you to your master, the devil, with the help of a tar-barrel and a torch!'

'I intend to delate mysell to the Presbytery,' said Steenie, 'and tell them all I have seen last night, whilk are things fitter for them to judge of than a borrel man like me.'

Sir John paused, composed himsell, and desired to hear the full history; and my gudesire told it him from point to point, as I have told it you – word for word, neither more nor less.

Sir John was silent again for a long time, and at last he said, very composedly, 'Steenie, this story of yours concerns the honour of many a noble family besides mine; and if it be a leasing-making, to keep yourself out of my danger, the least you can expect is to have a redhot iron driven through your tongue, and that will be as bad as scauding your fingers wi' a redhot chanter. But yet it may be true, Steenie; and if the money cast up, I shall not know what to think of it. But where shall we find the Cat's Cradle? There are cats enough about the old house, but I think they kitten without the ceremony of bed or cradle.'

'We were best ask Hutcheon,' said my gudesire; 'he kens a' the odd corners about as weel as – another serving-man that is now gane, and that I wad not like to name.'

Aweel, Hutcheon, when he was asked, told them, that a ruinous turret, lang disused, next to the clock-house, only accessible by a ladder, for the opening was on the outside, and far above the battlements, was called of old the Cat's Cradle.

'There will I go immediately,' said Sir John; and he took (with what purpose, Heaven kens) one of his father's pistols from the hall-table, where they had lain since the night he died, and hastened to the battlements.

It was a dangerous place to climb, for the ladder was auld and frail, and wanted ane or twa rounds. However, up got Sir John, and entered at the turret-door, where his body stopped the only little light that was in the bit turret. Something flees at him wi' a vengeance, maist dang him back ower – bang gaed the knight's pistol, and Hutcheon, that held the ladder, and my gudesire that stood beside him, hears a loud skelloch. A minute after, Sir John flings the body of the jackanape down to them, and cries that the siller is fund, and that they should come up and help him. And there was the bag of siller sure aneugh, and mony orra thing besides, that had been missing for mony a day. And Sir John, when he had riped the turret weel, led my gudesire into the dining-parlour, and took him by the hand and spoke kindly to him, and said he was sorry he should have doubted his word and that he would hereafter be a good master to him to make amends.

'And now, Steenie,' said Sir John, 'Although this vision of yours tend, on the whole, to my father's credit, as an honest man, that he should, even after his death, desire to see justice done to a poor man like you, yet you are sensible that ill-dispositioned men might make bad constructions upon it, concerning his soul's health. So, I think, we had better lay the haill dirdum on that ill-deedie creature, Major Weir, and say naething about your dream in the wood of Pitmurkie. You had taken ower muckle brandy to be very certain about onything; and, Steenie, this receipt' (his hand shook while he held it out), – 'it's but a queer kind of document, and we will do best, I think, to put it quietly in the fire.'

'Od, but for as queer as it is, it's a' the voucher I have for my rent,' said my gudesire, who was afraid, it may be, of losing the benefit of Sir Robert's discharge.

'I will bear the contents to your credit in the rental-book, and give you a discharge under my own hand,' said Sir John, 'and that on the spot. And, Steenie, if you can hold your tongue about this matter, you shall sit, from this term downward, at an easier rent.'

'Mony thanks to your honour,' said Steenie, who saw easily in what corner the wind was; 'doubtless I will be comformable to all your honour's commands; only I would willingly speak wi' some powerful minister on the subject, for I do not like the sort of soumons of appointment whilk your honour's father— '

'Do not call the phantom my father!' said Sir John, interrupting him.

'Weel, then, the thing that was so like him,' said my gudesire; 'he spoke of my coming back to see him this time twelvemonth, and it's a weight on my conscience.'

'Aweel, then,' said Sir John, 'if you be so much distressed in mind, you may speak to our miniater of the parish; he is a douce man, regards the honour of our family, and the mair that he may look for some patronage from me.'

Wi' that, my father readily agreed that the receipt should be burnt, and the laird threw it into the chimney with his ain hand. Burn it would not for them, though; but away it flew up the lum, wi' a lang train of sparks at its tail, and a hissing noise like a squib.

My gudesire gaed down to the Manse, and the minister, when he had heard the story, said it was his real opinion that though my gudesire had gaen very far in tampering with dangerous matters, yet, as he had refused the devil's arles (for such was the offer of meat and drink) and had refused to do homage by piping at his bidding, he hoped, that if he held a circumspect walk hereafter, Satan could take little advantage by what was come and gane. And, indeed, my gudesire, of his ain accord, lang foreswore baith the pipes and the brandy – it was not even till the year was out, and the fatal day past, that he would so much as take the fiddle, or drink usquebaugh or tippeny.

Sir John made up his story about the jackanape as he liked himsell; and some believe till this day there was no more in the matter than the filching nature of the brute. Indeed, ye'll no hinder some to threap that it was nane o' the auld Enemy that Dougal and my gudesire saw in the laird's room, but only that wanchancy creature, the major, capering on the coffin; and that, as to the blawing on the laird's whistle that was heard after he was dead, the filthy brute could do that as weel as the laird himsell, if no better. But Heaven kens the truth, whilk first came out by the minister's wife, after Sir John and her ain gudeman were baith in the moulds. And then my gudesire, wha was failed in his limbs, but not in his judgement or memory – at least nothing to speak of – was obliged to tell the real narrative to his friends, for the credit of his good name. He might else have been charged for a warlock.

The shades of evening were growing thicker around us as my conductor finished his long narrative with this moral – 'Ye see, birkie, it is nae chancy thing to tak a stranger traveller for a guide, when you are in an uncouth land.'

'I should not have made that inference,' said I. 'Your grandfather's adventure was fortunate for himself, whom it saved from ruin and distress; and fortunate for his landlord also, whom it prevented from committing a gross act of injustice.'

'Aye, but they had baith to sup the sauce o't sooner or later,' said Wandering Willie – 'what was fristed wasna forgiven. Sir John died before he was much over threescore; and it was just like of a moment's illness. And for my gudesire, though he departed in fullness of life, yet there was my father, a yauld of forty-five, fell down betwixt the stilts of his pleugh, and rase never again, and left nae bairn but me, a puir sightless, fatherless, motherless creature, could neither work nor want. Things gaed weel aneugh at first; for Sir Redwald Redgauntlet, the only son of Sir John, and the oye of auld Sir Robert, and, waes me! the last of the honourable house, took the farm aff our hands, and brought me into his household to have care of me. He liked music; and I had the best teachers baith England and Scotland could gie me. Mony a merry year was I wi' him; but waes me! he gaed out with other pretty men in the Forty-five – I'll say nae mair about it – my head never settled weel since I lost him; and if I say another word about it, deil a bar will I have the heart to play the night. – Look out, my gentle chap,' he resumed in a different tone, 'ye should see the lights at Brokenburn Glen by this time.'

The Monk (extract)

MATTHEW LEWIS

First published in 1796, The Monk *tells of the sinful fall of Ambrosio, proud and noble Abbot of the monastery of the Capuchins in medieval Madrid. Facing sentence of lingering death and torture for rape and murder, the Monk and his co-conspirator, Matilda, must make a hideous choice . . .*

The day of his second examination was at hand. He had been compelled to swallow cordials, whose virtues were calculated to restore his bodily strength, and enable him to support the question longer. On the night preceding this dreaded day, his fears for the morrow permitted him not to sleep. His terrors were so violent, as nearly to annihilate his mental powers. He sat like one stupefied near the table on which his lamp was burning dimly. Despair chained up his faculties in idiotism, and he remained for some hours, unable to speak or move, or indeed to think.

'Look up, Ambrosio!' said a voice in accents well-known to him –

The Monk started, and raised his melancholy eyes. Matilda stood before him. She had quitted her religious habit. She now wore a female dress, at once elegant and splendid: a profusion of diamonds blazed upon her robes, and her hair was confined by a coronet of roses. In her right hand she held a small book: a lively expression of pleasure beamed upon her countenance; but still it was mingled with a wild imperious majesty, which inspired the Monk with awe, and represt in some measure his transports at seeing her.

'You here, Matilda?' He at length exclaimed: 'How have you gained entrance? Where are your chains? What means this magnificence, and the joy which sparkles in your eyes? Have our judges relented? Is there a chance of my escaping? Answer me for pity, and tell me, what I have to hope, or fear.'

'Ambrosio!' She replied with an air of commanding dignity; 'I have baffled the Inquisition's fury. I am free: A few moments will place kingdoms between these dungeons and me. Yet I purchase my liberty at a dear, at a dreadful price! Dare you pay the same, Ambrosio? Dare you spring without fear over the bounds, which separate men from angels? – You are silent. – You look upon me with eyes of suspicion and alarm – I read your thoughts and confess their justice. Yes,

Ambrosio; I have sacrificed all for life and liberty. I am no longer a candidate for heaven! I have renounced God's service, and am enlisted beneath the banners of his foes. The deed is past recall: Yet were it in my power to go back, I would not. Oh! my friend, to expire in such torments! To die amidst curses and execrations! To bear the insults of an exasperated mob! To be exposed to all the mortifications of shame and infamy! Who can reflect without horror on such a doom? Let me then exult in my exchange. I have sold distant and uncertain happiness for present and secure: I have preserved a life, which otherwise I had lost in torture; and I have obtained the power of procuring every bliss, which can make that life delicious! The infernal spirits obey me as their sovereign: By their aid shall my days be past in every refinement of luxury and voluptuousness. I will enjoy unrestrained the gratification of my senses: Every passion shall be indulged, even to satiety; then will I bid my servants invent new pleasures, to revive and stimulate my glutted appetites! I go impatient to exercise my newly-gained dominion. I pant to be at liberty. Nothing should hold me one moment longer in this abhorred abode, but the hope of persuading you to follow my example. Ambrosio, I still love you: our mutual guilt and danger have rendered you dearer to me than ever and I would fain save you from impending destruction. Summon then your resolution to your aid; and renounce for immediate and certain benefits the hopes of a salvation, difficult to obtain, and perhaps altogether erroneous. Shake off the prejudice of vulgar souls: abandon a god, who has abandoned you, and raise yourself to the level of superior beings!'

She paused for the Monk's reply: he shuddered, while he gave it.

'Matilda!' he said after a long silence in a low and unsteady voice; 'What price gave you for liberty?'

She answered him firm and dauntless.

'Ambrosio, it was my soul!'

'Wretched woman, what have you done? Pass but a few years, and how dreadful will be your sufferings!'

'Weak man, pass but this night, and how dreadful will be your own! Do you remember what you have already endured? Tomorrow you must bear torments doubly exquisite. Do you remember the horrors of a fiery punishment? In two days you must be led a victim to the stake! What then will become of you? Still dare you hope for pardon? Still are you beguiled with visions of salvation? Think upon your crimes! Think upon your lust, your perjury, inhumanity, and hypocrisy! Think upon the innocent blood, which cries to the throne of God for vengeance, and then hope for mercy! Then dream of heaven, and sigh for worlds of light, and realms of peace and pleasure! Absurd! Open your eyes, Ambrosio, and be prudent. Hell is your lot; you are doomed to eternal perdition; nought lies beyond your grave, but a gulf of devouring flames. And will you then speed towards that hell? Will you clasp that perdition in your arms, ere 'tis needful? Will you plunge into those flames, while you still have the power to shun them? 'Tis a madman's action. No, no, Ambrosio: let us for awhile fly from divine vengeance. Be advised by me; purchase by one moment's courage the bliss of years; enjoy the present, and forget that a future lags behind.'

'Matilda, your counsels are dangerous: I dare not, I will not follow them. I must not give up my claim to salvation. Monstrous are my crimes; but God is merciful, and I will not despair of pardon.'

'Is such your resolution? I have no more to say. I speed to joy and liberty, and abandon you to death and eternal torments.'

'Yet stay one moment, Matilda! You command the infernal dæmons: You can force open these prison-doors; You can release me from these chains, which weigh me down. Save me, I conjure you, and bear me from these fearful abodes!'

'You ask the only boon beyond my power to bestow. I am forbidden to assist a churchman and a partisan of God: renounce those titles, and command me.'

'I will not sell my soul to perdition.'

'Persist in your obstinacy, till you find yourself at the stake: Then will you repent your error, and sigh for escape when the moment is gone by. I quit you. – Yet ere the hour of death arrives should wisdom enlighten you, listen to the means of repairing your present faith. I leave with you this book. Read the four first lines of the seventh page backwards: the spirit whom you have already once beheld, will immediately appear to you. If you are wise, we shall meet again: If not, farewell for ever!'

She let the book fall upon the ground. A cloud of blue fire wrapped itself round her: she waved her hand to Ambrosio, and disappeared. The momentary glare which the flames poured through the dungeon, on dissipating suddenly, seemed to have increased its natural gloom. The solitary lamp scarcely gave light sufficient to guide the Monk to a chair. He threw himself into his seat, folded his arms, and leaning his head upon the table, sank into reflections perplexing and unconnected.

He was still in this attitude, when the opening of the prison-door roused him from his stupor. He was summoned to appear before the Grand Inquisitor. He rose, and followed his gaoler with painful steps. He was led into the same hall, placed before the same examiners, and was again interrogated, whether he would confess. He replied as before, that having no crimes, he could acknowledge none: but when the executioners prepared to put him to the question, when he saw the engines of torture, and remembered the pangs, which they had already inflicted, his resolution failed him entirely. Forgetting the consequences, and only anxious to escape the terrors of the present moment, he made an ample confession. He disclosed every circumstance of his guilt, and owned not merely the crimes with which he was charged, but those of what he had never been suspected. Being interrogated as to Matilda's flight which had created much confusion, he confessed that she had sold herself to Satan, and that she was indebted to sorcery for her escape. He still assured his judges, that for his own part he had never entered into any compact with the infernal spirits; but the threat of being tortured made him declare himself to be a sorcerer, and heretic, and whatever other title the inquisitors chose to fix upon him. In consequence of this avowal, his sentence was immediately pronounced. He was ordered to prepare himself to perish in the *auto da fé*, which was to be solemnised at twelve o'clock that night. This hour was chosen from the idea, that the horror of the flames being heightened by the gloom of midnight, the execution would have a greater effect upon the mind of the people.

Ambrosio rather dead than alive was left alone in his dungeon. The moment in which this terrible decree was pronounced, had nearly proved that of his dissolution. He looked forward to the morrow with despair, and his terrors increased with the approach of midnight. Sometimes he was buried in gloomy silence: at others he raved with delirious passion, wrung his hands, and cursed the hour, when he first beheld the light. In one of these moments his eyes rested upon Matilda's mysterious gift. His transports of rage were instantly suspended. He looked earnestly at the book; he took it up, but immediately threw it from him with horror. He walked rapidly up and down his dungeon: then stopped, and again fixed his eyes on the spot where the book had fallen. He reflected, that here at least was a resource from the fate which he dreaded. He stooped, and took it up a second time. He remained for some time trembling and irresolute: he longed to try the charm, yet feared its consequences. The recollection of his sentence at length fixed his indecision. He opened the volume; but his agitation was so great, that he at first sought in vain for the page mentioned by Matilda. Ashamed of himself, he called all his courage to his aid. He turned to the seventh leaf. He began to read it aloud; but his eyes frequently wandered from the book, while he anxiously cast them round in search of the spirit, whom he wished, yet dreaded to behold. Still he persisted in his design; and with a voice unassured and frequent interruptions, he contrived to finish the four first lines of the page.

They were in a language, whose import was totally unknown to him. Scarce had he pronounced the last word, when the effects of the charm were evident. A loud burst of thunder was heard; the prison shook to its very foundations; a blaze of lightning flashed through the cell; and in the next moment, borne upon sulphurous whirl-winds, Lucifer stood before him a second time. But he came not, as when at Matilda's summons he borrowed the seraph's form to deceive Ambrosio. He appeared in all that ugliness, which since his fall from heaven had been his portion: his blasted limbs still bore marks of the Almighty's thunder: a swarthy darkness spread itself over his gigantic form: his hands and feet were armed with long talons: fury glared in his eyes, which might have struck the bravest heart with terror: over his huge shoulders waved two enormous sable wings; and his hair was supplied by living snakes, which twined themselves round his brows with frightful hissings. In one hand he held a roll of parchment, and in the other an iron pen. Still the lightning flashed around him, and the thunder with repeated bursts, seemed to announce the dissolution of nature.

Terrified at an apparition so different from what he had expected, Ambrosio remained gazing upon the fiend, deprived of the power of utterance. The thunder had ceased to roll: universal silence reigned through the dungeon.

'For what am I summoned hither?' said the dæmon, in a voice which sulphurous fogs had damped to hoarseness.

At the sound nature seemed to tremble: a violent earthquake rocked the ground, accompanied by a fresh burst of thunder, louder and more appalling than the first.

Ambrosio was long unable to answer the dæmon's demand.

'I am condemned to die;' he said with a faint voice, his blood running cold, while he gazed upon his dreadful visitor. 'Save me! Bear me from hence!'

'Shall the reward of my services be paid me? Dare you embrace my cause? Will you be mine, body and soul? Are you prepared to renounce him who made you, and him who died for you? Answer but "Yes" and Lucifer is your slave.'

'Will no less price content you? Can nothing satisfy you but my eternal ruin? Spirit, you ask too much. Yet convey me from this dungeon: be my servant for one hour, and I will be yours for a thousand years. Will not this offer suffice?'

'It will not. I must have your soul; must have it mine, and mine for ever.'

'Insatiate dæmon, I will not doom myself to endless torments. I will not give up my hopes of being one day pardoned.'

'You will not? On what chimæra rest then your hope? Short-sighted mortal! Miserable wretch! Are you not guilty? Are you not infamous in the eyes of men and angels? Can such enormous sins be forgiven? Hope you to escape my power? Your fate is already pronounced. The Eternal has abandoned you; mine you are marked in the book of destiny, and mine you must and shall be!'

'Fiend, 'tis false! Infinite is the Almighty's mercy, and the penitent shall meet his forgiveness. My crimes are monstrous, but I will not despair of pardon: Haply, when they have received due chastisement . . .'

'Chastisement? Was Purgatory meant for guilt like yours? Hope you that your offences shall be bought off by prayers of superstitious dotards and droning monks? Ambrosio, be wise! Mine you must be: you are doomed to flames, but may shun them for the present. Sign this parchment: I will be you from hence, and you may pass your remaining years in bliss and liberty. Enjoy your existence: indulge in every pleasure to which appetite may lead you: but from the moment that it quits your body, remember that your soul belongs to me, and that I will not be defrauded of my right.'

The Monk was silent; but his looks declared, that the tempter's words were not thrown away. He reflected on the conditions proposed with horror: on the other hand, he believed himself doomed to perdition, and that, by refusing the dæmon's succour, he only hastened tortures which he never could escape. The fiend saw, that his resolution was shaken: he renewed his instances, and endeavoured to fix the Abbot's indecision. He described the agonies of death in the most terrific colours; and he worked so powerfully upon Ambrosio's despair and fears, that he prevailed upon him to receive the parchment. He then struck the iron pen which he held into a vein of the Monk's left-hand. It pierced deep, and was instantly filled with blood; yet Ambrosio felt no pain from the wound. The pen was put into his hand: it trembled. The wretch placed the parchment on the table before him, and prepared to sign it. Suddenly he held his hand: he started away hastily, and threw the pen upon the table.

'What am I doing?' he cried – then turning to the fiend with a desperate air, 'Leave me! Begone! I will not sign the parchment.'

'Fool!' exclaimed the disappointed dæmon, darting looks so furious as penetrated the Friar's soul with horror; 'Thus am I trifled with? Go then! Rave in agony, expire in tortures, and then learn the extent of the Eternal's mercy! But beware how you make me again your mock! Call me no more, till resolved to accept my offers! Summon me a second time to dismiss me thus idly, and these talons shall rend you into a thousand pieces! Speak yet again; will you sign the parchment?'

'I will not! Leave me! Away!'

Instantly the thunder was heard to roll horribly: once more the earth trembled with violence: the dungeon resounded with loud shrieks, and the dæmon fled with blasphemy and curses.

At first, the Monk rejoiced at having resisted the seducer's arts, and obtained a triumph over mankind's enemy: but as the hour of punishment drew near, his former terrors revived in his heart. Their momentary repose seemed to have given fresh vigour. The nearer that the time approached, the more did he dread appearing before the throne of God. He shuddered to think how soon he must be plunged into eternity; how soon meet the eyes of his Creator, whom he had so grievously offended. The bell announced midnight: It was the signal for being led to the stake! As he listened to the first stroke, the blood ceased to circulate in the Abbot's veins: he heard death and torture murmured in each succeeding sound. He expected to see the archers entering his prison: and as the bell forbore to toll, he seized the magic volume in a fit of despair. He opened it, turned hastily to the seventh page, and as if fearing to allow himself a moment's thought ran over the fatal lines with rapidity. Accompanied by his former terrors, Lucifer again stood before the trembler.

'You have summoned me,' said the fiend; 'Are you determined to be wise? Will you accept my conditions? You know them already. Renounce your claim to salvation, make over to me your soul, and I bear you from this dungeon instantly. Yet is it time. Resolve, or it will be too late. Will you sign the parchment?'

'I must! – Fate urges me! – I accept your conditions.'

'Sign the parchment!' replied the dæmon in an exulting tone.

The contract and the bloody pen still lay upon the table. Ambrosio drew near it. He prepared to sign his name. A moment's reflection made him hesitate.

'Hark!' cried the tempter; 'They come! Be quick! Sign the parchment, and I bear you from hence this moment.'

In effect, the archers were heard approaching, appointed to lead Ambrosio to the stake. The sound encouraged the Monk in his resolution.

'What is the import of this writing?' said he.

'It makes your soul over to me for ever, and without reserve.'

'What am I to receive in exchange?'

'My protection, and release from this dungeon. Sign it, and this instant I bear you away.'

Ambrosio took up the pen; he set it to the parchment. Again his courage failed him: he felt a pang of terror at his heart, and once more threw the pen upon the table.

'Weak and puerile!' cried the exasperated fiend: 'Away with this folly! Sign the writing this instant, or I sacrifice you to my rage!'

At this moment the bolt of the outward door was drawn back. The prisoner heard the rattling of chains; The heavy bar fell; the archers were on the point of entering. Working up to frenzy by the urgent danger, shrinking from the approach of death, terrified by the dæmon's threats, and seeing no other means to escape destruction, the wretched Monk complied. He signed the fatal contract, and gave it hastily into the evil spirit's hands, whose eyes, as he received the gift, glared with malicious rapture.

'Take it!' said the God-abandoned; 'Now then save me! Snatch me from hence!'

'Hold! Do you freely and absolutely renounce your Creator and his Son?'

'I do! I do!'

'Do you make over your soul to me for ever?'

'For ever!'

'Without reserve or subterfuge? Without future appeal to the divine mercy?'

The last chain fell from the door of the prison: the key was heard turning in the lock: already the iron door grated heavily upon its rusty hinges.

'I am yours for ever and irrevocably!' cried the Monk wild with terror: 'I abandon all claim to salvation! I own no power but yours! Hark! Hark! They come! Oh! save me! Bear me away!'

'I have triumphed! You are mine past reprieve, and I fulfil my promise.'

While he spoke, the door unclosed. Instantly the dæmon grasped one of Ambrosio's arms, spread his broad pinions and sprang with him into the air. The roof opened as they soared upwards, and closed again when they had quitted the dungeon.

In the mean while, the gaoler was thrown into the utmost surprise by the disappearance of his prisoner. Though neither he nor the archers were in time to witness to Monk's escape, a sulphurous smell prevailing through the prison sufficiently informed them by whose aid he had been liberated. They hastened to make their report to the Grand Inquisitor. The story, how a sorcerer had been carried away by the Devil, was soon noised about Madrid; and for some days the whole city was employed in discussing the subject. Gradually it ceased to be the topic of conversation: other adventures arose whose novelty engaged universal attention; and Ambrosio was soon forgotten as totally, as if he never had existed. While this was passing, the Monk supported by his infernal guide, traversed the air with the rapidity of an arrow, and a few moments placed him upon a precipice's brink, the steepest in Sierra Morena.

Though rescued from the Inquisition, Ambrosio as yet was insensible of the blessings of liberty. The damning contract weighed heavy upon his mind; and the scenes in which he had been a principal actor, had left behind them such impressions, as rendered his heart the seat of anarchy and confusion. The objects now before his eyes, and which the full moon sailing through clouds permitted him to examine, were ill-calculated to inspire the calm, of which he stood so much in need. The disorder of his imagination was increased by the wildness of the surrounding scenery; by the gloomy caverns and steep rocks, rising above each other, and dividing the passing clouds; solitary clusters of trees scattered here and there, among whose thick-twined branches the wind of night sighed hoarsely and mournfully; the shrill cry of mountain eagles, who had built their nests among these lonely deserts; the stunning roar of torrents, as swelled by late rains they rushed violently down tremendous precipices; and the dark waters of a silent sluggish stream which faintly reflected the moon-beams, and bathed the rock's base on which Ambrosio stood. The Abbot cast round him a look of terror. His infernal conductor was still by his side, and eyed him with a look of mingled malice, exultation, and contempt.

'Whither have you brought me?' said the Monk at length in an hollow trembling voice: 'Why am I placed in this melancholy scene? Bear me from it quickly! Carry me to Matilda!'

The fiend replied not, but continued to gaze upon him in silence. Ambrosio could not sustain his glance; He turned away his eyes, while thus spoke the dæmon:

'I have him then in my power! This model of piety! This being without reproach! This mortal who placed his puny virtues on a level with those of angels. He is mine! Irrevocably, eternally mine! Companions of my sufferings! Denizens of hell! How grateful will be my present!'

He paused; then addressed himself to the Monk—

'Carry you to Matilda?' he continued, repeating Ambrosio's words: 'Wretch! you shall soon be with her! You well deserve a place near her, for hell boasts no miscreant more guilty than yourself. Hark, Ambrosio, while I unveil your crimes! You had shed the blood of two innocents; Antonia and Elvira perished by your hand. That Antonia whom you violated, was your sister! That Elvira whom you murdered, gave you birth! Tremble, abandoned hypocrite! Inhuman parricide! Incestuous ravisher! Tremble at the extent of your offences! And you it was who thought yourself proof against temptation, absolved from human frailties, and free from error and vice! Is pride then a virtue? Is inhumanity no fault? Know, vain man! That I long have marked you for my prey: I watched the movements of your heart; I saw that you were virtuous from vanity, not principle, and I seized the fit moment of seduction. I observed your blind idolatry of the Madonna's picture. I bad a subordinate but crafty spirit assume a similar form, and you eagerly yielded to the blandishments of Matilda. Your pride was gratified by her flattery; your lust only needed an opportunity to break forth; you ran into the snare blindly, and scrupled not to commit a crime, which you blamed in another with unfeeling severity. It was I who threw Matilda in your way; it was I who gave you entrance to Antonia's chamber; it was I who caused the dagger to be given you which pierced your sister's bosom; and it was I who warned Elvira in dreams of your designs upon her daughter, and thus, by preventing your profiting by her sleep, compelled you to add rape as well as incest to the catalogue of your crimes. Hear, hear, Ambrosio! Had you resisted me one minute longer, you have saved your body and soul. The guards whom you heard at your prison-door, came to signify your pardon. But I had already triumphed: my plots had already succeeded. Scarcely could I propose crimes so quick as you performed them. You are mine, and Heaven itself cannot rescue you from my power. Hope not that your penitence will make void our contract. Here is your bond signed with your blood; you have given up your claim to mercy, and nothing can restore to you the rights which you have foolishly resigned. Believe you, that your secret thoughts escaped me? No, no, I read them all! You trusted that you should still have time for repentence. I saw your artifice, knew its falsity, and rejoiced in deceiving the deceiver! You are mine beyond reprieve: I burn to possess my right, and alive you quit not these mountains.'

During the dæmon's speech, Ambrosio had been stupefied by terror and surprise. This last declaration roused him.

'Not quit these mountains alive?' he exclaimed: 'Perfidious, what mean you? Have you forgotten our contract?'

The fiend answered by a malicious laugh:

'Our contract? Have I not performed my part? What more did I promise than to save you from your prison? Have I not done so? Are you not safe from the Inquisition – safe from all but from me? Fool that you were to confide yourself to a devil! Why did you not stipulate for life, and power, and pleasure? Then all would have been granted: now, your reflections come too late. Miscreant, prepare for death; you have not many hours to live!'

On hearing this sentence, dreadful were the feelings of the devoted wretch! He sank upon his knees, and raised his hands towards heaven. The fiend read his intentions and prevented it—

'What?' He cried, darting at him a look of fury: 'Dare you still implore the Eternal's mercy? Would you feign penitence, and again act an hypocrite's part? Villain, resign your hopes of pardon. Thus I secure my prey!'

As he said this, darting his talons into the Monk's shaven crown, he sprang with him from the rock. The caves and mountains rang with Ambrosio's shrieks. The dæmon continued to soar aloft, till reaching a dreadful height, he released the sufferer. Headlong fell the Monk through the airy waste; the sharp point of a rock received him; and he rolled from precipice to precipice till bruised and mangled he rested on the river's banks. Life still existed in his miserable frame: He attempted in vain to raise himself; his broken and dislocated limbs refused to perform their office, nor was he able to quit the spot where he had first fallen. The sun now rose above the horizon; its scorching beams darted full upon the head of the expiring sinner. Myriads of insects were called forth by the warmth; they drank the blood which trickled from Ambrosio's wounds; he had no power to drive them from him, and they fastened upon his sores, darted their stings into his body, covered him with their multitudes, and inflicted on him tortures the most exquisite and insupportable. The eagles of the rock tore his flesh piecemeal, and dug out his eye-balls with their crooked beaks. A burning thirst tormented him; he heard the river's murmur as it rolled beside him, but strove in vain to drag himself towards the sound. Blind, maimed, helpless, and despairing, venting his rage in blasphemy and curses, execrating his existence, yet dreading the arrival of death destined to yield him up to greater torments, six miserable days did the villain languish. On the seventh a violent storm arose: the winds in fury rent up rocks and forests: the sky was now black with clouds, now sheeted with fire: the rain fell in torrents; it swelled the stream; the waves overflowed their banks; they reached the spot where Ambrosio lay, and when they abated carried with them into the river the corpse of the despairing Monk.

The White Wolf

CAPTAIN FREDERICK MARRYAT

I

Before noon Philip and Krantz had embarked, and made sail in the peroqua.

They had no difficulty in steering their course; the islands by day, and the clear stars by night, were their compass. It is true that they did not follow the more direct track, but they followed the more secure, working up the smooth waters, and gaining to the northward more than to the west. Many times they were chased by the Malay proas, which infested the islands, but the swiftness of their little peroqua was their security; indeed, the chase was, generally speaking, abandoned as soon as the smallness of the vessel was made out by the pirates, who expected that little or no booty was to be gained.

One morning, as they were sailing between the isles, with less wind than usual, Philip observed –

'Krantz, you said that there were events in your own life, or connected with it, which would corroborate the mysterious tale I confided to you. Will you now tell me to what you referred?'

'Certainly,' replied Krantz; 'I have often thought of doing so, but one circumstance or another has hitherto prevented me; this is, however, a fitting opportunity. Prepare therefore to listen to a strange story, quite as strange, perhaps, as your own.

'I take it for granted that you have heard people speak of the Hartz Mountains,' observed Krantz.

'I have never heard people speak of them, that I can recollect,' replied Philip; 'but I have read of them in some book, and of the strange things which have occurred there.'

'It is indeed a wild region,' rejoined Krantz, 'and many strange tales are told of it; but strange as they are, I have good reason for believing them to be true.

'My father was not born, or originally a resident, in the Hartz Mountains; he was a serf of an Hungarian nobleman, of great possessions, in Transylvania; but although a serf, he was not by any means a poor or illiterate man. In fact, he was rich, and his intelligence and respectability were such, that he had been raised by his lord to the stewardship; but whoever may happen to be born a serf, a serf must he remain, even though he become a wealthy man: such was the condition of my father. My father had been married for about five years; and by his marriage had three children – my eldest brother Cæsar, myself (Hermann), and a sister named Marcella. You know, Philip, that Latin is still the language spoken in that country; and that will account for our high-sounding names. My mother was a very beautiful woman, unfortunately more beautiful than virtuous: she was seen and admired by the lord of the soil; my father was sent away upon some mission; and during his absence, my mother, flattered by the attentions, and won by the assiduities, of this nobleman, yielded to his wishes. It so happened that my father returned very unexpectedly, and discovered the intrigue. The evidence of my mother's shame was positive: he surprised her in the company of her seducer! Carried away by the impetuosity of his feelings, he watched the opportunity of a meeting taking place between them, and murdered both his wife and her seducer. Conscious that, as a serf, not even the provocation which he had received would be allowed as a justification of his conduct, he hastily collected together what money he could lay his hands upon, and, as we were then in the depth of winter, he put his horses to the sleigh, and taking his children with him, he set off in the middle of the night, and was far away before the tragical circumstance had transpired. Aware that he would be pursued, and that he had no chance of escape if he remained in any portion of his native country (in which the authorities could lay hold of him), he continued his flight without intermission until he had buried himself in the intricacies and seclusion of the Hartz Mountains. Of course, all that I have now told you I learned afterwards. My oldest recollections are knit to a rude, yet comfortable cottage, in which I lived with my father, brother, and sister. It was on the confines of one of those vast forests which cover the northern part of Germany; around it were a few acres of ground, which, during the summer months, my father cultivated, and which, though they yielded a doubtful harvest, were sufficient for our support. In the winter we remained much indoors, for, as my father followed the chase, we were left alone, and the wolves during that season incessantly prowled about. My father had purchased the cottage, and land about it, of one of the rude foresters, who gain their livelihood partly by hunting, and partly by burning charcoal, for the purpose of smelting the ore from the neighbouring mines; it was distant about two miles from any other habitation. I can call to mind the whole landscape now; the tall pines which rose up on the mountain above us, and the wide expanse of the forest beneath, on the topmost boughs and heads of whose trees we looked down from our cottage, as the mountain below us rapidly descended into the distant valley. In summer time the prospect was beautiful: but during the severe winter a more desolate scene could not well be imagined.

'I said that, in the winter, my father occupied himself with the chase; every day he left us, and often would he lock the door, that we might not leave the cottage. He had no one to assist him, or to take care of us – indeed, it was not easy to find a female servant who would live in such a solitude; but, could he have found one, my father would not have received her, for he had imbibed a horror of the sex, as the difference of his conduct towards us, his two boys, and my poor little sister Marcella evidently proved. You may suppose we were sadly neglected; indeed, we suffered much, for my father, fearful that we might come to some harm, would not allow us fuel when he left the cottage; and we were obliged, therefore, to creep under the heaps of bears' skins, and there to keep ourselves as warm as we could until he returned in the evening, when a blazing fire was our delight. That my father chose this restless sort of life may appear strange, but the fact was, that he could not remain quiet; whether from the remorse for having committed murder, or from the misery consequent on his change of situation, or from both combined, he was never happy unless he was in a state of activity. Children, however, when left so much to themselves, acquire a thoughtfulness not common to their age. So it was with us; and during the short cold days of winter, we would sit silent, longing for the happy hours when the snow would melt and the leaves burst out, and the birds begin their songs, and when we should again be set at liberty.

'Such was our peculiar and savage sort of life until my brother Cæsar was nine, myself seven, and my sister five years old, when the circumstances occurred on which is based the extraordinary narrative which I am about to relate.

'One evening my father returned home rather later than usual; he had been unsuccessful, and as the weather was very severe, and many feet of snow were upon the ground, he was not only very cold, but in a very bad humour. He had brought in wood, and we were all three gladly assisting each other in blowing on the embers to create a blaze, when he caught poor little Marcella by the arm and threw her aside; the child fell, struck her mouth and bled very much. My brother ran to raise her up. Accustomed to ill-usage, and afraid of my father, she did not dare to cry, but looked up in his face very piteously. My father drew his stool nearer to the hearth, muttered something in abuse of women, and busied himself with the fire, which both my brother and I had deserted when our sister was so unkindly treated. A cheerful blaze was soon the result of his exertions; but we did not, as usual, crowd round it. Marcella, still bleeding, retired to a corner, and my brother and I took our seats beside her, while my father hung over the fire gloomily and alone. Such had been our position for about half an hour, when the howl of a wolf, close under the window of the cottage, fell on our ears. My father started up, and seized his gun; the howl was repeated; he examined the priming, and then hastily left the cottage, shutting the door after him. We all waited (anxiously listening), for we thought that if he succeeded in shooting the wolf, he would return in a better humour; and, although he was harsh to all of us, and particularly so to our little sister, still we loved our father, and loved to see him cheerful and happy, for what else had we to look up to? And I may here observe, that perhaps there never were three children who were fonder of each other; we did not, like other children, fight and dispute together; and if, by chance, any disagreement did arise, between my elder brother and me, little Marcella would run to us, and kissing us both, seal, through her entreaties, the peace between us. Marcella was a lovely, amiable child; I can recall her beautiful features even now. Alas! poor little Marcella.'

'She is dead, then?' observed Philip.

'Dead! yes, dead! but how did she die? – But I must not anticipate, Philip; let me tell my story.

'We waited for some time, but the report of the gun did not reach us, and my elder brother then said, "Our father has followed the wolf, and will not be back for some time. Marcella, let us wash the blood from your mouth, and then we will leave this corner and go to the fire to warm ourselves."

'We did so, and remained there until near midnight, every minute wondering, as it grew later, why our father did not return. We had no idea that he was in any danger, but we thought that he must have chased the wolf for a very long time. "I will look out and see if father is coming," said my brother Cæsar, going to the door. "Take care," said Marcella, "the wolves must be about now, and we cannot kill them, brother." My brother opened the door very cautiously, and but a few inches; he peeped out. "I see nothing," said he, after a time, and once more he joined us at the fire. "We have had no supper," said I, for my father usually cooked the meat as soon as he came home; and during his absence we had nothing but the fragments of the preceding day.

' "And if our father comes home, after his hunt, Cæsar," said Marcella, "he will be pleased to have some supper; let us cook it for him and for ourselves." Cæsar climbed upon the stool, and reached down some meat – I forget now whether it was venison or bear's meat, but we cut off the usual quantity, and proceeded to dress it, as we used to do under our father's superintendence. We were all busy putting it into the platters before the fire, to await his coming, when we heard the sound of a horn. We listened – there was a noise outside, and a minute afterwards my father entered, ushered in a young female and a large dark man in a hunter's dress.

'Perhaps I had better now relate what was only known to me many years afterwards. When my father had left the cottage, he perceived a large white wolf about thirty yards from him; as soon as the animal saw my father, it retreated slowly, growling and snarling. My father followed; the animal did not run, but always kept at some distance; and my father did not like to fire until he was pretty certain that his ball would take effect; thus they went on for some time, the wolf now leaving my father far behind, and then stopping and snarling defiance at him, and then, again, on his approach, setting off at speed.

'Anxious to shoot the animal (for the white wolf is very rare), my father continued the pursuit for several hours, during which he continually ascended the mountain.

'You must know, Philip, that there are peculiar spots on those mountains which are supposed, and, as my story will prove, truly supposed, to be inhabited by the evil influences: they are well known to the huntsmen, who invariably avoid them. Now, one of these spots, an open space in the pine forest above us, had been pointed out to my father as dangerous on that account. But whether he disbelieved these wild stories, or whether, in his eager pursuit of the chase, he disregarded them, I know not; certain, however, it is, that he was decoyed by the white wolf to this open space, when the animal appeared to slacken her speed. My father approached, came close up to her, raised his gun to his shoulder, and was about to fire, when the wolf suddenly disappeared. He thought that the snow on the ground must have dazzled his sight, and he let down his gun to look for the beast – but she was gone; how she could have escaped over the clearance, without his seeing her, was beyond his comprehension. Mortified at the ill-success of his chase, he was about to retrace his steps, when he heard the distant sound of a horn. Astonishment at such a sound – at such an hour – in such a wilderness, made him forget for the moment his disappointment, and he remained riveted to the spot. In a minute the horn was blown a second time, and at no great distance; my father stood still, and listened; a third time it was blown. I forget the term used to express it, but it was the signal which, my father well knew, implied that the party was lost in the woods. In a few minutes more my father beheld a man on horseback, with a female seated on the crupper, enter the cleared space, and ride up to him. At first, my father called to mind the strange stories which he had heard of the supernatural beings who were said to frequent these mountains; but the nearer approach of the parties satisfied him that they were mortals like himself. As soon as they came up to him, the man who guided the horse accosted him. "Friend hunter, you are out late, the better fortune for us; we have ridden far, and are in fear of our lives, which are eagerly sought after. These mountains have enabled us to elude our pursuers; but if we find not shelter and refreshment, that will avail us little, as we must perish from hunger and the inclemency of the night. My daughter, who rides behind me, is now more dead than alive – say, can you assist us in our difficulty?"

' "My cottage is some few miles distant," replied my father, "but I have little to offer you besides a shelter from the weather; to the little I have you are welcome. May I ask whence you come?"

' "Yes, friend, it is no secret now; we have escaped from Transylvania, where my daughter's honour and my life were equally in jeopardy!"

'This information was quite enough to raise an interest in my father's heart. He remembered his own escape: he remembered the loss of his wife's honour, and the tragedy by which it was wound up. He immediately, and warmly, offered all the assistance which he could afford them.

' "There is no time to be lost, then, good sir," observed the horseman; "my daughter is chilled with the frost, and cannot hold out much longer against the severity of the weather."

' "Follow me," replied my father, leading the way towards his home.

' "I was lured away in pursuit of a large white wolf," observed my father; "it came to the very window of my hut, or I should not have been out at this time of night."

' "The creature passed by us just as we came out of the wood," said the female, in a silvery tone.

' "I was nearly discharging my piece at it," observed the hunter; "but since it did us such good service, I am glad that I allowed it to escape."

'In about an hour and a half, during which my father walked at a rapid pace, the party arrived at the cottage, and, as I said before, came in.

' "We are in good time, apparently," observed the dark hunter, catching the smell of the roasted meat, as he walked to the fire and surveyed my brother and sister and myself. "You have young cooks here, Meinheer." "I am glad that we shall not have to wait," replied my father. "Come, mistress, seat yourself by the fire; you require warmth after your cold ride." "And where can I put up my horse, Meinheer?" observed the huntsman. "I will take care of him," replied my father, going out of the cottage door.

'The female must, however, be particularly described. She was young, and apparently twenty years of age. She was dressed in a travelling dress, deeply bordered with white fur, and wore a cap of white ermine on her head. Her features were very beautiful, at least I thought so, and so my father has since declared. Her hair was flaxen, glossy, and shining, and bright as a mirror; and her mouth, although somewhat large when it was open, showed the most brilliant teeth I have ever beheld. But there was something about her eyes, bright as they were, which made us children afraid; they were so restless, so furtive; I could not at that time tell why, but I felt as if there was cruelty in her eye; and when she beckoned us to come to her, we approached her with fear and trembling. Still she was beautiful, very beautiful. She spoke kindly to my brother and myself, patted our heads and caressed us; but Marcella would not come near her; on the contrary, she slunk away, and hid herself in the bed, and would not wait for the supper, which half an hour before she had been so anxious for.

'My father, having put the horse into a close shed, soon returned, and supper was placed on the table. When it was over, my father requested the young lady would take possession of the bed, and he would remain at the fire, and sit up with her father. After some hesitation on her part, this arrangement was agreed to, and I and my brother crept into the other bed with Marcella, for we had as yet always slept together.

'But we could not sleep; there was something so unusual, not only in seeing strange people, but in having those people sleep at the cottage, that we were bewildered. As for poor little Marcella, she was quiet, but I perceived that she trembled during the whole night, and sometimes I thought that she was checking a sob. My father had brought out some spirits, which he rarely used, and he and the strange hunter remained drinking and talking before the fire. Our ears were ready to catch the slightest whisper – so much was our curiosity excited.

' "You said you came from Transylvania?" observed my father.

' "Even so, Meinheer," replied the hunter. "I was a serf to the noble house of— ; my master would insist upon my surrendering up my fair girl to his wishes; it ended in my giving him a few inches of my hunting-knife."

' "We are countrymen and brothers in misfortune," replied my father, taking the huntsman's hand and pressing it warmly.

' "Indeed! Are you then from that country?"

' "Yes; and I too have fled for my life. But mine is a melancholy tale."

' "Your name?" inquired the hunter.

' "Krantz."

' "What! Krantz of— ? I have heard your tale; you need not renew your grief by repeating it now. Welcome, most welcome, Meinheer, and, I may say, my worthy kinsman. I am your second cousin, Wilfred of Barnsdorf," cried the hunter, rising up and embracing my father.

'They filled their horn-mugs to the brim and drank to one another after the German fashion. The conversation was then carried on in a low tone; all that we could collect from it was that our new relative and his daughter were to take up their abode in our cottage, at least for the present. In about an hour they both fell back in their chairs and appeared to sleep.

' "Marcella, dear, did you hear?" said my brother, in a low tone.

' "Yes," replied Marcella, in a whisper, "I heard all. Oh! brother, I cannot bear to look upon that woman – I feel so frightened."

'My brother made no reply, and shortly afterwards we were all three fast asleep.

'When we awoke the next morning, we found that the hunter's daughter had risen before us. I thought she looked more beautiful than ever. She came up to little Marcella and caressed her; the child burst into tears, and sobbed as if her heart would break.

'But not to detain you with too long a story, the huntsman and his daughter were accommodated in the cottage. My father and he went out hunting daily, leaving Christina with us. She performed all the household duties; was very kind to us children; and gradually the dislike even of little Marcella wore away. But a great change took place in my father; he appeared to have conquered his aversion to the sex, and was most attentive to Christina. Often, after her father and we were in bed, would he sit up with her, conversing in a low tone by the fire. I ought to have mentioned that my father and the huntsman Wilfred slept in another portion of the cottage, and that the bed which he formerly occupied, and which was in the same room as ours, had been given up to the use of Christina. These visitors had been about three weeks at the cottage, when, one night, after we children had been sent to bed, a consultation was held. My father had asked Christina in marriage, and had obtained both her own consent and that of Wilfred; after this, a conversation took place, which was, as nearly as I can recollect, as follows: –

' "You may take my child, Meinheer Krantz, and my blessing with her, and I shall then leave you and seek some other habitation – it matters little where."

' "Why not remain here, Wilfred?"

"No, no, I am called elsewhere; let that suffice, and ask no more questions. You have my child."

' "I thank you for her, and will duly value her; but there is one difficulty."

' "I know what you would say; there is no priest here in this wild country; true; neither is there any law to bind. Still must some ceremony pass between you, to satisfy a father. Will you consent to marry her after my fashion? if so, I will marry you directly."

' "I will," replied my father.

' "Then take her by the hand. Now, Meinheer, swear."

' "I swear," repeated my father. "'By all the spirits of the Hartz Mountains– "

' "Nay, why not by Heaven?" interrupted my father.

' "Because it is not my humour," rejoined Wilfred. "If I prefer that oath, less binding, perhaps, than another, surely you will not thwart me."

' "Well, be it so, then; have your humour. Will you make me swear by that in which I do not believe?"

' "Yet many do so, who in outward appearance are Christians," rejoined Wilfred; "say, will you be married, or shall I take my daughter away with me?"

' "Proceed," replied my father impatiently.

' "I swear by all the spirits of the Hartz Mountains, by all their power for good or for evil, that I take Christina for my wedded wife; that I will ever protect her, cherish her, and love her; that my hand shall never be raised against her to harm her."

'My father repeated the words after Wilfred.

' "And if I fail in this my vow, may all the vengeance of the spirits fall upon me and upon my children; may they perish by the vulture, by the wolf, or other beasts of the forest; may their flesh be torn from their limbs, and their bones blanch in the wilderness: all this I swear."

'My father hesitated, as he repeated the last words ; little Marcella could not restrain herself, and as my father repeated the last sentence, she burst into tears. This sudden interruption appeared to discompose the party, particularly my father; he spoke harshly to the child, who controlled her sobs, burying her face under the bedclothes.

'Such was the second marriage of my father. The next morning, the hunter Wilfred mounted his horse and rode away.

'My father resumed his bed, which was in the same room as ours; and things went on much as before the marriage, except that our new mother-in-law did not show any kindness towards us; indeed, during my father's absence, she would often beat us, particularly little Marcella, and her eyes would flash fire, as she looked eagerly upon the fair and lovely child.

'One night my sister awoke me and my brother.

' "What is the matter?" said Cæsar.

' "She has gone out," whispered Marcella.

' "Gone out!"

' "Yes, gone out at the door, in her night-clothes," replied the child; "I saw her get out of bed, look at my father to see if he slept, and then she went out at the door."

'What could induce her to leave her bed, and all undressed to go out, in such bitter wintry weather, with the snow deep on the ground, was to us incomprehensible; we lay awake, and in about an hour we heard the growl of a wolf close under the window.

' "There is a wolf," said Cæsar. "She will be torn to pieces."

' "Oh no!" cried Marcella.

'In a few minutes afterwards our mother-in-law appeared; she was in her night-dress, as Marcella had stated. She let down the latch of the door, so as to make no noise, went to a pail of water, and washed her face and hands, and then slipped into the bed where my father lay.

'We all three trembled – we hardly knew why; but we resolved to watch the next night. We did so; and not only on the ensuing night, but on many others, and always at about the same hour, would our mother-in-law rise from her bed and leave the cottage; and after she was gone we invariably heard the growl of a wolf under our window, and always saw her on her return wash herself before she retired to bed. We observed also that she seldom sat down to meals, and that when she did she appeared to eat with dislike; but when the meat was taken down to be prepared for dinner, she would often furtively put a raw piece into her mouth.

My brother Cæsar was a courageous boy; he did not like to speak to my father until he knew more. He resolved that he would follow her out, and ascertain what she did. Marcella and I endeavoured to dissuade him from the project; but he would not be controlled; and the very next night he lay down in his clothes, and as soon as our mother-in-law had left the cottage he jumped up, took down my father's gun, and followed her.

'You may imagine in what a state of suspense Marcella and I remained during his absence. After a few minutes we heard the report of a gun. It did not awaken my father; and we lay trembling with anxiety. In a minute afterwards we saw our mother-in-law enter the cottage – her dress was bloody. I put my hand to Marcella's mouth to prevent her crying out, although I was myself in great alarm. Our mother-in-law approached my father's bed, looked to see if he was asleep, and then went to the chimney and blew up the embers into a blaze.

' "Who is there?" said my father, waking up.

' "Lie still, dearest," replied my mother-in-law; "it is only me; I have lighted the fire to warm some water; I am not quite well."

'My father turned round, and was soon asleep; but we watched our mother-in-law. She changed her linen, and threw the garments she had worn into the fire; and we then perceived that her right leg was bleeding profusely, as if from a gunshot wound. She bandaged it up, and then dressing herself, remained before the fire until the break of day.

'Poor little Marcella, her heart beat quick as she pressed me to her side – so indeed did mine. Where was our brother Cæsar? How did my mother-in-law receive the wound unless from his gun? At last my father rose, and then for the first time I spoke, saying, "Father, where is my brother Cæsar?"

' "Your brother?" exclaimed he; "why, where can he be?"

' "Merciful Heaven! I thought as I lay very restless last night," observed our mother-in-law, "that I heard somebody open the latch of the door; and, dear me, husband, what has become of your gun?"

'My father cast his eyes up above the chimney, and perceived that his gun was missing. For a moment he looked perplexed; then, seizing a broad axe, he went out of the cottage without saying another word.

'He did not remain away from us long; in a few minutes he returned, bearing in his arms the mangled body of my poor brother; he laid it down, and covered up his face.

'My mother-in-law rose up, and looked at the body, while Marcella and I threw ourselves by its side, wailing and sobbing bitterly.

' "Go to bed again, children," said she sharply. "Husband," continued she, "your boy must have taken the gun down to shoot a wolf, and the animal has been too powerful for him. Poor boy! he has paid dearly for his rashness."

'My father made no reply. I wished to speak to tell all – but Marcella, who perceived my intention, held me by the arm, and looked at me so imploringly, that I desisted.

'My father, therefore, was left in his error; but Marcella and I, although we could not comprehend it, were conscious that our mother-in-law was in some way connected with my brother's death.

'That day my father went out and dug a grave; and when he laid the body in the earth, he piled up stones over it, so that the wolves should not be able to dig it up. The shock of this catastrophe was to my poor father very severe; for several days he never went to the chase, although at times he would utter bitter anathemas and vengeance against the wolves.

'But during this time of mourning on his part, my mother-in-law's nocturnal wanderings continued with the same regularity as before.

'At last my father took down his gun to repair to the forest; but he soon returned, and appeared much annoyed.

' "Would you believe it, Christina, that the wolves – perdition to the whole race! – have actually contrived to dig up the body of my poor boy, and now there is nothing left of him but his bones."

' "Indeed!" replied my mother-in-law. Marcella looked at me, and I saw in her intelligent eye all she would have uttered.

' "A wolf growls under our window every night, father," said I.

' "Ay, indeed! Why did you not tell me, boy? Wake me the next time you hear it."

'I saw my mother-in-law turn away; her eyes flashed fire, and she gnashed her teeth.

'My father went out again, and covered up with a larger pile of stones the little remains of my poor brother which the wolves had spared. Such was the first act of the tragedy.

'The spring now came on; the snow disappeared, and we were permitted to leave the cottage; but never would I quit for one moment my dear little sister, to whom, since the death of my brother, I was more ardently attached than ever; indeed, I was afraid to leave her alone with my mother-in-law, who appeared to have a particular pleasure in ill-treating the child. My father was now employed upon his little farm, and I was able to render him some assistance.

'Marcella used to sit by us while we were at work, leaving my mother-in-law alone in the cottage. I ought to observe that, as the spring advanced, so did my mother-in-law decrease her nocturnal rambles, and that we never heard the growl of the wolf under the window after I had spoken of it to my father.

'One day, when my father and I were in the field, Marcella being with us, my mother-in-law came out, saying that she was going into the forest to collect some herbs my father wanted, and that Marcella must go to the cottage and watch the dinner. Marcella went; and my mother-in-law soon disappeared in the forest, taking a direction quite contrary to that in which the cottage stood, and leaving my father and me, as it were, between her and Marcella.

'About an hour afterwards we were startled by shrieks from the cottage – evidently the shrieks of little Marcella. "Marcella has burnt herself, father," said I, throwing down my spade. My father threw down his, and we both hastened to the cottage. Before we could gain the door, out darted a large white wolf, which fled with the utmost celerity. My father had no weapon; he rushed into the cottage, and there saw poor little Marcella expiring. Her body was dreadfully mangled and the blood pouring from it had formed a large pool on the cottage floor. My father's first intention had been to seize his gun and pursue; but he was checked by this horrid spectacle; he knelt down by his dying child, and burst into tears. Marcella could just look kindly on us for a few seconds, and then her eyes were closed in death.

'My father and I were still hanging over my poor sister's body, when my mother-in-law came in. At the dreadful sight she expressed much concern; but she did not appear to recoil from the sight of blood, as most women do.

' "Poor child!" said she, "it must have been that great white wolf which passed me just now, and frightened me so. She's quite dead, Krantz."

' "I know it! – I know it!" cried my father, in agony.

'I thought my father would never recover from the effects of this second tragedy; he mourned bitterly over the body of his sweet child, and for several days would not consign it to its grave, although frequently requested by my mother-in-law to do so. At last he yielded, and dug a grave for her close by that of my poor brother, and took every precaution that the wolves should not violate her remains.

'I was now really miserable as I lay alone in the bed which I had formerly shared with my brother and sister. I could not help thinking that my mother-in-law was implicated in both their deaths, although I could not account for the manner; but I no longer felt afraid of her; my little heart was full of hatred and revenge.

'The night after my sister had been buried, as I lay awake, I perceived my mother-in-law get up and go out of the cottage. I waited some time, then dressed myself, and looked out through the door, which I half opened. The moon shone bright, and I could see the spot where my brother and my sister had been buried; and what was my horror when I perceived my mother-in-law busily removing the stones from Marcella's grave!

'She was in her white night-dress, and the moon shone full upon her. She was digging with her hands, and throwing away the stones behind her with all the ferocity of a wild beast. It was some time before I could collect my senses and decide what I should do. At last I perceived that she had arrived at the body, and raised it up to the side of the grave. I could bear it no longer: I ran to my father and awoke him.

"Father, father!" cried I, "dress yourself, and get your gun."

"What!" cried my father, "the wolves are there, are they?"

'He jumped out of bed, threw on his clothes, and in his anxiety did not appear to perceive the absence of his wife. As soon as he was ready I opened the door, he went out, and I followed him.

'Imagine his horror, when (unprepared as he was for such a sight) he beheld, as he advanced towards the grave, not a wolf, but his wife, in her night-dress, on her hands and knees, crouching by the body of my sister, and tearing off large pieces of the flesh, and devouring them with all the avidity of a wolf. She was too busy to be aware of our approach. My father dropped his gun; his hair stood on end, so did mine; he breathed heavily, and then his breath for a time stopped. I picked up the gun and put it into his hand. Suddenly he appeared as if concentrated rage had restored him to double vigour; he levelled his piece, fired, and with a loud shriek down fell the wretch whom he had fostered in his bosom.

' "God of heaven!" cried my father, sinking down upon the earth in a swoon, as soon as he had discharged his gun.

'I remained some time by his side before he recovered. "Where am I?" said he, "what has happened? Oh! – yes, yes! I recollect now. Heaven forgive me!"

'He rose and we walked up to the grave; what again was our astonishment and horror to find that, instead of the dead body of my mother-in-law, as we expected, there was lying over the remains of my poor sister a large white she-wolf.

' "The white wolf," exclaimed my father, "the white wolf which decoyed me into the forest – I see it all now – I have dealt with the spirits of the Hartz Mountains."

'For some time my father remained in silence and deep thought. He then carefully lifted up the body of my sister, replaced it in the grave, and covered it over as before, having struck the head of the dead animal with the heel of his boot, and raving like a madman. He walked back to the cottage, shut the door, and threw himself on the bed; I did the same, for I was in a stupor of amazement.

'Early in the morning we were both roused by a loud knocking at the door, and in rushed the hunter Wilfred.

' "My daughter – man – my daughter! – where is my daughter?" cried he in a rage.

' "Where the wretch, the fiend should be, I trust," replied my father, starting up, and displaying equal choler: "where she should be – in hell! Leave this cottage, or you may fare worse."

' "Ha – ha!" replied the hunter, "would you harm a potent spirit of the Hartz Mountains? Poor mortal, who must needs wed a werewolf."

' "Out, demon! I defy thee and thy power."

' "Yet shall you feel it; remember your oath – your solemn oath – never to raise your hand against her to harm her."

' "I made no compact with evil spirits."

' "You did, and if you failed in your vow, you were to meet the vengeance of the spirits. Your children were to perish by the vulture, the wolf— "

' "Out, out, demon!"

' "And their bones blanch in the wilderness. Ha – ha!"

'My father, frantic with rage, seized his axe and raised it over Wilfred's head to strike.

' "All this I swear," continued the huntsman mockingly.

'The axe descended; but it passed through the form of the hunter, and my father lost his balance, and fell heavily on the floor.

' "Mortal!" said the hunter, striding over my father's body, "we have power over those only who have committed murder. You have been guilty of a double murder: you shall pay the penalty attached to your marriage vow. Two of your children are gone, the third is yet to follow – and follow them he will, for your oath is registered. Go – it were kindness to kill thee – your punishment is, that you live!"

'With these words the spirit disappeared.

My father rose from the floor, embraced me tenderly, and knelt down in prayer.

'The next morning he quitted the cottage for ever. He took me with him, and bent his steps to Holland, where we safely arrived. He had some little money with him; but he had not been many days in Amsterdam before he was seized with a brain fever, and died raving mad. I was put into the asylum, and afterwards was sent to sea before the mast. You now know all my history. The question is, whether I am to pay the penalty of my father's oath? I am myself perfectly convinced that, in some way or another, I shall.'

II

On the twenty-second day the high land of the south of Sumatra was in view: as there were no vessels in sight, they resolved to keep their course through the Straits, and run for Pulo Penang, which they expected, as their vessel lay so close to the wind, to reach in seven or eight days. By constant exposure Philip and Krantz were now so bronzed, that with their long beards and Mussulman dresses, they might easily have passed off for natives. They had steered during the whole of the days exposed to a burning sun; they had lain down and slept in the dew of the night; but their health had not suffered. But for several days, since he had confided the history of his family to Philip, Krantz had become silent and melancholy; his usual flow of spirits had vanished, and Philip had often questioned him as to the cause. As they entered the Straits, Philip talked of what they should do upon their arrival at Goa; when Krantz gravely replied, 'For some days, Philip, I have had a presentiment that I shall never see that city.'

'You are out of health, Krantz,' replied Philip.

'No, I am in sound health, body and mind. I have endeavoured to shake off the presentiment but in vain; there is a warning voice that continually tells me that I shall not be long with you. Philip, will you oblige me by making me content on one point? I have gold about my person which may be useful to you; oblige me by taking it, and securing it on your own.'

'What nonsense, Krantz.'

'It is no nonsense, Philip. Have you not had your warnings? Why should I not have mine? You know that I have little fear in my composition, and that I care not about death; but I feel the presentiment which I speak of more strongly every hour. . . .'

'These are the imaginings of a disturbed brain, Krantz; why you, young, in full health and vigour, should not pass your days in peace, and live to a good old age, there is no cause for believing. You will be better tomorrow.'

'Perhaps so, replied Krantz; 'but still you must yield to my whim, and take the gold. If I am wrong, and we do arrive safe, you know, Philip, you can let me have it back,' observed Krantz, with a faint smile – 'but you forget, our water is nearly out, and we must look out for a rill on the coast to obtain a fresh supply.'

'I was thinking of that when you commenced this unwelcome topic. We had better look out for the water before dark, and as soon as we have replenished our jars, we will make sail again.'

At the time that this conversation took place, they were on the eastern side of the Strait, about forty miles to the northward. The interior of the coast was rocky and mountainous, but it slowly descended to low land of alternate forest and jungles, which continued to the beach; the country appeared to be uninhabited. Keeping close in to the shore, they discovered, after two hours' run, a fresh stream which burst in a cascade from the mountains, and swept its devious course through the jungle, until it poured its tribute into the waters of the Strait.

They ran close into the mouth of the stream, lowered the sails, and pulled the peroqua against the current, until they had advanced far enough to assure them that the water was quite fresh. The jars were soon filled, and they were again thinking of pushing off, when, enticed by the beauty of the spot, the coolness of the fresh water, and wearied with their long confinement on board of the peroqua, they proposed to bathe – a luxury hardly to be appreciated by those who have not been in a similar situation. They threw off their Mussulman dresses, and plunged into the stream, where they remained for some time. Krantz was the first to get out; he complained of feeling chilled, and he walked on to the banks where their clothes had been laid. Philip also approached nearer to the beach, intending to follow him.

'And now, Philip,' said Krantz, 'this will be a good opportunity for me to give you the money. I will open my sash and pour it out, and you can put it into your own before you put it on.'

Philip was standing in the water, which was about level with his waist.

'Well, Krantz,' said he, 'I suppose if it must be so, it must; but it appears to me an idea so ridiculous – however, you shall have your own way.'

Philip quitted the run, and sat down by Krantz, who was already busy in shaking the doubloons out of the folds of his sash; at last he said –

'I believe, Philip, you have got them all, now? – I feel satisfied.'

'What danger there can be to you, which I am not equally exposed to, I cannot conceive,' replied Philip; 'however— '

Hardly had he said these words, when there was a tremendous roar – a rush like a mighty wind through the air – a blow which threw him on his back – a loud cry – and a contention. Philip recovered himself, and perceived the naked form of Krantz carried off with the speed of an arrow by an enormous tiger through the jungle. He watched with distended eyeballs; in a few seconds the animal and Krantz had disappeared.

'God of heaven! would that thou hadst spared me this,' cried Philip, throwing himself down in agony on his face. 'O Krantz! my friend – my brother – too sure was your presentiment. Merciful God! have pity – but Thy will be done;' and Philip burst into a flood of tears.

For more than an hour did he remain fixed upon the spot, careless and indifferent to the danger by which he was surrounded. At last, somewhat recovered, he rose, dressed himself, and then again sat down – his eyes fixed upon the clothes of Krantz, and the gold which still lay on the sand.

'He would give me that gold. He foretold his doom. Yes! yes! it was his destiny, and it has been fulfilled. *His bones will bleach in the wilderness*, and the spirit-hunter and his wolfish daughter are avenged.'

Transformation

MARY SHELLEY

I have heard it said, that, when any strange, supernatural, and necromantic adventure has occurred to a human being, that being, however desirous he may be to conceal the same, feels at certain periods torn up as it were by intellectual earthquake and is forced to bare the inner depths of his spirit to another. I am a witness of the truth of this. I have dearly sworn to myself never to reveal to human ears the horrors to which I once, in excess of friendly pride, delivered myself over. The holy man who heard my confession, and reconciled me to the church, is dead. None knows that once –

Why should it not be thus? Why tell a tale of impious tempting of Providence, and soul-subduing humiliation? Why? answer me, ye who are wise in the secrets of human nature! I only know that so it is; and in spite of strong resolve – of a pride that too much masters me – of shame, and even of fear, so to render myself odious to my species – I must speak.

Genoa! my birthplace – proud city looking upon the blue Mediterranean – dost thou remember me in my boyhood, when thy cliffs and promontories, thy bright sky and gay vineyards, were my world? Happy time! when to the young heart the narrow-bounded universe, which leaves, by its very limitation, free scope to the imagination, enchains our physical energies, and, sole period in our lives, innocence and enjoyment are united. Yet, who can look back to childhood, and not remember its sorrows and its harrowing fears? I was born with the most imperious, haughty, tameless spirit. I quailed before my father only; and he, generous and noble, but capricious and tyrannical, at once fostered and checked the wild impetuosity of my character, making obedience necessary, but inspiring no respect for the motives which guided his commands. To be a man, free, independent; or, in better words, insolent and domineering, was the hope and prayer of my rebel heart.

My father had one friend, a wealthy Genoese noble, who in a political tumult was suddenly sentenced to banishment, and his property confiscated. The Marchese Torella went into exile alone. Like my father, he was a widower: he had one child, the almost infant Juliet, who was left under my father's guardianship. I should certainly have been unkind to the lovely girl, but that I was forced by my position to become her protector. A variety of childish incidents all tended to one point – to make Juliet see in me a rock of defence; I in her, one who must perish through the soft sensibility of her nature too rudely visited, but for my guardian care. We grew up together. The opening rose in May was not more sweet than this dear girl. An irradiation of beauty was spread over her face. Her form, her step, her voice – my heart weeps even now, to think of all of relying, gentle, loving, and pure, that she enshrined. When I was eleven and Juliet eight years of age, a cousin of mine, much older than either – he seemed to us a man – took great notice of my playmate; he called her his bride, and asked her to marry him. She refused, and he insisted, drawing her unwillingly towards him. With the countenance and emotions of a maniac I threw myself on him – I strove to draw his sword – I clung to his neck with the ferocious resolve to strangle him: he was obliged to call for assistance to disengage himself from me. On that night I led Juliet to the chapel of our house: I made her touch the sacred relics – I harrowed her child's heart, and profaned her child's lips with an oath, that she, would be mine, and mine only.

Well, those days passed away. Torella returned in a few years, and became wealthier and more prosperous than ever. When I was seventeen, my father died; he had been magnificent to prodigality; Torella rejoiced that my minority would afford an opportunity of repairing my fortunes. Juliet and I had been affianced beside my father's deathbed – Torella was to be a second parent to me.

I desired to see the world, and I was indulged. I went to Florence, to Rome, to Naples; thence I passed to Toulon, and at length reached what had long been a bourne of my wishes, Paris. There was wild work in Paris then. The poor king, Charles the Sixth, now sane, now mad, now a monarch, now an abject slave, was the very mockery of humanity. The queen, the dauphin, the Duke of Burgundy, alternately friends and foes – now meeting in prodigal feasts, now shedding blood in rivalry – were blind to the miserable state of their country, and the dangers that impended over it, and gave themselves wholly up to dissolute enjoyment or savage strife. My character still followed me. I was arrogant and self-willed; I loved display, and above all, I threw off all control. My young friends were eager to foster passions which furnished them with pleasures. I was deemed handsome – I was master of every knightly accomplishment. I was disconnected with any political party. I grew a favourite with all: my presumption and arrogance was pardoned in one so young: I became a spoiled child. Who could control me? not the letters and advice of Torella – only strong necessity visiting me in the abhorred shape of an empty purse. But there were means to refill this void. Acre after acre, estate after estate, I sold. My dress, my jewels, my horses and their caparisons, were almost unrivalled in gorgeous Paris, while the lands of my inheritance passed into possession of others.

The Duke of Orleans was waylaid and murdered by the Duke of Burgundy! Fear and tenor possessed all Paris. The dauphin and the queen shut themselves up; every pleasure was suspended. I grew weary of this state of things, and my heart yearned for my boyhood's haunts. I was nearly a beggar, yet still I would go there, claim my bride, and rebuild my fortunes. A few happy ventures as a merchant would make me rich again. Nevertheless, I would not return in humble guise. My last act was to dispose of my remaining estate near Albaro for half its worth, for ready money. Then I dispatched all kinds of artificers, arras, furniture to regal splendour, to fit up the last relic of my inheritance, my palace in Genoa. I lingered a little longer yet, ashamed at the part of the prodigal returned, which I feared I should play. I sent my horses. One matchless Spanish jannet I dispatched to my promised bride: its caparisons flamed with jewels and cloth of gold. In every part I caused to be entwined the initials of Juliet and her Guido. My present found favour in hers and in her father's eyes.

Still to return a proclaimed spendthrift, the mark of impertinent wonder, perhaps of scorn, and to encounter singly the reproaches or taunts of my fellow-citizens, was no alluring prospect. As a shield between me and censure, I invited some few of the most reckless of my comrades to accompany me: thus I went armed against the world, hiding a rankling feeling, half and half penitence, by bravado.

I arrived in Genoa. I trod the pavement of my ancestral palace. My proud step was no interpreter of my heart, for I deeply felt that, though surrounded by every luxury, I was a beggar. The first step I took in claiming Juliet must widely declare me such. I read contempt or pity in the looks of all. I fancied that rich and poor, young and old, all regarded me with derision. Torella came not near me. No wonder that my second father should expect a son's deference from me in waiting first on him. But, galled and stung by a sense of my follies and demerit, I strove to throw the blame on others. We kept nightly orgies in Palazzo Carega. To sleepless, riotous nights followed listless, supine mornings. At the Ave Maria we showed our dainty persons in the streets, scoffing at the sober citizens, casting insolent glances on the shrinking women. Juliet was not among them – no, no; if she had been there, shame would have driven me away, if love had not brought me to her feet.

I grew tired of this. Suddenly I paid the Marchese a visit. He was at his villa, one among the many which deck the suburb of San Pietro d'Arena. It was the month of May, the blossoms of the fruit-trees were fading among thick, green foliage; the vines were shooting forth; the ground strewed with the fallen olive blooms; the firefly was in the myrtle hedge; heaven and earth wore a mantle of surpassing beauty. Torella welcomed me kindly, though seriously; and even his shade of displeasure soon wore away. Some resemblance to my father – some look and tone of youthful ingenuousness, softened the good old man's heart. He sent for his daughter – he presented me to her as her betrothed. The chamber became hallowed by a holy light as she entered. Hers was that cherub look, those large, soft eyes, full dimpled cheeks, and mouth of infantine sweetness, that expresses the rare union of happiness and love. Admiration first possessed me; she is mine! was the second proud emotion, and my lips curled with haughty triumph. I had not been the *enfant gate* of the beauties of France not to have learnt the art of pleasing the soft heart of woman. If towards men I was overbearing, the deference I paid to them was more in contrast. I commenced my courtship by the display of a thousand gallantries to Juliet, who, vowed to me from infancy, had never admitted the devotion of others; and who, though accustomed to expressions of admiration, was uninitiated in the language of lovers.

For a few days all went well. Torella never alluded to my extravagance; he treated me as a favourite son. But the time came, as we discussed the preliminaries to my union with his daughter, when this fair face of things should be overcast. A contract had been drawn up in my father's lifetime. I had rendered this, in fact, void by having squandered the whole of the wealth which was to have been shared by Juliet and myself. Torella, in consequence, chose to consider this bond as cancelled, and proposed another, in which, though the wealth he bestowed was immeasurably increased, there were so many restrictions as to the mode of spending it, that I, who saw independence only in free career being given to my own imperious will, taunted him as taking advantage of my situation, and refused utterly to subscribe to his conditions. The old man mildly strove to recall me to reason. Roused pride became the tyrant of my thought: I listened with indignation – I repelled him with disdain.

'Juliet, thou art mine! Did we not interchange vows in our innocent childhood? Are we not one in the sight of God? and shall thy cold-hearted, cold-blooded father divide us? Be generous, my love, be just; take not away a gift, last treasure of thy Guido – retract not thy vows – let us defy the world, and, setting at nought the calculations of age, find in our mutual affection a refuge from every ill.'

Fiend I must have been with such sophistry to endeavour to poison that sanctuary of holy thought and tender love. Juliet shrank from me affrighted. Her father was the best and kindest of men, and she strove to show me how, in obeying him, every good would follow. He would receive my tardy submission with warm affection, and generous pardon would follow my repentance – profitless words for a young and gentle daughter to use to a man accustomed to make his will law, and to feel in his own heart a despot so terrible and stern that he could yield obedience to nought save his own imperious desires! My resentment grew with resistance; my wild companions were ready to add fuel to the flame. We laid a plan to carry off Juliet. At first it appeared to be crowned with success. Midway, on our return, we were overtaken by the agonized father and his attendants. A conflict ensued. Before the city guard came to decide the victory in favour of our antagonists, two of Torella's servitors were dangerously wounded.

This portion of my history weighs most heavily with me. Changed man as I am, I abhor myself in the recollection. May none who hear this tale ever have felt as I. A horse driven to fury by a rider armed with barbed spurs was not more a slave than I to the violent tyranny of my temper. A fiend possessed my soul, irritating it to madness. I felt the voice of conscience within me; but if I yielded to it for a brief interval, it was only to be a moment after torn, as by a whirlwind, away – borne along on the stream of desperate rag – the plaything of the storms engendered by pride. I was imprisoned, and, at the instance of Torella, set free. Again, I returned to carry off both him and his child to France, which hapless country, then preyed on by freebooters and gangs of lawless soldiery, offered a grateful refuge to a criminal like me. Our plots were discovered. I was sentenced to banishment; and, as my debts were already enormous, my remaining property was put in the hands of commissioners for their payment. Torella again offered his mediation, requiring only my promise not to renew my abortive attempts on himself and his daughter. I spurned his offers, and fancied that I triumphed when I was thrust out from Genoa, a solitary and penniless exile. My companions were gone: they had been dismissed from the city some weeks before, and were already in France. I was alone – friendless, with neither sword at my side, nor ducat in my purse.

I wandered along the sea-shore, a whirlwind of passion possessing and tearing my soul. It was as if a live coal had been set burning in my breast. At first I meditated on what *I should do*. I would join a band of freebooters. Revenge! – the word seemed balm to me; I hugged it, caressed it, till, like a serpent, it stung me. Then again I would abjure and despise Genoa, that little corner of the world. I would return to Paris, where so many of my friends swarmed; where my services would be eagerly accepted; where I would carve out a fortune with my sword, and make my paltry birthplace and the false Torella rue the day when they drove me, a new Coriolanus, from her walls. I would return to Paris – thus on foot – a beggar – and present myself in my poverty to those I had formerly entertained sumptuously? There was gall in the mere thought of it.

The reality of things began to dawn upon my mind, bringing despair in its train. For several months I had been a prisoner: the evils of my dungeon had whipped my soul to madness, but they subdued my corporeal frame. I was weak and wan. Torella had used a thousand artifices to administer to my comfort; I had detected and scorned them all, and I reaped the harvest of my obduracy. What was to be done? Should I crouch before my foe, and sue for forgiveness? – Die rather ten thousand deaths! – Never should they obtain that victory! Hate – I swore eternal hate! Hate from whom? – to whom! – From a wandering outcast – to a mighty noble! I and my feelings were nothing to them: already had they forgotten one so unworthy. And Juliet! – her angel face and sylph-like form gleamed among the clouds of my despair with vain beauty; for I had lost her – the glory and flower of the world! Another will call her his! – that smile of paradise will bless another!

Even now my heart fails within me when I recur to this rout of grimvisaged ideas. Now subdued almost to tears, now raving in my agony, still I wandered along the rocky shore, which grew at each step wilder and more desolate. Hanging rocks and hoar precipices overlooked the tideless ocean; black caverns yawned; and for ever, among the seaworn recesses, murmured and dashed the unfruitful waters. Now my way was almost barred by an abrupt promontory, now rendered nearly impracticable by fragments fallen from the cliff. Evening was at hand, when, seaward, arose, as if on the waving of a wizard's wand, a murky web of clouds, blotting the late azure sky, and darkening and disturbing the till now placid deep. The clouds had strange, fantastic shapes, and they changed and mingled and seemed to be driven about by a mighty spell. The waves raised their white crests; the thunder first muttered, then roared from across the waste of waters, which took a deep purple dye, flecked with foam. The spot where I stood looked, on one side, to the widespread ocean; on the other, it was barred by a rugged promontory. Round this cape suddenly came, driven by the wind, a vessel. In vain the mariners tried to force a path for her to the open sea – the gale drove her on the rocks. It will perish! – all on board will perish! Would I were among them! And to my young heart the idea of death came for the first time blended with that of joy. It was an awful sight to behold that vessel struggling with her fate. Hardly could I discern the sailors, but I heard them. It was soon all over! A rock, just covered by the tossing waves, and so unperceived, lay in wait for its prey. A crash of thunder broke over my head at the moment that, with a frightful shock, the vessel dashed upon her unseen enemy. In a brief space of time she went to pieces. There I stood in safety; and there were my fellow-creatures battling, how hopelessly, with annihilation. Methought I saw them struggling – too truly did I hear their shrieks, conquering the barking surges in their shrill agony. The dark breakers threw hither and thither the fragments of the wreck: soon it disappeared. I had been fascinated to gaze till the end: at last I sank on my knees – I covered my face with my hands. I again looked up; something was floating on the billows towards the shore. It neared and neared. Was that a human form? It grew more and more distinct; and at last a mighty wave, lifting the whole freight, lodged it upon a rock. A human being bestriding a sea chest! – a human being! Yet was it one? Surely never such had existed before – a misshapen dwarf, with squinting eyes, distorted features, and body deformed, till it became a horror to behold. My blood, lately warming towards a fellow – being so snatched from a watery tomb, froze in my heart. The dwarf got off his chest; lie tossed his straight, struggling hair from his odious visage.

'By St Beelzebub!' he exclaimed, 'I have been well bested.' He looked round and saw me. 'Oh, by the fiend! here is another ally of the mighty One. To what saint did you offer prayers, friend – if not to mine? Yet I remember you not on board.'

I shrank from the monster and his blasphemy. Again he questioned me, and I muttered some inaudible reply. He continued:

'Your voice is drowned by this dissonant roar. What a noise the big ocean makes! Schoolboys bursting from the prison are not louder than these waves set free to play. They disturb me. I will no more of their ill-timed brawling. Silence, hoary One! – Winds, avaunt! – to your homes! – Clouds, fly to the antipodes, and leave our heaven clear!'

As he spoke, he stretched out his two long, lank arms, that looked like spider's claws and seemed to embrace with them the expanse before him. Was it a miracle? The clouds became broken and fled; the azure sky first peeped out, and then was spread a calm field of blue above us; the stormy gale was exchanged to the softly breathing west; the sea grew calm; the waves dwindled to riplets.

'I like obedience even in these stupid elements,' said the dwarf. 'How much more in the tameless mind of man! It was a well-got-up storm, you must allow – and all of my own making.'

It was tempting Providence to interchange talk with this magician. But *Power*, in all its shapes, is respected by man. Awe, curiosity, a clinging fascination, drew me towards him.

'Come, don't be frightened, friend,' said the wretch: 'I am good humoured when pleased; and something does please me in your well-proportioned body and handsome face, though you look a little woebegone. You have suffered a land – I, a sea wreck. Perhaps I can allay the tempest of your fortunes as I did my own. Shall we be friends?' – And he held out his hand; I could not touch it. 'Well, then, companions – that will do as well. And now, while I rest after the buffeting I underwent just now, tell me why, young and gallant as you seem, you wander thus alone and downcast on this wild sea-shore.'

The voice of the wretch was screeching and horrid, and his contortions as he spoke were frightful to behold. Yet he did gain a kind of influence over me, which I could not master, and I told him my tale. When it was ended, he laughed long and loud: the rocks echoed back the sound: hell seemed yelling around me.

'Oh, thou cousin of Lucifer!' said he; 'so thou too hast fallen through thy pride; and, though bright as the son of Morning, thou art ready to give up thy good looks, thy bride, and thy well-being, rather than submit thee to the tyranny of good. I honour thy choice, by my soul! – So thou hast fled, and yield the day; and mean to starve on these rocks, and to let the birds peck out thy dead eyes, while thy enemy and thy bethrothed rejoice in thy ruin. Thy pride is strangely akin to humility, methinks.'

As he spoke, a thousand fanged thoughts stung me to the heart.

'What would you that I should do?' I cried.

'I! – Oh, nothing, but lie down and say your prayers before you die. But, were I you, I know the deed that should be done.'

I drew near him. His supernatural powers made him an oracle in my eyes; yet a strange unearthly thrill quivered through my frame as I said, 'Speak! – teach me – what act do you advise?'

'Revenge thyself, man! – humble thy enemies! – set thy foot on the old man's neck, and possess thyself of his daughter!'

'To the east and west I turn,' cried I, 'and see no means! Had I gold, much could I achieve; but, poor and single, I am powerless.'

The dwarf had been seated on his chest as he listened to my story. Now he got off; he touched a spring; it flew open! What a mine of wealth – of blazing jewels, beaming gold, and pale silver was displayed therein. A mad desire to possess this treasure was born within me.

'Doubtless,' I said, 'one so powerful as you could do all things.'

'Nay,' said the monster humbly, 'I am less omnipotent than I seem. Some things I possess which you may covet; but I would give them all for a small share, or even for a loan of what is yours.'

'My possessions are at your service,' I replied bitterly – 'my poverty, my exile, my disgrace – I make a free gift of them all.'

'Good! I thank you. Add one other thing to your gift, and my treasure is yours.'

'As nothing is my sole inheritence, what besides nothing would you have?'

'Your comely face and well-made limbs.'

I shivered. Would this all-powerful monster murder me? I had no dagger. I forgot to pray – but I grew pale.

'I ask for a loan, not a gift,' said the frightful thing: 'lend me your body for three days – you shall have mine to cage your soul the while, and in payment, my chest. What say you to the bargain? – Three short days.'

We are told that it is dangerous to hold unlawful talk; and well do I prove the same. Tamely written down, it may seem incredible that I should lend any ear to this proposition; but, in spite of his unnatural ugliness, there was something fascinating in a being whose voice could govern earth, air, and sea. I felt a keen desire to comply; for with that chest I could command the world. My only hesitation resulted from a fear that he would not be true to this bargain. Then I thought, I shall soon die here on these lonely sands, and the limbs he covets will be mine no more – it is worth the chance. And, besides, I knew that, by all the rules of art-magic, there were formula and oaths which none of its practisers dared break. I hesitated to reply; and he went on, now displaying his wealth, now speaking of the petty price he demanded, till it seemed madness to refuse. Thus is it – place our bark in the current of the stream, and down, over fall and cataract it is hurried; give up our conduct to the wild torrent of passion, and we are away, we know not whither.

He swore many an oath, and I adjured him by many a sacred name; till I saw this wonder of power, this ruler of the elements, shiver like an autumn leaf before my words; and as if the spirit spake unwillingly and perforce within him, at last, he, with broken voice, revealed the spell whereby he might be obliged, did he wish to play me false, to render up the unlawful spoil. Our warm life-blood must mingle to make and to mar the charm.

Enough of this unholy theme. I was persuaded – the thing was done. The morrow dawned upon me as I lay upon the shingles, and I knew not my own shadow as it fell from me. I felt myself changed to a shape of horror, and cursed my easy faith and blind credulity. The chest was there – there the gold and precious stones for which I had sold the frame of flesh which nature had given me. The sight a little stilled my emotions: three days would soon be gone.

They did pass. The dwarf had supplied me with a plenteous store of food. At first I could hardly walk, so strange and out of joint were all my limbs; and my voice – it was that of the fiend. But I kept silent, and turned my face to the sun, that I might not see my shadow, and counted the hours, and ruminated on my future conduct. To bring Torella to my feet – to possess my Juliet in spite of him – all this my wealth could easily achieve. During dark night I slept, and dreamt of the accomplishment of my desires. Two suns had set – the third dawned. I was agitated, fearful. Oh expectation, what a frightful thing art thou, when kindled more by fear than hope! How dost thou twist thyself round the heart, torturing its pulsations! How dost thou dart unknown pangs all through our feeble mechanism, now seeming to shiver us like broken glass, to nothingness – now giving us afresh strength, which can *do* nothing, and so torments us by a sensation, such as the strong man must feel who cannot break his fetters, though they bend in his grasp. Slowly paced the bright, bright orb up the eastern sky; long it lingered in the zenith, and still more slowly wandered down the west: it touched the horizon's verge – it was lost! Its glories were on the summits of the cliff – they grew dun and grey. The evening star shone bright. He will soon be here.

He came not! – By the living heavens, he came not! – and night dragged out its weary length, and, in its decaying age, 'day began to grizzle its dark hair'; and the sun rose again on the most miserable wretch that ever upbraided its light. Three days thus I passed. The jewels and the gold – oh, how I abhorred them!

Well, well – I will not blacken these pages with demoniac ravings. All too terrible were the thoughts, the raging tumult of ideas that filled my soul. At the end of that time I slept; I had not before since the third sunset; and I dreamt that I was at Juliet's feet, and she smiled, and then she shrieked – for she saw my transformation – and again she smiled, for still her beautiful lover knelt before her. But it was not I – it was he, the fiend, arrayed in my limbs, speaking with my voice, winning her with my looks of love. I strove to warn her, but my tongue refused its office; I strove to tear him from her, but I was rooted to the ground – I awoke with the agony. There were the solitary hoar precipices – there the splashing sea, the quiet strand, and the blue sky over all. What did it mean? was my dream but a mirror of the truth? was he wooing and winning my betrothed? I would on the instant back to Genoa – but I was banished. I laughed – the dwarf's yell burst from my lips – I banished! Oh no! they had not exiled the foul limbs I wore; I might with these enter, without fear of incurring the threatened penalty of death, my own, my native city.

I began to walk towards Genoa. I was somewhat accustomed to my distorted limbs; none were ever so ill-adapted for a straightforward movement; it was with infinite difficulty that I proceeded. Then, too, I desired to avoid all the hamlets strewed here and there on the sea-beach, for I was unwilling to make a display of my hideousness. I was not quite sure that, if seen, the mere boys would not stone me to death as I passed, for a monster; some ungentle salutations I did receive from the few peasants or fishermen I chanced to meet. But it was dark night before I approached Genoa. The weather was so balmy and sweet that it struck me that the Marchese and his daughter would very probably have quitted the city for their country retreat. It was from Villa Torella that I had attempted to carry off Juliet; I had spent many an hour reconnoitring the spot, and knew each inch of ground in its vicinity. It was beautifully situated, embosomed in trees, on the margin of a stream. As I drew near, it became evident that my conjecture was right; nay, moreover, that the hours were being then devoted to feasting and merriment. For the house was lighted up; strains of soft and gay music were wafted towards me by the breeze. My heart sank within me. Such was the generous kindness of Torella's heart that I felt sure that he would not have indulged in public manifestations of rejoicing just after my unfortunate banishment, but for a cause I dared not dwell upon.

The country people were all alive and flocking about; it became necessary that I should conceal myself; and yet I longed to address some one, or to hear others discourse, or in any way to gain intelligence of what was really going on. At length, entering the walks that were in immediate vicinity to the mansion, I found one dark enough to veil my excessive frightfulness; and yet others as well as I were loitering in its shade. I soon gathered all I wanted to know – all that first made my very heart die with horror, and then boil with indignation. Tomorrow Juliet was to be given to the penitent, reformed, beloved Guido – tomorrow my bride was to pledge her vows to a fiend from hell! And I did this! – my accursed pride – my demoniac violence and wicked self-idolatry had caused this act. For if I had acted as the wretch who had stolen my form had acted – if, with a mien at once yielding and dignified, I had presented myself to Torella, saying, I have done wrong, forgive me; I am unworthy of your angel-child, but permit me to claim her hereafter, when my altered conduct shall manifest that I abjure my vices, and endeavour to become in some sort worthy of her. I go to serve against the infidels; and when my zeal for religion and my true penitence for the past shall appear to you to cancel my crimes, permit me again to call myself your son. Thus had he spoken; and the penitent was welcomed even as the prodigal son of Scripture: the fatted calf was killed for him; and he, still pursuing the same path, displayed such open-hearted regret for his follies, so humble a concession of all his rights, and so ardent a resolve to reacquire them by a life of contrition and virtue, that he quickly conquered the kind old man; and full pardon, and the gift of his lovely child, followed in swift succession.

Oh, had an angel from Paradise whispered to me to act thus! But now, what would be the innocent Juliet's fate? Would God permit the foul union – or, some prodigy destroying it, link the dishonoured name of Carega with the worst of crimes? Tomorrow at dawn they were to be married: there was but one way to prevent this – to meet mine enemy, and to enforce the ratification of our agreement. I felt that this could only be done by a mortal struggle. I had no sword – if indeed my distorted arms could wield a soldier's weapon – but I had a dagger, and in that lay my hope. There was no time for pondering or balancing nicely the question: I might die in the attempt; but besides the burning jealousy and despair of my own heart, honour, mere humanity, demanded that I should fall rather than not destroy the machinations of the fiend.

The guests departed – the lights began to disappear; it was evident that the inhabitants of the villa were seeking repose. I hid myself among the trees – the garden grew deserted – the gates were closed – I wandered round and came upon a window – ah! well did I know the same! – a soft twilight glimmered in the room – the curtains were half withdrawn. It was the temple of innocence and beauty. Its magnificence was tempered, as it were, by the slight disarrangements occasioned by its being dwelt in, and all the objects scattered around displayed the taste of her who hallowed it by her presence. I saw her enter with a quick light step – I saw her approach the window – she drew back the curtain yet further, and looked out into the night. Its breezy freshness played among her ringlets, and wafted them from the transparent marble of her brow. She clasped her hands, she raised her eyes to heaven. I heard her voice. Guido! she softly murmured – mine own Guido! and then, as if overcome by the fullness of her own heart, she sank on her knees; – her upraised eyes – her graceful attitude – the beaming thankfulness that lighted up her face – oh, these are tame words! Heart of mine, thou imagest ever, though thou canst not portray, the celestial beauty of that child of light and love.

I heard a step – a quick firm step along the shady avenue. Soon I saw a cavalier, richly dressed, young and, methought, graceful to look on, advance. I hid myself yet closer. The youth approached; he paused beneath the window. She arose, and again looking out she saw him, and said – I cannot, no, at this distant time I cannot record her terms of soft silver tenderness; to me they were spoken, but they were replied to by him.

'I will not go,' he cried: 'here where you have been, where your memory glides like some heaven-visiting ghost, I will pass the long hours till we meet, never, my Juliet, again, day or night, to part. But do thou, my love, retire; the cold morn and fitfull breeze will make thy cheek pale, and fill with languor thy love-lighted eyes. Ah, sweetness! could I press one kiss upon them, I could, methinks, repose.'

And then he approached still nearer, and methought he was about to clamber into her chamber. I had hesitated, not to terrify her; now I was no longer master of myself. I rushed forward – I threw myself on him – I tore him away – I cried, 'O loathsome and foul-shaped wretch!'

I need not repeat epithets, all tending, as it appeared, to rail at a person I at present feel some partiality for. A shriek rose from Juliet's lips. I neither heard nor saw – I *felt* only mine enemy, whose throat I grasped, and my dagger's hilt;

he struggled, but could not escape. At length hoarsely he breathed these words: 'Do! – strike home! destroy this body – you will still live: may your life be long and merry!'

The descending dagger was arrested at the word, and he, feeling my hold relax, extricated himself and drew his sword, while the uproar in the house, and flying of torches from one room to the other, showed that soon we should be separated. In the midst of my frenzy there was much calculation – fall I might, and so that he did not survive, I cared not for the death-blow I might deal against myself. While still, therefore, he thought I paused, and while I saw the villainous resolve to take advantage of my hesitation, in the sudden thrust he made at me, I threw myself on his sword, and at the same moment plunged my dagger, with a true, desperate aim, in his side. We fell together, rolling over each other, and the tide of blood that flowed from the gaping wound of each mingled on the grass. More I know not – I fainted.

Again I returned to life: weak almost to death, I found myself stretched upon a bed – Juliet was kneeling beside it. Strange! my first broken request was for a mirror. I was so wan and ghastly, that my poor girl hesitated, as she told me afterwards; but, by the mass! I thought myself a right proper youth when I saw the dear reflection of my own well-known features. I confess it is a weakness, but I avow it, I do entertain a considerable affection for the countenance and limbs I behold, whenever I look at a glass; and have more mirrors in my house, and consult them oftener, than any beauty in Genoa. Before you too much condemn me, permit me to say that no one better knows than I the value of his own body; no one, probably, except myself, ever having had it stolen from him.

Incoherently I at first talked of the dwarf and his crimes, and reproached Juliet for her admission of his love. She thought me raving, as well she might; and yet it was some time before I could prevail on myself to admit that the Guido whose penitence had won her back for me was myself; and while I cursed bitterly the monstrous dwarf, and blest the well-directed blow that had deprived him of life, I suddenly checked myself when I heard her say, Amen! knowing that him whom she reviled was my very self. A little reflection taught me silence – a little practice enabled me to speak of that frightful night without any very excessive blunder. The wound I had given myself was no mockery of one – it was long before I recovered – and as the benevolent and generous Torella sat beside me, talking such wisdom as might win friends to repentance, and mine own dear Juliet hovered near me, administered to my wants, and cheering me by her smiles, the work of my bodily cure and mental reform went on together. I have never, indeed, wholly recovered my strength – my cheek is paler since – my person a little bent. Juliet sometimes ventures to allude bitterly to the malice that caused this change, but I kiss her on the moment, and tell her all is for the best. I am a fonder and more faithful husband, and true is this – but for that wound, never had I called her mine.

I did not revisit the sea-shore, nor seek for the fiend's treasure; yet, while I ponder on the past, I often think, and my confessor was not backward in favouring the idea, that it might be a good rather than an evil spirit, sent by my guardian angel, to show me the folly and misery of pride. So well at least did I learn this lesson, roughly taught as I was, that I am known by all my friends and fellow-citizens by the name of Guido il Cortese.

The Queen of Spades

Alexander Pushkin

I

When bleak was the weather
They would meet together
For cards – God forgive them!
Some would win, others lost,
And they chalked up the cost
In bleak autumn weather
When they met together.

There was a card party in the rooms of Narumov, an officer of the Horse Guards. The long winter night had passed unnoticed and it was after four in the morning when the company sat down to supper. Those who had won enjoyed their food; the others sat absent-mindedly in front of empty plates. But when the champagne appeared conversation became more lively and general.

'How did you fare, Surin?' Narumov asked.

'Oh I lost, as usual. I must confess, I have no luck: I stick to *mirandole*, never get excited, never lose my head, and yet I never win.'

'Do you mean to tell me you were not once tempted to back the red the whole evening? Your self-control amazes me.'

'But look at Hermann,' exclaimed one of the party, pointing to a young officer of the Engineers. 'Never held a card in his hands, never made a bet in his life, and yet he sits up till five in the morning watching us play.'

'Cards interest me very much,' said Hermann, 'but I am not in a position to risk the necessary in the hope of acquiring the superfluous.'

'Hermann is a German: he's careful, that's what that is!' remarked Tomsky. 'But if there is one person I can't understand it is my grandmother, Countess Anna Fedotovna.'

'Why is that?' the guests cried.

'I cannot conceive how it is that my grandmother does not play.'

'But surely there is nothing surprising in an old lady in her eighties not wanting to gamble?' said Narumov.

'Then you don't know about her?'

'No, nothing, absolutely nothing!'

'Well, listen then. I must tell you that some sixty years ago my grandmother went to Paris and was quite the rage there. People would run after her to catch a glimpse of *la Vénus moscovite*; Richelieu was at her beck and call, and grandmamma maintains that he very nearly blew his brains out because of her cruelty to him. In those days ladies used to play faro. One evening at the Court she lost a very considerable sum to the Duke of Orleans. When she got home she told my grandfather of her loss while removing the beauty spots from her face and untying her farthingale, and commanded him to pay her debt. My grandfather, so far as I remember, acted as a sort of major-domo to my grandmother. He feared her like fire; however, when he heard of such a frightful gambling loss he almost went out of his mind, fetched the bills they owed and pointed out to her that in six months they had spent half a million roubles and that in Paris they had neither their Moscow nor their Saratov estates upon which to draw, and flatly refused to pay. Grandmamma gave him a box on the ear and retired to bed without him as a sign of her displeasure. The following morning she sent for her husband, hoping that the simple punishment had had its effect, but she found him as obdurate as ever. For the first time in her life she went so far as to reason with him and explain, thinking to rouse his conscience and arguing with condescension, that there were debts and debts, and that a prince was different from a coach-builder. But it was not a bit of good – grandfather just would not hear of it. "Once and for all, no!" Grandmamma did not know what to do. Among her close acquaintances was a very remarkable man. You have heard of Count Saint-Germain, about whom so many marvellous stories are told. You know that he posed as the Wandering Jew and claimed to have discovered the elixir of life and the philosopher's stone, and so on. People laughed at him as a charlatan, and Casanova in his *Memoirs* says that he was a spy. Be that as it may, Saint-Germain, in spite of the mystery that surrounded him, had a most dignified appearance and was a very amiable person in society. Grandmamma is still to this day quite devoted to his memory and gets angry if anyone speaks of him with disrespect. Grandmamma knew that Saint-Germain had plenty of money at his disposal. She decided to appeal to him, and wrote a note asking him to come and see her immediately. The eccentric old man came at once and found her in terrible distress. She described in the blackest colours her husband's inhumanity, and ended by declaring that she laid all her hopes on his friendship and kindness. Saint-Germain pondered. "I could oblige you with the sum you want," he said, "but I know that you would not be easy until you had repaid me, and I should not like to involve you in fresh trouble. There is another way out – you could win it back."

' "But, my dear count," answered grandmamma, "I tell you I have no money at all."

' "That does not matter," Saint-Germain replied. "Listen now to what I am going to tell you."

'And he revealed to her a secret which all of us would give a great deal to know. . . .'

The young gamblers redoubled their attention. Tomsky lit his pipe, puffed away for a moment and continued:

'That evening grandmamma appeared at Versailles, at the *jeu de la reine*. The Duke of Orleans kept the bank. Grandmamma lightly excused herself for not having brought the money to pay off her debt, inventing some little story by way of explanation, and began to play against him. She selected three cards and played them one after the other: all three won, and grandmamma retrieved her loss completely.'

'Luck!' said one of the party.

'A fairy tale!' remarked Hermann.

'Marked cards, perhaps,' put in a third.

'I don't think so,' replied Tomsky impressively.

'What!' said Narumov. You have a grandmother who knows how to hit upon three lucky cards in succession, and you haven't learnt her secret yet?'

'That's the deuce of it!' Tomsky replied. 'She had four sons, one of whom was my father; all four were desperate gamblers, and yet she did not reveal her secret to a single one of them, though it would not have been a bad thing for them, or for me either. But listen to what my uncle, Count Ivan Ilyich, used to say, assuring me on his word of honour that it was true. Tchaplitsky – you know him, he died a pauper after squandering millions – as a young man once lost three hundred thousand roubles, to Zorich, if I remember rightly. He was in despair. Grandmamma was always very severe on the follies of young men, but somehow she took pity on Tchaplitsky. She gave him three cards, which he was to play one after the other, at the same time exacting from him a promise that he would never afterwards touch a card so long as he lived. Tchaplitsky went to Zorich's; they sat down to play. Tchaplitsky staked fifty thousand on his first card and won; doubled his stake and won; did the same again, won back his loss and ended up in pocket. . . .

'But, I say, it's time to go to bed: it is a quarter to six already.'

And indeed dawn was breaking. The young men emptied their glasses and went home.

II

'Il paraît que monsieur est décidément pour les suivantes'

'Que voulez-vous, madame? Elles sont plus fraîches.'

FROM A SOCIETY CONVERSATION

The old Countess X was seated before the looking-glass in her dressing-room. Three maids were standing round her. One held a pot of rouge, another a box of hairpins, and the third a tall cap with flame-coloured ribbons. The countess had not the slightest pretensions to beauty – it had faded long ago – but she still preserved all the habits of her youth, followed strictly the fashion of the seventies, and gave as much time and care to her toilette as she had sixty years before. A young girl whom she had brought up sat at an embroidery-frame by the window.

'Good morning, *grand'maman!*' said a young officer, coming into the room. '*Bonjour, Mademoiselle Lise. Grand'maman*, I have a favour to ask of you.'

'What is it, Paul?'

'I want you to let me introduce to you a friend of mine and bring him to your ball on Friday.'

'Bring him straight to the ball and introduce him to me then. Were you at the princess's last night?'

'Of course I was! It was most enjoyable: we danced until five in the morning. Mademoiselle Yeletsky looked enchanting!'

'Come, my dear! What is there enchanting about her? She isn't a patch on her grandmother, Princess Daria Petrovna. By the way, I expect Princess Daria Petrovna must have aged considerably?'

'How do you mean, aged?' Tomsky replied absentmindedly. 'She's been dead for the last seven years.'

The girl at the window raised her head and made a sign to the young man. He remembered that they concealed the deaths of her contemporaries from the old countess, and bit his lip. But the countess heard the news with the utmost indifference.

'Dead! I didn't know,' she said. 'We were maids of honour together, and as we were being presented the Empress . . .'

And for the hundredth time the countess repeated the story to her grandson.

'Well, Paul,' she said at the end; 'now help me to my feet. Lise, where is my snuff-box?'

And the countess went with her maids behind the screen to finish dressing. Tomsky was left *à deux* with the young girl.

'Who is it you want to introduce?' Lizaveta Ivanovna asked softly.

'Narumov. Do you know him?'

'No. Is he in the army?'

'Yes.'

'In the Engineers?'

'No, Horse Guards. What made you think he was in the Engineers?'

The girl laughed and made no answer.

'Paul!' the Countess called from behind the screen. 'Send me a new novel to read, only pray not one of those modern ones.'

'How do you mean, *grand'maman*?'

'I want a book in which the hero does not strangle either his father or his mother, and where there are no drowned corpses. I have a horror of drowned persons.'

'There aren't any novels of that sort nowadays. Wouldn't you like something in Russian?'

'Are there any Russian novels? . . . Send me something, my dear fellow, please send me something!'

'Excuse me, *grand'maman*: I must hurry. . . . Goodbye, Lizaveta Ivanovna! I wonder, what made you think Narumov was in the Engineers?'

And Tomsky departed from the dressing-room.

Lizaveta Ivanovna was left alone. She abandoned her work and began to look out of the window. Soon, round the corner of a house on the other side of the street, a young officer appeared. Colour flooded her cheeks; she took up her work again, bending her head over her embroidery-frame. At that moment the countess came in, having finished dressing.

'Order the carriage, Lise,' she said, 'and let us go for a drive.'

Lizaveta Ivanovna rose from her embroidery-frame and began putting away her work.

'What is the matter with you, my child, are you deaf?' the countess cried. 'Be quick and order the carriage.'

'I will go at once,' the young girl answered quietly, and ran into the ante-room.

A servant came in and handed the countess a parcel of books from Prince Paul Alexandrovich.

'Good! Tell him I am much obliged,' said the countess. 'Lise, Lise, where are you off to?'

'To dress.'

'There is plenty of time, my dear. Sit down here. Open the first volume and read to me.'

The girl took the book and read a few lines.

'Louder!' said the countess. 'What is the matter with you, my dear? Have you lost your voice, or what? Wait a minute . . . Give me that footstool. A little closer. That will do!'

Lizaveta Ivanovna read two more pages. The countess yawned.

'Throw that book away,' she said. 'What nonsense it is! Send it back to Prince Paul with my thanks. . . . What about the carriage?'

'The carriage is ready,' said Lizaveta Ivanovna, glancing out into the street.

'How is it you are not dressed?' the countess said. You always keep people waiting. It really is intolerable!'

Liza ran to her room. Hardly two minutes passed before the countess started ringing with all her might. Three maids rushed in at one door and a footman at the other.

'Why is it you don't come when you are called?' the countess said to them. 'Tell Lizaveta Ivanovna I am waiting.'

Lizaveta Ivanovna returned, wearing a hat and a pelisse.

'At last, my dear!' said the countess. 'Why the finery? What is it for? . . . For whose benefit? . . . And what is the weather like? Windy, isn't it?'

'No, your ladyship,' the footman answered, 'there is no wind at all.'

'You say anything that comes into your head! Open the window. Just as I thought: there is a wind, and a very cold one too! Dismiss the carriage. Lise, my child, we won't go out – you need not have dressed up after all.'

'And this is my life!' Lizaveta Ivanovna thought to herself.

Indeed, Lizaveta Ivanovna was a most unfortunate creature. 'Another's bread is bitter to the taste,' says Dante, 'and his staircase hard to climb;' and who should know the bitterness of dependence better than a orphan brought up by an old lady of quality? The countess was certainly not bad-hearted but she had all the caprices of a woman spoiled by society, she was stingy and coldly selfish, like all old people who have done with love and are out of touch with life around them. She took part in all the vanities of the fashionable world, dragged herself to balls, where she sat in a corner, rouged and attired after some bygone mode, like a misshapen but indispensable ornament of the ballroom. On their arrival the guests all went up to her and bowed low, as though in accordance with an old-established rite, and after that no one took any more notice of her. She received the whole town at her house, observing the strictest etiquette and not recognizing the faces of any of her guests. Her numerous servants, grown fat and grey in her entrance hall and the maids' quarters, did what they liked and vied with each other in robbing the decrepit old woman. Lizaveta Ivanovna was the household martyr. She poured out tea and was reprimanded for using too much sugar; she read novels aloud to the countess and was blamed for all the author's mistakes; she accompanied the countess on her drives and was answerable for the weather and the state of the roads. She was supposed to receive a salary, which was never paid in full and yet she was expected to be as well dressed as everyone else – that is, as very few indeed. In society she played the most pitiable role. Everybody knew her and nobody gave her any thought. At balls she danced only when someone was short of a partner, and the ladies would take her by the arm each time they wanted to go to the cloakroom to rearrange some detail of their toilette. She was sensitive and felt her position keenly, and looked about impatiently for a deliverer to come; but the young men, calculating in their empty-headed frivolity, honoured her with scant attention though Lizaveta Ivanovna was a hundred times more charming than the cold, brazen-faced heiresses they ran after. Many a time she crept away from the tedious, glittering drawing-room to go and weep in her humble little attic with its wallpaper screen, chest of drawers, small looking-glass and painted wooden bedstead, and where a tallow candle burned dimly in a brass candlestick.

One morning, two days after the card party described at the beginning of this story and a week before the scene we have just witnessed – one morning Lizaveta Ivanovna, sitting at her embroidery-frame by the window, happened to glance out into the street and see a young Engineers officer standing stock-still gazing at her window. She lowered her head and went on with her work. Five minutes afterwards she looked out again – the young officer was still on the same spot. Not being in the habit of coquetting with passing officers, she looked out no more and went on sewing for a couple of hours without raising her head. Luncheon was announced. She got up to put away her embroidery-frame and, glancing casually into the street, saw the officer again. This seemed to her somewhat strange. After luncheon she went to the window with a certain feeling of uneasiness, but the officer was no longer there, and she forgot about him. . . .

A day or so later, just as she was stepping into the carriage with the countess, she saw him again. He was standing right by the front door, his face hidden by his beaver collar; his dark eyes sparkled beneath his fur cap. Lizaveta Ivanovna felt alarmed, though she did not know why, and seated herself in the carriage, inexplicably agitated.

On returning home she ran to the window – the officer was standing in his accustomed place, his eyes fixed on her. She drew back, consumed with curiosity and excited by a feeling quite new to her.

Since then not a day had passed without the young man appearing at a certain hour beneath the windows of their house, and between him and her a sort of mute acquaintance was established. Sitting at her work she would sense his approach, and lifting her head she looked at him longer and longer every day. The young man seemed to be grateful to her for looking out: with the keen eyes of youth she saw the quick flush of his pale cheeks every time their glances met. By the end of a week she had smiled at him. . . .

When Tomsky asked the countess's permission to introduce a friend of his the poor girl's heart beat violently. But hearing that Narumov was in the Horse Guards, not the Engineers, she regretted the indiscreet question by which she had betrayed her secret to the irresponsible Tomsky.

Hermann was the son of a German who had settled in Russia and who left him some small capital sum. Being firmly convinced that it was essential for him to make certain of his independence, Hermann did not touch even the interest on his income but lived on his pay, denying himself the slightest extravagance. But since he was reserved and ambitious his companions rarely had any opportunity for making fun of his extreme parsimony. He had strong passions and an ardent imagination, but strength of character preserved him from the customary mistakes of youth. Thus, for instance, though a gambler at heart he never touched cards, having decided that his means did not allow him (as he put it) 'to risk the necessary in the hope of acquiring the superfluous'. And yet he spent night after night at the card tables, watching with feverish anxiety the vicissitudes of the game.

The story of the three cards had made a powerful impression upon his imagination and it haunted his mind all night. 'Supposing,' he thought to himself the following evening as he wandered about Petersburg, 'supposing the old countess were to reveal her secret to me? Or tell me the three winning cards! Why shouldn't I try my luck? . . . Get introduced to her, win her favour – become her lover, perhaps. But all that would take time, and she is eighty-seven. She might be dead next week, or the day after tomorrow even! . . . And the story itself? Is it likely? No, economy, moderation and hard work are my three winning cards. With them I can treble my capital – increase it sevenfold and obtain for myself leisure and independence!' Musing thus, he found himself in one of the main streets of Petersburg, in front of a house of old-fashioned architecture. The street was lined with carriages which followed one another up to the lighted porch. Out of the carriages stepped now the shapely little foot of a young beauty, now a military boot with clinking spur, or a diplomat's striped stockings and buckled shoes. Fur coats and cloaks passed in rapid procession before the majestic-looking concierge. Hermann stopped.

'Whose house is that?' he asked a watchman in his box at the corner.

'The Countess X's,' the man told him. It was Tomsky's grandmother.

Hermann started. The strange story of the three cards came into his mind again. He began walking up and down past the house, thinking of its owner and her wonderful secret. It was late when he returned to his humble lodgings; he could not get to sleep for a long time, and when sleep did come he dreamed of cards, a green baize table, stacks of bank-notes and piles of gold. He played card after card, resolutely turning down the corners, winning all the time. He raked in the gold and stuffed his pockets with bank-notes. Waking late in the morning, he sighed over the loss of his fantastic wealth, and then, sallying forth to wander about the town again, once more found himself outside the countess's house. It was as though some supernatural force drew him there. He stopped and looked up at the windows. In one of them he saw a dark head bent over a book or some needlework. The head was raised. Hermann caught sight of a rosy face and a pair of black eyes. That moment decided his fate.

III

Vous m'écrivez, mon ange, des lettres de quatre pages plus vite que je ne puis les lire.

FROM A CORRESPONDENCE

Lizaveta Ivanovna had scarcely taken off her hat and mantle before the countess sent for her and again ordered the carriage. They went out to take their seats. Just as the two footmen were lifting the old lady and helping her through the carriage door Lizaveta Ivanovna saw her Engineers officer standing by the wheel. He seized her hand; before she had recovered from her alarm the young man had disappeared, leaving a letter between her fingers. She hid it in her glove, and for the rest of the drive neither saw nor heard anything. It was the countess's habit when they were out in the carriage to ask a constant stream of questions: 'Who was that we met?' – 'What bridge is this?' – 'What does that signboard say?' This time Lizaveta Ivanovna returned such random and irrelevant answers that the countess grew angry with her.

'What is the matter with you, my dear? Have you taken leave of your senses? Don't you hear me or understand what I say? . . . I speak distinctly enough, thank heaven, and am not in my dotage yet!'

Lizaveta Ivanovna paid no attention to her. When they returned home she ran up to her room and drew the letter out of her glove: it was unsealed. She read it. The letter contained a declaration of love: it was tender, respectful and had been copied word for word from a German novel. But Lizaveta Ivanovna did not know any German and she was delighted with it.

For all that, the letter troubled her greatly. For the first time in her life she was embarking upon secret and intimate relations with a young man. His boldness appalled her. She reproached herself for her imprudent behaviour, and did not know what to do: ought she to give up sitting at the window and by a show of indifference damp the young man's inclination to pursue her further? Should she return his letter to him? Or answer it coldly and firmly? There was nobody to whom she could turn for advice: she had neither female friend nor preceptor. Lizaveta Ivanovna decided to reply to the letter.

She sat down at her little writing-table, took pen and paper – and began to ponder. Several times she made a start and then tore the paper across: what she had written seemed to her either too indulgent or too harsh. At last she succeeded in composing a few lines with which she felt satisfied. 'I am sure,' she wrote, 'that your intentions are honourable and that you had no wish to hurt me by any thoughtless conduct; but our acquaintance ought not to have begun in this manner. I return you your letter, and hope that in future I shall have no cause to complain of being shown a lack of respect which is undeserved.'

Next day, as soon as she saw Hermann approaching, Lizaveta Ivanovna got up from her embroidery-frame, went into the drawing-room, opened the little ventilating window and threw the letter into the street, trusting to the young officer's alertness. Hermann ran forward, picked the letter up and went into a confectioners shop. Breaking the seal, he found his own letter and Lizaveta Ivanovna's reply. It was just what he had expected and he returned home engrossed in his plot.

Three days after this a sharp-eyed young person brought Lizaveta Ivanovna a note from a milliner's establishment. Lizaveta Ivanovna opened it uneasily, fearing it was a demand for money, and suddenly recognized Hermann's handwriting.

'You have made a mistake, my dear,' she said. 'This note is not for me.

'Oh yes it is for you!' retorted the girl boldly, not troubling to conceal a knowing smile. 'Please read it.'

Lizaveta Ivanovna glanced at the letter. In it Hermann wanted her to meet him.

'Impossible!' she cried, alarmed at the request, at its coming so soon, and at the means employed to transmit it. 'I am sure this was not addressed to me.' And she tore the letter into fragments.

'If the letter was not for you, why did you tear it up?' said the girl. 'I would have returned it to the sender.'

'Be good enough, my dear,' said Lizaveta Ivanovna, flushing crimson at her remark, 'not to bring me any more letters. And tell the person who sent you that he ought to be ashamed. . . .'

But Hermann did not give in. Every day Lizaveta Ivanovna received a letter from him by one means or another. They were no longer translated from the German. Hermann wrote them inspired by passion and in a style which was his own: they reflected both his inexorable desire and the disorder of an unbridled imagination. Lizaveta Ivanovna no longer thought of returning them: she drank them in eagerly and took to answering – and the notes she sent grew longer and more affectionate every hour. At last she threw out of the window to him the following letter:

> There is a ball tonight at the Embassy. The countess will be there. We shall stay until about two o'clock. Here is an opportunity for you to see me alone. As soon as the countess is away the servants are sure to go to their quarters, leaving the concierge in the hall, but he usually retires to his lodge. Come at half past eleven. Walk straight up the stairs. If you meet anyone in the ante-room, ask if the countess is at home. They will say 'No,' but there will be no help for it – you will have to go away. But probably you will not meet anyone. The maids all sit together in the one room. Turn to the left out of the ante-room and keep straight on until you reach the countess's bedroom. In the bedroom, behind a screen, you will find two small doors: the one on the right leads into the study where the countess never goes; and the other on the left opens into a passage with a narrow winding staircase up to my room.

Hermann waited for the appointed hour like a tiger trembling for its prey. By ten o'clock in the evening he was already standing outside the countess's house. It was a frightful night: the wind howled, wet snow fell in big flakes; the street lamps burned dimly; the streets were deserted. From time to time a sledge drawn by a sorry-looking hack passed by, the driver on the watch for a belated fare. Hermann stood there without his great-coat, feeling neither the wind nor the snow. At last the countess's carriage was brought round. Hermann saw the old woman wrapped in sables being lifted into the vehicle by two footmen; then Liza in a light cloak, with natural flowers in her hair, flitted by. The carriage doors banged. The vehicle rolled heavily over the wet snow. The concierge closed the street-door. The lights in the windows went out. Hermann started to walk to and fro outside the deserted house; he went up to a street-lamp and glanced at his watch: it was twenty minutes past eleven. He stood still by the lamp-post, his eyes fixed on the hand of the watch. Precisely at half past eleven Hermann walked up the steps of the house and entered the brightly lit vestibule. The concierge was not there. Hermann ran up the stairs, opened the door of the ante-room and saw a footman asleep in a soiled, old-fashioned armchair by the side of a lamp. With a light, firm tread Hermann passed quickly by him. The ballroom and drawing-room were in darkness but the lamp in the ante-room shed a dim light into them. Hermann entered the bedroom. Ancient icons filled the icon-stand before which burned a golden lamp. Armchairs upholstered in faded damask and sofas with down cushions, the tassels of which had lost their gilt, were ranged with depressing symmetry round the walls hung with Chinese wallpaper. On one of the walls were two portraits painted in Paris by Madame Lebrun: the first of a stout, red-faced man of some forty years of age, in a light-green uniform with a star on his breast; the other – a beautiful young woman with an aquiline nose and a rose in the powdered hair drawn back over her temples. Every corner was crowded with porcelain shepherdesses, clocks made by the celebrated Leroy, little boxes, roulettes, fans and all the thousand and one playthings invented for ladies of fashion at the end of the last century together with Montgolfier's balloon and Mesmer's magnetism. Hermann stepped behind the screen. A small iron bedstead stood there; to the right was the door into the study – to the left, the other door into the passage. Hermann opened it and saw the narrow winding staircase leading to poor little Liza's room. But he turned about and went into the dark study.

The time passed slowly. Everything was quiet. The drawing-room clock struck twelve; the clocks in the other rooms chimed twelve, one after the other, and all was still again. Hermann stood leaning against the cold stove. He was quite calm: his heart beat evenly, like that of a man resolved upon a dangerous but inevitable undertaking, The clocks struck one, and then two, and he heard the distant rumble of a carriage. In spite of himself he was overcome with agitation. The carriage drove up to the house and stopped. He heard the clatter of the carriage-steps being lowered. In the house all was commotion. Servants ran to and fro, there was a confusion of voices, and lights appeared everywhere. Three ancient lady's maids bustled into the bedroom, followed by the countess who, half dead with fatigue, sank into a Voltaire armchair. Hermann watched through a crack in the door. Lizaveta Ivanovna passed close by him and he heard her footsteps hurrying up the stairs to her room. For a moment something akin to remorse assailed him but he quickly hardened his heart again.

The countess began undressing before the looking-glass. Her maids took off the cap trimmed with roses and lifted the powdered wig from her grey, close-cropped head. Pins showered about her. The silver-trimmed yellow dress fell at her puffy feet. Hermann witnessed the hideous mysteries of her toilet; at last the countess put on bed jacket and night-cap, and in this attire, more suited to her age, she seemed less horrible and ugly.

Like most old people the countess suffered from sleeplessness. Having undressed, she sat down in a big armchair by the window and dismissed her maids. They took away the candles, leaving only the lamp before the icons to light the room. The countess sat there, her skin sallow with age, her flabby lips twitching, her body swaying to and fro. Her dim eyes were completely vacant and looking at her one might have imagined that the dreadful old woman was rocking her body not from choice but owing to some secret galvanic mechanism.

Suddenly an inexplicable change came over the deathlike face. The lips ceased to move, the eyes brightened: before the countess stood a strange young man.

'Do not be alarmed, for heaven's sake, do not be alarmed!' he said in a low, clear voice. 'I have no intention of doing you any harm, I have come to beg a favour of you.'

The old woman stared at him in silence, as if she had not heard. Hermann thought she must be deaf and bending down to her ear he repeated what he had just said. The old woman remained silent as before.

'You can ensure the happiness of my whole life,' Hermann went on 'and at no cost to yourself. I know that you can name three cards in succession. . . .'

Hermann stopped The countess appeared to have grasped what he wanted and to be seeking words to frame her answer.

'It was a joke,' she said at last. 'I swear to you it was a joke.'

'No, madam,' Hermann retorted angrily. 'Remember Tchaplitsky, and how you enabled him to win back his loss.'

The countess was plainly perturbed. Her face expressed profound agitation; but soon she relapsed into her former impassivity.

'Can you not tell me those three winning cards?' Hermann went on.

The countess said nothing. Hermann continued:

'For whom would you keep your secret? For your grandsons? They are rich enough already: they don't appreciate the value of money. Your three cards would not help a spendthrift. A man who does not take care of his inheritance will die a beggar though all the demons of the world were at his command. I am not a spendthrift: I know the value of money. Your three cards would not be wasted on me. Well? . . .'

He paused, feverishly waiting for her reply. She was silent. Hermann fell on his knees.

'If your heart has ever known what it is to love, if you can remember the ecstasies of love, if you have ever smiled tenderly at the cry of your new-born son, if any human feeling has ever stirred in your breast, I appeal to you as wife, beloved one, mother – I implore you by all that is holy in life not to reject my prayer: tell me your secret. Of what use is it to you? Perhaps it is bound up with some terrible sin, with the loss of eternal salvation, with some bargain with the devil. . . . Reflect – you are old: you have not much longer to live, and I am ready to take your sin upon my soul. Only tell me your secret. Remember that a man's happiness is in your hands; that not only I, but my children and my children's children will bless your memory and hold it sacred. . . .'

The old woman answered not a word.

Hermann rose to his feet.

'You old hag!' he said, grinding his teeth. 'Then I will make you speak. . . .'

With these words he drew a pistol from his pocket. At the sight of the pistol the countess for the second time showed signs of agitation. Her head shook and she raised a hand as though to protect herself from the shot. . . . Then she fell back . . . and was still.

'Come, an end to this childish nonsense!' said Hermann, seizing her by the arm. 'I ask you for the last time – will you tell me those three cards? Yes or no?'

The countess made no answer. Hermann saw that she was dead.

IV

7 mai 18 –

Homme sans moeurs et sans religion!

FROM A CORRESPONDENCE

Lizaveta Ivanovna was sitting in her room, still in her ball dress, lost in thought. on returning home she had made haste to dismiss the sleepy maid who reluctantly offered to help her, saying that she would undress herself, and with trembling heart had gone to her own room, expecting to find Hermann and hoping that she would not find him. A glance convinced her he was not there, and she thanked fate for having prevented their meeting. She sat down without undressing and began to recall the circumstances that had led her so far in so short a time. It was not three weeks since she had first caught sight of the young man from the window – and yet she was carrying on a correspondence with him, and he had already succeeded in inducing her to agree to a nocturnal tryst! She knew his name only because he had signed some of his letters; she had never spoken to him, did not know the sound of his voice, had never heard him mentioned . . . until that evening. Strange to say, that very evening at the ball, Tomsky, piqued with the young Princess Pauline for flirting with somebody else instead of with him as she usually did, decided to revenge himself by a show of indifference. He asked Lizaveta Ivanovna to be his partner and danced the interminable mazurka with her. And all the time he kept teasing her about her partiality for officers of the Engineers, assuring her that he knew far more than she could suppose, and some of his sallies so found their mark that several times Lizaveta Ivanovna thought he must know her secret.

'Who told you all this?' she asked, laughing.

'A friend of someone you know,' Tomsky answered, 'a very remarkable person.'

'And who is this remarkable man?'

'His name is Hermann.'

Lizaveta Ivanovna said nothing; but her hands and feet turned to ice.

'This Hermann,' continued Tomsky, 'is a truly romantic figure: he has the profile of a Napoleon and the soul of a Mephistopheles. I think there must be at least three crimes on his conscience. How pale you look!'

'I have a bad headache. . . . Well, and what did this Hermann – or whatever his name is – tell you?'

'Hermann is very annoyed with his friend: he says that in his place he would act quite differently. . . . I suspect in fact that Hermann has designs upon you himself; at any rate he listens to his friend's ecstatic exclamations with anything but indifference.'

'But where has he seen me?'

'In church, perhaps, or when you were out walking . . . heaven only knows! – in your own room maybe, while you were asleep, for there is nothing he – '

Three ladies coming up to invite Tomsky to choose between *'oubli ou regret?'* interrupted the conversation which had become so painfully interesting to Lizaveta Ivanovna.

The lady chosen by Tomsky was the Princess Pauline herself. She succeeded in effecting a reconciliation with him while they danced an extra turn and spun round once more before she was conducted to her chair. When he returned to his place neither Hermann nor Lizaveta Ivanovna was in Tomsky's thoughts. Lizaveta Ivanovna longed to resume the interrupted conversation but the mazurka came to an end and shortly afterwards the old countess took her departure.

Tomsky's words were nothing more than the usual smalltalk of the ballroom; but they sank deep into the girl's romantic heart. The portrait sketched by Tomsky resembled the picture she had herself drawn, and thanks to the novels of the day the commonplace figure both terrified and fascinated her. She sat there with her bare arms crossed and with her head, still adorned with flowers, sunk upon her naked bosom . . . Suddenly the door opened and Hermann came in. . . . She shuddered.

'Where were you?' she asked in a frightened whisper.

'In the countess's bedroom,' Hermann answered. 'I have just left her. The countess is dead.'

'Merciful heavens! . . . what are you saying?'

'And I think,' added Hermann, 'that I am the cause of her death.'

Lizaveta darted a glance at him, and heard Tomsky's words echo in her soul: ' . . . there must be at least three crimes on his conscience'. Hermann sat down in the window beside her and related all that had happened.

Lizaveta Ivanovna listened to him aghast. So all those passionate letters, those ardent pleas, the bold, determined pursuit had not been inspired by love! Money!

– that was what his soul craved! It was not she who could satisfy his desires and make him happy! Poor child, she had been nothing but the blind tool of a thief, of the murderer of her aged benefactress! . . . She wept bitterly in a vain agony of repentance. Hermann watched in silence: he too was suffering torment; but neither the poor girl's tears nor her indescribable charm in her grief touched his hardened soul. He felt no pricking of conscience at the thought of the dead old woman. One thing only horrified him: the irreparable loss of the secret which was to have brought him wealth.

'You are a monster!' said Lizaveta Ivanovna at last.

'I did not mean her to die,' Hermann answered. 'My pistol was not loaded.'

Both were silent.

Morning came. Lizaveta Ivanovna blew out the candle which had burned down. A pale light illumined the room. She wiped her tear-stained eyes and looked up at Hermann: he was sitting on the window-sill with his arms folded, a menacing frown on his face. In this attitude he bore a remarkable likeness to the portrait of Napoleon. The likeness struck even Lizaveta Ivanovna.

'How shall I get you out of the house?' she said at last. 'I had thought of taking you down the street staircase but that means going through the bedroom, and I am afraid.'

'Tell me how to find this secret staircase – I will go alone.'

Lizaveta rose, took a key from the chest of drawers and gave it to Hermann with precise instructions. Hermann pressed her cold, unresponsive hand, kissed her bowed head and left her.

He walked down the winding stairway and entered the countess's bedroom again. The dead woman sat as though turned to stone. Her face wore a look of profound tranquillity. Hermann stood in front of her and gazed long and earnestly at her, as though trying to convince himself of the terrible truth. Then he went into the study, felt behind the tapestry for the door and began to descend the dark stairway, excited by strange emotions. 'Maybe some sixty years ago, at this very hour,' he thought, 'Some happy youth – long since turned to dust – was stealing up this staircase into that very bedroom, in an embroidered tunic, his hair dressed *à l'oiseau royal*, pressing his three-cornered hat to his breast; and today the heart of his aged mistress has ceased to beat. . . .'

At the bottom of the stairs Hermann saw a door which he opened with the same key, and found himself in a passage leading to the street.

V

That night the dead Baroness von W. appeared before me. She was all in white and said: 'How do you do, Mr Councillor?'

SWEDENBOURG

Three days after that fatal night, at nine o'clock in the morning, Hermann repaired to the Convent of ****, where the last respects were to be paid to the mortal remains of the dead countess. Though he felt no remorse he could not altogether stifle the voice of conscience which kept repeating to him: 'You are the old woman's murderer!' Having very little religious faith, he was exceedingly superstitious. Believing that the dead countess might exercise a malignant influence on his life, he decided to go to her funeral to beg and obtain her forgiveness.

The church was full. Hermann had difficulty in making his way through the crowd. The coffin rested on a rich catafalque beneath a canopy of velvet. The dead woman lay with her hands crossed on her breast, in a lace cap and a white satin robe. Around the bier stood the members of her household: servants in black clothes, with armorial ribbons on their shoulders and lighted candles in their hands; relatives in deep mourning – children, grandchildren and great-grandchildren. No one wept: tears would have been *une affectation*. The countess was so old that her death could not have taken anybody by surprise, and her family had long ceased to think of her as one of the living. A famous preacher delivered the funeral oration. In simple and touching phrases he described the peaceful passing of the saintly woman whose long life had been a quiet, touching preparation for a Christian end. 'The angel of death,' he declared, 'found her vigilant in devout meditation, awaiting the midnight coming of the bridegroom.' The service was concluded in melancholy decorum. First the relations went forward to bid farewell to the corpse. They were followed by a long procession of all those who had come to render their last homage to one who had for so many years been a participator in their frivolous amusements. Alter them came the members of the countess's household. The last of these was an old woman-retainer the same age as the deceased.

Two young girls supported her by the arms. She had not strength to prostrate herself – and she was the only one to shed tears as she kissed her mistress's cold hand. Hermann decided to approach the coffin after her. He knelt down on the cold stone strewed with branches of spruce-fir, and remained in that position for some minutes; at last he rose to his feet and, pale as the deceased herself, walked up the steps of the catafalque and bent over the corpse . . . At that moment it seemed to him that the dead woman darted a mocking look at him and winked her eye. Hermann drew back, missed his footing and crashed headlong to the floor. They picked him up. At the same time Lizaveta Ivanovna was carried out of the church in a swoon. This incident momentarily upset the solemnity of the mournful rite. There was a dull murmur among the congregation, and a tall thin man in the uniform of a court-chamberlain, a close relative of the deceased, whispered in the ear of an Englishman who was standing near him that the young officer was the natural son of the countess, to which the Englishman coldly replied, 'Oh?'

The whole of that day Hermann was strangely troubled. Repairing to a quiet little tavern to dine, he drank a great deal of wine, contrary to his habit, in the hope of stifling his inner agitation. But the wine only served to excite his imagination. Returning home, he threw himself on his bed without undressing, and fell heavily asleep.

It was night when he woke and the moon was shining into his room. He glanced at the time: it was a quarter to three. Sleep had left him; he sat on the bed and began thinking of the old countess's funeral.

Just then someone in the street looked in at him through the window and immediately walked on. Hermann paid no attention. A moment later he heard the door of his ante-room open. Hermann thought it was his orderly, drunk as usual, returning from some nocturnal excursion, but presently he heard an unfamiliar footstep: someone was softly shuffling along the floor in slippers. The door opened and a woman in white came in. Hermann mistook her for his old nurse and wondered what could have brought her at such an hour. But the woman in white glided across the room and stood before him – and Hermann recognized the countess!

'I have come to you against my will,' she said in a firm voice: 'but I am commanded to grant your request. The three, the seven and the ace will win for you if you play them in succession, provided that you do not stake more than one card in twenty-four hours and never play again as long as you live. I forgive you my death, on condition that you marry my ward, Lizaveta Ivanovna.'

With these words she turned softly, rustled to the door in her slippers, and disappeared. Hermann heard the street-door click and again saw someone peeping in at him through the window.

It was a long time before he could pull himself together and go into the next room. His orderly was asleep on the floor: Hermann had difficulty in waking him. The man was drunk as usual: there was no getting any sense out of him. The street-door was locked. Hermann returned to his room and, lighting a candle, wrote down all the details of his vision.

VI

'Attendez!'
How dare you say 'Attendez!' *to me?*'
'*Your Excellency, I said* "Attendez," *sir*.'

Two *idées fixes* cannot co-exist in the moral world any more than two physical bodies can occupy one and the same space. 'The three, the seven, the ace' soon drove all thought of the dead woman from Hermann's mind. Three, seven, ace were perpetually in his head and on his lips. If he saw a young girl he would say, 'How graceful she is! A regular three of hearts!' Asked the time, he would reply, 'Five minutes to seven.' Every stout man reminded him of the ace. 'Three, seven, ace haunted his dreams, assuming all sorts of shapes. The three blossomed before him like a luxuriant flower, the seven took the form of a Gothic portal, and aces became gigantic spiders. His whole attention was focused on one thought: how to make use of the secret which had cost him so dear. He began to consider resigning his commission in order to go and travel abroad. In the public gambling-houses in Paris he would compel fortune to give him his magical treasure. Chance spared him the trouble.

A circle of wealthy gamblers existed in Moscow, presided over by the celebrated Tchekalinsky, who had spent his life at the card-table and amassed millions, accepting promissory notes when he won and paying his losses in ready money. His long experience inspired the confidence of his fellow-players, while his open house, his famous chef and his gay and friendly manner secured for him the general respect of the public. He came to Petersburg. The young men of the capital flocked to his rooms, forsaking balls for cards and preferring the excitement of gambling to the seductions of flirting. Narumov brought Hermann to him.

They passed through a succession of magnificent rooms full of attentive servants. The place was crowded. Several generals and privy councillors were playing whist; young men smoking long pipes lounged about on sofas upholstered in damask. In the drawing-room some twenty gamblers jostled round a long table at which the master of the house was keeping bank. Tchekalinsky was a man of about sixty years of age and most dignified appearance; he had silvery-grey hair, a full, florid face with a kindly expression, and sparkling eyes which were always smiling. Narumov introduced Hermann. Shaking hands cordially, Tchekalinsky requested him not to stand on ceremony, and went on dealing.

The game continued for some while. On the table lay more than thirty cards. Tchekalinsky paused after each round to give the players time to arrange their cards and note their losses, listened courteously to their observations and more courteously still straightened the corner of a card that some careless hand had turned down. At last the game finished. Tchekalinsky shuffled the cards and prepared to deal again.

'Will you allow me to take a card?' said Hermann, stretching out his hand from behind a stout gentleman who was punting.

Tchekalinsky smiled and bowed graciously, in silent token of consent. Narumov laughingly congratulated Hermann on breaking his long abstention from cards and wished him a lucky start.

'There!' said Hermann, chalking some figures on the back of his card.

'How much?' asked the banker, screwing up his eyes. 'Excuse me, I cannot see.'

'Forty-seven thousand,' Hermann answered.

At these words every head was turned in a flash, and all eyes were fixed on Hermann.

'He has taken leave of his senses!' thought Narumov.

'Allow me to point out to you,' said Tchekalinsky with his unfailing smile, 'that you are playing rather high: nobody here has ever staked more than two hundred and seventy-five at a time.'

'Well?' returned Hermann. 'Do you accept my card or not?'

Tchekalinsky bowed with the same air of humble acquiescence.

'I only wanted to observe,' he said, 'that, being honoured with the confidence of my friends, I can only play against ready money. For my own part, of course, I am perfectly sure that your word is sufficient but for the sake of the rules of the game and our accounts I must request you to place the money on your card.'

Hermann took a bank-note from his pocket and handed it to Tchekalinsky, who after a cursory glance placed it on Hermann's card. He began to deal. On the right a nine turned up, and on the left a three.

'I win!' said Hermann, pointing to his card.

There was a murmur of astonishment among the company. Tchekalinsky frowned, but the smile quickly reappeared on his face.

'Would you like me to settle now?' he asked Hermann.

'If you please.'

Tchekalinsky took a number of bank-notes out of his pocket and paid there and then. Hermann picked up his money and left the table. Narumov could not believe his eyes. Hermann drank a glass of lemonade and departed home.

The following evening he appeared at Tchekalinsky's again. The host was dealing. Hermann walked up to the table; the players immediately made room for him. Tchekalinsky bowed graciously. Hermann waited for the next deal, took a card and placed on it his original forty-seven thousand together with his winnings of the day before. Tchekalinsky began to deal. A knave turned up on the right, a seven on the left.

Hermann showed his seven.

There was a general exclamation. Tchekalinsky was obviously disconcerted. He counted out ninety-four thousand and handed them to Hermann, who pocketed them in the coolest manner and instantly withdrew.

The next evening Hermann again made his appearance at the table. Everyone was expecting him; the generals and privy councillors left their whist to watch such extraordinary play. The young officers leaped up from their sofas and all the waiters collected in the drawing-room. Everyone pressed round Hermann. The other players left off punting, impatient to see what would happen. Hermann stood at the table, prepared to play alone against Tchekalinsky, who was pale but still smiling. Each broke the seal of a pack of cards. Tchekalinsky shuffled. Hermann took a card and covered it with a pile of bank-notes. It was like a duel. Deep silence reigned in the room.

Tchekalinsky began dealing; his hands trembled. A queen fell on the right, an ace on the left.

'Ace wins!' said Hermann, and showed his card.

'Your queen has lost,' said Tchekalinsky gently.

Hermann started: indeed, instead of an ace there lay before him the queen of spades. He could not believe his eyes or think how he could have made such a mistake.

At that moment it seemed to him that the queen of spades opened and closed her eye, and mocked him with a smile. He was struck by the extraordinary resemblance. . . .

'The old woman!' he cried in terror.

Tchekalinsky gathered up his winnings. Hermann stood rooted to the spot. When he left the table everyone began talking at once.

'A fine game, that!' said the players.

Tchekalinsky shuffled the cards afresh and the game resumed as usual.

Conclusion

Hermann went out of his mind. He is now in room number 17 of the Obukhov Hospital. He returns no answer to questions put to him but mutters over and over again, with incredible rapidity: 'Three, seven, ace! Three, seven, queen!'

Lizaveta Ivanovna has married a very pleasant young man; he is in the civil service somewhere and has a good income. He is the son of the old countess's former steward. Lizaveta Ivanovna in her turn is bringing up a poor relative.

And Tomsky, who has been promoted to the rank of captain, has married the Princess Pauline.

The Blue Room

PROSPER MÉRIMÉE

A young man was walking with an agitated air about the railway station. He had blue glasses, and although he had not a cold in his head, he kept putting his handkerchief to his nose. In his left hand he held a little black bag, containing, as I learnt later, a silk dressing-gown and some Turkish trousers.

From time to time he went to the entrance and looked up and down the street; then he drew out his watch and studied the timetable. It was an hour before the train went; but there are some folk who are always afraid of being late. The train was not one of those that busy people take – few first-class carriages. And the hour it went was not that which allows business men to leave as soon as their work is done, and arrive in time for dinner at their country-houses. When the passengers began to show themselves, a Parisian would have seen by their air that they were farmers or little traders of the suburbs.

Still, each time anyone entered the station, each time a cab stopped at the gate, the heart of the young man in blue glasses swelled out like a balloon; his knees trembled; his bag almost fell from his hand; and his glasses nearly tumbled from his nose, on which, it might be said in passing, they were placed wrong side round.

It was still worse when, after a long wait, there appeared through a side door, coming precisely from the only point that was not subjected to continual observation, a woman clad in black, with a thick veil over her face, holding in her hand a bag of brown morocco, containing, as I afterwards discovered, a wonderful dressing-gown and a pair of blue satin slippers. The woman and the young man came towards each other, looking to the right and the left, but never before them. They came together, touched hands, and stayed for some minutes without saying a word panting, trembling, overcome by one of those poignant emotions, for which I would give a hundred years of philosophic meditations.

'Léon,' said the young woman – I have forgotten to say she was young and pretty – 'Léon, what happiness! Never should I have known you in those blue glasses!'

'What joy!' said Léon. 'I should have never recognized you under that black veil!'

'What joy!' she continued. 'Let us get our seats quick. If the train started without us! . . . (And she squeezed his arm.) Nobody guesses what is happening. At this moment I am with Clara and her husband, going to their country-house, where I ought tomorrow to say goodbye! . . . And,' she added laughing and lowering her head, 'it is just an hour since I went away with Clara, and tomorrow . . . after having passed the last evening with her . . . (again she squeezed his arm), tomorrow, in the morning, she will leave me at the station, where I shall find Ursule, whom I have sent on ahead at my aunt's. . . . Oh! I have thought out everything! Let us get our tickets. . . . It is impossible we should be found out! Oh! If they want to know our names at the end ? I have already forgotten. . . .'

'Monsieur and Madame Duru.'

'No! not Duru. There was a shoemaker at the boarding school with that name.'

'Then, Dumont? . . .'

'Daumont!'

'Very well! But they will not question us!'

A bell rang, the door of the waiting-room opened, and the young woman, always carefully veiled, darted into a carriage with her young companion. For the second time the bell rang; a porter shut the door of their compartment.

'We are alone!' they cried joyfully.

But at that very moment a man of about fifty, dressed all in black, with a broad serious face, entered the carriage and settled down in a corner. The engine whistled and the train set off. The young couple, withdrawing as far as they could from their inconvenient neighbour, began to talk in whispers, and, as an extra precaution, in English.

'Sir,' said the other passenger in the same language and with a much purer English accent, 'if you want to talk secrets, you had better not use English before me. I am an Englishman. Sorry to trouble you; but in the other compartment there was only one man, and as a matter of principle I never travel with a single man. He looked to me like a Judas. And this might have tempted him.'

He pointed to his travelling-bag that he had thrown on a cushion before him.

'If I can't sleep, I will read.'

And he did loyally try to sleep. Opening his bag, he took out a travelling-cap, put it on his head, and kept his eyes shut for some minutes. Then opening them with a movement of impatience, he groped in his bag for spectacles, then for a Greek book. At last he began to read very attentively. In getting the book out of the bag he had overturned many things, all thrown in anyhow. Among other articles he drew out was a pretty thick bundle of Bank of England notes, placed them on the seat in front of him, and before putting them back in the bag he showed them to the young man and asked him if he could change bank-notes at a certain town.

'Probably. It is on the way to England,' said Léon.

It was to this town that the young couple were going. There is a little hotel there, fairly clean, where travellers usually stay only on Saturday evening. It is pretended that the rooms are good; but the landlord and his servants are not far enough removed from Paris to keep a really good inn. Léon had come across the place some time before, then he was not wearing blue glasses, and after the account he gave of it, his sweetheart felt she would like to see it.

Besides, on this day, she was in such a frame of mind that the walls of a prison would have seemed to her full of charm if she had been shut in there with Léon. However, the train went on, the Englishman read his Greek without turning to look at his companions, who chatted in such whispers that only lovers could have understood. Perhaps I shall not surprise my readers by admitting that they were eloping lovers. And what was really deplorable was that they were not married, and there were great difficulties in the way of their marriage.

They reached their stopping-place. The Englishman was the first to alight. While Leon was helping his sweetheart to get out of the carriage without showing her ankles, a man darted from a neighbouring compartment on to the platform. He was pale, even yellow, with sunken, blood-hot eyes and a straggling beard – quite a criminal in appearance. His suit was clean but threadworn. His frock-coat once black, now grey at the elbows and at the back, was buttoned to the chin, probably to hide a waistcoat still shabbier. He came up to the Englishman, and in a very humble voice:

'Uncle!' he said to him.

'Leave me alone, you wretch,' cried the Englishman, his grey eye lighting up with anger, as he began to walk out of the station.

'Don't drive me to despair,' said the other man, in a tone at once sorrowful and threatening.

'Will you be good enough to look after my bag a moment?' said the old Englishman, throwing his bag at the feet of Léon.

Seizing the arm of the man who had accosted him, he pushed him in a corner, where he hoped he would not be overheard, and there he spoke to him for a moment in a very harsh voice. Then, taking from his pocket some papers, he put them in the hand of the man who had called him uncle. The man took the papers without any thanks, and almost at once went away and disappeared.

There is only one hotel in the town, so you must not be astonished that, at the end of a few minutes, all the characters in this truthful tale met again there. In France every traveller who has the luck to have a well-dressed woman on his arm is sure of obtaining the best room in all the hotel: thus is it established that we are the most polished nation in Europe.

If the room given to Léon was the best, it would be rash to conclude that it was excellent. There was a great wooden bed, with curtains of chintz, on which was printed in violet the magical story of Pyramus and Thisbe. The walls were covered with a painted paper representing a view of Naples, and crowded with figures. Unhappily, idle and indiscreet travellers had added moustaches and pipes to all the figures, male and female; and many foolish remarks in prose and verse were written in pencil on the sky and on the sea. Against this background hung several engravings: *Louis Philippe swearing to the Charta* of 1830; *The First Meeting of Julie and Saint Preux*; the *Regrets* and the *Hope of Happiness* after Dubuffe. This room was called the Blue Room, because the two armchairs to the right and left of the fireplace were in Dutch velvet of this colour. But for many years past they had been hidden under coverings of grey, glazed cloth with amaranth frills.

While the maids of the hotel gathered round the young lady and offered her their services, Léon, who was not wanting in good sense, even when in love, went to the kitchen to order dinner. He had to use all his eloquence and resort to bribery to get the promise of a private dinner; but greatly was he disconcerted then he learnt that in the big dining-room adjoining the Blue Room the officers of the 3rd Hussars, who were about to relieve the officers of the 3rd Light Infantry, were joining the latter that very day in a farewell dinner that would take place with much cordiality.

The landlord swore by all his gods that, apart from the gaiety natural to all French soldiers, the Hussars and the Light Infantry were noted in the town for their gentleness and their good conduct, and that their presence would not inconvenience Madame in the least, the custom of the officers being to end the dinner before midnight.

As Léon went back to the Blue Room, worried over this affair, he saw that the old Englishman had taken the room next to his. The door was open. The Englishman, sitting before a table on which were placed a glass and a bottle, looked at the ceiling with deep attention, as though he were counting the flies that were walking there.

'What does it matter who our neighbours are?' said Léon to himself. 'The Englishman will soon be drunk, and the soldiers will have gone away before midnight.'

In entering the Blue Room his first care was to make sure that the communicating doors were properly closed and locked. On the side of the Englishman there was a double door; the wall was thick. On the side of the Hussars the partition was thinner; but the door had a lock and key. After all, it was a more effectual barrier against curiosity than the curtains of a cab are; and how many people think they are isolated from the world in a cab!

Certainly the richest imagination cannot picture a more complete happiness than that of two young lovers who, after long waiting, find themselves alone, far from the eyes of jealous and curious people, so that they can relate at leisure their bygone troubles and relish the delights of a perfect meeting. But the devil always finds some means of pouring his drop of bitterness into the cup of felicity. While eating a pretty poor dinner in the Blue Room, composed of some dishes stolen from the banquet of the officers, Léon and his lady had to suffer a good deal from the conversation that those gentlemen held in the neighbouring room. Their talk turned on matters that had nothing to do with strategy and tactics, and I cannot possibly report it.

It was a long string of coarse stories, accompanied by outbursts of laughter in which it was sometimes difficult for our lovers not to take part. Léon's sweetheart was not a prude, but there are some things a woman does not like to hear, even in company with the man she loves. The situation became more and more embarrassing; and when the officers were beginning their dessert, Léon went down to the kitchen to beg the landlord to tell the gentlemen there was a sick lady in the next room and to ask them to have the politeness to make a little less noise.

The landlord, as always happens in army dinners, was quite flurried, and did not know what to say. For at the moment when Léon gave him the message for the officers, a waiter asked him for champagne for the Hussars, and a maid for a bottle of port for the Englishman.

'I told him we had no port,' she added.

'You are a fool. I keep every kind of wine. I will find him his bottle of port! Bring me a bottle of ratafia, a bottle of fifteen, and a decanter of brandy.'

After having manufactured the port in a turn of the hand, the landlord entered the dining-room and gave the message from Léon. It first excited a furious storm. Then a bass voice, that dominated all the others, demanded what kind of woman they had for a neighbour.

'My faith, messieurs,' said the landlord, 'she is very pretty and she is very shy. Marie Jeanne says she has a wedding ring. So it may be a bride who has come here for her honeymoon, as they sometimes do.'

'A bride!' shouted forty voices. 'She must come and drink with us. We will toast her health, and teach her husband his duties!'

At these words there was a great clanking of spurs, and our couple trembled, thinking that their room was going to be taken by storm. But suddenly a voice stayed the movement. Evidently it was one of the chiefs that spoke. He reproached the officers with their impoliteness, and told them to sit down, and speak decently without shouting. Then he added some words in too low a voice to be heard in the Blue Room. They were received with deference, but not without exciting a certain restrained hilarity.

From this moment there was a comparative silence in the officers' room, and our loving pair blessed the salutary effects of discipline, and began to talk together with more ease. But after so much upset, it took some time to recover those tender emotions which anxieties, the fatigues of travelling, and above all the coarse merriment of their neighbours, had greatly troubled. At their age, however, the thing is not very difficult, and they soon forgot all the unpleasantness of their adventurous expedition, and began to think only of its pleasures.

They fancied they had made peace with the Hussars. Alas it was only a truce. The moment when they were least expecting it, when they were thousands of leagues away from this sublunary world, behold! twenty-four bugles, sustained by several trombones, poured out the air known to French soldiers, 'Ours is the victory!' How could any one resist such a tempest? The poor lovers were much to be pitied.

No, not very much. For in the end the officers came out of the dining-room, defiling before the door of the Blue Room with much clank of sabres and spurs, and shouting one after the other, 'Goodnight, madame, the bride.'

Then all sound ceased. No, I am mistaken. The Englishman came out into the corridor and cried:

'Waiter, bring me another bottle of that same port!'

Calmness settled at last on the little inn. The night was sweet, the moon at full. From time immemorial lovers have delighted to look at our satellite. Léon and his lady opened their window, that looked on a little garden, and breathed with joy the cool air, fragrant with the scent of clematis. They did not remain at the window very long. A man was walking in the garden, his head bowed, his arms crossed, a cigar in his mouth. Léon thought he recognised the nephew of the Englishman who loved the good wine of Portugal.

I hate useless details, and besides I am not obliged to tell the reader all that took place, hour by hour, in the inn. So I will only say that the candle, burning on the mantelpiece in the Blue Room, was more than half consumed, when, in the bedroom of the Englishman, hitherto silent, a strange noise was heard, such as a heavy body might produce in its fall. And with this noise there mingled a sort of cracking, not less strange, followed by a stifled cry and several indistinct words, resembling a curse. The young couple in the Blue Room were startled. Perhaps they had been aroused by the fall; for on both of them the mysterious noise produced an almost sinister impression.

'It is our Englishman dreaming,' said Léon, trying to smile. He wished to reassure his companion, but he shivered involuntarily. Two or three minutes afterwards, a door was opened in the corridor, very carefully it seemed, then it was shut very quietly. Some one could be heard walking slowly and uneasily, who, to all appearance, was trying to pass without being heard.

'What a cursed place!' cried Léon.

'Ah, it is like heaven! . . .' said the young lady letting her head fall on Léon's shoulder. 'I am so sleepy. . . .'

She sighed and fell asleep again almost at once. But Léon was worried, and his imagination began to dwell on several things that, in another frame of mind, he would have passed over. The sinister figure of the Englishman's nephew was recalled to his memory. There was hatred in the glance he gave his uncle, whilst speaking to him with humility, no doubt because he was asking for money. What could be easier than for a man, still young and vigorous, and desperate besides, to climb from the garden to the window of the next room? . . . Moreover, he was staying in the inn, since he was walking in the garden at night. Perhaps . . . even probably . . . indubitably, he knew that there was a thick bundle of bank-notes in his uncle's bag. . . . And that heavy blow, like a club falling on a bald head! . . . that stifled cry! . . . that frightful oath, and then the creeping steps afterwards! The nephew had the air of a murderer. . . . But a hotel full of officers is not a good place for a murderer. No doubt this Englishman, like a prudent man, had locked his door, especially knowing what sort of fellow was banging about. He mistrusted him, since he did not want to go up to him with his bag in his hand. . . . But why think of such hideous things when you are so happy?

That was what Léon said to himself. In the middle of his thoughts, which I refrain from analysing at length, and which came to him almost as confused as the visions of a dream, he had his eyes fixed mechanically on the communicating door between the Blue Room and the Englishman's room.

In France the doors do not shut well. Between this one and the floor there was an opening of nearly half an inch. Suddenly, through this opening, scarcely lighted by the reflection from the waxed floor, there appeared something blackish, flat, resembling the blade of a knife, for the edge, touched by the light from the candle, showed a thin brilliant line. This moved slowly in the direction of a little slipper of blue satin, thrown indiscreetly a little way from the door. Was it some insect like a centipede? . . . No; it was not an insect, it had no fixed shape. . . . Two or three brown trails, each with its line of light at the edge, penetrate into the Blue Room. There movement quickens, owing to the slope of the floor; they advance rapidly, and begin to touch the little slipper. No more doubt! It is a liquid, and its colour can now be seen distinctly by the light of the candle – it is blood! And while Léon, motionless, stared with horror at the frightful thing, the young lady slept on peacefully, and her regular breath warmed the neck and shoulder of the terrified man.

The care that Léon had taken to order dinner as soon as he arrived at the inn is sufficient to prove that he had a good head on his shoulders and was able to look ahead. He did not belie his character on this occasion. He made no movement, and all the force of his mind bent in an effort to come to some decision in the presence of the frightful misfortune that threatened him.

I imagine that most of my readers, and especially my lady readers, full themselves with the spirit of heroism, will blame Léon for his inactivity and his lack of courage. He ought, I shall be told, to have run to the Englishman's room and arrested the murderer. At the very least, he should have pulled his bell and aroused the people of the inn. To this I must answer, first, that in French inns the bell-rope is only an ornament in the bedrooms: there is no apparatus in metal attached to the other end of the cord. I will also add, respectfully but firmly, that, if it is wrong to let an Englishman die in the next room, it is not at all praiseworthy to sacrifice to an old foreigner the young and pretty woman who is sleeping with her head on your shoulder. What would have happened if Léon had shouted out and awakened everybody in the inn? Gendarmes, a magistrate and his clerk would soon have arrived. Before asking him what he had seen or heard, these gentlemen are so inquisitive by profession that they would have started by asking Léon:

'What is your name? Where are your papers? And madame? Why are you staying together in this Blue Room? You will both have to appear before the court of assize and give evidence that, on such a date, at such an hour at night, you have been witnesses to such and such things.'

Now, it was precisely this idea of the magistrate and the police that first presented itself to the mind of Léon. There are some problems in life that are difficult to solve. Is it better to let an unknown foreigner be murdered, or lose and bring dishonour upon a beloved woman? Léon did what most men would have done in his place. He did not stir. With his eyes fixed on the blue slipper, and the little red stream that touched it, he remained for some time as though he was fascinated, while a cold sweat came on his forehead, and his heart beat in his breast enough to break it open. A crowd of horrible thoughts and odd images beset him, and an inner voice said to him every minute, 'In an hour everything will be known, and it is your fault!' However, through continually asking himself,' Whatever shall I do in this affair?' a man often ends by finding some rays of hope.

'If we leave this accursed hotel,' said Léon to himself, 'before they discover what has happened in the next room, perhaps we shall be able to cover up our traces. Nobody knows us here. They have only seen me in blue glasses, and they have never seen her without her veil. We are only two steps from the station, and in an hour we shall be far away from this town.'

Then, as he had well studied the timetable in arranging his elopement, he remembered that a train to Paris passed at eight o'clock. Soon after that, he and his lady would he lost in the immensity of that city, that hides so many criminals. Who could there discover two innocent persons? But if any one entered the Englishman's room before eight o'clock? All the problem was there.

Well convinced there was nothing else he could do, he made a desperate effort to shake off the drowsiness that had long been gaining on him. But at his first movement his companion awoke and kissed him. At the touch of his icy cheek she gave a little cry.

'What's the matter? 'she said anxiously. 'Your forehead is like marble.'

'It is nothing,' he replied in a shaky voice. 'I heard a noise in the next room.'

Getting out of bed, he took the blue slipper away, and placed an arm-chair before the communicating door, so as to hide from his sweetheart the frightful stream which, having now ceased to spread, formed a large pool on the floor. Then he opened the door and listened in the corridor. He even dared to try the door of the Englishman's room. It was locked. There was already some stir in the inn. The day was dawning. Some stablemen were grooming the horses in the yard, and, on the second floor, an officer was coming downstairs with clanking spurs. He was going to see that the horses were properly looked after.

Léon returned to the Blue Room, and, with circumlocutions and euphemisms, and all the precautions that love could suggest, he told his lady in what situation they were.

It was dangerous to remain, and dangerous to go too soon, and still more dangerous to wait in the inn until the discovery was made in the next room. It is useless to describe the fright caused by this information; the tears that followed it; the wild proposals that were made; how many times the two unhappy creatures threw themselves in each other's arms, saying, 'Pardon me!' 'Pardon me!' Each blamed themselves. They promised to die together; for the young lady was sure they would be found guilty of the murder of the Englishman; and as they were not certain they would be permitted to kiss on the scaffold, they stifled each other with embraces, and watered each other with their tears.

At last, having said many absurdities and many loving things, they recognized, in the midst of a thousand kisses, that Léon's plan of departing by the eight o'clock train was the only practical one. But there were still two mortal hours to pass. At each step in the corridor they trembled in all their limbs. Each squeak of a boot announced to them the arrival of the police. Their little luggage was packed in the twinkling of an eye. The young lady wished to burn the blue slipper in the fireplace, but Léon took it and after wiping it on the under bedclothes, he kissed it, and put it in his pocket. He was surprised to find it had a vanilla fragrance: his lady liked the same perfume as the Empress Eugénie.

Already everybody was awake in the inn. They could hear the waiters laughing, the maids singing, the soldiers brushing the officers' clothes. Seven o'clock chimed. Léon wished to get his love to take a cup of coffee but she declared her throat was so tight that she would die if she tried to drink anything. Léon, putting on his blue glasses, went down to pay his bill. The landlord begged his pardon for the noise that had been made. He still could not understand it, for the officers were always so quiet. Léon assured him he had heard nothing, and had slept excellently.

'Now your neighbour in the other room,' continued the landlord, 'cannot have inconvenienced you, for he has not made much noise. I wager he is still sleeping like the dead.'

Léon leant heavily against the desk to prevent himself from falling, and his lady, who had resolved to come with him, clutched his arm, pressing her veil over her eyes.

'It is an English lord,' went on the landlord pitilessly. 'He always wants the best of everything. Ah, he is a gentleman! But all the English are not like him. There is another here who is a mean rascal. He finds everything too dear – the room and the dinner. He wanted me to give him a hundred and fifty francs for a Bank of England note of five pounds. But is it good? Here, sir, you ought to know that, for I heard you speaking English with Madame. Is it a good one?'

He held out a five pound bank-note. On one of the corners was a little red stain that Léon understood.

'I think it is quite good,' he said in a strangled voice.

'Oh, you have plenty of time,' continued the landlord. 'The train is not due till eight o'clock, and it is always late. Won't you sit down, Madame? you seem tired.'

At this moment a plump maid entered.

'Some warm water, quick,' she said, 'for the tea of milord! Get a sponge also! He has broken his bottle of port and all his room is flooded.'

Léon let himself fall into a chair; his companion did the same. A strong desire to laugh took them both, and they had some trouble not to give way. The young lady shook him joyfully by the hand.

'Decidely,' said Léon to the landlord, 'we will not go till the afternoon. Prepare a really good lunch for us at twelve.'

Young Goodman Brown

NATHANIEL HAWTHORNE

Young Goodman Brown came forth at sunset into the street of Salem village; but put his head back, after crossing the threshold, to exchange a parting kiss with his young wife. And Faith, as the wife was aptly named, thrust her own pretty head into the street, letting the wind play with the pink ribbons of her cap while she called to Goodman Brown.

'Dearest heart,' whispered she, softly and rather sadly, when her lips were close to his ear, 'prithee put off your journey until sunrise and sleep in your own bed tonight. A lone woman is troubled with such dreams and such thoughts that she's afeared of herself sometimes. Pray tarry with me this night, dear husband, of all nights in the year.'

'My love and my Faith,' replied young Goodman Brown, 'of all nights in the year, this one night must I tarry away from thee. My journey, as thou callest it, forth and back again, must needs be done 'twixt now and sunrise. What, my sweet, pretty wife, dost thou doubt me already, and we but three months married?'

'Then God bless you!' said Faith, with the pink ribbons; 'and may you find all well when you come back.'

'Amen!' cried Goodman Brown. 'Say thy prayers, dear Faith, and go to bed at dusk, and no harm will come to thee.'

So they parted; and the young man pursued his way until, being about to turn the corner by the meeting-house, he looked back and saw the head of Faith still peeping after him with a melancholy air, in spite of her pink ribbons.

'Poor little Faith!' thought he, for his heart smote him. 'What a wretch am I to leave her on such an errand! She talks of dreams, too. Methought as she spoke, there was trouble in her face, as if a dream had warned her what work is to be done tonight. But no, no; 'twould kill her to think it. Well, she's a blessed angel on earth; and after this one night I'll cling to her skirts and follow her to heaven.'

With this excellent resolve for the future, Goodman Brown felt himself justified in making more haste on his present evil purpose. He had taken a dreary road, darkened by all the gloomiest trees of the forest, which barely stood aside to let the narrow path creep through, and closed immediately behind. It was all as lonely as could be; and there is this peculiarity in such a solitude, that the traveler knows not who may be concealed by the innumerable trunks and the thick boughs overhead; so that with lonely footsteps he may yet be passing through an unseen multitude.

'There may be a devilish Indian behind every tree,' said Goodman Brown to himself; and he glanced fearfully behind him as he added, 'What if the Devil himself should be at my very elbow!'

His head being turned back, he passed a crook of the road, and, looking forward again, beheld the figure of a man, in grave and decent attire, seated at the foot of an old tree. He arose at Goodman Brown's approach and walked onward side by side with him.

'You are late, Goodman Brown,' said he. The clock of the Old South was striking as I came through Boston; and that is full fifteen minutes agone.'

'Faith kept me back awhile,' replied the young man, with a tremor in his voice, caused by the sudden appearance of his companion, though not wholly unexpected.

It was now deep dusk in the forest, and deepest in that part of it where these two were journeying. As nearly as could be discerned, the second traveler was about fifty years old, apparently in the same rank of life as Goodman Brown, and bearing a considerable resemblance to him, though perhaps more in expression than features. Still they might have been taken for father and son. And yet, though the elder person was as simply clad as the younger and as simple in manner too, he had an indescribable air of one who knew the world, and who would not have felt abashed at the governor's dinner-table or in King William's court, were it possible that his affairs should call him thither. But the only thing about him that could be fixed upon as remarkable was his staff, which bore the likeness of a great black snake, so curiously wrought that it might almost be seen to twist and wriggle itself like a living serpent. This, of course, must have been an ocular deception, assisted by the uncertain light.

'Come, Goodman Brown,' Cried his fellow-traveler, 'this is a dull face for the beginning of a journey. Take my staff, if you are so soon weary.'

'Friend,' said the other, exchanging his slow pace for a full stop, 'having kept covenant by meeting thee here, it is my purpose now to return whence I came. I have scruples touching the matter thou wot'st of.'

'Sayest thou so?' replied he of the serpent, smiling apart. 'Let us walk on, nevertheless, reasoning as we go; and if I convince thee not, thou shalt turn back. We are but a little way in the forest yet.'

'Too far! too far!' exclaimed the goodman, unconsciously resuming his walk. 'My father never went into the woods on such an errand, nor his father before him. We have been a race of honest men and good Christians since the days of the martyrs; and shall I be the first by the name of Brown that ever took this path and kept – '

'Such company, thou wouldst say,' observed the elder person, interpreting his pause. 'Well said, Goodman Brown! I have been as well acquainted with your family as with ever a one among the Puritans; and that's no trifle to say. I helped your grandfather, the constable, when he lashed the Quaker woman so smartly through the streets of Salem; and it was I that brought your father a pitch-pine knot, kindled at my own hearth, to set fire to an Indian village, in King Philip's war. They were my good friends both; and many a pleasant walk have we had along this path, and returned merrily after midnight. I would fain be friends with you for their sake.'

'If it be as thou sayest,' replied Goodman Brown, 'I marvel they never spoke of these matters; or, verily, I marvel not, seeing that the least rumor of the sort would have driven them from New England. We are a people of prayer, and good works to boot, and abide no such wickedness.'

'Wickedness or not,' said the traveler with the twisted staff, 'I have a very general acquaintance here in New England. The deacons of many a church have drunk the communion wine with me; the select men of divers towns make me their chairman; and a majority of the Great and General Court are firm supporters of my interest. The governor and I, too, – But these are state secrets.'

'Can this be so?' cried Goodman Brown, with a stare of amazement at his undisturbed companion. 'Howbeit, I have nothing to do with the governor and council; they have their own ways, and are no rule for a simple husbandman like me. But, were I to go on with thee, how should I meet the eye of that good old man, our minister, at Salem village? Oh, his voice would make me tremble both Sabbath day and lecture day!'

Thus far the elder traveler had listened with due gravity; but now burst into a fit of irrepressible mirth, shaking himself so violently that his snake-like staff actually seemed to wriggle in sympathy.

'Ha! ha! ha! shouted he again and again; then composing himself, 'Well, go on, Goodman Brown, go on; but, prithee, don't kill me with laughing.'

'Well, then, to end the matter at once,' said Goodman Brown, considerably nettled, 'there is my wife, Faith. It would break her dear little heart; and I'd rather break my own.'

'Nay, if that be the case,' answered the other, 'e'en go thy ways, Goodman Brown. I would not for twenty old women like the one hobbling before us that Faith should come to any harm.'

As he spoke, he pointed his staff at a female figure on the path, in whom Goodman Brown recognized a very pious and exemplary dame, who had taught him his catechism in youth, and was still his moral and spiritual adviser, jointly with the minister and Deacon Gookin.

'A marvel, truly, that Goody Cloyse should be so far in the wilderness at nightfall,' said he. 'But, with your leave, friend, I shall take a cut through the woods until we have left this Christian woman behind. Being a stranger to you, she might ask whom I was consorting with and whither I was going.'

'Be it so,' said his fellow-traveler. 'Betake you to the woods, and let me keep the path.'

Accordingly the young man turned aside, but took care to watch his companion, who advanced softly along the road until he had come within a staff's length of the old dame. She, meanwhile, was making the best of her way, with singular speed for so aged a woman, and mumbling some indistinct words – a prayer, doubtless – as she went. The traveler put forth his staff and touched her withered neck with what seemed the serpent's tail.

'The Devil!' screamed the pious old lady.

'Then Goody Cloyse knows her old friend?' observed the traveler, confronting her and leaning on his writhing stick.

'Ah, forsooth, and is it your worship indeed?' cried the good old dame. 'Yea, truly is it, and in the very image of my old gossip, Goodman Brown, the grandfather of the silly fellow that now is. But – would your worship believe it? – my broomstick hath strangely disappeared, stolen as I suspect, by that unhanged witch, Goody Cory, and that, too, when I was all anointed with the juice of smallage, and cinquefoil, and wolf's-bane – '

'Mingled with fine wheat and the fat of a newborn babe,' said the shape of old Goodman Brown.

'Ah, your worship knows the recipe,' cried the old lady, cackling aloud. 'So, as I was saying, being all ready for the meeting, and no horse to ride on, I made up my mind to foot it; for they tell me there is a nice young man to be taken into communion tonight. But now your good worship will lend me your arm, and we shall be there in a twinkling.'

'That can hardly be,' answered her friend. 'I may not spare you my arm, Goody Cloyse; but here is my staff, if you will.'

So saying, he threw it down at her feet, where, perhaps, it assumed life, being one of the rods which its owner had formerly lent to the Egyptian magi. Of this fact, however, Goodman Brown could not take cognizance. He had cast up his eyes in astonishment, and, looking down again, beheld neither Goody Cloyse nor the serpentine staff, but his fellow-traveler alone, who waited for him as calmly as if nothing had happened.

'That old woman taught me my catechism,' said the young man; and there was a world of meaning in this simple comment.

They continued to walk onward, while the elder traveller exhorted his companion to make good speed and persevere in the path, discoursing so aptly that his arguments seemed rather to spring up in the bosom of his auditor than to be suggested by himself. As they went, he plucked a branch of maple to serve for a walking-stick, and began to strip it of the twigs and little boughs, which were wet with evening dew. The moment his fingers touched them they became strangely withered and dried up as with a week's sunshine. Thus the pair proceeded at a good free pace, until suddenly, in a gloomy hollow of the road,

Goodman Brown sat himself down on the stump of a tree and refused to go any farther.

'Friend,' said he, stubbornly, 'my mind is made up. Not another step will I budge on this errand. What if a wretched old woman do choose to go to the Devil when I thought she was going to heaven: is that any reason why I should quit my dear Faith and go after her?'

'You will think better of this by and by,' said his acquaintance, composedly. 'Sit here and rest yourself awhile; and when you feel like moving again, there's my staff to help you along.'

Without more words, he threw his companion the maple-stick, and was as speedily out of sight as if he had vanished into the deepening gloom. The young man sat a few moments by the roadside, applauding himself greatly, and thinking with how clear a conscience he should meet the minister in his morning walk, nor shrink from the eye of good old Deacon Gookin. And what calm sleep would be his that very night, which was to have been spent so wickedly, but so purely and sweetly now, in the arms of Faith! Amidst these pleasant and praiseworthy meditations, Goodman Brown heard the tramp of horses along the road, and deemed it advisable to conceal himself within the verge of the forest, conscious of the guilty purpose that had brought him thither, though now so happily turned from it.

On came the hoof-tramps and the voices of the riders, two grave old voices, conversing soberly as they drew near. These mingled sounds appeared to pass along the road, within a few yards of the young man's hiding-place; but, owing doubtless to the depth of the gloom at that particular spot, neither the travelers nor their steeds were visible. Though their figures brushed the small boughs by the wayside, it could not be seen that they intercepted, even for a moment, the faint gleam from the strip of bright sky athwart which they must have passed. Goodman Brown alternately crouched and stood on tiptoe, pulling aside the branches and thrusting forth his head as far as he durst, without discerning so much as a shadow. It vexed him the more, because he could have sworn, were such a thing possible, that he recognized the voices of the minister and Deacon Gookin, jogging along quietly, as they were wont to do, when bound to some ordination or ecclesiastical council. While yet within hearing, one of the riders stopped to pluck a switch.

'Of the two, reverend sir,' said the voice like the deacon's, 'I had rather miss an ordination dinner than tonight's meeting. They tell me that some of our community are to be here from Falmouth and beyond, and others from Connecticut and Rhode Island, besides several of the Indian powwows, who, after their fashion, know almost as much deviltry as the best of us. Moreover, there is a goodly young woman to be taken into communion.'

'Mighty well, Deacon Gookin!' replied the solemn old tones of the minister. 'Spur up, or we shall be late. Nothing can be done, you know, until I get on the ground.'

The hoofs clattered again; and the voices, talking so strangely in the empty air, passed on through the forest, where no church had ever been gathered or solitary Christian prayed. Whither, then, could these holy men be journeying so deep into the heathen wilderness? Young Goodman Brown caught hold of a tree for support, being ready to sink down on the ground, faint and overburdened with the heavy sickness of his heart. He looked up to the sky, doubting whether there really was a heaven above him. Yet there was the blue arch, and the stars brightening in it.

'With heaven above and Faith below, I will yet stand firm against the Devil!' cried Goodman Brown.

While he still gazed upward into the deep arch of the firmament and had lifted his hands to pray, a cloud, though no wind was stirring, hurried across the zenith and hid the brightening stars. The blue sky was still visible except directly overhead, where this black mass of cloud was sweeping swiftly northward. Aloft in the air, as if from the depths of the cloud, came a confused and doubtful sound of voices. Once the listener fancied that he could distinguish the accents of townspeople of his own, men and women, both pious and ungodly, many of whom he had met at the communion-table, and had seen others rioting at the tavern. The next moment, so indistinct were the sounds, he doubted whether he had heard aught but the murmur of the old forest, whispering without a wind. Then came a stronger swell of those familiar tones, heard daily in the sunshine at Salem village, but never until now from a cloud of night. There was one voice, of a young woman, uttering lamentations, yet with an uncertain sorrow, and entreating for some favor, which, perhaps, it would grieve her to obtain; and all the unseen multitude, both saints and sinners, seemed to encourage her onward.

'Faith!' shouted Goodman Brown, in a voice of agony and desperation; and the echoes of the forest mocked him, crying, 'Faith! Faith!' as if bewildered wretches were seeking her all through the wilderness.

The cry of grief, rage, and terror was yet piercing the night, when the unhappy husband held his breath for a response. There was a scream, drowned immediately in a louder murmur of voices, fading into far-off laughter, as the dark cloud swept away, leaving the clear and silent sky above Goodman Brown. But something fluttered lightly down through the air and caught on the branch of a tree. The young man seized it, and beheld a pink ribbon.

'My Faith is gone! cried he, after one stupefied moment. 'There is no good on earth; and sin is but a name. Come, Devil; for to thee is this world given.'

And, maddened with despair, so that he laughed loud and long, did Goodman Brown grasp his staff and set forth again, at such a rate that he seemed to fly along the forest path rather than to walk or run. The road grew wilder and drearier and more faintly traced, and vanished at length, leaving him in the heart of the dark wilderness, still rushing onward with the instinct that guides mortal man to evil. The whole forest was peopled with frightful sounds, – the creaking of the trees, the howling of wild beasts, and the yell of Indians; while sometimes the wind tolled like a distant church-bell, and sometimes gave a broad roar around the traveler, as if all Nature were laughing him to scorn. But he was himself the chief horror of the scene, and shrank not from its other horrors.

'Ha! ha! ha!' roared Goodman Brown when the wind laughed at him. 'Let us hear which will laugh loudest. Think not to frighten me with your deviltry. Come witch, come wizard, come Indian powwow, come Devil himself, and here comes Goodman Brown. You may as well fear him as he fear you.'

In truth, all through the haunted forest there could be nothing more frightful than the figure of Goodman Brown. On he flew among the black pines, brandishing his staff with frenzied gestures, now giving vent to an inspiration of horrid blasphemy, and now shouting forth such laughter as set all the echoes of the forest laughing like demons around him. The fiend in his own shape is less hideous than when he rages in the breast of man. Thus sped the demoniac on his course, until, quivering among the trees, he saw a red light before him, as when the felled trunks and branches of a clearing have been set on fire, and throw up their lurid blaze against the sky, at the hour of midnight. He paused, in a lull of the tempest that had driven him onward, and heard the swell of what seemed a hymn rolling solemnly from a distance with the weight of many voices. He knew the tune; it was a familiar one in the choir of the village meeting-house. The verse died heavily away, and was lengthened by a chorus, not of human voices, but of all the sounds of the benighted wilderness pealing in awful harmony together. Goodman Brown cried out; and his cry was lost to his own ear by its unison with the cry of the desert.

In the interval of silence he stole forward until the light glared full upon his eyes. At one extremity of an open space, hemmed in by the dark wall of the forest, arose a rock, bearing some rude, natural resemblance either to an altar or a pulpit and surrounded by four blazing pines, their tops aflame, their stems untouched, like candles at an evening meeting. The mass of foliage that had overgrown the summit of the rock was all on fire, blazing high into the night and fitfully illuminating the whole field. Each pendent twig and leafy festoon was in a blaze. As the red light arose and fell, a numerous congregation alternately shone forth, then disappeared in shadow, and again grew, as it were, out of the darkness, peopling the heart of the solitary woods at once.

'A grave and dark-clad company,' quoth Goodman Brown.

In truth they were such. Among them, quivering to and fro between gloom and splendor, appeared faces that would be seen next day at the council board of the province, and others which, Sabbath after Sabbath, looked devoutly heavenward, and benignantly over the crowded pews, from the holiest pulpits in the land. Some affirm that the lady of the governor was there. At least there were high dames well known to her, and wives of honored husbands, and widows, a great multitude, and ancient maidens, all of excellent repute, and fair young girls, who trembled lest their mothers should espy them. Either the sudden gleams of light flashing over the obscure field bedazzled Goodman Brown, or he recognized a score of the church-members of Salem village famous for their especial sanctity. Good old Deacon Gookin had arrived, and waited at the skirts of that venerable saint, his revered pastor. But, irreverently consorting with these grave, reputable, and pious people, these elders of the church, these chaste dames and dewy virgins, there were men of dissolute lives and women of spotted fame, wretches given over to all mean and filthy vice, and suspected even of horrid crimes. It was strange to see that the good shrank not from the wicked, nor were the sinners abashed by the saints. Scattered also among their pale-faced enemies were the Indian priests, or powwows, who had often scared their native forest with more hideous incantations than any known to English witchcraft.'

'But where is Faith?' thought Goodman Brown; and, as hope came into his heart, he trembled.

Another verse of the hymn arose, a slow and mournful strain, such as the pious love, but joined to words which expressed all that our nature can conceive of sin, and darkly hinted at far more. Unfathomable to mere mortals is the lore of fiends. Verse after verse was sung; and still the chorus of the desert swelled between like the deepest tone of a mighty organ; and with the final peal of that dreadful anthem there came a sound, as if the roaring wind, the rushing streams, the howling beasts, and every other voice of the unconverted wilderness were mingling and according with the voice of guilty man in homage to the prince of all. The four blazing pines threw up a loftier flame, and obscurely discovered shapes and visages of horror on the smoke-wreaths above the impious assembly. At the same moment the fire on the rock shot redly forth and formed a glowing arch above its base, where now appeared a figure. With reverence be it spoken, the figure bore no slight similitude, both in garb and manner, to some grave divine of the New England churches.

'Bring forth the converts!' cried a voice that echoed through the field and rolled into the forest.

At the word, Goodman Brown stepped forth from the shadow of the trees and approached the congregation, with whom he felt a loathful brotherhood by the sympathy of all that was wicked in his heart. He could have wellnigh sworn that the shape of his own dead father beckoned him to advance, looking downward from a smoke-wreath, while a woman, with dim features of despair, threw out her hand to warn him back. Was it his mother? But he had no power to retreat one step, nor to resist, even in thought, when the minister and good old Deacon Gookin seized his arms and led him to the blazing rock. Thither came also the slender form of a veiled female, led between Goody Cloyse, that pious teacher of the catechism, and Martha Carrier, who had received the Devil's promise to be queen of hell. A rampant hag was she. And there stood the Proselytes beneath the canopy of fire.

'Welcome, my children,' said the dark figure, 'to the communion of your race.

Ye have found thus young your nature and your destiny. My children, look behind you!'

They turned; and flashing forth, as it were, in a sheet of flame, the fiend worshippers were seen; the smile of welcome gleamed darkly on every visage.

'There,' resumed the sable form, 'are all whom ye have reverenced from youth. Ye deemed them holier than yourselves, and shrank from your own sin, contrasting it with their lives of righteousness and prayerful aspirations heavenward. Yet here are they all in my worshiping assembly. This night it shall be granted you to know their secret deeds; how hoary-bearded elders of the church have whispered wanton words to the young maids of their households; how many a woman, eager for widow's weeds, has given her husband a drink at bedtime and let him sleep his last sleep in her bosom; how beardless youths have made haste to inherit their father's wealth; and how fair damsels – blush not, sweet ones – have dug little graves in the garden, and bidden me, the sole guest, to an infant's funeral. By the sympathy of your human hearts for sin ye shall scent out all the places – whether in church, bedchamber, street, field, or forest – where crime has been commited, and shall exult to behold the whole earth one stain of guilt, one mighty blood-spot. Far more than this. It shall be yours to penetrate, in every bosom, the deep mystery of sin, the fountain of all wicked arts, and which inexhaustibly supplies more evil impulses than human power – than my power at its utmost – can make manifest in deeds. And now, my children, look upon each other.'

They did so; and, by the blaze of the hell-kindled torches, the wretched man beheld his Faith, and the wife her husband, trembling before that unhallowed altar.

'Lo, there ye stand, my children,' said the figure, in a deep and solemn tone, almost sad with its despairing awfulness, as if his once angelic nature could yet mourn for our miserable race. 'Depending upon one another's hearts, ye had still hoped that virtue were not all a dream. Now are ye undeceived. Evil is the nature of mankind. Evil must be your only happiness. Welcome again, my children, to the communion of your race,'

'Welcome,' repeated the fiend worshippers, in one cry of despair and triumph.

And there they stood, the only pair, as it seemed, who were yet hesitating on the verge of wickedness in this dark world. A basin was hollowed, naturally, in the rock. Did it contain water, reddened by the lurid light? or was it blood? or, perchance, a liquid flame? Herein did the shape of evil dip his hand and prepare to lay the mark of baptism upon their foreheads, that they might be partakers of the mystery of sin, more conscious of the secret guilt of others, both in deed and thought, than they could now be of their own. The husband cast one look at his pale wife, and Faith at him. What polluted wretches would the next glance show them to each other, shuddering alike at what they disclosed and what they saw!

'Faith! Faith!' cried the husband, 'look up to Heaven, and resist the wicked one.'

Whether Faith obeyed, he knew not. Hardly had he spoken, when he found himself amid calm night and solitude, listening to a roar of the wind which died heavily away through the forest. He staggered against the rock, and felt it chill and damp; while a hanging twig, that had been all on fire, besprinkled his cheek with the coldest dew.

The next morning young Goodman Brown came slowly into the street of Salem village, staring around him like a bewildered man. The good old minister was taking a walk along the graveyard to get an appetite for breakfast and meditate his sermon, and bestowed a blessing, as he passed, on Goodman Brown. He shrank from the venerable saint as if to avoid an anathema. Old Deacon Gookin was at domestic worship, and the holy words of his prayer were heard through the open window. 'What God doth the wizard pray to?' quoth Goodman Brown. Goody Cloyse, that excellent old Christian, stood in the early sunshine at her own lattice, catechizing a little girl who had brought her a pint of morning's milk. Goodman Brown snatched away the child as from the grasp of the fiend himself. Turning the corner by the meeting-house, he spied the head of Faith, with the pink ribbons, gazing anxiously forth, and bursting into such joy at sight of him that she skipped along the street and almost kissed her husband before the whole village. But Goodman Brown looked sternly and sadly into her face, and passed on without a greeting.

Had Goodman Brown fallen asleep in the forest, and only dreamed a wild dream of a witch-meeting?

Be it so, if you will; but, alas! it was a dream of evil omen for young Goodman Brown. A stern, a sad, a darkly meditative, a distrustful, if not a desperate, man did he become from the night of that fearful dream. On the Sabbath day, when the congregation were singing a holy psalm, he could not listen, because an anthem of sin rushed loudly upon his ear and drowned all the blessed strain. When the minister spoke from the pulpit, with power and fervid eloquence, and with his hand on the open Bible, of the sacred truths of our religion, and of saint-like lives and triumphant deaths, and of future bliss or misery unutterable, then did Goodman Brown turn pale, dreading lest the roof should thunder down upon the grey blasphemer and his hearers. Often, awakening suddenly at midnight, he shrank from the bosom of Faith; and at morning or eventide, when the family knelt down to prayer, he scowled, and muttered to himself, and gazed sternly at his wife, and turned away. And when he had lived long, and was borne to his grave, a hoary corpse, followed by Faith, an aged woman, and children and grandchildren, a goodly procession, besides neighbours not a few, they carved no hopeful verse upon his tombstone; for his dying hour was gloom.

The Masque of the Red Death

Edgar Allan Poe

The 'Red Death' had long devastated the country. No pestilence had ever been so fatal, or so hideous. Blood was its Avatar and its seal – the redness and the horror of blood. There were sharp pains, and sudden dizziness, and then profuse bleeding at the pores, with dissolution. The scarlet stains upon the body and especially upon the face of the victim, were the pest ban which shut him out from the aid and from the sympathy of his fellow-men. And the whole seizure, progress, and termination of the disease, were the incidents of half an hour.

But the Prince Prospero was happy and dauntless and sagacious. When his dominions were half depopulated, he summoned to his presence a thousand hale and light-hearted friends from among the knights and dames of his court, and with these retired to the deep seclusion of one of his castellated abbeys. This was an extensive and magnificent structure, the creation of the prince's own eccentric yet august taste. A strong and lofty wall girdled it in. This wall had gates of iron. The courtiers, having entered, brought furnaces and massy hammers and welded the bolts. They resolved to leave means neither of ingress nor egress to the sudden impulses of despair or of frenzy from within. The abbey was amply provisioned. With such precautions the courtiers might bid defiance to contagion. The external world could take care of itself. In the meantime it was folly to grieve, or to think. The prince had provided all the appliances of pleasure. There were buffoons, there were improvisatori, there were ballet-dancers, there were musicians, there was Beauty, there was wine. All these and security were within. Without was the 'Red Death.'

It was toward the close of the fifth or sixth month of his seclusion, and while the pestilence raged most furiously abroad, that the Prince Prospero entertained his thousand friends at a masked ball of the most unusual magnificence.

It was a voluptuous scene, that masquerade. But first let me tell of the rooms in which it was held. There were seven – an imperial suite. In many palaces, however, such suites form a long and straight vista, while the folding doors slide back nearly to the walls on either hand, so that the view of the whole extent is scarcely impeded. Here the case was very different; as might have been expected from the duke's love of the *bizarre*. The apartments were so irregularly disposed that the vision embraced but little more than one at a time. There was a sharp turn at every twenty or thirty yards, and at each turn a novel effect. To the right and left, in the middle of each wall, a tall and narrow Gothic window looked out upon a closed corridor which pursued the windings of the suite. These windows were of stained glass whose color varied in accordance with the prevailing hue of the decorations of the chamber into which it opened. That at the eastern extremity was hung, for example, in blue – and vividly blue were its windows. The second chamber was purple in its ornaments and tapestries, and here the panes were purple. The third was green throughout, and so were the casements. The fourth was furnished and lighted with orange – the fifth with white – the sixth with violet. The seventh apartment was closely shrouded in black velvet tapestries that hung all over the ceiling and down the walls, falling in heavy folds upon a carpet of the same material and hue. But in this chamber only, the color of the windows failed to correspond with the decorations. The panes here were scarlet – a deep blood color. Now in no one of the seven apartments was there any lamp or candelabrum, amid the profusion of golden ornaments that lay scattered to and fro or descended from the roof. There was no light of any kind emanating from lamp or candle within the suite of chambers. But in the corridors that followed the suite, there stood, opposite to each window, a heavy tripod, bearing a brazier of fire, that projected its rays through the tinted glass and so glaringly illumined the room. And thus were produced a multitude of gaudy and fantastic appearances. But in the western or black chamber the effect of the fire-light that streamed upon the dark hangings through the blood-tinted panes was ghastly in the extreme, and produced so wild a look upon the countenances of those who entered, that there were few of the company bold enough to set foot within its precincts at all.

It was in this apartment, also, that there stood against the western wall, a gigantic clock of ebony. Its pendulum swung to and fro with a dull, heavy, monotonous clang; and when the minute-hand made the circuit of the face, and the hour was to be stricken, there came from the brazen lungs of the clock a sound which was clear and loud and deep and exceedingly musical, but of so peculiar a note and emphasis that, at each lapse of an hour, the musicians of the orchestra were constrained to pause, momentarily, in their performance, to hearken to the sound; and thus the waltzers perforce ceased their evolutions; and there was a brief disconcert of the whole gay company; and, while the chimes of the clock yet rang, it was observed that the giddiest grew pale, and the more aged and sedate passed their hands over their brows as if in confused revery or meditation. But when the echoes had fully ceased, a light laughter at once pervaded the assembly; the musicians looked at each other and smiled as if at their own nervousness and folly, and made whispering vows, each to the other, that the next chiming of the clock should produce in them no similar emotion; and then, after the lapse of sixty minutes (which embrace three thousand and six hundred seconds of the Time that flies), there came yet another chiming of the clock, and then were the same disconcert and tremulousness and meditation as before.

But, in spite of these things, it was a gay and magnificent revel. The tastes of the duke were peculiar. He had a fine eye for colors and effects. He disregarded the *decora* of mere fashion. His plans were bold and fiery, and his conceptions glowed with barbaric lustre. There are some who would have thought him mad. His followers felt that he was not. It was necessary to hear and see and touch him to be sure that he was not.

He had directed, in great part, the movable embellishments of the seven chambers, upon occasion of this great *fête*; and it was his own guiding taste which had given character to the masqueraders. Be sure they were grotesque. There were much glare and glitter and piquancy and phantasm – much of what has been since seen in 'Hernani'. There were arabesque figures with unsuited limbs and appointments. There were delirious fancies such as the madman fashions. There were much of the beautiful, much of the wanton, much of the *bizarre*, something of the terrible, and not a little of that which might have excited disgust. To and fro in the seven chambers there stalked, in fact, a multitude of dreams. And these – the dreams – writhed in and about, taking hue from the rooms, and causing the wild music of the orchestra to seem as the echo of their steps. And, anon, there strikes the ebony clock which stands in the hall of the velvet. And then, for a moment, all is still, and all is silent save the voice of the clock. The dreams are stiff – frozen as they stand. But the echoes of the chime die away – they have endured but an instant – and a light, half-subdued laughter floats after them as they depart. And now again the music swells, and the dreams live, and writhe to and fro more merrily than ever, taking hue from the many-tinted windows through which stream the rays from the tripods. But to the chamber which lies most westwardly of the seven there are now none of the maskers who venture; for the night is waning away; and there flows a ruddier light through the blood-colored panes; and the blackness of the sable drapery appals; and to him whose foot falls upon the sable carpet, there comes from the near clock of ebony a muffled peal more solemnly emphatic than any which reaches their ears who indulge in the more remote gaieties of the other apartments.

But these other apartments were densely crowded, and in them beat feverishly the heart of life. And the revel went whirlingly on, until at length there commenced the sounding of midnight upon the clock. And then the music ceased, as I have told; and the evolutions of the waltzers were quieted; and there was an uneasy cessation of all things as before. But now there were twelve strokes to be sounded by the bell of the clock; and thus it happened, perhaps that more of thought crept, with more of time, into the meditations of the thoughtful among those who reveled. And thus too, it happened, perhaps, that before the last echoes of the last chime had utterly sunk into silence, there were many individuals in the crowd who had found leisure to become aware of the presence of a masked figure which had arrested the attention of no single individual before. And the rumor of this new presence having spread itself whisperingly around, there arose at length from the whole company a buzz, or murmur, expressive of disapprobation and surprise – then, finally, of terror, of horror, and of disgust.

In an assembly of phantasms such as I have painted, it may well be supposed that no ordinary appearance could have excited such sensation. In truth the masquerade license of the night was nearly unlimited; but the figure in question had out-Heroded Herod, and gone beyond the bounds of even the prince's indefinite decorum. There are chords in the hearts of the most reckless which cannot be touched without emotion. Even with the utterly lost, to whom life and death are equally jests, there are matters of which no jest can be made. The whole company, indeed, seemed now deeply to feel that in the costume and bearing of the stranger neither wit nor propriety existed. The figure was tall and gaunt, and shrouded from head to foot in the habiliments of the grave. The mask which concealed the visage was made so nearly to resemble the countenance of a stiffened corpse that the closest scrutiny must have had difficulty in detecting the cheat. And yet all this might have been endured, if not approved, by the mad revelers around. But the mummer had gone so far as to assume the type of the Red Death. His vesture was dabbled in *blood* – and his broad brow, with all the features of the face, was besprinkled with the scarlet horror.

When the eyes of Prince Prospero fell upon this spectral image (which, with a slow and solemn movement, as if more fully to sustain its *rôle*, stalked to and fro among the waltzers) he was seen to be convulsed, in the first moment with a strong shudder either of terror or distaste; but, in the next, his brow reddened with rage.

'Who dares' – he demanded hoarsely of the courtiers who stood near him – 'who dares insult us with this blasphemous mockery? Seize him and unmask him – that we may know whom we have to hang, at sunrise, from the battlements!'

It was in the eastern or blue chamber in which stood the Prince Prospero as he uttered these words. They rang throughout the seven rooms loudly and clearly, for the prince was a bold and robust man, and the music had become hushed at the waving of his hand.

It was in the blue room where stood the prince, with a group of pale courtiers by his side. At first, as he spoke, there was a slight rushing movement of this group in the direction of the intruder, who, at the moment was also near at hand, and now, with deliberate and stately step, made closer approach to the speaker. But from a certain nameless awe with which the mad assumptions of the mummer had inspired the whole party, there were found none who put forth hand to seize him; so that, unimpeded, he passed within a yard of the prince's person; and, while the vast assembly, as if with one impulse, shrank from the centers of the rooms to the walls, he made his way uninterruptedly, but with the same solemn and measured step which had distinguished him from the first, through the blue chamber to the purple – through the purple to the green – through the green to the orange – through this again to the white – and even thence to the violet, ere a decided movement had been made to arrest him. It was then, however, that the Prince Prospero, maddening with rage and the shame of his own momentary cowardice, rushed hurriedly through the six chambers, while none followed him on account of a deadly terror that had seized upon all. He bore aloft a drawn dagger, and had approached, in rapid impetuosity, to within three or four feet of the retreating figure, when the latter, having attained the extremity of the velvet apartment, turned suddenly and confronted his pursuer. There was a sharp cry – and the dagger dropped gleaming upon the sable carpet, upon which, instantly afterward, fell prostrate in death the Prince Prospero. Then, summoning the wild courage of despair, a throng of the revelers at once threw themselves into the black apartment, and, seizing the mummer, whose tall figure stood erect and motionless within the shadow of the ebony clock, gasped in unutterable horror at finding the grave cerements and corpse-like mask, which they handled with so violent a rudeness, untenanted by any tangible form.

And now was acknowledged the presence of the Red Death. He had come like a thief in the night. And one by one dropped the revelers in the blood-bedewed halls of their revel, and died each in the despairing posture of his fall. And the life of the ebony clock went out with that of the last of the gay. And the flames of the tripods expired. And Darkness and Decay and the Red Death held illimitable dominion over all.

The Old Nurse's Story

Elizabeth Gaskell

You know, my dears that your mother was an orphan, and an only child; and I dare say you have heard that your grandfather was a clergyman up in Westmoreland, where I come from. I was just a girl in the village school, when, one day, your grandmother came in to ask the mistress if there was any scholar there who would do for a nursemaid; and mighty proud I was, I can tell ye, when the mistress called me up, and spoke to my being a good girl at my needle, and a steady honest girl, and one whose parents were very respectable, though they might be poor. I thought I should like nothing better than to serve the pretty young lady, who was blushing as deep as I was, as she spoke of the coming baby, and what I should have to do with it. However, I see you don't care so much for this part of my story, as for what you think is to come, so I'll tell you at once. I was engaged and settled at the parsonage before Miss Rosamond (that was the baby, who is now your mother) was born. To be sure, I had little enough to do with her when she came, for she was never out of her mother's arms, and slept by her all night long; and proud enough was I sometimes when missis trusted her to me. There never was such a baby before or since, though you've all of you been fine enough in your turns; but for sweet, winning ways, you've none of you come up to your mother. She took after her mother, who was a real lady born; a Miss Furnivall, a granddaughter of Lord Furnivall's in Northumberland. I believe she had neither brother nor sister, and had been brought up in my lord's family till she had married your grandfather, who was just a curate, son to a shopkeeper in Carlisle – but a clever, fine gentleman as ever was – and one who was a right-down hard worker in his parish, which was very wide, and scattered all abroad over the Westmoreland Fells. When your mother, little Miss Rosamond, was about four or five years old, both her parents died in a fortnight – one after the other. Ah! that was a sad time. My pretty young mistress and me was looking for another baby, when my master came home from one of his long rides, wet, and tired, and took the fever he died of; and then she never held up her head again, but just lived to see her dead baby; and have it laid on her breast before she sighed away her life. My mistress had asked me, on her deathbed, never to leave Miss Rosamond;

but if she had never spoken a word, I would have gone with the little child to the end of the world.

The next thing, and before we had well stilled our sobs, the executors and guardians came to settle the affairs. They were my poor young mistress's own cousin, Lord Furnivall, and Mr Esthwaite, my master's brother, a shopkeeper in Manchester; not so well-to-do then as he was afterwards, and with a large family rising about him. Well! I don't know if it were their settling, or because of a letter my mistress wrote on her deathbed to her cousin, my lord; but somehow it was settled that Miss Rosamond and me were to go to Furnivall Manor House, in Northumberland, and my lord spoke as if it had been her mother's wish that she should live with his family, and as if he had no objections, for that one or two more or less could make no difference in so grand a household. So, though that was not the way in which I should have wished the coming of my bright and pretty pet to have been looked at – who was like a sunbeam in any family, be it never so grand – I was well pleased that all the folks in the Dale should stare and admire, when they heard I was going to be young lady's maid at my Lord Furnivall's at Furnivall Manor.

But I made a mistake in thinking we were to go and live where my lord did. It turned out that the family had left Furnivall Manor House fifty years or more. I could not hear that my poor young mistress had ever been there, though she had been brought up in the family; and I was sorry for that, for I should have liked Miss Rosamond's youth to have passed where her mother's had been.

My lord's gentleman, from whom I asked as many questions as I durst, said that the Manor House was at the foot of the Cumberland Fells, and a very grand place; that an old Miss Furnivall, a great-aunt of my lord's, lived there, with only a few servants; but that it was a very healthy place, and my lord had thought that it would suit Miss Rosamond very well for a few years, and that her being there might perhaps amuse his old aunt.

I was bidden by my lord to have Miss Rosamond's things ready by a certain day. He was a stern proud man, as they say all the Lords Furnivall were; and he never spoke a word more than was necessary. Folk did say he had loved my young mistress, but that, because she knew his father would object, she would never listen to him, and married Mr Esthwaite; but I don't know. He never married at any rate. But he never took much notice of Miss Rosamond; which I thought he might have done if he had cared for her dead mother. He sent his gentleman with us to the Manor House, telling him to join him at Newcastle that same evening; so there was no great length of time for him to make us known to all the strangers before he, too, shook us off; and we were left, two lonely young things (I was not eighteen), in the great old Manor House. It seems like yesterday that we drove there. We had left our own dear parsonage very early, and we had both cried as if our hearts would break, though we were travelling in my lord's carriage, which I thought so much of. And now it was long past noon on a September day, and we stopped to change horses for the last time at a little smoky town, all full of colliers and miners. Miss Rosamond had fallen asleep, but Mr Henry told me to waken her, that she might see the park and the Manor House as we drove up. I thought it rather a pity; but I did what he bade me, for fear he should complain of me to my lord. We had left all signs of a town, or even a village, and were then inside the gates of a large wild park – not like the parks here in the south, but with rocks, and the noise of running water, and gnarled thorn trees, and old oaks, all white and peeled with age.

The road went up about two miles, and then we saw a great and stately house, with many trees close around it, so close that in some places their branches dragged against the walls when the wind blew; and some hung broken down; for no one seemed to take much charge of the place – to lop the wood, or to keep the moss-covered carriage-way in order. Only in front of the house all was clear. The great oval drive was without a weed; and neither tree nor creeper was allowed to grow over the long, many-windowed front; at both sides of which a wing projected, which were each the ends of other side fronts; for the house, although it was so desolate, was even grander than I expected. Behind it rose the Fells, which seemed unenclosed and bare enough; and on the left hand of the house, as you stood facing it, was a little, old-fashioned flower-garden, as I found out afterwards. A door opened out upon it from the west front; it had been scooped out of the thick dark wood for some old Lady Furnivall; but the branches of the great forest trees had grown and overshadowed it again, and there were very few flowers that would live there at that time.

When we drove up to the great front entrance and went into the hall I thought we should be lost – it was so large, and vast, and grand. There was a chandelier all of bronze, hung down from the middle of the ceiling; and I had never seen one before, and looked at it all in amaze. Then, at one end of the hall, was a great fireplace, as large as the sides of the houses in my country, with massy andirons and dogs to hold the wood; and by it were heavy old-fashioned sofas. At the opposite end of the hall, to the left as you went in – on the western side – was an organ built into the wall, and so large that it filled up the best part of that end. Beyond it, on the same side, was a door; and opposite, on each side of the fireplace, were also doors leading to the east front; but those I never went through as long as I stayed in the house, so I can't tell you what lay beyond.

The afternoon was closing in, and the hall, which had no fire lighted in it, looked dark and gloomy, but we did not stay there a moment. The old servant, who had opened the door for us, bowed to Mr Henry, and took us in through the door at the further side of the great organ, and led us through several smaller halls and passages into the west drawing-room, where he said that Miss Furnivall was sitting. Poor little Miss Rosamond held very tight to me, as if she were scared and lost in that great place, and as for myself, I was not much better. The west drawing-room was very cheerful-looking, with a warm fire in it, and plenty of good, comfortable furniture about. Miss Furnivall was an old lady not far from eighty, I should think, but do not know. She was thin and tall, and had a face as full of fine wrinkles if they had been drawn all over it with a needle's point. Her eyes were very watchful, to make up, I suppose, for her being so deaf as to be obliged to use a trumpet. Sitting with her, working at the same great piece of tapestry, was Mrs Stark, her maid and companion, and almost as old as she was. She had lived with Miss Furnivall ever since they both were young, and now she seemed more like a friend than a servant; she looked so cold and grey, and stony, as if she had never loved or cared for anyone; and I don't suppose she did care for anyone, except her mistress; and, owing to the great deafness of the latter, Mrs Stark treated her very much as if she were a child. Mr Henry gave some message from my lord, and then he bowed goodbye to us all – taking no notice of my sweet little Miss Rosamond's outstretched hand – and left us standing there, being looked at by the two old ladies through their spectacles.

I was right glad when they rung for the old footman who had shown us in at first, and told him to take us to our rooms. So we went out of the great drawing-room, and into another sitting-room, and out of that, and then up a great flight of stairs, and along a broad gallery – which was something like a library, having books all down one side, and windows and writing-tables all down the other – till we came to our rooms, which I was not sorry to hear were just over the kitchens; for I began to think I should be lost in that wilderness of a house. There was an old nursery, that had been used for all the little lords and ladies long ago, with a pleasant fire burning in the grate, and the kettle boiling on the hob, and tea-things spread out on the table; and out of that room was the night-nursery, with a little crib for Miss Rosamond close to my bed. And old James called up Dorothy, his wife, to bid us welcome; and both he and she were so hospitable and kind, that by and by Miss Rosamond and me felt quite at home; and by the time tea was over, she was sitting on Dorothy's knee, and chatting away as fast as her little tongue could go. I soon found out that Dorothy was from Westmoreland, and that bound her and me together, as it were; and I would never wish to meet with kinder people than were old James and his wife. James had lived pretty nearly all his life in my lord's family, and thought there was no one so grand as they. He even looked down a little on his wife; because, till he had married her, she had never lived in any but a farmer's household. But he was very fond of her, as well he might be. They had one servant under them, to do all the rough work. Bessy they called her; and she and me, and James and Dorothy, with Miss Furnivall and Mrs Stark, made up the family; always remembering my sweet little Miss Rosamond! I used to wonder what they had done before she came, they thought so much of her now. Kitchen and drawing-room, it was all the same. The hard, sad Miss Furnivall, and the cold Mrs Stark, looked pleased when she came fluttering in like a bird, playing and pranking hither and thither, with a continual murmur, and pretty prattle of gladness. I am sure, they were sorry many a time when she flittered away into the kitchen, though they were too proud to ask her to stay with them, and were a little surprised at her taste; though to be sure, as Mrs Stark said, it was not to be wondered at, remembering what stock her father had come of. The great, old rambling house was a famous place for little Miss Rosamond. She made expeditions all over it, with me at her heels; all, except the east wing, which was never opened, and whither we never thought of going, But in the western and northern part was many a pleasant room; full of things that were curiosities to us, though they might not have been to people who had seen more. The windows were darkened by the sweeping boughs of the trees, and the ivy which had overgrown them: but, in the green gloom, we could manage to see old china jars and carved ivory boxes, and great heavy books, and, above all, the old pictures!

Once, I remember, my darling would have Dorothy go with us to tell us who they all were; for they were all portraits of some of my lord's family, though Dorothy could not tell us the names of every one. We had gone through most of the rooms, when we came to the old state drawing-room over the hall, and there was a picture of Miss Furnivall; or, as she was called in those days, Miss Grace, for she was the younger sister. Such a beauty she must have been! but with such a set, proud look, and such scorn looking out of her handsome eyes, with her eyebrows just a little raised, as if she wondered how anyone could have the impertinence to look at her; and her lip curled at us, as we stood there gazing. She had a dress on, the like of which I had never seen before, but it was all the fashion when she was young: a hat of some soft white stuff like beaver, pulled a little over her brows, and a beautiful plume of feathers sweeping round it on one side; and her gown of blue satin was open in front to a quilted white stomacher.

'Well, to be sure!' said I; when I had gazed my fill. 'Flesh is grass, they do say; but who would have thought that Miss Furnivall had been such an out-and-out beauty, to see her now?'

'Yes,' said Dorothy. 'Folks change sadly. But if what my master's father used to say was true, Miss Furnivall, the elder sister, was handsomer than Miss Grace. Her picture is here somewhere; but, if I show it you, you must never let on, even to James, that you have seen it. Can the little lady hold her tongue, think you?' asked she.

I was not so sure, for she was such a little sweet, bold, open-spoken child, so I set her to hide herself; and then I helped Dorothy to turn a great picture, that leaned with its face towards the wall, and was not hung up as the others were. To be sure, it beat Miss Grace for beauty; and, I think, for scornful pride, too, though in that matter it might be hard to choose. I could have looked at it an hour, but Dorothy seemed half frightened at having shown it to me, and hurried it back again, and bade me run and find Miss Rosamond, for that there were some ugly places about the house, where she should like ill for the child to go. I was a brave, high-spirited girl, and thought little of what the old woman said, for I liked hide-and-seek as well as any child in the parish; so off I ran to find my little one.

As winter drew on, and the days grew shorter, I was sometimes almost certain that I heard a noise as if someone was playing on the great organ in the hall. I did not hear it every evening; but, certainly, I did very often; usually when I was sitting with Miss Rosamond; after I had put her to bed, and keeping quite still and silent in the bedroom. Then I used to hear it booming and swelling away in the distance. The first night, when I went down to my supper, I asked Dorothy who had been playing music, and James said very shortly that I was a gowk to take the wind soughing among the trees for music: but I saw Dorothy look at him very fearfully, and Bessy, the kitchenmaid, said something beneath her breath, and went quite white. I saw they did not like my question, so I held my peace till I was with Dorothy alone, when I knew I could get a good deal out of her. So, the next day, I watched my time, and I coaxed and asked her who it was that played the organ; for I knew that it was the organ and not the wind well enough, for all I had kept silence before James. But Dorothy had had her lesson, I'll warrant, and never a word could I get from her. So then I tried Bessy, though I had always held my head rather above her, as I was evened to James and Dorothy, and she was little better than their servant. So she said I must never, never tell; and if I ever told, I was never to say *she* had told me; but it was a very strange noise, and she had heard it many a time, but most of all on winter nights, and before storms; and folks did say, it was the old lord playing on the great organ in the hall, just as he used to do when he was alive, but who the old lord was, or why he played, and why he played on stormy winter evenings in particular, she either could not or would not tell me. Well! I told you I had a brave heart; and I thought it was rather pleasant to have that grand music rolling about the house, let who would be the player; for now it rose above the great gusts of wind, and wailed and triumphed just like a living creature, and then it fell to a softness most complete; only it was always music, and tunes, so it was nonsense to call it the wind. I thought at first that it might be Miss Furnivall who played, unknown to Bessy; but, one day when I was in the hall by myself, I opened the organ and peeped all about it and around it, as I had done to the organ in Crosthwaite Church once before, and I saw it was all broken and destroyed inside, though it looked so brave and fine; and then, though it was noonday, my flesh began to creep a little, and I shut it up, and run away pretty quickly to my own bright nursery; and I did not like hearing the music for some time after that, any more than James and Dorothy did. All this time Miss Rosamond was making herself more and more beloved. The old ladies liked her to dine with them at their early dinner; James stood behind Miss Furnivall's chair, and I behind Miss Rosamond's all in state; and, after dinner, she would play about in a corner of the great drawing-room, as still as any mouse, while Miss Furnivall slept, and I had my dinner in the kitchen. But she was glad enough to come to me in the nursery afterwards; for, as she said, Miss Furnivall was so sad, and Mrs Stark so dull; but she and I were merry enough; and, by-and-by, I got not to care for that weird rolling music, which did one no harm, if we did not know where it came from.

That winter was very cold. In the middle of October the frosts began, and lasted many, many weeks. I remembered, one day at dinner, Miss Furnivall lifted up her sad, heavy eyes, and said to Mrs Stark, 'I am afraid we shall have a terrible winter,' in a strange kind of meaning way. But Mrs Stark pretended not to hear, and talked very loud of something else. My little lady and I did not care for the frost; not we! As long as it was dry we climbed up the steep brows, behind the house, and went up on the Fells, which were bleak, and bare enough, and there we ran races in the fresh, sharp air; and once we came down by a new path that took us past the two old gnarled holly trees, which grew about halfway down by the east side of the house. But the days grew shorter and shorter; and the old lord, if it was he, played away more and more stormily and sadly on the great organ. One Sunday afternoon – it must have been towards the end of November – I asked Dorothy to take charge of little Missey when she came out of the drawing-room, after Miss Furnivall had had her nap; for it was too cold to take her with me to church, and yet I wanted to go. And Dorothy was glad enough to promise, and was so fond of the child that all seemed well; and Bessy and I set off very briskly, though the sky hung heavy and black over the white earth, as if the night had never fully gone away; and the air, though still, was very biting and keen.

'We shall have a fall of snow,' said Bessy to me. And sure enough, even while we were in church, it came down thick, in great large flakes, so thick it almost darkened the windows. It had stopped snowing before we came out, but it lay soft, thick and deep beneath our feet, as we tramped home. Before we got to the hall the moon rose, and I think it was lighter then – what with the moon, and what with the white dazzling snow – than it had been when we went to church, between two and three o'clock. I have not told you that Miss Furnivall and Mrs Stark never went to church: they used to read the prayers together, in their quiet gloomy way; they seemed to feel the Sunday very long without their tapestry-work to be busy at. So when I went to Dorothy in the kitchen, to fetch Miss Rosamond and take her upstairs with me, I did not much wonder when the old woman told me that the ladies had kept the child with them, and that she had never come to the kitchen, as I had bidden her, when she was tired of behaving pretty in the drawing-room. So I took off my things and went to find her and bring her to her supper in the nursery. But when I went into the best drawing-room, there sat the two old ladies, very still and quiet, dropping out a word now and then, but looking as if nothing so bright and merry as Miss Rosamond had ever been near them. Still I thought she might be hiding from me; it was one of her pretty ways; and that she had persuaded them to look as if they knew nothing about her; so I went softly peeping under this sofa, and behind that chair, making believe I was sadly frightened at not finding her.

'What's the matter, Hester?' said Mrs Stark, sharply. I don't know if Miss Furnivall had seen me, for, as I told you, she was very deaf, and she sat quite still, idly staring into the fire, with her hopeless face. 'I'm only looking for my little Rosy-Posy,' replied I, still thinking that the child was there, and near me, though I could not see her.

'Miss Rosamond is not here,' said Mrs Stark. 'She went away more than an hour ago to find Dorothy.' And she too turned and went on looking into the fire.

My heart sank at this, and I began to wish I had never left my darling. I went back to Dorothy and told her. James was gone out for the day, but she and me and Bessy took lights and went up into the nursery first, and then we roamed over the great large house, calling and entreating Miss Rosamond to come out of her hiding-place, and not frighten us to death in that way. But there was no answer; no sound.

'Oh!' said I at last. 'Can she have got into the east wing and hidden there?'

But Dorothy said it was not possible, for that she herself had never been in there; that the doors were always locked, and my lord's steward had the keys, she believed; at any rate, neither she nor James had ever seen them: so I said I would go back, and see if, after all, she was not hidden in the drawing-room, unknown to the old ladies; and if I found her there, I said, I would whip her well for the fright she had given me; but I never meant to do it. Well, I went back to the west drawing-room, and I told Mrs Stark we could not find her anywhere, and asked for leave to look all about the furniture there, for I thought now, that she might have fallen asleep in some warm hidden corner; but no! we looked, Miss Furnivall got up and looked, trembling all over, and she was nowhere there; then we set off again, everyone in the house, and looked in all the places we had searched before, but we could not find her. Miss Furnivall shivered and shook so much, that Mrs Stark took her back into the warm drawing-room; but not before they had made me promise to bring her to them when she was found. Well-a-day! I began to think she never would be found, when I bethought me to look out into the great front court, all covered with snow. I was upstairs when I looked out; but, it was such clear moonlight, I could see, quite plain, two little footprints, which might be traced from the hall door, and round the corner of the east wing. I don't know how I got down, but I tugged open the great, stiff hall door; and, throwing the skirt of my gown over my head for a cloak, I ran out. I turned the east corner, and there a black shadow fell on the snow; but when I came again into the moonlight, there were the little footmarks going up – up to the Fells. It was bitter cold; so cold that the air almost took the skin off my face as I ran, but I ran on, crying to think how my poor little darling must be perished, and frightened. I was within sight of the holly-trees when I saw a shepherd coming down the hill, bearing something in his arms wrapped in his maud. He shouted to me, and asked me if I had lost a bairn; and, when I could not speak for crying, he bore towards me, and I saw my wee bairnie lying still, and white, and stiff, in his arms, as if she had been dead. He told me he had been up the Fells to gather in his sheep, before the deep cold of night came on, and that under the holly-trees (black marks on the hillside, where no other bush was for miles around) he had found my little lady – my lamb – my queen – my darling – stiff and cold, in the terrible sleep which is frost-begotten. Oh! the joy, and the tears of having her in my arms once again! for I would not let him carry her; but took her, maud and all, into my own arms, and held her near my own warm neck and heart, and felt the life stealing slowly back again into her little gentle limbs. But she was still insensible when we reached the hall, and I had no breath for speech. We went in by the kitchen door.

'Bring the warming-pan,' said I; and I carried her upstairs and began undressing her by the nursery fire, which Bessy had kept up. I called my little lammie all the sweet and playful names I could think of – even while my eyes were blinded by my tears; and at last, oh! at length she opened her large blue eyes. Then I put her into her warm bed, and sent Dorothy down to tell Miss Furnivall that all was well; and I made up my mind to sit by my darling's bedside the live-long night. She fell away into a soft sleep as soon as her pretty head had touched the pillow, and I watched by her till morning light; when she wakened up bright and clear – or so I thought at first – and, my dears, so I think now.

She said that she had fancied that she should like to go to Dorothy, for that both the old ladies were asleep, and it was very dull in the drawing-room; and that, as she was going through the west lobby, she saw the snow through the high window falling – falling – soft and steady; but she wanted to see it lying pretty and white on the ground; so she made her way into the great hall; and then, going to the window, she saw it bright and soft upon the drive; but while she stood there, she saw a little girl, not so old as she was, 'but so pretty,' said my darling, 'and this little girl beckoned to me to come out; and oh, she was so pretty and so sweet, I could not choose but go.' And then this other little girl had taken her by the hand, and side by side the two had gone round the east corner.

'Now you are a naughty little girl, and telling stories,' said I. 'What would your good mamma, that is in heaven, and never told a story in her life, say to her little Rosamond, if she heard her – and I dare say she does – telling stories!'

'Indeed, Hester,' sobbed out my child, 'I'm telling you true. Indeed I am.'

'Don't tell me!' said I, very stern. 'I tracked you by your footmarks through the snow; there were only yours to be seen: and if you had had a little girl to go hand-in-hand with you up the hill, don't you think the footprints would have gone along with yours?'

'I can't help it, dear, dear Hester,' said she, crying, 'if they did not; I never looked at her feet, but she held my hand fast and tight in her little one, and it was very, very cold. She took me up the Fell-path, up to the holly-trees; and there I saw a lady weeping and crying; but when she saw me, she hushed her weeping, and smiled very proud and grand, and took me on her knee, and began to lull me to sleep; and that's all, Hester – but that is true; and my dear mamma knows it is,' said she, crying. So I thought the child was in a fever, and pretended to believe her, as she went over her story – over and over again, and always the same. At last Dorothy knocked at the door with Miss Rosamond's breakfast; and she told me the old ladies were down in the eating parlour, and that they wanted to speak to me. They had both been into the night-nursery the evening before, but it was after Miss Rosamond was asleep; so they had only looked at her – not asked me any questions.

'I shall catch it,' thought I to myself, as I went along the north gallery. 'And yet,' I thought taking courage, 'it was in their charge I left her; and it's they that's to blame for letting her steal away unknown and unwatched.' So I went in boldly, and told my story. I told it all to Miss Furnivall, shouting it close to her ear; but when I came to the mention of the other little girl out in the snow, coaxing and tempting her out, and willing her up to the grand and beautiful lady by the holly-tree, she threw her arms up – her old and withered arms – and cried aloud, 'Oh! Heaven, forgive! Have mercy!'

Mrs Stark took hold of her; roughly enough, I thought; but she was past Mrs Stark's management, and spoke to me, in a kind of wild warning and authority.

'Hester! keep her from that child! It will lure her to her death! That evil child! Tell her it is a wicked, naughty child.' Then Mrs Stark hurried me out of the room; where, indeed, I was glad enough to go; but Miss Furnivall kept shrieking out, 'Oh! have mercy! Wilt Thou never forgive! It is many a long year ago – '

I was very uneasy in my mind after that. I durst never leave Miss Rosamond, night or day, for fear lest she might slip off again, after some fancy or other; and all the more, because I thought I could make out that Miss Furnivall was crazy, from the odd ways about her; and I was afraid lest something of the same kind (which might be in the family, you know) hung over my darling. And the great frost never ceased all this time; and, whenever it was a more stormy night than usual, between the gusts, and through the wind, we heard the old lord playing on the great organ. But, old lord or not, wherever Miss Rosamond went, there I followed; for my love for her, pretty helpless orphan, was stronger than my fear for the grand and terrible sound. Besides, it rested with me to keep her cheerful and merry, as beseemed her age. So we played together, and wandered together, here and there, and everywhere; for I never dared to lose sight of her again in that large and rambling house. And so it happened, that one afternoon, not long before Christmas Day, we were playing together on the billiard-table in the great hall (not that we knew the right way of playing, but she liked to roll the smooth ivory balls with her pretty hands, and I liked to do whatever she did); and, by-and-by, without our noticing it, it grew dusk indoors, though it was still light in the open air, and I was thinking of taking her back into the nursery, when, all of a sudden, she cried out:

'Look, Hester! look! there is my poor little girl out in the snow!'

I turned towards the long narrow windows, and there, sure enough, I saw a little girl, less than my Miss Rosamond – dressed all unfit to be out-of-doors such a bitter night – crying, and beating against the window-panes, as if she wanted to be let in. She seemed to sob and wail, till Miss Rosamond could bear it no longer, and was flying to the door to open it, when, all of a sudden, and close upon us, the great organ pealed out so loud and thundering, it fairly made me tremble; and all the more, when I remembered me that, even in the stillness of that dead-cold weather, I had heard no sound of little battering hands upon the window-glass, although the Phantom Child had seemed to put forth all its force; and, although I had seen it wail and cry, no faintest touch of sound had fallen upon my ears. Whether I remembered all this at the very moment, I do not know; the great organ sound had so stunned me into terror; but this I know, I caught up Miss Rosamond before she got the hall-door opened, and clutched her, and carried her away, kicking and screaming into the large bright kitchen, where Dorothy and Bessy were busy with their mincepies.

'What is the matter with my sweet one?' cried Dorothy, as I bore in Miss Rosamond, who was sobbing as if her heart would break.

'She won't let me open the door for my little girl to come in; and she'll die if she is out on the Fells all night. Cruel, naughty Hester,' she said, slapping me; but she might have struck harder, for I had seen a look of ghastly terror on Dorothy's face, which made my very blood run cold.

'Shut the back-kitchen door fast, and bolt it well,' said she to Bessy. She said no more; she gave me raisins and almonds to quiet Miss Rosamond: but she sobbed about the little girl in the snow, and would not touch any of the good things. I was thankful when she cried herself to sleep in bed. Then I stole down to the kitchen, and told Dorothy I had made up my mind. I would carry my darling back to my father's house in Applethwaite; where, if we lived humbly, we lived at peace. I said I had been frightened enough with the old lord's organ-playing; but now that I had seen for myself this little moaning child, all decked out as no child in the neighbourhood could be, beating and battering to get in, yet always without any sound or noise – with the dark wound on its right shoulder; and that Miss Rosamond had known it again for the phantom that had nearly lured her to her death (which Dorothy knew was true); I would stand it no longer.

I saw Dorothy change colour once or twice. When I had done, she told me she did not think I could take Miss Rosamond with me, for that she was my lord's ward, and I had no right over her; and she asked me, would I leave the child that I was so fond of, just for sounds and sights that could do me no harm; and that they had all had to get used to in their turns? I was all in a hot, trembling passion; and I said it was very well for her to talk, that knew what these sights and noises betokened, and that had, perhaps, had something to do with the Spectre Child while it was alive. And I taunted her so, that she told me all she knew, at last; and then I wished I had never been told, for it only made me more afraid than ever.

She said she had heard the tale from old neighbours, that were alive when she was first married; when folks used to come to the hall sometimes, before it had got such a bad name in the countryside: it might not be true, or it might, what she had been told.

The old lord was Miss Furnivall's father – Miss Grace, as Dorothy called her, for Miss Maude was the elder, and Miss Furnivall by rights. The old lord was eaten up with pride. Such a proud man was never seen or heard of; and his daughters were like him. No one was good enough to wed them, although they had choice enough; for they were the great beauties of their day, as I had seen by their portraits, where they hung in the state drawing-room. But, as the old saying is, 'Pride will have a fall'; and these two haughty beauties fell in love with the same man, and he no better than a foreign musician, whom their father had down from London to play music with him at the Manor House. For, above all things, next to his pride, the old lord loved music. He could play on nearly every instrument that ever was heard of and it was a strange thing it did not soften him; but he was a fierce dour old man, and had broken his poor wife's heart with his cruelty, they said. He was mad after music, and would pay any money for it. So he got this foreigner to come; who made such beautiful music, that they said the very birds on the trees stopped their singing to listen. And, by degrees, this foreign gentleman got such a hold over the old lord, that nothing would serve him but that he must come every year; and it was he that had the great organ brought from Holland, and built up in the hall, where it stood now. He taught the old lord to play on it; but many and many a time, when Lord Furnivall was thinking of nothing but his fine organ, and his finer music, the dark foreigner was walking abroad in the woods with one of the young ladies; now Miss Maude, and then Miss Grace.

Miss Maude won the day and carried off the prize, such as it was; and he and she were married, all unknown to anyone; and before he made his next yearly visit, she had been confined of a little girl at a farm-house on the Moors, while her father and Miss Grace thought she was away at Doncaster Races. But though she was a wife and a mother, she was not a bit softened, but as haughty and as passionate as ever; and perhaps more so, for she was jealous of Miss Grace, to whom her foreign husband paid a deal of court – by way of blinding her – as he told his wife. But Miss Grace triumphed over Miss Maude, and Miss Maude grew fiercer and fiercer, both with her husband and with her sister; and the former – who could easily shake off what was disagreeable, and hide himself in foreign countries – went away a month before his usual time that summer, and half-threatened that he would never come back again. Meanwhile, the little girl was left at the farm-house, and her mother used to have her horse saddled and gallop wildly over the hills to see her once every week, at the very least – for where she loved, she loved; and where she hated, she hated. And the old lord went on playing – playing on his organ; and the servants thought the sweet music he made had soothed down his awful temper, of which (Dorothy said) some terrible tales could be told. He grew infirm too, and had to walk with a crutch; and his son – that was the present Lord Furnivall's father – was with the army in America, and the other son at sea; so Miss Maude had it pretty much her own way, and she and Miss Grace grew colder and bitterer to each other every day; till at last they hardly ever spoke, except when the old lord was by. The foreign musician came again the next summer, but it was for the last time; for they led him such a life with their jealousy and their passions, that he grew weary, and went away, and never was heard of again. And Miss Maude, who had always meant to have her marriage acknowledged when her father should be dead, was left now a deserted wife – whom nobody knew to have been married – with a child that she dared not own, although she loved it to distraction; living with a father whom she feared, and a sister whom she hated. When the next summer passed over and the dark foreigner never came, both Miss Maude and Miss Grace grew gloomy and sad; they had a haggard look about them, though they looked handsome as ever. But by-and-by Miss Maude brightened; for her father grew more and more infirm, and more than ever carried away by his music; and she and Miss Grace lived almost entirely apart, having separate rooms, the one on the west side, Miss Maude on the east – those very rooms which were now shut up. So she thought she might have her little girl with her, and no one need ever know except those who dared not speak about it, and were bound to believe that it was, as she said, a cottager's child she had taken a fancy to. All this, Dorothy said, was pretty well known; but what came afterwards no one knew, except Miss Grace, and Mrs Stark, who was even then her maid, and much more of a friend to her than ever her sister had been. But the servants supposed, from words that were dropped, that Miss Maude had triumphed over Miss Grace, and told her that all the time the dark foreigner had been mocking her with pretended love – he was her own husband; the colour left Miss Grace's cheek and lips that very day for ever, and she was heard to say many a time that sooner or later she would have her revenge; and Mrs Stark was forever spying about the east rooms.

One fearful night, just after the New Year had come in, when the snow was lying thick and deep, and the flakes were still falling – fast enough to blind anyone who might be out and abroad – there was a great and violent noise heard, and the old lord's voice above all, cursing and swearing awfully, – and the cries of a little child, – and the proud defiance of a fierce woman, – and the sound of a blow, – and a dead stillness, – and moans and wailings dying away on the hillside! Then the old lord summoned all his servants, and told them, with terrible oaths, and words more terrible, that his daughter had disgraced herself, and that he had turned her out of doors – her, and her child – and that if ever they gave her help, – or food, – or shelter, – he prayed that they might never enter Heaven. And, all the while, Miss Grace stood by him, white and still as any stone; and when he had ended she heaved a great sigh, as much as to say her work was done, and her end was accomplished. But the old lord never touched his organ again, and died within the year; and no wonder! for, on the morrow of that wild and fearful night, the shepherds, coming down the Fell side, found Miss Maude sitting, all crazy and smiling, under the holly-trees, nursing a dead child – with a terrible mark on its right shoulder. 'But that was not what killed it,' said Dorothy; 'it was the frost and the cold; every wild creature was in its hole, and every beast in its fold, while the child and its mother were turned out to wander on the Fells! And now you know all! and I wonder if you are less frightened now?'

I was more frightened than ever; but I said I was not. I wished Miss Rosamond and myself well out of that dreadful house for ever; but I would not leave her, and I dared not take her away. But oh! how I watched her, and guarded her! We bolted the doors, and shut the window-shutters fast, an hour or more before dark, rather than leave them open five minutes too late. But my little lady still heard the weird child crying and mourning; and not all we could do or say could keep her from wanting to go to her, and let her in from the cruel wind and the snow. All this time, I kept away from Miss Furnivall and Mrs Stark, as much as ever I could; for I feared them – I knew no good could be about them, with their grey hard faces, and their dreamy eyes, looking back into the ghastly years that were gone. But, even in my fear, I had a kind of pity – for Miss Furnivall, at least. Those gone down to the pit can hardly have a more hopeless look than that which was ever on her face. At last I even got so sorry for her – who never said a word but what was quite forced from her – that I prayed for her; and I taught Miss Rosamond to pray for one who had done a deadly sin; but often when she came to those words, she would listen, and start up from her knees, and say, 'I hear my little girl plaining and crying very sad – Oh! let her in, or she will die!'

One night – just after New Year's Day had come at last, and the long winter had taken a turn, as I hoped – I heard the west drawing-room bell ring three times, which was the signal for me. I would not leave Miss Rosamond alone, for all she was asleep – for the old lord had been playing wilder than ever – and I feared lest my darling should waken to hear the Spectre Child; see her I knew she could not. I had fastened the windows too well for that. So I took her out of her bed and wrapped her up in such outer clothes as were most handy, and carried her down to the drawing-room, where the old ladies sat at their tapestry-work as usual. They looked up when I came in, and Mrs Stark asked, quite astounded, 'Why did I bring Miss Rosamond there, out of her warm bed?' I had begun to whisper, 'Because I was afraid of her being tempted out while I was away, by the wild child in the snow,' when she stopped me short (with a glance at Miss Furnivall), and said Miss Furnivall wanted me to undo some work she had done wrong, and which neither of them could see to unpick. So I laid my pretty dear on the sofa, and sat down on a stool by them, and hardened my heart against them, as I heard the wind rising and howling.

Miss Rosamond slept on sound, for all the wind blew so; and Miss Furnivall said never a word, nor looked round when the gusts shook the windows. All at once she started up to her full height, and put up one hand, as if to bid us listen.

'I hear voices!' said she. 'I heard terrible screams – I hear my father's voice!'

Just at that moment my darling wakened with a sudden start: 'My little girl is crying, oh, how she is crying!' and she tried to get up and go to her, but she got her feet entangled in the blanket, and I caught her up; for my flesh had begun to creep at these noises, which they heard while we could catch no sound. In a minute or two the noises came, and gathered fast, and filled our ears; we, too, heard voices and screams, and no longer heard the winter's wind that raged abroad. Mrs Stark looked at me, and I at her, but we dared not speak. Suddenly Miss Furnivall went towards the door, out into the ante-room, through the west lobby, and opened the door into the great hall. Mrs Stark followed, and I durst not be left, though my heart almost stopped beating for fear. I wrapped my darling tight in my arms, and went out with them. In the hall the screams were louder than ever; they sounded to come from the east wing – nearer and nearer – close on the other side of the locked-up doors – close behind her. Then I noticed that the great bronze chandelier seemed all alight, though the hall was dim, and that a fire was blazing in the vast hearth-place, though it gave no heat; and I shuddered up with terror, and folded my darling closer to me. But as I did so, the east door shook, and she, suddenly struggling to get free from me, cried, 'Hester! I must go! My little girl is there; I hear her; she is coming! Hester, I must go!'

I held her tight with all my strength; with a set will, I held her. If I had died, my hands would have grasped her still, I was so resolved in my mind. Miss Furnivall stood listening, and paid no regard to my darling, who had got down to the ground, and whom I, upon my knees now, was holding with both my arms clasped round her neck; she still striving and crying to get free.

All at once the east door gave way with a thundering crash, as if torn in a violent passion, and there came into that broad and mysterious light, the figure of a tall old man, with grey hair and gleaming eyes. He drove before him, with many a relentless gesture of abhorrence, a stern and beautiful woman, with a little child clinging to her dress.

'Oh Hester! Hester!' cried Miss Rosamond. 'It's the lady! the lady below the holly-trees; and my little girl is with her. Hester! Hester! let me go to her; they are drawing me to them. I feel them – I feel them. I must go!'

Again she was almost convulsed by her efforts to get away; but I held her tighter and tighter, till I feared I should do her a hurt; but rather that than let her go towards those terrible phantoms. They passed along towards the great hall-door, where the winds howled and ravened for their prey; but before they reached that, the lady turned; and I could see that she defied the old man with a fierce and proud defiance; but then she quailed – and then she threw up her arms wildly and piteously to save her child – her little child – from a blow from his uplifted crutch.

And Miss Rosamond was torn as by a power stronger than mine, and writhed in my arms, and sobbed (for by this time the poor darling was growing faint).

'They want me to go with them on to the Fells – they are drawing me to them. Oh, my little girl! I would come, but cruel, wicked Hester holds me very tight.' But when she saw the uplifted crutch she swooned away, and I thanked God for it. Just at this moment – when the tall old man, his hair streaming as in the blast of a furnace, was going to strike the little shrinking child – Miss Furnivall, the old woman by my side, cried out, 'Oh, father! father! spare the little innocent child!' But just then I saw – we all saw – another phantom shape itself, and grow clear out of the blue and misty light that filled the hall; we had not seen her till now, for it was another lady who stood by the old man, with a look of relentless hate and triumphant scorn. That figure was very beautiful to look upon, with a soft white hat drawn down over the proud brows, and a red and curling lip. It was dressed in an open robe of blue satin. I had seen that figure before. It was the likeness of Miss Furnivall in her youth; and the terrible phantoms moved on, regardless of old Miss Furnivall's wild entreaty – and the uplifted crutch fell on the right shoulder of the little child, and the younger sister looked on, stony and deadly serene. But at that moment, the dim lights, and the fire that gave no heat, went out of themselves, and Miss Furnivall lay at our feet stricken down by the palsy – death-stricken.

Yes! she was carried to her bed that night never to rise again. She lay with her face to the wall, muttering low but muttering always: 'Alas! alas! what is done in youth can never be undone in age! What is done in youth can never be undone in age!'

The Dreamland Bride

THÉOPHILE GAUTIER

You ask me, brother, if I have loved. Yes, I have loved! The story is singular and terrible, and, for all my sixty-six years, I scarce dare stir the ashes of that memory.

To you I can refuse nothing; to a heart less hardened than yours this tale could never be told by me. For these things were so strange that I can scarce believe they came into my own existence. Three years was I the fool of a delusion of the devil. Three years was I a parish priest by day, while by night, in dreams (God grant they were but dreams!) I led the life of a child of this world, of a lost soul!

For one kind glance at a woman's face was my spirit to be doomed; but at length, with God to aid, and my patron saint, it was permitted to me to drive away the evil spirit that possessed me.

I lived a double life, by night and by day. All day long was I a pure priest of the Lord, concerned only with prayer and holy things; but when I closed my eyes in sleep then I was a young knight, a lover of women, of horses and hounds, a drinker, a dicer, a blasphemer, and, when I woke at dawn, meseemed that I was fallen on sleep, and did but dream that I was a priest. From those years of dreaming certain memories yet remain with me; memories of words and things that will not drown. Aye, though I have never left the walls of my vicarage, he who heard me would rather deem me one that had lived in the world and left it, to die in religion, and end in the breast of God his tumultuous day, than for a priest grown old in a forgotten church, deep in a wood, and far from the things of this earth.

Yes, I have loved as never man loved, with a wild love and a terrible one, so that I marvel my heart did not burst asunder. Oh, the nights of long ago! From my earliest childhood had I felt the call to be a priest. This was the end of all my studies, and, till I was twenty-four, my days were one long training. My theological course achieved, I took the lesser orders, and, at length, at the end of Holy Week was to be the hour of my ordination.

I had never entered the world; my world was the college close. Vaguely I knew that women existed, but of women I never thought. My heart was wholly pure.

Even my old and infirm mother I saw but twice a year; of other worldly relations I had none.

I had no regrets and no hesitations in taking the irrevocable vow; nay, I was full of an impatient joy. Never did a young bridegroom so eagerly count the hours to his wedding. In my sleep I dreamed of saying the Mass. To be a priest seemed to me the noblest thing in the world, and I would have disdained the estate of poet or of king. To be a priest! My ambition was nothing higher.

All this I tell you that you may know how little I deserved that which befell me; that you may know how inexplicable was the fascination by which I was overcome.

The great day came, and I walked to church as if I were winged or walked on air. I felt an angelic beatitude, and marvelled at the gloomy and thoughtful faces of my companions, for we were many.

The night I had passed in prayer. I was all but entranced in ecstasy. The bishop, a venerable old man, was in my eyes like a god, and I seemed to see heaven open beyond the arches of the minster.

You know the ceremony: the Benediction, the Communion in both kinds, the anointing of the palms of the hands with consecrated oil, and finally, the celebration of the holy rite, offered up in company with the bishop.

On these things I will not linger, but oh, how true is the word of Job, that he is foolish who maketh not a covenant with his eyes! I chanced to raise my head, and saw before me, so near that it seemed I could touch her, though in reality she was at some distance, and on the farther side of a railing, a young dame royally clad, and of incomparable beauty.

It was as if scales had fallen from my eyes; and I felt like a blind man who suddenly recovers his sight. The bishop, so splendid a moment ago, seemed to fade; through all the church was darkness, and the candles paled in their sconces of gold, like stars at dawn.

Against the gloom that lovely thing shone out like a heavenly revelation, seeming herself to be the fountain of light, and to give it rather than receive it.

I cast down my eyes, vowing that I would not raise them again; my attention was failing, and I scarce knew what I did. The moment afterwards I opened my eyes, for through my eyelids I saw her shining in a bright penumbra, as when one has stared at the sun. Ah, how beautiful she was!

The greatest painters, when they have sought in heaven for ideal beauty, and have brought to earth the portrait of Our Lady, came never near unto the glory of this vision! pen of poet, palette of painter, can give no vision of her. She was tall, with the bearing we give to a goddess. Her fair hair bowed about her brows in streams of gold. Like a crowned queen she stood there, with her broad, white brow and dark eyebrows; with her eyes of the brightness and life of the green sea, and one glance made or marred the destiny of a man. They were astonishingly clear and brilliant, shooting rays like arrows, which I could see winging straight for my heart. I know not if the flame that lighted them came from heaven or hell, but from one or other assuredly it came. Angel or devil, or both; this woman was no child of Eve, the mother of us all. White teeth shone in her smile, little dimples came and went with each movement of her mouth, among the roses of her cheeks. There was a lustre as of agate on the smooth and shining skin of her half-clad shoulders, and chains of great pearls no whiter than her neck fell over her breast.

From time to time she lifted her head in snake-like motion, and set the silvery ruffles of her raiment quivering. She wore a flame-coloured velvet robe, and from the ermine lining of her sleeves her delicate hands came and went, as transparent as the fingers of the dawn. As I gazed at her, I felt within me, as it were, the opening of gates that had ever been barred; I saw sudden vistas of an unknown future; all life seemed altered, new thoughts wakened in my heart. A horrible pain took possession of me; each minute seemed at once a moment and an age. The ceremony went on and on, and I was being carried far from the world, at whose gates my new desires were beating. I said, 'Yes,' when I wished to say 'No,' when my whole soul protested against the words my tongue was uttering. A hidden force seemed to drag them from me. This it is, perhaps, which makes so many young girls walk to the altar with the firm resolve to refuse the husband who is forced on them, and this is why not one of them does what she intends. This is why so many poor novices take the veil, though they are determined to tear it into shreds rather than speak the vows. None dare cause so great a scandal before so many observers, nor thus betray such general expectation. The will of all imposes itself upon you; the gaze of all presses upon you like a leaden cope. Again, all is so very clearly arranged in advance, so evidently irrevocable, that the intention to refuse is crushed out utterly, for ever.

The expression of the unknown lovely being changed as the ceremony advanced. Tender, caressing at first, it became contemptuous, disdainful. With an effort that might have moved a mountain, I strove to cry out that I would never be a priest; it was in vain, my tongue would not help in any cry, I could not refuse even by a sign. Though quite awake, I seemed to be in one of the nightmares wherein you cannot utter the word on which your life depends. She appeared to understand the torture which I endured, and cast on me a glance of divine pity and promise.

'Be mine,' she seemed to say, 'and I shall make thee happier than God, and heaven and His angels will be jealous of thee. Tear the shroud of death wherein thou art swathed, for I am Beauty, and Youth, and Life; come to me, together we shall be love. What can Jehovah offer thee in exchange for thy youth? Our life will flow like a dream in the eternity of a kiss. Cast but the wine from that chalice and thou art free, and I will carry thee to the Unknown Isles, and thou shalt sleep upon my breast in a bed of gold beneath a canopy of silver; for I love thee, and would fain take thee from thy God, before whom so many noble hearts offer up the incense of their love, which dies before it reaches the heaven where He dwells.'

These words I seemed to hear singing in the sweetest of tunes, the words which her eyes sent to me resounded in my heart as if they had been whispered in my soul. I was ready to forswear God, and yet I went through each rite of the ceremony. She cast me a second glance, so full of entreaty and despair that I felt more swords pierce me than ever pierced the heart of Our Lady of Sorrows.

It was over. I was a priest. Then never surely did human force declare so keen a sorrow: the girl who sees her bethrothed fall dead at her side, the mother by the empty cradle, Eve at the gate of Eden, the miser who seeks his treasure and finds but a stone, even they look less sorely smitten, less inconsolable. The blood left her sweet face pale; her lovely arms fell powerless, her feet failed her, and she leaned against a pillar. I staggered to the door with a white face and moist eyes breathless, and with all the weight of the dome upon my head. As I was crossing the threshold a hand seized one of mine. It was a woman's hand, and though cold, yet it seemed to burn me like a brand.

'Miserable man, what hast thou done?' she whispered, and was then absorbed into the crowd.

The old bishop paused, and gazed severely at me, who was a piteous spectacle, now red, now pale, dazed and faint. One of my colleagues had compassion on me and took me home. I could not have gone alone. At the corner of a street, while the young priest's head was turned, a black page, curiously clad, came up to me and gave me as he passed a little leathern case with corners of wrought gold, signing to me to hide it. I thrust it into my sleeve and kept it till I was alone in my cell. Then I unclasped it. There were but these words written in it –

Clarimonde
at the
Palazzo Concini

So little was I a worldling that I had never heard of Clarimonde despite her fame, nay, nor knew where the Palazzo Concini was. I made many guesses, but so that I did but see her again, I cared little whether Clarimonde were a noble lady or no better than one of the wicked. This love, thus born in an hour, had taken root too deep for me to dream of casting it from me. This woman had made me utterly her own, a glance had been enough to change me, her will swayed mine, I lived not for myself but for her.

Many mad things did I, kissing my hand where hers had touched it, repeating her name for hours – *Clarimonde, Clarimonde*. I had but to close my eyes and she stood before me again as distinctly as if she were present. Then I murmured the words that she had spoken under the porch of the church: 'Miserable man, what hast thou done?'

I felt the horror of the strait wherein I was, and the dead and terrible aspect of the life that I had chosen was now revealed. *To be a priest!* Never to love, to know not the call of youth and sex, to turn from beauty, to close the eyes and crawl in the chill shade of cloister or church, to see none but deathly men, to watch by corpses, to wear the cassock in which they would at last bury me!

Then life arose in me like a river in flood, my blood rioted in my veins, my youth burst and flowered forth in a moment. How was I again to have sight of Clarimonde? I had no excuse for leaving the seminary, for I knew nobody in the town, and indeed was only waiting there till I should be appointed to a parish.

I tried to remove the bars of the window, but to descend without a ladder was almost impossible. Then, again, I could only escape by night, when I should be lost in the labyrinth of streets. Those difficulties which might have been nothing to others were enormous to a poor priest, now first in love without experience, money or knowledge of the world.

Ah! Had I not been a priest I might have seen her every day, I might have been her lover, her husband, I said to myself in the blindness of my heart. In place of being swathed in a cassock I might have worn silk and velvet, chains of gold, a sword and feather like all the fair young knights. My locks would not be tonsured but would fall in perfumed curls around my throat. But one hour spent before an altar and some garbled words, had cut me off from the company of the living. With my own hands I had sealed the stone upon the tomb of my past life; I had turned the key in the lock of my prison.

I walked to the window. The sky was heavenly blue, the trees had clothed them in the raiment of spring, all nature smiled with mockery in her smile. The square was full of people coming and going: young exquisites, young beauties, two by two, were walking in the direction of the gardens.

Workmen sang songs as they passed. On all sides there was a life, a movement, a gaiety that did but increase my sorrow and my solitude. A young mother, on the steps of the gate, was playing with her child, kissing its rosy little mouth with a hundred caresses, the childlike and divine caresses that are the secret of mothers.

Near them the father, with folded arms above a happy heart, smiled softly as he watched them. I could not continue to look without pain, but closed the window and flung myself on the bed with a feeling of horrible jealousy and hatred, so that I gnawed my fingers and my coverlet like a starved and untamed beast.

How long I lay thus I know not, but at last, as I turned in a spasm of rage, I saw the Abbé Sérapion curiously regarding me. I bowed my head in shame and hid my face with my hands.

'Romuald, my friend,' said he, 'some strange thing hath befallen thee. Satan hath desired to have thee, that he may sift thee like wheat; he goeth about to devour thee as a raging lion. Beware and make thyself a breastplate of prayer, a shield of the mortifying of the flesh. Fight and thou shalt overcome. Be not afraid with any discouragement; for the firmest hearts and the most surely guarded have known hours like these. Pray, fast, meditate, and the evil spirit will pass away from thee.'

Sérapion told me that the priest of C— was dead, that the bishop had appointed me to this charge, and that I must be ready by the morrow. I nodded assent, and the Abbé departed. I opened my Missal and strove to read in it, but the lines wavered confusedly and the volume slipped unheeded from my hands.

Next day Sérapion came for me; two mules were waiting for us at the gate with our slender baggage, and we mounted as well as we could. As we traversed the streets I looked around for Clarimonde in each balcony and window. But it was too early, and the city was yet asleep. When we had passed the gates and were climbing the heights, I turned back for a last glance at the place that was the home of Clarimonde. The shadow of a cloud lay on the city, the red roofs and the blue were mingled in a mist, whence rose here and there white puffs of smoke. By some strange optical effect one house stood up golden in a ray of light far above the roofs that were mingled in the mist. A league away though it was, it seemed quite close to us – all was plain to see; turrets, balconies, parapets, the weathercocks even.

'What is that palace we see yonder in the sunlight?' said I to Sérapion. He shaded his eyes with his hands, looked and answered –

'That is the old palace which Prince Concini has given to Clarimonde the harlot. Therein dreadful things are done.'

Even at that moment, whether it were the actual or the ideal I know not, methought I saw a white and slender shape cross the terrace, glance and disappear. It was Clarimonde! . . .

Ah! did she know how in that hour, at the height of the rugged way which led me from her, even at the crest of the ascent I should never tread again, I was watching her, eager and restless, watching the palace where she dwelt? By a mystery of mirage or light and a shade the palace seemed very near as if inviting me to enter and be lord of all. Doubtless she knew it, so closely bound was her heart to mine; and this it was which had urged her, in the raiment of the night, to climb the palace terrace in the frosty dews of dawn. The shadow slipped over the palace and, anon, there was but a motionless sea of roofs, marked merely by a billowy undulation of forms. Sérapion pricked on his mule, mine also hastened, and a winding of the road hid from me for ever the city of S— , where I was to return no more. At the end of three days' journey through sad fields we saw the steeple of my parish church high above the trees. Some winding lanes, bordered by cottages and gardens, brought us to the building, which was certainly of no great splendour. A porch with a few mouldings, and two or three pillars rudely carved in sandstone, a tiled roof with counterforts of sandstone – that was all. To the left was the graveyard deep in tall grasses, with an iron cross in the centre. The priests' house was to the right in the shadow of the church. Simplicity could not be further used nor cleanliness made less lovely.

There was an old dog and an elderly housekeeper, and when she learned that both were to be retained in my service her joy was great.

When I had been installed Sérapion returned to the college. I was left alone.

Unsupported, uncomforted as I was, the thought of Clarimonde again beset me, nor could I drive her memory away for all my efforts. One evening, as I walked among the box-lined paths of my little garden, I fancied that I saw among the trees the form of a woman, who followed all my movements, and whose green eyes glistened through the leaves. Green as the sea shone her eyes, but it was no more than a vision, for when I crossed to the other side of the alley, nothing did I find but the print of a little foot on the sand – a foot like the foot of a child. Now the garden was girt with high walls, and, for all my search, I could find no living thing within them. I have never been able to explain this incident, which, after all, was nothing to the strange adventures that were to follow.

Thus did I live for a whole year, fulfilling every duty of the priesthood – preaching, praying, fasting, visiting the sick, denying myself necessaries that I might give to the poor. But within me all was dry and barren – the fountains of grace were sealed. I knew not the happiness which goes with the consciousness of a holy mission fulfilled. My heart was otherwhere; the words of Clarimonde dwelt on my lips like the ballad burden a man repeats against his will. Oh, my brother, consider this! For the lifting up of mine eyes to behold a woman have I been harried these many years, and my life hath been troubled for ever.

I shall not hold you longer with the story of these defeats and these victories; let me come to the beginning of the new life.

One night there was a violent knocking at my gate. The old housekeeper went to open it, and the appearance of a man richly clad, tawny of hue, armed with a long dagger, stood before her in the light of her lantern. She was terrified, but he soothed her, saying that he needs must see me instantly concerning a matter of my ministry. Barbara brought him upstairs to the room where I was about going to bed. There the man told me that his mistress, a lady of high degree, was on the point of death, and desired to see a priest. I answered that I was ready to follow him, and, taking with me such matters as are needful for extreme unction, I went down hastily. At the door were two horses, black as night, their breath rising in white clouds of vapour. The man held my stirrup while I mounted; then he laid one hand on the pommel, and vaulted on the other horse. Gripping his beast with his knees, he gave him his head, and we started with the speed of an arrow, my horse keeping pace with his own. We seemed in running to devour the way, the black trees fled in the darkness like an army in rout. A forest we crossed, so gloomy and so frozen cold that I felt in all my veins a shudder of superstitious dread. The sparks struck from the flints by our coursers' feet followed after us like a trail of fire, and whoever saw us must have deemed us two ghosts riding the nightmare. Will-o'-the-wisps glittered across our path, the night birds clamoured in the forest deeps, and now and again shone out the burning eyes of wild cats. The manes of the horses tossed more wildly on the wind, the sweat ran down their sides, their breath came thick and loud. But whenever they slackened the groom called on them with a cry like nothing that ever came from a human throat, and again they ran their furious course. At last the tempest of their flight reached its goal; suddenly there stood before us a great dark mass, with shining points of flame. Our horses' hoofs clattered louder on a drawbridge, and we thundered through the dark depths of a vaulted entrance which gaped between two monstrous towers. Within the castle all was confusion – servants with burning torches ran hither and thither through the courts; on the staircases lights rose and fell. I beheld a medley of vast buildings, columns, arches, parapet and balcony – a bewildering world of royal or of fancy palaces. The negro page who had given me the tablets of Clarimonde, and whom I recognized at a glance, helped me to alight. A seneschal in black velvet, with a golden chain about his neck, and an ivory wand in his hand, came forward to meet me, great tears rolling down his cheeks to his snowy beard.

'Too late,' he said, 'too late, sir priest! But if thou hast not come in time to save the soul, watch, I pray thee, with the unhappy body of the dead.'

He took me by the arm; he led me to the hall where the corpse was lying, and I wept as bitterly as he, deeming that the dead was Clarimonde, the well and wildly loved. There stood a *prie-dieu* by the bed: a blue flame flickering from a cup of bronze cast all about the chamber a doubtful light, and here and there set the shadows fluttering.

In a chiselled vase on the table was one white rose faded, a single petal clinging to the stem; the rest had fallen like fragrant tears, and lay beside the vase. A broken black mask, a fan, masquerading gear of every kind were huddled on the chairs, and showed that death had come, unlooked for and unheralded, to that splendid house. Not daring to cast mine eyes upon the bed, I kneeled, and fervently began to repeat the Psalms, thanking God that between this woman and me He had set the tomb, so that now her name might come like a thing enskied and sainted in my prayers.

By degrees this ardour slackened, and I fell a-dreaming. This chamber, after all, had none of the air of a chamber of death. In place of the corpse-laden atmosphere that I was wont to breathe in these vigils, there floated gently through the warmth a vapour of orient essences, a perfume of woman and of love. The pale glimmer of the lamp seemed rather the twilight of pleasure than the yellow burning of the taper that watches by the dead. I began to think of the rare hazard that brought me to Clarimonde in the moment when I had lost her for ever, and a sigh came from my breast. Then meseemed that one answered with a sigh behind me, and I turned unconsciously.'Twas but an echo but, as I turned, mine eyes fell on that which they had shunned – the bed where Clarimonde lay in state. The flowered and crimson curtains, bound up with loops of gold, left the dead woman plain to view, lying at her length, with hands folded on her breast. She was covered with a linen veil, very white and glistering, the more by reason of the dark purple hangings, and so fine was the shroud that her fair body shone through it, with those beautiful, soft, waving lines, as of the swan's neck, that not even death could harden. Fair she was as a statue of alabaster carved by some skilled man for the tomb of a queen; fair as a young maid asleep beneath new-fallen snow.

I could endure no longer. The air as of a bower of love, the scent of the faded rose intoxicated me, and I strode through the chamber, stopping at each turn to gaze at the beautiful dead beneath the transparent shroud. Strange thoughts haunted my brain. I fancied that she was not really gone, that it was but a device to draw me within her castle gates and to tell me all her love. Nay, one moment methought I saw her foot stir beneath its white swathings, and break the stiff lines of the shroud.

'Is she really Clarimonde?' I asked myself presently. 'What proof have I? The black page may have entered the household of some other lady. Mad must I be thus to disquiet myself.'

But the throbbing of my heart gave me an answer.

'It is she . . . It is she!'

I drew near to the bed and looked with fresh attention at that which thus perplexed me. Shall I confess it? The perfection of her beauty, though shadowed and sanctified by death, harassed my heart; and that long rest of hers was wondrous like a living woman's sleep. I forgot that I had come there to watch by a corpse, and I dreamed that I was a young bridegroom on the threshold of the chamber of the veiled, half-hidden bride!

Broken with sorrow, wild with joy, shuddering with dread and desire, I stooped toward the dreamland bride and raised a corner of the sheet. Gently I raised it, holding my breath as though I feared to waken her. My blood coursed so fearsomely that I heard it surging through the veins of my temples. My brow was moist with sweat, as if I had lifted not filmy linen, but weighty marble.

There lay Clarimonde, even (in the face) as she was upon the day I was ordained a priest. The pallor of her cheeks, her dead lips fading coral, her long, downcast eyelids with their brown lashes breaking the marble of her cheeks – all gave her an air of sadness and pureness, of pensive patience that had a winsome magic. Her long, loose hair, the small blue flowers yet strewn through it, pillowed her head and veiled the glory of the soft flesh of her shoulders. Her fair hands were crossed. The exquisite roundness and ivory sheen of her arms proved even in death a triumphant lure.

Long did I wait and watch her silently, and still the more I gazed the less I could deem that life had for ever left her beautiful body. I knew not if it were an illusion, or a reflection from the lamp, but it was as if the blood began to flow again beneath that dead white of her flesh, and yet she lay eternally, immovably still. I touched her arm; it was cold, but no colder than her hand had been on the day when it met mine beneath the church porch.

I fell into my old attitude, stooping my face above her face, while down upon her rained the warm dew of my tears. Oh, the bitterness of impotence and of despair; oh, wild agony of that death-watch! The night crept on, and as I felt that the eternal separation drew near, I could not deny myself the sad last delight of one kiss on the dead lips that held all my love.

Oh, miracle! A light breath mingled with my breath, and the mouth of Clarimonde answered to the touch of mine!

Her eyes opened, and softly shone. She sighed, she uncrossed her arms, and folding them about my neck in a ravished ecstasy, –

'Ah, Romuald, it is thou!' she said, in a voice as sweet and languishing as the last trembling of a lyre. 'Ah, Romuald, what makest thou here? So long have I waited for thee that I am dead. Yet now we are betrothed, now I may see thee and visit thee. Farewell, Romuald, farewell! I love thee. It is all that I had to tell thee, and I give thee again that life which thou gavest me with thy kiss. Soon shall we meet again.'

Her head sank down, but still her arms clung to me as if they would hold me for ever. A wild gust of wind burst open the window and broke into the room. The last leaf of the white rose fluttered like a bird's wing on the stem, and then fell and flew through the open casement, bearing with it the soul of Clarimonde.

The lamp went out, and I fell fainting on the breast of the beautiful corpse.

When I came to myself I was lying on my own bed in the little chamber of the priest's house; my hand had slipped from beneath the coverlet, the old dog was licking it. Barbara hobbled and trembled about the room, opening and shutting drawers, and shaking powders into glasses. The old woman gave a cry of delight when she saw me open my eyes. The dog yelped and wagged his tail, but I was too weak to utter a word or make the slightest movement. Later, I learned that for three days I had lain thus, with no sign of life but a scarce perceptible breathing. These three days do not count in my life; I know not where my spirit went wandering all that time, whereof I keep not the slightest memory. Barbara told me that the same bronzed man who had come for me at night, brought me back in a closed litter next morning, and instantly went his way. So soon as I could recall my thoughts, I reviewed each incident of that fatal night. At first I deemed that I had been duped by art magic, but presently actual, palpable circumstances destroyed that belief. I could not suppose that I had been dreaming, for Barbara, no less than myself, had seen the man with the two coal-black steeds, and she described them accurately. Yet no one knew of any castle in the neighbourhood at all like that in which I had found Clarimonde again.

One morning Sérapion entered my room; he had come with all haste in answer to Barbara's message about my illness.

Though this declared his affection for me, none the more did his visit give me pleasure. There was somewhat inquisitive and piercing, to my mind, in the very glance of Sérapion, and I felt like a criminal in his presence. He it was who first discovered my secret disquiet, and I bore him a grudge for being so clear-sighted.

While he was asking about my health in accents of honeyed hypocrisy, his eyes, as yellow as a lion's, were sounding the depths of my soul.

Presently, 'The famous harlot Clarimonde is dead,' says he in a piercing tone – 'dead at the close of an eight-days' revel. It was a feast of Belshazzar or of Cleopatra. Good God, what an age is ours! The guests were served by dusky slaves, who spoke no tongue known among men, and who seemed like spirits from the pit. The livery of the least of them might have beseemed an emperor on a coronation day. Wild tales are told of this same Clarimonde, and all her lovers have perished miserably or by violence. They say she was a ghost, a female vampire, but I believe she was Satan himself.'

He paused and watched me. I could not master a sudden movement at the name of Clarimonde.

'Satan's talons are long,' said Sérapion, with a stern look, 'and tombs ere now have given up their dead. Threefold should be the seal upon the grave of Clarimonde, for this is not – it is said – the first time she hath died. God be with thee, Romuald.'

So speaking, Sérapion departed with slow steps.

Time passed and I was well again. Nay, I deemed that the fears of Sérapion and my own terrors were too great, till one night I dreamed . . . Scarce had I tasted the first drops of the cup of sleep when I heard the curtains of my bed open, and the rings rang. I raised myself on my arm and saw the one whom straightaway I knew for Clarimonde.

She held in her hand a little lamp such as is placed in tombs, and the light touched her dainty fingers to a rosy hue that merged slowly into the milk-white of her arm.

She was clad with naught but the linen shroud in which she had lain in state. The folds were clasped about her breast as it were in pudency by a hand all too small. So white she was that her shroud and her body were blended in the pallid glow of the lamp.

Swathed thus in the fine tissue that betrayed every line of her figure, she seemed a marble image of some lady at the bath rainier than a living woman. Dead or living, statue or woman, spirit or flesh, her beauty was ever the same, only the glitter of her sea-green eye was dulled – only the mouth, so red of old, wore but a tender tint of rose, like the white rose of her cheeks. The little blue flowers that I had seen in her hair were sere now, and all but bloomless; yet so winning was she, so winning that, despite the strangeness of the adventure, and her inexplicable invasion of my chamber, I was not afraid for one moment.

She placed the lamp on the table, and sat down by my bed-foot. Then, in those soft and silver accents which I never heard from any lips but hers, –

'Long have I made thee wait for me,' she said, 'and thou must have deemed that I had forgotten thee quite. But lo! I come from far, very far – even from that land whence no traveller has returned. There is no sunlight nor moon in the country whence I wander, only shadow and space. There the foot finds no rest, nor the wandering wing any way; yet here am I – behold me, for Love can conquer Death. Ah, what sad faces and terrible eyes have I seen in my voyaging, and in what labour hath my soul been, to find my body and to make her home therein again! How hard to lift was the stone that they had laid on me for a covering! Lo, my hands are sorely wounded in that toil! Kiss them, my love, and heal them.' And she laid her chill palms on my mouth, that I kissed many times, she smiling on me with an inexpressible sweetness of delight.

To my shame be it spoken, I had wholly forgotten the counsels of the Abbé Sérapion, and the sacred character of my ministry. I fell unresisting at the first attack. Nay, I did not even try to bid the tempter avaunt, but succumbed without a struggle before the sweet freshness of Clarimonde's fair body. Poor child! for all that is come and gone, I can scarce believe that she was indeed a devil; surely there was naught of the devil in her aspect. Never hath Satan better concealed his claws and his horns! She was crouching on the side of my bed, her heels drawn up beneath her in an attitude of careless and provoking grace. Once and again she would pass her little hands among my locks, and curl them, as if to try what style suited my face. It is worth noting that I felt no astonishment at an adventure so marvellous – nay, as in a dream the strangest events fail to surprise us, even so the whole encounter seemed to me perfectly natural.

'I loved thee long before I saw thee, Romuald, my love, and I sought for thee everywhere. Thou wert my dream, and I beheld thee in the church at that fatal hour. "It is he," I whispered to myself and cast on thee a glance fulfilled of all the love wherewith I had loved, and did love, and shall love thee a glance that would have ruined the soul of a cardinal, or brought a king with all his court at my feet.

'But thou wert not moved, and before my love thou didst place the love of God.

'Ah, 'tis of God that I am jealous – God whom thou hast loved and lovest more than me.

'Miserable woman that I am! Never shall I have all thy heart for myself alone – for me, whom thou didst awaken with one kiss; for me, Clarimonde the dead; for me, who for thy sake have broken the portals of the grave, and am come to offer to thee a life that hath been taken up again for this one end to make thee happy.'

So she spoke; and every word was broken in on by maddening caresses, till my brain swam, and I feared not to console her by this awful blasphemy; namely – that my love of her passed my love of God.

Then the fire of her eyes was rekindled, and they blazed as it had been the chrysoprase stone.

'Verily thou lovest me with a love like thy love of God,' she cried, making her arms a girdle for my body. 'Then thou shalt come with me, and whithersoever I go there wilt thou follow. Thou wilt leave these ugly black robes, thou wilt follow. Thou wilt leave these ugly black robes, thou wilt be of all knights the proudest and the most envied. The acknowledged lover of Clarimonde shalt thou be, of her who refused a Pope! Ah, happy life, ah, golden days, that shall be ours! When do we mount and ride, my gentleman?'

'Tomorrow,' I cried in my madness.

'Tomorrow,' she answered. 'I shall have time to change this robe of mine that is somewhat scant, nor fit for voyaging. Also must I speak with my retainers, that think me dead in good earnest, and lament me as well as they may. Money, carriages, change of raiment, all shall be ready for thee; at this hour tomorrow will I seek thee. Goodbye, sweetheart.' She touched my brow with her lips, the lamp faded into darkness, the curtains closed, a sleep like lead came down on me, sleep without a dream. I wakened late, troubled by the memory of my dream, which at length I made myself believe was but a vision of the night. Yet it was not without dread that I sought rest again, praying Heaven to guard the purity of my slumber.

Anon I fell again into a deep sleep, and my dream began again. The curtains opened, and there stood Clarimonde, not pale in her pale shroud, nor with the violets of death upon her cheek; but gay, bright, splendid, in a travelling robe of green velvet with strappings of gold, and kilted upon one side to show a satin undercoat. Her fair, curled locks fell in great masses from under a large black beaver hat, with strange white plumes; in her hand she held a little riding-whip, topped with a golden whistle. With this she touched me gently, saying –

'Awake, fair sleeper! Is it thus you prepare for your voyage? I had thought to find you alert. Rise, rise quickly; we have no time to lose!'

I leaped out of bed.

'Come, dress, and let us begone,' she said, showing me a little packet she had brought. 'Our horses are fretting and champing at the gate. We should be ten leagues from here.'

I arrayed myself in haste, while she instructed me, handed me the various articles of a knight's attire, and laughed at my clumsiness. She dressed my hair, and when all was done, gave me a little Venice pocket-mirror in a silver frame, crying –

'What think you of yourself now? Will you take me for your *valet de chambre*?'

I did not know my own face in the glass, and was no more like myself than a statue is like the uncut stone. I was beautiful, and I was vain of the change. The gold embroidered gallant attire made me another man, and I marvelled at the magic of a few ells of cloth, fashioned to a certain device. The character of my clothes became my own, and in ten minutes I was sufficiently conceited. Clarimonde watched me with a kind of maternal fondness as I walked up and down the room, proving my new raiment, as it were; then –

'Come,' she cried, 'enough of this child's play! Up and away, my Romuald! We have far to go; we shall never arrive.'

She took my hand and led me forth. The gates opened at her touch; the dog did not waken as we passed.

At the gate we found the groom with three horses like those he had led before, Spanish horses that sped swift as the wind. Presently we came on a plain where a carriage and four horses waited for us. The postilion drove them to a mad gallop. My arm was around the waist of Clarimonde, her head upon my shoulder, her breast pressing against me. From then mine became a double life: within me were two men that knew each other not – the priest who dreamed that by night he was a noble, the noble who dreamed that by night he was a priest.

Certainly I was, or thought I was, in Venice, in a great palace on the Grand Canal. Clarimonde loved life in the great style. Custom could not make her common. To love her was to love a score of mistresses. She returned my love a hundredfold. One day, when she had been unwell for a time, I cut my hand, and she sucked the blood from the wound.

'I shall not die! I shall not die!' she exclaimed. 'I shall yet love thee long, for my life is in thine. Thy blood has given me back my life!'

This event and the strange fears it inspired haunted me long.

Sérapion often reproached me. One day he said –

'To drive away the demon that possesses thee, there is but one thing to do. I know where Clarimonde is buried. We must unearth her, and the sight of the worms and the dust of death will make thee thyself again.'

So weary was I of my double life that I accepted his plan and at midnight we found her gravestone. Thereon we read these words –

ICI GÎT CLARIMONDE,
QUI FUT DE SON VIVANT
LA PLUS BELLE DU MONDE.

At length the pick of Sérapion smote the coffin lid, which he then raised, and I saw Clarimonde—on her pale mouth shone one drop of blood.

Sérapion, breaking forth into fury, shouted—

'Ah, there thou art . . . Devil, Harlot, Vampire; thou that drainest the blood of men!'

With this he sprinkled holy water over her, and she straightaway crumbled into dust.

'There lies thy love, Sir Romuald,' he said. 'Go now and dally at the Lido with thy beauty.'

I bowed my head. Within me all was ruin. Back to my poor priest's house I went. Romuald the lover said farewell to the priest. *But, next night, I saw Clarimonde!*

'Wretched man that thou art,' she cried. 'What hast thou done? Why hast thou hearkened to that foolish priest? Wert thou not happy? What ill had I done thee that thou must violate my tomb? Henceforth the link between our souls and bodies is broken. Thou shalt desire me. Farewell!'

Then she fled into space and I saw her never more. . . . Alas! It was truth she spoke; I long for her still. Dearly bought hath my salvation been, and the love of my Lord hath not been too much to replace the love of her.

Behold, brother, the story of my youth.

Let not thine eyes gaze upon a woman. Walk with glances that only seek the earth. For, be ye chaste and calm as ye may, one minute may damn thee to all eternity.

Captain Murderer

CHARLES DICKENS

If we all knew our own minds (in a more enlarged sense than the popular acceptation of that phrase), I suspect we should find our nurses responsible for most of the dark corners we are forced to go back to, against our wills.

The first diabolical character who intruded himself on my peaceful youth was a certain Captain Murderer. This wretch must have been an offshoot of the Blue Beard family, but I had no suspicion of the consanguinity in those times. His warning name would seem to have awakened no general prejudice against him, for he was admitted into the best society and possessed immense wealth. Captain Murderer's mission was matrimony, and the gratification of a cannibal appetite with tender brides. On his marriage morning, he always caused both sides of the way to church to be planted with curious flowers; and when his bride said, 'Dear Captain Murderer, I never saw flowers like these before: what are they called?' he answered, 'They are called Garnish for house-lamb,' and laughed at his ferocious practical joke in a horrid manner, disquieting the minds of the noble bridal company, with a very sharp show of teeth, then displayed for the first time. He made love in a coach and six, and married in a coach and twelve, and all his horses were milk-white horses with one red spot on the back which he caused to be hidden by the harness. For, the spot *would* come there, though every horse was milk-white when Captain Murderer bought him. And the spot was young bride's blood. (To this terrific point I am indebted for my first personal experience of a shudder and cold beads on the forehead.) When Captain Murderer had made an end of feasting and revelry, and had dismissed the noble guests, and was alone with his wife on the day month after their marriage, it was his whimsical custom to produce a golden rolling-pin and a silver pie-board. Now, there was this special feature in the Captain's courtships, that he always asked if the young lady could make pie-crust; and if she couldn't by nature or education, she was taught. Well. When the bride saw Captain Murderer produce the golden rolling-pin and silver pie-board, she remembered this, and turned up her laced-silk sleeves to make a pie. The Captain brought out a silver pie-dish of immense capacity, and the Captain brought out flour and butter and eggs and all things needful, except the inside of the pie; of materials for the staple of the pie itself, the Captain brought out none. Then said the lovely bride, 'Dear Captain Murderer, what pie is this to be?' He replied, 'A meat pie.' Then said the lovely bride, 'Dear Captain Murderer, I see no meat.' The Captain humorously retorted, 'Look in the glass.' She looked in the glass, but still she saw no meat, and then the Captain roared with laughter, and suddenly frowning and drawing his sword, bade her roll out the crust. So she rolled out the crust, dropping large tears upon it all the time because he was so cross, and when she had lined the dish with crust and had cut the crust all ready to fit the top, the Captain called out, '*I* see the meat in the glass!' And the bride looked up at the glass, just in time to see the Captain cutting her head off; and he chopped her in pieces, and peppered her, and salted her, and put her in the pie, and sent it to the baker's, and ate it all, and picked the bones.

Captain Murderer went on in this way, prospering exceedingly, until he came to choose a bride from two twin sisters, and at first didn't know which to choose. For, though one was fair and the other dark, they were both equally beautiful. But the fair twin loved him, and the dark twin hated him, so he chose the fair one. The dark twin would have prevented the marriage if she could, but she couldn't; however, on the night before it, much suspecting Captain Murderer, she stole out and climbed his garden wall, and looked in at his window through a chink in the shutter, and saw him having his teeth filed sharp. Next day she listened all day, and heard him make his joke about the house-lamb. And that day month, he had the paste rolled out, and cut the fair twin's head off, and chopped her in pieces, and peppered her, and salted her, and put her in the pie, and sent it to the baker's, and ate it all, and picked the bones.

Now, the dark twin had had her suspicions much increased by the filing of the Captain's teeth, and again by the house-lamb joke. Putting all things together when he gave out that her sister was dead, she divined the truth, and determined to be revenged. So, she went up to Captain Murderer's house, and knocked at the knocker and pulled at the bell, and when the Captain came to the door, said: 'Dear Captain Murderer, marry me next, for I always loved you and was jealous of my sister.' The Captain took it as a compliment and made a polite answer, and the marriage was quickly arranged. On the night before it, the bride again climbed to his window, and again saw him having his teeth filed sharp. At this sight she laughed such a terrible laugh at the chink in the shutter, that the Captain's blood curdled, and he said: 'I hope nothing has disagreed with me!' At that, she laughed again, a still more terrible laugh, and the shutter was opened and search made, but she was nimbly gone, and there was no one. Next day they went to church in a coach and twelve, and were married. And that day month, she rolled the pie-crust out, and Captain Murderer cut her head off, and chopped her in pieces, and peppered her, and salted her, and put her in the pie, and sent it to the baker's, and ate it all, and picked the bones.

But before she began to roll out the paste she had taken a deadly poison of a most awful character, distilled from toads' eyes and spiders' knees; and Captain

Murderer had hardly picked her last bone, when he began to swell, and to turn blue, and to be all over spots, and to scream. And he went on swelling and turning bluer, and being more all over spots and screaming, until he reached from floor to ceiling and from wall to wall; and then, at one o'clock in the morning, he blew up with a loud explosion. At the sound of it, all the milk-white horses in the stables broke their halters and went mad, and then they galloped over everybody in Captain Murderer's house (beginning with the family blacksmith who had filed his teeth) until the whole were dead, and then they galloped away.

Mr Justice Harbottle

SHERIDAN LE FANU

Thirty years ago, an elderly man, to whom I paid quarterly a small annuity charged on some property of mine came on the quarter-day to receive it. He was a dry, sad, quiet man, who had known better days, and had always maintained an unexceptionable character. No better authority could be imagined for a ghost story.

He told me one, though with a manifest reluctance; he was drawn into the narration by his choosing to explain what I should not have remarked, that he had called two days earlier than that week after the strict day of payment, which he had usually allowed to elapse. His reason was a sudden determination to change his lodgings, and the consequent necessary of paying his rent a little before it was due.

He lodged in a dark street in Westminster, in a spacious old house, very warm, being wainscoted from top to bottom, and furnished with no undue abundance of windows, and those fitted with thick sashes and small panes.

This house was, as the bills upon the windows testified, offered to be sold or let. But no one seemed to care to look at it.

A thin matron, in rusty black silk, very taciturn, with large, steady, alarmed eyes, that seemed to look in your face, to read what you might have seen in the dark rooms and passages through which you had passed, was in charge of it, with a solitary 'maid-of-all-work' under her command. My poor friend had taken lodgings in this house, on account of their extraordinary cheapness. He had occupied them for nearly a year without the slightest disturbance; and was the only tenant, under rent, in the house. He had two rooms; a sitting-room and a bed-room with a closet opening from it, in which he kept his books and papers locked up. He had gone to his bed, having also locked the outer door. Unable to sleep, he had lighted a candle, and after having read for a time, had laid the book beside him. He heard the old clock at the stair-head strike one; and very shortly after, to his alarm, he saw the closet-door, which he thought he had locked, open stealthily, and a slight dark man, particularly sinister, and somewhere about fifty, dressed in mourning of a very antique fashion, such a suit as we see in Hogarth, entered the room on tiptoe. He was followed by an elder man, stout, and blotched with scurvy, and whose features, fixed as a corpse's, were stamped with dreadful force with a character of sensuality and villany.

This old man wore a flowered silk dressing-gown and ruffles, and he remarked a gold ring on his finger, and on his head a cap of velvet, such as, in the days of perukes, gentlemen wore in undress.

This direful old man carried in his ringed and ruffled hand a coil of rope; and these two figures crossed the floor diagonally, passing the foot of his bed, from the closet door at the farther end of the room, at the left, near the window, to the door opening upon the lobby, close to the bed's head, at his right.

He did not attempt to describe his sensations as these figures passed so near him. He merely said, that so far from sleeping in that room again, no consideration the world could offer would induce him so much as to enter it again alone, even in the daylight. He found both doors, that of the closet, and that of the room opening upon the lobby, in the morning fast locked as he had left them before going to bed.

In answer to a question of mine, he said that neither appeared the least conscious of his presence. They did not seem to glide, but walked as living men do, but without any sound, and he felt a vibration on the floor as they crossed it. He so obviously suffered from speaking about the apparitions, that I asked him no more questions.

There were in his description, however, certain coincidences so very singular, as to induce me, by that very post, to write to a friend much my senior, then living in a remote part of England, for the information which I knew he could give me. He had himself more than once pointed out that old house to my attention, and told me, though very briefly, the strange story which I now asked him to give me in greater detail.

His answer satisfied me; and the following pages convey its substance.

Your letter (he wrote) tells me you desire some particulars about the closing years of the life of Mr Justice Harbottle, one of the judges of the Court of Common Pleas. You refer, of course, to the extraordinary occurrences that made that period of his life long after a theme for 'winter tales' and metaphysical speculation. I happen to know perhaps more than any other man living of those mysterious particulars.

The old family mansion, when I revisited London, more than thirty years ago, I examined for the last time. During the years that have passed since then, I hear that improvement, with its preliminary demolitions, has been doing wonders for the quarter of Westminster in which it stood. If I were quite certain that the house had been taken down, I should have no difficulty about naming the street in which it stood. As what I have to tell, however, is not likely to improve its letting value, and as I should not care to get into trouble, I prefer being silent on that particular point.

How old the house was, I can't tell. People said it was built by Roger Harbottle, a Turkey merchant, in the reign of King James I. I am not a good opinion upon such questions; but having been in it, though in its forlorn and deserted state, I can tell you in a general way what it was like. It was built of dark-red brick, and the door and windows were faced with stone that had turned yellow by time. It receded some feet from the line of the other houses in the street; and it had a florid and fanciful rail of iron about the broad steps that invited your ascent to the hall-door, in which were fixed, under a file of lamps among scrolls and twisted leaves, two immense 'extinguishers;' like the conical caps of fairies, into which, in old times, the footmen used to thrust their flambeaux when their chairs or coaches had set down their great people, in the hall or at the steps, as the case might be. That hall is panelled up to the ceiling, and has a large fireplace. Two or three stately old rooms open from it at each side. The windows of these are tall, with many small panes. Passing through the arch at the back of the hall, you come upon the wide and heavy well-staircase. There is a back staircase also. The mansion is large, and has not as much light, by any means, in proportion to its extent, as modern houses enjoy. When I saw it, it had long been untenanted, and had the gloomy reputation beside of a haunted house. Cobwebs floated from the ceilings or spanned the corners of the cornices, and dust lay thick over everything. The windows were stained with the dust and rain of fifty years and darkness had thus grown darker.

When I made it my first visit, it was in company with my father, when I was still a boy, in the year 1808. I was about twelve years old, and my imagination impressible, as it always is at that age. I looked about me with great awe. I was here in the very centre and scene of those occurrences which I had heard recounted at the fireside at home, with so delightful a horror.

My father was an old bachelor of nearly sixty when he married. He had, when a child, seen Judge Harbottle on the bench in his robes and wig a dozen times at least before his death, which took place in 1748, and his appearance made a powerful and unpleasant impression, not only on his imagination, but upon his nerves.

The Judge was at that time a man of some sixty-seven years. He had a great mulberry-coloured face, a big, carbuncled nose, fierce eyes, and a grim and brutal mouth. My father, who was young at the time, thought it the most formidable face he had ever seen; for there were evidences of intellectual power in the formation and lines of the forehead. His voice was loud and harsh, and gave effect to the sarcasm which was his habitual weapon on the bench.

This old gentleman had the reputation of being about the wickedest man in England. Even on the bench he now and then showed his scorn of opinion. He had carried cases his own way, it was said, in spite of counsel, authorities, and even of juries, by a sort of cajolery, violence, and bamboozling, that somehow confused and overpowered resistance. He had never actually committed himself; he was too cunning to do that. He had the character of being, however, a dangerous and unscrupulous judge; but his character did not trouble him. The associates he chose for his hours of relaxation cared as little as he did about it.

One night during the session of 1746 this old Judge went down in his chair to wait in one of the rooms of the House of Lords for the result of a division in which he and his order were interested.

This over, he was about to return to his house close by, in his chair; but the night had become so soft and fine that he changed his mind, sent it home empty, and with two footmen, each with a flambeau, set out on foot in preference. Gout had made him rather a slow pedestrian. It took him some time to get through the two or three streets he had to pass before reaching his house,

In one of those narrow streets of tall houses, perfectly silent at that hour, he overtook, slowly as he was walking, a very singular-looking old gentleman.

He had a bottle-green coat on, with a cape to it, and large stone buttons, a broad-leafed low-crowned hat, from under which a big powdered wig escaped; he stooped very much, and supported his bending knees with the aid of a crutch-handled cane, and so shuffled and tottered along painfully.

'I ask your pardon, sir,' said this old man, in a very quavering voice, as the burly Judge came up with him, and he extended his hand feebly towards his arm.

Mr Justice Harbottle saw that the man was by no means poorly dressed, and his manner that of a gentleman.

The Judge stopped short, and said, in his harsh peremptory tones, 'Well, sir, how can I serve you?'

'Can you direct me to Judge Harbottle's house? I have some intelligence of the very last importance to communicate to him.'

'Can you tell it before witnesses?' asked the Judge.

'By no means; it must reach *his* ear only,' quavered the old man earnestly.

'If that be so sir, you have only to accompany me a few steps farther to reach my house, and obtain a private audience; for I am Judge Harbottle.'

With this invitation the infirm gentleman in the white wig complied very readily; and in another minute the stranger stood in what was then termed the front parlour of the Judge's house, *tête-à-tête* with that shrewd and dangerous functionary.

He had to sit down, being very much exhausted, and unable for a little time to speak; and then he had a fit of coughing, and after that a fit of gasping; and thus two or three minutes passed, during which the Judge dropped his roquelaure on an armchair, and threw his cocked-hat over that.

The venerable pedestrian in the white wig quickly recovered his voice. With closed doors they remained together for some time.

There were guests waiting in the drawing-rooms, and the sound of men's voices laughing, and then of a female voice singing to a harpsichord, were heard distinctly in the hall over the stairs; for old Judge Harbottle had arranged one of his dubious jollifications, such as might well make the hair of godly men's heads stand upright for that night.

This old gentleman in the powdered white wig, that rested on his stooped shoulders, must have had something to say that interested the Judge very much; for he would not have parted on easy terms with the ten minutes and upwards which that conference filched from the sort of revelry in which he most delighted, and in which he was the roaring king, and in some sort the tyrant also, of his company.

The footman who showed the aged gentleman out observed that the Judge's mulberry-coloured face, pimples and all, were bleached to a dingy yellow, and there was the abstraction of agitated thought in his manner, as he bid the stranger goodnight. The avant saw that the conversation had been of serious import, and that the Judge was frightened.

Instead of stumping upstairs forthwith to his scandalous hilarities, his profane company, and his great china bowl of punch – the identical bowl from which a bygone Bishop of London, good easy man, had baptized this Judge's grandfather, now clinking round the rim with silver ladles, and hung with scrolls of lemon-peel – instead, I say, of stumping and clambering up the great staircase to the cavern of his Circean enchantment, he stood with his big nose flattened against the window-pane, watching the progress of the feeble old man, who clung stiffly to the iron rail as he got down, step by step, to the pavement.

The hall-door had hardly closed, when the old Judge was in the hall bawling hasty orders, with such stimulating expletives as old colonels under excitement sometimes indulge in now-a-days, with a stamp or two of his big foot, and a waving of his clenched fist in the air. He commanded the footman to overtake the old gentleman in the white wig, to offer him his protection on his way home, and in no case to show his face again without having ascertained where he lodged, and who he was, and all about him.

'By— sirrah! if you fail me in this, you doff my livery to-night!'

Forth bounced the stalwart footman, with his heavy cane under his arm, and skipped down the steps, and looked up and down the street after the singular figure, so easy to recognize.

What were his adventures I shall not tell you just now.

The old man, in the conference to which he had been admitted in that stately panelled room, had just told the Judge a very strange story. He might be himself a conspirator; he might possibly be crazed; or possibly his whole story was straight and true.

The aged gentleman in the bottle-green coat, on finding himself alone with Mr Justice Harbottle, had become agitated. He said,

'There is, perhaps you are not aware, my lord, a prisoner in Shrewsbury jail, charged with having forged a bill of exchange for a hundred and twenty pounds, and his name is Lewis Pyneweck, a grocer of that town.'

'Is there?' says the Judge, who knew well that there was.

'Yes, my lord,' says the old man.

'Then you had better say nothing to affect this case. If you do, by— I'll commit you! for I'm to try it,' says the Judge, with his terrible look and tone.

'I am not going to do anything of the kind, my lord; of him or his case I know nothing, and care nothing. But a fact has come to my knowledge which it behoves you to well consider.'

'And what may that fact be?' inquired the Judge; 'I'm in haste, sir, and beg you will use dispatch.'

'It has come to my knowledge, my lord, that a secret tribunal is in process of formation, the object of which is to take cognizance of the conduct of the judges; and first, of *your* conduct, my lord: it is a wicked conspiracy.'

'Who are of it?' demands the Judge.

'I know not a single name as yet. I know but the fact, my lord; it is most certainly true.'

'I'll have you before the Privy Council, sir,' says the Judge.

'That is what I most desire; but not for a day or two, my lord.'

'And why so?'

'I have not as yet a single name, as I told your lordship; but I expect to have a list of the most forward men in it, and some other papers connected with the plot, in two or three days.'

'You said one or two just now.'

'About that time, my lord.'

'Is this a Jacobite plot?'

'In the main I think it is, my lord.'

'Why, then, it is political. I have tried no State prisoners, nor am like to try any such. How, then, doth it concern me?'

'From what I can gather, my lord, there are those in it who desire private revenges upon certain judges.'

'What do they call their cabal?'

'The High Court of Appeal, my lord.'

'Who are you, sir? What is your name?'

'Hugh Peters, my Lord.'

'That should be a Whig name?'

'It is, my lord.'

'Where do you lodge, Mr Peters?'

'In Thames Street, my lord, over against the sign of the "Three Kings."'

' "Three Kings?" Take care one be not too many for you, Mr Peters! How come you, an honest Whig, as you say, to be privy to a Jacobite plot? Answer me that.'

'My lord, a person in whom I take an interest has been seduced to take a part in it; and being frightened at the unexpected wickedness of their plans, he is resolved to become an informer for the Crown.'

'He resolves like a wise man, sir. What does he say of the persons? Who are in the plot? Doth he know them?'

'Only two, my lord; but he will be introduced to the club in a few days, and he will then have a list, and more exact information of their plans, and above all of their oaths, and their hours and places of meeting, with which he wishes to be acquainted before they can have any suspicions of his intentions. And being so informed, to whom, think you, my lord, had he best go then?'

'To the king's attorney-general straight. But you say this concerns me, sir, in particular? How about this prisoner, Lewis Pyneweck? Is he one of them?'

'I can't tell, my lord; but for some reason, it is thought your lordship will be well advised if you try him not. For if you do, it is feared 'twill shorten your days.'

'So far as I can learn, Mr Peters, this business smells pretty strong of blood and treason. The king's attorney-general will know how to deal with it. When shall I see you again, sir?'

'If you give me leave, my lord, either before your lordship's court sits, or after it rises, tomorrow. I should like to come and tell your lordship what has passed.'

'Do so, Mr Peters, at nine o'clock tomorrow morning. And see you play me no trick, sir, in this matter; if you do, by— , sir, I'll lay you by the heels!'

'You need fear no trick from me, my lord; had I not wished to serve you, and acquit my own conscience, I never would have come all this way to talk with your lordship.'

'I'm willing to believe you, Mr Peters; I'm willing to believe you, sir.'

And upon this they parted.

'He has either painted his face, or he is consumedly sick,' thought the old Judge.

The light had shone more effectually upon his features as he turned to leave the room with a low bow, and they looked, he fancied, unnaturally chalky.

'D— him!' said the Judge ungraciously, as he began to scale the stairs: 'he has half-spoiled my supper.'

But if he had, no one but the Judge himself perceived it, and the evidence was all, as any one might perceive, the other way.

In the meantime the footman dispatched in pursuit of Mr Peters speedily overtook that feeble gentleman. The old man stopped when he heard the sound of pursuing steps, but any alarms that may have crossed his mind seemed to disappear on his recognizing the livery. He very gratefully accepted the assistance, and placed his tremulous arm within the servant's for support. They had not gone far, however, when the old man stopped suddenly, saying,

'Dear me! as I live, I have dropped it. You heard it fall. My eyes, I fear, won't serve me, and I'm unable to stoop low enough; but if *you* look, you shall have half the find. It is a guinea; I carried it in my glove.'

The street was silent and deserted. The footman had hardly descended to what he termed his 'hunkers,' and begun to search the pavement about the spot which the old man indicated, when Mr Peters, who seemed very much exhausted, and breathed with difficulty, struck him a violent blow from above, over the back of the head with a heavy instrument, and then another; and leaving him bleeding and senseless in the gutter, ran like a lamp-lighter down a lane to the right, and was gone.

When, an hour later, the watchman brought the man in livery home, still stupid and covered with blood, Judge Harbottle cursed his servant roundly, swore he was drunk, threatened him with an indictment for taking bribes to betray his master, and cheered him with a perspective of the broad street leading from the Old Bailey to Tyburn, the cart's tail, and the hangman's lash.

Notwithstanding this demonstration, the Judge was pleased. It was a disguised 'affidavit man,' or footpad, no doubt, who had been employed to frighten him. The trick had fallen through.

A 'court of appeal,' such as the false Hugh Peters had indicated, with assassination for its sanction, would be an uncomfortable institution for a 'hanging judge' like the Honourable Justice Harbottle. That sarcastic and ferocious administrator of the criminal code of England, at that time a rather pharisaical, bloody and heinous system of justice, had reasons of his own for choosing to try that very Lewis Pyneweck, on whose behalf this audacious trick was devised. Try him he would. No man living should take that morsel out of his mouth.

Of Lewis Pyneweck, of course, so far as the outer world could see, he knew nothing. He would try him after his fashion, without fear, favour, or affection.

But did he not remember a certain thin man, dressed in mourning, in whose house, in Shrewsbury, the Judge's lodgings used to be, until a scandal of his ill-treating his wife came suddenly to light? A grocer with a demure look, a soft step, and a lean face as dark as mahogany, with a nose sharp and long, standing ever so little awry, and a pair of dark steady brown eyes under thinly-traced black brows – a man whose thin lips wore always a faint unpleasant smile.

Had not that scoundrel an account to settle with the Judge? had he not been troublesome lately? and was not his name Lewis Pyneweck, some time grocer in Shrewsbury, and now prisoner in the jail of that town?

The reader may take it, if he pleases, as a sign that Judge Harbottle was a good Christian, that he suffered nothing ever from remorse. That was undoubtedly true. He had, nevertheless, done this grocer, forger, what you will, some five or six years before, a grievous wrong; but it was not that, but a possible scandal, and possible complications, that troubled the learned Judge now.

Did he not, as a lawyer, know, that to bring a man from his shop to the dock, the chances must be at least ninety-nine out of a hundred that he is guilty.

A weak man like his learned brother Withershins was not a judge to keep the high-roads safe, and make crime tremble. Old Judge Harbottle was the man to make the evil-disposed quiver, and to refresh the world with showers of wicked blood, and thus save the innocent, to the refrain of the ancient saw he loved to quote:

Foolish pity
Ruins a city.

In hanging that fellow he could not be wrong. The eye of a man accustomed to look upon the dock could not fail to read 'villain' written sharp and clear in his plotting face. Of course he would try him, and no one else should.

A saucy-looking woman, still handsome, in a mob-cap gay with blue ribbons, in a saque of flowered silk, with lace and rings on, much too fine for the Judge's housekeeper, which nevertheless she was, peeped into his study next morning, and, seeing the Judge alone, stepped in.

'Here's another letter from him, come by the post this morning. Can't you do nothing for him?' she said wheedlingly, with her arm over his neck, and her delicate finger and thumb fiddling with the lobe of his purple ear.

'I'll try,' said Judge Harbottle, not raising his eyes from the paper he was reading.

'I knew you'd do what I asked you,' she said.

The Judge clapt his gouty claw over his heart, and made her an ironical bow.

'What,' she asked, 'will you do?'

'Hang him,' said the Judge with a chuckle.

'You don't mean to; no, you don't, my little man,' said she, surveying herself in a mirror on the wall.

'I'm d— d but I think you're falling in love with your husband at last!' said Judge Harbottle.

'I'm blest but I think you're growing jealous of him,' replied the lady with a laugh. 'But no; he was always a bad one to me; I've done with him long ago.'

'And he with you, by George! When he took your fortune, and your spoons, and your earrings, he had all he wanted of you. He drove you from his house; and when he discovered you had made yourself comfortable, and found a good situation, he'd have taken your guineas, and your silver, and your earrings over again, and then allowed you half-a-dozen years more to make a new harvest for his mill. You don't wish him good; if you say you do, you lie.'

She laughed a wicked, saucy laugh, and gave the terrible Rhadamanthus a playful tap on the chops.

'He wants me to send him money to fee a counsellor,' she said, while her eyes wandered over the pictures on the wall, and back again to the looking-glass; and certainly she did not look as if his jeopardy troubled her very much.

'Confound his impudence, the *scoundrel!*' thundered the old Judge, throwing himself back in his chair, as he used to do *in furore* on the bench, and the lines of his mouth looked brutal, and his eyes ready to leap from their sockets. 'If you answer his letter from my house to please yourself, you'll write your next from somebody else's to please me. You understand, my pretty witch, I'll not be pestered. Come, no pouting; whimpering won't do. You don't care a brass farthing for the villain, body or soul. You came here but to make a row. You are one of Mother Carey's chickens; and where you come, the storm is up. Get you gone, baggage! get you *gone!*' he repeated, with a stamp; for a knock at the hall-door made her instantaneous disappearance indispensable.

I need hardly say that the venerable Hugh Peters did not appear again. The Judge never mentioned him. But oddly enough, considering how he laughed to scorn the weak invention which he had blown into dust at the very first puff, his white-wigged visitor and the conference in the dark front parlour was often in his memory.

His shrewd eye told him that allowing for change of tints and such disguises as the playhouse affords every night, the features of this false old man, who had turned out too hard for his tall footman, were identical with those of Lewis Pyneweck.

Judge Harbottle made his registrar call upon the crown solicitor, and tell him that there was a man in own who bore a wonderful resemblance to a prisoner in Shrewsbury jail named Lewis Pyneweck, and to make inquiry through the post forthwith whether any one was personating Pyneweck in prison, and whether he had thus or otherwise made his escape.

The prisoner was safe, however, and no question as to his identity.

In due time Judge Harbottle went circuit; and in due time the judges were in Shrewsbury. News travelled slowly in those days, and newspapers, like the wagons and stage-coaches, took matters easily. Mrs Pyneweck, in the Judge's house, with a diminished household – the greater part of the Judge's servants having gone with him, for he had given up riding circuit, and travelled in his coach in state – kept house rather solitarily at home.

In spite of quarrels, in spite of mutual injuries – some of them, inflicted by herself, enormous – in spite of a married life of spited bickerings – a life in which there seemed no love or liking or forbearance, for years – now that Pyneweck stood in near danger of death, something like remorse came suddenly upon her. She knew that in Shrewsbury were transacting the scenes which were to determine his fate. She knew she did not love him; but she could not have supposed, even a fortnight, before, that the hour of suspense could have affected her so powerfully.

She knew the day on which the trial was expected to take place. She could not get it out of her head for a minute; she felt faint as it drew towards evening.

Two or three days passed; and then she knew that the trial must be over by this time. There were floods between London and Shrewsbury, and news was long delayed. She wished the floods would last for ever. It was dreadful waiting to hear; dreadful to know that the event was over, and that she could not hear till self-willed rivers subsided; dreadful to know that they must subside and the news come at last.

She had some vague trust in the Judge's good nature, and much in the resources of chance and accident. She had contrived to send the money he wanted. He would not be without legal advice and energetic and skilled support.

At last the news did come – a long arrear all in a gush: a letter from a female friend in Shrewsbury; a return of the sentences, sent up for the Judge; and most important, because most easily got at, being told with great aplomb and brevity, the long-deferred intelligence of the Shrewsbury Assizes in the *Morning Advertiser*. Like an impatient reader of a novel, who reads the last page first, she read with dizzy eyes the list of the executions.

Two were respited, seven were hanged; and in that capital catalogue was this line:

'Lewis Pyneweck – forgery.'

She had to read it half-a-dozen times over before she was sure she understood it. Here was the paragraph:

> *'Sentence, Death – 7.*
> 'Executed accordingly, on Friday the 13th instant, to wit:
> 'Thomas Primer, *alias* Duck—highway robbery.
> 'Flora Guy—stealing to the value of 11s. 6d.
> 'Arthur Pounden—burglary.
> 'Maltilda Mummery—riot.
> 'Lewis Pyneweck—forgery, bill of exchange."

And when she reached this, she read it over and over, feeling very cold and sick.

This buxom housekeeper was known in the house as Mrs Carwell—Carwell being her maiden name, which she had resumed.

No one in the house except its master knew her history. Her introduction had been managed craftily. No one suspected that it had been concerted between her and the old reprobate in scarlet and ermine.

Flora Carwell ran up the stairs now, and snatched her little girl, hardly seven years of age, whom she met on the lobby, hurriedly up in her arms, and carried her into her bedroom, without well knowing what she was doing, and sat down, placing the child before her. She was not able to speak. She held the child before her, and looked in the little girl's wondering face, and burst into tears of horror.

She thought the Judge could have saved him. I dare say he could. For a time she was furious with him, and hugged and kissed her bewildered little girl, who returned her gaze with large round eyes.

That little girl had lost her father, and knew nothing of the matter. She had been always told that her father was dead long ago.

A woman, coarse, uneducated, vain, and violent, does not reason, or even feel, very distinctly; but in these tears of consternation were mingling a self-upbraiding. She felt afraid of that little child.

But Mrs Carwell was a person who lived not upon sentiment, but upon beef and pudding; she consoled herself with punch; she did not trouble herself long even with resentments; she was a gross and material person, and could not mourn over the irrevocable for more than a limited number of hours, even if she would.

Judge Harbottle was soon in London again. Except the gout, this savage old epicurean never knew a day's sickness. He laughed, and coaxed, and bullied away the young woman's faint upbraidings, and in a little time Lewis Pyneweck troubled her no more; and the Judge secretly chuckled over the perfectly fair removal of a bore, who might have grown little by little into something very like a tyrant.

It was the lot of the Judge whose adventures I am now recounting to try criminal cases at the Old Bailey shortly after his return. He had commenced his charge to the jury in a case of forgery, and was, after his wont, thundering dead against the prisoner, with many a hard aggravation and cynical gibe, when suddenly all died away in silence, and, instead of looking at the jury, the eloquent Judge was gaping at some person in the body of the court.

Among the persons of small importance who stand and listen at the sides was one tall enough to show with a little prominence; a slight mean figure, dressed in seedy black, lean and dark of visage. He had just handed a letter to the crier, before he caught the Judge's eye.

That Judge descried, to his amazement, the features of Lewis Pyneweck. He has the usual faint thin-lipped smile; and with his blue chin raised in air, and as it seemed quite unconscious of the distinguished notice he had attracted, he was stretching his low cravat with his crooked fingers, while he slowly turned his head from side to side – a process which enabled the Judge to see distinctly a stripe of swollen blue round his neck, which indicated, he thought, the grip of the rope.

This man, with a few others, had got a footing on a step from which he could better see the court. He now stepped down, and the Judge lost sight of him.

His lordship signed energetically with his hand in the direction in which this man had vanished. He turned to the tipstaff. His first effort to speak ended in a gasp. He cleared his throat, and told the astounded official to arrest that man who had interrupted the court.

'He's but this moment gone down *there*. Bring him in custody before me, within ten minutes' time, or I'll strip your gown from your shoulders and fine the sheriff!' he thundered, while his eyes flashed round the court in search of the functionary.

Attorneys, counsellors, idle spectators, gazed in the direction in which Mr Justice Harbottle had shaken his gnarled old hand. They compared notes. Not one had seen anyone making a disturbance.

They asked one another if the Judge was losing his head.

Nothing came of the search. His lordship concluded his charge a great deal more tamely; and when the jury retired, he stared round the court with a wandering mind, and looked as if he would not have given sixpence to see the prisoner hanged.

The Judge had received the letter; had he known from whom it came, he would no doubt have read it intantaneously. As it was he simply read the direction:

To the Honourable
The Lord Justice
Elijah Harbottle,
One of his Majesty's Justices of
the Honourable Court of Common Pleas.

It remained forgotten in his pocket till he reached home.

When he pulled out that and others from the capacious pocket of his coat, it had its turn, as he sat in his library in his thick silk dressing-gown; and then he found its contents to be a closely-written letter, in a clerk's hand, and an enclosure in 'secretary hand,' as I believe the angular scrivinary of law writings in those days was termed, engrossed on a bit of parchment about the size of this page. The letter said:

MR JUSTICE HARBOTTLE, – MY LORD,

'I am ordered by the High Court of Appeal to acquaint your lordship, in order to your better preparing yourself for your trial, that a true bill hath been sent down, and the indictment lieth against your lordship for the murder of one Lewis Pyneweck of Shrewsbury, citizen, wrongfully executed for the forgery of a bill of exchange, on the –th day of— last, by reason of the wilful perversion of the evidence; and the undue pressure put upon the jury, together with the illegal admission of evidence by your lordship, well knowing the same to be illegal, by all which the promoter of the prosecution of the said indictment, before the High Court of Appeal, hath lost his life.

'And the trial of the said indictment, I am farther ordered to acquaint your lordship, is fixed for the 10th day of— next ensuing, by the right honourable the Lord Chief Justice Twofold, of the court aforesaid, to wit, the High Court of Appeal, on which day it will most certainly take place. And I am farther to acquaint your lordship, to prevent any surprise or miscarriage, that your case stands first for the said day, and that the said High Court of Appeal sits day and night, and never rises; and herewith, by order of the said court, I furnish your lordship with a copy (extract) of the record in this case, except of the indictment, whereof notwithstanding, the substance and effect is supplied to your lordship in this Notice. And farther I am to inform you, that in case the jury then to try your lordship should find you guilty, the right honourable the Lord Chief Justice will, in passing sentence of death upon you, fix the day of execution for the 10th day of— , being one calendar month from the day of your trial.'

It was signed by 'CALEB SEARCHER,
'Officer of the Crown Solicitor in the
'Kingdom of Life and Death.'

The Judge glanced through the parchment.

'Sblood! Do they think a man like me is to be bamboozled by their buffoonery?'

The Judge's coarse features were wrung into one of his sneers; but he was pale. Possibly, after all, there was a conspiracy on foot. It was queer. Did they mean to pistol him in his carriage? or did they only aim at frightening him?

Judge Harbottle had more than enough of animal courage. He was not afraid of highwaymen, and he had fought more than his share of duels, being a foul-mouthed advocate while he held briefs at the bar. No one questioned his fighting qualities. But with respect to this particular case of Pyneweck, he lived in a house of glass. Was there not his pretty, dark-eyed, over-dressed housekeeper, Mrs Flora Carwell? very easy for people who knew Shrewsbury to identify Mrs Pyneweck, if once put upon the scent; and had he not stormed and worked hard in that case? Had he not made it hard sailing for the prisoner? Did he not know very well what the bar thought of it? It would be the worst scandal that ever blasted Judge.

So much there was intimidating in the matter but nothing more. The Judge was a little bit gloomy for a day or two after, and more testy with every one than usual.

He locked up the papers; and about a week after he asked his housekeeper, one day, in the library:

'Had your husband never a brother?'

Mrs Carwell squalled on this sudden introduction of the funereal topic, and cried exemplary 'piggins full,' as the Judge used pleasantly to say. But he was in no mood for trifling now, and he said sternly:

'Come, madam! this wearies me. Do it another time; and give me an answer to my question.' So she did.

Pyneweck had no brother living. He once had one; but he died in Jamaica.

'How do you know he is dead?' asked the Judge.

'Because he told me so.'

'Not the dead man.'

'Pyneweck told me so.'

'Is that all?' sneered the Judge.

He pondered this matter; and time went on. The Judge was growing a little morose, and less enjoying. The subject struck nearer to his thoughts than he fancied it could have done. But so it is with most undivulged vexations, and there was no one to whom he could tell this one.

It was now the 9th; and Mr Justice Harbottle was glad. He knew nothing would come of it. Still it bothered him; and tomorrow would see it well over.

[What of the paper I have cited? No one saw it during his life; no one, after his death. He spoke of it to Dr Hedstone; and what purported to be 'a copy,' in the old Judge's handwriting, was found. The original was nowhere. Was it a copy of an illusion, incident to brain disease? Such is my belief.]

Judge Harbottle went this night to the play at Drury Lane. He was one of those old fellows who care nothing for late hours, and occasional knocking about in pursuit of pleasure. He had appointed with two cronies of Lincoln's Inn to come home in his coach with him to sup after the play.

They were not in his box, but were to meet him near the entrance, and get into his carriage there; and Mr Justice Harbottle, who hated waiting, was looking a little impatiently from the window.

The Judge yawned.

He told the footman to watch for Counsellor Thavies and Counsellor Beller, who were coming; and, with another yawn, he laid his cocked hat on his knees, closed his eyes, leaned back in his corner; wrapped his mantle closer about him, and began to think of pretty Mrs Abington.

And being a man who could sleep like a sailor, at a moment's notice, he was thinking of taking a nap. Those fellows had no business to keep a judge waiting.

He heard their voices now. Those rake-hell counsellors were laughing, and bantering, and sparring after their wont. The carriage swayed and jerked, as one got in, and then again as the other followed. The door clapped, and the coach was now jogging and rumbling over the pavement. The Judge was a little bit sulky. He did not care to sit up and open his eyes. Let them suppose he was asleep. He heard them laugh with more malice than good-humour, he thought, as they observed it. He would give them a d—d hard knock or two when they got to his door, and till then he would counterfeit his nap.

The clocks were chiming twelve. Beller and Thavies were silent as tombstones. They were generally loquacious and merry rascals.

The Judge suddenly felt himself roughly seized and thrust from his corner into the middle of the seat, and opening his eyes, instantly he found himself between his two companions.

Before he could blurt out the oath that was at his lips, he saw that they were two strangers – evil looking fellows, each with a pistol in his hand, and dressed like Bow Street officers.

The Judge clutched at the check-string. The coach pulled up. He stared about him. They were not among houses; but through the windows, under a broad moonlight, he saw a black moor stretching lifelessly from right to left, with rotting trees, pointing fantastic branches in the air, standing here and there in groups, as if they held up their arms and twigs like fingers, in horrible glee at the Judge's coming.

A footman came to the window. He knew his long face and sunken eyes. He knew it was Dingly Chuff, fifteen years ago a footman in his service, whom he had turned off at a moment's notice, in a burst of jealousy, and indicted for a missing spoon. The man had died in prison of the jail-fever.

The Judge drew back in utter amazement. His armed companions signed mutely; and they were again gliding over this unknown moor.

The bloated and gouty old man, in his horror considered the question of resistance. But his athletic days were long over. This moor was a desert. There was no help to be had. He was in the hands of strange servants, even if his recognition turned out to be a delusion, and they were under the command of his captors. There was nothing for it but submission, for the present.

Suddenly the coach was brought nearly to a standstill, so that the prisoner saw an ominous sight from the window.

It was a gigantic gallows beside the road; it stood three-sided, and from each of its three broad beams at top depended in chains some eight or ten bodies, from several of which the cere-clothes had dropped away, leaving the skeletons swinging lightly by their chains. A tall ladder reached to the summit of the structure, and on the peat beneath lay bones.

On top of the dark transverse beam facing the road, from which, as from the other two completing the triangle of death, dangled a row of these unfortunates in chains, a hangman, with a pipe in his mouth, much as we see him in the famous print of the 'Idle Apprentice,' though here his perch was ever so much higher, was reclining at his ease and listlessly shying bones, from a little heap at his elbow, at the skeletons that hung round, bringing down now a rib or two, now a hand, now half a leg. A long sighted man could have discerned that he was a dark fellow, lean; and from continually looking down on the earth from the elevation over which, in another sense, he always hung, his nose, his lips, his chin were pendulous and loose, and drawn down into a monstrous grotesque.

This fellow took his pipe from his mouth on seeing the coach, stood up, and cut some solemn capers high on his beam, and shook a new rope in the air, crying with a voice high and distant as the caw of a raven hovering over a gibbet, 'A rope for Judge Harbottle!'

The coach was now driving on at its old swift pace.

So high a gallows as that, the Judge had never, even in his most hilarious moments, dreamed of. He thought he must be raving. And the dead footman! He shook his ears and strained his eyelids; but if he was dreaming, he was unable to awake himself.

There was no good in threatening these scoundrels. A *brutum fulmen* might bring a real one on his head.

Any submission to get out of their hands; and then heaven and earth he would move to unearth and hunt them down.

Suddenly they drove round a corner of a vast white building, and under a *porte-cochère*.

The Judge found himself in a corridor lighted with dingy oil lamps, the walls of bare stone; it looked like a passage, in a prison. His guards placed him in the hands of other people. Here and there he saw bony and gigantic soldiers passing to and fro, with muskets over their shoulders. They looked straight before them, grinding their teeth, in bleak fury, with no noise but the clank of their shoes. He saw these by glimpses, round corners, and at the ends of passages, but he did not actually pass them by.

And now, passing under a narrow doorway, he found himself in the dock, confronting a judge in his scarlet robes, in a large court-house. There was nothing to elevate this Temple of Themis above its vulgar kind elsewhere. Dingy enough it looked, in spite of candles lighted in decent abundance. A case had just closed, and the last juror's back was seen escaping through the door in the wall of the jury-box. There were some dozen barristers, some fiddling with pen and ink, others buried in briefs, some beckoning, with the plumes of their pens, to their attorneys, of whom there were no lack; there were clerks to-ing and fro-ing, and the officers of the court, and the registrar, who was handing up a paper to the judge; and the tipstaff, who was presenting a note at the end of his wand to a king's counsel over the heads of the crowd between. If this was the High Court of Appeal, which never rose day or night, it might account for the pale and jaded aspect of everybody in it. An air of indescribable gloom hung upon the pallid features of all the people here; no one ever smiled; all looked more or less secretly suffering.

'The King against Elijah Harbottle!' shouted the officer.

'Is appellant Lewis Pyneweck in court?' asked Chief-Justice Twofold, in a voice of thunder, that shook the woodwork of the court, and boomed down the corridors.

Up stood Pyneweck from his place at the table.

'Arraign the prisoner!' roared the Chief: and Judge Harbottle felt the panels of the dock round him, and the floor, and the rails quiver in the vibrations of that tremendous voice.

The prisoner, *in limine*, objected to this pretended court, as being a sham, and non-existent in point of law; and then, that, even if it were a court constituted by law (the Judge was growing dazed), it had not and could not have any jurisdiction to try him for his conduct on the bench.

Whereupon the chief-justice laughed suddenly, and everyone in court, turning round upon the prisoner, laughed also, till the laugh grew and roared all round like a deafening acclamation; he saw nothing but glittering eyes and teeth, a universal stare and grin; but though all the voices laughed, not a single face of all those that concentrated their gaze upon him looked like a laughing face. The mirth subsided as suddenly as it began.

The indictment was read. Judge Harbottle actually pleaded! He pleaded 'Not Guilty.' A jury were sworn. The trial proceeded. Judge Harbottle was bewildered. This could not be real. He must be either mad, or *going* mad, he thought.

One thing could not fail to strike even him. This Chief-Justice Twofold, who was knocking him about at every turn with sneer and gibe, and roaring him down with his tremendous voice, was a dilated effigy of himself; an image of Mr Justice Harbottle, at least double his size, and with all his fierce colouring, and his ferocity of eye and visage, enhanced awfully.

Nothing the prisoner could argue, cite, or state, was permitted to retard for a moment the march of the case towards its catastrophe.

The chief-justice seemed to feel his power over the jury, and to exult and riot in the display of it. He glared at them, he nodded to them; he seemed to have established an understanding with them. The lights were faint in that part of the court. The jurors were mere shadows, sitting in rows; the prisoner could see a dozen pair of white eyes shining, coldly, out of the darkness; and whenever the judge in his charge, which was contemptuously brief, nodded and grinned and gibed, the prisoner could see, in the obscurity, by the dip of all these rows of eyes together, that the jury nodded in acquiescence.

And now the charge was over, the huge chief-justice leaned back panting and gloating on the prisoner. Everyone in the court turned about, and gazed with steadfast hatred on the man in the dock. From the jury-box where the twelve sworn brethren were whispering together, a sound in the general stillness like a prolonged 'hiss-s-s!' was heard; and then, in answer to the challenge of the officer, 'How say you, gentlemen of the jury, guilty or not guilty?' came in a melancholy voice the finding, 'Guilty.'

The place seemed to the eyes of the prisoner to grow gradually darker and darker, till he could discern nothing distinctly but the lumen of the eyes that were turned upon him from every bench and side and corner and gallery of the building. The prisoner doubtless thought that he had quite enough to say, and conclusive, why sentence of death should not be pronounced upon him; but the lord chief-justice puffed it contemptuously away, like so much smoke, and proceeded to pass sentence of death upon the prisoner, having named the 10th of the ensuing month for his execution.

Before he had recovered the stun of this ominous farce, in obedience to the mandate, 'Remove the prisoner,' he was led from the dock. The lamps seemed all to have gone out, and there were stoves and charcoal-fires here and there, that threw a faint crimson light on the walls of the corridors through which he passed. The stones that composed them looked now enormous, cracked and unhewn.

He came into a vaulted smithy, where two men, naked to the waist, with heads like bulls, round shoulders, and the arms of giants, were welding red-hot chains together with hammers that pelted like thunderbolts.

They looked on the prisoner with fierce red eyes, and rested on their hammers for a minute; and said the elder to his companion, 'Take out Elijah Harbottle's gyves;' and with a pincers he plucked the end which lay dazzling in the fire from the furnace.

'One end locks,' said he, taking the cool end of the iron in one hand, while with the grip of a vice he seized the leg of the Judge, and locked the ring round his ankle. 'The other,' he said with a grin, 'is welded.'

The iron band that was to form the ring for the other leg lay still red hot upon the stone floor, with brilliant sparks sporting up and down its surface.

His companion, in his gigantic hands, seized the old Judge's other leg, and pressed his foot immovably to the stone floor; while his senior, in a twinkling, with a masterly application of pincers and hammer, sped the glowing bar round his ankle so tight that the skin and sinews smoked and bubbled again, and old Judge Harbottle uttered a yell that seemed to chill the very stones, and make the iron chains quiver on the wall.

Chains, vaults, smiths, and smithy all vanished in a moment; but the pain continued. Mr Justice Harbottle was suffering torture all round the ankle on which the infernal smiths had just been operating.

His friends, Thavies and Beller were startled by the Judge's roar in the midst of their elegant trifling about a marriage *à-la-mode* case which was going on. The Judge was in panic as well as pain. The street lamps and the light of his own hall door restored him.

'I'm very bad,' growled he between his set teeth; 'my foot's blazing. Who was he that hurt my foot? 'Tis the gout – 'tis the gout!' he said, awaking completely. 'How many hours have we been coming from the playhouse? 'Sblood, what has happened on the way? I've slept half the night!'

There had been no hitch or delay, and they had driven home at a good pace.

The Judge, however, was in gout; he was feverish too; and the attack, though very short, was sharp; and when, in about a fortnight, it subsided, his ferocious joviality did not return. He could not get this dream, he chose to call it, out of his head.

People remarked that the Judge was in the vapours. His doctor said he should go for a fortnight to Buxton.

Whenever the Judge fell into a brown study, he was always conning over the terms of the sentence pronounced upon him in his vision – 'in one calendar month from the date of this day;' and then the usual form, 'and you shall be hanged by the neck till you are dead,' etc. 'That will be the 10th – I'm not much in the way of being hanged. I know what stuff dreams are, and I laugh at them; but this is continually in my thoughts, as if it forecast misfortune of some sort. I wish the day my dream gave me were passed and over. I wish I were well purged of my gout. I wish I were as I used to be.'Tis nothing but vapours, nothing but a maggot.' The copy of the parchment and letter which had announced his trial with many a snort and sneer he would read over and over again, and the scenery and people of his dream would rise about him in places the most unlikely, and steal him in a moment from all that surrounded him into a world of shadows.

The Judge had lost his iron energy and banter. He was growing taciturn and morose. The Bar remarked the change, as well they might. His friends thought him ill. The doctor said he was troubled with hypochondria, and that his gout was still lurking in his system, and ordered him to that ancient haunt of crutches and chalk-stones, Buxton.

The Judge's spirits were very low; he was frightened about himself; and he described to his housekeeper, having sent for her to his study to drink a dish of tea, his strange dream in his drive home from Drury Lane Playhouse. He was sinking into the state of nervous dejection in which men lose their faith in orthodox advice, and in despair consult quacks, astrologers and nursery story-tellers. Could such a dream mean that he was to have a fit, and so die on the 10th? She did not think so. On the contrary, it was certain some good luck must happen on that day.

The Judge kindled; and for the first time for many days, he looked for a minute or two like himself, and he tapped her on the cheek with the hand that was not in flannel.

'Odsbud! odsheart! you dear rogue! I had forgot. There is young Tom – yellow Tom, my nephew, you know, lies sick at Harrogate; why shouldn't he go that day as well as another, and if he does, I get an estate by it? Why, lookee, I asked Doctor Hedstone yesterday if I was like to take a fit any time, and he laughed, and swore I was the last man in town to go off that way.'

The Judge sent most of his servants down to Buxton to make his lodgings and all things comfortable for him. He was to follow in a day or two.

It was now the 9th; and the next day well over, he might laugh at his visions and auguries.

On the evening of the 9th, Dr Hedstone's footman knocked at the Judge's door. The Doctor ran up the dusky stairs to the drawing-room. It was a March evening, near the hour of sunset, with an east wind whistling sharply through the chimney-stacks. A wood fire blazed cheerily on the hearth. And Judge Harbottle, in what was then called a brigadier wig, with his red roquelaure on, helped the glowing effect of the darkened chamber, which looked red all over like a room on fire.

The Judge had his feet on a stool, and his huge grim purple face confronted the fire, and seemed to pant and swell, as the blaze alternately spread upward and collapsed. He had fallen again among his blue devils, and was thinking of retiring from the Bench, and of fifty other gloomy things.

But the Doctor, who was an energetic son of Æsculapius, would listen to no croaking, told the Judge he was full of gout, and in his present condition no judge even of his own case, but promised him leave to pronounce on all those melancholy questions, a fortnight later.

In the meantime the Judge must be very careful. He was over-charged with gout, and he must not provoke an attack, till the waters of Buxton should do that office for him in their own salutary way.

The Doctor did not think him perhaps quite so well as he pretended, for he told him he wanted rest, and would be better if he went forthwith to his bed.

Mr Gerningham, his valet, assisted him, and gave him his drops; and the Judge told him to wait in his bedroom till he should go to sleep.

Three persons that night had specially odd stories to tell.

The housekeeper had got rid of the trouble of amusing her little girl at this anxious time, by giving her leave to run about the sitting-rooms and look at the pictures and china, on the usual condition of touching nothing. It was not until the last gleam of sunset had for some time faded, and the twilight had so deepened that she could no longer discern the colours on the china figures on the chimneypiece or in the cabinets, that the child returned to the housekeeper's room to find her mother.

To her she related, after some prattle about the china, and the pictures, and the Judge's two grand wigs in the dressing-room off the library, an adventure of an extraordinary kind.

In the hall was placed, as was customary in those times, the sedan-chair which the master of the house occasionally used, covered with stamped leather, and studded with gilt nails, and with its red silk blinds down. In this case, the doors of this old-fashioned conveyance were locked, the windows up, and, as I said, the blinds down, but not so closely that the curious child could not peep underneath one of them, and see into the interior.

A parting beam from the setting sun, admitted through the window of a back room, shot obliquely through the open door, and lighting on the chair, shone with a dull transparency through the crimson blind.

To her surprise, the child saw in the shadow a thin man, dressed in black, seated in it; he had sharp dark features; his nose, she fancied, a little awry, and his brown eyes were looking straight before him; his hand was on his thigh, and he stirred no more than the waxen figure she had seen at Southwark fair.

A child is so often lectured for asking questions, and on the propriety of silence, and the superior wisdom of its elders, that it accepts most things at last in good faith; and the little girl acquiesced respectfully in the occupation of the chair by this mahogany-faced person as being all right and proper.

It was not until she asked her mother who this man was, and observed her scared face as she questioned her more minutely upon the appearance of the stranger that she began to understand that she had seen something unaccountable.

Mrs Carwell took the key of the chair from its nail over the footman's shelf, and led the child by the hand up to the hall, having a lighted candle in her other hand. She stopped at a distance from the chair, and placed the candlestick in the child's hand.

'Peep in, Margery, again, and try if there's anything there,' she whispered; 'hold the candle near the blind so as to throw its light through the curtain.'

The child peeped, this time with a very solemn face, and intimated at once that he was gone.

'Look again, and be sure,' urged her mother.

The little girl was quite certain; and Mrs Carwell, with her mob-cap of lace and cherry-coloured ribbons, and her dark brown hair, not yet powdered, over a very pale face, unlocked the door, looked in, and beheld emptiness.

'All a mistake, child, you see.'

'*There!* ma'am'! see there! He's gone round the corner,' said the child.

'Where?' said Mrs Carwell, stepping backward a step.

'Into that room.'

'Tut, child! 'twas the shadow,' cried Mrs Carwell, angrily, because she was frightened. 'I moved the candle.' But she clutched one of the poles of the chair, which leant against the wall in the corner, and pounded the floor furiously with one end of it, being afraid to pass the open door the child had pointed to.

The cook and two kitchen-maids came running upstairs, not knowing what to make of this unwonted alarm.

They all searched the room; but it was still and empty, and no sign of any one's having been there.

Some people may suppose that the direction given to her thoughts by this odd little incident will account for a very strange illusion which Mrs Carwell herself experienced about two hours later.

*

Mrs Flora Carwell was going up the great staircase with a posset for the Judge in a china bowl, on a little silver tray.

Across the top of the well-staircase there runs a massive oak rail; and, raising her eyes accidentally, she saw an extremely odd-looking stranger, slim and long, leaning carelessly over with a pipe between his finger and thumb. Nose, lips, and chin seemed all to droop downward into extraordinary length, as he leant his odd peering face over the banister. In his other hand he held a coil of rope, one end of which escaped from under his elbow and hung over the rail.

Mrs Çarwell, who had no suspicion at the moment, that he was not a real person, and fancied that he was someone employed in cording the Judge's luggage, called to know what he was doing there.

Instead of answering, he turned about, and walked across the lobby, at about the same leisurely pace at which she was ascending, and entered a room, into which she followed him. It was an uncarpeted and unfurnished chamber. An open trunk lay upon the floor empty, and beside it the coil of rope; but except herself there was no one in the room.

Mrs Carwell was very much frightened, and now concluded that the child must have seen the same ghost that had just appeared to her. Perhaps, when she was able to think it over, it was a relief to believe so; for the face, figure, and dress described by the child were awfully like Pyneweck; and this certainly was not he.

Very much scared and very hysterical, Mrs Carwell ran down to her room, afraid to look over her shoulder, and got some companions about her, and wept, and talked, and drank more than one cordial, and talked and wept again, and so on, until, in those early days, it was ten o'clock, and time to go to bed.

A scullery-maid remained up finishing some of her scouring and 'scalding' for some time after the other servants – who, as I said, were few in number – that night had got to their beds. This was a low-browed, broad-faced, intrepid wench with black hair, who did not 'vally a ghost not a button,' and treated the housekeeper's hysterics with measureless scorn.

The old house was quiet now. It was near twelve o'clock, no sounds were audible except the muffled wailing of the wintry winds, piping high among the roofs and chimneys, or rumbling at intervals, in under gusts, through the narrow channels of the street.

The spacious solitudes of the kitchen level were awfully dark, and this sceptical kitchen-wench was the only person now up and about in the house. She hummed tunes to herself, for a time; and then stopped and listened; and then resumed her work again. At last, she was destined to be more terrified than even was the housekeeper.

There was a back kitchen in this house, and from this she heard, as if coming from below its foundations, a sound like heavy strokes, that seemed to shake the earth beneath her feet. Sometimes a dozen in sequence, at regular intervals;

sometimes fewer. She walked out softly into the passage, and was surprised to see a dusky glow issuing from this room, as if from a charcoal fire.

The room seemed thick with smoke.

Looking in she very dimly beheld a monstrous figure, over a furnace, beating with a mighty hammer the rings and rivets of a chain.

The strokes, swift and heavy as they looked, sounded hollow and distant. The man stopped, and pointed to something on the floor, that, through the smoky haze, looked, she thought, like a dead body. She remarked no more; but the servants in the room close by, startled from their sleep by a hideous scream, found her in a swoon on the flags, close to the door, where she had just witnessed this ghastly vision.

Startled by the girl's incoherent asseverations that she had seen the Judge's corpse on the floor, two servants having first searched the lower part of the house, went rather frightened upstairs to inquire whether their master was well. They found him, not in his bed, but in his room. He had a table with candles burning at his bedside, and was getting on his clothes again; and he swore and cursed at them roundly in his old style, telling them that he had business, and that he would discharge on the spot any scoundrel who should dare to disturb him again.

So the invalid was left to his quietude.

In the morning it was rumoured here and there in the street that the Judge was dead. A servant was sent from the house three doors away, by Counsellor Traverse, to inquire at Judge Harbottle's hall door.

The servant who opened it was pale and reserved, and would only say that the Judge was ill. He had had a dangerous accident; Doctor Hedstone had been with him at seven o'clock in the morning.

There were averted looks, short answers, pale and frowning faces, and all the usual signs that there was a secret that sat heavily upon their minds, and the time for disclosing which had not yet come. That time would arrive when the coroner had arrived, the mortal scandal that had befallen the house could be no longer hidden. For that morning Mr Justice Harbottle been found hanging by the neck from the banister at the top of the great staircase, and quite dead.

There was not the smallest sign of any struggle or resistance. There had not been heard a cry or any other noise in the slightest degree indicative of violence. There was medical evidence to show that, in his atrabilious state, it was quite on the cards that he might have made away with himself. The jury found accordingly that it was a case of suicide. But to those who were acquainted with the strange story which Judge Harbottle had related to at least two persons, the fact that the catastrophe occurred on the morning of March 10th seemed a startling coincidence

A few days after, the pomp of a great funeral attended him to the grave; and so, in the language of Scripture, 'the rich man died, and was buried.'

A Terribly Strange Bed

WILLIAM WILKIE COLLINS

Shortly after my education at college was finished, I happened to be staying at Paris with an English friend. We were both young men then, and lived, I am afraid, rather a wild life, in the delightful city of our sojourn. One night we were idling about the neighbourhood of the Palais Royal, doubtful to what amusement we should next betake ourselves. My friend proposed a visit to Frascati's; but his suggestion was not to my taste. I knew Frascati's, as the French saying is, by heart; had lost and won plenty of five-franc pieces there, merely for amusement's sake, until it was amusement no longer, and was thoroughly tired, in fact, of all the ghastly respectabilities of such a social anomaly as a respectable gambling-house. 'For heaven's sake,' said I to my friend, 'let us go somewhere where we can see a little genuine, blackguard, poverty-stricken gaming, with no false gingerbread glitter thrown over it at all. Let us get away from fashionable Frascati's, to a house where they don't mind letting in a man with a ragged coat, or a man with no coat, ragged or otherwise.' – 'Very well,' said my friend, 'we needn't go out of the Palais Royal to find the sort of company you want. Here's the place just before us; as blackguard a place, by all report, as you could possibly wish to see.' In another minute we arrived at the door, and entered the house, the back of which you have drawn in your sketch.

When we got upstairs, and left our hats and sticks with the door-keeper, we were admitted into the chief gambling-room. We did not find many people assembled there. But, few as the men were who looked up at us on our entrance, they were all types – lamentably true types – of their respective classes.

We had come to see blackguards; but these men were something worse. There is a comic side, more or less appreciable, in all blackguardism – here there was nothing but tragedy – mute, weird tragedy. The quiet in the room was horrible. The thin, haggard, long-haired young man, whose sunken eyes firecely watched the turning up of the cards, never spoke; the flabby, fat-faced, pimply player, who pricked his piece of pasteboard perseveringly, to register how often black won, and how often red – never spoke; the dirty, wrinkled old man, with the vulture eyes and the darned greatcoat, who had lost his last *sou*, and still looked on desperately, after he could play no longer – never spoke. Even the voice of the croupier sounded as if it were strangely dulled and thickened in the atmosphere of the room. I had entered the place to laugh, but the spectacle before me was something to weep over. I soon found it necessary to take refuge in excitement from the depression of spirits which was fast stealing on me. Unfortunately I sought the nearest excitement, by going to the table, and beginning to play. Still more unfortunately, as the event will show, I won – won prodigiously; won incredibly; won at such a rate, that the regular players at the table crowded round me, and, staring at my stakes with hungry, superstitious eyes, whispered to one another that the English stranger was going to break the bank.

The game was *Rouge et Noir*. I had played at it in every city in Europe, without, however, the care or the wish to study the Theory of Chances – that philosopher's stone of all gamblers! And a gambler, in the strict sense of the word, I had never been. I was heart-whole from the corroding passion for play. My gaming was a mere idle amusement. I never resorted to it by necessity, because I never knew what it was to want money. I never practised it so incessantly as to lose more than I could afford, or to gain more than I could coolly pocket without being thrown off my balance by my good luck. In short, I had hitherto frequented gambling-tables – just as I frequented ballrooms and opera-houses – because they amused me, and because I had nothing better to do with my leisure hours.

But on this occasion it was very different – now, for the first time in my life, I felt what the passion for play really was. My success first bewildered, and then, in the most literal meaning of the word, intoxicated me. Incredible as it may appear, it is nevertheless true, that I only lost when I attempted to estimate chances, and played according to previous calculation. If I left everything to luck, and staked without any care or consideration, I was sure to win – to win in the face of every recognized probability in favour of the bank. At first, some of the men present ventured their money safely enough on my colour; but I speedily increased my stakes to sums which they dared not risk. One after another they left off playing, and breathlessly looked on at my game.

Still, time after time, I staked higher and higher, and still won. The excitement in the room rose to fever pitch. The silence was interrupted by a deep-muttered chorus of oaths and exclamations in different languages every time the gold was shovelled across to my side of the table – even the imperturbable croupier dashed his rake to the floor in a (French) fury of astonishment at my success. But one man present preserved his self-possession; and that man was my friend. He came to my side and, whispering in English, begged me to leave the place, satisfied with what I had already gained. I must do him the justice to say that he repeated his warnings and entreaties several times, and only left me and went away, after I had rejected his advice (I was to all intents and purposes gambling-drunk) in terms which rendered it impossible for him to address me again that night.

Shortly after he had gone, a hoarse voice behind me cried: 'Permit me, my dear sir! – permit me to restore to their proper place two Napoleons which you have dropped. Wonderful luck, sir! I pledge you my word of honour, as an old soldier, in the course of my long experience in this sort of thing, I never saw such luck as yours! – never! Go on, sir – *sacré mille bombes!* Go on boldly, and break the bank!'

I turned round and saw, nodding and smiling at me with inveterate civility, a tall man, dressed in a frogged and braided surtout.

If I had been in my senses, I should have considered him, personally, as being rather a suspicious specimen of an old soldier. He had goggling blood-shot eyes, mangy mustachios, and a broken nose. His voice betrayed a barrack-room intonation of the worst order, and he had the dirtiest pair of hands I ever saw – even in France. These little personal peculiarities exercised, however, no repelling influence on me. In the mad excitement, the reckless triumph of that moment, I was ready to 'fraternize' with anybody who encouraged me in my game. I accepted the old soldier's offered pinch of snuff; clapped him on the back, and swore he was the honestest fellow in the world – the most glorious relic of the Grand Army that I had ever met with. 'Go on!' cried my military friend, snapping his fingers in ecstasy – 'Go on, and win! Break the bank – *mille tonnerres!* my gallant English comrade, break the bank!'

And I *did* go on – went on at such a rate that in another quarter of an hour the croupier called out: 'Gentlemen! the bank has discontinued for tonight.' All the notes, and all the gold in that 'bank', now lay in a head under my hands; the whole floating capital of the gambling-house was waiting to pour into my pockets!

'Tie up the money in your pocket-handkerchief, my worthy sir,' said the old soldier, as I wildly plunged my hands into my heap of gold. 'Tie it up, as we used to tie up a bit of dinner in the Grand Army; your winnings are too heavy for any breeches pockets that ever were sewed. There! that's it! – shovel them in, notes and all! *Credié!* what luck! – Stop! another Napoleon on the floor! *Ah! – sacré petit polisson de Napoléon!* have I found thee at last? Now then, sir – two tight double knots each way with your honourable permission, and the money's safe. Feel it! feel it, fortunate sir! hard and round as a cannon ball – *ah, bah!* if they had only fired such cannon balls at us at Austerlitz – *nom d'une pipe!* if only they had! And now, as an ancient grenadier, as an ex-brave of the French Army, what remains for me to do? I ask what? Simply this: to entreat my valued English friend to drink a bottle of champagne with me, and toast the goddess Fortune in foaming goblets before we part!'

'Excellent ex-brave! Convivial ancient grenadier! Champagne by all means! An English cheer for an old soldier! Hurrah! hurrah! Another English cheer for the goddess Fortune! Hurrah! hurrah! hurrah!'

'Bravo! the Englishman; the amiable, gracious Englishman, in whose veins circulates the vivacious blood of France! Another glass? *Ah, bah!* – the bottle is empty! Never mind! *Vive le vin!* I, the old soldier, order another bottle, and half a pound of *bonbons* with it!'

'No, no, ex-brave; never – ancient grenadier! *Your* bottle last time; *my* bottle this. Behold it! Toast away! The French Army! – the great Napoleon! – the present company! the croupier! the honest croupier's wife and daughters – if he has any! the Ladies generally! Everybody in the world!'

By the time the second bottle of champagne was emptied, I felt as if I had been drinking liquid fire – my brain seemed all a-flame. No excess in wine ever had this effect on me before in my life. Was it the result of a stimulant acting upon my system when I was in a highly excited state? Was my stomach in a particularly disordered condition? Or was the champagne amazingly strong?

'Ex-brave of the French Army!' cried I, in a mad state of exhilaration, *'I am on fire! how are you*? You have set me on fire! Do you hear, my hero of Austerlitz? Let us have a third bottle of champagne to put the flame out!'

The old soldier wagged his head, rolled his goggle eyes, until I expected to see them slip out of their sockets; placed his dirty forefinger by the side of his broken nose; solemnly ejaculated 'Coffee!' and immediately ran off into an inner room.

The word pronounced by the eccentric veteran seemed to have a magical effect on the rest of the company present. With one accord they all rose to depart. Probably they had expected to profit by my intoxication; but finding that my new friend was benevolently bent on preventing me from getting dead drunk, had now abandoned all hope of thriving pleasantly on my winnings. Whatever their motive might be, at any rate they went away in a body. When the old soldier returned, and sat down again opposite to me at the table, we had the room to ourselves. I could see the croupier, in a sort of vestibule which opened out of it, eating his supper in solitude. The silence was now deeper than ever.

A sudden change, too, had come over the 'ex-brave'. He assumed a portentously solemn look! and when he spoke to me again, his speech was ornamented by no oaths, enforced by no finger-snapping, enlivened by no apostrophes or exclamations.

'Listen, my dear sir,' said he, in mysteriously confidential tones – 'listen to an old soldier's advice. I have been to the mistress of the house (a very charming woman, with a genius for cookery!) to impress on her the necessity of making us some particularly strong and good coffee. You must drain this coffee in order to get rid of your little amiable exaltation of spirits before you think of going home – you *must*, my good and gracious friend! With all that money to take home tonight, it is a sacred duty to yourself to have your wits about you. You are known to be a winner to an enormous extent by several gentlemen present tonight, who, in a certain point of view, are very worthy and excellent fellows, but they are mortal men, my dear sir, and they have their amiable weaknesses! Need I say more? Ah, no, no! you understand me! Now, this is what you must do – send for a cabriolet when you feel quite well again – draw up all the windows when you get into it – and tell the driver to take you home only through the large and well-lighted thoroughfares. Do this; and you and your money will be safe. Do this; and tomorrow you will thank an old soldier for giving you a word of honest advice.'

Just as the ex-brave ended his oration in very lachrymose tones, the coffe came in, ready poured out into two cups. My attentive friend handed me one of the cups with a bow. I was parched with thirst, and drank it off at a draught. Almost instantly afterwards, I was seized with a fit of giddiness, and felt more completely intoxicated than ever. The room whirled round and round furiously; the old soldier seemed to be regularly bobbing up and down before me like the piston of a steam-engine. I was half deafened by a violent singing in my ears; a feeling of utter bewilderment, helplessness, idiocy, overcame me. I rose from my chair, holding on by the table to keep my balance, and stammered out that I felt dreadfully unwell – so unwell that I did not know how I was to get home.

'My dear friend,' answered the old soldier – and even his voice seemed to be bobbing up and down as he spoke – 'my dear friend, it would be madness to go home in *your* state; you would be sure to lose your money; you might be robbed and murdered with the greatest ease. *I* am going to sleep here: do *you* sleep here, too – they make up capital beds in this house – take one; sleep off the effects of the wine, and go home safely with your winnings tomorrow – tomorrow, in broad daylight.'

I had but two ideas left: – one, that I must never let go hold of my handkerchief full of money; the other, that I must lie down somewhere immediately, and fall off into a comfortable sleep. So I agreed to the proposal about the bed, and took the offered arm of the old soldier, carrying my money with my disengaged hand. Preceded by the croupier, we passed alone some passages and up a flight of stairs into the bedroom which I was to occupy. The ex-brave shook me warmly by the hand, proposed that we should breakfast together, and then, followed by the croupier, left me for the night.

I ran to the wash-hand stand; drank some of the water in my jug; poured the rest out, and plunged my face into it; then sat down in a chair and tried to compose myself. I soon felt better. The change for my lungs, from the fetid atmosphere of the gambling-room to the cool air of the apartment I now occupied; the almost equally refreshing change for my eyes, from the glaring gas-lights of the 'salon' to the dim, quiet flicker of one bedroom candle, aided wonderfully the restorative effects of cold water. The giddiness left me, and I began to feel a little like a reasonable being again. My first thought was of the risk of sleeping all night in a gambling-house; my second, of the still greater risk of trying to get out after the house was closed, and of going home alone at night, through the streets of Paris, with a large sum of money about me. I had slept in worse places than this on my travels; so I determined to lock, bolt, and barricade the door, and take my chance till the next morning.

Accordingly, I secured myself against all intrusion; looked under the bed, and into the cupboard; tried the fastening of the window; and then, satisfied that I had taken every proper precaution, pulled off my upper clothing, put my light, which was a dim one, on the hearth among a feathery litter of wood ashes, and got into bed, with the handkerchief full of money under my pillow.

I soon felt not only that I could not go to sleep, but that I could not even close my eyes. I was wide awake, and in a high fever. Every nerve in my body trembled – every one of my senses seemed to be preternaturally sharpened. I tossed and rolled, and tried every kind of position, and perseveringly sought out the cold corners of the bed, and all to no purpose. Now, I thrust my arms over the clothes; now, I poked them under the clothes; now, I violently shot my legs straight out down to the bottom of the bed; now, I convulsively coiled them up as near my chin as they would go; now, I shook out my crumpled pillow, changed it to the cool side, patted it flat, and lay down quietly on my back; now, I fiercely doubled it in two, set it up on end, thrust it against the board of the bed, and tried a sitting posture. Every effort was in vain; I groaned with vexation, as I felt that I was in for a sleepless night.

What could I do? I had no book to read. And yet, unless I found out some method of diverting my mind, I felt certain that I was in the condition to imagine all sorts of horrors; to rack my brain with forebodings of every possible and impossible danger; in short, to pass the night in suffering all conceivable varieties of nervous terror.

I raised myself on my elbow, and looked about the room – which was brightened by a lovely moonlight pouring straight through the window – to see if it contained any pictures or ornaments that I could at all clearly distinguish. While my eyes wandered from wall to wall, a remembrance of Le Maistre's delightful little book, *Voyage autour de ma Chambre*, occurred to me. I resolved to imitate the French author, and find occupation and amusement enough to relieve the tedium of my wakefulness, by making a mental inventory of every article of furniture I could see, and by following up to their sources the multitude of associations which even a chair, a table, or a wash-hand stand may be made to call forth.

In the nervous unsettled state of my mind at that moment, I found it much easier to make my inventory than to make my reflections, and thereupon soon gave up all hope of thinking in Le Maistre's fanciful track – or, indeed, of thinking at all. I looked about the room at the different articles of furniture, and did nothing more.

There was, first, the bed I was lying in; a four-post bed, of all things in the world to meet with in Paris! – yes, a thoroughly clumsy British four-poster, with the regular top lined with chintz – the regular fringed valance all around – the reglar stifling unwholesome curtains, which I remembered having mechanically drawn back against the posts without particularly noticing the bed when I first got into the room. Then there was the marble-topped wash-hand stand, from which the water I had spilt, in my hurry to pour it out, was still dripping, slowly and more slowly, on to the brick floor. Then two small chairs, with my coat, waistcoat, and trousers flung on them. Then a large elbow-chair covered with dirty-white dimity, with my cravat and shirt-collar thrown over the back. Then a chest of drawers with two of the brass handles off, and a tawdry broken china inkstand placed on it by way of ornament for the top. Then the dressing-table, adorned by a very small looking-glass, and a very large pincushion. Then the window – an unusually large window. Then a dark old picture, which the feeble candle dimly showed me. It was the picture of a fellow in a high Spanish hat, crowned with a plume of towering feathers. A swarthy sinister ruffian, looking upward, shading his eyes with his hand, and looking intently upward – it might be at some tall gallows at which he was going to be hanged. At any rate, he had the appearance of thoroughly deserving it.

This picture put a kind of constraint upon me to look upward too – at the top of the bed. It was a gloomy and not an interesting object, and I looked back at the picture. I counted the feathers in the man's hat – they stood out in relief – three white, two green. I observed the crown of his hat, which was of a conical shape, according to the fashion supposed to have been favoured by Guido Fawkes. I wondered what he was looking up at. It couldn't be at the stars; such a desperado was neither astrologer nor astronomer. It must be at the high gallows, and he was going to be hanged presently. Would the executioner come into possession of his conical-crowned hat and plume of feathers? I counted the feathers again – three white, two green.

While I still lingered over this very improving intellectual employment, my thoughts insensibly began to wander. The moonlight shining into the room reminded me of a certain moonlight night in England – the night after a picnic party in a Welsh valley. Every incident of the drive homeward, through lovely scenery, which the moonlight made lovelier than ever, came back to my remembrance, though I had never given the picnic a thought for years; though, if I had *tried* to recollect it, I could certainly have recalled little or nothing of that scene long past. Of all the wonderful faculties that help to tell us we are immortal, which speaks the sublime truth more eloquently than memory? Here was I, in a strange house of the most suspicious character, in a situation of uncertainty, and even of peril, which might seem to make the cool exercise of my recollection almost out of the question; nevertheless, remembering, quite involuntarily, places, people, conversations, minute circumstances of every kind, which I had thought forgotten for ever; which I could not possibly have recalled at will, even under the most favourable auspices. And what cause had produced in a moment the whole of this strange, complicated, mysterious effect? Nothing but some rays of moonlight shining in at my bedroom window.

I was still thinking of the picnic – of our merriment on the drive home – of the sentimental young lady who *would* quote *Childe Harold* because it was moonlight. I was absorbed by these past scenes and past amusements, when, in an instant, the thread on which my memories hung snapped asunder; my attention immediately came back to present things more vividly than ever, and I found myself, I neither knew why nor wherefore, looking hard at the picture again.

Looking for what?

Good God! the man had pulled his hat down on his brows! – No! the hat itself was gone! Where was the conical crown? Where the feathers – three white, two green? Not there! In place of the hat and feathers, what dusky object was it that now hid his forehead, his eyes, his shading hand?

Was the bed moving?

I turned on my back and looked up. Was I mad? drunk? dreaming? giddy again? or was the top of the bed really moving down – sinking slowly, regularly, silently, horribly, right down throughout the whole of its length and breadth – right down upon me, as I lay underneath?

My blood seemed to stand still. A deadly paralysing coldness stole all over me, as I turned my head round on the pillow, and determined to test whether the bed-top was really moving or not by keeping my eye on the man in the picture.

The next look in that direction was enough. The dull, black, frowsy outline of the valance above me was within an inch of being parallel with his waist. I still looked breathlessly. And steadily, and slowly – very slowly – I saw the figure, and the line of frame below the figure, vanish, as the valance moved down before it.

I am, constitutionally, anything but timid. I have been on more than one occasion in peril of my life, and have not lost my self-possession for an instant; but when the conviction first settled on my mind that the bed-top was really moving, was steadily and continuously sinking down upon me, I looked up shuddering, helpless, panic-stricken, beneath the hideous machinery for murder, which was advancing closer and closer to suffocate me where I lay.

I looked up, motionless, speechless, breathless. The candle, fully spent, went out; but the moonlight still brightened the room. Down and down, without pausing and without sounding, came the bed-top, and still my panic-terror seemed to bind me faster and faster to the mattress on which I lay – down and down it sank, till the dusty odour from the lining of the canopy came stealing into my nostrils.

At that final moment, the instinct of self-preservation startled me out of my trance, and I moved at last. There was just room for me to roll myself sideways off the bed. As I dropped noiselessly to the floor, the edge of the murderous canopy touched me on the shoulder.

Without stopping to draw my breath, without wiping the cold sweat from my face, I rose instantly on my knees to watch the bed-top. I was literally spellbound by it. If I had heard footsteps behind me, I could not have turned round; if a means of escape had been miraculously provided for me, I could not have moved to take advantage of it. The whole life in me was, at that moment, concentrated in my eyes.

It descended – the whole canopy, with the fringe round it, came down – down – close down; so close that there was not room now to squeeze my finger between the bed-top and the bed. I felt at the sides, and discovered that what had appeared to me from beneath to be the ordinary light canopy of a four-post bed, was in reality a think, broad mattress, the substance of which was concealed by the valance and its fringe. I looked up and saw the four posts rising, hideously bare. In the middle of the bed-top was a huge wooden screw that had evidently worked it down through a hole in the ceiling, just as ordinary presses are worked down on the substance selected for compression. The frightful apparatus moved without making the faintest noise. There had been no creaking as it came down; there was now not the faintest sound from the room above. Amid a dead and awful silence I beheld before me – in the nineteenth century, and in the civilized capital of France – such a machine for secret murder by suffocation as might have existed in the worst days of the Inquisition, in the lonely inns among the Hartz Mountains, in the mysterious tribunals of Westphalia! Still, as I looked on it, I could not move, I could hardly breathe, but I began to recover the power of thinking, and in a moment I discovered the murderous conspiracy framed against me in all its horror.

My cup of coffee had been drugged, and drugged too strongly. I had been saved from being smothered by having taken an overdose of some narcotic. How I had chafed and fretted at the fever-fit which had preserved my life by keeping me awake! How recklessly I had confided myself to the two wretches who had led me into this room, determined, for the sake of my winnings, to kill me in my sleep by the surest and most horrible contrivance for secretly accomplishing my destruction! How many men, winners like me, had slept, as I had proposed to sleep, in that bed, and had never been seen or heard of more! I shuddered at the bare idea of it.

But, ere long, all thought was again suspended by the sight of the murderous canopy moving once more. After it had remained on the bed – as nearly as I could guess – about ten minutes, it began to move up again. The villains who worked it from above evidently believed that their purpose was now accomplished. Slowly and silently, as it had descended, that horrible bed-top rose towards its former place. When it reached the upper extremities of the four posts, it reached the ceiling too. Neither hole nor screw could be seen; the bed became in appearance an ordinary bed again – the canopy an ordinary canopy – even to the most suspicious eyes.

Now, for the first time, I was able to move – to rise from my knees – to dress myself in my upper clothing – and to consider of how I should escape. If I betrayed, by the smallest noise, that the attempt to suffocate me had failed, I was certain to be murdered. Had I made any noise already? I listened intently, looking towards the door.

No! no footsteps in the passage outside – no sound of a tread, light or heavy, in the room above – absolute silence everywhere. Besides locking and bolting the door, I had moved an old wooden chest against it, which I had found under the bed. To remove this chest (my blood ran cold as I thought of what it contents *might* be!) without making some disturbance was impossible; and, moreover, to think of escaping through the house, now barred up for the night, was sheer insanity. Only one chance was left me – the window, I stole to it on tiptoe.

My bedroom was on the first floor, above an *entresol*, and looked into the back street, which you have sketched in your view. I raised my hand to open the window knowing that on that action hung, by the merest hair's-breadth, my chance of safety. They keep vigilant watch in a House of Murder. If any part of the frame cracked, if the hinge creaked, I was a lost man! It must have occupied me at least five minutes, reckoning by time – five *hours*, reckoning by suspense – to open that window. I succeeded in doing it silently – in doing it with all the dexterity of a housebreaker – and then looked down into the street. To leap the distance beneath me would be almost certain destruction! Next, I looked round at the sides of the house. Down the left side ran the thick water-pipe which you have drawn – it passed close by the outer edge of the window. The moment I saw the pipe, I knew I was saved. My breath came and went freely for the first time since I had seen the canopy of the bed moving down upon me!

To some men the means of escape which I had discovered might have seemed difficult and dangerous enough – to *me* the prospect of slipping down the pipe into the street did not suggest even a thought of peril. I had always been accustomed, by the practice of gymnastics, to keep up my schoolboy powers as a daring and expert climber; and knew that my head, hands, and feet would serve me faithfully in any hazards of ascent or descent. I had already got one leg over the window-sill, when I remembered the handkerchief filled with money under my pillow. I could well have afforded to leave it behind me, but I was revengefully determined that the miscreants of the gambling-house should miss their plunder as well as their victim. So I went back to the bed and tied the heavy handkerchief at my back by my cravat.

Just as I had made it tight and fixed it in a comfortable place, I thought I heard a sound of breathing outside the door. The chill feeling of horror ran through me again as I listened. No! dead silence still in the passage – I had only heard the night air blowing softly into the room. The next moment I was on the window-sill – and the next I had a firm grip on the water-pipe with my hands and knees.

I slid down into the street easily and quietly, as I thought I should, and immediately set off at the top of my speed to a branch 'Prefecture' of Police, which I knew was situated in the immediate neighbourhood. A 'Sub-prefect', and several picked men among his subordinates, happened to be up, maturing. I believe, some scheme for discovering the perpetrator of a mysterious murder which all Paris was talking of just then. When I began my story, in a breathless hurry and in very bad French, I could see that the Sub-prefect suspected me of being a drunken Englishman who had robbed somebody; but he soon altered his opinion as I went on, and before I had anything like concluded, he shoved all the papers before him into a drawer, put on his hat, supplied me with another (for I was bare-headed), ordered a file of soldiers, desired his expert followers to get ready all sorts of tools for breaking open doors and ripping up brick-flooring, and took my arm, in the most friendly and familiar manner possible, to lead me with him out of the house. I will venture to say, that when the Sub-prefect was a little boy, and was taken for the first time to the play, he was not half as much pleased as he was now at the job in prospect for him at the gambling-house!

Away we went through the streets, the Sub-prefect cross-examining and congratulating me in the same breath as we marched at the head of our formidable *posse comitatus*. Sentinels were placed at the back and front of the house the moment we got to it; a tremendous battery of knocks was directed against the door; a light appeared at a window; I was told to conceal myself behind the police – then came more knocks, and a cry of 'Open in the name of the law!' At that terrible summons bolts and locks gave way before an invisible hand, and the moment after the Sub-prefect was in the passage, confronting a waiter half-dressed and ghastly pale. This was the short dialogue which immediately took place:

'We want to see the Englishman who is sleeping in this house.'

'He went away hours ago.'

'He did no such thing. His friend went away; *he* remained. Show us to his bedroom!'

'I swear to you, Monsieur le Sous-prefect, he is not here! he—'

'I swear to you, Monsieur le Garçon, he is. He slept here – he didn't find your bed comfortable – he came to us to complain of it – here he is among my men – and here am I ready to look for a flea or two in his bedstead. Renaudin!' (calling to one of the subordinates, and pointing to the waiter) 'collar that man, and tie his hands behind him. Now, then, gentlemen, let us walk upstairs!'

Every man and woman in the house was secured – the 'Old Soldier' the first. Then I identified the bed in which I had slept, and then we went into the room above.

No object that was at all extraordinary appeared in any part of it. The Sub-prefect looked round the place, commanded everybody to be silent, stamped twice on the floor, called for a candle, looked attentively at the spot he had stamped on, and ordered the flooring there to be carefully taken up. This was done in no time. Lights were produced, and we saw a deep raftered cavity between the floor of this room and the ceiling of the room beneath. Through this cavity there ran perpendicularly a sort of case of iron thickly greased; and inside the case appeared the screw, which communicated with the bed-top below. Extra lengths of screw, freshly oiled; levers covered with felt; all the complete upper works of a heavy press – constructed with infernal ingenuity so as to join the fixtures below, and when taken to pieces again to go into the smallest possible compass – were next discovered and pulled out on the floor. After some little difficulty, the Sub-prefect succeeded in putting the machinery together, and, leaving his men to work it, descended with me to the bedroom. The smothering canopy was then lowered, but not so noiselessly as I had seen it lowered. When I mentioned this to the Sub-prefect, his answer, simple as it was, had a terrible significance. 'My men,' said he, 'are working down the bed-top for the first time – the men whose money you won were in better practice.'

We left the house in the sole possession of two police agents – every one of the inmates being removed to prison on the spot. The Sub-prefect, after taking down my *procès-verbal* in his office, returned with me to my hotel to get my passport. 'Do you think,' I asked, as I gave it to him, 'that any men have really been smothered in that bed, as they tried to smother *me*?'

'I have seen dozens of drowned men laid out at the Morgue,' answered the Sub-prefect, 'in whose pocketbooks were found letters, stating that they had committed suicide in the Seine, because they had lost everything at the gaming-table. Do I know how many of those men entered the same gambling-house that *you* entered? won as *you* won? took that bed as *you* took it? slept in it? were smothered in it? and were privately thrown into the river, with a letter of explanation written by the murderers and placed in their pocket-books? No man can say how many or how few have suffered the fate from which you have escaped. The people of the gambling-house kept their bedstead machinery a secret from *us* – even from the police! The dead kept the rest of the secret for them. Goodnight, or rather good morning, Monsieur Faulkner! Be at my office again at nine o'clock – in the meantime, *au revoir!*'

The rest of my story is soon told. I was examined and re-examined; the gambling-house was strictly searched all through from top to bottom; the prisoners were separately interrogated; and two of the less guilty among them made a confession. *I* discovered that the old soldier was the master of the gambling-house – *justice* discovered that he had been drummed out of the army as a vagabond years ago; that he had been guilty of all sorts of villainies since; that he was in possession of stolen property, which the owners identified; and that he, the croupier, another accomplice, and the woman who had made a cup of coffee, were all in the secret of the bedstead. There appeared some reason to doubt whether the inferior persons attached to the house knew anything of the suffocating machinery; and they received the benefit of that doubt, by being treated simply as thieves and vagabonds. As for the old soldier and his two head-myrmidons, they went to the galleys; the woman who had drugged my coffee was imprisoned for I forget how many years; the regular attendants at the gambling-house were considered 'suspicious', and placed under 'surveillance'; and I became, for one whole week (which is a long time), the head 'lion' in Parisian society. My adventure was dramatized by three illustrious playmakers, but never saw theatrical daylight; for the censorship forbade the introduction on the stage of a correct copy of the gambling-house bedstead.

One good result was produced by my adventure, which any censorship must have approved: – it cured me of ever again trying *Rouge et Noir* as an amusement. The sight of a green cloth, with packs of cards and heaps of money on it, will henceforth be for ever associated in my mind with the sight of a bed-canopy descending to suffocate me in the silence and darkness of the night.

The Banshee's Warning

CHARLOTTE RIDDELL

Many a year, before chloroform was thought of, there lived in an old rambling house, in Gerrard Street, Soho, a clever Irishman called Hertford O'Donnell.

After Hertford O'Donnell he was entitled to write, M.R.C.S. for he had studied hard to gain this distinction, and the older surgeons at Guy's (his hospital) considered him one of the most rising operators of the day.

Having said chloroform was unknown at the time this story opens, it will strike my readers that, if Hertford O'Donnell were a rising and successful operator in those days, of necessity he combined within himself a larger number of striking qualities than are by any means necessary to form a successful operator in these.

There was more than mere hand skill, more than even thorough knowledge of his profession, then needful for the man, who, dealing with conscious subjects, essayed to rid them of some of the diseases to which flesh is heir. There was greater courage required in the manipulator of old than is altogether essential at present. Then, as now, a thorough mastery of his instruments, a steady hand, a keen eye, a quick dexterity were indispensable to a good operator; but, added to all these things, there formerly required a pulse which knew no quickening, a mental strength which never faltered, a ready power of adaptation in unexpected circumstances, fertility of resource in difficult cases, and a brave front under all emergencies.

If I refrain from adding that a hard as well as a courageous heart was an important item in the programme it is only out of deference to general opinion, which, amongst other strange delusions, clings to the belief that courage and hardness are antagonistic qualities.

Hertford O'Donnell, however, was hard as steel. He understood his work, and he did it thoroughly; but he cared no more for quivering nerves and shrinking muscles, for screams of agony, for faces white with pain, and teeth clenched in the extremity of anguish, than he did for the stony countenances of the dead, which so often in the dissecting room appalled younger and less experienced men.

He had no sentiment, and he had no sympathy. The human body was to him, merely an ingenious piece of mechanism, which it was at once a pleasure and a profit to understand. Precisely as Brunel loved the Thames Tunnel, or any other singular engineering feat, so O'Donnell loved a patient on whom he had operated successfully, more especially if the ailment possessed by the patient were of a rare and difficult character.

And for this reason he was much liked by all who came under his hands, since patients are apt to mistake a surgeon's interest in their cases for interest in themselves; and it was gratifying to John Dicks, plasterer, and Timothy Regan, labourer, to be the happy possessors of remarkable diseases, which produced a cordial understanding between them and the handsome Irishman.

If he had been hard and cool at the moment of hacking them to pieces, that was all forgotten or remembered only as a virtue, when, after being discharged from hospital like soldiers who have served in a severe campaign, they met Mr O'Donnell in the street, and were accosted by that rising individual just as though he considered himself nobody.

He had a royal memory, this stranger in a strange land, both for faces and cases; and like the rest of his countrymen, he never felt it beneath his dignity to talk cordially to corduroy and fustian.

In London, as a Calgillan, he never held back his tongue from speaking a cheery or a kindly word. His manners were pliable enough, if his heart were not; and the porters, and the patients, and the nurses, and the students at Guy's were all pleased to see Hertford O'Donnell.

Rain, hail, sunshine, it was all the same; there was a life and a brightness about the man which communicated itself to those with whom he came in contact. Let the mud in the Borough be a foot deep or the London fog as thick as pea-soup, Mr O'Donnell never lost his temper, never muttered a surly reply to the gatekeeper's salutation, but spoke out blithely and cheerfully to his pupils and his patients, to the sick and to the well, to those below and to those above him.

And yet, spite of all these good qualities, spite of his handsome face, his fine figure, his easy address, and his unquestionable skill as an operator, the dons, who acknowledged his talent, shook their heads gravely when two or three of them in private and solemn conclave, talked confidentially of their younger brother.

If there were many things in his favour, there were more in his disfavour. He was Irish – not merely by the accident of birth, which might have been forgiven, since a man cannot be held accountable for such caprices of Nature, but by every other accident and design which is objectionable to the orthodox and respectable and representative English mind.

In speech, appearance, manner, taste, modes of expression, habits of life, Hertford O'Donnell was Irish. To the core of his heart he loved the island which he declared he never meant to re-visit; and amongst the English he moved to all intents and purposes a foreigner, who was resolved, so said the great prophets at Guy's, to rush to destruction as fast as he could, and let no man hinder him.

'He means to go the whole length of his tether,' observed one of the ancient wiseacres to another; which speech implied a conviction that Hertford O'Donnell having sold himself to the Evil One, had determined to dive the full length of his rope into wickedness before being pulled to that shore where even wickedness is negative – where there are no mad carouses, no wild, sinful excitements, nothing but impotent wailing and gnashing of teeth.

A reckless, graceless, clever, wicked devil – going to his natural home as fast as in London anyone possibly speed thither; this was the opinion his superiors, held of the man who lived all alone with a housekeeper and her husband (who acted as butler) in his big house near Soho.

Gerrard Street – made famous by De Quincey, was not then an utterly shady and forgotten locality; carriage-patients found their way to the rising young surgeon – some great personages thought it not beneath them to fee an individual whose consulting rooms were situated on what was even then considered the wrong side of Regent Street. He was making money, and he was spending it; he was over head and ears in debt – useless, vulgar debt – senselessly contracted, never bravely faced. He had lived at an awful pace ever since he came to London, a pace which only a man who hopes and expects to die young can ever travel.

Life was good, was it? Death, was he a child, or a woman, or a coward, to be afraid of that hereafter? God knew all about the trifle which had upset his coach, better than the dons at Guy's.

Hertford O'Donnell understood the world pretty thoroughly, and the ways thereof were to him as roads often versed; therefore, when he said that at the Day of Judgment he felt certain he should come off as well as many of those who censured him, it may be assumed, that, although his views of post-mortem punishment were vague, unsatisfactory and infidel, still his information as to the peccadilloes of his neighbours was such as consoled himself.

And yet, living all alone in the old house near Soho Square, grave thoughts would intrude into the surgeon's mind – thoughts which were, so to say, italicised by peremptory letters, and still more peremptory visits from people who wanted money.

Although he had many acquaintances he had no single friend, and accordingly these thoughts were received and brooded over in solitude – in those hours when, after returning from dinner, or supper, or congenial carouse, he sat in his dreary rooms, smoking his pipe and considering means and ways, chances and certainties.

In good truth he had started in London with some vague idea that as his life in it would not be of long continuance, the pace at which he elected to travel could be of little consequence; but the years since his first entry into the Metropolis were now piled one on the top of another, his youth was behind him, his chances of longevity, spite of the way he had striven to injure his constitution, quite as good as ever. He had come to that period in existence, to that narrow strip of table-land, whence the ascent of youth and the descent of age are equally discernable – when, simply because he has lived for so many years, it strikes a man as possible he may have to live for just as many more, with the ability for hard work gone, with the boom companions scattered, with the capacity for enjoying convivial meetings a mere memory, with small means perhaps, with no bright hopes, with the pomp and the circumstance and the fairy carriages, and the glamour which youth flings over earthly objects, faded away like the pageant of yesterday, while the dreary ceremony of living has to be gone through today and tomorrow and the morrow after, as though the gay cavalcade and the martial music, and the glittering helmets and the prancing steeds were still accompanying the wayfarer to his journey's end.

Ah! my friends, there comes a moment when we must all leave the coach, with its four bright bays, its pleasant outside freight, its cheery company, its guard who blows the horn so merrily through villages and along lonely country roads.

Long before we reach that final stage, where the black business claims us for its own special property, we have to bid goodbye to all easy, thoughtless journeying, and betake ourselves, with what zest we may, to traversing the common of reality. There is no royal road across it that ever I heard of. From the king on his throne to the labourer who vaguely imagines what manner of being a king is, we have all to tramp across that desert at one period of our lives, at all events; and that period usually is when, as I have said, a man starts to find the hopes, and the strength, and the buoyancy of youth left behind, while years and years of life lie stretching out before him.

The coach he has travelled by drops him here. There is no appeal, there is no help; therefore, let him take off his hat and wish the new passengers good speed, without either envy or repining.

Behold, he has had his turn, and let whosoever will, mount on the box-seat of life again, and tip the coachman and handle the ribbons – he shall take that pleasant journey no more, no more for ever.

Even supposing a man's springtime to have been a cold and ungenial one, with bitter easterly winds and nipping frosts, biting the buds and retarding the blossoms, still it was spring for all that – spring with the sprouting forth, with the flowers unfolding tenderly, with the songs of the birds and the rush of waters, with the summer before and the autumn afar off, and winter remote as death and eternity, but when once the trees have donned their summer foliage, when the pure white blossoms have disappeared, and the gorgeous red and orange and purple blaze of many-coloured flowers fills the gardens, then if there come a wet, dreary day, the idea of autumn and winter is not so difficult to realise. When once twelve o'clock is reached, the evening and night become facts, not possibilities; and it was of the afternoon, and the evening, and the night, Hertford O'Donnell sat thinking on the Christmas Eve, when I crave permission to introduce him to my readers.

A good-looking man ladies considered him. A tall, dark-complexioned, black-haired, straight-limbed, deeply divinely blue-eyed fellow, with a soft voice, with a pleasant brogue, who had ridden like a centaur over the loose stone walls in Connemara, who had danced all night at the Dublin balls, who had walked across the Bennebeola Mountains, gun in hand, day after day, without weariness, who had fished in every one of the hundred lakes you can behold from the top of that mountain near the Recess Hotel, who had led a mad, wild life in Trinity College, and a wilder, perhaps, while 'studying for a doctor' – as the Irish phrase goes – in Edinburgh, and who, after the death of his eldest brother left him free to return to Calgillan, and pursue the usual utterly useless, utterly purposeless, utterly pleasant life of an Irish gentleman possessed of health, birth, and expectations, suddenly kicked over the paternal traces, bade adieu to Calgillan Castle and the blandishments of a certain beautiful Miss Clifden, beloved of his mother, and laid out to be his wife, walked down the avenue without even so much company as a Gossoon to carry his carpet-bag, shook the dust from his feet at the lodge gates, and took his seat on the coach, never once looking back at Calgillan, where his favourite mare was standing in the stable, his greyhounds chasing one another round the home paddock, his gun at half-cock in his dressing-room and his fishing-tackle all in order and ready for use.

He had not kissed his mother, or asked for his father's blessing; he left Miss Clifden, arrayed in her brand-new riding-habit, without a word of affection or regret; he had spoken no syllable of farewell to any servant about the place; only when the old woman at the lodge bade him good morning and God-blessed his handsome face, he recommended her bitterly to look at it well for she would never see it more.

Twelve years and a half had passed since then, without either Miss Clifden or any other one of the Calgillan people having set eyes on Master Hertford's handsome face.

He had kept his vow to himself; he had not written home; he had not been indebted to mother or father for even a tenpenny-piece during the whole of that time; he had lived without friends; and he had lived without God – so far as God ever lets a man live without him.

One thing only he felt to be needful – money; money to keep him when the evil days of sickness, or age, or loss of practice came upon him. Though a spendthrift, he was not a simpleton; around him he saw men, who, having started with fairer prospects that his own, were, nevertheless, reduced to indigence; and he knew that what had happened to others might happen to himself.

An unlucky cut, slipping on a piece of orange-peel in the street, the merest accident imaginable, is sufficient to change opulence to beggary in the life's programme of an individual, whose income depends on eye, on nerve, on hand;

and, besides the consciousness of this fact, Hertford O'Donnell knew that beyond a certain point in his profession, progress was not easy.

It did not depend quite on the strength of his own bow and shield whether he counted his earnings by hundreds or thousands. Work may achieve competence; but mere work cannot, in a profession, at all events, compass fortune.

He looked around him, and he perceived that the majority of great men – great and wealthy – had been indebted for their elevation, more to the accident of birth, patronage, connection, or marriage, than to personal ability.

Personal ability, no doubt, they possessed; but then, little Jones, who lived in Frith Street, and who could barely keep himself and his wife and family, had ability, too, only he lacked the concomitants of success.

He wanted something or someone to puff him into notoriety – a brother at Court – a lord's leg to mend – a rich wife to give him prestige in Society; and in his absence of this something or someone, he had grown grey-haired and faint-hearted while labouring for a world which utterly despises its most obsequious servants.

'Clatter along the streets with a pair of fine horses, snub the middle classes, and drive over the commonalty – that is the way to compass wealth and popularity in England,' said Hertford O'Donnell, bitterly; and as the man desired wealth and popularity, he sat before his fire, with a foot on each hob, and a short pipe in his mouth, considering how he might best obtain the means to clatter along the streets in his carriage, and splash plebeians with mud from his wheels like the best.

In Dublin he could, by means of his name and connection, have done well; but then he was not in Dublin, neither did he want to be. The bitterest memories of his life were inseparable from the very name of the Green Island, and he had no desire to return to it.

Besides, in Dublin, heiresses are not quite so plentiful as in London; and an heiress, Hertford O'Donnell had decided, would do more for him than years of steady work.

A rich wife could clear him of debt, introduce him to fashionable practice, afford him that measure of social respectability which a medical bachelor invariably lacks, deliver him from the loneliness of Gerrard Street, and the domination of Mr and Mrs Coles.

To most men, deliberately bartering away their independence for money seems so prosaic a business that they strive to gloss it over even to themselves, and to assign every reason for their choice, save that which is really the influencing one.

Not so, however, with Hertford O'Donnell. He sat beside the fire scoffing over his proposed bargain – thinking of the lady's age, her money bags, her desirable house in town, her seat in the country, her snobbishness, her folly.

'It could be a fitting ending,' he sneered, 'and why I did not settle the matter tonight passes my comprehension. I am not a fool, to be frightened with old women's tales; and yet I must have turned white. I felt I did, and she asked me whether I were ill. And then to think of my being such an idiot as to ask her if she had heard anything like a cry, as though she would be likely to hear *that*, she with her poor parvenu blood, which I often imagine must have been mixed with some of her father's strong pickling vinegar. What a deuce could I have been dreaming about? I wonder what it really was.' And Hertford O'Donnell pushed his hair back off his forehead, and took another draught from the too familiar tumbler, which was placed conveniently on the chimney-piece.

'After expressly making up my mind to propose, too!' he mentally continued. 'Could it have been conscience – that myth, which somebody, who knew nothing about the matter, said, "Makes cowards of us all"? I don't believe in conscience; and even if there be such a thing capable of being developed by sentiment and cultivation, why should it trouble me? I have no intention of wronging Miss Janice Price Ingot, not the least. Honestly and fairly I shall marry her; honestly and fairly I shall act by her. An old wife is not exactly an ornamental article of furniture in a man's house; and I do not know that the fact of her being well gilded makes her look any handsomer. But she shall have no cause for complaint; and I will go and dine with her tomorrow, and settle the matter.'

Having arrived at which resolution, Mr O'Donnell arose, kicked down the fire – burning hollow – with the heel of his boot, knocked the ashes out of his pipe, emptied his tumbler, and bethought him it was time to go to bed. He was not in the habit of taking his rest so early as a quarter to twelve o'clock; but he felt unusually weary – tired mentally and bodily – and lonely beyond all power of expression.

'The fair Janet would be better than this,' he said, half aloud; and then, with a start and a shiver, and a blanched face, he turned sharply round, whilst a low, sobbing, wailing cry echoed mournfully through the room. No form of words could give an idea of the sound. The plaintiveness of the Æolian harp – that plaintiveness which so soon affects and lowers the highest spirits – would have seemed wildly gay in comparison with the sadness of the cry which seemed floating in the air. As the summer wind comes and goes amongst the trees, so that mournful wail came and went – came and went. It came in a rush of sound, like a gradual crescendo managed by a skilful musician, and died away in a lingering note, so gently that the listener could scarcely tell the exact moment when it faded into utter silence.

I say faded, for it disappeared as the coast line disappears in the twilight, and there was total stillness in the apartment.

Then, for the first time, Hertford O'Donnell looked at his dog. and beholding the creature crouched into a corner beside the fireplace, called upon him to come out.

His voice sounded strange even to himself, and apparently the dog thought so too, for he made no effort to obey the summons.

'Come here, sir,' his master repeated, and then the animal came crawling reluctantly forward with his hair on end, his eyes almost starting from his head, trembling violently, as the surgeon, who caressed him, felt.

'So you heard it, Brian?' he said to the dog. 'And so your ears are sharper than Miss Ingot's, old fellow. It's a mighty queer thing to think of, being favoured with a visit from a Banshee in Gerrard Street; and as the lady has travelled so far, I only wish I knew whether there is any sort of refreshment she would like to take after her long journey.'

He spoke loudly, and with a certain mocking defiance, seeming to think the phantom he addressed would reply; but when he stopped at the end of his sentence, no sound came through the stillness. There was a dead silence in the room – a silence broken only by the falling of cinders on the hearth and the breathing of his dog.

'If my visitor would tell me,' he proceeded, 'for whom this lamentation is being made, whether for myself, or for for some member of my illustrious family, I should feel immensely obliged. It seems too much honour for a poor surgeon to have such attention paid him. Good Heavens! what is that?' he exclaimed, as a ring, loud and peremptory, woke all the echoes in the house, and brought his housekeeper, in a state of distressing dishabille 'out of her warm bed', as she subsequently stated, to the head of the staircase.

Across the hall Hertford O'Donnell strode, relieved at the prospect of speaking to any living being. He took no precaution of putting up the chain, but flung the door wide. A dozen burglars would have proved welcome in comparison with that ghostly intruder he had been interviewing; therefore, as has been said, he threw the door wide, admitting a rush of wet, cold air, which made poor Mrs Coles' few remaining teeth chatter in her head.

'Who is there? What do you want?' asked the surgeon, seeing no person, and hearing no voice. 'Who is there? Why the devil can't you speak?'

When even this polite exhortation failed to elicit an answer, he passed out into the night and looked up the street and down the street, to see nothing but the driving rain and the blinking lights.

'If this goes on much longer I shall soon think I must be either mad or drunk,' he muttered, as he re-entered the house and locked and bolted the door once more.

'Lord's sake! What is the matter, sir?' asked Mrs Coles, from the upper flight, careful only to reveal the borders of her night-cap to Mr O'Donnell's admiring gaze. 'Is anybody killed? Have you to go out, sir?'

'It was only a run-away ring,' he answered, trying to reassure himself with an explanation he did not in his heart believe.

'Run-away – I'd run away them!' murmured Mrs Coles, as she retired to the conjugal couch, where Coles was, to quote her own expression, 'snoring like a pig through it all'.

Almost immediately afterwards she heard her master ascend the stairs and close his bedroom door.

'Madam will surely be too much of a gentlewoman to intrude here,' thought the surgeon, scoffing even at his own fears; but when he lay down he did not put out his light, and made Brian leap up and crouch on the coverlet beside him.

The man was fairly frightened, and would have thought it no discredit to his manhood to acknowledge as much. He was not afraid of death, he was not afraid of trouble, he was not afraid of danger; but he was afraid of the Banshee; and as he lay with his hand on the dog's head, he recalled the many stories he had been told concerning this family retainer in the days of his youth.

He had not thought about her for years and years. Never before had he heard her voice himself. When his brother died she had not thought it necessary to travel up to Dublin and give him notice of the impending catastrophe. 'If she had, I would have gone down to Calgillan, and perhaps saved his life,' considered the surgeon. 'I wonder who this is for? If for me, that will settle my debts and my marriage. If I could be quite certain it was either of the old people, I would start tomorrow.'

Then vaguely his mind wandered on to think of every Banshee story he had ever heard in his life. About the beautiful lady with the wreath of flowers, who sat on the rocks below Red Castle, in the County Antrim, crying till one of the sons died for love of her; about the Round Chamber at Dunluce, which was swept clean by the Banshee every night; about the bed in a certain great house in Ireland, which was slept in constantly, although no human being ever passed in or out after dark; about that General Officer who, the night before Waterloo, said to a friend, 'I have heard the Banshee, and shall not come off the field alive tomorrow; break the news gently to poor Carry'; and who, nevertheless, coming safe off the field, had subsequently news about poor Carry broken tenderly and pitifully to him; about the lad, who, aloft in the rigging, hearing through the night a sobbing and wailing coming over the waters, went down to the captain and told him he was afraid they were somehow out of their reckoning, just in time to save the ship, which, when morning broke, they found but for his warning would have been on the rocks. It was blowing great guns, and the sea was all in a fret and turmoil, and they could sometimes see in the trough of the waves, as down a valley, the cruel black reefs they had escaped.

On deck the captain stood speaking to the boy who had saved them, and asking how he knew of their danger; and when the lad told him, the captain laughed, and said her ladyship had been outwitted that time.

But the boy answered, with a grave shake of his head, that the warning was either for him or his, and that if he got safe to port there would be bad tidings waiting for him from home; whereupon the captain bade him go below, and get some brandy and lie down.

He got the brandy, and he lay down, but he never rose again; and when the storm abated – when a great calm succeeded to the previous tempest – there was a very solemn funeral at sea; and on their arrival at Liverpool the captain took a journey to Ireland to tell a widowed mother how her only son died. and to bear his few effects to the poor desolate soul.

And Hertford O'Donnell thought again about his own father riding full-chase across country, and hearing, as he galloped by a clump of plantation, something like a sobbing and wailing. The hounds were in full cry, but he still felt, as he afterwards expressed it, that there was something among those trees he could not pass: and so he jumped off his horse, and hung the reins over the branch of a Scotch fir, and beat the cover well, but not a thing could he find in it.

Then for the first time in his life, Miles O'Donnell turned his horse's head *from* the hunt, and, within a mile of Calgillan, met a man running to tell him his brother's gun had burst, and injured him mortally.

And he remembered the story also, of how Mary O'Donnell, his great aunt, being married to a young Englishman, heard the Banshee as she sat one evening waiting for his return; and of how she, thinking the bridge by which he often came home unsafe for horse and man, went out in a great panic, to meet and entreat him to go round by the main road for her sake. Sir Edward was riding along in the moonlight, making straight for the bridge, when he beheld a figure dressed all in white crossing it. Then there was a crash, and the figure disappeared.

The lady was rescued and brought back to the hall; but next morning there were two dead bodies within its walls – those of Lady Eyreton and her still-born son.

Quicker than I write them, these memories chased one another through Hertford O'Donnell's brain; and there was one more terrible memory than any, which would recur to him, concerning an Irish nobleman who, seated alone in his great town-house in London, heard the Banshee, and rushed out to get rid of the phantom, which wailed in his ear, nevertheless, as he strode down Piccadilly. And then the surgeon remembered how that nobleman went with a friend to the Opera, feeling sure that there no Banshee, unless she had a box, could find admittance, until suddenly he heard her singing up amongst the highest part of the scenery, with a terrible mournfulness, and a pathos which made the prima donna's tenderest notes seem harsh by comparison.

As he came out, some quarrel arose between him and a famous fire-eater, against whom he stumbled; and the result was that the next afternoon there was a new Lord— vice Lord— , killed in a duel with Captain Bravo.

Memories like these are not the most enlivening possible; they are apt to make a man fanciful, and nervous, and wakeful; but as time ran on, Hertford O'Donnell fell asleep, with his candle still burning, and Brian's cold nose pressed against his hand.

He dreamt of his mother's family – the Hertfords of Artingbury, Yorkshire, far-off relatives of Lord Hertford – so far off that even Mrs O'Donnell held no clue to the genealogical maze.

He thought he was at Artingbury, fishing; that it was a misty summer morning, and the fish rising beautifully. In his dreams he hooked one after another, and the boy who was with him threw them into the basket.

At last there was one more difficult to land than the others; and the boy, in his eagerness to watch the sport, drew nearer and nearer to the brink, while the fisher, intent on his prey, failed to notice his companion's danger.

Suddenly there was a cry, a splash, and the boy disappeared from sight.

Next instance he rose again, however, and then, for the first time, Hertford O'Donnell saw his face.

It was one he knew well.

In a moment he plunged into the water, and struck out for the lad. He had him by the hair, he was turning to bring him back to land, when the stream suddenly changed into a wide, wild, shoreless sea, where the billows were chasing one another with a mad demoniac mirth.

For a while O'Donnell kept the lad and himself afloat. They were swept under the waves, and came up again, only to see larger waves rushing towards them; but through all, the surgeon never loosened his hold, until a tremendous billow, engulfing them both, tore the boy from his grasp.

With the horror of his dream upon him he awoke, to hear a voice quite distinctly:

'Go to the hospital – go at once!'

The surgeon started up in bed, rubbing his eyes, and looked around. The candle was flickering faintly in its socket. Brian, with his ears pricked forward, had raised his head at his master's sudden movement.

Everything was quiet, but still those words were ringing in his ear:

'Go to the hospital – go at once!'

The tremendous peal of the bell over night, and this sentence, seemed to be simultaneous.

That he was wanted at Guy's – wanted imperatively – came to O'Donnell like an inspiration. Neither sense nor reason had anything to do with the conviction that roused him out of bed, and made him dress as speedily as possible, and grope his way down the staircase, Brian following.

He opened the front door, and passed out into the darkness. The rain was over, and the stars were shining as he pursued his way down Newport Market, and thence, winding in and out in a south-easterly direction, through Lincoln's Inn Fields and Old Square to Chancery Lane, whence he proceeded to St Paul's.

Along the deserted streets he resolutely continued his walk. He did not know what he was going to Guy's for. Some instinct was urging him on, and he neither strove to combat nor control it. Only once did the thought of turning back cross his mind, and that was the archway leading into Old Square. There he had paused for a moment, asking himself whether he were not gone stark, staring mad; but Guy's seemed preferable to the haunted house in Gerrard Street, and he walked resolutely on, determined to say, if any surprise were expressed at his appearance, that he had been sent for.

Sent for? – yea, truly; but by whom?

On through Cannon Street; on over London Bridge, where the lights flickered in the river, and the sullen splash of the water flowing beneath the arches, washing the stone piers, could be heard, now the human din was hushed and lulled to sleep. On, thinking of many things: of the days of his youth; of his dead brother; of his father's heavily-encumbered estate; of the fortune his mother had vowed she would leave to some charity rather than to him, if he refused to marry according to her choice; of his wild life in London; of the terrible cry he had heard over-night – that unearthly wail which he could not drive from his memory even when he entered Guy's, and confronted the porter, who said:

'You have been sent for, sir; did you meet the messenger?'

Like one in a dream, Hertford O'Donnell heard him; like one in a dream, also, he asked what was the matter.

'Bad accident, sir; fire; fell off a balcony – unsafe – old building. Mother and child – a son; child with compound fracture of thigh.'

This, the joint information of porter and house-surgeon, mingled together, and made a boom in Mr O'Donnell's ears like the sound of the sea breaking on a shingly shore.

Only one sentence he understood properly – 'Immediate amputation necessary.' At this point he grew cool; he was the careful, cautious, successful surgeon, in a moment.

'The child you say?' he answered. 'Let me see him.'

The Guy's Hospital of today may be different to the Guy's Hertford O'Donnell knew so well. Railways have, I believe, swept away the old operating room; railways may have changed the position of the former accident ward, to reach which, in the days of which I am writing, the two surgeons had to pass a staircase leading to the opper stories.

On the lower step of this staircase, partially in shadow, Hertford O'Donnell beheld, as he came forward, an old woman seated.

An old woman with streaming grey hair, with attenuated arms, with head bowed forward, with scanty clothing, with bare feet; who never looked up at their approach, but sat unnoticing, shaking her head and wringing her hands in an extremity of despair.

'Who is that?' asked Mr O'Donnell, almost involuntarily

'Who is what?' demanded his companion.

'That – that woman,' was the reply.

'What woman?'

'There – are you blind? – seated on the bottom step of the staircase. What is she doing?' persisted Mr O'Donnell.

'There is no woman near us,' his companion answered, looking at the rising surgeon very much as though he suspected him of seeing double.

'No woman!' scoffed Hertford. 'Do you expect me to disbelieve the evidence of my own eyes?' and he walked up to the figure, meaning to touch it.

But as he assayed to do so, the woman seemed to rise in the air and float away, with her arms stretched high up – over her head, uttering such a wail of pain, and agony, and distress, as caused the Irishman's blood to curdle.

'My God! Did you hear that?' he said to his companion.

'What?' was the reply.

Then, although he knew the sound had fallen on deaf ears, he answered:

'The wail of the Banshee! Some of my people are doomed!'

'I trust not,' answered the house-surgeon, who had an idea nevertheless, that Hertford O'Donnell's Banshee lived in a whisky bottle, and would at some remote day make an end to the rising and clever operator,

With nerves utterly shaken, Mr O'Donnell walked forward to the accident ward. There with his face shaded from the light, lay his patient – a young boy, with a compound fracture of the thigh.

In that ward, in the face of actual danger or pain capable of relief the surgeon had never known faltering or fear; and now he carefully examined the injury, felt the pulse, inquired as to the treatment pursued, and ordered the sufferer to be carried to the operating room,

While he was looking out his instruments he heard the boy lying on the table murmur faintly:

'Tell her not to cry so – tell her not to cry.'

'What is he talking about?' Hertford O'Donnell inquired.

'The nurse says he has been speaking about some woman crying ever since he came in – his mother, most likely,' answered one of the attendants.

'He is delirious then?' observed the surgeon.

'No, sir,' pleaded the boy, excitedly, 'no; it is that woman – that woman with the grey hair. I saw her looking from the upper window before the balcony gave way. She has never left me since, and she won't be quiet, wringing her hands and crying.'

'Can you see her now?' Hertford O'Donnell inquired, stepping to the side of the table. 'Point out where she is.'

Then the lad stretched forth a feeble finger in the direction of the door, where clearly, as he had seen her seated on the stairs, the surgeon saw a woman standing – a woman with grey hair and scanty clothing, and upstretched arms and bare feet.

'A word with you, sir,' O'Donnell said to the house-surgeon, drawing him back from the table. 'I cannot perform this operation: send for some other person. I am ill; I am incapable.'

'But,' pleaded the other, 'there is no time to get anyone else. We sent for Mr West, before we troubled you, but he was out of town, and all the rest of the surgeons live so far away. Mortification may set in at any moment and— '.

'Do you think you require to teach me my business?' was the reply. 'I know the boy's life hangs on a thread, and that is the very reason I cannot operate. I am not fit for it. I tell you I have seen tonight that which unnerves me utterly.

My hand is not steady. Send for someone else without delay. Say I am ill – dead! – what you please. Heavens! There she is again, right over the boy! Do you hear her?' and Hertford O'Donnell fell fainting on the floor.

How long he lay in that death-like swoon I cannot say; but when he returned to consciousness, the principal physician of Guy's was standing beside him in the cold grey light of the Christmas morning.

'The boy?' murmured O'Donnell, faintly.

'Now, my dear fellow, keep yourself quiet.' was the reply.

'The boy?' he repeated, irritably. 'Who operated?'

'No one,' Dr Lanson answered. 'It would have been useless cruelty. Mortification had set in and – '

Hertford O'Donnell turned his face to the wall, and his friend could not see it.

'Do not distress yourself,' went on the physician. kindly. 'Allington says he could not have survived the operation in any case. He was quite delirious from the first, raving about a woman with grey hair and – '

'I know.' Hertford O'Donnell interrupted; 'and the boy had a mother, they told me, or I dreamt it.'

'Yes, she was bruised and shaken, but not seriously injured.'

'Has she blue eyes and fair hair – fair hair all rippling and wavy? Is she white as a lily, with just a faint flush of colour in her cheek? Is she young and trusting and innocent? No; I am wandering. She must be nearly thirty now. Go, for God's sake, and tell me if you can find a woman you could imagine having once been as a girl such as I describe.'

'Irish?' asked the doctor; and O'Donnell made a gesture of assent.

'It is she then,' was the reply, 'a woman with the face of an angel.'

'A woman who should have been my wife,' the surgeon answered; 'whose child was my son.'

'Lord help you!' ejaculated the doctor. Then Hertford O'Donnell raised himself from the sofa where they had laid him, and told his companion the story of his life – how there had been bitter feud between his people and her people – how they were divided by old animosities and by difference of religion – how they had met by stealth, and exchanged rings and vows, all for naught – how his family had insulted hers, so that her father, wishful for her to marry a kinsman of his own, bore her off to a far-away land, and made her write him a letter of eternal farewell – how his own parents had kept all knowledge of the quarrel from him till she was utterly beyond his reach – how they had vowed to discard him unless he agreed to marry according to their wishes – how he left home, and came to London, and sought his fortune. All this Hertford O'Donnell repeated; and when he had finished, the bells were ringing for morning service – ringing loudly, ringing joyfully, 'Peace on earth, goodwill towards men'.

But there was little peace that morning for Hertford O'Donnell. He had to look on the face of his dead son, wherein he beheld, as though reflected, the face of the boy in his dream.

Afterwards stealthily he followed his friend, and beheld, with her eyes closed, her cheeks pale and pinched, her hair thinner but still falling like a veil over her, the love of his youth, the only woman he had ever loved devotedly and unselfishly.

There is little space left her to tell of how the two met at last – of how the stone of the years seemed suddenly rolled away from the tomb of their past, and their youth arose and returned to them, even amid their tears.

She had been true to him, through persecution, through contumely, through kindness, which was more trying; through shame, and grief, and poverty, she had been loyal to the lover of her youth; and before the New Year dawned there came a letter from Calgillan, saying that the Banshee's wail had been heard there, and praying Hertford, if he were still alive, to let bygones be bygones, in consideration of the long years of estrangement – the anguish and remorse of his afflicted parents.

More than that. Hertford O'Donnell, if a reckless man, was honourable; and so, on the Christmas Day when he was to have proposed for Miss Ingot, he went to that lady, and told her how he had wooed and won, in the years of his youth, one who after many days was miraculously restored to him; and from the hour in which he took her into his confidence, he never thought her either vulgar or foolish, but rather he paid homage to the woman who, when she had heard the whole tale repeated, said, simply, 'Ask her to come to me till you can claim her – and God bless you both!'

The Bird Woman

HENRY SPICER

The events of this strange tale, though they actually occurred in England but a short while since would scarcely be out of place in a book of German dreams and fancies.

The narrator, a girl of the servant class, but of rather superior education and manners, had called on the writer's sister on the subject of a place to which she had been recommended, and in the course of conversation, related the following as a recent experience.

The advertisement in which she set forth her willingness to take charge of an invalid, infirm, or lunatic person, or to assume any office demanding unusual steadiness of nerve, was replied to by a lady whose letter was dated from a certain locality on the outskirts of a large commercial city, and who requested her attendance there at an appointed time.

The house proved to be a dingy, deserted looking mansion, and was not rendered more cheerful by the fact that the adjoining tenements on either side were unoccupied. It wore altogether a haunted and sinister aspect, and the girl, as she rang the bell, was sensible of a kind of misgiving for which she could not account. A timid person might have hesitated. This girl possessed unusual firmness and courage, and, in spite of the presentiment we have mentioned, she determined, at all events to see *what* she would be called on to encounter.

A lady-like person, the mistress herself, opened the door, and conducting the applicant into a vacant apartment, informed her in a few words that the service that would be required of her was of a very peculiar nature imperatively demanding those precise qualities she conceived her to possess. It was right, she added, to mention that the family lived in great seclusion, partly from choice, partly from necessity, an impression having gone abroad that there existed something strange and evil in connection with the residence, which was, in reality, known in the vicinity by the title of the 'haunted house.'

With these preliminary warnings, the lady suggested that the applicant might wish to reconsider her purpose. The latter, however, having little fear of anything human, and none at all of apparitions, at once agreed to the terms proposed stipulating only that the cause of the strange reports affecting the mansion should be a little more clearly explained, and her own particular duties defined.

The mistress readily assented to both conditions, and, leading the way to a ground floor apartment at the back, unlocked the door and turned the handle as about to enter, but checking herself suddenly, warned her companion, without sinking her voice below its ordinary tone, that she was about to be brought face to face with a spectacle that might well try the strongest nerves; nevertheless, there was nothing to fear so long as she retained her self-command. With this not very reassuring preface, they entered the room.

It was rather dark, for the lower half of the windows were boarded up; but in one corner, on the floor was plainly distinguishable what looked like a heap of clothes flung together in disorder. It appeared to be in motion, however, and the mistress of the house once more turning to her follower had just time to utter the mysterious words –

'Don't be frightened. If she likes you she'll hoot; if she doesn't she'll scream.'

When from the apex of the seeming heap of clothes there rose a head that made the stranger's blood run chill. It was human, indeed, in general structure, but exhibited, in place of a nose, a huge beak curved and pointed like that of an owl. Two large staring yellow eyes increased the bizarre resemblance, while numerous tufts of some feathery substance, sprouting from a hard skin and black as a parrot's tongue, completed this horrible intermingling of bird and woman.

As they approached, the unhappy being rose and sunk with the measured motion of a bird upon a perch, and presently, opening its mouth, gave utterance to a hideous and prolonged 'tu-whoo.'

'All right,' said the lady quietly, 'she likes you!'

They were now standing as it were over the unfortunate freak of nature.

'Have you the courage to lift her?' enquired the lady. 'Try.'

The girl, though recoiling instinctively from the contact, nerved herself to the utmost, and, putting her arms beneath those of the still hooting creature, strove to raise it up. In doing so, the hands became disengaged from the clothes. They were black, and armed with long curved talons, like those of a bird of prey.

Even this new discovery might not have made the girl's courage quail, had she not, in raising the creature, observed that she was not, as had seemed to be the case, crouched on the ground, but balanced on an actual perch, or rail, round which her feet closed and clung by means of talons similar to those which adorned her hands.

So inexpressible was the feeling of horror that now overcame the visitor, that, after one desperate effort of self control, she was forced to let go of the thing she held. A wild, unearthly scream that rang through the house marked the creature's change of mood. The baleful eyes shot yellow fire, and scream after scream pursued her as she fairly fled from the apartment, followed at a steadier pace, by the lady.

The latter took her into another room, did all in her power to soothe her agitation, but expressed no surprise when the girl declared that ten times the liberal amount already offered, would not tempt her to undertake such a charge.

Eveline's Visitant

MARY ELIZABETH BRADDON

It was at a masked ball at the Palais Royal that my fatal quarrel with my first cousin André de Brissac began. The quarrel was about a woman. The women who followed the footsteps of Philip of Orleans were the causes of many such disputes; and there was scarcely one fair head in all that glittering throng which, to a man versed in social histories and mysteries, might not have seemed bedabbled with blood.

I shall not record the name of her for love of whom André de Brissac and I crossed one of the bridges, in the dim August dawn on our way to the waste ground beyond the church of Saint-Germain des Prés.

There were many beautiful vipers in those days, and she was one of them. I can feel the chill breath of that August morning blowing in my face, as I sit in my dismal chamber at my chateau of Puy Verdun tonight, alone in the stillness, writing the strange story of my life. I can see the white mist rising from the river, the grim outline of the Châtelet, and the square towers of Notre Dame black against the pale-grey sky. Even more vividly can I recall André's fair young face, as he stood opposite me with his two friends – scoundrels both, and like eager for that unnatural fray. We were a strange group to be seen in a summer sunrise, all of us fresh from the heat and clamour of the Regent's saloons – André in a quaint hunting-dress copied from a family portrait at Puy Verdun, I costumed as one of Law's Mississippi Indians; the other men in like garish frippery adorned with broideries and jewels that looked wan in the pale light of dawn.

Our quarrel had been a fierce one – a quarrel which could have but one result, and that the direst. I had struck him; and the welt raised by my open hand was crimson upon his fair, womanish face as he stood opposite to me. The eastern sun shone on the face presently, and dyed the cruel mark with a deeper red; but the sting of my own wrongs was fresh, and I had not yet learned to despise myself for that brutal outrage.

To André de Brissac such an insult was most terrible. He was the favourite of Fortune, the favourite of woman; and I was nothing – a rough soldier who had done my country good service, but in the boudoir of a Parabère a mannerless boor.

We fought, and I wounded him mortally. Life had been very sweet to him; and I think that a frenzy of despair took possession of him when he felt the life-blood ebbing away. He beckoned me to him as he lay on the ground. I went, and knelt at his side.

'Forgive me, André!' I murmured.

He took no more heed of my words than if that piteous entreaty had been the idle ripple of the river near at hand.

'Listen to me, Hector de Brissac,' he said. 'I am not one who believes that a man has done with earth because his eyes glaze and his jaw stiffens. They will bury me in the old vault at Puy Verdun; and you will be master of the château. Ah, I know how lightly they take things in these days, and how Dubois will laugh when he hears that *Ca* has been killed in a duel. They will bury me, and sing masses for my soul; but you and I have not finished our affair yet, my cousin. I will be with you when you least look to see me – I, with this ugly scar upon the face that women have praised and loved. I will come to you when your life seems brightest. I will come between you and all that you hold fairest and dearest. My ghostly hand shall drop a poison in your cup of joy. My shadowy form shall shut the sunlight from your life. Men with such iron will as mine can do what they please, Hector de Brissac. It is my will to haunt you when I am dead.'

All this in short, broken sentences he whispered into my ear. I had need to bend my ear close to his dying lips; but the iron will of André de Brissac was strong enough to do battle with Death, and I believe he said all he wished to say before his head fell back upon the velvet cloak they had spread beneath him, never to be lifted again.

As he lay there, you would have fancied him a fragile stripling, too fair and frail for the struggle called life; but there are those who remember the brief manhood of André de Brissac, and who can bear witness to the terrible force of that proud nature.

I stood looking down at the young face with that foul mark upon it and God knows I was sorry for what I had done.

Of these blasphemous threats which he had whispered in my ear I took no heed. I was a soldier, and a believer. There was nothing absolutely dreadful to me in the thought that I had killed this man. I had killed many men on the battlefield; and this one had done me a cruel wrong.

My friends would have had me cross the frontier to escape the consequences of my act; but I was ready to face those consequences, and I remained in France. I kept aloof from the court, and received a hint that I had best confine myself to my own province. Many masses were chanted in the little chapel of Puy Verdun for the soul of my dead cousin, and his coffin filled a niche in the vault of our ancestors.

His death had made me a rich man; and the thought that it was so made my newly acquired wealth very hateful to me. I lived a lonely existence in the old château, where I rarely held converse with any but the servants of the household, all of whom had served my cousin, and none of whom liked me.

It was a hard and bitter life. It galled me, when I rode through the village, to see the peasant children shrink away from me. I have seen old women cross themselves stealthily as I passed by. Strange reports had gone forth about me; and there were those who whispered that I had given my soul to the Evil One as the price of my cousin's heritage. From my boyhood I had been dark of visage and stern of manner; and hence, perhaps no woman's love had ever been mine. I remembered my mother's face in all its changes of expression; but I can remember no look of affection that ever shone on me. The other woman, beneath whose feet I laid my heart, was pleased to accept my homage, but she never loved me; and the end was treachery.

I had grown hateful to myself, and had well-nigh begun to hate my fellow-creatures, when a feverish desire seized upon me, and I pined to be back in the press and throng of the busy world once again. I went back to Paris, where I kept myself aloof from the court, and where an angel took compassion on me.

She was the daughter of an old comrade, a man whose merits had been neglected, whose achievements had been ignored, and who sulked in his shabby lodging like a rat in a hole, while all Paris went mad with the Scotch Financier, and gentlemen and lackeys were trampling one another to death in the Rue Quincampoix. The only child of this little cross-grained old captain of dragoons was an incarnate sunbeam, whose mortal name was Eveline Duchalet.

She loved me. The richest blessings of our lives are often those which cost us least. I wasted the best years of my youth in the worship of a wicked woman, who jilted and cheated me at last. I gave this meek angel but a few courteous words – a little fraternal tenderness – and lo, she loved me. The life which had been so dark and desolate grew bright beneath her influence; and I went back to Puy Verdun with a fair young bride for my companion.

Ah, how sweet a change there was in my life and in my home! The village children no longer shrank appalled as the dark horseman rode by, the village crones no longer crossed themselves; for a woman rode by his side – a woman whose charities had won the love of all those ignorant creatures, and whose companionship had transformed the gloomy lord of the château into a loving husband and gentle master. The old retainers forgot the untimely fate of my cousin, and served me with cordial willingness, for love of their young mistress.

There are no words which can tell the pure and perfect happiness of that time. I felt like a traveller who had traversed the frozen seas of an arctic region, remote from human love or human companionship, to find himself all of a sudden in the bosom of a verdant valley, in the sweet atmosphere of home. The change seemed too bright to be real; and I strove in vain to put away from my mind the vague suspicion that my new life was but some fantastic dream.

So brief were those halcyon hours, that, looking back on them now, it is scarcely strange if I am still half inclined to fancy the first days of my married life could have been no more than a dream.

Neither in my days of gloom nor in my days of happiness had I been troubled by the recollection of André's blasphemous oath. The words which with his last breath he had whispered in my ear were vain and meaningless to me. He had vented his rage in those idle threats, as he might have vented it in idle execrations. That he will haunt the footsteps of his enemy after death is the one revenge which a dying man can promise himself; and if men had power thus to avenge themselves the earth would be peopled with phantoms.

I had lived for three years at Puy Verdun; sitting alone in the solemn midnight by the hearth where he had sat, pacing the corridors that had echoed his footfall; and in all that time my fancy had never so played me false as to shape the shadow of the dead. Is it strange, then, if I had forgotten André's horrible promise?

There was no portrait of my cousin at Puy Verdun. It was the age of boudoir art, and a miniature set in the lid of a gold bonbonnière, or hidden artfully in a massive bracelet, was more fashionable than a clumsy life-size image, fit only to hang on the gloomy walls of a provincial château rarely visited by its owner. My cousin's fair face had adorned more than one bonbonnière, and had been concealed in more than one bracelet; but it was not among the faces that looked down from the pannelled walls of Puy Verdun.

In the library I found a picture which awoke painful associations. It was the portrait of a de Brissac, who had flourished in the time of Francis I; and it was from this picture that my cousin André had copied the quaint hunting dress he wore at the Regent's ball. The library was a room in which I spent a good deal of my life; and I ordered a curtain to be hung before this picture.

We had been married three months, when Eveline one day asked: 'Who is the lord of the château nearest to this?'

I looked at her in astonishment.

'My dearest,' I answered, 'do you not know that there is no other château within forty miles of Puy Verdun?'

'Indeed!' she said. 'That is strange.'

I asked her why the fact seemed strange to her; and after much entreaty I obtained from her the reason of her surprise.

In her walks about the park and woods during the last month she had met a man who, by his dress and bearing, was obviously of noble rank. She had imagined that he occupied some château near at hand, and that his estate adjoined ours. I was at a loss to imagine who this stranger could be; for my estate at Puy Verdun lay in the heart of a desolate region, and unless when some traveller's coach went lumbering and jingling through the village, one had little more chance of encountering a gentlemen than of meeting a demigod.

'Have you seen this man often, Eveline?' I asked.

She answered, in a tone which had a touch of sadness: 'I see him every day.'

'Where, dearest?'

'Sometimes in the park, sometimes in the wood. You know the little cascade, Hector, where there is some old neglected rock-work that forms a kind of cavern. I have taken a fancy to that spot, and have spent many mornings there reading. Of late I have seen the stranger there every morning.'

'He has never dared to address you?'

'Never. I have looked up from my book, and have seen him standing at a little distance, watching me silently. I have continued reading; and when I have raised my eyes again I have found him gone. He must approach and depart with a stealthy tread, for I never hear his footfall. Sometimes I have almost wished that he would speak to me. It is so terrible to see him standing silently there.'

'He is some insolent peasant who seeks to frighten you.'

My wife shook her head.

'He is no peasant,' she answered. 'It is not by his dress alone I judge, for that is strange to me. He has an air of nobility which it is impossible to mistake.'

'Is he young or old?'

'He is young and handsome.'

I was much disturbed by the idea of this stranger's intrusion on my wife's solitude; and I went straight to the village to inquire if any stranger had been seen there. I could hear of no one. I questioned the servants closely, but without result. Then I determined to accompany my wife in her walks, and to judge for myself of the rank of the stranger.

For a week I devoted all my mornings to rustic rambles with Eveline in the park and woods; and in all that week we saw no one but the occasional peasant in *sabos*, or one of our own household returning from a neighbouring farm.

I was a man of studious habits, and those summer rambles disturbed the even current of my life. My wife perceived this, and untreated me to trouble myself no further.

'I will spend my mornings in the pleasaunce, Hector,' she said 'The stranger cannot intrude upon me there.'

'I began to think the stranger is only a phantasm of your own romantic brain,' I replied, smiling at the earnest face lifted to mine. 'A châtelaine who is always reading romances may well meet handsome cavaliers in the woodlands. I dare say I have Mademoiselle Scuderi to thank for this noble stranger, and that he is only the great Cyrus in modern costume.'

'Ah, that is the point which mystifies me, Hector,' she said. 'The stranger's costume is not modern. He looks as an old picture might look if it could descend from its frame.'

Her words pained me, for they reminded me of that hidden picture in the library, and the quaint hunting costume of orange and purple, which André de Brissac wore at the Regent's ball.

After this my wife confined her walks to the pleasaunce; and for many weeks I heard no more of the nameless stranger. I dismissed all thought of him from my mind, for a graver and heavier care had come upon me. My wife's health began to droop. The change in her was so gradual as to be almost imperceptible to those who watched her day by day. It was only when she put on a rich gala dress which she had not worn for months that I saw how wasted the form must be on which the embroidered bodice hung so loosely, and how wan and dim were the eyes which had once been brilliant as the jewels she wore in her hair.

I sent a messenger to Paris to summon one of the court physicians; but I knew that many days must needs elapse before he could arrive at Puy Verdun.

In the interval I watched my wife with unutterable fear.

It was not her health only that had declined. The change was more painful to behold than any physical alteration. The bright and sunny spirit had vanished, and in the place of my joyous young bride I beheld a woman weighed down by rooted melancholy. In vain I sought to fathom the cause of my darling's sadness. She assured me that she had no reason for sorrow or discontent, and that if she seemed sad without a motive, I must forgive her sadness, and consider it as a misfortune rather than a fault.

I told her that the court physician would speedily find some cure for her despondency, which needs must arise from physical causes, since she had no real ground for sorrow. But although she said nothing, I could see she had no hope or belief in the healing powers of medicine.

One day, when I wished to beguile her from that pensive silence in which she was wont to sit an hour at a time, I told her, laughing, that she appeared to have forgotten her mysterious cavalier in the wood, and it seemed also as if he had forgotten her.

To my wonderment, her pale face became a sudden crimson; and from crimson changed to pale again in a breath.

'You have never seen him since you deserted your woodland grotto?' I said.

She turned to me with a heart-rending look.

'Hector,' she cried, 'I see him every day; and it is that which is killing me.'

She burst into a passion of tears when she had said this. I took her in my arms as if she had been a frightened child, and tried to comfort her.

'My darling, this is madness,' I said. 'You know that no stranger can come to you in the pleasaunce. The moat is ten feet wide and always full of water, and the gates are kept locked day and night by old Massou. The châtelaine of a medieval fortress need fear no intruder in her antique garden.'

My wife shook her head sadly.

'I see him every day,' she said.

On this I believed that my wife was mad. I shrank from questioning her more closely concerning her mysterious visitant. It would be ill, I thought, to give form and substance to the shadow that tormented her, by too close inquiry about its looks and manner, its coming and going.

I took care to assure myself that no stranger to the household could by any possibility penetrate to the pleasaunce. Having done this, I was fain to await the coming of the physician.

He came at last. I revealed to him the conviction which was my misery. I told him that I believed my wife to be mad. He saw her – spent an hour alone with her, and then came to me. To my unspeakable relief he assured me of her sanity.

'It is just possible that she may be affected by one delusion' he said 'but she is so reasonable upon all other points that I can scarcely bring myself to believe her the subject of a monomania. I am rather inclined to think that she really sees the person of whom she speaks. She described him to me with a perfect minuteness. The descriptions of scenes or individuals given by patients afflicted with monomania are always more or less disjointed; but your wife spoke to me as clearly and calmly as I am now speaking to you. Are you sure there is no one who can approach her in that garden where she walks?'

'I am quite sure.'

'Is there any kinsman of your steward, or hanger-on of your household – a young man with a fair, womanish face, very pale and rendered remarkable by a crimson scar, which looks like the mark of a blow?'

'My God!' I cried, as the light broke in upon me all at once. 'And the dress – the strange, old-fashioned dress?'

'The man wears a hunting costume of purple and orange,' answered the doctor.

I knew then that André de Brissac had kept his word, and that in the hour when my life was brightest his shadow had come between me and happiness.

I showed my wife the picture in the library, for I would fain assure myself that there was some error in my fancy about my cousin. She shook like a leaf when she beheld it, and clung to me convulsively.

'This is witchcraft Hector,' she said. 'The dress in that picture is the dress of the man I see in the pleasaunce; but the face is not his.'

Then she described to me the face of the stranger; and it was my cousin's face line for line – André de Brissac, whom she had never seen in the flesh. Most vividly of all did she describe the cruel mark upon his face, the trace of a fierce blow from an open hand.

After this I carried my wife away from Puy Verdun. We wandered far – through the southern provinces, and into the very heart of Switzerland. I thought to distance the ghastly phantom, and I fondly hoped that change of scene would bring peace to my wife.

It was not so. Go where we would, the ghost of André de Brissac followed us. To my eyes that fatal shadow never revealed itself. *That* would have been too poor a vengeance. It was my wife's innocent heart which André made the instrument of his revenge. The unholy presence destroyed her life. My constant companionship could not shield her from the horrible intruder. In vain did I watch her; in vain did I strive to comfort her.

'He will not let me be at peace,' she said. 'He comes between us, Hector. He is standing between us now. I can see his face with the red mark upon it plainer than I see yours.'

One fair moonlight night, when we were together in a mountain village in the Tyrol, my wife cast herself at my feet, and told me she was the worst and vilest of women. 'I have confessed all to my Director,' she said; 'from the first I have not hidden my sin from heaven. But I feel that death is near me; and before I die I would fain reveal my sin to you.'

'What sin, my sweet one?'

'When first the stranger came to me in the forest, his presence bewildered and distressed me, and I shrank from him as from something strange and terrible. He came again and again; by and by I found myself thinking of him, and watching for his coming. His image haunted me perpetually; I strove in vain to shut his face out of my mind. Then followed an interval in which I did not see him; and, to my shame and anguish, I found that life seemed dreary and desolate without him. After that came the time in which he haunted the pleasaunce; and – oh, Hector, kill me if you will, for I deserve no mercy at your hands – I grew in those days to count the hours that must elapse before his coming, to take no pleasure save in the sight of that pale face with the red brand upon it. He plucked all old familiar joys out of my heart, and left in it but one weird, unholy pleasure – the delight of his presence. For a year I lived but to see him. And now curse me, Hector; for this is my sin. Whether it comes of the baseness of my own heart, or is the work of witchcraft, I know not; but I know that I have striven against this wickedness in vain.'

I took my wife to my breast, and forgave her. In sooth, what had I to forgive? Was the fatality that overshadowed us any work of hers? On the next night she died, with her hand in mine; and at the very last she told me, sobbing and affrighted, that *he* was by her side.

A Torture by Hope

VILLIERS DE L'ISLE-ADAM

Below the vaults of the *Oficial* of Saragossa one nightfall long ago, the venerable Pedro Arbuez d'Espila, sixth Prior of the Dominicans of Segovia, third Grand Inquisitor of Spain – followed by a *fra redemptor* (master-torturer), and preceded by two familiars of the Holy Office holding lanterns – descended towards a secret dungeon. The lock of a massive door creaked; they entered a stifling *in pace*, where the little light that came from above revealed an instrument of torture blackened with blood, a chafing-dish, and a pitcher. Fastened to the wall by heavy iron rings, on a mass of filthy straw, secured by fetters, an iron circlet about his neck, sat a man in rags: it was impossible to guess at his age.

This prisoner was no other than Rabbi Aser Abarbanel, a Jew of Aragon who, on an accusation of usury and pitiless contempt of the poor, had for more than a year undergone daily torture. In spite of all, 'his blind obstinacy being as tough as his skin', he had refused to abjure.

Proud of his descent and his ancestors – for all Jews worthy of the name are jealous of their race – he was descended, according to the Talmud, from Othoniel, and consequently from Ipsiboe, wife of this last Judge of Israel, a circumstance which had sustained his courage under the severest of the incessant tortures.

It was, then, with tears in his eyes at the thought that so steadfast a soul was excluded from salvation, that the venerable Pedro Arbuez d'Espila, approaching the quivering Rabbi, pronounced the following words:

'My son, be of good cheer; your trials here below are about to cease. If, in presence of such obstinacy, I have had to permit, though with sighs, the employment of severe measures, my task of paternal correction has its limits. You are the barren fig-tree, that, found so oft without fruit, incurs the danger of being dried up by the roots . . . but it is for God alone to decree concerning your soul. Perhaps the Infinite Mercy will shine upon you at the last moment! Let us hope so. There *are* instances. May it be so! Sleep, then, this evening in peace. Tomorrow you will take part in the *auto da fé*, that is to say, you will be exposed to the *quemadero*, the brazier premonitory of the eternal flame. It burns, you are aware, at a certain distance, my son; and death takes, in coming, two hours at least, often three, thanks to the moistened and frozen clothes with which we take care to preserve the forehead and the heart of the holocausts. You will be only forty-three. Consider, then, that, placed in the last rank, you will have the time needful to invoke God, to offer unto Him that baptism of fire which is of the Holy Spirit. Hope, then, in the Light, and sleep.'

As he ended this discourse, Dom Arbuez – who had motioned the wretched man's fetters to be removed – embraced him tenderly. Then came the turn of the *fra redemptor*, who, in a low voice, prayed the Jew to pardon what he had made him endure in the effort to redeem him; then the two familiars clasped him in their arms: their kiss, through their cowls, was unheard. The ceremony at an end, the captive was left alone in the darkness. Rabbi Aser Abarbanel, his lips parched, his face stupefied by suffering, stared, without any particular attention, at the closed door. Closed? The word, half unknown to himself, awoke a strange delusion in his confused thoughts. He fancied he had seen, for one second, the light of the lanterns through the fissure between the sides of this door. A morbid idea of hope, due to the enfeeblement of his brain, took hold on him. He dragged himself towards this strange thing he had seen; and, slowly inserting a finger, with infinite precautions, into the crack, he pulled the door towards him. Wonder of wonders! By some extraordinary chance the familiar who had closed it had turned the great key a little before it had closed upon its jambs of stone. So, the rusty bolt not having entered its socket, the door rolled back into the cell.

The Rabbi ventured to look out.

By means of a sort of livid obscurity he distinguished, first of all, a half-circle of earthy walls, pierced by spiral stairways, and, opposite to him, five or six stone steps, dominated by a sort of black porch, giving access to a vast corridor, of which he could only see, from below, the nearest arches.

Stretching himself along, he crawled to the level of this threshold. Yes, it was indeed a corridor, but of boundless length. A faint light – a sort of dream-light – was cast over it; lamps suspended to the arched roof, turned, by intervals, the wan air blue; the far distance was lost in shadow. Not a door visible along all this length! On one side only, to the left, small holes, covered with a network of bars, let a feeble twilight through the depths of the wall – the light of sunset apparently, for red gleams fell at long intervals on the flagstones. And how fearful a silence! . . . Yet there – there in the depths of the dim distance – the way might lead to liberty! The wavering hope of the Jew was dogged, for it was the last.

Without hesitation he ventured forth, keeping close to the side of the light-holes, hoping to render himself indistinguishable from the darksome colour of the long walls. He advanced slowly, dragging himself along the ground, forcing himself not to cry out when one of his wounds, recently opened, sent a sharp pang through him.

All of a sudden the beat of a sandal, coming in his direction, echoed along the stone passage. A trembling fit seized him. he choked with anguish, his sight grew dim. So this, no doubt, was to be the end! He squeezed himself, doubled up on his hands and knees, into a recess, and, half dead with terror, waited.

It was a familiar hurrying along. He passed rapidly, carrying an instrument for tearing out the muscles, his cowl lowered: he disappeared. The violent shock which the Rabbi had received had half suspended the functions of life; he remained for nearly an hour unable to make a single movement. In the fear of an increase of torments if he were caught, the idea came to him of returning to his cell. But the old hope chirped in his soul – the divine 'Perhaps', the comforter in the worst of distresses. A miracle had taken place! There was no more room for doubt. He began again to crawl towards the possible escape. Worn out with suffering and with hunger, trembling with anguish, he advanced. The sepulchral corridor seemed to lengthen out mysteriously. And he, never ceasing his slow advance, gazed forward through the darkness, on, on, where there *must* be an outlet that should save him.

But, oh! steps sounding again; steps, this time, slower, more sombre. The forms of two Inquisitors, robed in black and white, and wearing their large hats with rounded brims, emerged into the faint light. They talked in low voices, and seemed to be in controversy on some important point, for their hands gesticulated.

At this sight Rabbi Aser Abarbanel closed his eyes, his heart beat as if it would kill him, his rags were drenched with the cold sweat of agony; motionless, gasping, he lay stretched along the wall, under the light of one of the lamps – motionless, imploring the God of David.

As they came opposite to him the two Inquisitors stopped under the light of the lamp, through a mere chance, no doubt, in their discussion. One of them, listening to his interlocutor, looked straight at the Rabbi. Under this gaze – of which he did not at first notice the vacant expression – the wretched man seemed to feel the hot pincers biting into his poor flesh; so he was again to become a living wound, a living woe! Fainting, scarce able to breathe, his eyelids quivering, he shuddered as the robe grazed him. But – strange at once and natural – the eyes of the Inquisitor were evidently the eyes of a man profoundly preoccupied with what he was going to say in reply, absorbed by what he was listening to; they were fixed, and seemed to look at the Jew *without seeing him*.

And, indeed, in a few minutes, the two sinister talkers went on their way, slowly, still speaking in low voices, in the direction from which the prisoner had come. They had not seen him! And it was so, that, in the horrible disarray of his sensations, his brain was traversed by this thought: 'Am I already dead, so that no one sees me?' A hideous impression drew him from his lethargy. On gazing at the wall, exactly opposite to his face, he fancied he saw, over against his, two ferocious eyes observing him! He flung back his head in a blind and sudden terror; the hair started upright upon his head. But no, no. He put out his hand, and felt along the stones. What he saw was the *reflection* of the eyes of the Inquisitor still left upon his pupils, and which he had refracted upon two spots of the wall.

Forward! He must hasten towards that end that he imagined (fondly, no doubt) to mean deliverance; towards those shadows from which he was no more than thirty paces, or so, distant. He started once more – crawling on hands and knees and stomach – upon his dolorous way, and he was soon within the dark part of the fearful corridor.

All at once the wretched man felt the sensation of cold *upon* his hands that he placed on the flagstones; it was a strong current which came from under a little door at the end of the passage. O God, if this door opened on the outer world! The whole being of the poor prisoner was overcome by a sort of vertigo of hope. He examined the door from top to bottom without being able to distinguish it completely on account of the dimness around him. He felt over it. No lock, not a bolt! A latch! He rose to his feet: the latch yielded beneath his finger; the silent door opened before him.

'Hallelujah!' murmured the Rabbi, in an immense sigh, as he gazed at what stood revealed to him from the threshold.

The door opened upon gardens, under a night of stars – upon spring, liberty, life! The gardens gave access to the neighbouring country that stretched away to the sierras, whose sinuous white lines stood out in profile on the horizon. There lay liberty! Oh, to fly! He would run all night under those woods of citrons, whose perfume intoxicated him. Once among the mountains, he would be saved. He breathed the dear, holy air: the wind reanimated him, his lungs found free play. He heard, in his expanding heart, the 'Lazarus, come forth!' And, to give thanks to God who had granted him this mercy, he stretched forth his arms before him, lifting his eyes to the firmament in an ecstasy.

And then he seemed to see the shadow of his arms returning upon himself; he seemed to feel those shadow-arms surround, enlace him, and himself pressed tenderly against some breast. A tall figure, indeed, was opposite to him. Confidently he lowered his eyes upon this figure, and remained gasping, stupefied, with staring eyes and mouth drivelling with fright.

Horror! He was in the arms of the Grand Inquisitor himself, the venerable Pedro Arbuez d'Espila, who gazed at him with eyes full of tears, like a good shepherd who has found the lost sheep.

The sombre priest clasped the wretched Jew against his heart with so fervent a transport of charity that the points of the monacal hair-cloth rasped against the chest of the Dominican. And, while the Rabbi Aser Abarbanel, his eyes convulsed beneath his eyelids, choked with anguish between the arms of the ascetic Dom Arbuez, realizing confusedly *that all the phases of the fatal evening had been only a calculated torture, that of Hope!* the Grand Inquisitor, with a look of distress, an accent of poignant reproach, murmured in his ear, with the burning breath of much fasting: 'What! my child! on the eve, perhaps, of salvation . . . you would then leave us?'

Barbara of the House of Grebe

THOMAS HARDY

It was apparently an idea, rather than a passion, that inspired Lord Uplandtowers' resolve to win her. Nobody ever knew when he formed it, or whence he got his assurance of success in the face of her manifest dislike of him. Possibly not until after that first important act of her life which I shall presently mention. His matured and cynical doggedness at the age of nineteen, when impulse mostly rules calculation, was remarkable, and might have owed its existence as much to his succession to the earldom and its accompanying local honours in childhood, as to the family character; an elevation which jerked him into maturity, so to speak, without his having known adolescence. He had only reached his twelfth year when his father, the fourth Earl, died, after a course of the Bath waters.

Nevertheless, the family character had a great deal to do with it. Determination was hereditary in the bearers of that escutcheon, sometimes for good, sometimes for evil.

The seats of the two families were about ten miles apart, the way between them lying along the now old, then new, turnpike-road connecting Havenpool and Warborne with the city of Melchester; a road which, though only a branch from what was known as the Great Western Highway, is probably, even at present, as it has been for the last hundred years, one of the finest examples of a macadamized turnpike-track that can be found in England.

The mansion of the Earl, as well as that of his neighbour, Barbara's father, stood back about a mile from the highway, with which each was connected by an ordinary drive and lodge. It was along this particular highway that the young Earl drove on a certain evening at Christmastide some twenty years before the end of the last century, to attend a ball at Chene Manor, the home of Barbara and her parents Sir John and Lady Grebe. Sir John's was a baronetcy created a few years before the breaking out of the Civil War, and his lands were even more extensive than those of Lord Uplandtowers himself, comprising this Manor of Chene, another on the coast near, half the Hundred of Cockdene, and well-enclosed lands in several other parishes, notably Warborne and those contiguous. At this time Barbara was barely seventeen, and the ball is the first occasion on which we have any tradition of Lord Uplandtowers attempting tender relations with her; it was early enough, God knows.

An intimate friend – one of the Drenkhards – is said to have dined with him that day, and Lord Uplandtowers had, for a wonder, communicated to his guest the secret design of his heart.

'You'll never get her – sure; you'll never get her!' this friend had said at parting. 'She's not drawn to your lordship by love: and as for thought of a good match, why, there's no more calculation in her than in a bird.'

'We'll see,' said Lord Uplandtowers impassively.

He no doubt thought of his friend's forecast as he travelled along the highway in his chariot; but the sculptural repose of his profile against the vanishing daylight on his right hand would have shown his friend that the Earl's equanimity was undisturbed. He reached the solitary wayside tavern called Lornton Inn – the rendezvous of many a daring poacher for operations in the adjoining forest; and he might have observed, if he had taken the trouble, a strange post-chaise standing in the halting-space before the inn. He duly sped past it, and half-an-hour after through the little town of Warborne. Onward, a mile further, was the house of his entertainer.

At this date it was an imposing edifice – or, rather, congeries of edifices – as extensive as the residence of the Earl himself, though far less regular. One wing showed extreme antiquity, having huge chimneys, whose substructures projected from the external walls like towers; and a kitchen of vast dimensions, in which (it was said) breakfasts had been cooked for John of Gaunt. Whilst he was yet in the forecourt he could hear the rhythm of french horns and clarionets, the favourite instruments of those days at such entertainments.

Entering the long parlour, in which the dance had just been opened by Lady Grebe with a minuet – it being now seven o'clock, according to the tradition – he was received with a welcome befitting his rank, and looked round for Barbara. She was not dancing, and seemed to be preoccupied – almost, indeed, as though she had been waiting for him. Barbara at this time was a good and pretty girl, who never spoke ill of anyone, and hated other pretty women the very least possible. She did not refuse him for the country-dance which followed, and soon after was his partner in a second.

The evening wore on, and the horns and clarionets tootled merrily. Barbara evinced towards her lover neither distinct preference nor aversion; but old eyes would have seen that she pondered something. However, after supper she pleaded a headache, and disappeared. To pass the time of her absence, Lord Uplandtowers went into a little room adjoining the long gallery, where some elderly ones were sitting by the fire – for he had a phlegmatic dislike of dancing for its own sake – and, lifting the window-curtains, he looked out of the window into the park and wood, dark now as a cavern. Some of the guests appeared to be leaving even so soon as this, two lights showing themselves as turning away from the door and sinking to nothing in the distance.

His hostess put her head into the room to look for partners for the ladies, and Lord Uplandtowers came out. Lady Grebe informed him that Barbara had not returned to the ballroom: she had gone to bed in sheer necessity.

'She has been so excited over the ball all day,' her mother continued, 'that I feared she would be worn out early. . . . But sure, Lord Uplandtowers, you won't be leaving yet?'

He said that it was near twelve o'clock, and that some had already left.

'I protest nobody has gone yet,' said Lady Grebe.

To humour her he stayed till midnight, and then set out. He had made no progress in his suit; but he had assured himself that Barbara gave no other guest the preference, and nearly everybody in the neighbourhood was there.

''Tis only a matter of time,' said the calm young philosopher.

The next morning he lay till near ten o'clock, and he had only just come out upon the head of the staircase when he heard hoofs upon the gravel without; in a few moments the door had been opened, and Sir John Grebe met him in the hall, as he set foot on the lowest stair.

'My lord – where's Barbara – my daughter?'

Even the Earl of Uplandtowers could not repress amazement. 'What's the matter, my dear Sir John,' says he.

The news was startling, indeed. From the Baronet's disjointed explanation Lord Uplandtowers gathered that after his own and the other guests' departure Sir John and Lady Grebe had gone to rest without seeing any more of Barbara; it being understood by them that she had retired to bed when she sent word to say that she could not join the dancers again. Before then she had told her maid that she would dispense with her services for this night; and there was evidence to show that the young lady had never lain down at all, the bed remaining unpressed. Circumstances seemed to prove that the deceitful girl had feigned indisposition to get an excuse for leaving the ballroom, and that she had left the house within ten minutes, presumably during the first dance after supper.

'I saw her go,' said Lord Uplandtowers.

'The devil you did!' says Sir John.

'Yes.' And he mentioned the retreating carriage-lights, and how he was assured by Lady Grebe that no guest had departed.

'Surely that was it!' said the father. 'But she's not gone alone, d'ye know!'

'Ah – who is the young man?'

'I can on'y guess. My worst fear is my most likely guess. I'll say no more. I thought – yet I would not believe – it possible that you was the sinner. Would that you had been! But 'tis t'other, 'tis t'other, by Heaven! I must e'en up and after 'em!'

'Whom do you suspect?'

Sir John would not give a name, and, stultified rather than agitated, Lord Uplandtowers accompanied him back to Chene. He again asked upon whom were the Baronet's suspicions directed; and the impulsive Sir John was no match for the insistence of Uplandtowers.

He said at length, 'I fear 'tis Edmond Willowes.'

'Who's he?'

'A young fellow of Shottsford-Forum – a widow-woman's son,' the other told him, and explained that Willowes's father, or grandfather, was the last of the old glass-painters in that place, where (as you may know) the art lingered on when it had died out in every other part of England.

'By God that's bad – mighty bad!' said Lord Uplandtowers, throwing himself back in the chaise in frigid despair.

They despatched emissaries in all directions; one by the Melchester Road, another by Shottsford-Forum, another coastwards.

But the lovers had a ten-hours' start; and it was apparent that sound judgement had been exercised in choosing as their time of flight the particular night when the movements of a strange carriage would not be noticed, either in the park or on the neighbouring highway, owing to the general press of vehicles. The chaise which had been seen waiting at Lornton Inn was, no doubt, the one they had escaped in; and the pair of heads which had planned so cleverly thus far had probably contrived marriage ere now.

The fears of her parents were realized. A letter sent by special messenger from Barbara, on the evening of that day, briefly informed them that her lover and herself were on the way to London, and before this communication reached her home they would be united as husband and wife. She had taken this extreme step because she loved her dear Edmond as she could love no other man, and because she had seen closing round her the doom of marriage with Lord Uplandtowers, unless she put that threatened fate out of possibility by doing as she had done. She had well considered the step beforehand, and was prepared to live like any other country-townsman's wife if her father repudiated her for her action.

'Damn her!' said Lord Uplandtowers, as he drove homeward that night. 'Damn her for a fool!' – which shows the kind of love he bore her.

Well; Sir John had already started in pursuit of them as a matter of duty, driving like a wild man to Melchester, and thence by the direct highway to the capital. But he soon saw that he was acting to no purpose; and by and by, discovering that the marriage had actually taken place, he forebore all attempts to unearth them in the City, and returned and sat down with his lady to digest the event as best they could.

To proceed against this Willowes for the abduction of our heiress was, possibly, in their power; yet, when they considered the now unalterable facts, they refrained from violent retribution. Some six weeks passed, during which time Barbara's parents, though they keenly felt her loss, held no communication with the truant, either for reproach or condonation. They continued to think of the disgrace she had brought upon herself; for, though the young man was an honest fellow, and the son of an honest father, the latter had died so early, and his widow had had such struggles to maintain herself, that the son was very imperfectly educated. Moreover, his blood was, as far as they knew, of no distinction whatever, whilst hers, through her mother, was compounded of the best juices of ancient baronial distillation, containing tinctures of Maundeville, and Mohun, and Syward, and Peverell, and Culliford, and Talbot, and Plantagenet, and York, and Lancaster, and God knows what besides, which it was a thousand pities to throw away.

The father and mother sat by the fireplace that was spanned by the four-centred arch bearing the family shields on its haunches, and groaned aloud – the lady more than Sir John.

'To think this should have come upon us in our old age!' said he.

'Speak for yourself!' she snapped through her sobs, 'I am only one-and-forty! . . . Why didn't ye ride faster and overtake 'em!'

In the meantime the young married lovers, caring no more about their blood than about ditch-water, were intensely happy – happy, that is in the descending scale which, as we all know, Heaven in its wisdom has ordained for such rash cases; that is to say, the first week they were in the seventh heaven, the second in the sixth, the third week temperate, the fourth reflective, and so on; a lover's heart after possession being comparable to the earth in its geologic stages, as described to us sometimes by our worthy President; first a hot coal, then a warm one, then a cooling cinder, then chilly – the simile shall be pursued no further. The long and the short of it was that one day a letter, sealed with their daughter's own little seal, came into Sir John and Lady Grebe's hands; and, on opening it, they found it to contain an appeal from the young couple to Sir John to forgive them for what they had done, and they would fall on their naked knees and be most dutiful children for evermore.

Then Sir John and his lady sat down again by the fireplace with the four-centred arch, and consulted, and re-read the letter. Sir John Grebe, if the truth must be told, loved his daughter's happiness far more, poor man, than he loved his name and lineage; he recalled to his mind all her little ways, gave vent to a sigh; and, by this time acclimatized to the idea of the marriage, said that what was done could not be undone, and that he supposed they must not be too harsh with her. Perhaps Barbara and her husband were in actual need; and how could they let their only child starve?

A slight consolation had come to them in an unexpected manner. They had been credibly informed that an ancestor of plebeian Willowes was once honoured with intermarriage with a scion of the aristocracy who had gone to the dogs. In short, such is the foolishness of distinguished parents, and sometimes of others also, that they wrote that very day to the address Barbara had given them, informing her that she might return home and bring her husband with her; they would not object to see him, would not reproach her, and would endeavour to welcome both, and to discuss with them what could best be arranged for their future.

In three or four days a rather shabby post-chaise drew up at the door of Chene Manor-house, at sound of which the tender-hearted baronet and his wife ran out as if to welcome a prince and princess of the blood. They were overjoyed to see their spoilt child return safe and sound – though she was only Mrs Willowes, wife of Edmond Willowes of nowhere. Barbara burst into penitential tears, and both husband and wife were contrite enough, as well they might be, considering that they had not a guinea to call their own.

When the four had calmed themselves, and not a word of chiding had been uttered to the pair, they discussed the position soberly, young Willowes sitting in the background with great modesty till invited forward by Lady Grebe in no frigid tone.

'How handsome he is!' she said to herself. 'I don't wonder at Barbara's craze for him.'

He was, indeed, one of the handsomest men who ever set his lips on a maid's. A blue coat, murrey waistcoat, and breeches of drab set off a figure that could scarcely be surpassed. He had large dark eyes, anxious now, as they glanced from Barbara to her parents and tenderly back again to her; observing whom, even now in her trepidation, one could see why the *sang froid* of Lord Uplandtowers had been raised to more than lukewarmness. Her fair young face (according to the tale handed down by old women) looked out from under a grey conical hat, trimmed with white ostrich-feathers, and her little toes peeped from a buff petticoat worn under a puce gown. Her features were not regular: they were almost infantine, as you may see from miniatures in possession of the family, her mouth showing much sensitiveness, and one could be sure that her faults would not lie on the side of bad temper unless for urgent reasons.

Well, they discussed their state as became them, and the desire of the young couple to gain the goodwill of those upon whom they were literally dependent for everything induced them to agree to any temporizing measure that was not too irksome. Therefore, having been nearly two months united, they did not oppose Sir John's proposal that he should furnish Edmond Willowes with funds sufficient for him to travel a year on the Continent in the company of a tutor, the young man undertaking to lend himself with the utmost diligence to the tutor's instructions, till he became polished outwardly and inwardly to the degree required in the husband of such a lady as Barbara. He was to apply himself to the study of languages, manners, history, society, ruins, and everything else that came under his eyes, till he should return to take his place without blushing by Barbara's side.

'And by that time,' said worthy Sir John, 'I'll get my little place out at Yewsholt ready for you and Barbara to occupy on your return. The house is small and out of the way; but it will do for a young couple for a while.'

'If 'twere no bigger than a summer-house it would do!' says Barbara.

'If 'twere no bigger than a sedan-chair!' says Willowes. 'And the more lonely the better.'

'We can put up with the loneliness,' said Barbara, with less zest. 'Some friends will come, no doubt.'

All this being laid down, a travelled tutor was called in – a man of many gifts and great experience, – and on a fine morning away tutor and pupil went. A great reason urged against Barbara accompanying her youthful husband was that his attentions to her would naturally be such as to prevent his zealously applying every hour of his time to learning and seeing – an argument of wise prescience, and unanswerable. Regular days for letter-writing were fixed, Barbara and her Edmond exchanged their last kisses at the door, and the chaise swept under the archway into the drive.

He wrote to her from Le Havre, as soon as he reached that port, which was not for seven days, on account of adverse winds; he wrote from Rouen, and from Paris; described to her his sight of the King and Court at Versailles, and the wonderful marblework and mirrors in that palace; wrote next from Lyons; then, after a comparatively long interval, from Turin, narrating his fearful adventures in crossing Mont Cenis on mules, and how he was overtaken with a terrific snowstorm, which had well-nigh been the end of him, and his tutor, and.his guides. Then he wrote glowingly of Italy; and Barbara could see the development of her husband's mind reflected in his letters month by month; and she much admired the forethought of her father in suggesting this education for Edmond. Yet she sighed sometimes – her husband being no longer in evidence to fortify her in her choice of him – and timidly dreaded what mortifications might be in store for her by reason of this *mésalliance*. She went out very little; for on the one or two occasions on which she had shown herself to former friends she noticed a distinct difference in their manner, as though they should say, 'Ah, my happy swain's wife; you're caught!'

Edmond's letters were as affectionate as ever; even more affectionate, after a while, than hers were to him. Barbara observed this growing coolness in herself, and like a good and honest lady was horrified and grieved, since her only wish was to act faithfully and uprightly. It troubled her so much that she prayed for a warmer heart, and at last wrote to her husband to beg him, now that he was in the land of Art, to send her his portrait, ever so small, that she might look at it all day and every day, and never for a moment forget his features.

Willowes was nothing loath, and replied that he would do more than she wished: he had made friends with a sculptor in Pisa, who was much interested in him and his history; and he had commissioned this artist to make a bust of himself in marble, which when finished he would send her. What Barbara had wanted was something immediate; but she expressed no objection to the delay; and in his next communication Edmond told her that the sculptor, of his own choice, had decided to extend the bust to a full-length statue, so anxious was he to get a specimen of his skill introduced to the notice of the English aristocracy. It was progressing well, and rapidly.

Meanwhile, Barbara's attention began to be occupied at home with Yewsholt Lodge, the house that her kind-hearted father was preparing for her residence when her husband returned. It was a small place on the plan of a large one – a cottage built in the form of a mansion, having a central hall with a wooden gallery running round it, and rooms no bigger than closets to support this introduction. It stood on a slope so solitary, and surrounded by trees so dense, that the birds who inhabited the boughs sang at strange hours, as if they hardly could distinguish night from day.

During the progress of repairs at this bower Barbara frequently visited it. Though so secluded by the dense growth, it was near the high road, and one day while looking over the fence she saw Lord Uplandtowers riding past. He saluted her courteously, yet with mechanical stiffness, and did not halt. Barbara went home, and continued to pray that she might never cease to love her husband. After that she sickened, and did not come out of doors again for a long time.

The year of education had extended to fourteen months, and the house was in order for Edmond's return to take up his abode there with Barbara, when, instead of the accustomed letter for her, came one to Sir John Grebe in the handwriting of the said tutor, informing him of a terrible catastrophe that had occurred to them at Venice. Mr Willowes and himself had attended the theatre one night during the Carnival of the preceding week, to witness the Italian comedy, when, owing to the carelessness of one of the candle-snuffers, the theatre had caught fire, and been burnt to the ground. Few persons had lost their lives, owing to the superhuman exertions of some of the audience in getting out the senseless sufferers; and, among them all, he who had risked his own life the most heroically was Mr Willowes. In re-entering for the fifth time to save his fellow-creatures some fiery beams had fallen upon him, and he had been given up for lost. He was, however, by the blessing of Providence, recovered, with the life still in him, though he was fearfully burnt; and by almost a miracle he seemed likely to survive, his constitution being wondrously sound. He was, of course, unable to write, but he was receiving the attention of several skilful surgeons. Further report would be made by the next mail or by private hand.

The tutor said nothing in detail of poor Willowes's sufferings, but as soon as the news was broken to Barbara she realized how intense they must have been, and her immediate instinct was to rush to his side, though, on consideration, the journey seemed impossible to her. Her health was by no means what it had been, and to post across Europe at that season of the year, or to traverse the Bay of Biscay in a sailing-craft, was an undertaking that would hardly be justified by the result. But she was anxious to go till, on reading to the end of the letter, her husband's tutor was found to hint very strongly against such a step if it should be contemplated, this being also the opinion of the surgeons. And though

Willowes's comrade refrained from giving his reasons, they disclosed themselves plainly enough in the sequel.

The truth was that the worst of the wounds resulting from the fire had occurred to his head and face – that handsome face which had won her heart from her, – and both the tutor and the surgeons knew that for a sensitive young woman to see him before his wounds had healed would cause more misery to her by the shock than happiness to him by her ministrations.

Lady Grebe blurted out what Sir John and Barbara had thought, but had had too much delicacy to express.

'Sure, 'tis mighty hard for you, poor Barbara, that the one little gift he had to justify your rash choice of him – his wonderful good looks – should be taken away like this, to leave 'ee no excuse at all for your conduct in the world's eyes. . . . Well, I wish you'd married t'other – that do I!' And the lady sighed.

'He'll soon get right again,' said her father soothingly.

Such remarks as the above were not often made; but they were frequent enough to cause Barbara an uneasy sense of self-stultification. She determined to hear them no longer; and the house at Yewsholt being ready and furnished, she withdrew thither with her maids, where for the first time she could feel mistress of a home that would be hers and her husband's exclusively, when he came.

After long weeks Willowes had recovered sufficiently to be able to write himself, and slowly and tenderly he enlightened her upon the full extent of his injuries. It was a mercy, he said, that he had not lost his sight entirely; but he was thankful to say that he still retained full vision in one eye, though the other was dark for ever. The sparing manner in which he meted out particulars of his condition told Barbara how appalling had been his experience. He was grateful for her assurance that nothing could change her; but feared she did not fully realize that he was so sadly disfigured as to make it doubtful if she would recognize him. However, in spite of all, his heart was as true to her as it ever had been.

Barbara saw from his anxiety how much lay behind. She replied that she submitted to the decrees of Fate, and would welcome him in any shape as soon as he could come. She told him of the pretty retreat in which she had taken up her abode, pending their joint occupation of it, and did not reveal how much she had sighed over the information that all his good looks were gone. Still less did she say that she felt a certain strangeness in awaiting him, the weeks they had lived together having been so short by comparison with the length of his absence.

Slowly drew on the time when Willowes found himself well enough to come home. He landed at Southampton, and posted thence towards Yewsholt. Barbara arranged to go out to meet him as far as Lornton Inn – the spot between the Forest and the Chase at which he had waited for night on the evening of their elopement. Thither she drove at the appointed hour in a little pony-chaise, presented her by her father on her birthday for her especial use in her new house; which vehicle she sent back on arriving at the inn, the plan agreed upon being that she should perform the return journey with her husband in his hired coach.

There was not much accommodation for a lady at this wayside tavern; but, as it was a fine evening in early summer, she did not mind – walking about outside, and straining her eyes along the highway for the expected one. But each cloud of dust that enlarged in the distance and drew near was found to disclose a conveyance other than his post-chaise. Barbara remained till the appointment was two hours passed, and then began to fear that owing to some adverse wind in the Channel he was not coming that night.

While waiting she was conscious of a curious trepidation that was not entirely solicitude, and did not amount to dread; her tense state of incertitude bordered both on disappointment and on relief. She had lived six or seven weeks with an imperfectly educated yet handsome husband whom now she had not seen for seventeen months, and who was so changed physically by an accident that she was assured she would hardly know him. Can we wonder at her compound state of mind?

But her immediate difficulty was to get away from Lornton Inn, for her situation was becoming embarrassing. Like too many of Barbara's actions, this drive had been undertaken without much reflection. Expecting to wait no more than a few minutes for her husband in his post-chaise, and to enter it with him, she had not hesitated to isolate herself by sending back her own little vehicle. She now found that, being so well known in this neighbourhood, her excursion to meet her long-absent husband was exciting great interest. She was conscious that more eyes were watching her from the inn-windows than met her own gaze. Barbara had decided to get home by hiring whatever kind of conveyance the tavern afforded, when, straining her eyes for the last time over the now darkening highway, she perceived yet another dust-cloud drawing near. She paused; a chariot ascended to the inn, and would have passed had not its occupant caught sight of her standing expectantly. The horses were checked on the instant.

'You here – and alone, my dear Mrs Willowes?' said Lord Uplandtowers, whose carriage it was.

She explained what had brought her into this lonely situation; and, as he was going in the direction of her own home, she accepted his offer of a seat beside him. Their conversation was embarrassed and fragmentary at first; but when they had driven a mile or two she was surprised to find herself talking earnestly and warmly to him: her impulsiveness was in truth but the natural consequence of her late existence – a somewhat desolate one by reason of the strange marriage she had made; and there is no more indiscreet mood than that of a woman surprised into talk who has long been imposing upon herself a policy of reserve. Therefore her ingenuous heart rose with a bound into her throat when, in response to his leading questions, or rather hints, she allowed her troubles to leak out of her. Lord Uplandtowers took her quite to her own door, although he had driven three miles out of his way to do so; and in handing her down she heard from him a whisper of stern reproach: 'It need not have been thus if you had listened to me!'

She made no reply, and went indoors. There, as the evening wore away, she regretted more and more that she had been so friendly with Lord Uplandtowers. But he had launched himself upon her so unexpectedly: if she had only foreseen the meeting with him, what a careful line of conduct she would have marked out! Barbara broke into a perspiration of disquiet when she thought of her unreserve, and, in self-chastisement, resolved to sit up till midnight on the bare chance of Edmond's return; directing that supper should be laid for him, improbable as his arrival till the morrow was.

The hours went past, and there was dead silence in and round about Yewsholt Lodge, except for the soughing of the trees; till, when it was near upon midnight, she heard the noise of hoofs and wheels approaching the door. Knowing that it could only be her husband, Barbara instantly went into the hall to meet him. Yet she stood there not without a sensation of faintness, so many were the changes since their parting! And, owing to her casual encounter with Lord Uplandtowers, his voice and image still remained with her, excluding Edmond, her husband, from the inner circle of her impressions.

But she went to the door, and the next moment a figure stepped inside, of which she knew the outline, but little besides. Her husband was attired in a flapping black cloak and slouched hat, appearing altogether as a foreigner, and not as the young English burgess who had left her side. When he came forward into the light of the lamp, she perceived with surprise, and almost with fright, that he wore a mask. At first she had not noticed this – there being nothing in its colour which would lead a casual observer to think he was looking on anything but a real countenance.

He must have seen her start of dismay at the unexpectedness of his appearance, for he said hastily: 'I did not mean to come in to you like this – I thought you would have been in bed. How good you are, dear Barbara!' He put his arm round her, but he did not attempt to kiss her.

'O Edmond – it *is* you? – it must be?' she said, with clasped hands, for though his figure and movement were almost enough to prove it, and the tones were not unlike the old tones, the enunciation was so altered as to seem that of a stranger.

'I am covered like this to hide myself from the curious eyes of the inn-servants and others,' he said, in a low voice. 'I will send back the carriage and join you in a moment.'

'You are quite alone?'

'Quite. My companion stopped at Southampton.'

The wheels of the post-chaise rolled away as she entered the dining-room, where the supper was spread; and presently he rejoined her there. He had removed his cloak and hat, but the mask was still retained; and she could now see that it was of special make, of some flexible material like silk, coloured so as to represent flesh; it joined naturally to the front hair, and was otherwise cleverly executed.

'Barbara – you look ill,' he said, removing his glove, and taking her hand.

'Yes – I have been ill,' said she.

'Is this pretty little house ours?'

'O – yes.' She was hardly conscious of her words, for the hand he had ungloved in order to take hers was contorted, and had one or two of its fingers missing; while through the mask she discerned the twinkle of one eye only.

'I would give anything to kiss you, dearest, now at this moment!' he continued, with mournful passionateness. 'But I cannot – in this guise. The servants are abed, I suppose?'

'Yes,' said she. 'But I can call them? You will have some supper?'

He said he would have some, but that it was not necessary to call anybody at that hour. Thereupon they approached the table, and sat down, facing each other.

Despite Barbara's scared state of mind, it was forced upon her notice that her husband trembled, as if he feared the impression he was producing, or was about to produce, as much as, or more than, she. He drew nearer, and took her hand again.

'I had this mask made at Venice,' he began, in evident embarrassment. 'My darling Barbara – my dearest wife – do you think you – will mind when I take it off? You will not dislike me – will you?'

'O Edmond, of course I shall not mind,' said she. 'What has happened to you is our misfortune; but I am prepared for it.'

'Are you sure you are prepared?'

'O yes! You are my husband.'

'You really feel quite confident that nothing external can affect you?' he said again, in a voice rendered uncertain by his agitation.

'I think I am – quite,' she answered faintly.

He bent his head. 'I hope, I hope you are,' he whispered.

In the pause which followed, the ticking of the clock in the hall seemed to grow loud; and he turned a little aside to remove the mask. She breathlessly awaited the operation, which was one of some tediousness, watching him one moment, averting her face the next; and when it was done she shut her eyes at the dreadful spectacle that was revealed. A quick spasm of horror had passed through her; but though she quailed she forced herself to regard him anew, repressing the cry that would naturally have escaped from her ashy lips. Unable to look at him longer, Barbara sank down on the floor beside her chair, covering her eyes.

'You cannot look at me!' he groaned in a hopeless way. 'I am too terrible an object even for you to bear! I knew it; yet I hoped against it. O, this is a bitter fate – curse the skill of those Venetian surgeons who saved me alive! . . . Look up, Barbara,' he continued beseechingly; 'view me completely; say you loathe me, if you do loathe me, and settle the case between us for ever!'

His unhappy wife pulled herself together for a desperate strain. He was her Edmond; he had done her no wrong; he had suffered. A momentary devotion to him helped her, and lifting her eyes as bidden she regarded this human remnant, this *écorché* a second time. But the sight was too much. She again involuntarily looked aside and shuddered.

'Do you think you can get used to this?' he said. 'Yes or no! Can you bear such a thing of the charnel-house near you? Judge for yourself, Barbara. Your Adonis, your matchless man, has come to this!'

The poor lady stood beside him motionless, save for the restlessness of her eyes. All her natural sentiments of affection and pity were driven clean out of her by a sort of panic; she had just the same sense of dismay and fearfulness that she would have had in the presence of an apparition. She could nohow fancy this to be her chosen one – the man she had loved; he was metamorphosed to a specimen of another species. 'I do not loathe you,' she said with trembling. 'But I am so horrified – so overcome! Let me recover myself. Will you sup now? And while you do so may I go to my room to – regain my old feeling for you? I will try, if I may leave you awhile? Yes, I will try!'

Without waiting for an answer from him, and keeping her gaze carefully averted, the frightened woman crept to the door and out of the room. She heard him sit down to the table, as if to begin supper; though, Heaven knows, his appetite was slight enough after a reception which had confirmed his worst surmises. When Barbara had ascended the stairs and arrived in her chamber she sank down, and buried her face in the coverlet of the bed.

Thus she remained for some time. The bedchamber was over the dining-room, and presently as she knelt Barbara heard Willowes thrust back his chair, and rise to go into the hall. In five minutes that figure would probably come up the stairs and confront her again; it, – this new and terrible form, that was not her husband's. In the loneliness of this night, with neither maid nor friend beside her, she lost all self-control, and at the first sound of his footstep on the stairs, without so much as flinging a cloak round her, she flew from the room, ran along the gallery to the back staircase, which she descended, and, unlocking the back door, let herself out. She scarcely was aware what she had done till she found herself in the greenhouse, crouching on a flower-stand.

Here she remained, her great timid eyes strained through the glass upon the garden without, and her skirts gathered up, in fear of the field-mice which sometimes came there. Every moment she dreaded to hear footsteps which she ought by law to have longed for, and a voice that should have been as music to her soul. But Edmond Willowes came not that way. The nights were getting short at this season, and soon the dawn appeared, and the first rays of the sun.

By daylight she had less fear than in the dark. She thought she could meet him, and accustom herself to the spectacle.

So the much-tried young woman unfastened the door of the hothouse, and went back by the way she had emerged a few hours ago. Her poor husband was probably in bed and asleep, his journey having been long; and she made as little noise as possible in her entry. The house was just as she had left it, and she looked about in the hall for his cloak and hat, but she could not see them; nor did she perceive the small trunk which had been all that he brought with him, his heavier baggage having been left at Southampton for the road-waggon. She summoned courage to mount the stairs; the bedroom-door was open as she had left it. She fearfully peeped round; the bed had not been pressed. Perhaps he had lain down on the dining-room sofa. She descended and entered; he was not there. On the table beside his unsoiled plate lay a note, hastily written on the leaf of a pocketbook. It was something like this:

> MY EVER-BELOVED WIFE. – The effect that my forbidding appearance has produced upon you was one which I foresaw as quite possible. I hoped against it, but foolishly so. I was aware that no *human* love could survive such a catastrophe. I confess I thought yours *divine*; but, after so long an absence, there could not be left sufficient warmth to overcome the too natural first aversion. It was an experiment, and it has failed. I do not blame you; perhaps, even, it is better so. Good-bye. I leave England for one year. You will see me again at the expiration of that time, if I live. Then I will ascertain your true feeling; and, if it be against me, go away for ever.
>
> E.W.

On recovering from her surprise, Barbara's remorse was such that she felt herself absolutely unforgiveable. She should have regarded him as an afflicted being, and not been this slave to mere eyesight, like a child. To follow him and entreat him to return was her first thought. But on making inquiries she found that nobody had seen him: he had silently disappeared.

More than this, to undo the scene of last night was impossible. Her terror had been too plain, and he was a man unlikely to be coaxed back by her efforts to do her duty. She went and confessed to her parents all that had occurred; which, indeed, soon became known to more persons than those of her own family.

The year passed, and he did not return; and it was doubted if he were alive. Barbara's contrition for her unconquerable repugnance was now such that she longed to build a church-aisle, or erect a monument, and devote herself to deeds of charity for the remainder of her days. To that end she made inquiry of the excellent parson under whom she sat on Sundays, at a vertical distance of a dozen feet. But he could only adjust his wig and tap his snuffbox; for such was the lukewarm state of religion in those days, that not an aisle, steeple, porch, east window, Ten-Commandment board, lion-and-unicorn, or brass candlestick, was required anywhere at all in the neighbourhood as a votive offering from a distracted soul – the last century contrasting greatly in this respect with the happy times in which we live, when urgent appeals for contributions to such objects pour in by every morning's post, and nearly all churches have been made to look like new pennies. As the poor lady could not ease her conscience this way, she determined at least to be charitable, and soon had the satisfaction of finding her porch thronged every morning by the raggedest, idlest, most drunken, hypocritical, and worthless tramps in Christendom.

But human hearts are as prone to change as the leaves of the creeper on the wall, and in the course of time, hearing nothing of her husband, Barbara could sit unmoved whilst her mother and friends said in her hearing, 'Well, what has happened is for the best.' She began to think so herself, for even now she could not summon up that lopped and mutilated form without a shiver, though whenever her mind flew back to her early wedded days, and the man who had stood beside her then, a thrill of tenderness moved her, which if quickened by his living presence might have become strong. She was young and inexperienced, and had hardly on his late return grown out of the capricious fancies of girlhood.

But he did not come again, and when she thought of his word that he would return once more, if living, and how unlikely he was to break his word, she gave him up for dead. So did her parents; so also did another person – that man of silence, of irresistible incisiveness, of still countenance, who was as awake as seven sentinels when he seemed to be as sound asleep as the figures on his family monument. Lord Uplandtowers, though not yet thirty, had chuckled like a caustic fogey of threescore when he heard of Barbara's terror and flight at her husband's return, and of the latter's prompt departure. He felt pretty sure, however, that Willowes, despite his hurt feelings, would have reappeared to claim his bright-eyed property if he had been alive at the end of the twelve months.

As there was no husband to live with her, Barbara had relinquished the house prepared for them by her father, and taken up her abode anew at Chene Manor, as in the days of her girlhood. By degrees the episode with Edmond Willowes seemed but a fevered dream, and as the months grew to years Lord Uplandtowers' friendship with the people at Chene – which had somewhat cooled after Barbara's elopement – revived considerably, and he again became a frequent visitor there. He could not make the most trivial alteration or improvement at Knollingwood Hall, where he lived, without riding off to consult with his friend Sir John at Chene; and thus putting himself frequently under her eyes, Barbara grew accustomed to him, and talked to him as freely as to a brother. She even began to look up to him as a person of authority, judgement, and prudence; and though his severity on the bench towards poachers, smugglers, and turnip-stealers was matter of common notoriety, she trusted that much of what was said might be misrepresentation.

Thus they lived on till her husband's absence had stretched to years, and there could be no longer any doubt of his death. A passionless manner of renewing his addresses seemed no longer out of place in Lord Uplandtowers. Barbara did not love him, but hers was essentially one of those sweet-pea or with-wind natures which require a twig of stouter fibre than its own to hang upon and bloom. Now, too, she was older, and admitted to herself that a man whose ancestor had run scores of Saracens through and through in fighting for the site of the Holy Sepulchre was a more desirable husband, socially considered, than one who could only claim with certainty to know that his father and grandfather were respectable burgesses.

Sir John took occasion to inform her that she might legally consider herself a widow; and, in brief, Lord Uplandtowers carried his point with her, and she married him, though he could never get her to own that she loved him as she had loved Willowes. In my childhood I knew an old lady whose mother saw the wedding, and she said that when Lord and Lady Uplandtowers drove away from her father's house in the evening it was in a coach-and-four, and that my lady was dressed in green and silver, and wore the gayest hat and feather that ever were seen; though whether it was that the green did not suit her complexion, or otherwise, the Countess looked pale, and the reverse of blooming. After their marriage her husband took her to London, and she saw the gaieties of a season there; then they returned to Knollingwood Hall, and thus a year passed away.

Before their marriage her husband had seemed to care but little about her inability to love him passionately. 'Only let me win you,' he had said, 'and I will submit to all that.' But now her lack of warmth seemed to irritate him, and he conducted himself towards her with a resentfulness which led to her passing many hours with him in painful silence. The heir-presumptive to the title was a remote relative, whom Lord Uplandtowers did not exclude from the dislike he entertained towards many persons and things besides, and he had set his mind upon a lineal successor. He blamed her much that there was no promise of this, and asked her what she was good for.

On a particular day in her gloomy life a letter, addressed to her as Mrs Willowes, reached Lady Uplandtowers from an unexpected quarter. A sculptor in Pisa, knowing nothing of her second marriage, informed her that the long-delayed life-size statue of Mr Willowes, which, when her husband left that city, he had been directed to retain till it was sent for, was still in his studio. As his commission had not wholly been paid, and the statue was taking up room he could ill spare, he should be glad to have the debt cleared off, and directions where to forward the figure. Arriving at a time when the Countess was beginning to have little secrets (of a harmless kind, it is true) from her husband, by reason of their growing estrangement, she replied to this letter without saying a word to Lord Uplandtowers, sending off the balance that was owing to the sculptor, and telling him to dispatch the statue to her without delay.

It was some weeks before it arrived at Knollingwood Hall, and, by a singular coincidence, during the interval she received the first absolutely conclusive tidings of her Edmond's death. It had taken place years before, in a foreign land, about six months after their parting, and had been induced by the sufferings he had already undergone, coupled with much depression of spirit, which had caused him to succumb to a slight ailment. The news was sent her in a brief and formal letter from some relative of Willowes's in another part of England.

Her grief took the form of passionate pity for his misfortunes, and of reproach to herself for never having been able to conquer her aversion to his latter image by recollection of what Nature had originally made him. The sad spectacle that had gone from earth had never been her Edmond at all to her. O that she could have met him as he was at first! Thus Barbara thought. It was only a few days later that a waggon with two horses, containing an immense packing-case, was seen at breakfast-time both by Barbara and her husband to drive round to the back of the house, and by-and-by they were informed that a case labelled 'Sculpture' had arrived for her ladyship.

'What can that be?' said Lord Uplandtowers.

'It is the statue of poor Edmond, which belongs to me, but has never been sent till now,' she answered.

'Where are you going to put it?' asked he.

'I have not decided,' said the Countess. 'Anywhere, so that it will not annoy you.'

'Oh, it won't annoy me,' says he.

When it had been unpacked in a back room of the house, they went to examine it. The statue was a full-length figure, in the purest Carrara marble, representing Edmond Willowes in all his original beauty, as he had stood at parting from her when about to set out on his travels; a specimen of manhood almost perfect in every line and contour. The work had been carried out with absolute fidelity.

'Phoebus-Apollo, sure,' said the Earl of Uplandtowers, who had never seen Willowes, real or represented, till now.

Barbara did not hear him. She was standing in a sort of trance before the first husband, as if she had no consciousness of the other husband at her side. The mutilated features of Willowes had disappeared from her mind's eye; this perfect being was really the man she had loved, and not that later pitiable figure; in whom tenderness and truth should have seen this image always, but had not done so.

It was not till Lord Uplandtowers said roughly, 'Are you going to stay here all the morning worshipping him?' that she roused herself.

Her husband had not till now the least suspicion that Edmond Willowes originally looked thus, and he thought how deep would have been his jealousy years ago if Willowes had been known to him. Returning to the Hall in the afternoon he found his wife in the gallery, whither the statue had been brought.

She was lost in reverie before it, just as in the morning.

'What are you doing?' he asked.

She started and turned. 'I am looking at my husb – my statue, to see if it is well done,' she stammered. 'Why should I not?'

'There's no reason why,' he said. 'What are you going to do with the monstrous thing? It can't stand here for ever.'

'I don't wish it,' she said. 'I'll find a place.'

In her boudoir there was a deep recess, and while the Earl was absent from home for a few days in the following week, she hired joiners from the village, who under her directions enclosed the recess with a panelled door. Into the tabernacle thus formed she had the statue placed, fastening the door with a lock, the key of which she kept in her pocket.

When her husband returned he missed the statue from the gallery, and, concluding that it had been put away out of deference to his feelings, made no remark. Yet at moments he noticed something on his lady's face which he had never noticed there before. He could not construe it; it was a sort of silent ecstasy, a reserved beatification. What had become of the statue he could not divine, and growing more and more curious, looked about here and there for it till, thinking of her private room, he went towards that spot. After knocking he heard the shutting of a door, and the click of a key; but when he entered his wife was sitting at work, on what was in those days called knotting. Lord Uplandtowers' eye fell upon the newly-painted door where the recess had formerly been.

'You have been carpentering in my absence then, Barbara,' he said carelessly.

'Yes, Uplandtowers.'

'Why did you go putting up such a tasteless enclosure as that – spoiling the handsome arch of the alcove?'

'I wanted more closet-room; and I thought that as this was my own apartment – '

'Of course,' he returned. Lord Uplandtowers knew now where the statue of young Willowes was.

One night, or rather in the smallest hours of the morning, he missed the Countess from his side. Not being a man of nervous imaginings he fell asleep again before he had much considered the matter, and the next morning had forgotten the incident. But a few nights later the same circumstances occurred. This time he fully roused himself, but before he had moved to search for her she returned to the chamber in her dressing-gown, carrying a candle, which she extinguished as she approached, deeming him asleep. He could discover from her breathing that she was strangely moved; but not on this occasion either did he reveal that he had seen her. Presently, when she had lain down, affecting to wake, he asked her some trivial questions. 'Yes, Edmond,' she replied absently.

Lord Uplandtowers became convinced that she was in the habit of leaving the chamber in this queer way more frequently than he had observed, and he determined to watch. The next midnight he feigned deep sleep, and shortly after perceived her stealthily rise and let herself out of the room in the dark. He slipped on some clothing and followed. At the further end of the corridor, where the clash of flint and steel would be out of the hearing of one in the bedchamber, she struck a light. He stepped aside into an empty room till she had lit a taper and had passed on to her boudoir. In a minute or two he followed. Arrived at the door of the boudoir, he beheld the door of the private recess open, and Barbara within it, standing with her arms clasped tightly round the neck of her Edmond, and her mouth on his. The shawl which she had thrown round her nightclothes had slipped from her shoulders, and her long white robe and pale face lent her the blanched appearance of a second statue embracing the first. Between her kisses, she apostrophized it in a low murmur of infantine tenderness:

'My only love – how could I be so cruel to you, my perfect one – so good and true – I am ever faithful to you, despite my seeming infidelity! I always think of you – dream of you – during the long hours of the day, and in the night-watches! O Edmond, I am always yours!' Such words as these, intermingled with sobs, and streaming fears, and dishevelled hair, testified to an intensity of feeling in his wife which Lord Uplandtowers had not dreamed of her possessing.

'Ha, ha!' says he to himself. 'This is where we evaporate – this is where my hopes of a successor in the title dissolve – ha! ha! This must be seen to, verily!'

Lord Uplandtowers was a subtle man when once he set himself to strategy; though in the present instance he never thought of the simple stratagem of constant tenderness. Nor did he enter the room and surprise his wife as a blunderer would have done, but went back to his chamber as silently as he had left it. When the Countess returned thither, shaken by spent sobs and sighs, he appeared to be soundly sleeping as usual. The next day he began his countermoves by making inquiries as to the whereabouts of the tutor who had travelled with his wife's first husband; this gentleman, he found, was now master of a grammar-school at no great distance from Knollingwood. At the first convenient moment Lord Uplandtowers went thither and obtained an interview with the said gentleman. The schoolmaster was much gratified by a visit from such an influential neighbour, and was ready to communicate anything that his lordship desired to know.

After some general conversation on the school and its progress, the visitor observed that he believed the schoolmaster had once travelled a good deal with the unfortunate Mr Willowes, and had been with him on the occasion of his accident. He, Lord Uplandtowers, was interested in knowing what had really happened at that time, and had often thought of inquiring. And then the Earl not only heard by word of mouth as much as he wished to know, but, their chat becoming more intimate, the schoolmaster drew upon paper a sketch of the disfigured head, explaining with bated breath various details in the representation.

'It was very strange and terrible!' said Lord Uplandtowers, taking the sketch in his hand. 'Neither nose nor ears, nor lips scarcely!'

A poor man in the town nearest to Knollingwood Hall, who combined the art of sign-painting with ingenious mechanical occupations, was sent for by Lord Uplandtowers to come to the Hall on a day in that week when the Countess had gone on a short visit to her parents. His employer made the man understand that the business in which his assistance was demanded was to be considered private, and money insured the observance of this request. The lock of the cupboard was picked, and the ingenious mechanic and painter, assisted by the schoolmaster's sketch, which Lord Uplandtowers had put in his pocket, set to work upon the god-like countenance of the statue under my lord's direction. What the fire had maimed in the original the chisel maimed in the copy. It was a fiendish disfigurement, ruthlessly carried out, and was rendered still more shocking by being tinted to the hues of life, as life had been after the wreck.

Six hours after, when the workman was gone, Lord Uplandtowers looked upon the result, and smiled grimly, and said:

'A statue should represent a man as he appeared in life, and that's as he appeared. Ha! ha! But 'tis done to good purpose, and not idly.'

He locked the door of the closet with a skeleton key, and went his way to fetch the Countess home.

That night she slept, but he kept awake. According to the tale, she murmured soft words in her dream; and he knew that the tender converse of her imaginings was held with one whom he had supplanted but in name. At the end of her dream the Countess of Uplandtowers awoke and arose, and then the enactment of former nights was repeated. Her husband remained still and listened. Two strokes sounded from the clock in the pediment without, when, leaving the chamber-door ajar, she passed along the corridor to the other end, where, as usual, she obtained a light. So deep was the silence that he could even from his bed hear her softly blowing the tinder to a glow after striking the steel. She moved on into the boudoir, and he heard, or fancied he heard, the turning of the key in the closet-door. The next moment there came from that direction a loud and prolonged shriek, which resounded to the furthest corners of the house. It was repeated, and there was the noise of a heavy fall.

Lord Uplandtowers sprang out of bed. He hastened along the dark corridor to the door of the boudoir, which stood ajar, and, by the light of the candle within, saw his poor young Countess lying in a heap in her nightdress on the floor of the closet. When he reached her side he found that she had fainted, much to the relief of his fears that matters were worse. He quickly shut up and locked in the hated image which had done the mischief, and lifted his wife in his arms, where in a few instants she opened her eyes. Pressing her face to his without saying a word, he carried her back to her room, endeavouring as he went to disperse her terrors by a laugh in her ear, oddly compounded of causticity, predilection, and brutality.

'Ho-ho-ho!' says he: 'Frightened, dear one, hey? What a baby 'tis! Only a joke, sure, Barbara – a splendid joke! But a baby should not go to closets at midnight to look for the ghost of the dear departed! If it do it must expect to be terrified at his aspect – ho-ho-ho!'

When she was in her bed-chamber, and had quite come to herself, though her nerves were still much shaken, he spoke to her more sternly. 'Now, my lady, answer me: do you love him – eh?'

'No – no!' she faltered, shuddering, with her expanded eyes fixed on her husband. 'He is too terrible – no, no!'

'You are sure?'

'Quite sure!' replied the poor broken-spirited Countess.

But her natural elasticity asserted itself. Next morning he again inquired of her: 'Do you love him now?' She quailed under his gaze, but did not reply.

'That means that you do still, by God!' he continued.

'It means that I will not tell an untruth, and do not wish to incense my lord,' she answered, with dignity.

'Then suppose we go and have another look at him?' As he spoke, he suddenly took her by the wrist, and turned as if to lead her towards the ghastly closet.

'No – no! O – no!' she cried, and her desperate wriggle out of his hand revealed that the fright of the night had left more impression upon her delicate soul than superficially appeared.

'Another dose or two, and she will be cured,' he said to himself.

It was now so generally known that the Earl and Countess were not in accord, that he took no great trouble to disguise his deeds in relation to this matter. During the day he ordered four men with ropes and rollers to attend him in the boudoir. When they arrived, the closet was open, and the upper part of the statue tied up in canvas. He had it taken to the sleeping-chamber. What followed is more or less matter of conjecture. The story, as told to me, goes on to say that, when Lady Uplandtowers retired with him that night, she saw facing the foot of the heavy oak four-poster, a tall dark wardrobe, which had not stood there before; but she did not ask what its presence meant.

'I have had a little whim,' he explained when they were in the dark.

'Have you?' says she.

'To erect a little shrine, as it may be called.'

'A little shrine?'

'Yes; to one whom we both equally adore – eh? I'll show you what it contains.'

He pulled a cord which hung covered by the bedcurtains, and the doors of the wardrobe slowly opened, disclosing that the shelves within had been removed throughout, and the interior adapted to receive the ghastly figure, which stood there as it had stood in the boudoir, but with a wax candle burning on each side of it to throw the cropped and distorted features into relief. She clutched him, uttered a low scream, and buried her head in the bedclothes. 'O, take it away – please take it away!' she implored.

'All in good time; namely, when you love me best,' he returned calmly. 'You don't quite yet – eh?'

'I don't know – I think – O Uplandtowers, have mercy – I cannot bear it – O, in pity, take it away!'

'Nonsense; one gets accustomed to anything. Take another gaze.'

In short, he allowed the doors to remain unclosed at the foot of the bed, and the wax-tapers burning; and such was the strange fascination of the grisly exhibition that a morbid curiosity took possession of the Countess as she lay, and, at his repeated request, she did again look out from the coverlet, shuddered, hid her eyes, and looked again, all the while begging him to take it away, or it would drive her out of her senses. But he would not do so yet, and the wardrobe was not locked till dawn.

The scene was repeated the next night. Firm in enforcing his ferocious correctives, he continued the treatment till the nerves of the poor lady were quivering in agony under the virtuous tortures inflicted by her lord, to bring her truant heart back to faithfulness.

The third night, when the scene had opened as usual, and she lay staring with immense wild eyes at the horrid fascination, on a sudden she gave an unnatural laugh; she laughed more and more, staring at the image, till she literally shrieked with laughter: then there was silence, and he found her to have become insensible. He thought she had fainted, but soon saw that the event was worse: she was in an epileptic fit. He started up, dismayed by the sense that, like many other subtle personages, he had been too exacting for his own interests. Such love as he was capable of, though rather a selfish gloating than a cherishing solicitude, was fanned into life on the instant. He closed the wardrobe with the pulley, clasped her in his arms, took her gently to the window, and did all he could to restore her.

It was a long time before the Countess came to herself, and when she did so, a considerable change seemed to have taken place in her emotions. She flung her arms around him, and with gasps of fear abjectly kissed him many times, at last bursting into tears. She had never wept in this scene before.

'You'll take it away, dearest – you will!' she begged plaintively.

'If you love me.'

'I do – oh, I do!'

'And hate him, and his memory?'

'Yes – yes!'

'Thoroughly?'

'I cannot endure recollection of him!' cried the poor Countess slavishly. 'It fills me with shame – how could I ever be so depraved! I'll never behave badly again, Uplandtowers; and you will never put the hated statue again before my eyes?'

He felt that he could promise with perfect safety. 'Never,' said he.

'And then I'll love you,' she returned eagerly, as if dreading lest the scourge should be applied anew. 'And I'll never, never dream of thinking a single thought that seems like faithlessness to my marriage vow.'

The strange thing now was that this fictitious love wrung from her by terror took on, through mere habit of enactment, a certain quality of reality. A servile mood of attachment to the Earl became distinctly visible in her contemporaneously with an actual dislike for her late husband's memory. The mood of attachment grew and continued when the statue was removed. A permanent revulsion was operant in her, which intensified as time wore on. How fright could have effected such a change of idiosyncrasy learned physicians alone can say; but I believe such cases of reactionary instinct are not unknown.

The upshot was that the cure became so permanent as to be itself a new disease. She clung to him so tightly that she would not willingly be out of his sight for a moment. She would have no sitting-room apart from his, though she could not help starting when he entered suddenly to her. Her eyes were well-nigh always fixed upon him. If he drove out, she wished to go with him; his slightest civilities to other women made her frantically jealous; till at length her very fidelity became a burden to him, absorbing his time, and curtailing his liberty, and causing him to curse and swear. If he ever spoke sharply to her now, she did not revenge herself by flying off to a mental world of her own; all that affection for another, which had provided her with a resource, was now a cold black cinder.

From that time the life of this scared and enervated lady – whose existence might have been developed to so much higher purpose but for the ignoble ambition of her parents and the conventions of the time – was one of obsequious amativeness towards a perverse and cruel man. Little personal events came to her in quick succession – half a dozen, eight, nine, ten such events, in brief, she bore him no less than eleven children in the nine following years, but half of them came prematurely into the world, or died a few days old; only one, a girl, attained to maturity; she in after years became the wife of the Honourable Mr Beltonleigh, who was created Lord d'Almaine, as may be remembered.

There was no living son and heir. At length, completely worn out in mind and body, Lady Uplandtowers was taken abroad by her husband, to try the effect of a more genial climate upon her wasted frame. But nothing availed to strengthen her and she died at Florence, a few months after her arrival in Italy.

Contrary to expectation, the Earl of Uplandtowers did not marry again. Such affection as existed in him – strange, hard, brutal as it was – seemed untransferable, and the title, as is known, passed at his death to his nephew. Perhaps it may not be so generally known that, during the enlargement of the Hall for the sixth Earl, while digging in the grounds for the new foundations, the broken fragments of a marble statue were unearthed. They were submitted to various antiquaries, who said that, so far as the damaged pieces would allow them to form an opinion, the statue seemed to be that of a mutilated Roman satyr; or, if not, an allegorical figure of Death. Only one or two old inhabitants guessed whose statue those fragments had composed.

I should have added that, shortly after the death of the Countess, an excellent sermon was preached by the Dean of Melchester, the subject of which, though names were not mentioned, was unquestionably suggested by the aforesaid events. He dwelt upon the folly of indulgence in sensuous love for a handsome form merely; and showed that the only rational and virtuous growths of that affection were those based upon intrinsic worth. In the case of the tender but somewhat shallow lady whose life I have related, there is no doubt that an infatuation for the person of young Willowes was the chief feeling that induced her to marry him; which was the more deplorable in that his beauty, by all tradition, was the least of his recommendations, every report bearing out the inference that he must have been a man of steadfast nature, bright intelligence, and promising life.

The Man and The Snake

AMBROSE BIERCE

It is of veritabyll report, and attested of so many that there be nowe of wyse and learned none to gaynsaye it, that ye serpente hys eye hath a magnetick propertie that whosoe falleth into its suasion is drawn forwards in despyte of his wille, and perisheth miserabyll by ye creature hys byte.

Stretched at ease upon a sofa, in gown and slippers, Harker Brayton smiled as he read the foregoing sentence in old Morryster's 'Marvells of Science.' 'The only marvel in the matter,' he said to himself, 'is that the wise and learned in Morryster's day should have believed such nonsense as is rejected by most of even the ignorant in ours.'

A train of reflections followed – for Brayton was a man of thought – and he unconsciously lowered his book without altering the direction of his eyes. As soon as the volume had gone below the line of sight, something in an obscure corner of the room recalled his attention to his surroundings. What he saw, in the shadow under his bed, were two small points of light, apparently about an inch part. They might have been reflections of the gas jet above him, in metal nail heads; he gave them but little thought and resumed his reading. A moment later something – some impulse which it did not occur to him to analyze – impelled him to lower the book again and seek for what he saw before. The points of light were still there. They seemed to have become brighter than before, shining with a greenish luster which he had not at first observed. He thought, too, that they might have moved a trifle – were somewhat nearer. They were still too much in shadow, however, to reveal their nature and origin to an indolent attention, and he resumed his reading. Suddenly something in the text suggested a thought which made him start and drop the book for the third time to the side of the sofa, whence, escaping from his hand, it fell sprawling to the floor, back upward. Brayton, half risen, was staring intently into the obscurity beneath the bed, where the points of light shone with, it seemed to him, an added fire. His attention was now fully aroused, his gaze eager and imperative. It disclosed, almost directly beneath the foot-rail of the bed, the coils of a large serpent – the points of lights were its eyes! Its horrible head, thrust flatly forth from the innermost coil and resting upon the outermost, was directed straight toward him, the definition of the wide, brutal jaw and the idiot-like forehead serving to show the direction of its malevolent gaze. The eyes were no longer merely luminous points; they looked into his own with a meaning, a malign significance.

A snake in a bedroom of a modern city dwelling of the better sort is, happily, not so common a phenomenon as to make explanation altogether needless. Harker Brayton, a bachelor of thirty-five, a scholar, idler, and something of an athlete, rich, popular, and of sound health, had returned to San Francisco from all manner of remote and unfamiliar countries. His tastes, always a trifle luxurious, had taken on an added exuberance from long privation; and the resources of even the Castle Hotel being inadequate to their perfect gratification, he had gladly accepted the hospitality of his friend, Dr Druring, the distinguished scientist. Dr Druring's house, a large, old-fashioned one in what was now an obscure quarter of the city, had an outer and visible aspect of proud reserve. It plainly would not associate with the contiguous elements of its altered environment, and appeared to have developed some of the eccentricities which come of isolation. One of these was a 'wing,' conspicuously irrelevant in point of architecture, and no less rebellious in the matter of purpose; for it was a combination of laboratory, menagerie, and museum. It was here that the doctor indulged the scientific side of his nature in the study of such forms of animal life as engaged his interest and comforted his taste – which, it must be confessed, ran rather to the lower forms. For one of the higher types nimbly and sweetly to recommend itself unto his gentle senses, it had at least to retain certain rudimentary characteristics allying it to such 'dragons of the prime' as toads and snakes. His scientific sympathies were distinctly reptilian; he loved nature's vulgarians and described himself as the Zola of zoology. His wife and daughters, not having the advantage to share his enlightened curiosity regarding the works and ways of our ill-starred fellow-creatures, were, with needless austerity, excluded from what he called the Snakery, and doomed to companionship with their own kind, though, to soften the rigors of their lot, he had permitted them, out of his great wealth, to outdo the reptiles in the gorgeousness of their surroundings and to shine with a superior slendor.

Architecturally, and in point of 'furnishing,' the Snakery had a severe simplicity befitting the humble circumstances of its occupants, many of whom, indeed, could not safely have been intrusted with the liberty which is necessary to the full enjoyment of luxury, for they had the troublesome peculiarity of being alive. In their own apartments, however, they were under as little personal restraint as was compatible with their protection from the baneful habit of swallowing one another; and, as Brayton had thoughtfully apprised, it was more than a tradition that some of them had at divers times been found in parts of the premises where it would have embarrassed them to explain their presence.

Despite the Snakery and its uncanny associations – to which, indeed, he gave little attention – Brayton found life at the Druring mansion very much to his mind.

Beyond a smart shock of surprise and a shudder of mere loathing, Mr Brayton was not greatly affected. His first thought was to ring the call-bell and bring a servant; but, although the bell-cord dangled within easy reach, he made no movement toward it; it had occurred to his mind that the act might subject him to the suspicion of fear, which he certainly did not feel. He was more keenly conscious of the incongruous nature of the situation than affected by its perils; it was revolting, but absurd.

The reptile was of a species with which Brayton was unfamiliar. Its length he could only conjecture; the body at the largest visible part seemed about as thick as his forearm. In what way was it dangerous, if in any way? Was it venomous? Was it a constrictor? His knowledge of nature's danger signals did not enable him to say; he had never deciphered the code.

If not dangerous, the creature was at least offensive. It was *de trop* – 'matter out of place' – an impertinence. The gem was unworthy of the setting. Even the barbarous taste of our time and country, which had loaded the walls of the room with pictures the floor with furniture and the furniture with bric-a-brac, had not quite fitted the place for this bit of the savage life of the jungle. Besides – insupportable thought! – the exhalations of its breath mingled with the atmosphere which he himself was breathing!

These thoughts shaped themselves with greater or less definition in Brayton's mind, and begot action. The process is what we call consideration and decision. It is thus that we are wise and unwise. It is thus that the withered leaf in an autumn breeze shows greater or less intelligence than its fellows, falling upon the land or upon the lake. The secret of human action is an open one: something contracts our muscles. Does it matter if we give to the preparatory molecular changes the name of will?

Brayton rose to his feet and prepared to back softly away from the snake, without disturbing it, if possible, and through the door. People retire so from the presence of the great, for greatness is power, and power is a menace. He knew that he could walk backward without obstruction, and find the door without error. Should the monster follow, the taste which had plastered the walls with paintings had consistently supplied a rack of murderous Oriental weapons from which he could snatch one to suit the occasion. In the meantime the snake's eyes burned with a more pitiless malevolence than ever.

Brayton lifted his right foot free of the floor to step backward. That moment he felt a strong aversion to doing so.

'I am accounted brave,' he murmured; 'is bravery, then, no more than pride? Because there are none to witness the shame shall I retreat?'

He was steadying himself with his right hand upon the back of a chair, his foot suspended.

'Nonsense!' he said aloud; 'I am not so great a coward as to fear to seem to myself afraid.'

He lifted the foot a little higher by slightly bending the knee, and thrust it sharply to the floor – an inch in front of the other! He could not think how that had occurred. A trial with the left foot had the same result; it was again in advance of the right. The hand upon the chair-back was grasping it; the arm was straight, reaching somewhat backward. One might have seen that he was reluctant to lose his hold. The snake's malignant head was still thrust forth from the inner coil as before, the neck level. It had not moved, but its eyes were now electric sparks, radiating an infinity of luminous needles.

The man had an ashy pallor. Again he took a step forward, and another, partly dragging the chair, which, when finally released, fell upon the floor with a crash. The man groaned; the snake made neither sound nor motion, but its eyes were two dazzling suns. The reptile itself was wholly concealed by them. They gave off enlarging rings of rich and vivid colours, which at their greatest expansion successively vanished like soap bubbles; they seemed to approach his very face, and anon were an immeasurable distance away. He heard, somewhere, the continuous throbbing of a great drum, with desultory bursts of far music, inconceivably sweet, like the tones of an æolian harp. He knew it for the sunrise melody of Memmon's statue, and thought he stood in the Nileside reeds, hearing, with exalted sense, that immortal anthem through the silence of the centuries.

The music ceased; rather, it became by insensible degrees that distant roll of a retreating thunderstorm. A landscape, glittering with sun and rain, stretched before him, arched with a vivid rainbow, framing in its giant curve a hundred visible cities. In the middle distance a vast serpent, wearing a crown, reared its head out of voluminous convolutions and looked at him with his dead mother's eyes. Suddenly this enchanting landscape seemed to rise swiftly upward, like the drop-scene at a theatre, and vanished in a blank. Something struck him a hard blow upon the face and breast. He had fallen to the floor; the blood ran from his broken nose and his bruised lips. For a moment he was dazed and stunned, and lay with closed eyes, his face against the floor. In a few moments he had recovered, and then realized that his fall, by withdrawing his eyes, had broken the spell which held him. He felt that now, by keeping his gaze averted, he would be able to retreat. But the thought of the serpent within a few feet of his head, yet unseen – perhaps in the very act of springing upon him and throwing its coils about his throat – was too horrible. He lifted his head, stared again into those baleful eyes, and was again in bondage.

The snake had not moved, and appeared somewhat to have lost its power upon the imagination; the gorgeous illusions of a few moments before were not repeated. Beneath that flat and brainless brow its black, beady eyes simply glittered, as at first, with an expression unspeakably malignant. It was as if the creature, knowing its triumph assured, had determined to practise no more alluring wiles.

Now ensued a fearful scene. The man, prone upon the floor, within a yard of his enemy, raised the upper part of his body upon his elbows, his head thrown back, his legs extended to their full length. His face was white between its gouts of blood; his eyes were strained open to their uttermost expansion. There was froth upon his lips; it dropped off in flakes. Strong convulsions ran through his body, making almost serpentine undulations. He bent himself at the waist, shifting his legs from side to side. And every movement left him a little nearer to the snake. He thrust his hands forward to brace himself back, yet constantly advanced upon his elbows.

Dr Druring and his wife sat in the library. The scientist was in rare good humour.

'I have just obtained, by exchange with another collector,' he said, 'a splendid specimen of the *ophiophagus*.'

'And what may that be?' the lady inquired with a somewhat languid interest.

'Why, bless my soul, what profound ignorance! My dear, a man who ascertains after marriage that his wife does not know Greek, is entitled to a divorce. The *ophiophagus* is a snake which eats other snakes.'

'I hope it will eat all yours,' she said, absently shifting the lamp. 'But how does it get the other snakes? By charming them, I suppose.'

'That is just like you, dear,' said the doctor, with an affection of petulance. 'You know how irritating to me is any allusion to that vulgar superstition about the snake's power of fascination.'

The conversation was interrupted by a mighty cry, which rang through the silent house like the voice of a demon shouting in a tomb! Again and yet again it sounded, with terrible distinctness. They sprang to their feet, the man confused, the lady pale and speechless with fright. Almost before the echoes of the last cry had died away, the doctor was out of the room, springing up the staircase two steps at a time. In the corridor, in front of Brayton's chamber, he met some servants who had come from the upper floor. Together they rushed at the door without knocking. It was unfastened and gave way. Brayton lay upon his stomach on the floor, dead. His head and arms were partly concealed under the foot-rail of the bed. They pulled the body away, turning it upon the back. The face was daubed with blood and froth, the eyes were wide open, staring – a dreadful sight!

'Died in a fit,' said the scientist, bending his knee and placing his hand upon the heart. While in that position, he happened to glance under the bed. 'Good God!' he added, 'how did this thing get in here?'

He reached under the bed, pulled out the snake, and flung it, still coiled, to the centre of the room, whence, with a harsh, shuffling sound, it slid across the polished floor till stopped by the wall, where it lay without motion. It was a stuffed snake; its eyes were two shoe buttons.

The Romance of Certain Old Clothes

HENRY JAMES

I

Towards the middle of the eighteenth century there lived in the Province of Massachusetts a widowed gentlewoman, the mother of three children, by name Mrs Veronica Wingrave. She had lost her husband early in life, and had devoted herself to the care of her progeny. These young persons grew up in a manner to reward her tenderness and to gratify her highest hopes. The first-born was a son, whom she had called Bernard, after his father. The others were daughters born at an interval of three years apart. Good looks were traditional in the family, and this youthful trio were not likely to allow the tradition to perish. The boy was of that fair and ruddy complexion and that athletic structure which in those days (as in these) were the sign of good English descent – a frank, affectionate young fellow, a deferential son, a patronizing brother, a steadfast friend. Clever, however, he was not; the wit of the family had been apportioned chiefly to his sisters. The late Mr Wingrave had been a great reader of Shakespeare, at a time when this pursuit implied more freedom of thought than at the present day, and in a community where it required much courage to patronize the drama even in the closet: and he had wished to call attention to his admiration of the great poet by calling his daughters out of his favourite plays. Upon the elder he had bestowed the romantic name of Rosalind, and the younger he had called Perdita, in memory of a little girl born between them, who had lived but a few weeks.

When Bernard Wingrave came to his sixteenth year his mother put a brave face upon it and prepared to execute her husband's last injunction. This had been a formal command that, at the proper age, his son should be sent out to England, to complete his education at the university of Oxford, where he himself had acquired his taste for elegant literature. It was Mrs Wingrave's belief that the lad's equal was not to be found in the two hemispheres, but she had the old traditions of literal obedience. She swallowed her sobs, and made up her boy's trunk and his simple provincial outfit, and sent him on his way across the seas. Bernard presented himself at his father's college, and spent five years in England, without great honour, indeed, but with a vast deal of pleasure and no discredit. On leaving the university he made the journey to France. In his twenty-fourth year he took ship for home, prepared to find poor little New England (New England was very small in those days) a very dull, unfashionable residence. But there had been changes at home, as well as in Mr Bernard's opinions. He found his mother's house quite habitable, and his sisters grown into two very charming young ladies, with all the accomplishments and graces of the young women of Britain, and a certain native-grown originality and wildness, which, if it was not an accomplishment, was certainly a grace the more. Bernard privately assured his mother that his sisters were fully a match for the most genteel young women in the old country; whereupon poor Mrs Wingrave, you may be sure, bade them hold up their heads. Such was Bernard's opinion; and such, in a tenfold higher degree, was the opinion of Mr Arthur Lloyd. This gentleman was a college-mate of Mr Bernard, a young man of reputable family, of a good person and a handsome inheritance; which latter appurtenance he proposed to invest in trade in the flourishing colony. He and Bernard were sworn friends; they had crossed the ocean together, and the young American had lost no time in presenting him at his mother's house, where he had made quite as good an impression as that which he had received and of which I have just given a hint.

The two sisters were at this time in all the freshness of their youthful bloom; each wearing, of course, this natural brilliancy in the manner that became her best. They were equally dissimilar in appearance and character. Rosalind, the elder – now in her twenty-second year – was tall and white, with calm grey eyes and auburn tresses; a very faint likeness to the Rosalind of Shakespeare's comedy, whom I imagine a brunette (if you will), but a slender, airy creature, full of the softest, quickest impulses. Miss Wingrave, with her slightly lymphatic fairness, her fine arms, her majestic height, her slow utterance, was not cut out for adventures. She would never have put on a man's jacket and hose; and, indeed, being a very plump beauty, she may have had reasons apart from her natural dignity. Perdita, too, might very well have exchanged the sweet melancholy of her name against something more in consonance with her aspect and disposition. She had the cheek of a gypsy and the eye of an eager child, as well as the smallest waist and lightest foot in all the country of the Puritans. When you spoke to her she never made you wait, as her handsome sister was wont to do (while she looked at you with a cold fine eye), but gave you your choice of a dozen answers before you had uttered half your thought.

The young girls were very glad to see their brother once more; but they found themselves quite able to spare part of their attention for their brother's friend. Among the young men their friends and neighbours, the *belle jeunesse* of the Colony, there were many excellent fellows, several devoted swains, and some two or three who enjoyed the reputation of universal charmers and conquerors. But the homebred arts and somewhat boisterous gallantry of these honest colonists were completely eclipsed by the good looks, the fine clothes, the punctilious courtesy, the perfect elegance, the immense information, of Mr Arthur Lloyd. He was in reality no paragon; he was a capable, honorable, civil youth, rich in pounds sterling, in his health and complacency and his little capital of uninvested affections. But he was a gentleman; he had a handsome person; he had studied and traveled; he spoke French, he played the flute, and he read verses aloud with very great taste. There were a dozen reasons why Miss Wingrave and her sister should have thought their other male acquaintance made but a poor figure before such a perfect man of the world. Mr Lloyd's anecdotes told our little New England maidens a great deal more of the ways and means of people of fashion in European capitals than he had any idea of doing. It was delightful to sit by and hear him and Bernard talk about the fine people and fine things they had seen. They would all gather round the fire after tea, in the little wainscoted parlour, and the two young men would remind each other, across the rug, of this, that and the other adventure. Rosalind and Perdita would often have given their ears to know exactly what adventure it was, and where it happened, and who was there, and what the ladies had on; but in those days a well-bred young woman was not expected to break into the conversation of her elders, or to ask too many questions; and the poor girls used therefore to sit fluttering behind the more languid or more discreet curiosity of their mother.

II

That they were both very fine girls Arthur Lloyd was not slow to discover; but it took him some time to make up his mind whether he liked the big sister or the little sister best. He had a strong presentiment – an emotion of a nature entirely too cheerful to be called a foreboding – that he was destined to stand up before the parson with one of them; yet he was unable to arrive at a preference, and for such a consummation a preference was certainly necessary, for Lloyd had too much young blood in his veins to make a choice by lot and be cheated of the satisfaction of falling in love. He resolved to take things as they came – to let his heart speak. Meanwhile he was on a very pleasant footing. Mrs Wingrave showed a dignified indifference to his 'intentions', equally remote from a carelessness of her daughter's honor and from that sharp alacrity to make him come to the point, which, in his quality of young man of property, he had too often encountered in the worldly matrons of his native islands. As for Bernard, all that he asked was that his friend should treat his sisters as his own; and as for the poor girls themselves, however each may have secretly longed that their visitor should do or say something 'marked', they kept a very modest and contented demeanor.

Towards each other, however, they were somewhat more on the offensive. They were good friends enough, and accommodating bedfellows (they shared the same four-poster), betwixt whom it would take more than a day for the seeds of jealousy to sprout and bear fruit; but they felt that the seeds had been sown on the day that Mr Lloyd came into the house. Each made up her mind that, if she should be slighted, she would bear her grief in silence, and that no one should be any the wiser; for if they had a great deal of ambition, they had also a large share of pride. But each prayed in secret, nevertheless, that upon *her* the selection, the distinction, might fall. They had need of a vast deal of patience, of self-control, of dissimulation. In those days a young girl of decent breeding could make no advances whatever, and barely respond, indeed, to those that were made. She was expected to sit still in her chair, with her eyes on the carpet, watching the spot where the mystic handkerchief should fall. Poor Arthur Lloyd was obliged to carry on his wooing in the little wainscoted parlor, before the eyes of Mrs Wingrave, her son, and his prospective sister-in-law. But youth and love are so cunning that a hundred signs and tokens might travel to and fro, and not one of these three pairs of eyes detect them in their passage. The two maidens were almost always together, and had plenty of chances to betray themselves. That each knew she was being watched, made not a grain of difference in the little offices they mutually rendered, or in the various household tasks they performed in common. Neither flinched nor fluttered beneath the silent battery of her sister's eyes. The only apparent change in their habits was that they had less to say to each other. It was impossible to talk about Mr Lloyd, and it was ridiculous to talk about anything else. By tacit agreement they began to wear all their choice finery, and to devise such little implements of conquest, in the way of ribbons and top-knots and kerchiefs, as were sanctioned by indubitable modesty. They executed in the same inarticulate fashion a contract of fair play in this exciting game. 'Is it better so?' Rosalind would ask, tying a bunch of ribbons on her bosom, and turning about from her glass to her sister. Perdita would look up gravely from her work and examine the decoration. 'I think you had better give it another loop,' she would say, with great solemnity, looking hard at her sister with eyes that added, 'upon my honor!' So they were for ever stitching and trimming their petticoats, and pressing out their muslins, and contriving washes and ointments and cosmetics, like the ladies in the household of the vicar of Wakefield. Some three or four months went by; it grew to be midwinter, and as yet Rosalind knew that if Perdita had nothing more to boast of than she, there was not much to be feared from her rivalry. But Perdita by this time – the charming Perdita – felt that her secret had grown to be tenfold more precious than her sister's.

One afternoon Miss Wingrave sat alone – that was a rare accident – before her toilet-glass, combing out her long hair. It was getting too dark to see; she lit the two candles in their sockets, on the frame of her mirror, and then went to the window to draw her curtains. It was a grey December evening; the landscape was bare and bleak, and the sky heavy with snow-clouds. At the end of the large garden into which her window looked was a wall with a little postern door, opening into a lane. The door stood ajar, as she could vaguely see in the gathering darkness, and moved slowly to and fro, as if someone were swaying it from the lane without. It was doubtless a servant-maid who had been having a tryst with her sweetheart. But as she was about to drop her curtain Rosalind saw her sister step into the garden and hurry along the path which led to the house. She dropped the curtain, all save a little crevice for her eyes. As Perdita came up the path she seemed to be examining something in her hand, holding it close to her eyes. When she reached the house she stopped a moment, looked intently at the object, and pressed it to her lips.

Poor Rosalind slowly came back to her chair and sat down before her glass where, if she had looked at it less abstractedly, she would have seen her handsome features sadly disfigured by jealousy. A moment afterwards the door opened behind her and her sister came into the room, out of breath, her cheeks aglow with the chilly air.

Perdita started. 'Ah,' said she, 'I thought you were with our mother.' The ladies were to go to a tea-party, and on such occasions it was the habit of one of the girls to help their mother to dress. Instead of coming in, Perdita lingered at the door.

'Come in, come in,' said Rosalind. 'We have more than an hour yet. I should like you very much to give a few strokes to my hair.' She knew that her sister wished to retreat, and that she could see in the glass all her movements in the room. 'Nay, just help me with my hair,' she said, and I will go to mamma.'

Perdita came reluctantly, and took the brush. She saw her sister's eyes, in the glass, fastened hard upon her hands. She had not made three passes when Rosalind clapped her own right hand upon her sister's left, and started out of her chair. 'Whose ring is that?' she cried, passionately, drawing her towards the light.

On the young girl's third finger glistened a little gold ring, adorned with a very small sapphire. Perdita felt that she need no longer keep her secret, yet that she must put a bold face on her avowal. 'It's mine,' she said proudly.

'Who gave it to you?' cried the other.

Perdita hesitated a moment. 'Mr Lloyd.'

'Mr Lloyd is generous, all of a sudden.'

'Ah no,' cried Perdita, with spirit, 'not all of a sudden! He offered it to me a month ago.'

'And you needed a month's begging to take it?' said Rosalind, looking at the little trinket, which indeed was not especially elegant, although it was the best that the jeweller of the Province could furnish. 'I wouldn't have taken it in less than two.'

'It isn't the ring,' Perdita answered, 'it's what it means!'

'It means that you are not a modest girl!' cried Rosalind. 'Pray, does your mother know of your intrigue? does Bernard?'

'My mother has approved my "intrigue", as you call it. Mr Lloyd has asked for my hand, and mamma has given it. Would you have had him apply to you, dearest sister?'

Rosalind gave her companion a long look, full of passionate envy and sorrow. Then she dropped her lashes on her pale cheeks and turned away. Perdita felt that it had not been a pretty scene; but it was her sister's fault. However, the elder girl rapidly called back her pride, and turned herself about again. 'You have my very best wishes,' she said, with a low curtsey. 'I wish you every happiness, and a very long life.'

Perdita gave a bitter laugh. 'Don't speak in that tone!' she cried. 'I would rather you should curse me outright. Come, Rosy,' she added, 'he couldn't marry both of us.'

'I wish you very great joy,' Rosalind repeated, mechanically, sitting down to her glass again, 'and a very long life, and plenty of children.'

There was something in the sound of these words not at all to Perdita's taste. 'Will you give me a year to live at least?' she said. 'In a year I can have one little boy – or one little girl at least. If you will give me your brush again I will do your hair.'

'Thank you,' said Rosalind. 'You had better go to mamma. It isn't becoming that a young lady with a promised husband should wait on a girl with none.'

'Nay,' said Perdita good-humoredly, 'I have Arthur to wait upon me. You need my service more than I need yours.'

But her sister motioned her away, and she left the room. When she had gone poor Rosalind fell on her knees before her dressing-table, buried her head in her arms, and poured out a flood of tears and sobs. She felt very much the better for this effusion of sorrow. When her sister came back she insisted on helping her to dress – on her wearing her prettiest things. She forced upon her acceptance of a bit of lace of her own, and declared that now that she was to be married she should do her best to appear worthy of her lover's choice. She discharged these offices in stern silence: but, such as they were, they had to do duty as an apology and an atonement; she never made any other.

Now that Lloyd was received by the family as an accepted suitor nothing remained but to fix the wedding-day. It was appointed for the following April, and in the interval preparations were diligently made for the marriage. Lloyd, on his side, was busy with his commercial arrangements, and with establishing a correspondence with the great mercantile house to which he had attached himself in England. He was therefore not so frequent a visitor at Mrs Wingrave's as during the months of his diffidence and irresolution, and poor Rosalind had less to suffer than she had feared from the sight of the mutual endearments of the young lovers. Touching his future sister-in-law Lloyd had a perfectly clear conscience. There had not been a particle of love-making between them, and he had not the slightest suspicion that he had dealt her a terrible blow. He was quite at his ease; life promised so well, both domestically and financially. The great revolt of the Colonies was not yet in the air, and that his connubial felicity should take a tragic turn it was absurd, it was blasphemous, to apprehend. Meanwhile, at Mrs Wingrave's, there was a greater rustling of silks, a more rapid clicking of scissors and flying of needles, than ever. The good lady had determined that her daughter should carry from home the genteelest outfit that her money could buy or that the country could furnish. All the sage women in the Province were convened, and their united taste was brought to bear on Perdita's wardrobe. Rosalind's situation, at this moment, was assuredly not to be envied. The poor girl had an inordinate love of dress, and the very best taste in the world, as her sister perfectly well knew. Rosalind was tall, she was stately and sweeping, she was made to carry stiff brocade and masses of heavy lace, such as belong to the toilet of a rich man's wife. But Rosalind sat aloof with her beautiful arms folded and her head averted, while her mother and sister and the venerable women aforesaid worried and wondered over their materials, oppressed by the multitude of their resources. One day there came in a beautiful piece of white silk, brocaded with heavenly blue and silver sent by the bridegroom himself – it not being thought amiss in those days that the husband-elect should contribute to the bride's trousseau. Perdita could think of no form or fashion which would do sufficient honor to the splendor of the material.

'Blue's your color, sister, more than mine,' she said, with appealing eyes. 'It's a pity it's not for you. You would know what to do with it.'

Rosalind got up from her place and looked at the great shining fabric, as it lay spread over the back of a chair. Then she took it up in her hands and felt it lovingly, as Perdita could see – and turned about towards the mirror with it. She let it roll down to her feet, and flung the other end over her shoulder, gathering it in about her waist with her white arm, which was bare to the elbow. She threw back her head, and looked at her image, and a hanging tress of her auburn hair fell upon the gorgeous surface of the silk. It made a dazzling picture. The women standing about uttered a little 'Look, look!' of admiration. 'Yes, indeed – ' said Rosalind, quietly, 'blue is my color.' But Perdita could see that her fancy had been stirred, and that she would now fall to work and solve all their silken riddles. And indeed she behaved very well, as Perdita, knowing her insatiable love of millinery, was quite ready to declare. Innumerable yards of lustrous silk and satin, of muslin, velvet and lace, passed through her cunning hands, without a jealous word coming from her lips. Thanks to her industry, when the wedding-day came Perdita was prepared to espouse more of the vanities of life than any fluttering young bride who had yet received the sacramental blessing of a New England divine.

It had been arranged that the young couple should go out and spend the first days of their wedded life at the country-house of an English gentleman – a man of rank and a very kind friend to Arthur Lloyd. He was a bachelor; he declared he should be delighted to give up the place to the influence of Hymen. After the ceremony at church – it had been performed by an English clergyman – young Mrs Lloyd hastened back to her mother's house to change her nuptial robes for a riding-dress. Rosalind helped her to effect the change, in the little homely room in which they had spent their undivided younger years. Perdita then hurried off to bid farewell to her mother, leaving Rosalind to follow. The parting was short; the horses were at the door, and Arthur was impatient to start. But Rosalind had not followed, and Perdita hastened back to her room, opening the door abruptly. Rosalind, as usual, was before the glass, but in a position which caused the other to stand still, amazed. She had dressed herself in Perdita's cast-off wedding veil and wreath, and on her neck she had hung the full string of pearls which the young girl had received from her husband as a wedding-gift. These things had been hastily laid aside, to await their possessor's disposal on her return from the country. Bedizened by this unnatural garb Rosalind stood before the mirror, plunging a long look into its depths and reading heaven knows what audacious visions. Perdita was horrified. It was a hideous image of their old rivalry come to life again. She made a step towards her sister, as if to pull off the veil and the flowers. But catching her eyes in the glass, she stopped.

'Farewell, sweetheart,' she said. 'You might at least have waited till I had got out of the house!' And she hurried away from the room.

Mr Lloyd had purchased in Boston a house which to the taste of those days appeared as elegant as it was commodious; and here he very soon established himself with his young wife. He was thus separated by a distance of twenty miles from the residence of his mother-in-law. Twenty miles, in that primitive era of roads and conveyances, were as serious a matter as a hundred at the present day, and Mrs Wingrave saw but little of her daughter during the first twelvemonth of her marriage. She suffered in no small degree from Perdita's absence; and her affliction was not diminished by the fact that Rosalind had fallen into terribly low spirits and was not to be roused or cheered but by change of air and company. The real cause of the young lady's dejection the reader will not be slow to suspect. Mrs Wingrave and her gossips, however, deemed her complaint a mere bodily ill, and doubted not that she would obtain relief from the remedy just mentioned. Her mother accordingly proposed, on her behalf, a visit to certain relatives on the paternal side, established in New York, who had long complained that they were able to see so little of their New England cousins. Rosalind was dispatched to these good people, under a suitable escort, and remained with them for several months. In the interval her brother Bernard, who had begun the practice of the law, made up his mind to take a wife. Rosalind came home to the wedding, apparently cured of her heartache, with bright roses and lilies in her face and a proud smile on her lips. Arthur Lloyd came over from Boston to see his brother-in-law married, but without his wife, who was expecting very soon to present him with an heir. It was nearly a year since Rosalind had seen him. She was glad – she hardly knew why – that Perdita had stayed at home. Arthur looked happy, but he was more grave and important than before his marriage. She thought he looked 'interesting' – for although the word, in its modern sense, was not then invented, we may be sure that the idea was. The truth is, he was simply anxious about his wife and her coming ordeal. Nevertheless, he by no means failed to observe Rosalind's beauty and splendor, and to note how she effaced the poor little bride. The allowance that Perdita had enjoyed for her dress had now been transferred to her sister, who turned it to wonderful account. On the morning after the wedding he had a lady's saddle put on the horse of the servant who had come with him from town, and went out with the young girl for a ride. It was a keen, clear morning in January; the ground was bare and hard, and the horses in good condition – to say nothing of Rosalind, who was charming in her hat and plume, and her dark blue riding coat, trimmed with fur. They rode all the morning, lost their way and were obliged to stop for dinner at a farm-house. The early winter dusk had fallen when they got home. Mrs Wingrave met them with a long face. A messenger had arrived at noon from Mrs Lloyd; she was beginning to be ill, she desired her husband's immediate return. The young man, at the thought that he had lost several hours, and that by hard riding he might already have been with his wife, uttered a passionate oath. He barely consented to stop for a mouthful of supper, but mounted the messenger's horse and started off at a gallop.

He reached home at midnight. His wife had been delivered of a little girl. 'Ah, why weren't you with me?' she said, as he came to her bedside.

'I was out of the house when the man came. I was with Rosalind,' said Lloyd, innocently.

Mrs Lloyd made a little moan, and turned away. But she continued to do very well, and for a week her improvement was uninterrupted. Finally, however, through some indiscretion in the way of diet or exposure, it was checked, and the poor lady grew rapidly worse. Lloyd was in despair. It very soon became evident that she was breathing her last. Mrs Lloyd came to a sense of her approaching end, and declared that she was reconciled with death. On the third evening after the change took place she told her husband that she felt she should not get through the night. She dismissed her servants, and also requested her mother to withdraw – Mrs Wingrave having arrived on the preceding day. She had had her infant placed on the bed beside her, and she lay on her side, with the child against her breast, holding her husband's hands. The night-lamp was hidden behind the heavy curtains of the bed, but the room was illumined with a red glow from the immense fire of logs on the hearth.

'It seems strange not to be warmed into life by such a fire as that,' the young woman said, feebly trying to smile. 'If I had but a little of it in my veins! But I have given all *my* fire to this little spark of mortality.' And she dropped her eyes on her child. Then raising them she looked at her husband with a long, penetrating gaze. The last feeling which lingered in her heart was one of suspicion. She had not recovered from the shock which Arthur had given her by telling her that in the hour of her agony he had been with Rosalind. She trusted her husband very nearly as well as she loved him; but now that she was called away for ever she felt a cold horror of her sister. She felt in her soul that Rosalind had never ceased to be jealous of her good fortune; and a year of happy security had not effaced the young girl's image, dressed in her wedding-garments, and smiling with simulated triumph. Now that Arthur was to be alone, what might not Rosalind attempt? She was beautiful, she was engaging; what arts might she not use, what impression might she not make upon the young man's saddened heart? Mrs Lloyd looked at her husband in silence. It seemed hard, after all, to doubt of his constancy. His fine eyes were filled with tears; his face was convulsed with weeping; the clasp of his hands was warm and passionate. How noble he looked, how tender, how faithful and devoted! 'Nay,' thought Perdita, 'he's not for such a one as Rosalind. He'll never forget me. Nor does Rosalind truly care for him; she cares only for vanities and finery and jewels.' And she lowered her eyes on her white hands, which her husband's liberality had covered with rings, and on the lace ruffles which trimmed the edge of her nightdress. 'She covets my rings and my laces more than she covets my husband.'

At this moment the thought of her sister's rapacity seemed to cast a dark shadow between her and the helpless figure of her little girl. 'Arthur,' she said, 'you must take off my rings. I shall not be buried in them. One of these days my daughter shall wear them – my rings and my laces and silks. I had them all brought out and shown me today. It's a great wardrobe – there's not such another in the Province; I can say it without vanity, now that I have done with it. It will be a great inheritance for my daughter when she grows into a young woman. There are things there that a man never buys twice, and if they are lost you will never again see the like. So you will watch them well. Some dozen things I have left to Rosalind; I have named them to my mother. I have given her that blue and silver; it was meant for her; I wore it only once, I looked ill in it. But the rest are to be sacredly kept for this little innocent. It's such a providence that she should be my color; she can wear my gowns; she has her mother's eyes. You know the same fashions come back every twenty years. She can wear my gowns as they are. They will lie there quietly waiting till she grows into them – wrapped in camphor and rose-leaves, and keeping their colors in the sweet-scented darkness. She shall have black hair, she shall wear my carnation satin. Do you promise me, Arthur?'

'Promise you what, dearest?'

'Promise me to keep your poor little wife's old gowns.'

'Are you afraid I shall sell them?'

'No, but that they may get scattered. My mother will have them properly wrapped up, and you shall lay them away under a double-lock. Do you know the great chest in the attic, with the iron bands? There is no end to what it will hold. You can put them all there. My mother and the housekeeper will do it, and give you the key. And you will keep the key in your secretary, and never give it to anyone but your child. Do you promise me?'

'Ah, yes, I promise you,' said Lloyd, puzzled at the intensity with which his wife appeared to cling to this idea.

'Will you swear?' repeated Perdita.

'Yes, I swear.'

'Well – I trust you – I trust you,' said the poor lady, looking into his eyes with eyes in which, if he had suspected her vague apprehensions, he might have read an appeal quite as much as an assurance.

Lloyd bore his bereavement rationally and manfully. A month after his wife's death, in the course of business, circumstances arose which offered him an opportunity of going to England. He took advantage of it, to change the current of his thoughts. He was absent nearly a year, during which his little girl was tenderly nursed and guarded by her grandmother. On his return he had his house again thrown open, and announced his intention of keeping the same state as during his wife's lifetime. It very soon came to be predicted that he would marry again, and there were at least a dozen young women of whom one may say that it was by no fault of theirs that, for six months after his return, the prediction did not come true. During this interval he still left his little daughter in Mrs Wingrave's hands, the latter assuring him that a change of residence at so tender an age would be full of danger for her health. Finally, however, he declared that his heart longed for his daughter's presence and that she must be brought up to town. He sent his coach and his housekeeper to fetch her home. Mrs Wingrave was in terror lest something should befall her on the road; and, in accordance with this feeling, Rosalind offered to accompany her. She could return the next day. So she went up to town with her little niece, and Mr Lloyd met her on the threshold of his house, overcome with her kindness and with paternal joy. Instead of returning the next day Rosalind stayed out the week; and when at last she reappeared, she had only come for her clothes. Arthur would not hear of her coming home, nor would the baby. That little person cried and choked if Rosalind left her; and at the sight of her grief Arthur lost his wits, and swore that she was going to die. In fine, nothing would suit them but that the aunt should remain until the little niece had grown used to strange faces.

It took two months to bring this consummation about; for it was not until this period had elapsed that Rosalind took leave of her brother-in-law. Mrs Wingrave had shaken her head over her daughter's absence; she had declared that it was not becoming, that it was the talk of the whole country. She had reconciled herself to it only because, during the girl's visit, the household enjoyed an unwonted term of peace. Bernard Wingrave had brought his wife home to live, between whom and her sister-in-law there was as little love as you plead. Rosalind was perhaps no angel; but in the daily practice of life she was a sufficiently good-natured girl, and if she quarrelled with Mrs Bernard, it was not without provocation. Quarrel, however, she did, to the great annoyance not only of her antagonist, but of the two spectators of these constant altercations. Her stay in the household of her brother-in-law, therefore, would have been delightful, if only because it removed her from contact with the object of her antipathy at home. It was doubly – it was ten times – delightful, in that it kept her near the object of her early passion. Mrs Lloyd's sharp suspicions had fallen very far short of the truth. Rosalind's sentiment had been a passion at first, and a passion it remained – a passion of whose radiant heat, tempered to the delicate state of his feelings, Mr Lloyd very soon felt the influence. Lloyd, as I have hinted, was not a modern Petrarch; it was not in his nature to practise an ideal constancy. He had not been many days in the house with his sister-in-law before he began to assure himself that she was, in the language of that day, a devilish fine woman. Whether Rosalind really practised those insidious arts that her sister had been tempted to impute to her it is needless to inquire. It is enough to say that she found means to appear to the very best advantage. She used to seat herself every morning before the big fireplace in the dining-room, at work upon a piece of tapestry, with her little niece disporting herself on the carpet at her feet, or on the train of her dress, and playing with her woollen balls. Lloyd would have been a very stupid fellow if he had remained insensible to the rich suggestions of this charming picture. He was exceedingly fond of his little girl, and was never weary of taking her in his arms and tossing her up and down, and making her crow with delight. Very often, however, he would venture upon greater liberties than the young lady was yet prepared to allow, and then she would suddenly vociferate her displeasure. Rosalind, at this, would drop her tapestry, and put out her handsome hands with the serious smile of the young girl whose virgin fancy has revealed to her all a mother's healing arts. Lloyd would give up the child, their eyes would meet, their hands would touch, and Rosalind would extinguish the little girl's sobs upon the snowy folds of the kerchief that crossed her bosom. Her dignity was perfect, and nothing could be more discreet than the manner in which she accepted her brother-in-law's hospitality. It may almost be said, perhaps, that there was something harsh in her reserve. Lloyd had a provoking feeling that she was in the house and yet was unapproachable. Half-an-hour after supper, at the very outset of the long winter evenings, she would light her candle, make the young man a most respectful curtsey, and march off to bed. If these were arts, Rosalind was a great artist. But their effect was so gentle, so gradual, they were calculated to work upon the young widower's fancy with a *crescendo* so finely shaded, that, as the reader has seen, several weeks elapsed before Rosalind began to feel sure that her returns would cover her outlay. When this became morally certain she packed up her trunk and returned to her mother's house. For three days she waited: on the fourth Mr Lloyd made his appearance – a respectful but pressing suitor. Rosalind heard him to the end, with great humility, and accepted him with infinite modesty. It is hard to imagine that Mrs Lloyd would have forgiven her husband: but if anything might have disarmed her resentment it would have been the ceremonious continence of this interview. Rosalind imposed upon her lover but a short probation. They were married, as was becoming, with great privacy – almost with secrecy – in the hope perhaps, as was waggishly remarked at the time, that the late Mrs Lloyd wouldn't hear of it.

The marriage was to all appearance a happy one, and each party obtained what each had desired – Lloyd 'a devilish fine woman', and Rosalind – but Rosalind's desires, as the reader will have observed, had remained a good deal of a mystery. There were, indeed, two blots upon their felicity, but time would perhaps efface them. During the first three years of her marriage Mrs Lloyd failed to become a mother, and her husband on his side suffered heavy losses of money. This latter circumstance compelled a material retrenchment in his expenditure, and Rosalind was perforce less of a fine lady than her sister had been. She contrived, however, to carry it like a woman of considerable fashion. She had long since ascertained that her sister's copious wardrobe had been sequestrated for the benefit of her daughter, and that it lay languishing in thankless gloom in the dusty attic. It was a revolting thought that these exquisite fabrics should await the good pleasure of a little girl who sat in a high chair and ate bread-and-milk with a wooden spoon. Rosalind had the good taste, however, to say nothing about the matter until several months had expired. Then, at last, she timidly broached it to her husband. Was it not a pity that so much finery should be lost? – for lost it would be, what with colors fading, and moths eating it up, and the change of fashions. But Lloyd gave her so abrupt and peremptory a refusal, that she saw, for the present, her attempt was vain. Six months went by, however, and brought with them new needs and new visions. Rosalind's thoughts hovered lovingly about her sister's relics. She went up and looked at the chest in which they lay imprisoned. There was a sullen defiance in its three great padlocks and its iron bands which only quickened her cupidity. There was something exasperating in its incorruptible immobility. It was like a grim and grizzled old household servant, who locks his jaws over a family secret. And then there was a look of capacity in its vast extent, and a sound as of dense fullness, when Rosalind knocked its side with the toe of her little shoe, which caused her to flush with baffled longing. 'It's absurd,' she cried; 'it's improper, it's wicked'; and she forthwith resolved upon another attack upon her husband. On the following day, after dinner, when he had had his wine, she boldly began it. But he cut her short with great sternness.

'Once for all, Rosalind,' said he, 'it's out of the question. I shall be gravely displeased if you return to the matter.'

'Very good,' said Rosalind. 'I am glad to learn the esteem in which I am held. Gracious heaven,' she cried, 'I am a very happy woman! It's an agreeable thing to feel one's self sacrificed to a caprice!' And her eyes filled with tears of anger and disappointment.

Lloyd had a good-natured man's horror of a woman's sobs, and he attempted – I may say he condescended – to explain. 'It's not a caprice, dear, it's a promise,' he said – 'an oath.'

'An oath? It's a pretty matter for oaths! and to whom, pray?'

'To Perdita,' said the young man, raising his eyes for an instant and immediately dropping them.

'Perdita – ah, Perdita!' and Rosalind's tears broke forth. Her bosom heaved with stormy sobs – sobs which were the long-deferred sequel of the violent fit of weeping in which she had indulged herself on the night when she discovered her sister's betrothal. She had hoped, in her better moments, that she had done with her jealousy, but her temper, on that occasion, had taken an ineffaceable hold. 'And pray, what right had Perdita to dispose of my future?' she cried. 'What right had she to bind you to meanness and cruelty? Ah, I occupy a dignified place, and I make a very fine figure! I am welcome to what Perdita has left! And what has she left? I never knew till now how little! Nothing, nothing, nothing.'

This was very poor logic, but it was very good as a 'scene'. Lloyd put his arm around his wife's waist and tried to kiss her, but she shook him off with magnificent scorn. Poor fellow! he had coveted a 'devilish fine woman, and he had got one. Her scorn was intolerable. He walked away with his ears tingling – irresolute, distracted. Before him was his secretary, and in it the sacred key which with his own hand he had turned in the triple lock. He marched up and opened it, and took the key from a secret drawer, wrapped in a little packet which he had sealed with his own honest bit of glazonry. *Je garde,* said the motto – 'I keep.' But he was ashamed to put it back. He flung it upon the table beside his wife.

'Put it back!' she cried. 'I want it not. I hate it!'

'I wash my hands of it,' cried her husband. 'God forgive me!'

Mrs Lloyd gave an indignant shrug of her shoulders, and swept out of the room, while the young man retreated by another door. Ten minutes later Mrs Lloyd returned, and found the room occupied by her little step-daughter and the nursery-maid. The key was not on the table. She glanced at the child. Her little niece was perched on a chair, with the packet in her hands. She had broken the seal with her own small fingers. Mrs Lloyd hastily took possession of the key.

At the habitual supper-hour Arthur Lloyd came back from his counting-room. It was the month of June, and supper was served by daylight. The meal was placed on the table, but Mrs Lloyd failed to make her appearance. The servant whom his master sent to call her came back with the assurance that her room was empty, and that the women informed him that she had not been seen since dinner. They had, in truth, observed her to have been in tears, and, supposing her to be shut up in her chamber, had not disturbed her. Her husband called her name in various parts of the house, but without response. At last it occurred to him that he might find her by taking the way to the attic. The thought gave him a strange feeling of discomfort, and he bade his servants remain behind, wishing no witness in his quest. He reached the foot of the staircase leading to the topmost flat, and stood with his hand on the banisters, pronouncing his wife's name. His voice trembled. He called again louder and more firmly. The only sound which disturbed the absolute silence was a faint echo of his own tones, repeating his question under the great eaves. He nevertheless felt irresistibly moved to ascend the staircase. It opened upon a wide hall, lined with wooden closets, and terminating in a window which looked westward, and admitted the last rays of the sun. Before the window stood the great chest. Before the chest, on her knees, the young man saw with amazement and horror the figure of his wife. In an instant he crossed the interval between them, bereft of utterance. The lid of the chest stood open, exposing, amid their perfumed napkins, its treasure of stuffs and jewels. Rosalind had fallen backward from a kneeling posture, with one hand supporting her on the floor and the other pressed to her heart. On her limbs was the stiffness of death, and on her face, in the fading light of the sun, the terror of something more than death. Her lips were parted in entreaty, in dismay, in agony; and on her blanched brow and cheeks there glowed the marks of ten hideous wounds from two vengeful ghostly hands.

Ken's Mystery

JULIAN HAWTHORNE

One cool October evening – it was the last day of the month, and unusually cool for the time of year – I made up my mind to go and spend an hour or two with my friend Keningale. Keningale was an artist (as well as a musical amateur and poet), and had a very delightful studio built onto his house, in which he was wont to sit of an evening. The studio had a cavernous fireplace, designed in imitation of the old-fashioned fireplaces of Elizabethan manor-houses, and in it, when the temperature out-doors warranted, he would build up a cheerful fire of dry logs. It would suit me particularly well, I thought, to go and have a quiet pipe and chat in front of that fire with my friend.

I had not had such a chat for a very long time – not, in fact, since Keningale (or Ken, as his friends called him) had returned from his visit to Europe the year before. He went abroad, as he affirmed at the time, 'for purposes of study', whereat we all smiled, for Ken, so far as we knew him, was more likely to do anything else than to study. He was a young fellow of buoyant temperament, lively and social in his habits, of a brilliant and versatile mind, and possessing an income of twelve or fifteen thousand dollars a year; he could sing, play, scribble, and paint very cleverly, and some of his heads and figure-pieces were really well done. considering that he never had any regular training in art; but he was not a worker. Personally he was fine-looking, of good height and figure, active, healthy, and with a remarkably fine brow, and clear, full-gazing eye. Nobody was surprised at his going to Europe, nobody expected him to do anything there except amuse himself, and few anticipated that he would be soon again seen in New York. He was one of the sort that find Europe agrees with them. Off he went, therefore; and in the course of a few months the rumor reached us that he was engaged to a handsome and wealthy New York girl whom he had met in London. This was nearly all we did hear of him until, not very long afterward, he turned up again on Fifth Avenue, to everyone's astonishment; made no satisfactory answer to those who wanted to know how he happened to tire so soon of the Old World; while, as to the reported engagement, he cut short all allusion to that in so peremptory a manner as to show that it was not a permissible topic of conversation with him. It was surmised that the lady had jilted him; but on the other hand, she herself returned home not a great while after, and, though she had plenty of opportunities, she has never married to this day.

Be the rights of that matter what they may, it was soon remarked that Ken was no longer the careless and merry fellow he used to be; on the contrary, he appeared grave, moody, averse from general society, and habitually taciturn and undemonstrative even in the company of his most intimate friends. Evidently something had happened to him, or he had done something. What? Had he committed a murder? or joined the Nihilists? or was his unsuccessful love affair at the bottom of it? Some declared that the cloud was only temporary, and would soon pass away. Nevertheless, up to the period of which I am writing, it had not passed away, but had rather gathered additional gloom, and threatened to become permanent.

Meanwhile I had met him twice or thrice at the club, at the opera, or in the street, but had as yet had no opportunity of regularly renewing my acquaintance with him. We had been on a footing of more than common intimacy in the old days, and I was not disposed to think that he would refuse to renew the former relations now. But what I had heard and myself seen of his changed condition imparted a stimulating tinge of suspense or curiosity to the pleasure with which I looked forward to the prospects of this evening. His house stood at a distance of two or three miles beyond the general range of habitations in New York at this time, and as I walked briskly along in the clear twilight air I had leisure to go over in my mind all that I had known of Ken and had divined of his character. After all, had there not always been something in his nature – deep down, and held in abeyance by the activity of his animal spirits – but something strange and separate, and capable of developing under suitable conditions into – into what? As I asked myself this question I arrived at his door; and it was with a feeling of relief that I felt the next moment the cordial grasp of his hand, and his voice bidding me welcome in a tone that indicated unaffected gratification at my presence. He drew me at once into the studio, relieved me of my hat and cane, and then put his hand on my shoulder.

'I am glad to see you,' he repeated, with singular earnestness – glad to see you and to feel you; and tonight of all nights in the year.'

'Why tonight especially?'

'Oh, never mind. It's just as well, too, you didn't let me know beforehand you were coming; the unreadiness is all, to paraphrase the poet. Now, with you to help me, I can drink a glass of whisky and water and take a bit draw of the pipe. This would have been a grim night for me if I'd been left to myself.'

'In such a lap of luxury as this, too!' said I, looking round at the glowing fireplace, the low, luxurious chairs, and all the rich and sumptuous fittings of the room. 'I should have thought a condemned murderer might make himself comfortable here.'

'Perhaps; but that's not exactly my category at present. But have you forgotten what night this is? This is November-eve, when, as tradition asserts, the dead arise and walk about, and fairies, goblins, and spiritual beings of all kinds have more freedom and power than on any other day of the year. One can see you've never been in Ireland.'

'I wasn't aware till now that you had been there, either.'

'Yes, I have been in Ireland. Yes – ' He paused, sighed, and fell into a reverie, from which, however, he soon roused himself by an effort, and went to a cabinet in a corner of the room for the liquor and tobacco. While he was thus employed I sauntered about the studio, taking note of the various beauties, grotesquenesses, and curiosities that it contained. Many things were there to repay study and arouse admiration; for Ken was a good collector, having excellent taste as well as means to back it. But, upon the whole, nothing interested me more than some studies of a female head, roughly done in oils, and, judging from the sequestered positions in which I found them, not intended by the artist for exhibition or criticism. There were three or four of these studies, all of the same face, but in different poses and costumes. In one the head was enveloped in a dark hood, overshadowing and partly concealing the features; in another she seemed to be peering duskily through a latticed casement, lit by a faint moonlight; a third showed her splendidly attired in evening costume, and jewels in her hair and ears, and sparkling on her snowy bosom. The expressions were as various as the poses; now it was demure penetration, now a subtle inviting glance, now burning passion, and again a look of elfish and elusive mockery. In whatever phase, the countenance possessed a singular and poignant fascination, not of beauty merely, though that was very striking, but of character and quality likewise.

'Did you find this model abroad?' I inquired at length. 'She has evidently inspired you, and I don't wonder at it.'

Ken, who had been mixing the punch, and had not noticed my movements, now looked up, and said: 'I didn't mean those to be seen. They don't satisfy me, and I am going to destroy them; but I couldn't rest till I'd made some attempts to reproduce – What was it you asked? Abroad? Yes – or no. They were all painted here within the last six weeks.'

'Whether they satisfy you or not, they are by far the best things of yours I have ever seen.'

'Well, let them alone, and tell me what you think of this beverage. To my thinking, it goes to the right spot. It owes its existence to your coming here. I can't drink alone, and those portraits are not company, though, for aught I know, she might have come out of the canvas tonight and sat down in that chair.' Then, seeing my inquiring look, he added, with a hasty laugh, 'It's November-eve, you know, when anything may happen, provided it's strange enough. Well, here's to ourselves.'

We each swallowed a deep draught of the smoking and aromatic liquor, and set down our glasses with approval. The punch was excellent. Ken now opened a box of cigars, and we seated ourselves before the fireplace.

'All we need now,' I remarked, after a short silence, 'is a little music. By-the-by, Ken, have you still got the banjo I gave you before you went abroad?'

He paused so long before replying that I supposed he had not heard my question. 'I have got it,' he said, at length, 'but it will never make any more music.'

'Got broken, eh? Can't it be mended? It was a fine instrument.'

'It's not broken, but it's past mending. You shall see for yourself.'

He arose as he spoke, and going to another part of the studio, opened a black oak coffer, and took out of it a long object wrapped up in a piece of faded yellow silk. He handed it to me, and when I had unwrapped it, there appeared a thing that might once have been a banjo, but had little resemblance to one now. It bore every sign of extreme age. The wood of the handle was honeycombed with the gnawings of worms, and dusty with dry-rot. The parchment head was green with mould, and hung in shrivelled tatters. The hoop, which was of solid silver, was so blackened and tarnished that it looked like dilapidated iron. The strings were gone, and most of the tuning-screws had dropped out of their decayed sockets. Altogether it had the appearance of having been made before the Flood, and been forgotten in the forecastle of Noah's Ark ever since.

'It is a curious relic, certainly,' I said. 'Where did you come across it? I had no idea that the banjo was invented so long ago as this. It certainly can't be less than two hundred years old, and may be much older than that.'

Ken smiled gloomily. 'You are quite right,' he said; 'it is at least two hundred years old, and yet it is the very same banjo that you gave me a year ago.'

'Hardly,' I returned, smiling in my turn, 'since that was made to my order with a view to presenting it to you.'

'I know that; but the two hundred years have passed since then. Yes: it is absurd and impossible, I know, but nothing is truer. That banjo, which was made last year, existed in the sixteenth century, and has been rotting ever since. Stay. Give it to me a moment, and I'll convince you. You recollect that your name and mine, with the date, were engraved on the silver hoop?'

'Yes; and there was a private mark of my own there, also.'

'Very well,' said Ken, who had been rubbing a place on the hoop with a corner of the yellow silk wrapper; 'look at that.'

I took the decrepit instrument from him, and examined the spot which he had rubbed. It was incredible, sure enough; but there were the names and the date precisely as I had caused them to be engraved; and there, moreover, was my own private mark, which I had idly made with an old etching point not more than eighteen months before. After convincing myself that there was no mistake, I laid the banjo across my knees, and stared at my friend in bewilderment. He sat smoking with a kind of grim composure, his eyes fixed upon the blazing logs.

'I'm mystified, I confess,' said I. 'Come; what is the joke? What method have you discovered of producing the decay of centuries on this unfortunate banjo in a few months? And why did you do it? I have heard of an elixir to counteract the effects of time, but your recipe seems to work the other way – to make time rush forward at two hundred times his usual rate, in one place, while he jogs on at his usual gait elsewhere. Unfold your mystery, magician. Seriously, Ken, how on earth did the thing happen?'

'I know no more about it than you do,' was his reply. 'Either you and I and all the rest of the living world are insane, or else there has been wrought a miracle as strange as any in tradition. How can I explain it? It is a common saying – a common experience, if you will – that we may, on certain trying or tremendous occasions, live years in one moment. But that's a mental experience, not a physical one, and one that applies, at all events, only to human beings, not to senseless things of wood and metal. You imagine the thing is some trick or jugglery. If it be, I don't know the secret of it. There's no chemical appliance that I ever heard of that will get a piece of solid wood into that condition in a few months, or a few years. And it wasn't done in a few years, or a few months either. A year ago today at this very hour that banjo was as sound as when it left the maker's hands, and twenty-four hours afterward – I'm telling you the simple truth – it was as you see it now.'

The gravity and earnestness with which Ken made this astounding statement were evidently not assumed. He believed every word that he uttered. I knew not what to think. Of course my friend might be insane, though he betrayed none of the ordinary symptoms of mania; but, however that might be, there was the banjo, a witness whose silent testimony there was no gainsaying. The more I meditated on the matter the more inconceivable did it appear. Two hundred years – twenty-four hours; these were the terms of the proposed equation. Ken and the banjo both affirmed that the equation had been made; all worldly knowledge and experience affirmed it to be impossible. What was the explanation? What is time? What is life? I felt myself beginning to doubt the reality of all things. And so this was the mystery which my friend had been brooding over since his return from abroad. No wonder it had changed him. More to be wondered at was it that it had not changed him more.

'Can you tell me the whole story?' I demanded at length.

Ken quaffed another draught from his glass of whisky and water and rubbed his hand through his thick brown beard. 'I have never spoken to anyone of it heretofore,' he said, 'and I had never meant to speak of it. But I'll try and give you some idea of what it was. You know me better than anyone else; you'll understand the thing as far as it can ever be understood, and perhaps I may be relieved of some of the oppression it has caused me. For it is rather a ghastly memory to grapple with alone, I can tell you.'

Hereupon, without further preface, Ken related the following tale. He was, I may observe in passing, a naturally fine narrator. There were deep, lingering tones in his voice, and he could strikingly enhance the comic or pathetic effect of a sentence by dwelling here and there upon some syllable. His features were equally susceptible of humorous and of solemn expressions, and his eyes were in form and hue wonderfully adapted to showing great varieties of emotion. Their mournful aspect was extremely earnest and affecting; and when Ken was giving utterance to some mysterious passage of the tale they had a doubtful, melancholy, exploring look which appealed irresistibly to the imagination. But the interest of his story was too pressing to allow of noticing these incidental embellishments at the time, though they doubtless had their influence upon me all the same.

'I left New York on an Inman Line steamer, you remember,' began Ken, 'and landed at Havre. I went the usual round of sight-seeing on the Continent, and got round to London in July, at the height of the season. I had good introductions, and met any number of agreeable and famous people. Among others was a young lady, a countrywoman of my own – you know whom I mean – who interested me very much, and before her family left London she and I were engaged. We parted there for the time, because she had the Continental trip still to make, while I wanted to take the opportunity to visit the north of England and Ireland. I landed at Dublin about the 1st of October, and, zigzagging about the country, I found myself in County Cork about two weeks later.

'There is in that region some of the most lovely scenery that human eyes ever rested on, and it seems to be less known to tourists than many places of infinitely less picturesque value. A lonely region too: during my rambles I met not a single stranger like myself and few enough natives. It seems incredible that so beautiful a country should be so deserted. After walking a dozen Irish miles you come across a group of two or three one-roomed cottages, and, like as not, one or more of those will have the roof off and the walls in ruins. The few peasants whom one sees, however, are affable and hospitable, especially when they hear you are from that terrestrial heaven whither most of their friends and relatives have gone before them. They seem simple and primitive enough at first sight, and yet they are as strange and incomprehensible a race as any in the world. They are as superstitious, as credulous of marvels, fairies, magicians, and omens, as the men whom St Patrick preached to, and at the same time they are shrewd, sceptical, sensible, and bottomless liars. Upon the whole, I met with no nation on my travels whose company I enjoyed so much, or who inspired me with so much kindliness, curiosity, and repugnance.

'At length I got to a place on the sea-coast, which I will not further specify than to say that it is not many miles from Ballymacheen, on the south shore. I have seen Venice and Naples, I have driven along the Cornice Road, I have spent a month at our own Mount Desert, and say that all of them together are not so beautiful as this glowing, deep-hued, soft-gleaming, silvery-lighted, ancient harbor and town, with the tall hills crowding round it and the black cliffs and headlands planting their iron feet in the blue, transparent sea. It is a very old place, and has had a history which it has outlived ages since. It may once have had two or three thousand inhabitants; it has scarce five or six hundred today. Half the houses are in ruins or have disappeared; many of the remainder are standing empty. All the people are poor, most of them abjectly so; they saunter about with bare feet and uncovered heads, the women in quaint black or dark-blue cloaks, the men in such anomalous attire as only an Irishman knows how to get together, the children half naked. The only comfortable-looking people are the monks and the priests, and the soldiers in the fort. For there is a fort there, constructed on the huge ruins of one which may have done duty in the reign of Edward the Black Prince, or earlier, in whose mossy embrasures are mounted a couple of cannon, which occasionally sent a practice-shot or two at the cliff on the other side of the harbor. The garrison consists of a dozen men and three or four officers and non-commissioned officers. suppose they are relieved occasionally, but those I saw seemed to have become component parts of their surroundings.

'I put up at a wonderful little old inn, the only one in the place, and took my meals in a dining-saloon fifteen feet by nine, with a portrait of George I (a print varnished to preserve it) hanging over the mantelpiece. On the second evening after dinner a young gentleman came in – the dining-saloon being public property of course – and ordered some bread and cheese and a bottle of Dublin stout. We presently fell into talk; he turned out to be an officer from the fort, Lieutenant O'Connor, and a fine young specimen of the Irish soldier he was. After telling me all he knew about the town, the surrounding country, his friends, and himself, he intimated a readiness to sympathize with whatever tale I might choose to pour into his ear; and I had pleasure in trying to rival his own outspokenness. We became excellent friends; we had up a half-pint of Kinahan's whisky, and the lieutenant expressed himself in terms of high praise of my countrymen, my country, and my own particular cigars. When it became time for him to depart I accompanied him – for there was a splendid moon abroad – and bade him farewell at the fort entrance, having promised to come over the next day and make the acquaintance of the other fellows. "And mind your eye, now, going back, my dear boy," he called out, as I turned my face homeward. "Faith, 'tis a spooky place, that graveyard, and you'll as likely meet the black woman there as anywhere else!"

'The graveyard was a forlorn and barren spot on the hillside, just the hither side of the fort: thirty or forty rough headstones, few of which retained any semblance of the perpendicular, while many were so shattered and decayed as to seem nothing more than irregular natural projections from the ground. Who the black woman might be I knew not, and did not stay to inquire. I had never been subject to ghostly apprehensions, and as a matter of fact, though the path I had to follow was in places very bad going, not to mention a haphazard scramble over a ruined bridge that covered a deep-lying brook, I reached my inn without any adventure whatever.

'The next day I kept my appointment at the fort, and found no reason to regret it; and my friendly sentiments were abundantly reciprocated, thanks more especially, perhaps, to the success of my banjo, which I carried with me, and which was as novel as it was popular with those who listened to it. The chief personages in the social circle besides my friend the lieutenant were Major Molloy, who was in command, a racy and juicy old campaigner, with a face like a sunset, and the surgeon, Dr Dudeen, a long, dry, humorous genius, with a wealth of anecdotical and traditional lore at his command that I have never seen surpassed. We had a jolly time of it, and it was the precursor of many more like it. The remains of October slipped away rapidly, and I was obliged to remember that I was a traveler in Europe, and not a resident in Ireland. The major, the surgeon, and the lieutenant all protested cordially against my proposed departure, but, as there was no help for it, they arranged a farewell dinner to take place in the fort on All-halloween.

'I wish you could have been at that dinner with me! It was the essence of Irish good-fellowship. Dr Dudeen was in great force; the major was better than the best of Lever's novels; the lieutenant was overflowing with hearty good-humor, merry chaff, and sentimental rhapsodies anent this or the other pretty girl of the neighborhood. For my part I made the banjo ring as it had never rung before, and the others joined in the chorus with a mellow strength of lungs such as you don't often hear outside of Ireland. Among the stories that Dr Dudeen regaled us with was one about the Kern of Querin and his wife, Ethelind Fionguala – which being interpreted signifies "the white-shouldered". The lady, it appears, was originally betrothed to one O'Connor (here the lieutenant smacked his lips), but was stolen away on the wedding night by a party of vampires, who, it would seem, were at that period a prominent feature among the troubles of Ireland. But as they were bearing her along – she being unconscious – to that supper where she was not to eat but to be eaten, the young Kern of Querin, who happened to be out duck-shooting, met the party, and emptied his gun at it. The vampires fled, and the Kern carried the fair lady, still in a state of insensibility, to his house. "And by the same token, Mr Keningale," observed the doctor, knocking the ashes out of his pipe, "ye're after passing that very house on your way here. The one with the dark archway underneath it, and the big mullioned window at the corner, ye recollect, hanging over the street as I might say – "

' "Go 'long wid the house, Dr Dudeen, dear," interrupted the lieutenant; "sure can't you see we're all dying to know what happened to sweet Miss Fionguala, God be good to her, when I was after getting her safe upstairs – "

' "Faith, then, I can tell ye that myself, Mr O'Connor," exclaimed the major, imparting a rotary motion to the remnants of whisky in his tumbler. "'Tis a question to be solved on general principles, as Colonel O'Halloran said that time he was asked what he'd do if he'd been the Dook o' Wellington, and the Prussions hadn't come up in the nick o' time at Waterloo. 'Faith,' says the colonel, 'I'll tell ye – '

' "Arrah, then, major, why would ye be interruptin' the doctor, and Mr Keningale there lettin' his glass stay empty till he hears – The Lord save us! the bottle's empty!"

'In the excitement consequent upon this discovery, the thread of the doctor's story was lost; and before it could be recovered the evening had advanced so far that I felt obliged to withdraw. It took some time to make my proposition heard and comprehended; and a still longer time to put it in execution; so that it was fully midnight before I found myself standing in the cool pure air outside the fort, with the farewells of my boon companions ringing in my ears.

'Considering that it had been rather a wet evening indoors, I was in a remarkably good state of preservation, and I therefore ascribed it rather to the roughness of the road than to the smoothness of the liquor, when, after advancing a few rods, I stumbled and fell. As I picked myself up I fancied I had heard a laugh, and supposed that the lieutenant, who had accompanied me to the gate, was making merry over my mishap; but on looking round I saw that the gate was closed and no one was visible. The laugh, moreover, had seemed to be close at hand, and to be even pitched in a key that was rather feminine than masculine. Of course I must have been deceived; nobody was near me: my imagination had played me a trick, or else there was more truth than poetry in the tradition that Halloween is the carnival-time of disembodied spirits. It did not occur to me at the time that a stumble is held by the superstitious Irish to be an evil omen, and had I remembered it it would only have been to laugh at it. At all events, I was physically none the worse for my fall, and I resumed my way immediately.

'But the path was singularly difficult to find, or rather the path I was following did not seem to be the right one. I did not recognize it; I could have sworn (except I knew the contrary) that I had never seen it before. The moon had risen, though her light was as yet obscured by clouds, but neither my immediate surroundings nor the general aspect of the region appeared familiar. Dark, silent hill-sides mounted up on either hand, and the road, for the most part, plunged downward, as if to conduct me into the bowels of the earth. The place was alive with strange echoes, so that at times I seemed to be walking through the midst of muttering voices and mysterious whispers, and a wild, faint sound of laughter seemed ever and anon to reverberate among the passes of the hills. Currents of colder air sighing up through narrow defiles and dark crevices touched my face as with airy fingers. A certain feeling of anxiety and insecurity began to take possession of me, though there was no definable cause for it, unless that I might be belated in getting home. With the perverse instinct of those who are lost I hastened my steps, but was impelled now and then to glance back over my shoulder, with a sensation of being pursued. But no living creature was in sight. The moon, however, had now risen higher, and the clouds that were drifting slowly across the sky flung into the naked valley dusky shadows, which occasionally assumed shapes that looked like the vague semblance of gigantic human forms.

'How long I had been hurrying onward I know not, when, with a kind of suddenness, I found myself approaching a graveyard. It was situated on the spur of a hill, and there was no fence around it, nor anything to protect it from the incursions of passers-by. There was something in the general appearance of this spot that made me half fancy I had seen it before; and I should have taken it to be the same that I had often noticed on my way to the fort, but that the latter was only a few hundred yards distant therefrom, whereas I must have traversed several miles at least. As I drew near, moreover, I observed that the headstones did not appear so ancient and decayed as those of the other. But what chiefly attracted my attention was the figure that was leaning or half sitting upon one of the largest of the upright slabs near the road. It was a female figure draped in black, and a closer inspection – for was soon within a few yards of her – showed that she wore the calla, or long hooded cloak, the most common as well as the most ancient garment of Irish women, and doubtless of Spanish origin.

'I was a trifle startled by this apparition, so unexpected as it was, and so strange did it seem that any human creature should be at that hour of the night in so desolate and sinister a place. Involuntarily I paused as I came opposite her, and gazed at her intently. But the moonlight fell behind her, and the deep hood of her cloak so completely shadowed her face that I was unable to discern anything but the sparkle of a pair of eyes, which appeared to be returning my gaze with much vivacity.

' "You seem to be at home here," I said, at length. "Can you tell me where I am?"

'Hereupon the mysterious personage broke into a light laugh, which, though in itself musical and agreeable, was of a timbre and intonation that caused my heart to beat rather faster than my late pedestrian exertions warranted; for it was the identical laugh (or so my imagination persuaded me) that had echoed in my ears as I arose from my tumble an hour or two ago. For the rest, it was the laugh of a young woman, and presumably of a pretty one; and yet it had a wild, airy, mocking quality, that seemed hardly human at all, or not, at any rate, characteristic of a being of affections and limitations like unto ours. But this impression of mine was fostered, no doubt, by the unusual and uncanny circumstances of the occasion.

' "Sure, sir," said she, "you're at the grave of Ethelind Fionguala."

'As she spoke she rose to her feet, and pointed to the inscription on the stone. I bent forward, and was able, without much difficulty, to decipher the name, and a date which indicated that the occupant of the grave must have entered the disembodied state between two and three centuries ago.

' "And who are you?" was my next question.

' "I'm called Elsie," she replied. "But where would your honor be going November-eve?"

'I mentioned my destination, and asked her whether she could direct me thither.

' "Indeed, then, 'tis there I'm going myself," Elsie replied; "and if your honor'll follow me, and play me a tune on the pretty instrument, 'tisn't long we'll be on the road."

'She pointed to the banjo which I carried wrapped up under my arm. How she knew that it was a musical instrument I could not imagine; possibly, I thought, she may have seen me playing on it as I strolled about the environs of the town. Be that as it may, I offered no opposition to the bargain, and further intimated that I would reward her more substantially on our arrival. At that she laughed again, and made a peculiar gesture with her hand above her head. I uncovered my banjo, swept my fingers across the strings, and struck into a fantastic dance-measure, to the music of which we proceeded along the path, Elsie slightly in advance, her feet keeping time to the airy measure. In fact, she trod so lightly, with an elastic, undulating movement, that with a little more it seemed as if she might float onward like a spirit. The extreme whiteness of her feet attracted my eye, and I was surprised to find that instead of being bare, as I had supposed, these were incased in white satin slippers quaintly embroidered with gold thread.

' "Elsie," said I, lengthening my steps so as to come up with her, "where do you live, and what do you do for a living?"

' "Sure, I live by myself," she answered; "and if you'd be after knowing how, you must come and see for yourself."

' "Are you in the habit of walking over the hills at night in shoes like that?"

' "And why would I not?" she asked, in her turn. "And where did your honor get the pretty gold ring on your finger?"

'The ring, which was of no great intrinsic value, had struck my eye in an old curiosity-shop in Cork. It was an antique of very old-fashioned design, and might have belonged (as the vendor assured me was the case) to one of the early kings or queens of Ireland.

' "Do you like it?" said I.

' "Will your honor be after making a present of it to Elsie?" she returned, with an insinuating tone and turn of the head.

' "Maybe I will, Elsie, on one condition. I am an artist; I make pictures of people. If you will promise to come to my studio and let me paint your portrait, I'll give you the ring, and some money besides."

' "And will you give me the ring now?" said Elsie.

' "Yes, if you'll promise."

' "And will you play the music to me?" she continued.

' "As much as you like."

' "But maybe I'll not be handsome enough for ye,' said she, with a glance of her eyes beneath the dark hood.

' "I'll take the risk of that," I answered, laughing, "though, all the same, I don't mind taking a peep beforehand to remember you by." So saying, I put forth a hand to draw back the concealing hood. But Elsie eluded me, I scarce know how, and laughed a third time, with the same airy, mocking cadence.

' "Give me the ring first, and then you shall see me," she said, coaxingly.

' "Stretch out your hand, then," returned I, removing the ring from my finger. "When we are better acquainted, Elsie, you won't be so suspicious."

'She held out a slender, delicate hand, on the forefinger of which I slipped the ring. As I did so, the folds of her cloak fell a little apart, affording me a glimpse of a white shoulder and of a dress that seemed in that deceptive semi-darkness to be wrought of rich and costly material; and I caught, to, or so I fancied, the frosty sparkle of precious stones.

' "Arrah, mind where ye tread!" said Elsie, in a sudden, sharp tone.

'I looked round, and became aware for the first time that we were standing near the middle of a ruined bridge which spanned a rapid stream that flowed at a considerable depth below. The parapet of the bridge on one side was broken down, and I must have been, in fact, in imminent danger of stepping over into empty air. I made my way cautiously across the decaying structure; but, when I turned to assist Elsie, she was nowhere to be seen.

'What had become of the girl? I called, but no answer came. I gazed about on every side, but no trace of her was visible. Unless she had plunged into the narrow abyss at my feet, there was no place where she could have concealed herself – none at least that I could discover. She had vanished, nevertheless; and since her disappearance must have been premeditated, I finally came to the conclusion that it was useless to attempt to find her. She would present herself again in her own good time, or not at all. She had given me the slip very cleverly, and I must make the best of it. The adventure was perhaps worth the ring.

'On resuming my way, I was not a little relieved to find that I once more knew where I was. The bridge that I had just crossed was none other than the one I mentioned some time back; I was within a mile of the town, and my way lay clear before me. The moon, moreover, had now quite dispersed the clouds, and shone down with exquisite brilliance. Whatever her other failings, Elsie had been a trustworthy guide; she had brought me out of the depth of elf-land into the material world again. It had been a singular adventure, certainly; and I mused over it with a sense of mysterious pleasure as I sauntered along, humming snatches of airs, and accompanying myself on the strings. Hark! what light step was that behind me? It sounded like Elsie's; but no, Elsie was not there. The same impression or hallucination, however, recurred several times before I reached the outskirts of the town – the tread of an airy foot behind or beside my own. The fancy did not make me nervous; on the contrary, I was pleased with the notion of being thus haunted, and gave myself up to a romantic and genial vein of reverie.

'After passing one or two roofless and moss-grown cottages, I entered the narrow and rambling street which leads through the town. This street a short distance down widens a little, as if to afford the wayfarer space to observe a remarkable old house that stands on the northern side. The house was built of stone, and in a noble style of architecture; it reminded me somewhat of certain palaces of the old Italian nobility that I had seen on the Continent, and it may very probably have been built by one of the Italian or Spanish immigrants of the sixteenth or seventeenth century. The moulding of the projecting windows and arched doorway was richly carved, and upon the front of the building was an escutcheon wrought in high relief, though I could not make out the purport of the device. The moonlight falling upon this picturesque pile enhanced all its beauties, and at the same time made it seem like a vision that might dissolve away when the light ceased to shine. I must often have seen the house before, and yet I retained no definite recollection of it; I had never until now examined it with my eyes open, so to speak. Leaning against the wall on the opposite side of the street, I contemplated it for a long while at my leisure. The window at the corner was really a very fine and massive affair. It projected over the pavement below, throwing a heavy shadow aslant; the frames of the diamond-paned lattices were heavily mullioned. How often in past ages had that lattice been pushed open by some fair hand, revealing to a lover waiting beneath in the moonlight the charming countenance of his high-born mistress! Those were brave days. They had passed away long since. The great house had stood empty for who could tell how many years; only bats and vermin were its inhabitants. Where now were those who had built it? and who were they? Probably the very name of them was forgotten.

'As I continued to stare upward, however, a conjecture presented itself to my mind which rapidly ripened into a conviction. Was not this the house that Dr Dudeen had described that very evening as having been formerly the abode of the Kern of Querin and his mysterious bride? There was the projecting window, the arched doorway. Yes, beyond a doubt this was the very house. I emitted a low exclamation of renewed interest and pleasure, and my speculations took a still more imaginative, but also a more definite turn.

'What had been the fate of that lovely lady after the Kern had brought her home insensible in his arms? Did she recover, and were they married and made happy ever after; or had the sequel been a tragic one? I remembered to have read that the victims of vampires generally became vampires themselves. Then my thoughts went back to that grave on the hillside. Surely that was unconsecrated ground. Why had they buried her there? Ethelind of the white shoulder! Ah! why had not I lived in those days; or why might not some magic cause them to live again for me? Then would I seek this street at midnight, and standing here beneath her window, I would lightly touch the strings of my bandore until the casement opened cautiously and she looked down. A sweet vision indeed! And what prevented my realizing it? Only a matter of a couple of centuries or so. And was time, then, at which poets and philosophers sneer, so rigid and real a matter that a little faith and imagination might not overcome it? At all events, I had my banjo, the bandore's legitimate and lineal descendant, and the memory of Fionguala should have the love-ditty.

'Hereupon, having retuned the instrument, I launched forth into an old Spanish love-song, which I had met with in some mouldy library during my travels, and had set to music of my own. I sang low, for the deserted street re-echoed the lightest sound, and what I sang must reach only my lady's ears. The words were warm with the fire of the ancient Spanish chivalry, and I threw into their expression all the passion of the lovers of romance. Surely Fionguala, the white-shouldered, would hear, and awaken from her sleep of centuries, and come to the latticed casement and look down! Hist! see yonder! What light – what shadow is that that seems to flit from room to room within the abandoned house, and now approaches the mullioned window? Are my eyes dazzled by the play of the moonlight, or does the casement move – does it open! Nay, this is no delusion; there is no error of the senses here. There is simply a woman, young, beautiful, and richly attired, bending forward from the window, and silently beckoning me to approach.

'Too much amazed to be conscious of amazement, I advanced until I stood directly beneath the casement, and the lady's face, as she stooped toward me, was not more than twice a man's height from my own. She smiled and kissed her finger-tips; something white fluttered in her hand, then fell through the air to the ground at my feet. The next moment she had withdrawn, and I heard the lattice close.

'I picked up what she had let fall; it was a delicate lace handkerchief, tied to the handle of an elaborately wrought bronze key. It was evidently the key of the house, and invited me to enter. I loosened it from the handkerchief, which bore a faint, delicious perfume, like the aroma of flowers in an ancient garden, and turned to the arched doorway. I felt no misgiving, and scarcely any sense of strangeness. All was as I had wished it to be, and as it should be; the medieval age was alive once more, and as for myself, I almost felt the velvet cloak hanging from my shoulder and the long rapier dangling at my belt. Standing in front of the door I thrust the key into the lock, turned it, and felt the bolt yield. The next instant the door was opened, apparently from within; I stepped across the threshold, the door closed again, and was alone in the house, and in darkness.

'Not alone, however! As I extended my hand to grope my way it was met by another hand, soft, slender, and cold, which insinuated itself gently into mine and drew me forward. Forward I went, nothing loath; the darkness was impenetrable, but I could hear the light rustle of a dress close to me, and the same delicious perfume that had emanated from the handkerchief enriched the air that I breathed, while the little hand that clasped and was clasped by my own alternately tightened and half relaxed the hold of its soft cold fingers. In this manner, and treading lightly, we traversed what I presumed to be a long, irregular passageway, and ascended a staircase. Then another corridor, until finally we paused, a door opened, emitting a flood of soft light, into which we entered, still hand in hand. The darkness and the doubt were at an end.

'The room was of imposing dimensions, and was furnished and decorated in a style of antique splendor. The walls were draped with mellow hues of tapestry; clusters of candles burned in polished silver sconces, and were reflected and multiplied in tall mirrors placed in the four corners of the room. The heavy beams of the dark oaken ceiling crossed each other in squares, and were laboriously carved; the curtains and the drapery of the chairs were of heavy-figured damask. At one end of the room was a broad ottoman, and in front of it a table, on which was set forth, in massive silver dishes, a sumptuous repast, with wines in crystal beakers. At the side was a vast and deep fire-place, with space enough on the broad hearth to burn whole trunks of trees. No fire, however, was there, but only a great heap of dead embers; and the room, for all its magnificence, was cold-cold as a tomb, or as my lady's hand – and it sent a subtle chill creeping to my heart.

'But my lady! how fair she was! I gave but a passing glance at the room; my eyes and my thoughts were all for her. She was dressed in white, like a bride; diamonds sparkled in her dark hair and on her snowy bosom; her lovely face and slender lips were pale, and all the paler for the dusky glow of her eyes. She gazed at me with a strange, elusive smile; and yet there was, in her aspect and bearing, something familiar in the midst of strangeness, like the burden of a song heard long ago and recalled among other conditions and surroundings. It seemed to me that something in me recognized her and knew her, had known her always. She was the woman of whom I had dreamed, whom I had beheld in visions, whose voice and face had haunted me from boyhood up. Whether we had ever met before, as human beings meet, I knew not; perhaps I had been blindly seeking her all over the world, and she had been awaiting me in this splendid room, sitting by those dead embers until all the warmth had gone out of her blood, only to be restored by the heat with which my love might supply her.

' "I thought you had forgotten me," she said, nodding as if in answer to my thought. "The night was so late – our one night of the year! How my heart rejoiced when I heard your dear voice singing the song I know so well! Kiss me – my lips are cold!"

'Cold indeed they were – cold as the lips of death. But the warmth of my own seemed to revive them. They were now tinged with a faint color, and in her cheeks also appeared a delicate shade of pink. She drew fuller breath, as one who recovers from a long lethargy. Was it my life that was feeding her? I was ready to give her all. She drew me to the table and pointed to the viands and the wine.

' "Eat and drink," she said. "You have traveled far, and you need food."

' "Will you eat and drink with me?" said I, pouring out the wine.

' "You are the only nourishment I want," was her answer. "This wine is thin and cold. Give me wine as red as your blood and as warm, and I will drain a goblet to the dregs."

'At these words, I know not why, a slight shiver passed through me. She seemed to gain vitality and strength at every instant, but the chill of the great room struck into me more and more.

'She broke into a fantastic flow of spirits, clapping her hands, and dancing about me like a child. Who was she? And was I myself, or was she mocking me when she implied that we had belonged to each other of old? At length she stood still before me, crossing her hands over her breast. I saw upon the forefinger of her right hand the gleam of an antique ring.

' "Where did you get that ring?" I demanded.

'She shook her head and laughed. "Have you been faithful?" she asked. "It is my ring; it is the ring that unites us; it is the ring you gave me when you loved me first. It is the ring of the Kern – the fairy ring, and I am your Ethelind – Ethelind Fionguala."

' "So be it," I said, casting aside all doubt and fear, and yielding myself wholly to the spell of her inscrutable eyes and wooing lips. "You are mine, and I am yours, and let us be happy while the hours last.

' "You are mine, and I am yours," she repeated, nodding her head with an elfish smile. "Come and sit beside me, and sing that sweet song again that you sang to me so long ago. Ah, now I shall live a hundred years.'

'We seated ourselves on the ottoman, and while she nestled luxuriously among the cushions, I took my banjo and sang to her. The song and the music resounded through the lofty room, and came back in throbbing echoes. And before me as I sang I saw the face and form of Ethelind Fionguala, in her jewelled bridal dress, gazing at me with burning eyes. She was pale no longer, but ruddy and warm, and life was like a flame within her. It was I who had become cold and bloodless, yet with the last life that was in me I would have sung to her of love that can never die. But at length my eyes grew dim, the room seemed to darken, the form of Ethelind alternately brightened and waxed indistinct, like the last flickerings of a fire; I swayed toward her, and felt myself lapsing into unconsciousness, with my head resting on her white shoulder.'

Here Keningale paused a few moments in his story, flung a fresh log upon the fire, and then continued:

'I awoke, I know not how long afterward. I was in a vast, empty room in a ruined building. Rotten shreds of drapery depended from the walls, and heavy festoons of spiders' webs gray with dust covered the windows, which were destitute of glass or sash; they had been boarded up with rough planks which had themselves become rotten with age, and admitted through their holes and crevices pallid rays of light and chilly draughts of air. A bat, disturbed by these rays or by my own movement, detached himself from his hold on a remnant of mouldy tapestry near me, and after circling dizzily around my head, wheeled the flickering noiselessness of his flight into a darker corner. As I arose unsteadily from the heap of miscellaneous rubbish on which I had been lying, something which had been resting across my knees fell to the floor with a rattle. I picked it up, and found it to be my banjo – as you see it now.

'Well, that is all I have to tell. My health was seriously impaired; all the blood seemed to have been drawn out of my veins; I was pale and haggard, and the chill – Ah, that chill,' murmured Keningale, drawing nearer to the fire, and spreading out his hands to catch the warmth – 'I shall never get over it; I shall carry it to my grave.'

The Squaw

BRAM STOKER

Nurnberg at the time was not so much exploited as it has been since then. Irving had not been playing *Faust*, and the very name of the old town was hardly known to the great bulk of the travelling public. My wife and I being in the second week of our honeymoon, naturally wanted someone else to join our party, so that when the cheery stranger, Elias P. Hutcheson, hailing from Isthmain City, Bleeding Gulch, Maple Tree County, Neb., turned up at the station at Frankfurt, and casually remarked that he was going on to see the most all-fired old Methusaleh of a town in Yurrup, and that he guessed that so much travelling alone was enough to send an intelligent, active citizen into the melancholy ward of a daft house, we took the pretty broad hint and suggested that we should join forces. We found, on comparing notes afterwards, that we had each intended to speak with some diffidence or hesitation so as not to appear too eager, such not being a good compliment to the success of our married life; but the effect was entirely marred by our both beginning to speak at the same instant – stopping simultaneously and then going together again. Anyhow, no matter how, it was done; and Elias P. Hutcheson became one of our party. Straightway Amelia and I found the pleasant benefit; instead of quarrelling, as we had been doing, we found that the restraining influence of a third party was such that we took every opportunity of spooning in odd corners. Amelia declares that ever since she has, as the result of that experience, advised all her friends to take a friend on the honeymoon. Well we 'did' Nurnberg together, and much enjoyed the racy remarks of our Transatlantic friend, who, from his quaint speech and his wonderful stock of adventures, might have stepped out of a novel. We kept for the last object of interest in the city to be visited the Burg, and on the day appointed for the visit strolled round the outer wall of the city by the eastern side.

The Burg is seated on a rock dominating the town, and an immensely deep fosse guards it on the northern side. Nurnberg has been happy in that it was never sacked; had it been it would certainly not be so spick and span perfect as it is at present. The ditch has not been used for centuries, and now its base is spread with tea-gardens and orchards, of which some of the trees are of quite respectable growth. As we wandered round the wall, dawdling in the hot July sunshine, we often paused to admire the views spread before us, and in especial the great plain covered with towns and villages and bounded with a blue line of hills, like a landscape of Claude Lorraine. From this we always turned with new delight to the city itself with its myriad of quaint old gables and acre-wide red roofs dotted with dormer windows, tier upon tier. A little to our right rose the towers of the Burg, and nearer still, standing grim, the Torture Tower, which was, and is, perhaps, the most interesting place in the city. For centuries the tradition of the Iron Virgin of Nurnberg has been handed down as an instance of the horrors of cruelty of which man is capable; we had long looked forward to seeing it; and here at last was its home.

In one of our pauses we leaned over the wall of the moat and looked down. The garden seemed quite fifty or sixty feet below us, and the sun pouring into it with an intense, moveless heat like that of an oven. Beyond rose the grey, grim wall seemingly of endless height, and losing itself right and left in the angles of bastion and counter-scarp. Trees and bushes crowned the wall, and above again towered the lofty houses on whose massive beauty Time has only set the hand of approval. The sun was hot and we were lazy; time was our own, and we lingered, leaning on the wall. Just below us was a pretty sight – a great black cat lying stretched in the sun, whilst round her gambolled prettily a tiny black kitten. The mother would wave her tail for the kitten to play with, or would raise her feet and push away the little one as an encouragement to further play. They were just at the foot of the wall, and Elias P. Hutcheson, in order to help the play, stooped and took from the walk a moderate-sized pebble.

'See!' he said 'I will drop it near the kitten, and they will both wonder where it came from.'

'Oh, be careful,' said my wife; 'you might hit the dear little thing!'

'Not me, ma'am,' said Elias P. 'Why I'm as tender as a Maine cherry-tree. Lor, bless ye, I wouldn't hurt the poor pooty little critter more'n I'd scalp a baby. An' you may bet your variegated socks on that! See, I'll drop it fur away on the outside so's not to go near her!' Thus saying, he leaned over and held his arm out at full length and dropped the stone. It may be that there is some attractive force which draws lesser matters to greater; or more probably that the wall was not plumb but sloped to its base – we not noticing the inclination from above; but the stone fell with a sickening thud that came up to us through the hot air, right on the kitten's head, and shattered out its little brains then and there. The black cat cast a swift upward glance, and we saw her eyes like green fire fixed an instant on Elias P. Hutcheson; and then her attention was given to the kitten, which lay still with just a quiver of her tiny limbs, whilst a thin red stream trickled from a gaping wound. With a muffled cry, such as a human being might give, she bent over the kitten, licking its wound and moaning. Suddenly she seemed to realize that it was dead, and again threw her eyes up at us. I shall never forget the sight, for she looked the perfect incarnation of hate. Her green eyes blazed with lurid fire, and the white, sharp teeth seemed to almost shine through the blood which dabbled her mouth and whiskers. She gnashed her teeth, and her claws stood out stark and at full length on every paw. Then she made a wild rush up the wall as if to reach us, but when the momentum ended fell back, and further added to her horrible appearance for she fell on the kitten, and rose with her back fur smeared with its brains and blood. Amelia turned quite faint, and I had to lift her back from the wall. There was a seat close by in the shade of a spreading plane-tree, and here I placed her whilst she composed herself. Then I went back to Hutcheson, who stood without moving, looking down on the angry cat below.

As I joined him he said:

'Wall, I guess that air the savagest beast I ever see – 'cept once when an Apache squaw had an edge on a half-breed what they nicknamed 'Splinters' 'cos of the way he fixed up her papoose which he stole on a raid just to show that he appreciated the way they had given his mother the fire torture. She got that kinder look so set on her face that it just seemed to grow there. She followed Splinters more'n three years till at last the braves got him and handed him over to her. They did say that no man, white or Injun, had ever been so long a-dying under the tortures of the Apaches. The only time I ever see her smile was when I wiped her out. I kem on the cam just in time to see Splinters pass in his checks, and he wasn't sorry to go either. He was a hard citizen, and though I never could shake with him after that papoose business – for it was bitter bad, and he should have been a white man, for he looked like one – I see he had got paid out in full. Durn me, but I took a piece of his hide from one of his skinnin' posts an' had it made into a pocket-book. It's here now!' and he slapped the breast pocket of his coat.

Whilst he was speaking, the cat was continuing her frantic efforts to get up the wall. She would take a run back and then charge up, sometimes reaching an incredible height. She did not seem to mind the heavy fall which she got each time but started with renewed vigour; and at every tumble her appearance became more horrible. Hutcheson was a kindhearted man – my wife and I had both noticed little acts of kindness to animals as well as to persons – and he seemed concerned at the state of fury to which the cat had wrought herself.

'Wall now!' he said, 'I du declare that that poor critter seems quite desperate. There! there! poor thing, it was all an accident though that won't bring back your little one to you. Say! I wouldn't have had such a thing happen for a thousand! Just shows what a clumsy fool of a man can do when he tries to play! Seems I'm darned slipperhanded to even play with a cat. Say Colonel!' – it was a pleasant way he had to bestow titles freely – 'I hope your wife don't hold no grudge against me on account of this unpleasantness? Why, I wouldn't have had it occur on no account.'

He came over to Amelia and apologized profusely, and she with her usual kindness of heart hastened to assure him that she quite understood that it was an accident. Then we all went again to the wall and looked over.

The cat missing Hutcheson's face had drawn back across the moat, and was sitting on her haunches as though ready to spring. Indeed, the very instant she saw him she did spring, and with a blind unreasoning fury, which would have been grotesque, only that it was so frightfully real. She did not try to run up the wall, but simply launched herself at him as though hate and fury could lend her wings to pass straight through the great distance between them. Amelia, womanlike, got quite concerned, and said to Elias P. in a warning voice:

'Oh! You must be careful. That animal would try to kill you if she were here; her eyes look like positive murder.'

He laughed out jovially. 'Excuse me, ma'am,' he said, 'but I can't help laughin'. Fancy a man that has fought grizzlies an' Injuns bein' careful of bein' murdered by a cat!'

When the cat heard him laugh, her whole demeanour seemed to change. She no longer tried to jump or run up the wall, but went quietly over, and sitting again beside the dead kitten began to lick and fondle it as though it were alive.

'See!' said I, 'the effect of a really strong man. Even that animal in the mids't of her fury recognizes the voice of a master, and bows to him!'

'Like a squaw!' was the only comment of Elias P. Hutcheson, as we moved over the wall and each time saw the cat following us. At first she had kept going back to the dead kitten, and then as the distance grew greater took it in her mouth and so followed. After a while, however, she abandoned this, for we saw her following all alone; she had evidently hidden the body somewhere. Amelia's alarm grew at the cat's persistence, and more than once she repeated her warning; but the American always laughed with amusement, till finally, seeing that she was beginning to be worried he said:

'I say ma'am, you needn't be skeered over that cat. I go heeled, I du!' Here he slapped his pistol pocket at the back of his lumbar region. 'Why soener'n have you worried, I'll shoot the critter, right here an' risk the police interferin' with a citizen of the United States for carryin' arms contrairy to reg'lations!' As he spoke he looked over the wall, but the cat, on seeing him, retreated, with a growl, into a bed of tall flowers, and was hidden. He went on: 'Blest if that ar critter ain't got more sense of what's good for her than most Christians. I guess we've seen the last of her! You bet, she'll go back now to that busted kitten and have a private funeral of it, all to herself!'

Amelia did not like to say more, lest he might, in mistaken kindness to her, fulfil his threat of shooting the cat: and so went on and crossed the little wooden bridge leading to the gateway whence ran the steep paved roadway between the Burg and the pentagonal Torture Tower. As we crossed the bridge we saw the cat again down below us. When she saw us her fury seemed to return, and she made frantic efforts to get up the steep wall. Hutcheson laughed as he looked down at her, and said:

'Goodbye, old girl. Sorry I injured your feelin's, but you'll get over it in time! So long!' And then we passed through the long, dim archway and came to the gate of the Burg.

When we came out again after our survey of this most beautiful old place which not even the well-intended efforts of the Gothic restorers of forty years ago have been able to spoil – though their restoration was then glaring white – we seemed to have quite forgotten the unpleasant episode of the morning. The old lime tree with its great trunk gnarled with the passing of nearly nine centuries, the deep well cut through the heart of the rock by those captives of old, and the lovely view from the city wall whence we heard, spread over almost a full quarter of an hour, the multitudinous chimes of the city, had all helped to wipe out from our minds the incident of the slain kitten.

We were the only visitors who had entered the Torture Tower that morning – so at least said the old custodian – and as we had the place all to ourselves were able to make a minute and more satisfactory survey than would have otherwise been possible. The custodian, looking to us as the sole source of his gains for the day, was willing to meet our wishes in any way. The Torture Tower is truly a grim place, even now when many thousands of visitors have sent a stream of life, and the joy that follows life, into the place; but at the time I mention it wore its primmest and most gruesome aspect. The dust of ages seemed to have settled on it, and the darkness and the horror of its memories seem to have become sentient in a way that would have satisfied the Pantheistic soul of Philo or Spinoza. The lower chamber where we entered was seemingly, in its normal state, filled with incarnate darkness; even the hot sunlight streaming in through the door seemed to be lost in the vast thickness of the walls, and only showed the masonry rough as when the builder's scaffolding had come down, but coated with dust and marked here and there with patches of dark stain which, if walls could speak, could have given their own dread memories of fear and pain. We were glad to pass up the dusty wooden staircase, the custodian leaving the outer door open to light us somewhat on our way; for to our eyes the one long-wick'd, evil-smelling candle stuck in a sconce on the wall gave an inadequate light. When we came up through the open trap in the corner of the chamber overhead, Amelia held on to me so tightly that I could actually feel her heart beat. I must say for my own part that I was not surprised at her fear, for this room was even more gruesome that that below. Here there was certainly more light, but only just sufficient to realize the horrible surroundings of the place. The builders of the tower had evidently intended that only they who should gain the top should have any of the joys of light and prospect. There, as we had noticed from below, were ranges of windows, albeit of mediaeval smallness, but elsewhere in the tower were only a very few narrow slits such as were habitual in places of mediaeval defence. A few of these only lit the chamber, and these so high up in the wall that from no part could the sky be seen through the thickness of the walls. In racks, and leaning in disorder against the walls, were a number of headsmen's swords, great double-handed weapons with broad blade and keen edge. Hard by were several blocks whereon the necks of the victims had lain, with here and there deep notches where the steel had bitten through the guard of flesh and shored into the wood. Round the chamber, placed in all sorts of irregular ways, were many implements of torture which made one's heart ache to see – chairs full of spikes which give instant and excruciating pain; chairs and couches with dull knobs whose torture was seemingly less, but which, though slower, were equally efficacious; racks, belts, boots, gloves, collars, all made for compressing at will; steel baskets in which the head could be slowly crushed into pulp if necessary; watchmen's hooks with long handle and knife that cut at resistance – this a specialty of the old Nurnberg police system; and many, many other devices for man's injury to man. Amelia grew quite pale with the horror of the things, but fortunately did not faint, for being a little overcome she sat down on a torture chair, but jumped up again with a shriek, all tendency to faint gone. We both pretended that it was the injury done to her dress by the dust of the chair, and the rusty spikes which had upset her, and Mr Hutcheson acquiesced in accepting the explanation with a kind-hearted laugh.

But the central object in the whole of this chamber of horrors was the engine known as the Iron Virgin, which stood near the centre of the room. It was a rudely-shaped figure of a woman, something of the bell order, or, to make a closer comparison, of the figure of Mrs Noah in the children's Ark, but without that slimness of waist and perfect *rondeur* of hip which marks the aesthetic type of the Noah family. One would hardly have recognized it as intended for a human figure at all had not the founder shaped on the forehead a rude semblance of a woman's face. This machine was coated with rust without, and covered with dust; a rope was fastened to a ring in the front of the figure, about where the waist should have been, and was drawn through a pulley, fastened on the wooden pillar which sustained the flooring above. The custodian pulling this rope showed that a section of the front was hinged like a door at one side; we then saw that the engine was of considerable thickness, leaving just room enough inside for a man to be placed. The door was of equal thickness and of great weight, for it took the custodian all his strength, aided though he was by the contrivance of the pulley, to open it. This weight was partly due to the fact that the door was of manifest purpose hung so as to throw its weight downwards, so that it might shut of its own accord when the strain was released. The inside was honeycombed with rust – nay more, the rust alone that comes through time would hardly have eaten so deep into the iron walls; the rust of the cruel stains was deep indeed! It was only, however, when we came to look at the inside of the door that the diabolical intention was manifest to the full. Here were several long spikes, square and massive, broad at the base and sharp at the points, placed in such a position that when the door should close the upper ones would pierce the eyes of the victim, and the lower ones his heart and vitals. The sight was too much for poor Amelia, this time she fainted dead off, and I had to carry her down the stairs, and place her on a bench outside till she recovered. That she felt it to the quick was afterwards shown by the fact that my eldest son bears to this day a rude birthmark on his breast, which has, by family consent, been accepted as representing the Nurnberg Virgin.

When we got back to the chamber we found Hutcheson still opposite the Iron Virgin; he had been evidently philosophizing, and now gave us the benefit of his thought in the shape of a sort of exordium.

'Wall I guess I've been learnin' somethin' here while madam has been gettin' over her faint. 'Pears to me that we're a long way behind the times on our side of the big drink. We uster think out on the plains that the Injun could give us points in tryin' to make a man oncomfortable; but I guess you old mediaeval law-and-order party could raise him every time. Splinters was pretty good in his bluff on the squaw, but this here young miss held a straight flush all high on him. The points of them spikes air sharp enough still, though even the edges air eaten out by what uster be on them. It'd be a good thing for our Indian section to get some specimens of this here play-toy to send round to the Reservations jest to knock the stuffin' out of the bucks, and the squaws too, by showing them as how old civilization lays over them at their best. Guess but I'll get in that box a minute jest to see how it feels!'

'Oh no! no!' said Amelia. 'It is too terrible!'

'Guess, ma'am nothin's too terrible to the explorin' mind. I've been in some queer places in my time. Spent a night inside a dead horse while a prairie fire swept over me in Montana Territory – an' another time slept inside a dead buffler when the Comanches was on the war path an' I didn't keer to leave my kyard on them. I've been two days in a caved-in tunnel in the Billy Broncho gold mine in New Mexico, an' was one of the four shut up for three parts of a day in the caisson what slid over her side when we was settin' the foundations of the Buffalo Bridge. I've not funked an odd experience yet, an' I don't propose to begin now!'

We saw that he was set on the experiment, so I said: 'Well, hurry up, old man, and get through it quick!'

'All right, General,' said he, 'But I calculate we ain't quite ready yet. The gentlemen, my predecessors, what stood in that thar canister, didn't volunteer for the office not much! And I guess there was some ornamental tyin' up before the big stroke was made. I want to go into this thing fair and square, so I must get fixed up proper first. I dare say this old galoot can rise some string and tie me up accordin' to sample?'

This was said interrogatively to the old custodian, but the latter, who understood the drift of his speech, though perhaps not appreciating to the full the niceties of dialect and imagery, shook his head. His protest was, however, only formal and made to be overcome. The American thrust a gold piece into his hand saying, 'Take it, pard; it's your pot; and don't be skeer'd. This ain't no necktie party that you're asked to assist in!' He produced some thin frayed rope and proceeded to bind our companion, with sufficient strictness for the purpose. When the upper part of his body was bound, Hutcheson said:

'Hold on a moment, Judge. Guess I'm too heavy for you to tote into the canister. You jest let me walk in, and then you can wash up regardin' my legs!'

Whilst speaking he had backed himself into the opening which was just enough to hold him. It was a close fit and no mistake. Amelia looked on with fear in her eyes, but she evidently did not like to say anything. Then the custodian completed his task by tying the American's feet together so that he was now absolutely helpless and fixed in his voluntary prison. He seemed to really enjoy it, and the incipient smile which was habitual to his face blossomed into actuality as he said:

'Guess this here Eve was made out of the rib of a dwarf! There ain't much room for a full-grown citizen of the United States to hustle. We uster make our coffins more roomier in Idaho territory. Now, Judge, you just begin to let this door down, slow on me. I want to feel the same pleasure as the other jays had when those spikes began to move toward their eyes!'

'Oh no! no! no!' broke in Amelia hysterically, 'It is too terrible! I can't bear to see it! I can't! I can't!'

But the American was obdurate. 'Say, Colonel,' said he, 'why not take Madame for a little promenade? I wouldn't hurt her feelin's for the world; but now that I am here, havin' kem eight thousand miles, wouldn't it be too hard to give up the very experience I've been pinin' an' pantin' fur? A man can't get to feel like canned goods every time! Me and the Judge here'll fix up this thing in no time an' then you'll come back, an' we'll all laugh together!'

Once more the resolution that is born of curiosity triumphed, and Amelia stayed holding tight to my arm and shivering whilst the custodian began to slacken slowly inch by inch the rope that held back the iron door. Hutcheson's face was positively radiant as his eyes followed the first movements of the spikes.

'Wall!' he said, 'I guess I've not had enjoyment like this since I left Noo York. Bar a scrap with a French sailor at Wapping – an' that warn't much of a picnic neither – I've not had a show fur real pleasure in this dodrotted Continent, where there ain't no b'ars nor no Injuns, an' wheer nary man goes unheeled. Slow there, Judge! Don't you rush this business! I want a show for my money this game – I du!'

The custodian must have had in him some of the blood of his predecessors in that ghastly tower, for he worked the engine with a deliberate and excruciating slowness which after five minutes, in which the outer edge of the door had not moved half as many inches, began to overcome Amelia. I saw her lips whiten, and felt her hold upon my arm relax. I looked around an instant for a place whereon to lay her, and when I looked at her again found that her eye had become fixed on the side of the Virgin. Following its direction I saw the black cat crouching out of sight. Her green eyes shone like danger lamps in the gloom of the place, and their colour was heightened by the blood which still smeared her coat and reddened her mouth. I cried out:

'The cat! look out for the cat!' for even then she sprang out before the engine. At this moment she looked like a triumphant demon. Her eyes blazed with ferocity, her hair bristled out till she seemed twice her normal size, and her tail lashed about as does a tiger's when the quarry is before it. Elias P. Hutcheson when he saw her was amused, and his eyes positively sparkled with fun as he said:

''Darned if the squaw hain't got on all her war paint! Jest give her a shove off if she comes any of her tricks on me, for I'm so fixed everlastingly by the boss, that durn my skin if I can keep my eyes from her if she wants them! Easy there Judge! Don't you slack that ar rope or I'm euchered!'

At this moment Amelia completed her faint, and I had to clutch hold of her round the waist or she would have fallen to the floor. Whilst attending to her I saw the black cat crouching for a spring, and jumped up to turn the creature out.

But at that instant, with, a sort of hellish scream, she hurled herself, not as we expected at Hutcheson, but straight at the face of the custodian. Her claws seemed to be tearing wildly as one sees in the Chinese drawings of the dragon rampant, and as I looked I saw one of them light on the poor man's eye, and actually tear through it and down his cheek, leaving a wide band of red where the blood seemed to spurt from every vein.

With a yell of sheer terror which came quicker than even his sense of pain, the man leaped back, dropping as he did so the rope which held back the iron door. I jumped for it, but was too late, for the cord ran like lightening through the pulley-block, and the heavy mass fell forward from its own weight.

As the door closed I caught a glimpse of our poor companion's face. He seemed frozen with terror. His eyes stared with a horrible anguish as if dazed, and no sound came from his lips.

And then the spikes did their work. Happily the end was quick, for when I wrenched open the door they had pierced so deep that they had locked in the bones of the skull through which they had crushed, and actually tore him – it – out of his iron prison till, bound as he was, he fell at full length with a sickly thud upon the floor, the face turning upward as he fell.

I rushed to my wife, lifted her up and carried her out, for I feared for her very reason if she should wake from her faint to such a scene. I laid her on the bench outside and ran back. Leaning against the wooden column was the custodian moaning in pain whilst he held his reddening handkerchief to his eyes. And sitting on the head of the poor American was the cat, purring loudly as she licked the blood which trickled through the gashed sockets of his eyes.

I think no one will call me cruel because I seized one of the old executioner's swords and shore her in two as she sat.

The Wind in the Rose-Bush

MARY E. WILKINS

Ford Village has no railroad station, being on the other side of the river from Porter's Falls, and accessible only by the ford which gives it its name, and a ferry line.

The ferry-boat was waiting when Rebecca Flint got off the train with her bag and lunch basket. When she and her small trunk were safely embarked she sat stiff and straight and calm in the ferry-boat as it shot swiftly and smoothly across stream. There was a horse attached to a light country wagon on board, and he pawed the deck uneasily. His owner stood near, with a wary eye upon him, although he was chewing, with as dully reflective an expression as a cow. Beside Rebecca sat a woman of about her own age, who kept looking at her with furtive curiosity; her husband, short and stout and saturnine, stood near her. Rebecca paid no attention to either of them. She was tall and spare and pale, the type of a spinster, yet with rudimentary lines and expressions of matronhood. She all unconsciously held her shawl, rolled up in a canvas bag, on her left hip, as if it had been a child. She wore a settled frown of dissent at life, but it was the frown of a mother who regarded life as a froward child, rather than as an overwhelming fate.

The other woman continued staring at her; she was mildly stupid, except for an overdeveloped curiosity which made her at times sharp beyond belief. Her eyes glittered, red spots came on her flaccid cheeks; she kept opening her mouth to speak, making little abortive motions. Finally she could endure it no longer; she nudged Rebecca boldly.

'A pleasant day,' said she.

Rebecca looked at her and nodded coldly.

'Yes, very,' she assented.

'Have you come far?'

'I have come from Michigan.'

'Oh!' said the woman, with awe. 'It's a long way,' she remarked, presently.

'Yes, it is,' replied Rebecca, conclusively.

Still the other woman was not daunted; there was something which she determined to know, possibly roused thereto by a vague sense of incongruity in the other's appearance. 'It's a long ways to come and leave a family,' she remarked with painful slyness.

'I ain't got any family to leave,' returned Rebecca, shortly.

'Then you ain't—'

'No, I ain't.'

'Oh!' said the woman.

Rebecca looked straight ahead at the race of the river.

It was a long ferry. Finally Rebecca herself waxed unexpectedly loquacious. She turned to the older woman and inquired if she knew John Dent's widow who lived in Ford Village. 'Her husband died about three years ago,' said she, by way of detail.

The woman started violently. She turned pale, then she flushed; she cast a strange glance at her husband, who was regarding both women with a sort of stolid keenness.

'Yes, I guess I do,' faltered the woman, finally.

'Well, his first wife was my sister,' said Rebecca with the air of one imparting important intelligence.

'Was she?' responded the other woman, feebly. She glanced at her husband with an expression of doubt and terror, and he shook his head forbiddingly.

'I'm going to see her and take my niece Agnes home with me,' said Rebecca.

Then the woman gave such a violent start that she noticed it.

'What is the matter?' she asked.

'Nothin', I guess,' replied the woman, with eyes on her husband, who was slowly shaking his head, like a Chinese toy.

'Is my niece sick?' asked Rebecca with quick suspicion.

'No, she ain't sick,' replied the woman with alacrity, then she caught her breath with a gasp.

'When did you see her?'

'Let me see; I ain't seen her for some little time,' replied the woman. Then she caught her breath again.

'She ought to have grown up real pretty, if she takes after my sister. She was a real pretty woman,' Rebecca said, wistfully.

'Yes, I guess she did grow up pretty,' replied the woman in a trembling voice.

'What kind of a woman is the second wife?'

The woman glanced at her husband's warning face. She continued to gaze at him while she replied in a choking voice to Rebecca:

'I – guess she's a nice woman,' she replied. 'I – don't know, I – guess so. I – don't see much of her.'

'I felt kind of hurt that John married again so quick,' said Rebecca; 'but I suppose he wanted his house kept, and Agnes wanted care. I wasn't so situated that I could take her when her mother died. I had my own mother to care for, and I was school-teaching. Now mother has gone, and my uncle died six months ago and left me quite a little property, and I've given up my school and I've come for Agnes. I guess she'll be glad to go with me, though I suppose her stepmother is a good woman and has always done for her.'

The man's warning shake at his wife was fairly portentous.

'I guess so,' said she.

'John always wrote that she was a beautiful woman,' said Rebecca.

Then the ferry-boat grated on the shore.

John Dent's widow had sent a horse and wagon to meet her sister-in-law. When the woman and her husband went down the road, on which Rebecca in the wagon with her trunk soon passed them, she said, reproachfully:

'Seems as if I'd ought to have told her, Thomas.'

'Let her find it out herself,' replied the man. 'Don't you go to burnin' your fingers in other folks' puddin', Maria.'

'Do you s'pose she'll see anything?' asked the woman with a spasmodic shudder and a terrified roll of her eyes.

'See!' returned her husband with stolid scorn. 'Better be sure there's anything to see.'

'Oh, Thomas, they say—'

'Lord, ain't you found out that what they say is mostly lies?'

'But if it should be true, and she's a nervous woman, she might be scared enough to lose her wits,' said his wife, staring uneasily after Rebecca's erect figure in the wagon disappearing over the crest of the hilly road.

'Wits that's so easy upset ain't worth much,' declared the man. 'You keep out of it, Maria.'

Rebecca in the meantime rode on in the wagon, beside a flaxen-headed boy, who looked, to her understanding, not very bright. She asked him a question, and he paid no attention. She repeated it, and he responded with a bewildered and incoherent grunt. Then she let him alone, after making sure that he knew how to drive straight.

They had traveled about half a mile, passed the village square, and gone a short distance beyond, when the boy drew up with a sudden Whoa! before a very prosperous-looking house. It had been one of the aboriginal cottages of the vicinity, small and white, with a roof extending on one side over a piazza, and a tiny 'L' jutting out in the rear, on the right hand. Now the cottage was transformed by dormer windows, a bay window on the piazzaless side, a carved railing down the front steps, and a modern hardwood door.

'Is this John Dent's house?' asked Rebecca.

The boy was as sparing of speech as a philosopher. His only response was in flinging the reins over the horse's back, stretching out one foot to the shaft, and leaping out of the wagon, then going around to the rear for the trunk. Rebecca got out and went toward the house. Its white paint had a new gloss; its blinds were an immaculate apple green; the lawn was trimmed as smooth as velvet, and it was dotted with scrupulous groups of hydrangeas and cannas.

'I always understood that John Dent was well-to-do,' Rebecca reflected, comfortably. 'I guess Agnes will have considerable. I've got enough, but it will come in handy for her schooling. She can have advantages.'

The boy dragged the trunk up the fine gravel walk, but before he reached the steps leading up to the piazza, for the house stood on a terrace, the front door opened and a fair, frizzled head of a very large and handsome woman appeared. She held up her black silk skirt, disclosing voluminous ruffles of starched embroidery, and waited for Rebecca. She smiled placidly, her pink, double-chinned face widened and dimpled, but her blue eyes were wary and calculating. She extended her hand as Rebecca climbed the steps.

'This is Miss Flint, I suppose,' said she.

'Yes, ma'am,' replied Rebecca, noticing with bewilderment a curious expression compounded of fear and defiance on the other's face.

'Your letter only arrived this morning,' said Mrs Dent, in a steady voice. Her great face was a uniform pink, and her china-blue eyes were at once aggressive and veiled with secrecy.

'Yes, I hardly thought you'd get my letter,' replied Rebecca. 'I felt as if I could not wait to hear from you before I came. I supposed you would be situated that you could have me a little while without putting you out too much, from what John used to write me about his circumstances, and when I had that money so unexpected I felt as if I must come for Agnes. I suppose you will be willing to give her up. You know she's my own blood, and of course she's no relation to you, though you must have got attached to her. I know from her picture what a sweet girl she must be, and John always said she looked like her own mother, and Grace was a beautiful woman, if she was my sister.'

Rebecca stopped and stared at the other woman in amazement and alarm. The great handsome blonde creature stood speechless, livid, gasping, with her hand to her heart, her lips parted in a horrible caricature of a smile.

'Are you sick!' cried Rebecca, drawing near. 'Don't you want me to get you some water!'

Then Mrs Dent recovered herself with a great effort. 'It is nothing,' she said. 'I am subject to – spells. I am over it now. Won't you come in, Miss Flint?'

As she spoke, the beautiful deep-rose color suffused her face, her blue eyes met her visitor's with the opaqueness of turquoise – with a revelation of blue, but a concealment of all behind.

Rebecca followed her hostess in, and the boy, who had waited quiescently, climbed the steps with the trunk. But before they entered the door a strange thing happened. On the upper terrace, close to the piazza post, grew a great rose-bush, and on it, late in the season though it was, one small red, perfect rose.

Rebecca looked at it, and the other woman extended her hand with a quick gesture. 'Don't you pick that rose!' she brusquely cried.

Rebecca drew herself up with stiff dignity.

'I ain't in the habit of picking other folks' roses without leave,' said she.

As Rebecca spoke she started violently and lost sight of her resentment, for something singular happened. Suddenly the rosebush was agitated violently as if by a gust of wind, yet it was a remarkably still day. Not a leaf of the hydrangea standing on the terrace close to the rose trembled.

'What on earth—' began Rebecca; then she stopped with a gasp at the sight of the other woman's face. Although a face, it gave somehow the impression of a desperately clutched hand of secrecy.

'Come in!' said she in a harsh voice, which seemed to come forth from her chest with no intervention of the organs of speech. 'Come into the house. I'm getting cold out here.'

'What makes that rose-bush blow so when there isn't any wind?' asked Rebecca, trembling with vague horror, yet resolute.

'I don't see as it is blowing,' returned the woman, calmly. And as she spoke, indeed, the bush was quiet.

'It was blowing,' declared Rebecca.

'It isn't now,' said Mrs Dent. 'I can't try to account for everything that blows out-of-doors. I have too much to do.'

She spoke scornfully and confidently, with defiant, unflinching eyes, first on the bush, then on Rebecca, and led the way into the house.

'It looked queer,' persisted Rebecca, but she followed, and also the boy with the trunk.

Rebecca entered an interior, prosperous, even elegant, according to her simple ideas. There were Brussels carpets, lace curtains, and plenty of brilliant upholstery and polished wood.

'You're real nicely situated,' remarked Rebecca after she had become a little accustomed to her new surroundings and the two women were seated at the tea-table.

Mrs Dent stared with a hard complacency from behind her silver-plated service. 'Yes, I be,' said she.

'You got all the things new?' said Rebecca, hesitatingly, with a jealous memory of her dead sister's bridal furnishings.

'Yes,' said Mrs Dent. 'I was never one to want dead folks' things, and I had money enough of my own, so I wasn't beholden to John. I had the old duds put up at auction. They didn't bring much.'

'I suppose you saved some for Agnes. She'll want some of her poor mother's things when she is grown up,' said Rebecca with some indignation.

The defiant stare of Mrs Dent's blue eyes waxed more intense. 'There's a few things up garret,' said she.

'She'll be likely to value them,' remarked Rebecca. As she spoke she glanced at the window. 'Isn't it 'most time for her to be coming home?' she asked.

''Most time,' answered Mrs Dent, carelessly; 'but when she gets over to Addie Slocum's she never knows when to come home.'

'Is Addie Slocum her intimate friend?'

'Intimate as any.'

'Maybe we can have her come out to see Agnes when she's living with me,' said Rebecca, wistfully. 'I suppose she'll be likely to be homesick at first.'

'Most likely,' answered Mrs Dent.

'Does she call you mother?' Rebecca asked.

'No, she calls me Aunt Emeline,' replied the other woman, shortly. 'When did you say you were going home?'

'In about a week, I thought, if she can be ready to go soon,' answered Rebecca with a surprised look.

She reflected that she would not remain a day longer than she could help after such an inhospitable look and question.

'Oh, as far as that goes,' said Mrs Dent, 'it wouldn't make any difference about her being ready. You could go home whenever you felt that you must, and she could come afterward.'

'Alone?'

'Why not? She's a big girl now, and you don't have to change cars.'

'My niece will go home when I do, and not travel alone; and if I can't wait here for her, in the house that used to be her mother's and my sister's home, I'll go and board somewhere,' returned Rebecca with warmth.

'Oh, you can stay here as long as you want to. You're welcome,' said Mrs Dent.

Then Rebecca started. 'There she is!' she declared in a trembling, exultant voice. Nobody knew how she longed to see the girl.

'She isn't as late as I thought she'd be,' said Mrs Dent, and again that curious, subtle change passed over her face, and again it settled into that stony impassiveness.

Rebecca stared at the door, waiting for it to open. 'Where is she?' she asked, presently.

'I guess she's stopped to take off her hat in the entry,' suggested Mrs Dent.

Rebecca waited. 'Why don't she come? It can't take her all this time to take off her hat.'

For answer Mrs Dent rose with a stiff jerk and threw open the door.

'Agnes!' she called. 'Agnes!' Then she turned and eyed Rebecca. 'She ain't there.'

'I saw her pass the window,' said Rebecca in bewilderment.

'You must have been mistaken.'

'I know I did,' persisted Rebecca.

'You couldn't have.'

'I did. I saw first a shadow go over the ceiling, then I saw her in the glass there' – she pointed to a mirror over the sideboard opposite – 'and then the shadow passed the window.'

'How did she look in the glass?'

'Little and light-haired, with the light hair kind of tossing over her forehead.'

'You couldn't have seen her.'

'Was that like Agnes?'

'Like enough; but of course you didn't see her. You've been thinking so much about her that you thought you did.'

'You thought *you* did.'

'I thought I saw a shadow pass the window, but I must have been mistaken. She didn't come in, or we would have seen her before now. I knew it was too early for her to get home from Addie Slocum's, anyhow.'

When Rebecca went to bed Agnes had not returned. Rebecca had resolved that she would not retire until the girl came, but she was very tired, and she reasoned with herself that she was foolish. Besides, Mrs Dent suggested that Agnes might go to the church social with Addie Slocum. When Rebecca suggested that she be sent for and told that her aunt had come, Mrs Dent laughed meaningly.

'I guess you'll find out that a young girl ain't so ready to leave a sociable, where there's boys, to see her aunt,' said she.

'She's too young,' said Rebecca, incredulously and indignantly.

'She's sixteen,' replied Mrs Dent; 'and she's always been great for the boys.'

'She's going to school four years after I get her before she thinks of boys,' declared Rebecca.

'We'll see,' laughed the other woman.

After Rebecca went to bed, she lay awake a long time listening for the sound of girlish laughter and a boy's voice under her window; then she fell asleep.

The next morning she was down early. Mrs Dent, who kept no servants, was busily preparing breakfast.

'Don't Agnes help you about breakfast?' asked Rebecca.

'No, I let her lay,' replied Mrs Dent, shortly.

'What time did she get home last night?'

'She didn't get home.'

'What?'

'She didn't get home. She stayed with Addie. She often does.'

'Without sending you word?'

'Oh, she knew I wouldn't worry.'

'When will she be home?'

'Oh, I guess she'll be along pretty soon.'

Rebecca was uneasy, but she tried to conceal it, for she knew of no good reason for uneasiness. What was there to occasion alarm in the fact of one young girl staying overnight with another? She could not eat much breakfast. Afterward she went out on the little piazza, although her hostess strove furtively to stop her.

'Why don't you go out back of the house? It's real pretty – a view over the river,' she said.

'I guess I'll go out here,' replied Rebecca. She had a purpose – to watch for the absent girl.

Presently Rebecca came hustling into the house through the sitting room, into the kitchen where Mrs Dent was cooking.

'That rose-bush!' she gasped.

Mrs Dent turned and faced her.

'What of it?'

'It's a-blowing.'

'What of it?'

'There isn't a mite of wind this morning.'

Mrs Dent turned with an inimitable toss of her fair head. 'If you think I can spend my time puzzling over such nonsense as—' she began, but Rebecca interrupted her with cry and a rush to the door.

'There she is now!' she cried.

She flung the door wide open, and curiously enough a breeze came in and her own gray hair tossed, and a paper blew off the table to the floor with a loud rustle, but there was nobody in sight.

'There's nobody here,' Rebecca said.

She looked blankly at the other woman, who brought her rolling-pin down on a slab of pie crust with a thud.

'I didn't hear anybody,' she said, calmly.

'I saw somebody pass that window!'

'You were mistaken again.'

'I *know* I saw somebody.'

'You couldn't have. Please shut that door.'

Rebecca shut the door. She sat down beside the window and looked out on the autumnal yard, with its little curve of footpath to the kitchen door.

'What smells so strong of roses in this room?' she said, presently. She sniffed hard.

'I don't smell anything but these nutmegs.'

'It is not nutmeg.'

'I don't smell anything else.'

'Where do you suppose Agnes is?'

'Oh, perhaps she has gone over the ferry to Porter's Falls with Addie. She often does. Addie's got an aunt over there, and Addie's got a cousin, a real pretty boy.'

'You suppose she's gone over there?'

'Mebbe. I shouldn't wonder.'

'When should she be home?'

'Oh, not before afternoon.'

Rebecca waited with all the patience she could muster. She kept reassuring herself, telling herself that it was all natural, that the other woman could not help it, but she made up her mind that if Agnes did not return that afternoon she should be sent for.

When it was four o'clock she started up with resolution. She had been furtively watching the onyx clock on the sitting-room mantel; she had timed herself. She had said that if Agnes was not home by that time she should demand that she be sent for. She rose and stood before Mrs Dent, who looked up coolly from her embroidery.

'I've waited just as long as I'm going to,' she said. 'I've come 'way from Michigan to see my own sister's daugher and take her home with me. I've been here ever since yesterday – twenty-four hours – and I haven't seen her. Now I'm going to. I want her sent for.'

Mrs Dent folded her embroidery and rose.

'Well, I don't blame you,' she said. 'It is high time she came home. I'll go right over and get her myself.'

Rebecca heaved a sigh of relief. She hardly knew what she had suspected or feared, but she knew that her position had been one of antagonism if not accusation, and she was sensible of relief.

'I wish you would,' she said, gratefully, and went back to her chair, while Mrs Dent got her shawl and her little white head-tie. 'I wouldn't trouble you, but I do feel as if I couldn't wait any longer to see her,' she remarked, apologetically.

'Oh, it ain't any trouble at all,' said Mrs Dent as she went out. 'I don't blame you; you have waited long enough.'

Rebecca sat at the window watching breathlessly until Mrs Dent came stepping through the yard alone. She ran to the door and saw, hardly noticing it this time, that the rose-bush was again violently agitated, yet with no wind evident elsewhere.

'Where is she?' she cried.

Mrs Dent laughed with stiff lips as she came up the steps over the terrace. 'Girls will be girls,' said she. 'She's gone with Addie to Lincoln. Addie's got an uncle who's conductor on the train, and lives there, and he got 'em passes, and they're goin' to stay to Addie's Aunt Margaret's a few days. Mrs Slocum said Agnes didn't have time to come over and ask me before the train went, but she took it on herself to say it would be all right, and—'

'Why hadn't she been over to tell you?' Rebecca was angry, though not suspicious. She even saw no reason for her anger.

'Oh, she was putting up grapes. She was coming over just as soon as she got the black off her hands. She heard I had company, and her hands were a sight. She was holding them over sulphur matches.'

'You say she's going to stay a few days?' repeated Rebecca, dazedly.

'Yes; till Thursday, Mrs Slocum said.'

'How far is Lincoln from here?'

'About fifty miles. It'll be a real treat to her. Mrs Slocum's sister is a real nice woman.'

'It is goin' to make it pretty late about my goin' home.'

'If you don't feel as if you could wait, I'll get her ready and send her on just as soon as I can,' Mrs Dent said, sweetly.

'I'm going to wait,' said Rebecca, grimly.

The two women sat down again, and Mrs Dent took up her embroidery.

'If there any sewing I can do for her?' Rebecca asked, finally, in a desperate way. 'If I can get her sewing along some—'

Mrs Dent arose with alacrity and fetched a mass of white from the closet. 'Here,' she said, 'if you want to sew the lace on this nightgown. I was going to put her to it, but she'll be glad enough to get rid of it. She ought to have this and one more before she goes. I don't like to send her away without some good underclothing.'

Rebecca snatched at the little white garment and sewed feverishly.

That night she wakened from a deep sleep a little after midnight and lay a minute trying to collect her faculties and explain to herself what she was listening to. At last she discovered that it was the then popular strains of 'The Maiden's Prayer' floating up through the floor from the piano in the sitting room below. She jumped up, threw a shawl over her nightgown, and hurried downstairs trembling. There was nobody in the sitting room; the piano was silent. She ran to Mrs Dent's bedroom and called hysterically:

'Emeline! Emeline!'

'What is it?' asked Mrs Dent's voice from the bed. The voice was stern, but had a note of consciousness in it.

'Who – who was that playing "The Maiden's Prayer" in the sitting room, on the piano?'

'I didn't hear anybody.'

'There was some one.'

'I didn't hear anything.'

'I tell you there was some one. But – *there ain't anybody there.*'

'I didn't hear anything.'

'I did – somebody playing "The Maiden's Prayer" on the piano. Has Agnes got home? I want to know.'

'Of course Agnes hasn't got home,' answered Mrs Dent with rising inflection. 'Be you gone crazy over that girl? The last boat from Porter's Falls was in before we went to bed. Of course she ain't come.'

'I heard—'

'You were dreaming.'

'I wasn't; I was broad awake.'

Rebecca went back to her chamber and kept her lamp burning all night.

The next morning her eyes upon Mrs Dent were wary and blazing with suppressed excitement. She kept opening her mouth as if to speak, then frowning, and setting her lips hard. After breakfast she went upstairs, and came down presently with her coat and bonnet.

'Now, Emeline,' she said, 'I want to know where the Slocums live.'

Mrs Dent gave a strange, long, half-lidded glance at her. She was finishing her coffee.

'Why?' she asked.

'I'm going over there and find out if they have heard anything from her daughter and Agnes since they went away. I don't like what I heard last night.'

'You must have been dreaming.'

'It don't make any odds whether I was or not. Does she play "The Maiden's Prayer" on the piano? I want to know.'

'What if she does? She plays it a little, I believe. I don't know. She don't half play it, anyhow; she ain't got an ear.'

'That wasn't half played last night. I don't like such things happening. I ain't superstitious, but I don't like it. I'm going. Where do the Slocums live?'

'You go down the road over the bridge past the old grist mill, then you turn to the left; it's the only house for half a mile. You can't miss it. It has a barn with a ship in full sail on the cupola.'

'Well, I'm going. I don't feel easy.'

About two hours later Rebecca returned. There were red spots on her cheeks. She looked wild. 'I've been there,' she said, 'and there isn't a soul at home. Something *has* happened.'

'What has happened?'

'I don't know. Something. I had a warning last night. There wasn't a soul there. They've been sent for to Lincoln.'

'Did you see anybody to ask?' asked Mrs Dent with thinly concealed anxiety.

'I asked the woman that lives on the turn of the road. She's stone deaf. I suppose you know. She listened while I screamed at her to know where the Slocums were, and then she said, 'Mrs Smith don't live here.' I didn't see anybody on the road, and that's the only house. What do you suppose it means?'

'I don't suppose it means much of anything,' replied Mrs Dent, coolly. 'Mr Slocum is conductor on the railroad, and he'd be away, anyway, and Mrs Slocum often goes early when he does, to spend the day with her sister in Porter's Falls. She'd be more likely to go away than Addie.'

'And you don't think anything has happened?' Rebecca asked with diminishing distrust before the reasonableness of it.

'Land, no!'

Rebecca went upstairs to lay aside her coat and bonnet. But she came hurrying back with them still on.

'Who's been in my room?' she gasped. Her face was pale as ashes.

Mrs Dent also paled as she regarded her.

'What do you mean?' she asked, slowly.

'I found when I went upstairs that – little nightgown of – Agnes's on – the bed, laid out. It was – *laid out*. The sleeves were folded across the bosom, and there was that little red rose between them. Emeline, what is it? Emeline, what's the matter? Oh!'

Mrs Dent was struggling for breath in great, choking gasps. She clung to the back of a chair. Rebecca, trembling herself so she could scarcely keep on her feet, got her some water.

As soon as she recovered herself Mrs Dent regarded her with eyes full of the strangest mixture of fear and horror and hostility.

'What do you mean talking so?' she said in a hard voice.

'It *is there*.'

'Nonsense. You threw it down and it fell that way.'

'It was folded in my bureau drawer.'

'It couldn't have been.'

'Who picked that red rose?'

'Look on the bush,' Mrs Dent replied shortly.

Rebecca looked at her; her mouth gaped. She hurried out of the room. When she came back her eyes seemed to protrude. (She had in the meantime hastened upstairs, and come down with tottering steps, clinging to the banister.)

'Now I want to know what all this means?' she demanded.

'What what means?'

'The rose is on the bush, and it's gone from the bed in my room! Is this house haunted, or what?'

'I don't know anything about a house being haunted. I don't believe in such things. Be you crazy?' Mrs Dent spoke with gathering force. The color flashed back to her cheeks.

'No,' said Rebecca, shortly. 'I ain't crazy yet, but I shall be if this keeps on much longer. I'm going to find out where that girl is before night.'

Mrs Dent eyed her.

'What be you going to do?'

'I'm going to Lincoln.'

A faint triumphant smile overspread Mrs Dent's large face.

'You can't,' said she; 'there ain't any train.'

'No train?'

'No; there ain't any afternoon train from the Falls to Lincoln.'

'Then I'm going over to the Slocum's again tonight.'

However, Rebecca did not go; such a rain came up as deterred even her resolution, and she had only her best dresses with her. Then in the evening came the letter from the Michigan village which she had left nearly a week ago. It was from her cousin, a single woman, who had come to keep her house while she was away. It was a pleasant unexciting letter enough, all the first of it, and related mostly how she missed Rebecca; how she hoped she was having pleasant weather and kept her health; and how her friend, Mrs Greenaway, had come to stay with her since she had felt lonesome the first night in the house; how she hoped Rebecca would have no objections to this, although nothing had been said about it, since she had not realized that she might be nervous alone. The cousin was painfully conscientious, hence the letter. Rebecca smiled in spite of her disturbed mind as she read it; then her eyes caught the postscript. That was in a different land, purporting to be written by the friend, Mrs Hannah Greenaway, informing her that the cousin had fallen down the cellar stairs and broken her hip, and was in a dangerous condition, and begging Rebecca to return at once, as she herself was rheumatic and unable to nurse her properly, and no one else could be obtained.

Rebecca looked at Mrs Dent, who had come to her room with the letter quite late; it was half-past nine, and she had gone upstairs for the night.

'Where did this come from?' she asked.

'Mr Amblecrom brought it,' she replied.

Who's he?'

'The postmaster. He often brings the letters that come on the late mail. He knows I ain't anybody to send. He brought yours about your coming. He said he and his wife came over on the ferry-boat with you.'

'I remember him,' Rebecca replied, shortly. 'There's bad news in this letter.'

Mrs Dent's face took on an expression of serious inquiry.

'Yes, my Cousin Harriet has fallen down the cellar stairs – they were always dangerous – and she's broken her hip, and I've got to take the first train home tomorrow.'

'You don't say so. I'm dreadfully sorry.'

'No, you ain't sorry!' said Rebecca with a look as if she leaped. 'You're glad. I don't know why, but you're glad. You've wanted to get rid of me for some reason ever since I came. I don't know why. You're a strange woman. Now you've got your way, and I hope you're satisfied.'

'How you talk.'

Mrs Dent spoke in a faintly injured voice, but there was a light in her eyes.

'I talk the way it is. Well, I'm going tomorrow morning, and I want you, just as soon as Agnes Dent comes home, to send her out to me. Don't you wait for anything. You pack what clothes she's got, and don't wait even to mend them, and you buy her ticket. I'll leave the money, and you send her along. She don't have to change cars. You start her off, when she gets home, on the next train!'

'Very well,' replied the other woman. She had an expression of covert amusement.

'Mind you do it.'

'Very well, Rebecca.'

Rebecca started on her journey the next morning. When she arrived, two days later, she found her cousin in perfect health. She found, moreover, that the friend had not written the postscript in the cousin's letter. Rebecca would have returned to Ford Village the next morning, but the fatigue and nervous strain had been too much for her. She was not able to move from her bed. She had a species of low fever induced by anxiety and fatigue. But she could write, and she did, to the Slocums, and she received no answer. She also wrote to Mrs Dent; she even sent numerous telegrams, with no response. Finally she wrote to the postmaster, and an answer arrived by the first possible mail. The letter was short, curt, and to the purpose. Mr Ambelcrom, the postmaster, was a man of few words, and especially wary as to his expression in a letter.

'Dear madam,' he wrote, 'your favor rec'ed. No Slocums in Ford's Village. All dead. Addie ten years ago, her mother two years later, her father five. House vacant. Mrs John Dent said to have neglected stepdaughter. Girl was sick. Medicine not given. Talk of taking action. Not enough evidence. House said to be haunted. Strange sights and sounds. Your niece, Agnes Dent, died a year ago, about this time.

Yours truly,

'THOMAS AMBLECROM.'

The Golem

ISAAC LOEB PERETZ

Great men were once capable of great miracles.

When the ghetto of Prague was being attacked, and they were about to rape the women, roast the children, and slaughter the rest; when it seemed that the end had finally come, the great Rabbi Loeb put aside his *Gemarah*, went into the street, stopped before a heap of clay in front of the teacher's house, and molded a clay image. He blew into the nose of the *golem* – and it began to stir; then he whispered the Name into its ear, and our *golem* left the ghetto. The rabbi returned to the House of Prayer, and the *golem* fell upon our enemies, threshing them as with flails. Men fell on all sides.

Prague was filled with corpses. It lasted, so they say, through Wednesday and Thursday. Now it is already Friday, the clock strikes twelve, and the *golem* is still busy at its work.

'Rabbi,' cries the head of the ghetto, 'the *golem* is slaughtering all of Prague! There will not be a gentile left to light the Sabbath fires or take down the Sabbath lamps.'

Once again the rabbi left his study. He went to the altar and began singing the psalm 'A song of the Sabbath.'

The *golem* ceased its slaughter. It returned to the ghetto, entered the House of Prayer, and waited before the rabbi. And again the rabbi whispered into its ear. The eyes of the golem closed, the soul that had dwelt in it flew out, and it was once more a *golem* of clay.

To this day the *golem* lies hidden in the attic of the Prague synagogue, covered with cobwebs that extend from wall to wall. No living creature may look at it, particularly women in pregnancy. No one may touch the cobwebs, for whoever touches them dies. Even the oldest people no longer remember the *golem*, though the wise man Zvi, the grandson of the great Rabbi Loeb, ponders the problem: may such a *golem* be included in a congregation of worshipers or not?

The *golem*, you see, has not been forgotten. It is still here! But the Name by which it could be called to life in a day of need, the Name has disappeared. And the cobwebs grow and grow, and no one may touch them.

What are we to do?

Only a Dream

H. RIDER HAGGARD

Footprints – footprints – the footprints of one dead. How ghastly they look as they fall before me! Up and down the long hall they go, and I follow them. *Pit, pat* they fall, those unearthly steps, and beneath them starts up that awful impress. I can see it grow upon the marble, a damp and dreadful thing.

Tread them down; tread them out; follow after them with muddy shoes, and cover them up. In vain. See how they rise through the mire! Who can tread out the footprints of the dead?

And soon, up and down the dim vista of the past, following the sound of the dead feet that wander so restlessly, stamping upon the impress that will not be stamped out. Rave on, wild wind, eternal voice of human misery; fall, dead footsteps, eternal echo of human memory; stamp, miry feet; stamp into forgetfulness that which will not be forgotten.

And so on, on to the end.

Pretty ideas these for a man about to be married, especially when they float into his brain at night like ominous clouds into a summer sky, and he is going to be married tomorrow. There is no mistake about it – the wedding, I mean. To be plain and matter-of-fact, why there stand the presents, or some of them, and very handsome presents they are, ranged in solemn rows upon the long table. It is a remarkable thing to observe when one is about to make a really satisfactory marriage how scores of unsuspected or forgotten friends crop up and send little tokens of their esteem. It was very different when I married my first wife, I remember, but then that marriage was not satisfactory – just a love-match, no more.

There they stand in solemn rows, as I have said, and inspire me with beautiful thoughts about the innate kindness of human nature, especially the human nature of our distant cousins. It is possible to grow almost poetical over a silver teapot when one is going to be married tomorrow. On how many future mornings shall I be confronted with that teapot? Probably for all my life; and on the other side of the teapot will be the cream jug, and the electro-plated urn will hiss away behind them both. Also, the chased sugar basin will be in front, full of sugar, and behind everything will be my second wife.

'My dear,' she will say, 'will you have another cup of tea?' and probably I shall have another cup.

Well, it is very curious to notice what ideas will come into a man's head sometimes. Sometimes something waves a magic wand over his being, and from the recesses of his soul dim things arise and walk. At unexpected moments they come, and he grows aware of the issues of his mysterious life, and his heart shakes and shivers like a lightning-shattered tree. In that drear light all earthly things seem far, and all unseen things draw near and take shape and awe him, and he knows not what is true and what is false, neither can he trace the edge that marks off the Spirit from the Life. Then it is that the footsteps echo, and the ghostly footprints will not be stamped out.

Pretty thoughts again! and how persistently they come! It is one o'clock and I will go to bed. The rain is falling in sheets outside. I can hear it lashing against the window panes, and the wind wails through the tall wet elms at the end of the garden. I could tell the voice of those elms anywhere; I know it as well as the voice of a friend. What a night it is; we sometimes get them in this part of England in October. It was just such a night when my first wife died, and that is three years ago. I remember how she sat up in her bed.

'Ah! those horrible elms,' she said; 'I wish you would have them cut down, Frank; they cry like a woman,' and I said I would and just after that she died, poor dear. And so the old elms stand, and I like their music. It is a strange thing; I was half broken-hearted, for I loved her dearly, and she loved me with all her life and strength, and now – I am going to be married again.

'Frank, Frank, don't forget me!' Those were my wife's last words; and, indeed, though I am going to be married again tomorrow, I have not forgotten her. Nor shall I forget how Annie Guthrie (whom I am going to marry now) came to see her the day before she died. I know that Annie always liked me more or less, and I think that my dear wife guessed it. After she had kissed Annie and bid her a last goodbye, and the door had closed, she spoke quite suddenly: 'There goes your future wife, Frank,' she said; 'You should have married her at first instead of me; she is very handsome and very good, and she has two thousand a year; *she* would never have died of a nervous illness.' And she laughed a little, and then added:

'Oh, Frank dear, I wonder if you will think of me before you marry Annie Guthrie. Wherever I am I shall be thinking of you.'

And now that time which she foresaw has come, and Heaven knows that I have thought of her, poor dear. Ah! those footsteps of one dead that will echo through our lives, those woman's footprints on the marble flooring which will not be stamped out. Most of us have heard and seen them at some time or other, and I hear and see them very plainly tonight. Poor dead wife, I wonder if there are any doors in the land where you have gone through which you can creep out to look at me tonight? I hope that there are none. Death must indeed be a hell if the dead can see and feel and take measure of the forgetful faithlessness of their beloved. Well, I will go to bed and try to get a little rest. I am not so young or so strong as I was, and this wedding wears me out. I wish that the whole thing were done or had never been begun.

What was that? It was not the wind, for it never makes that sound here, and it was not the rain, since the rain has ceased its surging for a moment; nor was it the howling of a dog, for I keep none. It was more like the crying of a woman's voice; but what woman can be abroad on such a night or at such an hour – half-past one in the morning?

There it is again – a dreadful sound; it makes the blood turn chill, and yet has something familiar about it. It is a woman's voice calling round the house. There, she is at the window now, and rattling it, and, great heavens! she is calling me.

'Frank! Frank! Frank!' she calls.

I strive to stir and unshutter that window, but before I can get there she is knocking and calling at another.

Gone again, with her dreadful wail of 'Frank! Frank!' Now I hear her at the front door, and, half mad with a horrible fear, I run down the long, dark hall and unbar it. There is nothing there – nothing but the wild rush of the wind and the drip of the rain from the portico. But I can hear the wailing voice going round the house, past the patch of shrubbery. I close the door and listen. There, she has got through the little yard, and is at the back door now. Whoever it is, she must know the way about the house. Along the hall I go again, through a swing door, through the servants hall, stumbling down some steps into the kitchen, where the embers of the fire are still alive in the grate, diffusing a little warmth and light into the dense gloom.

Whoever it is at the door is knocking now with her clenched hand against the hard wood, and it is wonderful, though she knocks so low, how the sound echoes through the empty kitchen.

There I stood and hesitated, trembling in every limb; I dared not open the door. No words of mine can convey the sense of utter desolation that overpowered me. I felt as though I were the only living man in the whole world.

'Frank! Frank!' cried the voice with the dreadful familiar ring in it. 'Open the door; I am so cold. I have so little time.'

My heart stood still, and yet my hands were constrained to obey. Slowly, slowly I lifted the latch and unbarred the door, and, as I did so, a great rush of air snatched it from my hands and swept it wide. The black clouds had broken a little overhead, and there was a patch of blue, rain-washed sky and with just a star or two glimmering in it fitfully. For a moment I could only see this bit of sky, but by degrees I made out the accustomed outline of the great trees swinging furiously against it, and the rigid line of the coping of the garden wall beneath them. Then a whirling leaf hit me smartly on the face, and instinctively I dropped my eyes on to something that as yet I could not distinguish – something small and black and wet.

'What are you?' I gasped. Somehow I seemed to feel that it was not a person – I could not say, *Who* are you?

'Don't you know me?' wailed the voice, with the far-off familiar ring about it. 'And I mayn't come in and show myself. I haven't the time. You were so long opening the door, Frank, and I am so cold – oh, so bitterly cold! Look there, the moon is coming out, and you will be able to see me. I suppose that you long to see me, as I have longed to see you.'

As the figure spoke, or rather wailed, a moonbeam struggled through the watery air and fell on it. It was short and shrunken, the figure of a tiny woman. Also it was dressed in black and wore a black covering over the whole head, shrouding it, after the fashion of a bridal veil. From every part of this veil and dress the water fell in heavy drops.

The figure bore a small basket on her left arm, and her hand – such a poor thin little hand – gleamed white in the moonlight. I noticed that on the third finger was a red line, showing that a wedding-ring had once been there. The other hand was stretched towards me as though in entreaty.

All this I saw in an instant, as it were, and as I saw it, horror seemed to grip me by the throat as though it were a living thing, for as the voice had been familiar, so was the form familiar, though the churchyard had received it long years ago. I could not speak – I could not even move.

'Oh, don't you know me yet?' wailed the voice; 'and I have come from so far to see you, and I cannot stop. Look, look,' and she began to pluck feverishly with her poor thin hand at the black veil that enshrouded her. At last it came off, and, as in a dream, I saw what in a dim frozen way I had expected to see – the white face and pale yellow hair of my dead wife. Unable to speak or to stir, I gazed and gazed. There was no mistake about it, it was she, ay, even as I had last seen her, white with the whiteness of death, with purple circles round her eyes and the grave-cloth yet beneath her chin. Only her eyes were wide open and fixed upon my face; and a lock of the soft yellow hair had broken loose, and the wind tossed it.

'You know me now, Frank – don't you, Frank? It has been so hard to come to see you, and so cold! But you are going to be married tomorrow, Frank; and I promised – oh, a long time ago – to think of you when you were going to be married wherever I was, and I have kept my promise, and I have come from whence I am and brought a present with me. It was bitter to die so young! I was so young to die and leave you, but I had to go. Take it – take it; be quick, I cannot stay any longer. *I could not give you my life, Frank, so I brought you my death – take it!'*

The figure thrust the basket into my hand, and as it did so the rain came up again, and began to obscure the moonlight.

'I must go, I must go,' went on the dreadful, familiar voice, in a cry of despair. 'Oh, why were you so long opening the door? I wanted to talk to you before you married Annie; and now I shall never see you again – never! never! *never!* I have lost you for ever! ever! *ever!*'

As the last wailing notes died away the wind came down with a rush and a whirl and the sweep as of a thousand wings, and threw me back into the house, bringing the door to with a crash after me.

I staggered into the kitchen, the basket in my hand, and set it on the table. Just then some embers of the fire fell in, and a faint little flame rose and glimmered on the bright dishes on the dresser, even revealing a tin candlestick, with a box of matches by it. I was well-nigh mad with the darkness and fear, and, seizing the matches, I struck one, and held it to the candle. Presently it caught, and I glanced round the room. It was just as usual, just as the servants had left it, and above the mantelpiece the eight-day clock ticked away solemnly. While I looked at it it struck two, and in a dim fashion I was thankful for its friendly sound.

Then I looked at the basket. It was of very fine white plaited work with black bands running up it, and a chequered black-and-white handle. I knew it well. I have never seen another like it. I bought it years ago at Madeira, and gave it to my poor wife. Ultimately it was washed overboard in a gale in the Irish Channel. I remember that it was full of newspapers and library books, and I had to pay for them. Many and many is the time that I have seen that identical basket standing there on that very kitchen table, for my dear wife always used it to put flowers in, and the shortest cut from that part of the garden where her roses grew was through the kitchen. She used to gather the flowers, and then come in and place her basket on the table, just where it stood now, and order the dinner.

All this passed through my mind in a few seconds as I stood there with the candle in my hand, feeling indeed half dead, and yet with my mind painfully alive, I began to wonder if I had gone asleep, and was the victim of a nightmare. No such thing. I wish it had only been a nightmare. A mouse ran out along the dresser and jumped on to the floor, making quite a crash in the silence.

What was in the basket? I feared to look, and yet some power within me forced me to it. I drew near to the table and stood for a moment listening to the sound of my own heart. Then I stretched out my hand and slowly raised the lid of the basket.

'I could not give you my life, so I have brought you my death!' Those were her words. What could she mean – what could it all mean? I must know or I should go mad. There it lay, whatever it was, wrapped up in linen.

Ah, heaven help me! It was a small bleached human skull!

A dream! After all, only a dream by the fire, but what a dream. And I am to be married tomorrow.

Can I be married tomorrow?

Marsyas in Flanders

VERNON LEE

I

'You are right. This is not the original crucifix at all. Another one has been put instead. *Il y a eu substitution,'* and the little old Antiquary of Dunes nodded mysteriously, fixing his ghostseer's eyes upon mine.

He said it in a scarce audible whisper. For it happened to be the vigil of the Feast of the Crucifix, and the once famous church was full of semi-clerical persons decorating it for the morrow, and of old ladies in strange caps, clattering about with pails and brooms. The Antiquary had brought me there the very moment of my arrival, lest the crowd of faithful should prevent his showing me everything next morning.

The famous crucifix was exhibited behind rows and rows of unlit candles, and surrounded by strings of paper flowers and coloured muslin, and garlands of sweet resinous maritime pine; and two lighted chandeliers illumined it.

'There has been an exchange,' he repeated, looking around that no one might hear him. 'Il y a eu substitution.'

For I had remarked, as anyone would have done, at the first glance, that the crucifix had every appearance of French work of the thirteenth century, boldly realistic, whereas the crucifix of the legend, which was a work of St Luke, which had hung for centuries in the Holy Sepulchre at Jerusalem and been miraculously cast ashore at Dunes in 1195, would surely have been a more or less Byzantine image, like its miraculous companion of Lucca.

'But why should there have been a substitution?' I inquired innocently.

'Hush, hush,' answered the Antiquary, frowning, 'not here – later, later – '

He took me all over the church, once so famous for pilgrimages; but from which, even like the sea which has left it in a salt marsh beneath the cliffs, the tide of devotion has receded for centuries. It is a very dignified little church, of charmingly restrained and shapely Gothic, built of a delicate pale stone, which the sea damp has picked out, in bases and capitals and carved foliation, with stains of a lovely bright green. The Antiquary showed me where the transept and belfry had been left unfinished when the miracles had diminished in the fourteenth century. And he took me up to the curious warder's chamber, a large room up some steps in the triforium; with a fireplace and stone seats for the men who guarded the precious crucifix day and night. There had even been beehives in the window, he told me, and he remembered seeing them still as a child.

'Was it usual, here in Flanders, to have a guardroom in churches containing important relics?' I asked, for I could not remember having seen anything similar before.

'By no means,' he answered, looking round to make sure we were alone, 'but it was necessary here. You have never heard in what the chief miracles of this church consisted?'

'No,' I whispered back, gradually infected by his mysteriousness, 'unless you allude to the legend that the figure of the Saviour broke all the crosses until the right one was cast up by the sea?'

He shook his head but did not answer, and descended the steep stairs into the nave, while I lingered a moment looking down into it from the warder's chamber. I have never had so curious an impression of a church. The chandeliers on either side of the crucifix swirled slowly round, making great pools of light which were broken by the shadows of the clustered columns; and among the pews of the nave moved the flicker of the sacristan's lamp. The place was full of the scent of resinous pine branches, evoking dunes and mountainsides; and from the busy groups below rose a subdued chatter of women's voices, and a splash of water and clatter of pattens. It vaguely suggested preparations for a witches' sabbath.

'What sort of miracles did they have in this church?' I asked, when we had passed into the dusky square, 'and what did you mean about their having exchanged the crucifix – about a *substitution?*'

It seemed quite dark outside. The church rose black, a vague lopsided mass of buttresses and high-pitched roofs, against the watery, moonlit sky; the big trees of the churchyard behind out in the seawind ; and the windows like flaming portals, in the darkness.

'Please remark the bold effect of the gargoyles,' said the Antiquary pointing upwards.

They jutted out, vague wild beasts, from the roof-line; and, what was positively frightening, you saw the moonlight, yellow and blue through the open jaws of some of them. A gust swept through the trees, making the weathercock clatter and groan.

'Why, those gargoyle wolves seem positively to howl,' I exclaimed.

The old Antiquary chuckled. 'Aha,' he answered, 'did I not tell you that this church has witnessed things like no other church in Christendom? And it still remembers them! There – have you ever known such a wild, savage church before?'

And as he spoke there suddenly mingled with the sough of the wind and the groans of the weather-vane, a shrill quavering sound as of pipers inside.

'The organist trying his vox humana for to-morrow,' remarked the Antiquary.

II

Next day I bought one of the printed histories of the miraculous crucifix which they were hawking all round the church; and next day also, my friend the Antiquary was good enough to tell me all that he knew of the matter. Between my two informants, the following may be said to be the true story.

In the autumn of 1195, after a night of frightful storm, a boat was found cast upon the shore of Dunes, which was at that time a fishing village at the mouth of the Nys, and exactly opposite a terrible sunken reef.

The boat was broken and upset; and close to it, on the sand and bent grass, lay a stone figure of the crucified Saviour, without its cross and, as seems probable, also without its arms, which had been made of separate blocks. A variety of persons immediately came forward to claim it; the little church of Dunes, on whose glebe it was found; the Barons of Croy, who had the right of jetsam on that coast, and also the great Abbey of St Loup of Arras, as possessing the spiritual overlordship of the place. But a holy man who lived close by in the cliffs, had a vision which settled the dispute. St Luke in person appeared and told him that he was the original maker of the figure; that it had been one of three which had hung round the Holy Sepulchre of Jerusalem; that three knights, a Norman, a Tuscan, and a man of Arras, had with the permission of Heaven stolen them from the Infidels and placed them on unmanned boats; that one of the images had been cast upon the Norman coast near Salenelles; that the second had run aground not far from the city of Lucca, in Italy; and that this third was the one which had been embarked by the knight from Artois. As regarded its final resting place, the hermit, on the authority of St Luke, recommended that the statue should be left to decide the matter itself. Accordingly, the crucified figure was solemnly cast back into the sea. The very next day it was found once more in the same spot, among the sand and bent grass at the mouth of the Nys. It was therefore deposited in the little church of Dunes; and very soon indeed the flocks of pious persons who brought it offerings from all parts made it necessary and possible to rebuild the church thus sanctified by its presence.

The Holy Effigy of Dunes – *Sacra Dunarum Effigies* as it was called – did not work the ordinary sort of miracles. But its fame spread far and wide by the unexampled wonders which became the constant accompaniment of its existence. The Effigy, as above mentioned, had been discovered without the cross to which it had evidently been fastened, nor had any researches or any subsequent storms brought the missing blocks to light, despite the many prayers which were offered for the purpose. After some time therefore, and a deal of discussion, it was decided that a new cross should be provided for the effigy to hang upon. And certain skilful stonemasons of Arras were called to Dunes for this purpose. But behold! the very day after the cross had been solemnly erected in the church, an unheard of and terrifying fact was discovered. The Effigy, which had been hanging perfectly straight the previous evening, had shifted its position, and was bent violently to the right, as if in an effort to break loose.

This was attested not merely by hundreds of laymen, but by the priests of the place, who notified the fact in a document, existing in the episcopal archives of Arras until 1790, to the Abbot of St Loup their spiritual overlord.

This was the beginning of a series of mysterious occurrences which spread the fame of the marvellous crucifix all over Christendom. The Effigy did not remain in the position into which it had miraculously worked itself: it was found, at intervals of time, shifted in some other manner upon its cross, and always as if it had gone through violent contortions. And one day, about ten years after it had been cast up by the sea, the priests of the church and the burghers of Dunes discovered the Effigy hanging in its original outstretched, symmetrical attitude, but, O wonder! with the cross, broken in three pieces, lying on the steps of its chapel.

Certain persons, who lived in the end of the town nearest the church, reported to have been roused in the middle of the night by what they had taken for a violent clap of thunder, but which was doubtless the crash of the cross falling down; or perhaps, who knows? the noise with which the terrible Effigy had broken loose and spurned the alien cross from it. For that was the secret: the Effigy, made by a saint and come to Dunes by miracle, had evidently found some trace of unholiness in the stone to which it had been fastened. Such was the ready explanation afforded by the Prior of the church, in answer to an angry summons of the Abbot of St Loup, who expressed his disapproval of such unusual miracles. Indeed, it was discovered that the piece of marble had not been cleaned from sinful human touch with the necessary rites before the figure was fastened on; a most grave, though excusable oversight. So a new cross was ordered, although it was noticed that much time was lost about it; and the consecration took place only some years later.

Meanwhile the Prior had built the warder's chamber, with the fireplace and recess, and obtained permission from the Pope himself that a clerk in orders should watch day and night, on the score that so wonderful a relic might be stolen. For the relic had by this time entirely cut out all similar crucifixes, and the village of Dunes, through the concourse of pilgrims, had rapidly grown into a town, the property of the now fabulously wealthy Priory of the Holy Cross.

The Abbots of St Loup, however, looked upon the matter with an unfavourable eye. Although nominally remaining their vassals, the Priors of Dunes had contrived to obtain gradually from the Pope privileges which rendered them virtually independent, and in particular, immunities which sent to the treasury of St Loup only a small proportion of the tribute money brought by the pilgrims. Abbot

Walterius in particular, showed himself actively hostile. He accused the Prior of Dunes of having employed his warders to trump up stories of strange movements and sounds on the part of the still crossless Effigy, and of suggesting, to the ignorant, changes in its attitude which were more credulously believed in now that there was no longer the straight line of the cross by which to verify. So finally the new cross was made, and consecrated, and on Holy Cross Day of the year, the Effigy was fastened to it in the presence of an immense concourse of clergy and laity. The Effigy, it was now supposed, would be satisfied, and no unusual occurrences would increase or perhaps fatally compromise its reputation for sanctity.

These expectations were violently dispelled. In November, 1293, after a year of strange rumours concerning the Effigy, the figure was again discovered to have moved, and continued moving, or rather (judging from the position on the cross) writhing; and on Christmas Eve of the same year, the cross was a second time thrown down and dashed in pieces. The priest on duty was, at the same time, found, it was thought, dead, in his warder's chamber. Another cross was made and this time privately consecrated and put in place, and a hole in the roof made a pretext to close the church for a while, and to perform the rites of purification necessary after its pollution by workmen. Indeed, it was remarked that on this occasion the Prior of Dunes took as much trouble to diminish and if possible to hide away the miracles, as his predecessor had done his best to blazon the preceding ones abroad. The priest who had been on duty on the eventful Christmas Eve disappeared mysteriously, and it was thought by many persons that he had gone mad and was confined in the Prior's prison, for fear of the revelations he might make. For by this time, and not without some encouragement from the Abbots at Arras, extraordinary stories had begun to circulate about the goings-on in the church of Dunes. This church, be it remembered, stood a little above the town, isolated and surrounded by big trees. It was surrounded by the precincts of the Priory and, save on the water side, by high walls. Nevertheless, persons there were who affirmed that, the wind having been in that direction, they had heard strange noises come from the church of nights. During storms, particularly, sounds had been heard which were variously described as howls, groans, and the music of rustic dancing. A master mariner affirmed that one Hallow Even, as his boat approached the mouth of the Nys, he had seen the church of Dunes brilliantly lit up, its immense windows flaming. But he was suspected of being drunk and of having exaggerated the effect of the small light shining from the warder's chamber. The interest of the townfolk of Dunes coincided with that of the Priory, since they prospered greatly by the pilgrimages, so these tales were promptly hushed up. Yet they undoubtedly reached the ear of the Abbot of St Loup. And at last there came an event which brought them all back to the surface.

For, on the Vigil of All Saints, 1299, the church was struck by lightning. The new warder was found dead in the middle of the nave, the cross broken in two;

and oh, horror! the Effigy was missing. The indescribable fear which overcame everyone was merely increased by the discovery of the Effigy lying behind the high altar, in an attitude of frightful convulsion, and, it was whispered, blackened by lightning.

This was the end of the strange doings at Dunes.

An ecclesiastical council was held at Arras, and the church shut once more for nearly a year. It was opened this time and re-consecrated by the Abbot of St Loup, whom the Prior of Holy Cross served humbly at mass. A new chapel had been built, and in it the miraculous crucifix was displayed, dressed in more splendid brocade and gems than usual, and its head nearly hidden by one of the most gorgeous crowns ever seen before; a gift, it was said, of the Duke of Burgundy.

All this new splendour, and the presence of the great Abbot himself, was presently explained to the faithful, when the Prior came forward to announce that a last and greatest miracle had now taken place. The original cross, on which the figure had hung in the Church of the Holy Sepulchre, and for which the Effigy had spurned all others made by less holy hands, had been cast on the shore of Dunes, on the very spot where, a hundred years before, the figure of the Saviour had been discovered in the sands. 'This,' said the Prior, 'was the explanation of the terrible occurrences which had filled all hearts with anguish. The Holy Effigy was now satisfied, it would rest in peace and its miraculous powers would be engaged only in granting the prayers of the faithful.'

One-half of the forecast came true: from that day forward the Effigy never shifted its position; but from that day forward also, no considerable miracle was ever registered; the devotion of Dunes diminished, other relics threw the Sacred Effigy into the shade; and the pilgrimages dwindling to mere local gatherings, the church was never brought to completion.

What had happened? No one ever knew, guessed, or perhaps even asked. But, when in 1790 the Archiepiscopal palace of Arras was sacked, a certain notary of the neighbourhood bought a large portion of the archives at the price of waste paper, either from historical curiosity, or expecting to obtain thereby facts which might gratify his aversion to the clergy. These documents lay unexamined for many years, till my friend the Antiquary bought them. Among them, taken helter skelter from the Archbishop's palace, were sundry papers referring to the suppressed Abbey of St Loup of Arras, and among these latter, a series of notes concerning the affairs of the church of Dunes; they were, so far as their fragmentary nature explained, the minutes of an inquest made in 1309, and contained the deposition of sundry witnesses. To understand their meaning it is necessary to remember that this was the time when witch trials had begun, and when the proceedings against the Templars had set the fashion of inquests which again could help the finances of the country while furthering the interests of religion.

What appears to have happened is that after the catastrophe of the Vigil of All

Saints, October, 1299, the Prior, Urbain de Luc, found himself suddenly threatened with a charge of sacrilege and witchcraft, of obtaining the miracles of the Effigy by devilish means, and of converting his church into a chapel of the Evil One.

Instead of appealing to high ecclesiastical tribunals, as the privileges obtained from the Holy See would have warranted, Prior Urbain guessed that this charge came originally from the wrathful Abbey of St Loup, and, dropping all his pretensions in order to save himself, he threw himself upon the mercy of the Abbot whom he had hitherto flouted. The Abbot appears to have been satisfied by his submission, and the matter to have dropped after a few legal preliminaries, of which the notes found among the archiepiscopal archives of Arras represented a portion. Some of these notes my friend the Antiquary kindly allowed me to translate from the Latin, and I give them here, leaving the reader to make what he can of them.

'Item. The Abbot expresses himself satisfied that His Reverence the Prior has had no personal knowledge of or dealings with the Evil One (Diabolus). Nevertheless, the gravity of the charge requires . . .' – here the page is torn.

'Hugues Jacquot, Simon le Couvreur, Pierre Denis, burghers of Dunes, being interrogated, witness :

'That the noises from the Church of the Holy Cross always happened on nights of bad storms, and foreboded shipwrecks on the coast; and were very various, such as terrible rattling, groans, howls as of wolves, and occasional flute playing. A certain Jehan, who has twice been branded and flogged for lighting fires on the coast and otherwise causing ships to wreck at the mouth of the Nys, being promised immunity, after two or three slight pulls on the rack, witnesses as follows: That the band of wreckers to which he belongs always knew when a dangerous storm was brewing, on account of the noises which issued from the church of Dunes. Witness has often climbed the walls and prowled round in the churchyard, waiting to hear such noises. He was not unfamiliar with the howlings and roarings mentioned by the previous witnesses. He has heard tell by a countryman who passed in the night that the howling was such that the countryman thought himself pursued by a pack of wolves, although it is well known that no wolf has been seen in these parts for thirty years. But the witness himself is of opinion that the most singular of all the noises, and the one which always accompanied or foretold the worst storms, was a noise of flutes and pipes (quod vulgo dicuntur flustes et musettes) so sweet that the King of France could not have sweeter at his Court. Being interrogated whether he had ever seen anything? the witness answers: "That he has seen the church brightly lit up from the sands; but on approaching found all dark, save the light from the warder's chamber. That once, by moonlight, the piping and fluting and howling being uncommonly loud, he thought he had seen wolves, and a human figure on the roof, but that he ran away from fear, and cannot be sure."

'Item. His Lordship the Abbot desires the Right Reverend Prior to answer truly, placing his hand on the Gospels, whether or not he had himself heard such noises.

'The Right Reverend Prior denies ever having heard anything similar. But, being threatened with further proceedings (the rack?) acknowledges that he had frequently been told of these noises by the Warder on duty.

'*Query*: Whether the Right Reverend Prior was ever told anything else by the Warder?

'*Answer*: Yes; but under the seal of confession. The last Warder, moreover, the one killed by lightning – had been a reprobate priest, having committed the greatest crimes and obliged to take asylum, whom the Prior had kept there on account of the difficulty of finding a man sufficiently courageous for the office.'

'*Query*: Whether the Prior has ever questioned previous Warders?

'*Answer*: That the Warders were bound to reveal only in confession whatever they had heard; that the Prior's predecessors had kept the seal of confession inviolate, and that though unworthy, the Prior himself desired to do alike.

'*Query*: What had become of the Warder who had been found in a swoon after the occurrences of Hallow Even?

'*Answer*: That the Prior does not know. The Warder was crazy. The Prior believes he was secluded for that reason.'

A disagreeable surprise had been, apparently, arranged for Prior Urbain de Luc, For the next entry states that :

'Item. By order of His Magnificence the Lord Abbot, certain servants of the Lord Abbot aforesaid introduce Robert Baudouin, priest, once Warder in the Church of the Holy Cross, who has been kept ten years in prison by His Reverence the Prior, as being of unsound mind. Witness manifests great terror on finding himself in the presence of their Lordships, and particularly of His Reverence the Prior. And refuses to speak, hiding his face in his hands and uttering shrieks. Being comforted with kind words by those present, nay even most graciously by My Lord the Abbot himself, *etiam* threatened with the rack if he continue obdurate, this witness deposes as follows, not without much lamentation, shrieking and senseless jabber after the manner of mad men.

'*Query*: Can he remember what happened on the Vigil of All Saints, in the church of Dunes, before he swooned on the floor of the church?

'*Answer*: He cannot. It would be sin to speak of such things before great spiritual Lords. Moreover he is but an ignorant man, and also mad. Moreover his hunger is great.

'Being given white bread from the Lord Abbot's own table, witness is again cross-questioned.

'*Query*: What can he remember of the events of the Vigil of All Saints?

'*Answer*: Thinks he was not always mad. Thinks he has not always been in prison. Thinks he once went in a boat on sea, etc.

'*Query*: Does witness think he has ever been in the church of Dunes?

'*Answer*: Cannot remember. But is sure that he was not always in prison.

'*Query*: Has witness ever heard anything like that? (My Lord the Abbot having secretly ordered that a certain fool in his service, an excellent musician, should suddenly play the pipes behind the Arras.)

'At which sound witness began to tremble and sob and fall on his knees, and catch hold of the robe even of My Lord the Abbot, hiding his head therein.

'*Query*: Wherefore does he feel such terror, being in the fatherly presence of so clement a prince as the Lord Abbot?

'*Answer*: That witness cannot stand that piping any longer. That it freezes his blood. That he has told the Prior many times that he will not remain any longer in the warder's chamber. That he is afraid for his life. That he dare not make the sign of the Cross nor say his prayers for fear of the Great Wild Man. That the Great Wild Man took the Cross and broke it in two and played at quoits with it in the nave. That all the wolves trooped down from the roof howling, and danced on their hind legs while the Great Wild Man played the pipes on the high altar. That witness had surrounded himself with a hedge of little crosses, made of broken rye straw, to keep off the Great Wild Man from the warder's chamber. Ah – ah – ah! He is piping again! The wolves are howling! He is raising the tempest.

'Item: That no further information can be extracted from witness, who falls on the floor like one possessed and has to be removed from the presence of His Lordship the Abbot and His Reverence the Prior.'

III

Here the minutes of the inquest break off. Did those great spiritual dignitaries ever get to learn more about the terrible doings in the church of Dunes? Did they ever guess at their cause?

'For there was a cause,' said the Antiquary, folding his spectacles after reading me these notes, 'or more strictly the cause still exists. And you will understand, though those learned priests of six centuries ago could not.'

And rising, he fetched a key from a shelf and preceded me into the yard of his house, situated on the Nys, a mile below Dunes.

Between the low steadings one saw the salt marsh, lilac with sea lavender, the Island of Birds, a great sandbank at the mouth of the Nys, where every kind of sea fowl gathers; and beyond, the angry white-crested sea under an angry orange afterglow. On the other side, inland, and appearing above the farm roofs, stood the church of Dunes, its pointed belfry and jagged outlines of gables and buttresses and gargoyles and wind-warped pines black against the easterly sky of ominous livid red.

'I told you,' said the Antiquary, stopping with the key in the lock of a big outhouse,' that there had been a *substitution*; that the crucifix at present at Dunes is not the one miraculously cast up by the storm of 1195. I believe the present one may be identified as a life-size statue, for which a receipt exists in the archives of Arras, furnished to the Abbot of St Loup by Estienne Le Mas and Guillaume Pernel, stone masons, in the year 1299, that is to say the year of the inquest and of the cessation of all supernatural occurrences at Dunes. As to the original effigy, you shall see it and understand everything.'

The Antiquary opened the door of a sloping, vaulted passage, lit a lantern and led the way. It was evidently the cellar of some mediaeval building; and a scent of wine, of damp wood, and of fir branches from innumerable stacked up faggots, filled the darkness among thickset columns.

'Here,' said the Antiquary, raising his lantern, 'he was buried beneath this vault, and they had run an iron stake through his middle, like a vampire, to prevent his rising.'

The Effigy was erect against the dark wall, surrounded by brushwood. It was more than life-size, nude, the arms broken off at the shoulders, the head, with stubbly beard and clotted hair, drawn up with an effort, the face contracted with agony; the muscles dragged as of one hanging crucified, the feet bound together with a rope. The figure was familiar to me in various galleries. I came forward to examine the ear: it was leaf-shaped.

'Ah, you have understood the whole mystery,' said the Antiquary.

'I have understood,' I answered, not knowing how far his thought really went, 'that this supposed statue of Christ is an antique satyr, a Marsyas awaiting his punishment.'

The Antiquary nodded. 'Exactly,' he said drily, 'that is the whole explanation. Only I think the Abbot and the Prior were not so wrong to drive the iron stake through him when they removed him from the church.'

The Witch of the Marsh

ETHEL MARRIOTT-WATSON

It was nigh upon dusk when I drew close to the Great Marsh, and already the white vapours were about, riding across the sunken levels like ghosts in a churchyard. Though I had set forth in a mood of wild delight, I had sobered in the lonely ride across the moor and was now uneasily alert. As my horse jerked down the grassy slopes that fell away to the jaws of the swamp I could see thin streams of mist rise slowly, hover like wraiths above the long rushes, and then, turning gradually more material, go blowing heavily away across the flat. The appearance of the place at this desolate hour, so remote from human society and so darkly significant of evil presences, struck me with a certain wonder that she should have chosen this spot for our meeting. She was a familiar of the moors, where I had invariably encountered her; but it was like her caprice to test my devotion by some such dreary assignation.

The prospect depressed me beyond reason, but the fact of her neighbourhood drew me on, and my spirits mounted at the thought that at last she was to put me in possession of herself. Tethering my horse upon the verge of the swamp, I soon discovered the path that crossed it, and entering struck out boldly for the heart. The track could have been little used, for the reeds, which stood high above the level of my eyes upon either side, straggled everywhere across in low arches, through which I dodged, and broke my way with some inconvenience and much impatience. A full half hour I was solitary in that wilderness, and when at last a sound other than my own footsteps broke the silence the dusk had fallen.

I was moving very slowly at the time, with a mind half disposed to turn from the expedition, which it seemed to me now must surely be a jest she had played upon me. While some such reluctance held me, I was suddenly arrested by a hoarse croaking which broke out upon my left, sounding somewhere from the reeds in the black mire. A little farther it came again from close at hand, and when I had passed on a few more steps in wonder and perplexity, I heard it for the third time. I stopped and listened, but the marsh was as a grave, and so taking the noise for the signal of some raucous frog, I resumed my way. But in a little the croaking was repeated, and coming quickly to a stand I pushed the reeds aside and peered into the darkness.

I could see nothing, but at the immediate moment of my pause I thought I detected the sound of somebody trailing me through the rushes. My distaste for the adventure grew with this suspicion, and had it not been for my infatuation I would have assuredly turned back and ridden home. The sound pursued me at intervals along the track, until at last, irritated beyond endurance by the sense of this persistent and invisible company, I broke into a sort of run. This, it seemed, the creature (whatever it was) could not achieve, for I heard no more of it, and continued my way in peace. My path at length ran out from among the reeds upon the smooth flat of which she had spoken, and here my heart quickened, and the gloom of the place lifted.

The flat lay in the very centre of the marsh, and here and there in it a gaunt brush or withered tree rose like a spectre against the white mists. At the further end I fancied some kind of building loomed but the fog which had been gathering ever since my entrance upon the passage sailed down upon me at that moment and the prospect went out with suddenness. As I stood waiting for the clouds to pass, a voice cried to me out of its centre, and I saw her next second with bands of mist swirling about her body, come rushing to me from the darkness. She put her long arms about me, and, drawing her close I looked into her deep eyes. Far down in them, it seemed to me, I could discern a mystic laughter dancing in the wells of light.

'At last,' she said, 'at last, my beloved!' I caressed her.

'Why,' said I, tingling at the nerves, 'why have you put this journey between us? And what mad freak is your presence in this swamp?'

She uttered her silver laugh, and nestled to me again.

'I am the creature of this place,' she answered. 'This is my home. I have sworn you should behold me in my native sin ere you ravished me away.'

'Come, then,' said I, 'I have seen; let there be an end of this. I know you, what you are. This marsh chokes up my heart. God forbid you should spend more of your days here. Come.'

'You are in haste,' she cried. 'There is yet much to learn. Look my friend,' she said, 'you who know me, what I am. This is my prison, and I have inherited its properties. Have you no fear?'

For answer I pulled her to me, and her warm lips drove out the horrid humours of the night; but the swift passage of a flickering mockery over her eyes struck me as a flash of lightning, and I grew chill again.

'I have the marsh in my blood,' she whispered; 'the marsh and the fog of it. Think ere you vow to me, for I am the cloud in a starry night.'

A lithe and lovely creature, palpably of warm flesh, she lifted her magic face to mine and besought me plaintively with these words. The dews of the nightfall hung on her lashes, and seemed to plead with me for her forlorn and solitary plight.

'Behold!' I cried, 'witch or devil of the marsh, you shall come with me! I have known you on the moors, a roving apparition of beauty; nothing more I know, nothing more I ask. I care not what this dismal haunt means, nor again these strange and mystic eyes. You have powers and senses above me; your sphere and habits are as mysterious and incomprehensible as your beauty. But that,' I said, 'is mine, and the world that is mine shall be yours also.'

She moved her head nearer to me with an antic gesture, and her gleaming eyes glanced up at me with a sudden flash, the similitude (great heavens!) of a hooded snake. Starting, I fell away, but at that moment she turned her face and set it fast towards the fog that came rolling in thick volumes over the flat. Noiselessly the great cloud crept down upon us, and all dazed and troubled I watched her watching it in silence. It was as if she awaited some omen, and I too trembled in the fear of its coming.

Then suddenly out of the night issued the hoarse and hideous croaking I had head upon my journey here. I reached out my arm to take her hand, but in an instant the mists broke over us, and I was groping in the vacancy. Something like panic took hold of me, and, beating through the blind obscurity, I rushed over the flat, calling upon her. In a little the swirl went by, and I perceived her upon the margin of the swamp, her arm raised as in imperious command, I ran to her, but stopped, amazed and shaken by a fearful sight. Low by the dripping reeds crouched a small squat thing, in the likeness of a monstrous frog, coughing and choking in its throat. As I stared, the creature rose upon its legs and disclosed a human resemblance. Its face was white and thin, with long black hair; its body gnarled and twisted as with the ague of a thousand years. In a flash of horror I realized this monster had once been a man!

Shaking, the creature whined in a breathless voice, pointing a skeleton finger at the woman by my side.

'Your eyes were my guide,' it quavered. 'Do you think that after all these years I have no knowledge of your eyes? Lo, is there aught of evil in you I am not instructed in? This is the Hell you designed for me, and now you would leave me to a greater one still.'

The wretch paused, and panting leaned upon a bush, while she stood silent, mocking him with her eyes, and soothing my terror with her soft touch.

'Hear!' he cried, turning to me, 'hear the tale of this woman that you may know her as she is. She is the witch of the marshes. Woman or Devil I know not, but only that the accursed marsh has crept into her soul and she herself has become its Evil Spirit; she herself, that lives and grows young and beautiful by it, has its full power to blight and chill and slay. I, who was once as you are, have this knowledge. What bones lie deep in this swamp who can say but she? She has drained of health, she has drained of mind and of soul; what is between her and her desire that she should not drain also of life? She has made me a devil in her Hell, and now she would leave me to my solitary pain, and go search for another victim. But she shall not!' he screamed through his chattering teeth; 'she shall not! My Hell is also hers! She shall not!'

Her smiling untroubled eyes left his face and turned to me: she put out her arms, swaying towards me, and so fervid and so great a light glowed in her face that, as one distraught of superhuman means, I took her into my embrace. And then the madness seized me.

'Woman or witch,' I said, 'I will go with you! Of what account this pitiful past? Blight me even as that wretch, so long as you are with me!'

She laughed, and, disengaging herself, leaned, half-clinging to me, towards the coughing creature by the mire.

'Come,' I cried, catching her by the waist. 'Come!' She laughed again a silver-ringing laugh. She moved with me slowly across the flat to where the track started for the portals of the marsh. She laughed and clung to me.

But at the edge of the track I was startled by a shrill, hoarse screaming; and behold, from my very feet, that loathsome creature rose up and wound his long black arms about her, shrieking and crying in his pain. Stooping I pushed him from her skirts, and with one sweep of my arm drew her across the pathway; as her face passed mine her eyes were wide and smiling.

Then of a sudden the still mist enveloped us once more; but ere it descended I had a glimpse of that contorted figure trembling on the margin, the white face drawn and full of desolate pain. At the sight an icy shiver ran through me. And then through the yellow gloom the shadow of her darted past me to the further side. I heard the hoarse cough, the dim noise of a struggle, a swishing sound, a thin cry, and then the sucking of the slime over something in the rushes. I leapt forward: and once again the fog thinned, and I beheld her, woman or devil, standing upon the verge, and peering with smiling eyes into the foul and sickly bog.

With a sharp cry wrung from my nerveless soul, I turned and fled down the narrow way from that accursed spot; and as I ran the thickening fog closed round me, and I heard far off, yet never lessening, the silver sound of her mocking laughter.

The Power of Darkness

E. NESBIT

It was an enthusiastic send-off. Half the students from her atelier were there, and twice as many more from other studios. She had been the belle of the Artists' Quarter in Montparnasse for three golden months. Now she was off to the Riviera to meet her people, and everyone she knew was at the Gare de Lyon to catch the last glimpse of her. And, as had been more than once said late of an evening, 'to see her was to love her'. She was one of those agitating blondes, with the naturally rippled hair, the rounded rose-leaf cheeks, the large violet-blue eyes, that looked all things and meant Heaven alone knew how little. She held her court like a queen, leaning out of the carriage window and receiving bouquets, books, journals, long last words, and last longing looks. All eyes were on her, and her eyes were for all – and her smile. For all but one, that is. Not a single glance went Edward's way, and Edward – tall, lean, gaunt, with big eyes, straight nose, and the mouth somewhat too small, too beautiful – seemed to grow thinner and paler before one's eyes. One pair of eyes at least saw the miracle worked, the paling of what had seemed absolute pallor, the revelation of the bones of a face that seemed already covered but by the thinnest possible veil of flesh.

And the man whose eyes saw this rejoiced, for he loved her, like the rest, or not like the rest, and he had had Edward's face before him for the last month, in that secret shrine where we set the loved and the hated, the shrine that is lighted by a million lamps kindled at the soul's flame, the shrine that leaps into dazzling glow when the candles are out and one lies alone on hot pillows to outface the night and the light as best one may.

'Oh, goodbye; goodbye, all of you,' said Rose. 'I shall miss you. Oh, you don't know how I shall miss you all!'

She gathered the eyes of her friends and her worshippers in a glance, as one gathers jewels on a silken string. The eyes of Edward alone seemed to escape her.

'En voiture, messieurs et dames!'

Folk drew back from the train. There was a whistle.

And then at the very last little moment of all, as the train pulled itself together for the start, her eyes met Edward's eyes. And the other man saw the meeting, and he knew – which was more than Edward did.

So when, the light of life having been borne away in the retreating train, the broken-hearted group dispersed, the other man – whose name, by the way, was Vincent – linked his arm in Edward's and asked, cheerily:

'Whither away, sweet nymph?'

'I'm off home,' said Edward. 'The seven-twenty to Calais.'

'Sick of Paris?'

'One has to see one's people sometimes, don't you know, hang it all!' was Edward's way of expressing the longing that tore him for the old house among the brown woods of Kent.

'No attraction here now, eh?'

'The chief attraction has gone, certainly,' Edward made himself say.

'But there are as good fish in the sea— .'

'Fishing isn't my trade,' said Edward.

'The beautiful Rose!' said Vincent.

Edward raised hurriedly the only shield he could find. It happened to be the truth as he saw it.

'Oh,' he said, 'of course, we're all in love with her – and all hopelessly.'

Vincent perceived that this was truth, as Edward saw it.

'What are you going to do till your train goes?' he asked.

'I don't know. Café', I suppose, and a vilely early dinner.'

'Let's look in at the Musée Grévin,' said Vincent.

The two were friends. They had been schoolfellows, and this is a link that survives many a strain too strong to be resisted by more intimate and vital bonds. And they were fellow-students, though that counts for little or much – as you take it. Besides, Vincent knew something about Edward that no one else of their age and standing even guessed. He knew that Edward was afraid of the dark, and why. He had found it out that Christmas which the two had spent at an English country house. The house was full; there was a dance. There were to be theatricals. Early in the new year the hostess meant to 'move house' to an old convent, built in Tudor times, a beautiful palace with terraces and clipped yew trees, castellated battlements, a moat, swans, and a ghost story.

'You boys,' she said, 'must put up with a shakedown in the new house. I hope the ghost won't worry you. She's an old lady in a figured satin dress. Comes and breathes softly on the back of your neck when you're shaving. Then you see her in the glass, and as often as not you cut your throat.' She laughed. So did Edward and Vincent and the other young men. There were seven or eight of them.

But that night, when sparse candles had lighted 'the boys' to their rooms, when the last pipe had been smoked, the last 'Goodnight' said, there came a fumbling with the handle of Vincent's door. Edward came in, an unwieldy figure, clasping pillows, trailing blankets.

'What the deuce?' queried Vincent, in natural amazement.

'I'll turn in here on the floor if you don't mind,' said Edward. 'I know it's beastly rot, but I can't stand it. The room they've put me into, it's an attic as big as a barn – and there's a great door at the end, eight feet high, and it leads into a sort of horror hole – bare beams and rafters, and black as night. I know I'm an abject duffer, but there it is – I can't face it.'

Vincent was sympathetic; though he had never known a night terror that could not be exorcized by pipe, book, and candle.

'I know, old chap. There's no reasoning about these things,' said he, and so on.

'You can't despise me more than I despise myself,' Edward said. 'I feel a crawling hound. But it is so. I had a scare when I was a kid, and it seems to have left a sort of brand on me. I'm branded "coward", old man, and the feel of it's not nice.'

Again Vincent was sympathetic, and the poor little tale came out. How Edward, eight years old, and greedy as became his little years, had sneaked down, night-clad, to pick among the outcomings of a dinner party, and how, in the hall, dark with the light of an 'artistic' coloured glass lantern, a white figure had suddenly faced him – leaned towards him, it seemed, pointed lead-white hands at his heart. That next day, finding him weak from his fainting fit, had shown the horror to be but a statue, a new purchase of his father's, had mattered not one whit.

Edward shared Vincent's room, and Vincent, alone of all men, shared Edward's secret.

And now, in Paris, Rose speeding away towards Cannes, Vincent said:

'Let's look in at the Musée Grévin.'

The Musée Grévin is a waxwork show. Your mind, at the word, flies instantly to the excellent exhibition founded by the worthy Mme Tussaud. And you think you know what waxworks mean. But you are wrong. The Musée Grévin contains the work of artists for a nation of artists. Wax-modelled and retouched till it seems as near life as death is: this is what one sees at the Musée Grévin.

'Let's look in at the Musée Grévin,' said Vincent. He remembered the pleasant thrill the Musée had given him, and wondered what sort of a thrill it would give his friend.

'I hate museums,' said Edward.

'This isn't a museum,' Vincent said, and truly; 'it's just waxworks.'

'All right,' said Edward, indifferently. And they went.

They reached the doors of the Musée in the grey-brown dusk of a February evening.

One walks along a bare, narrow corridor, much like the entrance to the stalls of the Standard Theatre, and such daylight as there may be fades away behind one, and one finds oneself in a square hall, heavily decorated, and displaying with its electric lights Loie Fuller in her accordion-pleated skirts, and one or two other figures not designed to quicken the pulse.

'It's very like Mme Tussaud's,' said Edward.

'Yes,' Vincent said; 'isn't it?'

Then they passed through an arch, and beheld a long room with waxen groups life-like behind glass – the *coulisses* of the Opera, Kitchener at Fashoda – this last with a desert background lit by something convincingly like desert sunlight.

'By Jove!' said Edward. 'That's jolly good.'

'Yes,' said Vincent again; 'isn't it?'

Edward's interest grew.

The things were so convincing, so very nearly alive. Given the right angle, their glass eyes met one's own, and seemed to exchange with one meaning glances.

Vincent led the way to an arched door labelled 'Galerie de la Révolution.'

There one saw – almost in the living, suffering body – poor Marie Antoinette in prison in the Temple, her little son on his couch of rags, the rats eating from his platter, the brutal Simon calling to him from the grated window. One almost heard the words: 'Hola, little Capet! – are you asleep?'

One saw Marat bleeding in his bath, the brave Charlotte eyeing him; the very tiles of the bathroom, the glass of the windows, with, outside, the very sunlight, as it seemed, of 1793, on that 'yellow July evening, the thirteenth of the month'.

The spectators did not move in a public place among waxwork figures. They peeped through open doors into rooms where history seemed to be relived. The rooms were lighted each by its own sun or lamp or candle. The spectators walked among shadows that might have oppressed a nervous person.

'Fine, eh?' said Vincent.

'Yes,' said Edward; 'it's wonderful.'

A turn of a corner brought them to a room. Marie Antoinette fainting, supported by her ladies; poor, fat Louis by the window looking literally sick.

'What's the matter with them all?' said Edward.

'Look at the window,' said Vincent.

There was a window to the room. Outside was sunshine – the sunshine of 1792 – and gleaming in it, blonde hair flowing, red mouth half-open, what seemed the just-severed head of a beautiful woman. It was raised on a pike, so that it seemed to he looking in at the window.

'I say,' said Edward, and the head on the pike seemed to sway before his eyes.

'Mme de Lamballe. Good thing, isn't it?' said Vincent.

'It's altogether too much of a good thing,' said Edward. 'Look here – I've had enough of this.'

'Oh, you must just see the Catacombs,' said Vincent; 'nothing gruesome, you know. Only early Christians being married and baptized, and all that.'

He led the way down some clumsy steps to the cellars which the genius of a great artist has transformed into the exact semblance of the old Catacombs at

Rome. The same rough hewing of rock, the same sacred tokens engraved strongly and simply; and among the arches of these subterranean burrowings the life of the early Christians, their sacraments, their joys, their sorrows – all expressed in groups of waxwork as like life as death is.

'But this is very fine, you know,' said Edward, getting his breath again after Mme de Lamballe, and his imagination loved the thought of the noble sufferings and refrainings of these first lovers of the crucified Christ.

'Yes,' said Vincent, for the third time; 'isn't it?'

They passed the baptism and the burying and the marriage. The tableaux were sufficiently lighted, but little light strayed to the narrow passage where the two men walked, and the darkness seemed to press, tangible as a bodily presence, against Edward's shoulder. He glanced backward.

'Come,' he said; 'I've had enough.'

'Come on, then,' said Vincent.

They turned the corner, and a blaze of Italian sunlight struck at their eyes with positive dazzlement. There lay the Coliseum – tier on tier of eager faces under the blue sky of Italy. They were level with the arena. In the arena were crosses; from them drooped bleeding figures. On the sand beasts prowled, bodies lay. They saw it all through bars. They seemed to be in the place where the chosen victims waited their turn, waited for the lions and the crosses, the palm and the crown. Close by Edward was a group – an old man, a woman, and children. He could have touched them with his hand. The woman and the man stared in an agony of terror straight in the eyes of a snarling tiger, ten feet long, that stood up on its hind feet and clawed through the bars at them. The youngest child only, unconscious of the horror, laughed in the very face of it. Roman soldiers, unmoved in military vigilance, guarded the group of martyrs. In a low cage to the left more wild beasts cringed and seemed to growl, unfed. Within the grating, on the wide circle of yellow sand, lions and tigers drank the blood of Christians. Close against the bars a great lion sucked the chest of a corpse, on whose bloodstained face the horror of the death-agony was printed plain.

'Good heavens!' said Edward. Vincent took his arm suddenly, and he started with what was almost a shriek.

'What a nervous chap you are!' said Vincent, complacently as they regained the street where the lights were, and the sound of voices and the movement of live human beings – all that warms and awakens nerves almost paralysed by the life in death of waxen immobility.

'I don't know,' said Edward. 'Let's have a vermouth, shall we? There's something uncanny about those wax things. They're like life – but they're much more like death. Suppose they moved? I don't feel at all sure that they don't move, when the lights are all out and there's no one there.'

He laughed.

'I suppose you were never frightened, Vincent?'

'Yes, I was once, said Vincent, sipping his absinthe. 'Three other men and I were taking turns by twos to watch by a dead man. It was a fancy of his mother's. Our time was up, and the other watch hadn't come. So my chap – the one who was watching with me, I mean – went to fetch them. I didn't think I should mind. But it was just like you say.'

'How?'

'Why, I kept thinking, "Suppose it should move." It was so like life. And if it did move, of course it would have been because it was alive, and I ought to have been glad, because the man was my friend. But all the same, if he had moved I should have gone mad.'

'Yes,' said Edward, 'that's just exactly it.'

Vincent called for a second absinthe.

'But a dead body's different to waxworks,' he said. 'I can't understand anyone being frightened of *them*.'

'Oh, can't you?' The contempt in the other's tone stung him. 'I bet you wouldn't spend a night alone in that place.'

'I bet you five pounds I do!'

'Done,' said Edward, briskly. 'At least, I would if you'd got five pounds.'

'But I have. I'm simply rolling. I've sold my Dejanira; didn't you know? I shall win your money though, anyway. But *you* couldn't do it, old man. I suppose you'll never outgrow that childish scare.'

'You might shut up about that,' said Edward, shortly.

'Oh, it's nothing to be ashamed of; some women are afraid of mice or spiders. I say, does Rose know you're a coward?'

'Vincent!'

'No offence, old boy. One may as well call a spade a spade. Of course, you've got tons of moral courage and all that. But you *are* afraid of the dark – and waxworks!'

'Are you trying to quarrel with me?'

'Heaven in its mercy forbid. But I bet *you* wouldn't spend a night in the Musée Grévin and keep your senses.'

'What's the stake?'

'Anything you like.'

'Make it that if I do you'll never speak to Rose again, and, what's more, that you'll never speak to me,' said Edward, white-hot, knocking down a chair as he rose.

'Done,' said Vincent. 'But you'll never do it. Keep your hair on. Besides, you're off home.'

'I shall be back in ten days. I'll do it then,' said Edward, and was off before the other could answer.

Then Vincent, left alone, sat still, and over his third absinthe remembered how, before she had known Edward, Rose had smiled on him more than the others, he thought. He thought of her wide, lovely eyes, her wild-rose cheeks, the scented curves of her hair, and then and there the devil entered into him.

In ten days Edward would undoubtedly try to win his wager. He would try to spend the night in the Musée Grévin. Perhaps something could be arranged before that. If one knew the place thoroughly! A little scare would serve Edward right for being the man to whom that last glance of Rose's had been given.

Vincent dined lightly, but with conscientious care – and as he dined he thought. Something might be done by tying a string to one of the figures and making it move when Edward was going through that impossible night among the effigies that are so like life – so like death. Something that was not the devil said:

'You may frighten him out of his wits.'

And the devil answered: 'Nonsense; do him good. He oughtn't to be such a schoolgirl.'

Anyway, the five pounds might as well be won tonight as any other night. He would take a greatcoat, sleep sound in the place of horrors, and the people who opened it in the morning to sweep and dust would bear witness that he had passed the night there. He thought he might trust to the French love of a sporting wager to keep him from any bother with the authorities.

So he went in among the crowd, and looked about among the waxworks for a place to hide in. He was not in the least afraid of these lifeless images. He had always been able to control his nervous tremors in his time. He was not even afraid of being frightened, which, by the way, is the worst fear of all.

As one looks at the room of the poor little Dauphin one sees a door to the left. It opens out of the room on to blackness. There were few people in the gallery. Vincent watched, and, in a moment when he was alone, stepped over the barrier and through this door. A narrow passage ran round behind the wall of the room. Here he hid, and when the gallery was deserted he looked out across the body of little Capet to the gaoler at the window. There was a soldier at the window too. Vincent amused himself with the fancy that this soldier might walk round the passage at the back of the room and tap him on the shoulder in the darkness. Only the head and shoulders of the soldier and the gaoler showed, so, of course, they could not walk, even if they were something that was not waxwork.

Presently he himself went along the passage and round to the window where they were. He found that they had legs. They were full-sized figures, dressed completely in the costume of the period.

'Thorough the beggars are, even the parts that don't show – artists, upon my word,' said Vincent, and went back to his doorway, thinking of the hidden carving behind the capitals of Gothic cathedrals.

But the idea of the soldier who might come behind him in the dark stuck in his mind. Though still a few visitors strolled through the gallery, the closing hour was near. He supposed it would be quite dark. Then – and now he had allowed himself to be amused by the thought of something that should creep up behind him in the dark – he might possibly be nervous in that passage round which, if waxworks could move, the soldier might have come.

'By Jove!' he said; 'one might easily frighten oneself by just fancying things.

Suppose there were a back way from Marat's bathroom, and instead of the soldier Marat came out of his bath with his wet towels stained with blood and dabbed them against your neck!'

When next the gallery was deserted he crept out. Not because he was nervous, he told himself, but because one might be, and because the passage was draughty, and he meant to sleep.

He went down the steps into the Catacombs, and here he spoke the truth to himself.

'Hang it all,' he said, 'I was nervous. That fool Edward must have infected me. Mesmeric influences or something.'

'Chuck it and go home,' said common sense.

'I'm hanged if I do,' said Vincent.

There were a good many people in the Catacombs at the moment. Live people. He sucked confidence from their nearness, and went up and down looking for a hiding place.

Through rock-hewn arches he saw a burial scene – a corpse on a bier surrounded by mourners; a great pillar cut off half the still lying figure. It was all still and unemotional as a Sunday-school oleograph. He waited till no one was near, then slipped quickly through the mourning group and hid behind the pillar. Surprising – heartening, too, to find a plain rush-chair there, doubtless set for the resting of tired officials. He sat down in it, comforted his hand with the commonplace lines of its rungs and back. A shrouded waxen figure just behind him to the left of his pillar worried him a little, but the corpse left him unmoved as itself. A far better place, this, than that draughty passage where the soldier with legs kept intruding on the darkness that is always behind one.

Custodians went along the passages issuing orders. A stillness fell. Then, suddenly, all the lights went out.

'That's all right,' said Vincent, and composed himself to sleep.

But he seemed to have forgotten what sleep was like. He firmly fixed his thoughts on pleasant things – the sale of his picture, dances with Rose, merry evenings with Edward and the others. But the thoughts rushed by him like motes in sunbeams – he could not hold a single one of them, and presently it seemed that he had thought of every pleasant thing that had ever happened to him, and that now, if he thought at all, he must think of the things one wants most to forget. And there would be time in this long night to think much of many things. But now he found that he could no longer think.

The draped effigy just behind him worried him again. He had been trying, at the back of his mind, behind the other thoughts, to strangle the thought of it. But it was there, very close to him. Suppose it put out its hand, its wax hand, and touched him? But it was of wax. It could not move. No, of course not. But suppose it *did*?

He laughed aloud, a short, dry laugh, that echoed through the vaults. The cheering effect of laughter has been overestimated perhaps. Anyhow, he did not laugh again.

The silence was intense, but it was a silence thick with rustlings and breathings, and movements that his ear, strained to the uttermost, could just not hear. Suppose, as Edward had said, when all the lights were out these things did move. A corpse was a thing that had moved, given a certain condition – life. What if there were a condition, given which these things could move? What if such conditions were present now? What if all of them – Napoleon, yellow-white from his death sleep; the beasts from the amphitheatre, gore dribbling from their jaws; that soldier with the legs – all were drawing near to him in this full silence? Those death masks of Robespierre and Mirabeau – they might float down through the darkness till they touched his face. That head of Mme de Lamballe on the pike might be thrust at him from behind the pillar. The silence throbbed with sounds that could not quite be heard.

'You fool,' he said to himself; 'your dinner has disagreed with you with a vengeance. Don't be an ass. The whole lot are only a set of big dolls.'

He felt for his matches and lighted a cigarette. The gleam of the match fell on the face of the corpse in front of him. The light was brief, and it seemed, somehow, impossible to look by its light in every corner where one would have wished to look. The match burnt his fingers as it went out. And there were only three more matches in the box.

It was dark again, and the image left on the darkness was that of the corpse in front of him. He thought of his dead friend. When the cigarette was smoked out he thought of him more and more, till it seemed that what lay on the bier was not wax. His hand reached forward and drew back more than once. But at last he made it touch the bier and through the blackness travel up along a lean, rigid arm to the wax face that lay there so still. The touch was not reassuring. Just so, and not otherwise, had his dead friend's face felt, to the last touch of his lips. Cold, firm, waxen. People always said the dead were 'waxen'. How true that was! He had never thought of it before. He thought of it now.

He sat still – so still that every muscle ached; because if you wish to hear the sounds that infest silence you must be very still indeed. He thought of Edward, and of the string he had meant to tie to one of the figures.

'That wouldn't be needed,' he told himself. And his ears ached with listening, listening for the sound that, it seemed, must break at last from that crowded silence.

He never knew how long he sat there. To move, to go up, to batter at the door and clamour to be let out – that one could have done if one had had a lantern or even a full matchbox. But in the dark, not knowing the turnings, to feel one's way among these things that were so like life and yet were not alive – to touch, perhaps, these faces that were not dead and yet felt like death! His heart beat heavily in his throat at the thought.

No; he must sit still till morning. He had been hypnotized into this state, he told himself, by Edward, no doubt; it was not natural to him.

Then, suddenly, the silence was shattered. In the dark something moved, and, after those sounds that the silence teemed with, the noise seemed to him thunder-loud. Yet it was only a very, very little sound, just the rustling of drapery, as though something had turned in its sleep. And there was a sigh – not far off.

Vincent's muscles and tendons tightened like fine-drawn wire. He listened. There was nothing more. Only the silence, the thick silence.

The sound had seemed to come from a part of the vault where long ago, when there was light, he had seen a grave being dug for the body of a young girl martyr.

'I will get up and go out,' said Vincent. 'I have three matches. I am off my head. I shall really be nervous presently if I don't look out.'

He got up and struck a match, refused his eyes the sight of the corpse whose waxen face he had felt in the blackness, and made his way through the crowd of figures. By the match's flicker they seemed to make way for him, to turn their heads to look after him. The match lasted till he got to a turn of the rock-hewn passage. His next match showed him the burial scene. The little, thin body of the martyr, palm in hand, lying on the rock-floor in patient waiting, the grave-digger, the mourners. Some standing, some kneeling, one crouched on the ground.

This was where that sound had come from, that rustle, that sigh. He had thought he was going away from it. Instead he had come straight to the spot where, if anywhere, his nerves might be expected to play him false.

'Bah!' he said, and he said it aloud. 'The silly things are only wax. Who's afraid?'

His voice sounded loud in the silence that lives with the wax people.

'They're only wax,' he said again, and touched with his foot contemptuously the crouching figure in the mantle.

And, as he touched it, it raised its head and looked vacantly at him, and its eyes were bright and alive. He staggered back against another figure and dropped the match. In the new darkness he heard the crouching figure move towards him. Then the darkness fitted in round him very closely.

'What was it exactly that sent poor Vincent mad – you've never told me?' Rose asked the question. She and Edward were looking out over the pines and tamarisks across the blue Mediterranean. They were very happy, because it was their honeymoon.

He told her about the Musée Grévin and the wager, but he did not state the terms of it.

'But why did he think you would be afraid?'

He told her why.

'And then what happened?'

'Why, I suppose he thought there was no time like the present – for his five pounds, you know – and he hid among the waxworks. And I missed my train, and, *I* thought, there was no time like the present. In fact, dear, I thought if I waited I should have time to make certain of funking it. So I hid there, too. And I put on my big black capuchon, and sat down right in one of the waxwork groups – they couldn't see me from the gallery where you walk. And after they put the lights out I simply went to sleep. And I woke up – and there was a light, and I heard someone say:

"They're only wax," and it was Vincent. He thought I was one of the wax people till I looked at him; and I expect he thought I was one of them even then, poor chap. And his match went out, and while I was trying to find my railway reading lamp that I'd got near me he began to scream. And the night-watchman came running. And now he thinks everyone in the asylum is made of wax, and he screams if they come near him. They have to put his food near him while he's asleep. It's horrible. I can't help feeling as if it were my fault somehow.'

'Of course it's not,' said Rose. 'Poor Vincent! Do you know, I never *really* liked him.'

There was a pause. Then she said:

'But how was it *you* weren't frightened?'

'I was,' he said, 'horribly frightened. It – it – sounds idiotic, but I was really. And yet I *had* to go through with it. And then I got among the figures of the people in the Catacombs, the people who died for – for things, don't you know, died in such horrible ways. And there they were, so calm – and believing it was all right. So I thought about what they'd gone through. It sounds awful rot, I know, dear, but I expect I was sleepy. Those wax people, they sort of seemed as if they were alive, and were telling me there wasn't anything to be frightened about. I felt as if I was one of them – and they were all my friends, and they'd wake me if anything went wrong. So I just went to sleep.'

'I think I understand,' she said. But she didn't.

'And the odd thing is,' he went on, 'I've never been afraid of the dark since. Perhaps his calling me a coward had something to do with it.'

'I don't think so,' said she. And she was right. But she would never have understood how, nor why.

Lot No. 249

ARTHUR CONAN DOYLE

Of the dealings of Edward Bellingham with William Monkhouse Lee, and of the cause of the great terror of Abercrombie Smith, it may be that no absolute and final judgment will ever be delivered. It is true that we have the full and clear narrative of Smith himself, and such corroboration as he could look for from Thomas Styles the servant, from the Reverend Plumptree Peterson, Fellow of Old's, and from such other people as chanced to gain some passing glance at this or that incident in a singular chain of events. Yet, in the main, the story must rest upon Smith alone, and the most will think that it is more likely that one brain, however outwardly sane, has some subtle warp in its texture, some strange flaw in its workings, than that the path of Nature has been overstepped in open day in so famed a centre of learning and light as the University of Oxford. Yet when we think how narrow and how devious this path of Nature is, how dimly we can trace it, for all our lamps of science, and how from the darkness which girds it round great and terrible possibilities loom ever shadowly upwards, it is a bold and confident man who will put a limit to the strange bypaths into which the human spirit may wander.

In a certain wing of what we will call Old College in Oxford there is a corner turret of an exceeding great age. The heavy arch which spans the open door has bent downwards in the centre under the weight of its years, and the grey, lichen-blotched blocks of stone are bound and knitted together with withes and strands of ivy, as though the old mother had set herself to brace them up against wind and weather. From the door a stone stair curves upward spirally, passing two landings, and terminating in a third one, its steps all shapeless and hollowed by the tread of so many generations of the seekers after knowledge. Life has flowed like water down this winding stair, and, waterlike, has left these smooth-worn grooves behind it. From the long-gowned, pedantic scholars of Plantagenet days down to the young bloods of a later age, how full and strong had been that tide of young, English life. And what was left now of all those hopes, those strivings, those fiery energies, save here and there in some old-world churchyard a few scratches upon a stone, and perchance a handful of dust in a mouldering coffin? Yet here were the silent stair and the grey, old wall, with bend and saltire and many another heraldic device still to be read upon its surface, like grotesque shadows thrown back from the days that had passed.

In the month of May, in the year 1884, three young men occupied the sets of rooms which opened on to the separate landings of the old stair. Each set consisted simply of a sitting-room and of a bedroom, while the two corresponding rooms upon the ground-floor were used, the one as a coal-cellar, and the other as the living-room of the servant, or scout, Thomas Styles, whose duty it was to wait upon the three men above him. To right and to left was a line of lecture-rooms and of offices, so that the dwellers in the old turret enjoyed a certain seclusion, which made the chambers popular among the more studious undergraduates. Such were the three who occupied them now – Abercrombie Smith above, Edward Bellingham beneath him, and William Monkhouse Lee upon the lowest storey.

It was ten o'clock on a bright, spring night, and Abercrombie Smith lay back in his armchair, his feet upon the fender, and his briar-root pipe between his lips. In a similar chair, and equally at his ease, there lounged on the other side of the fireplace his old school friend Jephro Hastie. Both men were in flannels, for they had spent their evening upon the river, but apart from their dress no one could look at their hard-cut, alert faces without seeing that they were open-air men – men whose minds and tastes turned naturally to all that was manly and robust. Hastie, indeed, was stroke of his college boat, and Smith was an even better oar, but a coming examination had already cast its shadow over him and held him to his work, save for the few hours a week which health demanded. A litter of medical books upon the table, with scattered bones, models, and anatomical plates, pointed to the extent as well as the nature of his studies, while a couple of single-sticks and a set of boxing-gloves above the mantelpiece hinted at the means by which, with Hastie's help, he might take his exercise in its most compressed and least-distant form. They knew each other very well – so well that they could sit now in that soothing silence which is the very highest development of companionship.

'Have some whisky,' said Abercrombie Smith at last between two cloudbursts. 'Scotch in the jug and Irish in the bottle.'

'No, thanks, I'm in for the sculls. I don't liquor when I'm training. How about you?'

'I'm reading hard. I think it best to leave it alone.'

Hastie nodded, and they relapsed into a contended silence.

'By the way, Smith,' asked Hastie, presently, 'have you made the acquaintance of either of the fellows on your stair yet?'

'Just a nod when we pass. Nothing more.'

'Hum! I should be inclined to let it stand at that. I know something of them both. Not much, but as much as I want. I don't think I should take them to my bosom if I were you. Not that there's much amiss with Monkhouse Lee.'

'Meaning the thin one?'

'Precisely. He is a gentlemanly little fellow. I don't think there is any vice in him. But then you can't know him without knowing Bellingham.'

'Meaning the fat one?'

'Yes, the fat one. And he's a man whom I, for one, would rather not know.'

Abercrombie Smith raised his eyebrows and glanced across at his companion.

'What's up, then?' he asked. 'Drink? Cards? Cad? You used not to be censorious.'

'Ah! you evidently don't know the man, or you wouldn't ask. There's something damnable about him – something reptilian. My gorge always rises at him. I should put him down as a man with secret vices – an evil liver. He's no fool, though. They say that he is one of the best men in his line that they have ever had in the college.'

'Medicine or classics?'

'Eastern languages. He's a demon at them. Chillingworth met him somewhere above the second cataract last long, and he told me that he just prattled to the Arabs as if he had been born and nursed and weaned among them. He talked Coptic to the Copts, and Hebrew to the Jews, and Arabic to the Bedouins, and they were all ready to kiss the hem of his frock-coat. There are some old hermit Johnnies up in those parts who sit on rocks and scowl and spit at the casual stranger. Well, when they saw this chap Bellingham, before he had said five words they just lay down on their bellies and wriggled. Chillingworth said that he never saw anything like it. Bellingham seemed to take it as his right, too, and strutted about among them and talked down to them like a Dutch uncle. Pretty good for an undergrad. of Old's, wasn't it?'

'Why do you say you can't know Lee without knowing Bellingham?'

'Because Bellingham is engaged to his sister Eveline. Such a bright little girl, Smith! I know the whole family well. It's disgusting to see that brute with her. A toad and a dove, that's what they always remind me of.'

Abercrombie Smith grinned and knocked his ashes out against the side of the grate.

'You show every card in your hand, old chap,' said he. 'What a prejudiced, green-eyed, evil-thinking old man it is! You have really nothing against the fellow except that.'

'Well, I've known her ever since she was as long as that cherry-wood pipe, and I don't like to see her taking risks. And it is a risk. He looks beastly. And he has a beastly temper, a venomous temper. You remember his row with Long Norton?'

'No; you always forget that I am a freshman.'

'Ah, it was last winter. Of course. Well, you know the towpath along by the river. There were several fellows going along it, Bellingham in front, when they came on an old market-woman coming the other way. It had been raining – you know what those fields are like when it has rained – and the path ran between the river and a great puddle that was nearly as broad. Well, what does this swine do but keep the path, and push the old girl into the mud, where she and her marketings came to terrible grief. It was a blackguard thing to do, and Long Norton, who is as gentle a fellow as ever stepped, told him what he thought of it. One word led to another, and it ended in Norton laying his stick across the fellow's shoulders. There was the deuce of a fuss about it, and it's a treat to see the way in which Bellingham looks at Norton when they meet now. By Jove, Smith, it's nearly eleven o'clock!'

'No hurry. Light your pipe again.'

'Not I. I'm supposed to be in training. Here I've been sitting gossiping when I ought to have been safely tucked up. I'll borrow your skull, if you can share it. Williams has had mine for a month. I'll take the little bones of your ear, too, if you are sure you won't need them. Thanks very much. Never mind a bag, I can carry them very well under my arm. Good night, my son, and take my tip as to your neighbour.'

When Hastie, bearing his anatomical plunder, had clattered off down the winding stair, Abercrombie Smith hurled his pipe into the wastepaper basket, and drawing his chair nearer to the lamp, plunged into a formidable, green-covered volume, adorned with great, coloured maps of that strange, internal kingdom of which we are the hapless and helpless monarchs. Though a freshman at Oxford, the student was not so in medicine, for he had worked for four years at Glasgow and at Berlin, and this coming examination would place him finally as a member of his profession. With his firm mouth, broad forehead, and clear-cut, somewhat hard-featured face, he was a man who, if he had no brilliant talent, was yet so dogged, so patient, and so strong that he might in the end overtop a more showy genius. A man who can hold his own among Scotchmen and North Germans is not a man to be easily set back. Smith had left a name at Glasgow and at Berlin, and he was bent now upon doing as much at Oxford, if hard work and devotion could accomplish it.

He had sat reading for about an hour, and the hands of the noisy carriage clock upon the side-table were rapidly closing together upon the twelve, when a sudden sound fell upon the student's ear – a sharp, rather shrill sound, like the hissing intake of a man's breath who gasps under some strong emotion. Smith laid down his book and slanted his ear to listen. There was no one on either side or above him, so that the interruption came certainly from the neighbour beneath – the same neighbour of whom Hastie had given so unsavoury an account. Smith knew him only as a flabby, pale-faced man of silent and studious habits, a man whose lamp threw a golden bar from the old turret even after he had extinguished his own. This community in lateness had formed a certain silent bond between them. It was soothing to Smith when the hours stole on towards dawning to feel that there was another so close who set as small a value upon his sleep as he did. Even now, as his thoughts turned towards him, Smith's feelings were kindly. Hastie was a good fellow, but he was rough, strong-fibred, with no imagination or sympathy. He could not tolerate departures from what he looked upon as the model type of manliness. If a man could not be measured by a public-school standard, then he was beyond the pale with Hastie. Like so many who are themselves robust, he was apt to confuse the constitution with the character, to ascribe to want of principle what was really a want of circulation. Smith, with his stronger mind, knew his friend's habit, and made allowance for it now as his thoughts turned towards the man beneath him.

There was no return of the singular sound, and Smith was about to turn to his work once more, when suddenly there broke out in the silence of the night a hoarse cry, a positive scream – the call of a man who is moved and shaken beyond all control. Smith sprang out of his chair and dropped his book. He was a man of fairly firm fibre, but there was something in this sudden, uncontrollable shriek of horror which chilled his blood and pringled in his skin. Coming in such a place and at such an hour, it brought a thousand fantastic possibilities into his head. Should he rush down, or was it better to wait? He had all the national hatred of making a scene, and he knew so little of his neighbour that he would not lightly intrude upon his affairs. For a moment he stood in doubt and even as he balanced the matter there was a quick rattle of footsteps upon the stairs, and young Monkhouse Lee, half-dressed and as white as ashes, burst into his room.

'Come down!' he gasped. 'Bellingham's ill.'

Abercrombie Smith followed him closely downstairs into the sitting-room which was beneath his own, and intent as he was upon the matter in hand, he could not but take an amazed glance around his as he crossed the threshold. It was such a chamber as he had never seen before – a museum rather than a study. Walls and ceiling were thickly covered with a thousand strange relics from Egypt and the East. Tall, angular figures bearing burdens or weapons stalked in an uncouth frieze round the apartments. Above were bull-headed, stork-headed, cat-headed, owl-headed statues, with viper-crowned, almond-eyed monarchs, and strange, beetle-like deities cut out of the blue Egyptian lapis lazuli. Horus and Isis and Osiris peeped down from every niche and shelf, while across the ceiling a true son of Old Nile, a great, hanging-jawed crocodile, was slung in a double noose.

In the centre of this singular chamber was a large, square table, littered with papers, bottles, and the dried leaves of some graceful, palm-like plant. These varied objects had all been heaped together in order to make room for a mummy case, which had been conveyed from the wall, as was evident from the gap there, and laid across the front of the table. The mummy itself, a horrid, black, withered thing, like a charred head on a gnarled bush, was lying half out of the case, with its claw-like hand and bony forearm resting upon the table. Propped up against the sarcophagus was an old, yellow scroll of papyrus, and in front of it, in a wooden armchair, sat the owner of the room, his head thrown back, his widely opened eyes directed in a horrified stare to the crocodile above him, and his blue, thick lips puffing loudly with every expiration.

'My God! he's dying!' cried Monkhouse Lee, distractedly.

He was a slim, handsome young fellow, olive-skinned and dark-eyed, of a Spanish rather than of an English type, with a Celtic intensity of manner which contrasted with the Saxon phlegm of Abercrombie Smith.

'Only a faint, I think,' said the medical student. 'Just give me a hand with him. You take his feet. Now on to the sofa. Can you kick all those little wooden devils off? What a litter it is! Now he will be all right if we undo his collar and give him some water. What has he been up to at all?'

'I don't know. I heard him cry out. I ran up. I know him pretty well, you know. It is very good of you to come down.'

'His heart is going like a pair of castanets,' said Smith, laying his hand on the breast of the unconscious man. 'He seems to me to be frightened all to pieces. Chuck the water over him! What a face he has got on him!'

It was indeed a strange and most repellent face, for colour and outline were equally unnatural. It was white, not with the ordinary pallor of fear, but with an absolutely bloodless white, like the under side of a sole. He was very fat, but gave the impression of having at some time been considerably fatter, for his skin hung loosely in creases and folds, and was shot with a meshwork of wrinkles. Short, stubbly brown hair bristled up from his scalp, with a pair of thick, wrinkled ears protruding at the sides. His light-grey eyes were still open, the pupils dilated and the balls projecting in a fixed and horrid stare. It seemed to Smith as he looked down upon him that he had never seen Nature's danger signals flying so plainly upon a man's countenance, and his thoughts turned more seriously to the warning which Hastie had given him an hour before.

'What the deuce can have frightened him so?' he asked.

'It's the mummy.'

'The mummy? How, then?'

'I don't know. It's beastly and morbid. I wish he would drop it. It's the second fright he has given me. It was the same last winter. I found him just like this, with that horrid thing in front of him.'

'What does he want with the mummy, then?'

'Oh, he's a crank, you know. It's his hobby. He knows more about these things than any man in England. But I wish he wouldn't! Ah, he's beginning to come to.'

A faint tinge of colour had begun to steal back into Bellingham's ghastly cheeks, and his eyelids shivered like a sail after a calm. He clasped and unclasped his hands, drew a long, thin breath between his teeth, and suddenly jerking up his head, threw a glance of recognition around him. As his eyes fell upon the mummy, he sprang off the sofa, seized the roll of papyrus, thrust it into a drawer, turned the key, and then staggered back on to the sofa.

'What's up?' he asked. 'What do you chaps want?'

'You've been shrieking out and making no end of a fuss,' said Monkhouse

Lee. 'If our neighbour here from above hadn't come down, I'm sure I don't know what I should have done with you.'

'Ah, it's Abercrombie Smith,' said Bellingham, glancing up at him. 'How very good of you to come in! What a fool I am! Oh, my God, what a fool I am!'

He sank his head on to his hands, and burst into peal after peal of hysterical laughter.

'Look here! Drop it!' cried Smith, shaking him roughly by the shoulder.

'Your nerves are all in a jangle. You must drop these little midnight games with mummies, or you'll be going off your chump. You're all on wires now.'

'I wonder,' said Bellingham, 'whether you would be as cool as I am if you had seen – '

'What then?'

'Oh, nothing. I meant that I wonder if you could sit up at night with a mummy without trying your nerves. I have no doubt that you are quite right. I dare say that I have been taking it out of myself too much lately. But I am all right now. Please don't go, though. Just wait for a few minutes until I am quite myself.'

'The room is very close,' remarked Lee, throwing open the window and letting in the cool night air.

'It's balsamic resin,' said Bellingham. He lifted up one of the dried palmate leaves from the table and frizzled it over the chimney of the lamp. It broke away into heavy smoke wreaths, and a pungent, biting odour filled the chamber. 'It's a sacred plant – the plant of the priests,' he remarked. 'Do you know anything of Eastern languages, Smith?'

'Nothing at all. Not a word.'

The answer seemed to lift a weight from the Egyptologist's mind.

'By the way,' he continued, 'how long was it from the time that you ran down, until I came to my senses?'

'Not long. Some four or five minutes.'

'I thought it could not be very long,' said he, drawing a long breath. 'But what a strange thing unconsciousness is! There is no measurement to it. I could not tell from my own sensations if it were seconds or weeks. Now that gentleman on the table was packed up in the days of the eleventh dynasty, some forty centuries ago, and yet if he could find his tongue, he would tell us that this lapse of time has been but a closing of the eyes and a reopening of them. He is a singularly fine mummy, Smith.'

Smith stepped over to the table and looked down with a professional eye at the black and twisted form in front of him. The features, though horribly discoloured, were perfect, and two little nut-like eyes still lurked in the depths of the black, hollow sockets. The blotched skin was drawn tightly from bone to bone, and a tangled wrap of black, coarse hair fell over the ears. Two thin teeth, like those of a rat, overlay the shrivelled, lower lip. In its crouching position, with bent joints and craned head, there was a suggestion of energy about the horrid thing which made Smith's gorge rise. The gaunt ribs, with their parchment-like covering, were exposed, and the sunken, leaden-hued abdomen, with the long slit where the embalmer had left his mark; but the lower limbs were wrapped round with coarse, yellow bandages. A number of little clove-like pieces of myrrh and of cassia were sprinkled over the body, and lay scattered on the inside of the case.

'I don't know his name,' said Bellingham, passing his hand over the shrivelled head. 'You see the outer sarcophagus with the inscriptions is missing. Lot 249 is all the title he has now. You see it printed on his case. That was his number in the auction at which I picked him up.'

'He has been very pretty sort of fellow in his day,' remarked Abercrombie Smith.

'He has been a giant. His mummy is six feet seven in length, and that would be a giant over there, for they were never a very robust race. Feel these great, knotted bones, too. He would be a nasty fellow to tackle.'

'Perhaps these very hands helped to build the stones into the pyramids,' suggested Monkhouse Lee, looking down with disgust in his eyes at the crooked, unclean talons.

'No fear. This fellow has been pickled in natron, and looked after in the most approved style. They did not serve hodsmen in that fashion. Salt or bitumen was enough for them. It has been calculated that this sort of thing cost about seven hundred and thirty pounds in our money. Our friend was a noble at the least. What do you make of that small inscription near his feet, Smith?'

'I told you that I know no Eastern tongue.'

'Ah, so you did. It is the name of the embalmer, I take it. A very conscientious worker he must have been. I wonder how many modern works will survive four thousand years?'

He kept on speaking lightly and rapidly, but it was evident to Abercrombie Smith that he was still palpitating with fear. His hands shook, his lower lip trembled, and look where he would, his eye always came sliding round to his gruesome companion. Through all his fear, however, there was a suspicion of triumph in his tone and manner. His eyes shone, and his footstep, as he paced the room, was brisk and jaunty. He gave the impression of a man who has gone through an ordeal, the marks of which he still bears upon him, but which has helped him to his end.

'You're not going yet?' he cried, as Smith rose from the sofa.

At the prospect of solitude, his fears seemed to crowd back upon him, and he stretched out a hand to detain him.

'Yes, I must go. I have my work to do. You are all right now. I think that with your nervous system you should take up some less morbid study.'

'Oh, I am not nervous as a rule; and I have unwrapped mummies before.'

'You fainted last time,' observed Monkhouse Lee.

'Ah, yes, so I did. Well, I must have a nerve tonic or a course of electricity. You are not going, Lee?'

'I'll do whatever you wish, Ned.'

Then I'll come down with you and have a shakedown on your sofa. Good-night, Smith. I am so sorry to have disturbed you with my foolishness.'

They shook hands, and as the medical student stumbled up the spiral and irregular stair he heard a key turn in a door, and the steps of his two new acquaintances as they descended to the lower floor.

In this strange way began the acquaintance between Edward Bellingham and Abercrombie Smith, an acquaintance which the latter, at least, had no desire to push further. Bellingham, however, appeared to have taken a fancy to his rough-spoken neighbour, and made his advances in such a way that he could hardly be repulsed without absolute brutality. Twice he called to thank Smith for his assistance, and many times afterwards he looked in with books, papers and such other civilities as two bachelor neighbours can offer each other. He was, as Smith soon found, a man of wide reading, with catholic tastes and an extraordinary memory. His manner, too, was so pleasing and suave that one came, after a time, to overlook his repellent appearance. For a jaded and wearied man he was no unpleasant companion, and Smith found himself, after a time, looking forward to his visits, and even returning them.

Clever as he undoubtedly was, however, the medical student seemed to detect a dash of insanity in the man. He broke out at times into a high, inflated style of talk which was in contrast with the simplicity of his life.

'It is a wonderful thing,' he cried, 'to feel that one can command powers of good and of evil – a ministering angel or a demon of vengeance.' And again, of Monkhouse Lee, he said, 'Lee is a good fellow, an honest fellow, but he is without strength or ambition. He would not make a fit partner for a man with a great enterprise. He would not make a fit partner for me.'

At such hints and innuendoes stolid Smith, puffing solemnly at his pipe, would simply raise his eyebrows and shake his head, with little interjections of medical wisdom as to earlier hours and fresher air.

One habit Bellingham had developed of late which Smith knew to be a frequent herald of a weakening mind. He appeared to be for ever talking to himself. At late hours of the night, when there could be no visitor with him, Smith could still hear his voice beneath him in a low, muffled monologue, sunk almost to a whisper, and yet very audible in the silence. This solitary babbling annoyed and distracted the student, so that he spoke more than once to his neighbour about it. Bellingham, however, flushed up at the charge, and denied curtly that he had uttered a sound; indeed, he showed more annoyance over the matter than the occasion seemed to demand.

Had Abercrombie Smith had any doubt as to his own ears he had not to go far to find corroboration. Tom Styles, the little wrinkled man-servant who had attended to the wants of the lodgers in the turret for a longer time than any man's memory could carry him, was sorely put to it over the same matter.

'If you please, sir,' said he, as he tidied down the top chamber one morning, 'do you think Mr Bellingham is all right, sir?'

'All right, Styles?'

'Yes, sir. Right in his head, sir.'

'Why should he not be, then?'

'Well, I don't know, sir. His habits has changed of late. He's not the same man he used to be, though I make free to say that he was never quite one of my gentlemen, like Mr Hastie or yourself, sir. He's took to talkin' to himself something awful. I wonder it don't disturb you. I don't know what to make of him, sir.'

'I don't know what business it is of yours, Styles.'

'Well, I takes an interest, Mr Smith. It may be forward of me, but I can't help it. I feel sometimes as if I was mother and father to my young gentlemen. It all falls on me when things go wrong and the relations come. But Mr Bellingham, sir. I want to know what it is that walks about his room sometimes when he's out and when the door's locked on the outside.'

'Eh? you're talking nonsense, Styles.'

'Maybe so, sir; but I heard it more'n once with my own ears.'

'Rubbish, Styles.'

'Very good, sir. You'll ring the bell if you want me.'

Abercrombie Smith gave little heed to the gossip of the old man-servant, but a small incident occurred a few days later which left an unpleasant effect upon his mind, and brought the words of Styles forcibly to his memory.

Bellingham had come up to see him late one night, and was entertaining him with an interesting account of the rock tombs of Beni Hassan in Upper Egypt, when Smith, whose hearing was remarkably acute, distinctly heard the sound of a door opening on the landing below.

'There's some fellow gone in or out of your room,' he remarked.

Bellingham sprang up and stood helpless for a moment, with the expression of a man who is half-incredulous and half-afraid.

'I surely locked it. I am almost positive that I locked it,' he stammered. 'No one could have opened it.'

'Why, I hear someone coming up the steps now,' said Smith.

Bellingham rushed out through the door, slammed it loudly behind him, and hurried down the stairs. About half-way down Smith heard him stop, and thought he caught the sound of whispering. A moment later the door beneath him shut, a key creaked in a lock, and Bellingham, with beads of moisture upon his pale face, ascended the stairs once more, and re-entered the room.

'It's all right,' he said, throwing himself down in a chair. 'It was that fool of a dog. He had pushed the door open. I don't know how I came to forget to lock it.'

'I didn't know you kept a dog,' said Smith, looking very thoughtfully at the disturbed face of his companion.

'Yes, I haven't had him long. I must get rid of him. He's a great nuisance.'

'He must be, if you find it so hard to shut him up. I should have thought that shutting the door would have been enough, without locking it.'

'I want to prevent old Styles from letting him out. He's of some value, you know, and it would be awkward to lose him.'

'I am a bit of a dog-fancier myself,' said Smith, still gazing hard at his companion from the corner of his eyes. 'Perhaps you'll let me have a look at it.'

'Certainly. But I am afraid it cannot be tonight; I have an appointment. Is that clock right? Then I am a quarter of an hour late already. You'll excuse me, I am sure.'

He picked up his cap and hurried from the room. In spite of his appointment, Smith heard him re-enter his own chamber and lock his door upon the inside.

This interview left a disagreeable impression upon the medical student's mind. Bellingham had lied to him, and lied so clumsily that it looked as if he had desperate reasons for concealing the truth. Smith knew that his neighbour had no dog. He knew, also, that the step which he had heard upon the stairs was not the step of an animal. But if it were not, then what could it be? There was old Style's statement about the something which used to pace the room at times when the owner was absent. Could it be a woman? Smith rather inclined to the view. If so, it would mean disgrace and expulsion to Bellingham if it were discovered by the authorities, so that his anxiety and falsehoods might be accounted for. And yet it was inconceivable that an undergraduate could keep a woman in his rooms without being instantly detected. Be the explanation what it might, there was something ugly about it, and Smith determined, as he turned to his books, to discourage all further attempts at intimacy on the part of his softspoken and ill-favoured neighbour.

But his work was destined to interruption that night. He had hardly caught up the broken threads when a firm, heavy footfall came three steps at a time from below, and Hastie, in blazer and flannels, burst into the room.

'Still at it!' said he, plumping down into his wonted armchair. 'What a chap you are to stew! I believe an earthquake might come and knock Oxford into a cocked hat, and you would sit perfectly placid with your books among the ruins. However, I won't bore you long. Three whiffs of baccy, and I am off.'

'What's the news, then?' asked Smith, cramming a plug of bird's-eye into his briar with his forefinger.

'Nothing very much. Wilson made 70 for the freshmen against the eleven. They say that they will play him instead of Buddicomb, for Buddicomb is clean off colour. He used to be able to bowl a little, but it's nothing but half-volleys and long hops now.'

'Medium right,' suggested Smith, with the intense gravity which comes upon a 'varsity man when he speaks of athletics.

'Inclining to fast, with a work from leg. Comes with the arm about three inches or so. He used to be nasty on a wet wicket. Oh, by the way, have you heard about Long Norton?'

'What's that?'

'He's been attacked.'

'Attacked?'

'Yes, just as he was turning out of the High Street, and within a hundred yards of the gate of Old's.'

'But who – '

'Ah, that's the rub! If you said "what," you would be more grammatical. Norton swears that it was not human, and, indeed, from the scratches on his throat, I should be inclined to agree with him.'

'What, then? Have we come down to spooks?'

Abercrombie Smith puffed his scientific contempt.

'Well, no; I don't think that is quite the idea, either. I am inclined to think that if any showman has lost a great ape lately, and the brute is in these parts, a jury would find a true bill against it. Norton passes that way every night, you know, about the same hour. There's a tree that hangs low over the path – the big elm from Rainy's garden. Norton thinks the thing dropped on him out of the tree. Anyhow, he was nearly strangled by two arms, which, he says, were as strong and as thin as steel bands. He saw nothing; only those beastly arms that tightened and tightened on him. He yelled his head nearly off, and a couple of chaps came running, and the thing went over the wall like a cat. He never got a fair sight of it the whole time. It gave Norton a shake up, I can tell you. I tell him it has been as good as a change at the seaside for him.'

'A garrotter, most likely,' said Smith.

'Very possibly. Norton says not; but we don't mind what he says. The garrotter had long nails, and was pretty smart at swinging himself over walls. By the way, your beautiful neighbour would be pleased if he heard about it. He had a grudge against Norton, and he's not a man, from what I know of him, to forget his little debts. But hallo, old chap, what have you got in your noddle?'

'Nothing,' Smith answered curtly.

He had started in his chair, and the look had flashed over his face which comes upon a man who is struck suddenly by some unpleasant idea.

'You looked as if something I had said had taken you on the raw. By the way, you have made the acquaintance of Master B. since I looked in last, have you not? Young Monkhouse Lee told me something to that effect.'

'Yes; I know him slightly. He has been up here one or twice.'

'Well, you're big enough and ugly enough to take care of yourself. He's not what I should call exactly a healthy sort of Johnny, though, no doubt, he's very clever, and all that. But you'll soon find out for yourself. Lee is all right; he's a very decent little fellow. Well, so long, old chap! I row Mullins for the Vice-Chancellor's pot on Wednesday week, so mind you come down, in case I don't see you before.'

Bovine Smith laid down his pipe and turned stolidly to his books once more. But with all the will in the world, he found it very hard to keep his mind upon his work. It would slip away to brood upon the man beneath him, and upon the little mystery which hung round his chambers. Then his thoughts turned to this singular attack of which Hastie had spoken, and to the grudge which Bellingham was said to owe the object of it. The two ideas would persist in rising together in his mind, as though there were some close and intimate connection between them. And yet the suspicion was so dim and vague that it could not be put down in words.

'Confound the chap!' cried Smith, as he shied his book on pathology across the room. 'He has spoiled my night's reading, and that's reason enough, if there were no other, why I should steer clear of him in the future.'

For ten days the medical student confined himself so closely to his studies that he neither saw nor heard anything of either of the men beneath him. At the hours when Bellingham had been accustomed to visit him, he took care to sport his oak, and though he more than once heard a knocking at his outer door, he resolutely refused to answer it. One afternoon, however, he was descending the stairs when, just as he was passing it, Bellingham's door flew open, and young Monkhouse Lee came out with his eyes sparkling and a dark flush of anger upon his olive cheeks. Close at his heels followed Bellingham, his fat, unhealthy face all quivering with malignant passion.

'You fool!' he hissed. 'You'll be sorry.'

'Very likely,' cried the other. 'Mind what I say. It's off! I won't hear of it!'

'You've promised, anyhow.'

'Oh, I'll keep that! I won't speak. But I'd rather little Eva was in her grave. Once for all, it's off. She'll do what I say. We don't want to see you again.'

So much Smith could not avoid hearing, but he hurried on, for he had no wish to be involved in their dispute. There had been a serious breach between them, that was clear enough, and Lee was going to cause the engagement with his sister to be broken off. Smith thought of Hastie's comparison of the toad and the dove, and was glad to think that the matter was at an end. Bellingham's face when he was in a passion was not pleasant to look upon. He was not a man to whom an innocent girl could be trusted for life. As he walked, Smith wondered languidly what could have caused the quarrel, and what the promise might be which Bellingham had been so anxious that Monkhouse Lee should keep.

It was the day of the sculling match between Hastie and Mullins, and a stream of men were making their way down to the banks of the Isis. A May sun was shining brightly, and the yellow path was barred with the black shadows of the tall elm-trees. On either side the grey colleges lay back from the road, the hoary old mothers of minds looking out from their high, mullioned windows at the tide of young life which swept so merrily past them. Blackclad tutors, prim officials, pale, reading men, brown-faced, straw-hatted young athletes in white sweaters or many-coloured blazers, all were hurrying towards the blue, winding river which curves through the Oxford meadows.

Abercrombie Smith, with the intuition of an old oarsman, chose his position at the point where he knew that the struggle, if there were a struggle, would come. Far off he heard the hum which announced the start, the gathering roar of the approach, the thunder of running feet, and the shouts of the men in the boats beneath him. A spray of half-clad, deep-breathing runners shot past him, and craning over their shoulders, he saw Hastie pulling a steady thirty-six, while his opponent, with a jerky forty, was a good boat's length behind him. Smith gave a cheer for his friend, and pulling out his watch, was starting off again for his chambers, when he felt a touch upon his shoulder, and found that young Monkhouse Lee was beside him.

'I saw you there,' he said, in a timid, deprecating way. 'I wanted to speak to you, if you could spare me a half-hour. This cottage is mine. I share it with Harrington of King's. Come in and have a cup of tea.'

'I must be back presently,' said Smith. 'I am hard on the grind at present. But I'll come in for a few minutes with pleasure. I wouldn't have come out only Hastie is a friend of mine.'

'So he is of mine. Hasn't he a beautiful style? Mullins wasn't in it. But come into the cottage. It's a little den of a place, but it is pleasant to work in during the summer months.'

It was a small, square, white building, with green doors and shutters, and a rustic trellis-work porch, standing back some fifty yards from the river's bank. Inside, the main room was roughly fitted up as a study – deal table, unpainted shelves with the books, and a few cheap oleographs upon the wall. A kettle sang upon a spirit-stove, and there were tea things upon a tray on the table.

'Try that chair and have a cigarette,' said Lee. 'Let me pour you out a cup of tea. It's so good of you to come in, for I know that your time is a good deal taken up. I wanted to say to you that, if I were you, I should change my rooms at once.'

'Eh?'

Smith sat staring with a lighted match in one hand and his unlit cigarette in the other.

'Yes; it must seem very extraordinary, and the worst of it is that I cannot give my reasons, for I am under a solemn promise – a very solemn promise. But I may go so far as to say that I don't think Bellingham is a very safe man to live near. I intend to camp out here as much as I can for a time.'

'Not safe! What do you mean?'

'Ah, that's what I mustn't say. But do take my advice and move your rooms. We had a grand row today. You must have heard us, for you came down the stairs.'

'I saw that you had fallen out.'

'He's a horrible chap, Smith. That is the only word for him. I have had doubts about him ever since that night when he fainted – you remember, when you came down. I taxed him to-day, and he told me things that made my hair rise, and wanted me to stand in with him. I'm not straight-laced, but I am a clergyman's son, you know, and I think there are some things which are quite beyond the pale. I only thank God that I found him out before it was too late, for he was to have married into my family.'

'This is all very fine, Lee,' said Abercrombine Smith curtly. 'But either you are saying a great deal too much or a great deal too little.'

'I give you a warning.'

'If there is real reason for warning, no promise can bind you. If I see a rascal about to blow a place up with dynamite no pledge will stand in my way of preventing him.'

'Ah, but I cannot prevent him, and I can do nothing but warn you.'

'Without saying what you warn me against.'

'Against Bellingham.'

'But that is childish. Why should I fear him, or any man?'

'I can't tell you. I can only entreat you to change your rooms. You are in danger where you are. I don't even say that Bellingham would wish to injure you. But it might happen, for he is a dangerous neighbour just now.'

'Perhaps I know more than you think,' said Smith, looking keenly at the young man's boyish, earnest face. 'Suppose I tell you that someone else shares Bellingham's rooms.'

Monkhouse Lee sprang from his chair in uncontrollable excitement.

'You know, then?' he gasped.

'A woman.'

Lee dropped back again with a groan.

'My lips are sealed,' he said. 'I must not speak.'

'Well, anyhow,' said Smith, rising, 'it is not likely that I should allow myself to be frightened out of rooms which suit me very nicely. It would be a little too feeble for me to move out all my goods and chattels because you say that Bellingham might in some unexplained way do me an injury. I think that I'll just take my chance, and stay where I am, and as I see that it's nearly five o'clock, I must ask you to excuse me.'

He bade the young student adieu in a few curt words, and made his way homeward through the sweet spring evening, feeling half-ruffled, half-amused, as any other strong, unimaginative man might who has been menaced by a vague and shadowy danger.

There was one little indulgence which Abercrombie Smith always allowed himself, however closely his work might press upon him. Twice a week, on the Tuesday and the Friday, it was his invariable custom to walk over to Farlingford, the residence of Doctor Plumptree Peterson, situated about a mile and a half out of Oxford. Peterson had been a close friend of Smith's elder brother, Francis, and as he was a bachelor, fairly well-to-do, with a good cellar and a better library, his house was a pleasant goal for a man who was in need of a brisk walk. Twice a week, then, the medical student would swing out there along the dark country roads and spend a pleasant hour in Peterson's comfortable study, discussing, over a glass of old port, the gossip of the 'varsity or the latest developments of medicine or of surgery.

On the day which followed his interview with Monkhouse Lee, Smith shut up his books at a quarter past eight, the hour when he usually started for his friend's house. As he was leaving his room, however, his eyes chanced to fall upon one of the books which Bellingham had lent him, and his conscience pricked him for not having returned it. However repellent the man might be, he should not be treated with discourtesy. Taking the book, he walked downstairs and knocked at his neighbour's door. There was no answer; but on turning the handle he found that it was unlocked. Pleased at the thought of avoiding an interview, he stepped inside, and placed the book with his card upon the table.

The lamp was turned half down, but Smith could see the details of the room plainly enough. It was all much as he had seen it before – the frieze, the animal-headed gods, the hanging crocodile, and the table littered over with papers and dried leaves. The mummy case stood upright against the wall, but the mummy itself was missing. There was no sign of any second occupant of the room, and he felt as he withdrew that he had probably done Bellingham an injustice. Had he a guilty secret to preserve, he would hardly leave his door open so that all the world might enter.

The spiral stair was as black as pitch, and Smith was slowly making his way down its irregular steps, when he was suddenly conscious that something had passed him in the darkness. There was a faint sound, a whiff of air, a light brushing past his elbow, but so slight that lie could scarcely be certain of it. He stopped and listened, but the wind was rustling among the ivy outside, and he could hear nothing else.

'Is that you, Styles?' he shouted.

There was no answer, and all was still behind him. It must have been a sudden gust of air, for there were crannies and cracks in the old turret. And yet he could almost have sworn that he heard a footfall by his very side. He had emerged into the quadrangle, still turning the matter over in his head, when a man came running swiftly across the smooth-cropped lawn.

'Is that you, Smith?'

'Hullo, Hastie!'

'For God's sake come at once! Young Lee is drowned! Here's Harrington of King's with the news. The doctor is out. You'll do, but come along at once. There may be life in him.'

'Have you brandy?'

'No.'

'I'll bring some. There's a flask on my table.'

Smith bounded up the stairs, taking three at a time, seized the flask, and was rushing down with it, when, as he passed Bellingham's room, his eyes fell upon something which left him gasping and staring upon the landing.

The door, which he had closed behind him, was now open, and right in front of him, with the lamp-light shining upon it, was the mummy case. Three minutes ago it had been empty. He could swear to that. Now it framed the lank body of its horrible occupant, who stood, grim and stark, with his black, shrivelled face towards the door. The form was lifeless and inert, but it seemed to Smith as he gazed that there still lingered a lurid spark of vitality, some faint sign of consciousness in the little eyes which lurked in the depths of the hollow sockets. So astounded and shaken was he that he had forgotten his errand, and was still staring at the lean, sunken figure when the voice of his friend below recalled him to himself.

'Come on, Smith!' he shouted. 'It's life and death, you know. Hurry up! Now, then,' he added, as the medical student reappeared, 'let us do a sprint. It is well under a mile, and we should do it in five minutes. A human life is better worth running for than a pot.'

Neck and neck they dashed through the darkness, and did not pull up until panting and spent, they had reached the little cottage by the river. Young Lee, limp and dripping like a broken waterplant, was stretched upon the sofa, the green scum of the river upon his black hair, and a fringe of white foam upon his leaden-hued lips. Beside him knelt his fellow-student, Harrington, endeavouring to chafe some warmth back into his rigid limbs.

'I think there's life in him,' said Smith, with his hand to the lad's side. 'Put your watch glass to his lips. Yes, there's dimming on it. You take one arm, Hastie. Now work it as I do, and we'll soon pull him round.'

For ten minutes they worked in silence, inflating and depressing the chest of the unconscious man. At the end of that time a shiver ran through his body, his lips trembled, and he opened his eyes. The three students burst out into an irrepressible cheer.

'Wake up, old chap. You've frightened us quite enough.'

'Have some brandy. Take a sip from the flask.'

'He's all right now,' said his companion Harrington. 'Heavens, what a fright I got! I was reading here, and he had gone out for a stroll as far as the river, when I heard a scream and a splash. Out I ran, and by the time I could find him and fish him out, all life seemed to have gone. Then Simpson couldn't get a doctor, for he has a game-leg, and I had to run, and I don't know what I'd have done without you fellows. That's right, old chap. Sit up.'

Monkhouse Lee had raised himself on his hands, and looked wildly about him.

'What's up?' he asked. 'I've been in the water. Ah, yes; I remember.'

A look of fear came into his eyes, and he sank his face into his hands.

'How did you fall in?'

'I didn't fall in.'

'How then?'

'I was thrown in. I was standing by the bank, and something from behind picked me up like a feather and hurled me in. I heard nothing, and I saw nothing. But I know what it was, for all that.'

'And so do I,' whispered Smith.

Lee looked up with a quick glance of surprise.

'You've learned, then?' he said. 'You remember the advice I gave you?'

'Yes, and I begin to think that I shall take it.'

'I don't know what the deuce you fellows are talking about,' said Hastie, 'but I think, if I were you, Harrington, I should get Lee to bed at once. It will be time enough to discuss the why and the wherefore when he is a little stronger. I think, Smith, you and I can leave him alone now. I am walking back to college; if you are coming in that direction, we can have a chat.'

But it was little chat that they had upon their homeward path. Smith's mind was too full of the incidents of the evening, the absence of the mummy from his neighbour's rooms, the step that passed him on the stair, the reappearance – the extraordinary, inexplicable reappearance of the grisly thing – and then this attack upon Lee, corresponding so closely to the previous outrage upon another man against whom Bellingham bore a grudge. All this settled in his thoughts, together with the many little incidents which had previously turned him against his neighbour, and the singular circumstances under which he was first called in to him. What had been a dim suspicion, a vague, fantastic conjecture, had suddenly taken form, and stood out in his mind as a grim fact, a thing not to be denied. And yet, how monstrous it was! how unheard of! how entirely beyond all bounds of human experience. An impartial judge, or even the friend who walked by his side, would simply tell him that his eyes had deceived him, that the mummy had been there all the time, that young Lee had tumbled into the river as any other man tumbles into a river, and the blue pill was the best thing for a disordered liver. He felt that he would have said as much if the positions had been reversed. And yet he could swear that Bellingham was a murderer at heart, and that he wielded a weapon such as no man had ever used in all the grim history of crime.

Hastie had branched off to his rooms with a few crisp and emphatic comments upon his friend's unsociability, and Abercrombie Smith crossed the quadrangle to his corner turret with a strong feeling of repulsion for his chambers and their associations. He would take Lee's advice, and move his quarters as soon as possible, for how could a man study when his ear was ever straining for every murmur or footstep in the room below? He observed, as he crossed over the lawn, that the light was still shining in Bellingham's window, and as he passed up the staircase the door opened, and the man himself looked out at him. With his fat, evil face he was like some bloated spider fresh from the weaving of his poisonous web.

'Good evening,' said he. 'Won't you come in?'

'No,' cried Smith fiercely.

'No? You are as busy as ever? I wanted to ask you about Lee. I was sorry to hear that there was a rumour that something was amiss with him.'

His features were grave, but there was the gleam of a hidden laugh in his eyes as he spoke. Smith saw it, and he could have knocked him down for it.

'You'll be sorrier still to hear that Monkhouse Lee is doing very well, and is out of all danger,' he answered. 'Your hellish tricks have not come off this time. Oh, you needn't try to brazen it out. I know all about it.'

Bellingham took a step back from the angry student, and half-closed the door as if to protect himself.

'You are mad,' he said. 'What do you mean? Do you assert that I had anything to do with Lee's accident?'

'Yes,' thundered Smith, 'You and that bag of bones behind you; you worked it between you. I tell you what it is, Master B., they have given up burning folk like you, but we still keep a hangman, and, by George! if any man in this college meets his death while you are here, I'll have you up, and if you don't swing for it, it won't be my fault. You'll find that your filthy Egyptian tricks won't answer in England.'

'You're a raving lunatic,' said Bellingham.

'All right. You just remember what I say, for you'll find that I'll be better than my word.'

The door slammed, and Smith went fuming up to his chamber, where he locked the door upon the inside, and spent half the night in smoking his old briar and brooding over the strange events of the evening.

Next morning Abercrombie Smith heard nothing of his neighbour, but Harrington called upon him in the afternoon to say that Lee was almost himself again. All day Smith stuck fast to his work, but in the evening he determined to pay the visit to his friend Doctor Peterson upon which he had started the night before. A good walk and a friendly chat would be welcome to his jangled nerves.

Bellingham's door was shut as he passed, but glancing back when he was some distance from the turret, he saw his neighbour's head at the window outlined against the lamp-light, his face pressed apparently against the glass as he gazed out into the darkness. It was a blessing to be away from all contact with him, if but for a few hours, and Smith stepped out briskly and breathed the soft spring air into his lungs. The half-moon lay in the west between two Gothic pinnacles, and threw upon the silvered street a dark tracery from the stone-work above. There was a brisk breeze, and light, fleecy clouds drifted swiftly across the sky. Old's was on the very border of the town, and in five minutes Smith found himself beyond the houses and between the hedges of a May-scented, Oxfordshire lane.

It was a lonely and little-frequented road which led to his friend's house. Early as it was, Smith did not meet a single soul upon his way. He walked briskly along until he came to the avenue gate, which opened into the long, gravel drive leading up to Farlingford. In front of him he could see the cosy, red light of the windows glimmering through the foliage. He stood with his hand upon the iron latch of the swinging gate, and he glanced back at the road along which he had come. Something was coming swiftly down it.

It moved in the shadow of the hedge, silently and furtively, a dark, crouching figure, dimly visible against the black background. Even as he gazed back at it, it had lessened its distance by twenty paces, and was fast closing upon him. Out of the darkness he had a glimpse of a scraggy neck, and of two eyes that will ever haunt him in his dreams. He turned, and with a cry of terror he ran for his life up the avenue. There were the red lights, the signals of safety, almost within a stone's-throw of him. He was a famous runner, but never had he run as he ran that night.

The heavy gate had swung into place behind him but he heard it dash open again before his pursuer. As he rushed madly and wildly through the night, he could hear a swift, dry patter behind him, and could see, as he threw back a glance, that this horror was bounding like a tiger at his heels, with blazing eyes and one stringy arm out-thrown. Thank God, the door was ajar. He could see the thin bar of light which shot from the lamp in the hall. Nearer yet sounded the clatter from behind. He heard a hoarse gurgling at his very shoulder. With a shriek he flung himself against the door, slammed and bolted it behind him, and sank half-fainting on to the hall chair.

'My goodness, Smith, what's the matter?' asked Peterson, appearing at the door of his study.

'Give me some brandy.'

Peterson disappeared, and came rushing out again with a glass and a decanter.

'You need it,' he said, as his visitor drank off what he poured out for him. 'Why, man, you are as white as a cheese.'

Smith laid down his glass, rose up, and took a deep breath.

'I am my own man again now,' said he. 'I was never so unmanned before. But, with your leave, Peterson, I will sleep here tonight, for I don't think I could face that road again except by daylight. It's weak, I know, but I can't help it.'

Peterson looked at his visitor with a very questioning eye.

'Of course you shall sleep here if you wish. I'll tell Mrs Burney to make up the spare bed. Where are you off to now?'

'Come up with me to the window that overlooks the door. I want you to see what I have seen.'

They went up to the window of the upper hall whence they could look down upon the approach to the house. The drive and the fields on either side lay quiet and still, bathed in the peaceful moonlight.

'Well, really, Smith,' remarked Peterson, 'it is well that I know you to be an abstemious man. What in the world can have frightened you?'

'I'll tell you presently. But where can it have gone? Ah, now, look, look! See the curve of the road just beyond your gate.'

'Yes, I see; you needn't pinch my arm off. I saw someone pass. I should say a man, rather thin, apparently, and tall, very tall. But what of him? And what of yourself? You are still shaking like an aspen leaf.'

'I have been within hand-grip of the devil, that's all. But come down to your study, and I shall tell you the whole story.'

He did so. Under the cheery lamp-light with a glass of wine on the table beside him, and the portly form and florid face of his friend in front, he narrated, in their order, all the events, great and small, which had formed so singular a chain, from the night on which he had found Bellingham fainting in front of the mummy case until this horrid experience of an hour ago.

'There now,' he said as he concluded, 'that's the whole, black business. It is monstrous and incredible, but it is true.'

Doctor Plumptree Peterson sat for some time in silence with a very puzzled expression upon his face.

'I never heard of such a thing in my life, never!' he said at last. 'You have told me the facts. Now tell me your inferences.'

'You can draw your own.'

'But I should like to hear yours. You have thought over the matter, and I have not.'

'Well, it must be a little vague in detail, but the main points seem to me to be clear enough. This fellow Bellingham, in his Eastern studies, has got hold of some infernal secret by which a mummy – or possibly only this particular mummy – can be temporarily brought to life. He was trying this disgusting business on the night when he fainted. No doubt the sight of the creature moving had shaken his nerve, even though he had expected it. You remember that almost the first words he said were to call out upon himself as a fool. Well, he got more hardened afterwards, and carried the matter through without fainting. The vitality which he could put into it was evidently only a passing thing, for I have seen it continually in its case as dead as this table. He has some elaborate process, I fancy, by which he brings the thing to pass. Having done it, he naturally bethought him that he might use the creature as an agent. It has intelligence and it has strength. For some purpose he took Lee into his confidence; but Lee, like a decent Christian, would have nothing to do with such a business. Then they had a row, and Lee vowed that he would tell his sister of Bellingham's true character. Bellingham's game was to prevent him, and he nearly managed it, by setting this creature of his on his track. He had already tried its powers upon another man – Norton – towards whom he had a grudge. It is the merest chance that he has not two murders upon his soul. Then, when I taxed him with the matter, he had the strongest reasons for wishing to get me out of the way before I could convey my knowledge to anyone else. He got his chance when I went out, for he knew my habits and where I was bound for. I have had a narrow shave, Peterson, and it is mere luck you didn't find me on your doorstep in the morning. I'm not a nervous man as a rule, and I never thought to have the fear of death put upon me as it was tonight.'

'My dear boy, you take the matter too seriously,' said his companion. 'Your nerves are out of order with your work, and you make too much of it. How could such a thing as this stride about the streets of Oxford, even at night, without being seen?'

'It has been seen. There is quite a scare in the town about an escaped ape, as they imagine the creature to be. It is the talk of the place.'

'Well, it's a striking chain of events. And yet, my dear fellow, you must allow that each incident in itself is capable of a more natural explanation.'

'What! even my adventure of tonight?'

'Certainly. You come out with your nerves all unstrung, and your head full of this theory of yours. Some gaunt, half-famished tramp steals after you, and seeing you run, is emboldened to pursue you. Your fears and imagination do the rest.'

'It won't do, Peterson: it won't do.'

'And again, in the instance of your finding the mummy case empty, and then a few moments later with an occupant, you know that it was lamp-light, that the lamp was half turned down, and that you had no special reason to look hard at the case. It is quite possible that you may have overlooked the creature in the first instance.'

'No, no; It is out of the question.'

'And then Lee may have fallen into the river, and Norton been garrotted. It is certainly a formidable indictment that you have against Bellingham; but if you were to place it before a police magistrate, he would simply laugh in your face.'

'I know he would. That is why I mean to take the matter into my own hands.'

'Eh?'

'Yes; I feel that a public duty rests upon me, and, besides, I must do it for my own safety, unless I choose to allow myself to be hunted by this beast out of the college, and that would be a little too feeble. I have quite made up my mind what I shall do. And first of all, may I use your paper and pens for an hour?'

'Most certainly. You will find all that you want upon that side-table.'

Abercrombie Smith sat down before a sheet of foolscap, and for an hour, and then for a second hour his pen travelled swiftly over it. Page after page was finished and tossed aside while his friend leaned back in his armchair, looking across at him with patient curiosity. At last, with an exclamation of satisfaction, Smith sprang to his feet, gathered his papers up into order, and laid the last one upon Peterson's desk.

'Kindly sign this as a witness,' he said.

'A witness? Of what?'

'Of my signature, and of the date. The date is the most important. Why, Peterson, my life might hang upon it.'

'My dear Smith, you are talking wildly. Let me beg you to go to bed.'

'On the contrary, I never spoke so deliberately in my life. And I will promise to go to bed the moment you have signed it.'

'But what is it?'

'It is a statement of all that I have been telling you tonight. I wish you to witness it.'

'Certainly,' said Peterson, signing his name under that of his companion. 'There you are! But what is the idea?'

'You will kindly retain it, and produce it in case I am arrested.'

'Arrested? For what?'

'For murder. It is quite on the cards. I wish to be ready for every event. There is only one course open to me, and I am determined to take it.'

'For Heaven's sake, don't do anything rash!'

'Believe me, it would be far more rash to adopt any other course. I hope that we won't need to bother you, but it will ease my mind to know that you have this statement of my motives. And now I am ready to take your advice and to go to roost, for I want to be at my best in the morning.'

Abercrombie Smith was not an entirely pleasant man to have as an enemy. Slow and easy-tempered, he was formidable when driven to action. He brought to every purpose in life the same deliberate resoluteness which had distinguished him as a scientific student. He had laid his studies aside for a day, but he intended that the day should not be wasted. Not a word did he say to his host as to his plans, but by nine o'clock he was well on his way to Oxford.

In the High Street he stopped at Clifford's, the gunmakers, and bought a heavy revolver, with a box of central-fire cartridges. Six of them he slipped into the chambers, and half-cocking the weapon, placed it in the pocket of his coat. He then made his way to Hastie's rooms, where the big oarsman was lounging over his breakfast, with the *Sporting Times* propped up against the coffeepot.

'Hullo! What's up?' he asked. 'Have some coffee?'

'No, thank you. I want you to come with me, Hastie, and do what I ask you.'

'Certainly, my boy.'

'And bring a heavy stick with you.'

'Hullo!' Hastie stared. 'Here's a hunting crop that would fell an ox.'

'One other thing. You have a box of amputating knives. Give me the longest of them.'

'There you are. You seem to be fairly on the war trail. Anything else?'

'No; that will do.' Smith placed the knife inside his coat, and led the way to the quadrangle. 'We are neither of us chickens, Hastie,' said he. 'I think I can do this job alone, but I take you as a precaution. I am going to have a little talk with Bellingham. If I have only him to deal with, I won't, of course, need you. If I shout, however, up you come, and lam out with your whip as hard as you can lick. Do you understand?'

'All right. I'll come if I hear you bellow.'

'Stay here, then. I may be a little time, but don't budge until I come down.'

'I'm a fixture.'

Smith ascended the stairs, opened Bellingham's door and stepped in. Bellingham was seated behind his table, writing. Beside him, among his litter of strange possessions, towered the mummy case, with its sale number 249 still stuck upon its front, and its hideous occupant stiff and stark within it. Smith looked very deliberately round him, closed the door, and then, stepping across to the fireplace, struck a match and set the fire alight. Bellingham sat staring, with amazement and rage upon his bloated face.

'Well, really now, you make yourself at home,' he gasped.

Smith sat himself deliberately down, placing his watch upon the table, drew out his pistol, cocked it, and laid it in his lap. Then he took the long amputating knife from his bosom, and threw it down in front of Bellingham.

'Now, then,' said he, 'just get to work and cut up that mummy.'

'Oh, is that it?' said Bellingham with a sneer.

'Yes, that is it. They tell me that the law can't touch you. But I have a law that will set matters straight. If in five minutes you have not set to work, I swear by the God who made me that I will put a bullet through your brain!'

'You would murder me?'

Bellingham had half-risen, and his face was the colour of putty.

'Yes.'

'And for what?'

'To stop your mischief. One minute has gone.'

'But what have I done?'

'I know and you know.'

'This is mere bullying.'

'Two minutes are gone.'

'But you must give reasons. You are a madman – a dangerous madman. Why should I destroy my own property? It is a valuable mummy.'

'You must cut it up, and you must burn it.'

'I will do no such thing.'

'Four minutes are gone.'

Smith took up the pistol and he looked towards Bellingham with an inexorable face. As the secondhand stole round, he raised his hand, and the finger twitched upon the trigger.

'There! there! I'll do it!' screamed Bellingham.

In frantic haste he caught up the knife and hacked at the figure of the mummy, ever glancing round to see the eye and the weapon of his terrible visitor bent upon him. The creature crackled and snapped under every stab of the keen blade. A thick, yellow dust rose up from it. Spices and dried essences rained down upon the floor. Suddenly, with a rending crack, its backbone snapped asunder, and it fell, a brown heap of sprawling limbs, upon the floor.

'Now into the fire!' said Smith.

The flames leaped and roared as the dried and tinder-like debris was piled upon it. The little room was like the stoke-hole of a steamer and the sweat ran down the faces of the two men; but still the one stooped and worked, while the other sat watching him with a set face. A thick, fat smoke oozed out from the fire, and a heavy smell of burned resin and singed hair filled the air. In a quarter of an hour a few charred and brittle sticks were all that was left of Lot No. 249.

'Perhaps that will satisfy you,' snarled Bellingham, with hate and fear in his little grey eyes as he glanced back at his tormentor.

'No; I must make a clean sweep of all your materials. We must have no more devil's tricks. In with all these leaves! They may have something to do with it.'

'And what now?' asked Bellingham, when the leaves also had been added to the blaze.

'Now the roll of papyrus which you had on the table that night. It is in that drawer, I think.'

'No, no,' shouted Bellingham. 'Don't burn that! Why, man, you don't know what you do. It is unique; it contains wisdom which is nowhere else to be found.'

'Out with it!'

'But look here, Smith, you can't really mean it. I'll share the knowledge with you. I'll teach you all that is in it. Or, stay, let me only copy it before you burn it!'

Smith stepped forward and turned the key in the drawer. Taking out the yellow, curled roll of paper, he threw it into the fire, and pressed it down with his heel. Bellingham screamed, and grabbed at it; but Smith pushed him back and stood over it until it was reduced to a formless, grey ash.

'Now, Master B.,' said he, 'I think I have pretty well drawn your teeth. You'll hear from me again, if you return to your old tricks. And now good morning, for I must go back to my studies.'

And such is the narrative of Abercrombie Smith as to the singular events which occurred in Old College, Oxford, in the spring of '84. As Bellingham left the university immediately afterwards, and was last heard of in the Soudan, there is no one who can contradict his statement. But the wisdom of men is small, and the ways of Nature are strange, and who shall put a bound to the dark things which may be found by those who seek for them?

The Yellow Wallpaper

CHARLOTTE PERKINS STETSON

It is very seldom that mere ordinary people like John and myself secure ancestral halls for the summer.

A colonial mansion, a hereditary estate, I would say a haunted house, and reach the height of romantic felicity – but that would be asking too much of Fate!

Still I will proudly declare that there is something queer about it.

Else, why should it be let so cheaply? And why have stood so long untenanted?

John laughs at me, of course, but one expects that in marriage.

John is practical in the extreme. He has no patience with faith, an intense horror of superstition, and he scoffs openly at any talk of things not to be felt and seen and put down in figures.

John is a physician, and *perhaps* – (I would not say it to a living soul, of course, but this is dead paper and a great relief to my mind) – *perhaps* that is one reason I do not get well faster.

You see he does not believe I am sick!

And what can one do?

If a physician of high standing, and one's own husband, assures friends and relatives that there is really nothing the matter with one but temporary nervous depression – a slight hysterical tendency – what is one to do?

My brother is also a physician, and also of high standing, and he says the same thing.

So I take phosphates or phosphites – whichever it is, and tonics, and journeys, and air, and exercise, and am absolutely forbidden to work until I am well again.

Personally, I disagree with their ideas.

Personally, I believe that congenial work, with excitement and change, would do me good.

But what is one to do?

I did write for a while in spite of them; but it *does* exhaust me a good deal – having to be so sly about it, or else meet with heavy opposition.

I sometimes fancy that in my condition if I had less opposition and more society and stimulus – but John says the very worst thing I can do is to think about my condition, and I confess it always makes me feel bad.

So I will let it alone and talk about the house.

The most beautiful place! It is quite alone, standing well back from the road, quite three miles from the village. It makes me think of English places that you read about, for there are hedges and walls and gates that lock, and lots of separate little houses for the gardeners and people.

There is a *delicious* garden! I never saw such a garden – large and shady, full of box-bordered paths, and lined with long grape-covered arbors with seats under them.

There were greenhouses, too, but they are all broken now.

There was some legal trouble, I believe, something about the heirs and coheirs; anyhow, the place has been empty for years.

That spoils my ghostliness, I am afraid, but I don't care – there is something strange about the house – I can feel it.

I even said so to John one moonlight evening but he said what I felt was a *draught*, and shut the window.

I get unreasonably angry with John sometimes. I'm sure I never used to be so sensitive. I think it is due to this nervous condition.

But John says if I feel so, I shall neglect proper self-control; so I take pains to control myself – before him, at least, and that makes me very tired.

I don't like our room a bit. I wanted one downstairs that opened on the piazza and had roses all over the window, and such pretty old-fashioned chintz hangings! but John would not hear of it.

He said there was only one window and not room for two beds, and no near room for him if he took another.

He is very careful and loving, and hardly lets me stir without special direction.

I have a schedule prescription for each hour in the day; he takes all care from me, and so I feel basely ungrateful not to value it more.

He said we came here solely on my account, that I was to have perfect rest and all the air I could get. 'Your exercise depends on your strength, my dear,' said he, 'and your food somewhat on your appetite; but air you can absorb all the time.' So we took the nursery at the top of the house.

It is a big, airy room, the whole floor nearly, with windows that look all ways, and air and sunshine galore. It was nursery first and then playroom and gymnasium, I should judge; for the windows are barred for little children, and there are rings and things in the walls.

The paint and paper look as if a boys' school had used it. It is stripped off – the paper – in great patches all around the head of my bed, about as far as I can reach, and in a great place on the other side of the room low down. I never saw a worse paper in my life.

One of those sprawling flamboyant patterns committing every artistic sin.

It is dull enough to confuse the eye in following, pronounced enough to constantly irritate and provoke study, and when you follow the lame uncertain curves for a little distance they suddenly commit suicide – plunge off at outrageous angles, destroy themselves in unheard of contradictions.

The color is repellent, almost revolting; a smouldering unclean yellow strangely faded by the slow-turning sunlight.

It is a dull yet lurid orange in some places, a sickly sulphur tint in others.

No wonder the children hated it! I should hate it myself if I had to live in this room long.

There comes John, and I must put this away – he hates to have me write a word.

We have been here two weeks, and I haven't felt like writing before, since that first day.

I am sitting by the window now, up in this atrocious nursery, and there is nothing to hinder my writing as much as I please, save lack of strength.

John is away all day, and even some nights when his cases are serious.

I am glad my case is not serious!

But these nervous troubles are dreadfully depressing.

John does not know how much I really suffer. He knows there is no *reason* to suffer, and that satisfies him.

Of course it is only nervousness. It does weigh on me so not to do my duty in any way!

I meant to be such a help to John, such a real rest and comfort, and here I am a comparative burden already!

Nobody would believe what an effort it is to do what little I am able, – to dress and entertain, and order things.

It is fortunate Mary is so good with the baby. Such a dear baby!

And yet I *cannot* be with him, it makes me so nervous.

I suppose John never was nervous in his life. He laughs at me so about this wallpaper!

At first he meant to repaper the room, but afterwards he said that I was letting it get the better of me, and that nothing was worse for a nervous patient than to give way to such fancies.

He said that after the wallpaper was changed it would be the heavy bedstead, and then the barred windows, and then that gate at the head of the stairs, and so on.

'You know the place is doing you good,' he said, 'and really, dear, I don't care to renovate the house just for a three months' rental.'

'Then do let us go downstairs,' I said, 'there are such pretty rooms there.'

Then he took me in his arms and called me a blessed little goose, and said he would go down to the cellar, if I wished, and have it whitewashed into the bargain.

But he is right enough about the beds and windows and things.

It is an airy and comfortable room as anyone need wish, and, of course, I would not be so silly as to make him uncomfortable just for a whim.

I'm really getting quite fond of the big room, all but that horrid paper.

Out of one window I can see the garden, those mysterious deep-shaded arbors, the riotous old-fashioned flowers, and bushes and gnarly trees.

Out of another I get a lovely view of the bay and a little private wharf belonging to the estate. There is a beautiful shaded lane that runs down there from the house. I always fancy I see people walking in these numerous paths and arbors, but John has cautioned me not to give way to fancy in the least. He says that with my imaginative power and habit of story-making, a nervous weakness like mine is sure to lead to all manner of excited fancies, and that I ought to use my will and good sense to check the tendency. So I try.

I think sometimes that if I were only well enough to write a little it would relieve the press of ideas and rest me.

But I find I get pretty tired when I try.

It is so discouraging not to have any advice and companionship about my work. When I get really well, John says we will ask Cousin Henry and Julia down for a long visit; but he says he would as soon put fireworks in my pillow-case as to let me have those stimulating people about now.

I wish I could get well faster.

But I must not think about that. This paper looks to me as if it *knew* what a vicious influence it had!

There is a recurrent spot where the pattern lolls like a broken neck and two bulbous eyes stare at you upside down.

I get positively angry with the impertinence of it and the everlastingness. Up and down and sideways they crawl, and those absurd, unblinking eyes are everywhere. There is one place where two breadths didn't match, and the eyes go all up and down the line, one a little higher than the other.

I never saw so much expression in an inanimate thing before, and we all know how much expression they have! I used to lie awake as a child and get more entertainment and terror out of blank walls and plain furniture than most children could find in a toy-store.

I remember what a kindly wink the knobs of our big, old bureau used to have, and there was one chair that always seemed like a strong friend.

I used to feel that if any of the other things looked too fierce I could always hop into that chair and be safe.

The furniture in this room is no worse than inharmonious, however, for we had to bring it all from downstairs. I suppose when this was used as a playroom they had to take the nursery things out, and no wonder! I never saw such ravages as the children have made here.

The wallpaper as I said before, is torn off in spots, and it sticketh closer than a brother – they must have had perseverance as well as hatred.

Then the floor is scratched and gouged and splintered, the plaster itself is dug out here and there, and this great heavy bed which is all we found in the room, looks as if it had been through the wars.

But I don't mind it a bit – only the paper.

There comes John's sister. Such a dear girl as she is, and so careful of me! I must not let her find me writing.

She is a perfect and enthusiastic housekeeper, and hopes for no better profession. I verily believe she thinks it is the writing which made me sick!

But I can write when she is out, and see her a long way off from these windows.

There is one that commands the road, a lovely shaded winding road, and one that just looks off over the country. A lovely country, too, full of great elms and velvet meadows.

This wallpaper has a kind of sub-pattern in a different shade, a particularly irritating one, for you can only see it in certain lights, and not clearly then.

But in the places where it isn't faded and where the sun is just so – I can see a strange, provoking, formless sort of figure, that seems to skulk about behind that silly and conspicuous front design.

There's sister on the stairs!

Well, the Fourth of July is over! The people are all gone and I am tired out. John thought it might do me good to see a little company, so we just had mother and Nellie and the children down for a week.

Of course I didn't do a thing. Jennie sees to everything now. But it tired me all the same.

John says if I don't pick up faster he shall send me to Weir Mitchell in the Fall.

But I don't want to go there at all. I had a friend who was in his hands once, and she says he is just like John and my brother, only more so!

Besides, it is such an undertaking to go so far.

I don't feel as if it was worth while to turn my hand over for anything, and I'm getting dreadfully fretful and querulous.

I cry at nothing and cry most of the time.

Of course I don't when John is here, or anybody else, but when I am alone.

And I am alone a good deal just now. John is kept in town very often by serious cases, and Jennie is good and lets me alone when I want her to.

So I walk a little in the garden or down that lovely lane, sit on the porch under the roses, and lie down up here a good deal.

I'm getting really fond of the room in spite of the wallpaper. Perhaps *because* of the wallpaper.

It dwells in my mind so!

I lie here on this great immovable bed – it is nailed down, I believe – and follow that pattern about by the hour. It is as good as gymnastics, I assure you. I start, we'll say, at the bottom, down in the corner over there where it has not been touched and I determine for the thousandth time that I will follow that pointless pattern to some sort of a conclusion.

I know a little of the principle of design, and I know this thing was not arranged on any laws of radiation, or alternation, or repetition, or symmetry, or anything else that I ever heard of.

It is repeated of course, by the breadths, but not otherwise.

Looked at in one way each breadth stands alone, the bloated curves and flourishes – a kind of 'debased Romanesque' with *delirium tremens* – go waddling up and down in isolated columns of fatuity.

But, on the other hand, they connect diagonally, and the sprawling outlines run off in great slanting waves of optic horror, like a lot of wallowing seaweeds in full chase.

The whole thing goes horizontally, too, at least it seems so, and I exhaust myself in trying to distinguish the order of its going in that direction.

They have used a horizontal breadth for a frieze, and that adds wonderfully to the confusion.

There is one end of the room where it is almost intact, and there, when the crosslights fade and the low sun shines directly upon it, I can almost fancy radiation after all, – the interminable grotesques seem to form around a common center and rush off in headlong plunges of equal distraction.

It makes me tired to follow it. I will take a nap I guess.

I don't know why I should write this.

I don't want to.

I don't feel able.

And I know John would think it absurd. But I *must* say what I feel and think in some way – it is such a relief!

But the effort is getting to be greater than the relief.

Half the time now I am awfully lazy, and lie down ever so much.

John says I mustn't lose my strength, and has me take cod liver oil and lots of tonics and things, to say nothing of ale and wine and rare meat.

Dear John! He loves me very dearly, and hates to have me sick. I tried to have a real earnest reasonable talk with him the other day, and tell him how I wish he would let me go and make a visit to Cousin Henry and Julia.

But he said I wasn't able to go, nor able to stand it after I got there; and I did not make out a very good case for myself, for I was crying before I had finished.

It is getting to be a great effort for me to think straight. Just this nervous weakness I suppose.

And dear John gathered me up in his arms, and just carried me upstairs and laid me on the bed, and sat by me and read to me till it tired my head.

He said I was his darling and his comfort and all he had, and that I must take care of myself for his sake, and keep well.

He says no one but myself can help me out of it, that I must use my will and self-control and not let any silly fancies run away with me.

There's one comfort, the baby is well and happy, and does not have to occupy this nursery with the horrid wallpaper.

If we had not used it, that blessed child would have! What a fortunate escape! Why, I wouldn't have a child of mine, an impressionable little thing, live in such a room for worlds.

I never thought of it before, but it is lucky that John kept me here after all, I can stand it so much easier than a baby, you see.

Of course I never mention it to them any more – I am too wise, – but I keep watch of it all the same.

There are things in that paper that nobody knows but me, or ever will.

Behind that outside pattern the dim shapes get clearer even day.

It is always the same shape, only very numerous.

And it is like a woman stooping down and creeping about behind that pattern. I don't like it a bit. I wonder – I begin to think – I wish John would take me away from here!

It is so hard to talk with John about my case, because he is so wise, and because he loves me so.

But I tried it last night.

It was moonlight. The moon shines in all around just as the sun does.

I hate to see it sometimes, it creeps so slowly, and always comes in by one window or another.

John was asleep and I hated to waken him, so I kept still and watched the moonlight on that undulating wallpaper till I felt creepy.

The faint figure behind seemed to shake the pattern, just as if she wanted to get out.

I got up softly and went to feel and see if the paper *did* move, and when I came back John was awake.

'What is it, little girl?' he said. 'Don't go walking about like that – you'll get cold.'

I thought it was a good time to talk, so I told him that I really was not gaining here, and that I wished he would take me away.

'Why darling!' said he, 'our lease will be up in three weeks, and I can't see how to leave before.'

'The repairs are not done at home, and I cannot possibly leave town just now. Of course if you were in any danger, I could and would, but you really are better, dear, whether you can see it or not. I am a doctor, dear, and I know. You are gaining flesh and color, your appetite is better, I feel really much easier about you.'

'I don't weigh a bit more,' said I, 'nor as much; and my appetite may be better in the evening when you are here, but it is worse in the morning when you are away!'

'Bless her little heart!' said he with a big hug, 'she shall be as sick as she pleases! But now let's improve the shining hours by going to sleep, and talk about it in the morning!'

'And you won't go away?' I asked gloomily.

'Why, how can I, dear? It is only three weeks more and then we will take a nice little trip of a few days while Jennie is getting the house ready. Really dear you are better!'

'Better in body perhaps – ' I began, and stopped short, for he sat up straight and looked at me with such a stern, reproachful look that I could not say another word.

'My darling,' said he, 'I beg of you, for my sake and for our child's sake, as well as for your own, that you will never for one instant let that idea enter your mind! There is nothing so dangerous, so fascinating, to a temperament like yours. It is a false and foolish fancy. Can you not trust me as a physician when I tell you so?'

So of course I said no more on that score, and we went to sleep before long. He thought I was asleep first, but I wasn't, and lay there for hours trying to decide whether that front pattern and the back pattern really did move together or separately.

On a pattern like this, by daylight, there is a lack of sequence, a defiance of law, that is a constant irritant to a normal mind.

The color is hideous enough, and unreliable enough, and infuriating enough, but the pattern is torturing.

You think you have mastered it, but just as you get well underway in following, it turns a back-somersault and there you are. It slaps you in the face, knocks you down, and tramples upon you. It is like a bad dream.

The outside pattern is a florid arabesque reminding one of a fungus. If you can imagine a toadstool in joints, an interminable string of toadstools, budding and sprouting in endless convolutions – why, that is something like it.

That is, sometimes!

There is one marked peculiarity about this paper, a thing nobody seems to notice but myself, and that is that it changes as the light changes.

When the sun shoots in through the east window – I always watch for that first long, straight ray – it changes so quickly that I never can quite believe it.

That is why I watch it always.

By moonlight – the moon shines in all night when there is a moon – I wouldn't know it was the same paper.

At night in any kind of light, in twilight, candlelight, lamplight, and worst of all by moonlight, it becomes bars! The outside pattern I mean, and the woman behind it is as plain as can be.

I didn't realize for a long time what the thing was that showed behind, that dim sub-pattern, but now I am quite sure it is a woman.

By daylight she is subdued, quiet. I fancy it is the pattern that keeps her so still. It is so puzzling. It keeps me quiet by the hour.

I lie down ever so much now. John says it is good for me, and to sleep all I can.

Indeed he started the habit by making me lie down for an hour after each meal.

It is a very bad habit I am convinced, for you see I don't sleep.

And that cultivates deceit, for I don't tell them I'm awake – O no!

The fact is I am getting a little afraid of John.

He seems very queer sometimes, and even Jennie has an inexplicable look.

It strikes me occasionally, just as a scientific hypothesis, – that perhaps it is the paper!

I have watched John when he did not know I was looking, and come into the room suddenly on the most innocent excuses, and I've caught him several times *looking at the paper!* and Jennie too. I caught Jennie with her hand on it once.

She didn't know I was in the room, and when I asked her in a quiet, a very quiet voice, with the most restrained manner possible, what she was doing with the paper – she turned around as if she had been caught stealing, and looked quite angry – asked me why I should frighten her so!

Then she said that the paper stained everything it touched, that she had found yellow smooches on all my clothes and John's, and she wished we would be more careful!

Did not that sound innocent? But I know she was studying that pattern, and I am determined that nobody shall find it out but myself!

Life is very much more exciting now than it used to be. You see I have something more to expect, to look forward to, to watch. I really do eat better, and am more quiet than I was.

John is so pleased to see me improve! He laughed a little the other day, and said I seemed to be flourishing in spite of my wallpaper.

I turned it off with a laugh. I had no intention of telling him it was *because* of the wallpaper – he would make fun of me. He might even want to take me away.

I don't want to leave now until I have found it out. There is a week more, and I think that will be enough.

I'm feeling ever so much better! I don't sleep much at night, for it is so interesting to watch developments; but I sleep a good deal in the daytime.

In the daytime it is tiresome and perplexing.

There are always new shoots on the fungus, and new shades of yellow all over it. I cannot keep count of them, though I have tried conscientiously.

It is the strangest yellow, that wallpaper! It makes me think of all the yellow things I ever saw – not beautiful ones like buttercups, but old foul, bad yellow things.

But there is something else about that paper – the smell! I noticed it the moment we came into the room, but with so much air and sun it was not bad. Now we have had a week of fog and rain, and whether the windows are open or not, the smell is here.

It creeps all over the house.

I find it hovering in the dining-room, skulking in the parlor, hiding in the hall, lying in wait for me on the stairs.

It gets into my hair.

Even when I go to ride, if I turn my head suddenly and surprise it – there is that smell!

Such a peculiar odor, too! I have spent hours in trying to analyze it, to find what it smelled like.

It is not bad – at first, and very gentle, but quite the subtlest, most enduring odor I ever met.

In this damp weather it is awful, I wake up in the night and find it hanging over me.

It used to disturb me at first. I thought seriously of burning the house – to reach the smell.

But now I am used to it. The only thing I can think of that it is like is the *color* of the paper! A yellow smell.

There is a very funny mark on this wall, low down, near the mopboard. A streak that runs round the room. It goes behind every piece of furniture, except the bed, a long, straight, even *smooch,* as if it had been rubbed over and over.

I wonder how it was done and who did it, and what they did it for. Round and round and round – round and round and round – it makes me dizzy!

I really have discovered something at last.

Through watching so much at night, when it changes so, I have finally found out.

The front pattern does move – and no wonder! The woman behind shakes it!

Sometimes I think there are a great many women behind, and sometimes only one, and she crawls around fast, and her crawling shakes it all over.

Then in the very bright spots she keeps still, and in the very shady spots she just takes hold of the bars and shakes them hard.

And she is all the time trying to climb through. But nobody could climb through that pattern – it strangles so; I think that is why it has so many heads.

They get through and then the pattern strangles them off and turns them upside down, and makes their eyes white!

If those heads were covered or taken off it would not be half so bad.

I think that woman gets out in the daytime!

And I'll tell you why – privately – I've seen her!

I can see her out of every one of my windows!

It is the same woman, I know, for she is always creeping, and most women do not creep by daylight.

I see her on that long road under the trees, creeping along, and when a carriage comes she hides under the blackberry vines.

I don't blame her a bit. It must be very humiliating to be caught creeping by daylight!

I always lock the door when I creep by daylight. I can't do it at night, for I know John would suspect something at once.

And John is so queer now, that I don't want to irritate him. I wish he would take another room! Besides, I don't want anybody to get that woman out at night but myself.

I often wonder if I could see her out of all the windows at once.

But, turn as fast as I can, I can only see out of one at one time.

And though I always see her, she *may* be able to creep faster than I can turn!

I have watched her sometimes away off in the open country, creeping as fast as a cloud shadow in a high wind.

If only that top pattern could be gotten off from the under one! I mean to try it, little by little.

I have found out another funny thing, but I shan't tell it this time! It does not do to trust people too much.

There are only two more days to get this paper off, and I believe John is beginning to notice. I don't like the look in his eyes.

And I heard him ask Jennie a lot of professional questions about me. She had a very good report to give.

She said I slept a good deal in the daytime.

John knows I don't sleep very well at night, for all I'm so quiet!

He asked me all sorts of questions, too, and pretended to be very loving and kind.

As if I couldn't see through him!

Still, I don't wonder he acts so, sleeping under this paper for three months.

It only interests me, but I feel sure John and Jennie are secretly affected by it.

Hurrah! This is the last day, but it is enough. John to stay in town over night, and won't be out until this evening.

Jennie wanted to sleep with me – the sly thing! but I told her I should undoubtedly rest better for a night all alone.

That was clever, for really I wasn't alone a bit! As soon as it was moonlight and that poor thing began to crawl and shake the pattern, I got up and ran to help her.

I pulled and she shook, I shook and she pulled, and before morning we had peeled off yards of that paper.

A strip about as high as my head and half around the room.

And then when the sun came and that awful pattern began to laugh at me, I declared I would finish it today!

We go away tomorrow, and they are moving all my furniture down again to leave things as they were before.

Jennie looked at the wall in amazement, but I told her merrily that I did it out of pure spite at the vicious thing.

She laughed and said she wouldn't mind doing it herself, but I must not get tired.

How she betrayed herself that time!

But I am here, and no person touches this paper but me, – not *alive!*

She tried to get me out of the room – it was too patent! But I said it was so quiet and empty and clean now that I believed I would lie down again and sleep all I could; and not to wake me even for dinner – I would call when I woke.

So now she is gone, and the servants are gone, and the things are gone and there is nothing left but that great bedstead nailed down, with the canvas mattress we found on it.

We shall sleep downstairs tonight, and take the boat home tomorrow.

I quite enjoy the room, now it is bare again.

How those children did tear about here!

This bedstead is fairly gnawed!

But I must get to work.

I have locked the door and thrown the key down into the front path.

I don't want to go out, and I don't want to have anybody come in, till John comes.

I want to astonish him.

I've got a rope up here that even Jennie did not find. If that woman does get out, and tries to get away, I can tie her!

But I forgot I could not reach far without anything to stand on!

This bed will *not* move!

I tried to lift and push it until I was lame, and then I got so angry I bit off a little piece at one corner – but it hurt my teeth.

Then I peeled off all the paper I could reach standing on the floor. It sticks horribly and the pattern just enjoys it! All those strangled heads and bulbous eyes and waddling fungus growths just shriek with derision!

I am getting angry enough to do something desperate. To jump out of the window would be admirable exercise, but the bars are too strong even to try.

Besides I wouldn't do it. Of course not. I know well enough that a step like that is improper and might be misconstrued.

I don't like to *look* out of the windows even – there are so many of those creeping women, and they creep so fast.

I wonder if they all come out of that wallpaper as I did?

But I am securely fastened now by my well-hidden rope – you don't get *me* out in the road there!

I suppose I shall have to get back behind the pattern when it comes night, and that is hard!

It is so pleasant to be out in this great room and creep around as I please!

I don't want to go outside. I won't, even if Jennie asks me to.

For outside you have to creep on the ground, and everything is green instead of yellow.

But here I can creep smoothly on the floor, and my shoulder just fits in that long smooch around the wall, so I cannot lose my way.

Why there's John at the door!

It is no use, young man, you can't open it!

How he does call and pound!

Now he's crying for an ax.

It would be a shame to break down that beautiful door!

'John dear!' said I in the gentlest voice, 'the key is down by the front steps, under a plantain leaf!'

That silenced him for a few moments.

Then he said – very quietly indeed, 'Open the door, my darling!'

'I can't,' said I. 'The key is down by the front door under a plantain leaf!'

And then I said it again, several times, very gently and slowly, and said it so often that he had to go and see, and he got it of course, and came in. He stopped short by the door.

'What is the matter?' he cried. 'For God's sake, what are you doing!'

I kept on creeping just the same, but I looked at him over my shoulder.

'I've got out at last,' said I, 'in spite of you and Jane. And I've pulled off most of the paper, so you can't put me back!'

Now why should that man have fainted? But he did, and right across my path by the wall, so that I had to creep over him every time!

The Mezzotint

M. R. JAMES

Some time ago I believe I had the pleasure of telling you the story of an adventure which happened to a friend of mine by the name of Dennistoun, during his pursuit of objects of art for the museum at Cambridge.

He did not publish his experiences very widely upon his return to England; but they could not fail to become known to a good many of his friends, and among others to the gentleman who at that time presided over an art museum at another University. It was to be expected that the story should make a considerable impression on the mind of a man whose vocation lay in lines similar to Dennistoun's, and that he should be eager to catch at any explanation of the matter which tended to make it seem improbable that he should ever be called upon to deal with so agitating an emergency. It was, indeed, somewhat consoling to him to reflect that he was not expected to acquire ancient MSS. for his institution; that was the business of the Shelburnian Library. The authorities of that institution might, if they pleased, ransack obscure corners of the Continent for such matters. He was glad to be obliged at the moment to confine his attention to enlarging the already unsurpassed collection of English topographical drawings and engravings possessed by his museum. Yet, as it turned out, even a department so homely and familiar as this may have its dark corners, and to one of these Mr Williams was unexpectedly introduced.

Those who have taken even the most limited interest in the acquisition of topographical pictures are aware that there is one London dealer whose aid is indispensable to their researches. Mr J. W. Britnell publishes at short intervals very admirable catalogues of a large and constantly changing stock of engravings, plans, and old sketches of mansions, churches, and towns in England and Wales. These catalogues were, of course, the ABC of his subject to Mr Williams: but as his museum already contained an enormous accumulation of topographical pictures, he was a regular, rather than a copious, buyer; and he rather looked to Mr Britnell to fill up gaps in the rank and file of his collection than to supply him with rarities.

Now, in February of last year there appeared upon Mr Williams's desk at the museum a catalogue from Mr Britnell's emporium, and accompanying it was a typewritten communication from the dealer himself. This latter ran as follows:

> DEAR SIR, – We beg to call your attention to No. 978 in our accompanying catalogue, which we shall be glad to send on approval. – Yours faithfully,
> J. W. BRITNELL.

To turn to No. 978 in the accompanying catalogue was with Mr Williams (as he observed to himself) the work of a moment, and in the place indicated he found the following entry:

> 978. – *Unknown*. Interesting mezzotint: View of a manor-house, early part of the century. 15 by 10 inches; black frame. £2, 2s.

It was not specially exciting, and the price seemed high. However, as Mr Britnell, who knew his business and his customer, seemed to set store by it, Mr Williams wrote a postcard asking for the article to be sent on approval, along with some other engravings and sketches which appeared in the same catalogue. And so he passed without much excitement or anticipation to the ordinary labours of the day.

A parcel of any kind always arrives a day later than you expect it, and that of Mr Britnell proved, as I believe the right phrase goes, no exception to the rule. It was delivered at the museum by the afternoon post of Saturday, after Mr Williams had left his work, and it was accordingly brought round to his rooms in college by the attendant, in order that he might not have to wait over Sunday before looking through it and returning such of the contents as he did not propose to keep. And here he found it when he came in to tea, with a friend.

The only item with which I am concerned was the rather large, black-framed mezzotint of which I have already quoted the short description given in Mr Britnell's catalogue. Some more details of it will have to be given, though I cannot hope to put before you the look of the picture as clearly as it is present to my own eye. Very nearly the exact duplicate of it may be seen in a good many old inn parlours, or in the passages of undisturbed country mansions at the present moment. It was a rather indifferent mezzotint, and an indifferent mezzotint is, perhaps, the worst form of engraving known. It presented a full-face view of a not very large manor-house of the last century, with three rows of plain sashed windows with rusticated masonry about them, a parapet with balls or vases at the angles, and a small portico in the centre. On either side were trees, and in front a considerable expanse of lawn. The legend 'A. W. F. sculpsit' was engraved on the narrow margin; and there was no further inscription. The whole thing gave the impression that it was the work of an amateur. What in the world Mr Britnell could mean by affixing the price of £2, 2s. to such an object was more than Mr Williams could imagine. He turned it over with a good deal of contempt;

upon the back was a paper label, the left-hand half of which had been torn off. All that remained were the ends of two lines of writing: the first had the letters – *ngley Hall*; the second, – *ssex*.

It would, perhaps, be just worth while to identify the place represented, which he could easily do with the help of a gazetteer, and then he would send it back to Mr Britnell, with some remarks reflecting upon the judgment of that gentleman.

He lighted the candles, for it was now dark, made the tea, and supplied the friend with whom he had been playing golf (for I believe the authorities of the University I write of indulge in that pursuit by way of relaxation); and tea was taken to the accompaniment of a discussion which golfing persons can imagine for themselves, but which the conscientious writer has no right to inflict upon any non-golfing persons.

The conclusion arrived at was that certain strokes might have been better, and that in certain emergencies neither player had experienced that amount of luck which a human being has a right to expect. It was now that the friend – let us call him Professor Binks – took up the framed engraving, and said:

'What's this place, Williams?'

'Just what I am going to try to find out,' said Williams, going to the shelf for a gazetteer. 'Look at the back. Something— ley Hall, either in Sussex or Essex. Half the name's gone, you see. You don't happen to know it, I suppose?'

'It's from that man Britnell, I suppose, isn't it?' said Binks. 'Is it for the museum?'

'Well, I think I should buy it if the price was five shillings,' said Williams; 'but for some unearthly reason he wants two guineas for it. I can't conceive why. It's a wretched engraving, and there aren't even any figures to give it life.'

'It's not worth two guineas, I should think,' said Binks; 'but I don't think it's so badly done. The moonlight seems rather good to me; and I should have thought there *were* figures, or at least a figure, just on the edge in front.'

'Let's look,' said Williams. 'Well, it's true the light is rather cleverly given. Where's your figure? Oh yes! Just the head, in the very front of the picture.'

And indeed there was – hardly more than a black blot on the extreme edge of the engraving – the head of a man or woman, a good deal muffled up, the back turned to the spectator, and looking towards the house.

Williams had not noticed it before.

'Still,' he said, 'though it's a cleverer thing than I thought, I can't spend two guineas of museum money on a picture of a place I don't know.'

Professor Binks had his work to do, and soon went; and very nearly up to Hall time Williams was engaged in a vain attempt to identify the subject of his picture. 'If the vowel before the *ng* had only been left, it would have been easy enough,' he thought; 'but as it is, the name may be any thing from Guestingley to Langley, and there are many more names ending like this than I thought; and this rotten book has no index of terminations.'

Hall in Mr Williams's college was at seven. It need not be dwelt upon; the less so as he met there colleagues who had been playing golf during the afternoon, and words with which we have no concern were freely bandied across the table – merely golfing words, I would hasten to explain.

I suppose an hour or more to have been spent in what is called common-room after dinner. Later in the evening some few retired to Williams's rooms, and I have little doubt that whist was played and tobacco smoked. During a lull in these operations Williams picked up the mezzotint from the table without looking at it, and handed it to a person mildly interested in art, telling him where it had come from, and the other particulars which we already know.

The gentleman took it carelessly, looked at it, then said, in a tone of some interest:

'It's really a very good piece of work, Williams; it has quite a feeling of the romantic period. The light is admirably managed, it seems to me, and the figure, though it's rather too grotesque, is somehow very impressive.'

'Yes, isn't it?' said Williams, who was just then busy giving whisky and soda to others of the company, and was able to come across the room to look at the view again.

It was by this time rather late in the evening, and the visitors were on the move. After they went Williams was obliged to write a letter or two and clear up some odd bits of work. At last, some time past midnight, he was disposed to turn in, and he put out his lamp after lighting his bedroom candle. The picture lay face upwards on the table where the last man who looked at it had put it, and it caught his eye as he turned the lamp down. What he saw made him very nearly drop the candle on the floor, and he declares now that if he had been left in the dark at that moment he would have had a fit. But, as that did not happen, he was able to put down the light on the table and take a good look at the picture. It was undubitable – rankly impossible, no doubt, but absolutely certain. In the middle of the lawn in front of the unknown house there was a figure where no figure had been at five o'clock that afternoon. It was crawling on all-fours towards the house, and it was muffled in a strange black garment with a white cross on the back.

I do not know what is the ideal course to pursue in a situation of this kind. I can only tell you what Mr Williams did. He took the picture by one corner and carried it across the passage to a second set of rooms which he possessed. There he locked it up in a drawer, sported the doors of both sets of rooms, and retired to bed; but first he wrote out and signed an account of the extraordinary change which the picture had undergone since it had come into his possession.

Sleep visited him rather late; but it was consoling to reflect that the behaviour of the picture did not depend upon his own unsupported testimony. Evidently the man who had looked at it the night before had seen something of the same kind as he had, otherwise he might have been tempted to think that something gravely wrong was happening either to his eyes or his mind. This possibility being fortunately precluded, two matters awaited him on the morrow. He must take stock of the picture very carefully, and call in a witness for the purpose, and he must make a determined effort to ascertain what house it was that was represented. He would therefore ask his neighbour Nisbet to breakfast with him, and he would subsequently spend a morning over the gazetteer.

Nisbet was disengaged, and arrived about 9.30. His host was not quite dressed, I am sorry to say, even at this late hour. During breakfast nothing was said about the mezzotint by Williams, save that he had a picture on which he wished for Nisbet's opinion. But those who are familiar with University life can picture for themselves the wide and delightful range of subjects over which the conversation of two Fellows of Canterbury College is likely to extend during a Sunday morning breakfast. Hardly a topic was left unchallenged, from golf to lawn-tennis. Yet I am bound to say that Williams was rather distraught; for his interest naturally centred in that very strange picture which was now reposing, face downwards, in the drawer in the room opposite.

The morning pipe was at last lighted, and the moment had arrived for which he looked. With very considerable – almost tremulous excitement, he ran across, unlocked the drawer, and, extracting the picture – still face downwards – ran back, and put it into Nisbet's hands.

'Now,' he said, 'Nisbet, I want you to tell me exactly what you see in that picture. Describe it, if you don't mind, rather minutely. I'll tell you why afterwards.'

'Well,' said Nisbet, 'I have here a view of a country house – English, I presume – by moonlight.'

'Moonlight? You're sure of that?'

'Certainly. The moon appears to be on the wane, if you wish for details, and there are clouds in the sky.'

'All right. Go on. I'll swear,' added Williams in an aside, 'there was no moon when I saw it first.'

'Well, there's not much more to be said,' Nisbet continued. 'The house has one – two – three rows of windows, five in each row, except at the bottom, where there's a porch instead of the middle one, and— '

But what about figures?' said Williams, with marked interest.

'There aren't any,' said Nisbet; 'but— '

'What! No figure on the grass in front?'

'Not a thing.'

'You'll swear to that?'

'Certainly I will. But there's just one other thing.'

'What?'

'Why, one of the windows on the ground floor – left of the door – is open.'

'Is it really so? My goodness! he must have got in,' said Williams, with great excitement; and he hurried to the back of the sofa on which Nisbet was sitting, and, catching the picture from him, verified the matter for himself.

It was quite true. There was no figure, and there was the open window. Williams, after a moment of speechless surprise, went to the writing-table and scribbled for a short time. Then he brought two papers to Nisbet, and asked him first to sign one – it was his own description of the picture, which you have just heard – and then to read the other which was Williams's statement written the night before.

'What can it all mean? 'said Nisbet.

'Exactly,' said Williams. 'Well, one thing I must do – or three things, now I think of it. I must find out from Garwood '– this was his last night's visitor – 'what he saw, and then I must get the thing photographed before it goes further, and then I must find out what the place is.'

'I can do the photographing myself,' said Nisbet, 'and I will. But, you now, it looks very much as if we were assisting at the working out of a tragedy somewhere. The question is, has it happened already, or is it going to come off? You must find out what the place is. Yes,' he said, looking at the picture again, 'I expect you're right: he has got in. And if I don't mistake there'll be the devil to pay in one of the rooms upstairs.'

I'll tell you what,' said Williams: 'I'll take the picture across to old Green' (this was the senior Fellow of the College, who had been Bursar for many years). 'It's quite likely he'll know it. We have property in Essex and Sussex, and he must have been over the two counties a lot in his time.'

'Quite likely he will,' said Nisbet; 'but just let me take my photograph first. Rut look here, I rather think Green isn't up today. He wasn't in Hall last night, and I think I heard him say he was going down for the Sunday.'

'That's true, too,' said Williams; 'I know he's gone to Brighton. Well, if you'll photograph it now, I'll go across to Garwood and get his statement, and you keep an eye on it while I'm gone. I'm beginning to think two guineas is not a very exorbitant price for it now.'

In a short time he had returned, and brought Mr Garwood with him. Garwood's statement was to the effect that the figure, when he had seen it, was clear of the edge of the picture but had not got far across the lawn. He remembered a white mark on the back of its drapery, but could not have been sure it was a cross. A document to this effect was then drawn up and signed, and Nisbet proceeded to photograph the picture.

'Now what do you mean to do?' he said. 'Are you going to sit and watch it all day?'

'Well no, I think not,' said Williams. 'I rather imagine we're meant to see the whole thing. You see, between the time I saw it last night and this morning there was time for lots of things to happen, but the creature only got into the house. It could easily have got through its business in the time and gone to its own place again; but the fact of the window being open, I think, must mean that it's in there now. So I feel quite easy about leaving it. And, besides, I have a kind of idea that it wouldn't change much, if at all, in the daytime. We might go out for a walk this afternoon, and come in to tea, or whenever it gets dark. I shall leave it out on the table here, and sport the door. My skip can get in, but no one else.'

The three agreed that this would be a good plan; and, further, that if they spent the afternoon together they would be less likely to talk about the business to other people; for any rumour of such a transaction as was going on would bring the whole of the Phasmatological Society about their ears.

We may give them a respite until five o'clock.

At or near that hour the three were entering Williams's staircase. They were at first slightly annoyed to see that the door of his rooms was unsported; but in a moment it was remembered that on Sunday the skips came for orders an hour or so earlier than on week-days. However, a surprise was awaiting them. The first thing they saw was the picture leaning up against a pile of books on the table, as it had been left, and the next thing was Williams's skip, seated on a chair opposite, gazing at it with undisguised horror. How was this? Mr Filcher (the name is not my own invention) was a servant of considerable standing, and set the standard of etiquette to all his own college and to several neighbouring ones, and nothing could be more alien to his practice than to be found sitting on his master's chair, or appearing to take any particular notice of his master's furniture or pictures. Indeed, he seemed to feel this himself. He started violently when the three men were in the room, and got up with a marked effort. Then he said:

'I ask your pardon, sir, for taking such a freedom as to set down.'

'Not at all, Robert,' interposed Mr Williams. 'I was meaning to ask you some time what you thought of that picture.'

'Well, sir, of course I don't set up my opinion again yours, but it ain't the picture I should 'ang where my little girl could see it, sir.'

'Wouldn't you; Robert? Why not?'

'No sir. Why, the pore child, I recollect once she see a Door Bible, with pictures not 'alf what that is, and we 'ad to set up with her three or four nights afterwards, if you'll believe me; and if she was to ketch a sight of this skelinton here, or whatever it is, carrying off the pore baby, she would be in a taking. You know 'ow it is with children; 'ow nervish they git with a little thing and all. But what I should say, it don't seem a right picture to be laying about, sir, not where any one that's liable to be startled could come on it. Should you be wanting anything this evening, sir? Thank you, sir.'

With these words the excellent man went to continue the round of his masters, and you may be sure the gentlemen whom he left lost no time in gathering round the engraving. There was the house, as before, under the waning moon and the drifting clouds. The window that had been open was shut, and the figure was once more on the lawn: but not this time crawling cautiously on hands and knees. Now it was erect and stepping swiftly, with long strides, towards the front of the picture. The moon was behind it, and the black drapery hung down over its face so that only hints of that could be seen, and what was visible made the spectators profoundly thankful that they could see no more than a white dome-like forehead and a few straggling hairs. The head was bent down, and the arms were tightly clasped over an object which could be dimly seen and identified as a child, whether dead or living it was not possible to say. The legs of the appearance alone could be plainly discerned, and they were horribly thin.

From five to seven the three companions sat and watched the picture by turns. But it never changed. They agreed at last that it would be safe to leave it, and that they would return after Hall and await further developments.

When they assembled again, at the earliest possible moment, the engraving was there, but the figure was gone, and the house was quiet under the moonbeams. There was nothing for it but to spend the evening over gazetteers and guide-books. Williams was the lucky one at last, and perhaps he deserved it. At 11.30 p.m. he read from Murray's *Guide to Essex* the following lines:

> 16½ miles, *Anningley*. The church has been an interesting building of Norman date, but was extensively classicized in the last century. It contains the tomb of the family of Francis, whose mansion, Anningley Hall, a solid Queen Anne house, stands immediately beyond the churchyard in a park of about 80 acres. The family is now extinct, the last heir having disappeared mysteriously in infancy in the year 1802. The father, Mr Arthur Francis, was locally known as a talented amateur engraver in mezzotint. After his son's disappearance he lived in complete retirement at the Hall, and was found dead in his studio on the third anniversary of the disaster, having just completed an engraving of the house, impressions of which are of considerable rarity.

This looked like business, and, indeed, Mr Green on his return at once identified the house as Anningley Hall.

'Is there any kind of explanation of the figure, Green?' was the question which Williams naturally asked.

'I don't know, I'm sure, Williams. What used to be said in the place when I first knew it, which was before I came up here, was just this: old Francis was always very much down on these poaching fellows, and whenever he got a chance he used to get a man whom he suspected of it turned off the estate, and by degrees he got rid of them all but one. Squires could do a lot of things then that they daren't think of now. Well, this man that was left was what you find pretty often in that country – the last remains of a very old family. I believe they were Lords of the Manor at one time. I recollect just the same thing in my own parish.'

'What, like the man in *Tess o' the Durbervilles*?' Williams put in.

'Yes, I dare say; it's not a book I could ever read myself. But this fellow could show a row of tombs in the church there that belonged to his ancestors, and all that went to sour him a bit; but Francis, they said, could never get at him – he always kept just on the right side of the law – until one night the keepers found him at it in a wood right at the end of the estate. I could show you the place now; it marches with some land that used to belong to an uncle of mine. And you can imagine there was a row; and this man Gawdy (that was the name, to be sure – Gawdy; I thought I should get it – Gawdy), he was unlucky enough, poor chap! to shoot a keeper. Well, that was what Francis wanted, and grand juries – you know what they would have been then – and poor Gawdy was strung up in double-quick time; and I've been shown the place he was buried in, on the north side of the church – you know the way in that part of the world: anyone that's been hanged or made away with themselves, they bury them that side. And the idea was that some friend of Gawdy's – not a relation, because he had none, poor devil! he was the last of his line: kind of *spes ultima gentis* – must have planned to get hold of Francis's boy and put an end to *his* line, too. I don't know – it's rather an out-of-the-way thing for an Essex poacher to think of but, you know, I should say now it looks more as if old Gawdy had managed the job himself. Booh! I hate to think of it! have some whisky, Williams!'

The facts were communicated by Williams to Dennistoun, and by him to a mixed company, of which I was one, and the Sadducean Professor of Ophiology another. I am sorry to say that the latter when asked what he thought of it, only remarked: 'Oh, those Bridgeford people will say anything' – a sentiment which met with the reception it deserved.

I have only to add that the picture is now in the Ashleian Museum; that it has been treated with a view to discovering whether sympathetic ink has been used in it, but without effect; that Mr Britnell knew nothing of it save that he was sure it was uncommon; and that, though carefully watched, it has never been known to change again.

The Courting of Dinah Shadd

RUDYARD KIPLING

What did the colonel's lady think?
  Nobody never knew.
Somebody asked the sergeant's wife
  An' she told 'em true.
When you git to a man in the case
  They're like a row o' pins,
For the colonel's lady an' Judy O'Grady
  Are sisters under their skins.

Barrack Room Ballad.

All day I had followed at the heels of a pursuing army engaged on one of the finest battles that ever camp of exercise beheld. Thirty thousand troops, had, by the wisdom of the Government of India been turned loose over a few thousand square miles of country to practise in peace what they would never attempt in war. Consequently cavalry charged unshaken infantry at the trot. Infantry captured artillery by frontal attacks delivered in line of quarter columns, and mounted infantry skirmished up to the wheels of an armoured train which carried nothing more deadly than a twenty-five pounder Armstrong, two Nordenfeldts, and a few score volunteers all cased in three-eighths-inch boiler-plate. Yet it was a very lifelike camp. Operations did not cease at sundown; nobody knew the country and nobody spared man or horse. There was unending cavalry scouting and almost unending forced work over broken ground. The Army of the South had finally pierced the centre of the Army of the North, and was pouring through a gap hot-foot to capture a city of strategic importance. Its front extended fanwise, the sticks being represented by regiments strung out along the line of route backwards to the divisional transport columns and all the lumber that trails behind an army on the move. On its right the broken left of the Army of the North was flying in mass, chased by the Southern horse and hammered by the Southern guns till these had been pushed far beyond the limits of their last support. Then the flying sat down to rest, while the elated commandant of the pursuing force telegraphed that he held all in check and observation.

Unluckily he did not observe that three miles to his right flank a flying column of Northern horse with a detachment of Ghoorkhas and British troops had been pushed round as fast as the failing light allowed, to cut across the entire rear of the Southern Army, – to break, as it were, all the ribs of the fan where they converged by striking at the transport, reserve ammunition, and artillery supplies. Their instructions were to go in, avoiding the few scouts who might not have been drawn off by the pursuit, and create sufficient excitement to impress the Southern Army with the wisdom of guarding their own flank and rear before they captured cities. It was a pretty manœuvre neatly carried out.

Speaking for the second division of the Southern Army, our first intimation of the attack was at twilight, when the artillery were labouring in deep sand, most of the escort were trying to help them out, and the main body of the infantry had gone on. A Noah's Ark of elephants, camels, and the mixed menagerie of an Indian transport-train bubbled and squealed behind the guns, when there appeared from nowhere in particular British infantry to the extent of three companies, who sprang to the head of the gun-horses and brought all to a standstill amid oaths and cheers.

'How's that, umpire?' said the major commanding the attack, and with one voice the drivers and limber gunners answered 'Hout!' while the colonel of artillery sputtered.

'All your scouts are charging our main body,' said the major. 'Your flanks are unprotected for two miles. I think we've broken the back of this division. And listen, – there go the Ghoorkhas!'

A weak fire broke from the rear-guard more than a mile away, and was answered by cheerful howlings. The Ghoorkhas, who should have swung clear of the second division, had stepped on its tail in the dark, but drawing off hastened to reach the next line of attack, which lay almost parallel to us five or six miles away.

Our column swayed and surged irresolutely – three batteries, the divisional ammunition reserve, the baggage, and a section of the hospital and bearer corps. The commandant ruefully promised to report himself 'cut up' to the nearest umpire, and commending his cavalry and all other cavalry to the special care of Eblis, toiled on to resume touch with the rest of the division.

'We'll bivouac here tonight,' said the major. 'I have a notion that the Ghoorkhas will get caught. They may want us to re-form on. Stand easy till the transport gets away.'

A hand caught my beast's bridle and led him out of the choking dust; a larger hand deftly canted me out of the saddle; and two of the hugest hands in the world received me sliding. Pleasant is the lot of the special correspondent who falls into such hands as those of Privates Mulvaney, Ortheris, and Learoyd.

'An' that's all right,' said the Irishman calmly. 'We thought we'd find you somewheres here by. Is there anything av yours in the transport? Orth'ris'll fetch ut out.'

Ortheris did 'fetch ut out', from under the trunk of an elephant, in the shape of a servant and an animal both laden with medical comforts. The little man's eyes sparkled.

'If the brutil an' licentious soldiery av these parts gets sight av the thruck,' said Mulvaney, making practised investigation, 'they'll loot ev'rything. They're bein' fed on iron-filin's an' dog-biscuit these days, but glory's no compensation for a belly-ache. Praise be, we're here to protect you, sorr. Beer, sausage, bread (soft an' that's a cur'osity), soup in a tin, whisky by the smell av ut, an' fowls! Mother av Moses, but ye take the field like a confectioner! 'Tis scand'lus.'

'Ere's a orficer,' said Ortheris significantly. 'When the sergent's done lushin' the privit may clean the pot.'

I bundled several things into Mulvaney's haversack before the major's hand fell on my shoulder and he said tenderly, 'Requisitioned for the Queen's service. Wolsey was quite wrong about special correspondents: they are the soldier's best friends. Come and take pot-luck with us tonight.'

And so it happened amid laughter and shoutings that my well-considered commissariat melted away to reappear later at the mess-table, which was a waterproof sheet spread on the ground. The flying column had taken three days' rations with it, and there be few things nastier than Government rations – especially when Government is experimenting with German toys. Erbswurst, tinned beef of surpassing tinniness, compressed vegetables, and meat-biscuits may be nourishing, but what Thomas Atkins needs is bulk in his inside. The major, assisted by his brother officers, purchased goats for the camp, and so made the experiment of no effect. Long before the fatigue-party sent to collect brushwood had returned, the men were settled down by their valises, kettles and pots had appeared from the surrounding country, and were dangling over fires as the kid and the compressed vegetable bubbled together; there rose a cheerful clinking of mess-tins; outrageous demands for 'a little more stuffin' with that there liverwing;' and gust on gust of chaff as pointed as a bayonet and as delicate as a gun-butt.

'The boys are in a good temper,' said the major. 'They'll be singing presently. Well, a night like this is enough to keep them happy.'

Over our heads burned the wonderful Indian stars, which are not all pricked in on one plane, but, preserving an orderly perspective, draw the eye through the velvet of the void up to the barred doors of heaven itself. The earth was a grey shadow more unreal than the sky. We could hear her breathing lightly in the pauses between the howling of the jackals, the movement of the wind in the tamarisks, and the fitful mutter of musketry-fire leagues away to the left. A native woman from some unseen hut began to sing, the mail-train thundered past on its way to Delhi, and a roosting crow cawed drowsily. Then there was a belt-loosening silence about the fires, and the even breathing of the crowded earth took up the story.

The men, full fed, turned to tobacco and song, – their officers with them. The subaltern is happy who can win the approval of the musical critics in his regiment, and is honoured among the more intricate step-dancers. By him, as by him who plays cricket cleverly, Thomas Atkins will stand in time of need, when he will let a better officer go on alone. The ruined tombs of forgotten Mussulman saints heard the ballad of *Agra Town, The Buffalo Battery, Marching to Kabul, The Long, Long Indian Day, The Place Where the Punkah-coolie Died*, and the crashing chorus which announces,

> Youth's daring spirit, manhood's fire,
> Firm hand and eagle eye,
> Must he acquire, who would aspire
> To see the grey boar die.

To-day, of all those jovial thieves who appropriated my commissariat and lay and laughed round that waterproof sheet, not one remains. They went to camps that were not of exercise and battles without umpires. Burmah, and Soudan, and the frontier, – fever and fight, – took them in their time.

I drifted across to the men's fires in search of Mulvaney, whom I found strategically greasing his feet by the blaze. There is nothing particularly lovely in the sight of a private thus engaged after a long day's march, but when you reflect on the exact proportion of the 'might, majesty, dominion, and power' of the British Empire which stands on those feet you take an interest in the proceedings.

'There's a blister, bad luck to ut, on the heel,' said Mulvaney. 'I can't touch ut. Prick ut out, little man.'

Ortheris took out his house-wife, eased the trouble with a needle, stabbed Mulvaney in the calf with the same weapon, and was swiftly kicked into the fire.

'I've bruk the best av my toes over you, ye grinnin' child av disruption,' said Mulvaney, sitting cross-legged and nursing his feet; then seeing me, 'Oh, ut's you, sorr! Be welkim, an' take that maraudin' scutt's place. Jock, hold him down on the cindhers for a bit.'

But Ortheris escaped and went elsewhere, as I took possession of the hollow he had scraped for himself and lined with his greatcoat. Learoyd on the other side of the fire grinned affably and in a minute fell fast asleep.

'There's the height av politeness for you,' said Mulvaney, lighting his pipe with a flaming branch. 'But Jock's eaten half a box av your sardines at wan gulp, an' I think the tin too. What's the best wid you, sorr, an' how did you happen to be on the losin' side this day whin we captured you?'

'The Army of the South is winning all along the line,' I said.

'Then that line's the hangman's rope, savin' your presence. You'll learn tomorrow how we rethreated to dhraw thim on before we made thim trouble, an' that's what a woman does. By the same tokin, we'll be attacked before the dawnin' an' ut would be betther not to slip your boots. How do I know that? By the light av pure reason. Here are three companies av us ever so far inside av the enemy's flank an' a crowd av roarin', tarin', squealin' cavalry gone on just to turn out the whole hornet's nest av them. Av course the enemy will pursue, by brigades like as not, an' thin we'll have to run for ut. Mark my words. I am av the opinion av Polonius whin he said, 'Don't fight wid ivry scutt for the pure joy av fightin', but if you do, knock the nose av him first an' frequint.' We ought to ha' gone on an' helped the Ghoorkhas.'

'But what do you know about Polonius?' I demanded. This was a new side of Mulvaney's character.

'All that Shakespeare iver wrote an' a dale more that the gallery shouted,' said the man of war, carefully lacing his boots. 'Did I not tell you av Silver's theatre in Dublin whin I was younger than I am now an' a patron av the drama? Ould Silver wud never pay actor-man or woman their just dues, an' by consequince his comp'nies was collapsible at the last minut. Thin the bhoys wud clamour to take a part, an' oft as not ould Silver made them pay for the fun. Faith, I've seen Hamlut played wid a new black eye an' the queen as full as a cornucopia. I remimber wanst Hogin that 'listed in the Black Tyrone an' was shot in South Africa, he sejuced ould Silver into givin' him Hamlut's part instid av me that had a fine fancy for rhetoric in those days. Av course I wint into the gallery an' began to fill the pit wid other people's hats, an' I passed the time av day to Hogin walkin' through Denmark like a hamstrung mule wid a pall on his back. "Hamlut," sez I, "there's a hole in your heel. Pull up your shtockin's, Hamlut," sez I. "Hamlut, Hamlut, for the love av decincy dhrop that skull an' pull up your shtockin's." The whole house begun to tell him that. He stopped his soliloquishms mid-between. "My shtockin's may be comin' down or they may not," sez he, screwin' his eyes into the gallery, for well he knew who I was. "But afther this performince is over me an' the Ghost'll trample the tripes out av you, Terence, wid your ass's bray!" An' that's how I come to know about Hamlut. Eyah! Those days, those days! Did you iver have onendin' devilmint an' nothin' to pay for it in your life, sorr?'

'Never, without having to pay,' I said.

'That's thrue! 'Tis mane whin you considher on ut; but ut's the same wid horse or fut. A headache if you dhrink, an' a belly-ache if you eat too much, an' a heart-ache to kape all down. Faith, the beast only gets the colic, an' he's the lucky man.'

He dropped his head and stared into the fire, fingering his moustache the while. From the far side of the bivouac the voice of Corbet-Nolan, senior subaltern of B company, uplifted itself in an ancient and much appreciated song of sentiment, the men moaning melodiously behind him.

The north wind blew coldly, she drooped from that hour,
My own little Kathleen, my sweet little Kathleen,
Kathleen, my Kathleen, Kathleen O'Moore!

With forty-five O's in the last word: even at that distance you might have cut the soft South Irish accent with a shovel.

'For all we take we must pay, but the price is cruel high,' murmured Mulvaney when the chorus had ceased.

'What's the trouble?' I said gently, for I knew that he was a man of an extinguishable sorrow.

'Hear now,' said he. 'Ye know what I am now. *I* know what I mint to be at the beginnin' av my service. I've tould you time an' again, an' what I have not Dinah Shadd has. An' what am I? Oh, Mary Mother av Hiven, an ould dhrunken, untrustable baste av a privit that has seen the reg'ment change out from colonel to drummer-boy, not wanst or twice, but scores av times! Ay, scores! An' me not so near gettin' promotion as in the first! An' me livin' on an' kapin' clear av clink, not by my own good conduck, but the kindness av some orf'cer-bhoy young enough to be son to me? Do I not know ut? Can I not tell whin I'm passed over at p'rade, tho' I'm rockin' full av liquor an' ready to fall all in wan piece, such as even a suckin' child might see, bekaze, "Oh, 'tis only ould Mulvaney!" An' whin I'm let off in ord'ly-room through some thrick of the tongue an' a ready answer an' the ould man's mercy, is ut smilin' I feel whin I fall away an' go back to Dinah Shadd, thryin' to carry ut all off as a joke? Not I! 'Tis hell to me, dumb hell through ut all; an' next time whin the fit comes I will be as bad again. Good cause the reg'ment has to know me for the best soldier in ut. Better cause have I to know mesilf for the worst man. I'm only fit to tache the new drafts what I'll niver learn myself; an' I am sure, as tho' I heard ut, that the minut wan av these pink-eyed recruities gets away from my "Mind ye now," an' "Listen to this, Jim, bhoy," – sure I am that the sergint houlds me up to him for a warnin'. So I tache, as they say at musketry-instruction, by direct and ricochet fire. Lord be good to me, for I have stud some throuble!'

'Lie down and go to sleep,' said I, not being able to comfort or advise. 'You're the best man in the regiment, and, next to Ortheris, the biggest fool. Lie down and wait till we're attacked. What force will they turn out? Guns, think you?'

'Try that wid your lorrds an' ladies, twistin' an' turnin' the talk, tho' you mint ut well. Ye cud say nothin' to help me, an' yet ye niver knew what cause I had to be what I am.'

'Begin at the beginning and go on to the end,' I said royally. 'But rake up the fire a bit first.'

I passed Ortheris's bayonet for a poker.

'That shows how little we know what we do,' said Mulvaney, putting it aside. "Fire takes all the heart out av the steel, an' the next time, may be, that our little man is fighting for his life his bradawl'll break, an' so you'll ha' killed him, manin' no more than to kape yourself warm.'Tis a recruity's thrick that. Pass the clanin'-rod, sorr.'

I snuggled down abashed; and after an interval the voice of Mulvaney began. 'Did I iver tell you how Dinah Shadd came to be wife av mine?'

I dissembled a burning anxiety that I had felt for some months – ever since Dinah Shadd, the strong, the patient, and the infinitely tender, had of her own good love and free will washed a shirt for me, moving in a barren land where washing was not.

'I can't remember,' I said casually. 'Was it before or after you made love to Annie Bragin and got no satisfaction?'

The story of Annie Bragin is written in another place. It is one of the many less respectable episodes in Mulvaney's chequered career.

'Before – before – long before, was that business av Annie Bragin an' the corp'ril's ghost. Niver woman was the worse for me whin I had married Dinah. There's a time for all things, an' I know how to kape all things in place – barrin' the dhrink, that kapes me in my place wid no hope av comin' to be aught else.'

'Begin at the beginning,' I insisted. 'Mrs Mulvaney told me that you married her when you were quartered in Krab Bokhar barracks.'

'An' the same is a cess-pit,' said Mulvaney piously. 'She spoke thrue, did Dinah.'Twas this way. Talkin' av that, have ye iver fallen in love, sorr?'

I preserved the silence of the damned. Mulvaney continued –

'Thin I will assume that ye have not. *I* did. In the days av my youth, as I have no more than wanst tould you, I was a man that filled the eye an' delighted the sowl av women. Niver man was hated as I have bin. Niver man was loved as I – no, not within half a day's march av ut! For the first five years av my service, whin I was what I wud give my sowl to be now, I tuk whatever was within my reach an' digested ut – an' that's more than most men can say. Dhrink I tuk, an' ut did me no harm. By the Hollow av Hiven, I cud play wid four women at wanst, an' kape them from findin out anythin' about the other three, an' smile like a fullblown marigold through ut all. Dick Coulhan, av the battery we'll have down on us tonight, could drive his team no better than I mine, an' I hild the worser cattle! An' so I lived, an' so I was happy till afther that business wid Annie Bragin – she that turned me off as cool as a meat-safe, an' taught me where I stud in the mind av an honest woman.'Twas no sweet dose to swallow.

'Afther that I sickened awhile an' tuk thought to my reg'mental work; conceiting mesilf I wud study an' be a sargint, an' a major-gineral twinty minutes afther that. But on top av my ambitiousness there was an empty place in my sowl, an' me own opinion av mesilf cud not fill ut. Ses I to mesilf, "Terence, you're a great man an' the best set-up in the reg'mint. Go on an' get promotion." Sez mesilf to me, "What for?" Sez I to, mesilf, "For the glory av ut!" Sez mesilf to me, "Will that fill these two strong arrums av yours, Terence?" – "Go to the devil," sez I to mesilf. "Go to the married lines," sez mesilf to me. "'Tis the same thing," sez I to mesilf. "Av you're the same man, ut is," said mesilf to me; an' wid that I considhered on ut a long while. Did you iver feel that way, sorr?'

I snored gently, knowing that if Mulvaney were uninterrupted he would go on. The clamour from the bivouac fires beat up to the stars, as the rival singers of the companies were pitted against each other.

'So I felt that way an' a bad time ut was. Wanst, bein' a fool, I wint into the married lines more for the sake av spakin' to our ould colour-sergint Shadd than for any thruck wid women-folk. I was a corp'ril then – rejuced aftherwards, but a corp'ril then. I've got a photograft av mesilf to prove ut. "You'll take a cup av tay wid us?" sez Shadd. "I will that," I sez, "tho' tay is not my divarsion."

' "'Twud be better for you if ut were," sez ould Mother Shadd, an' she had ought to know, for Shadd, in the ind av his service, dhrank bungfull each night.

'Wid that I tuk off my gloves – there was pipeclay in thim, so that they stud alone – an' pulled up my chair, lookin' round at the china ornaments an' bits av things in the Shadds' quarters. They were things that belonged to a man, an' no camp-kit, here today an' dishipated next. "You're comfortable in this place, sergint," sez I. "'Tis the wife that did ut, boy," sez he, pointin' the stem av his pipe to ould Mother Shadd, an' she smacked the top av his bald head apon the compliment. "That manes you want money," sez she.

'An' thin – an' thin whin the kettle was to be filled, Dinah came in – my Dinah – her sleeves rowled up to the elbow an' her hair in a winkin' glory over her forehead, the big blue eyes beneath twinklin' like stars on a frosty night, an' the tread av her two feet lighter than waste-paper from the colonel's basket in ord'ly-room whin ut's emptied. Bein' but a shlip av a girl she went pink at seein' me, an' I twisted me moustache an' looked at a picture forninst the wall. Niver show a woman that ye care the snap av a finger for her, an' begad she'll come bleatin' to your boot-heels!'

'I suppose that's why you followed Annie Bragin till everybody in the married quarters laughed at you,' said I, remembering that unhallowed wooing and casting off the disguise of drowsiness.

'I'm layin' down the gin'ral theory av the attack,' said Mulvaney, driving his boot into the dying fire. 'If you read the *Soldier's Pocket Book,* which niver any soldier reads, you'll see that there are exceptions. Whin Dinah was out av the door (an' 'twas as tho' the sunlight had shut too) – "Mother av Hiven, sergint," sez I, "but is that your daughter?" – "I've believed that way these eighteen years," sez ould Shadd, his eyes twinklin'; "but Mrs Shadd has her own opinion like iv'ry woman." – ' "Tis wid yours this time, for a mericle," sez Mother Shadd. "Thin why in the name av fortune did I niver see her before?" sez I. "Bekaze you've been thrapesin' round wid the married women these three years past. She was a bit av a child till last year, an' she shot up wid the spring," sez ould Mother Shadd. "I'll thrapese no more," sez I. "D'you mane that?" sez ould Mother Shadd, lookin' at me sideways like a hen looks at a hawk whin the chickens are runnin' free. "Try me, an' tell," sez I. Wid that I pulled on my gloves, dhrank off the tay, an' went out av the house as stiff as a gin'ral p'rade, for well I knew that Dinah Shadd's eyes were in the small av my back out av the scullery window. Faith! that was the only time I mourned I was not a cav'l'ry man for the pride av the spurs to jingle.

'I want out to think, an' I did a powerful lot av thinkin', but ut all came round to that shlip av a girl in the dotted blue dhress, wid the blue eyes an' the sparkil in them. Thin I kept off canteen, an' I kept to the married quarthers or near by, on the chanst av meetin' Dinah. Did I meet her? Oh, my time past, did I not; wid a lump in my throat as big as my valise an' my heart goin' like a farrier's forge on a Saturday morning? 'Twas "Good day to ye, Miss Dinah," an' "Good day t'you, corp'ril," for a week or two, and divil a bit further could I get bekaze av the respect I had to that girl that I cud' ha' broken betune finger an' thumb.'

Here I giggled as I recalled the gigantic figure of Dinah Shadd when she handed me my shirt.

'Ye may laugh,' grunted Mulvaney. 'But I'm speakin' the trut,' an' 'tis you that are in fault. Dinah was a girl that wud ha' taken the imperiousness out av the Duchess av Clonmel in those days. Flower hand, foot av shod air, an' the eyes av the livin' mornin' she had that is my wife today – ould Dinah, and niver aught else than Dinah Shadd to me.

''Twas after three weeks standin' off an' on, an' niver makin' headway excipt through the eyes, that a little drummer-boy grinned in me face whin I had admonished him wid the buckle av my belt for riotin' all over the place. "An' I'm not the only wan that doesn't kape to barricks," sez he. I tuk him by the scruff av his neck, – my heart was hung on a hair-thrigger those days, you will onderstand – an' "Out wid ut," sez I, "or I'll lave no bone av you unbreakable." "Speak to Dempsey," sez he howlin'. "Dempsey which?" sez I, "ye unwashed limb av Satan." – "Av the Bobtailed Dhragoons," sez he. "He's seen her home from her aunt's house in the civil lines four times this fortnight." – "Child!" sez I, dhroppin' him, "your tongue's stronger than your body. Go to your quarters. I'm sorry I dhressed you down."

'At that I went four ways to wanst huntin' Dempsey. I was mad to think that wid all my airs among women I shud ha' been chated by a basin-faced fool av a cav'lryman not fit to trust on a trunk. Presintly I found him in our lines – the Bobtails was quartered next us – an' a tallowy, topheavy son av a she-mule he was wid his big brass spurs an' his plastrons on his epigastrons an' all. But he niver flinched a hair.

' "A word wid you, Dempsey," sez I. "You've walked wid Dinah Shadd four times this fortnight gone."

' "What's that to you?" sez he. "I'll walk forty times more, an forty on top av that, ye shovel-futted clod-breakin' infantry lance-corp'ril."

'Before I cud gyard he had his gloved fist home on my cheek an' down I went full-sprawl. "Will that content you?" sez he, blowin' on his knuckles for all the world like a Scots Greys orf'cer. "Content!" sez I. "For your own sake, man, take off your spurs, peel your jackut, an' onglove.'Tis the beginnin' av the overture; stand up!"

'He stud all he know, but he niver peeled his jacket, an' his shoulders had no fair play. I was fightin' for Dinah Shadd an' that cut on my cheek. What hope had he forninst me? "Stand up," sez I, time an' again whin he was beginnin' to quarter the ground an' gyard high an' go large. "This isn't ridin'-school," I sez. "O man, stand up an' let me get in at ye." But whin I saw he wud be runnin' about, I grup his shtock in my left an' his waist-belt in my right an' swung him clear to my right front, head undher, he hammerin' my nose till the wind was knocked out av him on the bare ground. "Stand up," sez I, "or I'll kick your head into your chest!" and I wud ha' done ut too, so ragin' mad I was.

' "My collar bone's bruk," sez he. "Help me back to lines. I'll walk wid her no more." So I helped him back.'

'And was his collar-bone broken?' I asked, for I fancied that only Learoyd could neatly accomplish that terrible throw.

'He pitched on his left shoulder-point. Ut was. Next day the news was in both barricks, an' whin I met Dinah Shadd wid a cheek on me like all the reg'mintal tailor's samples there was no "Good mornin', corp'ril" or aught else. "An' what have I done, Miss Shadd," sez I, very bould, plantin' mesilf forninst her, "that ye should not pass the time of day?"

' "Ye've half-killed rough-rider Dempsey," sez she, her dear blue eyes fillin' up.

' "May be," sez I. "Was he a friend av yours that saw ye home four times in the fortnight?"

' "Yes," sez she, but her mouth was down at the corners. "An' – an' what's that to you?" she sez.

' "Ask Dempsey," sez I, purtendin' to go away.

' "Did you fight for me then, ye silly man?" she sez, tho' she knew ut all along.

' "Who else?" sez I, an' I tuk wan pace to the front.

' "I wasn't worth ut," sez she, fingerin' in her apron.

' "That's for me to say," sez I. "Shall I say ut?"

' "Yes," sez she in a saint's whisper, an' at that I explained mesilf; and she tould me what ivry man that is a man, an' many that is a woman, hears wanst in his life.

' "But what made ye cry at startin', Dinah, darlin'?" sez I.

' "Your – your bloody cheek," sez she, duckin' her little head down on my sash (I was on duty for the day) an' whimperin' like a sorrowful angil.

'Now a man cud take that two ways. I tuk ut as pleased me best an' my first kiss wid ut. Mother av Innocence! but I kissed her on the tip av the nose an' undher the eye; an' a girl that lets a kiss come tumbleways like that has never been kissed before. Take note av that, sorr. Thin we wint hand in hand to ould Mother Shadd like two little childher, an' she said 'twas no bad thing, an' ould

Shadd nodded behind his pipe, an' Dinah ran way to her own room. That day I throd on rollin' clouds. All earth was too small to hould me. Begad, I cud ha' hiked the sun out av the sky for a live coal to my pipe so magnificent I was. But I tuk recruities at squad-drill instid, an' began wid general battalion advance whin I shud ha' been balance-steppin' them. Eyah! that day! that day!'

A very long pause. 'Well?' said I.

''Twas all wrong,' said Mulvaney, with an enormous sigh. 'An I know that ev'ry bit av ut was my own foolishness. That night I tuk maybe the half av three pints – not enough to turn the hair of a man in his natural senses. But I was more than half drunk wid pure joy, an' that canteen beer was so much whisky to me. I can't tell how it came about, but *bekaze* I had no thought for anywan except Dinah, *bekaze* I hadn't slipped her little white arms from my neck five minuts, *bekaze* the breath of her kiss was not gone from my mouth, I must go through the married lines on my way to quarters, an' I must stay talkin' to a red-headed Mullingar heifer av a girl, Judy Sheehy, that was daughter to Mother Sheehy, the wife of Nick Sheehy, the canteen-sergint – the Black Curse av Shielygh be on the whole brood that are above groun' this day!

' "An' what are ye houldin' your head that high for, corp'ril?" sez Judy. "Come in an' thry a cup av tay," she sez, standin' in the doorway. Bein' an ontrustable fool, an' thinkin' av anything but tay, I wint.

' "Mother's at canteen," sez Judy, smoothin' the hair av hers that was like red snakes, an' lookin' at me corner-ways out av her green cats' eyes. "Ye will not mind, corp'ril?"

' "I can endure," sez I; ould Mother Sheehy bein' no divarsion av mine, nor her daughter too. Judy fetched the tea things an' put thim on the table, leanin' over me very close to get thim square. I dhrew back, thinkin' av Dinah.

' "Is ut afraid you are av a girl alone?" sez Judy.

' "No," sez I. "Why should I be?"

' "That rests wid the girl," sez Judy, dhrawin' her chair next to mine.

' "Thin there let ut rest," sez I; an' thinkin' I'd been a trifle onpolite, I sez, "The tay's not quite sweet enough for my taste. Put your little finger in the cup, Judy. 'Twill make ut necthar."

"What's necthar?" sez she.

' "Somethin' very sweet," sez I; an' for the sinful life av me I cud not help lookin' at her out av the corner av my eye, as I was used to look at a woman.

' "Go on wid ye, corp'ril,' sez she. 'You're a flirrt."

' "On me sowl I'm not," sez I.

' "Then you're a cruel handsome man, an' that's worse," sez she, heaving big sighs an' lookin' crossways.

' "You know your own mind," sez I.

' "'Twud be better for me if I did not," she sez.

' "There's a dale to be said on both sides av that," sez I, unthinkin'.

' "Say your own part av ut, then, Terence, darlin'," sez she; "for begad I'm thinkin' I've said too much or too little for an honest girl," an' wid that she put her arms round my neck an' kissed me. ' "There's no more to be said afther that," sez I, kissin' her back again – Oh the mane scutt that I was, my head ringin' wid Dinah Shadd! How does ut come about, sorr, that when a man has put the comether on wan woman, he's sure bound to put it on another? 'Tis the same thing at musketry. Wan day ivry shot goes wide or into the bank, an' the next, lay high lay low, sight or snap, ye can't get off the bull's-eye for ten shots runnin'.'

'That only happens to a man who has had a good deal of experience. He does it without thinking,' I replied.

'Thankin' you for the complimint, sorr, ut may be so. But I'm doubtful whether you mint ut for a complimint. Hear now; I sat there wid Judy on my knee tellin' me all manner av nonsinse an only sayin "yes" an' "no", when I'd much better ha' kept tongue betune teeth. An' that was not an hour afther I had left Dinah! What I was thinkin' av I cannot say. Presintly, quiet as a cat, ould Mother Sheehy came in velvet-dhrunk. She had her daughter's red hair, but 'twas bald in patches, an' I cud see in her wicked ould face, clear as lightnin', what Judy wud be twenty years to come. I was for jumpin' up, but Judy niver moved.

' "Terence has promust, mother," sez she, an' the could sweat bruk out all over me. Ould Mother Sheehy sat down of a heap an' began playin' wid the cups. "Thin you're a well-matched pair," she sez very thick. "For he's the biggest rogue that iver spoiled the Queen's shoe-leather, an' – "

' "I'm off, Judy," sez I. "Ye should not talk nonsinse to your mother. Get her to bed, girl."

' "Nonsinse!" sez the ould woman, prickin' up her ears like a cat an' grippin' the table-edge. ' "Twill be the most non-sinsical nonsinse for you, ye grinnin' badger, if nonsinse 'tis. Git clear, you. I'm goin' to bed."

'I ran out into the dhark, my head in a stew an' my heart sick, but I had sinse enough to see that I'd brought ut all on mysilf. "It's this to pass the time av day to a panjandhrum av hellcats," sez I. "What I've said, an' what I've not said do not matther. Judy an' her dam will hould me for a promust man, an Dinah will give me the go, an' I desarve ut. I will go an' get dhrunk," sez I, "an' forget about ut, for 'tis plain I'm not a marrin' man."

'On my way to canteen I ran against Lascelles, colour-sergeant that was av E Comp'ny, a hard, hard man, wid a torment av a wife. "You've the head av a drowned man on your shoulders," sez he; "an' you're goin' where you'll get a worse wan. Come back," sez he. "Let me go," sez I. "I've thrown my luck over the wall wid my own hand!" – "Then that's not the way to get ut back again," sez he. "Have out wid your throuble, ye fool-bhoy." An' I tould him how the matther was.

'He sucked in his lower lip. "You've been thrapped," sez he. "Ju Sheehy wud be the betther for a man's name to hers as soon as can. An' ye thought ye'd put the comether on her, – that's the natural vanity of the baste. Terence, you're a big born fool, but you're not bad enough to marry into that comp'ny. If you said anythin', an' for all your protestations I'm sure ye did – or did not, which is worse, – eat ut all – lie like the father of all lies, but come out av ut free av Judy. Do I not know what ut is to marry a woman that was the very spit an' image av Judy whin she was young? I'm gettin' old an' I've larnt patience, but you, Terence, you'd raise hand on Judy an' kill her in a year. Never mind if Dinah gives you the go, you've desarved ut; never mind if the whole reg'mint laughs you all day. Get shut av Judy an' her mother. They can't dhrag you to church, but if they do, they'll dhrag you to hell. Go back to your quarters and lie down," sez he. Thin over his shoulder, "You *must* ha' done with thim."

'Next day I wint to see Dinah, but there was no tucker in me as walked. I knew the throuble wud come soon enough widout any handlin' av mine, an I dreaded ut sore.

'I heard Judy callin' me, but I hild straight on to the Shadd's quarthers, an' Dinah wud ha' kissed me but I put her back.

' "Whin all's said, darlin'," sez I, "you can give ut me if ye will, tho' I misdoubt 'twill be so easy to come by then."

'I had scarce begun to put the explanation into shape before Judy an' her mother came to the door. I think there was a verandah, but I'm forgettin'.

' "Will ye not step in?" sez Dinah, pretty and polite, though the Shadds had no dealin's with the Sheehys. Old Mother Shadd looked up quick, an' she was the fust to see the throuble; for Dinah was her daughter.

' "I'm pressed for time today," sez Judy as bould as brass; "an' I've only come for Terence, – my promust man.'Tis strange to find him here the day afther the day."

'Dinah looked at me as though I had hit her, an' I answered straight.

' "There was some nonsinse last night at the Sheehys' quarthers, an' Judy's carryin' on the joke, darlin'," sez I.

' "At the Sheehys' quarthers?" sez Dinah very slow an' Judy cut in wid: "He was there from nine till ten, Dinah Shadd, an' the betther half av that time I was sittin' on his knee, Dinah Shadd. Ye may look and ye may look an' ye may look me up an' down, but ye won't look away that Terence is my promust man. Terence, darlin', 'tis time for us to be comin' home."

'Dinah Shadd niver said word to Judy. "Ye left me at half-past eight," she sez to me, "an' I niver thought that ye'd leave me for Judy, – promises or no promises. Go back wid her, you that have to be fetched by a girl! I'm done with you," sez she, and she ran into her own room, her mother followin'. So I was alone wid those two women and at liberty to spake my sentiments."

' "Judy Sheehy," sez I, "if you made a fool av me betune the lights you shall not do ut in the day. I niver promised you words or lines."

' "You lie," sez ould Mother Sheehy, "an' may ut choke you where you stand!" She was far gone in dhrink.

' "An, tho' ut choked me where I stud I'd not change," sez I. "Go home, Judy.

I take shame for a decent girl like you dhraggin' your mother out bare-headed on this errand. Hear now, and have ut for an answer. I gave my word to Dinah Shadd yesterday, an', more blame on me, I was wid you last night talkin' nonsinse but nothin' more. You've chosen to thry to hould me on ut. I will not be held thereby for anythin' in the world. Is that enough?"

'Judy wint pink all over. "An' I wish you joy av the perjury," sez she, duckin' a curtsey. "You've lost a woman that would ha' wore her hand to the bone for your pleasure; an' 'deed, Terence, ye were not thrapped. . . ." Lascelles must ha' spoken plain to her. "I am such as Dinah is – 'deed I am! Ye've lost a fool av a girl that'll niver look at you again, an' ye've lost what ye niver had, – your common honesty. If you manage your men as you manage your love-makin', small wondher they call you the worst corp'ril in the comp'ny. Come away, mother," sez she.

'But divil a fut would the ould woman budge! "D'you hould by that?" sez she, peerin' up under her thick grey eyebrows.

' "Ay, an' wud," sez I, "tho' Dinah gave me the go twinty times. I'll have no thruck with you or yours," sez I. "Take your child away, ye shameless woman."

' "An' am I shameless?" sez she, bringin' her hands up above her head. "Thin what are you, ye lyin', schamin', weak-kneed, dhirty-souled son av a sutler? Am *I* shameless? Who put the open shame on me an' my child that we shud go beggin' through the lines in the broad daylight for the broken word of a man? Double portion of my shame be on you, Terence Mulvaney, that think yourself so strong! By Mary and the saints, by blood and water an' by ivry sorrow that came into the world since the beginnin', the black blight fall on you and yours, so that you may niver be free from pain for another when ut's not your own! May your heart bleed in your breast drop by drop wid all your friends laughin' at the bleedin'! Strong you think yourself? May your strength be a curse to you to dhrive you into the divil's hands against your own will! Clear-eyed you are? May your eyes see clear evry step av the dark path you take till the hot cindhers av hell put thim out! May the ragin' dry thirst in my own ould bones go to you that you shall niver pass bottle full nor glass empty. God preserve the light av your onderstandin' to you, my jewel av a bhoy, that ye may niver forget what you mint to be an' do, whin you're wallowin' in the muck! May ye see the betther and follow the worse as long as there's breath in your body; an' may ye die quick in a strange land, watchin' your death before ut takes you, an' onable to stir hand or foot!"

'I heard a scufflin' in the room behind, and thin Dinah Shadd's hand dhropped into mine like a rose-leaf into a muddy road.

' "The half av that I'll take," sez she, "an' more too if I can. Go home, ye silly talkin' woman, – go home an' confess."

' "Come away! Come away!" sez Judy, pullin' her mother by the shawl. " 'Twas none av Terence's fault. For the love av Mary stop the talkin'!"

' "An' you!" said ould Mother Sheehy, spinnin' round forninst Dinah. "Will ye take the half av that man's load? Stand off from him, Dinah Shadd, before he takes you down too – you that look to be a quarther-master-sergeant's wife in five years. You look too high, child. You shall *wash* for the quarther-master-sergeant, whin he plases to give you the job out av charity; but a privit's wife you shall be to the end, an' evry sorrow of a privit's wife you shall know and niver a joy but wan, that shall go from you like the running tide from a rock. The pain av bearin' you shall know but niver the pleasure av giving the breast; an' you shall put away manchild into the common ground wid niver a priest to say a prayer over him, an' on that man-child ye shall think ivry day av your life. Think long, Dinah Shadd, for you'll niver have another tho' you pray till your knees are bleedin'. The mothers av childer shall mock you behind your back when you're wringing over the wash-tub. You shall know what ut is to help a dhrunken husband home an' see him go to the gyard-room. Will that plase you, Dinah Shadd, that won't be seen talkin' to my daughter? You shall talk to worse than Judy before all's over. The sergints' wives shall look down on you contemptuous, daughter av a sergint, an' you shall cover ut all up wid a smiling face whin your heart's burstin'. Stand off av him, Dinah Shadd, for I've put the Black Curse of Shielygh upon him an' his own mouth shall make ut good."

'She pitched forward on her head an' began foamin' at the mouth. Dinah Shadd ran out wid water, an' Judy dhragged the ould woman into the verandah till she sat up.

' "I'm old an' forlore," she sez, thremblin' an' cryin', "and 'tis like I say a dale more than I mane."

' "When you're able to walk, – go," says ould Mother Shadd "This house has no place for the likes av you that have cursed my daughter."

' "Eyah!" said the ould woman. "Hard words break no bones, an' Dinah Shadd'll kape the love av her husband till my bones are green corn. Judy darlin', I misremember what I came here for. Can you lend us the bottom av a taycup av tay Mrs Shadd?"

'But Judy dhragged her off cryin' as tho' her heart wud break. An' Dinah Shadd an' I, in ten minutes we had forgot ut all.'

'Then why do you remember it now?' said I.

'Is ut like I'd forget? Ivry word that wicked ould woman spoke fell thrue in my life aftherwards, an' I cud ha' stud ut all – stud ut all, – excipt when my little Shadd was born. That was on the line av march three months afther the regiment was taken with cholera. We were betune Umballa an' Kalka thin, an' I was on picket. Whin I came off duty the women showed me the child, an' ut turned on uts side an' died as I looked. We buried him by the road, an' Father Victor was a day's march behind wid the heavy baggage, so the comp'ny captain read a prayer. An' since then I've been a childless man, an' all else that ould Mother Sheehy put upon me an' Dinah Shadd. What do you think, sorr?'

I thought a good deal, but it seemed better then to reach out for Mulvaney's hand. The demonstration nearly cost me the use of three fingers. Whatever he knows of his weaknesses, Mulvaney is entirely ignorant of his strength.

'But what do you think?' he repeated, as I was straightening out the crushed fingers.

My reply was drowned in yells and outcries from the next fire, where ten men were shouting for 'Orth'ris,' 'Privit Orth'ris,' 'Mistah Or-ther-ris!' 'Deah boy,' 'Cap'n Orth'ris,' 'Field-Marshal Orth'ris,' 'Stanley, you pen'north o' pop, come 'ere to your own comp'ny!' And the cockney, who had been delighting another audience with recondite and Rabelaisian yarns, was shot down among his admirers by the major force.

'You've crumpled my dress-shirt 'orrid,' said he, 'an' I shan't sing no more to this 'ere bloomin' drawin'-room.'

Learoyd, roused by the confusion, uncoiled himself, crept behind Ortheris, and slung him aloft on his shoulders.

'Sing, ye bloomin' hummin' bird!' said he, and Ortheris, beating time on Learoyd's skull, delivered himself, in the raucous voice of the Ratcliffe Highway, of this song: –

My girl she give me the go onst,
  When I was a London lad,
An' I went on the drink for a fortnight,
  An' then I went to the bad.
The Queen she give me a shillin'
  To fight for 'er over the seas;
But Guv'ment built me a fever-trap,
  An' Injia give me disease.

Chorus.

Ho! don't you 'eed what a girl says,
  An' don't you go for the beer;
But I was an ass when I was at grass,
  An' that is why I'm here.

I fired a shot at a Afghan,
  The beggar 'e fired again,
An' I lay on my bed with a 'ole in my 'ed,
  An' missed the next campaign!
I up with my gun at a Burman
  Who carried a bloomin' *dah*,
But the cartridge stuck and the bay'nit brink,
  An' all I got was the scar.

Chorus.

Ho! don't you aim at a Afghan,
When you stand on the sky-line clear;
An' don't you go for a Burman
If none o' your friends is near.

I served my time for a corp'ral,
An' wetted my stripes with pop,
For I went on the bend with a intimate friend,
An' finished the night in the 'shop'.
I served my time for a sergeant;
The colonel 'e sez 'No!
The most you'll see is full C.B.'[1]
An' . . . very next night 'twas so.

Chorus.

Ho! don't you go for a corp'ral
Unless your 'ed is clear;
But I was an ass when I was at grass,
An' that is why I'm 'ere.

I've tasted the luck o' the army
In barrack an' camp an' clink,
An' I lost my tip through the bloomin' trip
Along o' the women an' drink.
I'm down at the heel o' my service,
An, when I am laid on the shelf,
My very wust friend from beginning to end
By the blood of a mouse was myself!

Chorus.

Ho! don't you 'eed what a girl says,
An' don't you go for the beer;
But I was an ass when I was at grass
An' that is why I'm 'ere.

'Ay, listen to our little man now, singin' an' shoutin' as tho' trouble had niver touched him. D'you remember when he went mad with the home-sickness?' said Mulvaney, recalling a never-to-be-forgotten season when Ortheris waded through the deep waters of affliction and behaved abominably. 'But he's talkin' bitter truth, though. Eyah!

[1]confined to barracks.

'My very worst frind from beginnin' to ind
By the blood av a mouse was mesilf!'

'Harkout' he continued, jumping to his feet.

'What did I tell you, sorr?'

Fttl', spttl', whttl' went the rifles of the picket in the darkness, and we heard their feet rushing towards us as Ortheris tumbled past me and into his great-coat. It is an impressive thing, even in peace, to see an armed camp spring to life with clatter of accoutrements, click of Martini levers, and blood curdling speculations as to the fate of missing boots. "Pickets dhriven in", said Mulvaney, staring like a buck at bay into the soft, clinging gloom. "Stand by an' kape close to us. If 'tis cav'lry, they may blundher into the fires".

Tr-ra-ra' -ta-ra-la' sung the thrice blessed bugle, and the rush to form square began. There is much rest and peace in the heart of a square if you arrive in time, and are not trodden upon too frequently. The smell of leather belts, fatigue uniform and packed humanity is comforting.

A dull grumble, that seemed to come from every point of the compass, at once, struck our listening ears, and little thrills of excitement ran down the faces of the square. Those who write so learnedly about judging distance by sound should hear cavalry on the move at night. A high-pitched yell on the left told us that the disturbers were friends, the cavalry of the attack, who had missed their direction, in the darkness, and were feeling blindly for some sort of support and camping-ground. The difficulty explained, they jingled on.

'Double pickets out there; by your arms lie down and sleep the rest', said the major, and the square melted away as the men scrambled for their places by the fire.

When I woke I saw Mulvaney, the night-dew gemming his moustache, leaning on his rifle at picket, lonely as Prometheus on his rock, with I know not what vultures tearing his liver.

The Red Room

H. G. WELLS

'I can assure you,' said I, 'that it will take a very tangible ghost to frighten me.' And I stood up before the fire with my glass in my hand.

'It is your own choosing,' said the man with the withered arm, and glanced at me askance.

'Eight-and-twenty years,' said I, 'I have lived, and never a ghost have I seen as yet.'

The old woman sat staring hard into the fire, her pale eyes wide open. 'Ah,' she broke in: 'and eight-and-twenty years you have lived and never seen the likes of this house, I reckon. There's a many things to see, when one's still but eight-and-twenty.' She swayed her head slowly from side to side. 'A many things to see and sorrow for.'

I half suspected the old people were trying to enhance the spiritual terrors of their house by their droning insistence. I put down my empty glass on the table and looked about the room, and caught a glimpse of myself, abbreviated and broadened to an impossible sturdiness, in the queer old mirror at the end of the room. 'Well,' I said, 'if I see anything tonight, I shall be so much the wiser. For I come to the business with an open mind.'

'It's your own choosing,' said the man with the withered arm once more.

I heard the sound of a stick and a shambling step on the flags in the passage outside, and the door creaked on its hinges as a second old man entered, more bent, more wrinkled, more aged even than the first. He supported himself by a single crutch, his eyes were covered by a shade, and his lower lip, half averted, hung pale and pink from his decaying yellow teeth. He made straight for an armchair on the opposite side of the table, sat down clumsily, and began to cough. The man with the withered arm gave this newcomer a short glance of positive dislike; the old woman took no notice of his arrival, but remained with her eyes fixed steadily on the fire.

'I said – it's your own choosing,' said the man with the withered arm, when the coughing had ceased for a while.

'It's my own choosing,' I answered.

The man with the shade became aware of my presence for the first time, and threw his head back for a moment and sideways, to see me. I caught a momentary glimpse of his eyes, small and bright and inflamed. Then he began to cough and splutter again.

'Why don't you drink?' said the man with the withered arm, pushing the beer towards him. The man with the shade poured out a glassful with a shaky arm that splashed half as much again on the deal table. A monstrous shadow of him crouched upon the wall and mocked his action as he poured and drank. I must confess I had scarce expected these grotesque custodians. There is to my mind something inhuman in senility, something crouching and atavistic; the human qualities seem to drop from old people insensibly day by day. The three of them made me feel uncomfortable, with their gaunt silences, their bent carriage, their evident unfriendliness to me and to one another.

'If,' said I, 'you will show me to this haunted room of yours, I will make myself comfortable there.'

The old man with the cough jerked his head back so suddenly that it startled me, and shot another glance of his red eyes at me from under the shade; but no one answered me. I waited a minute, glancing from one to the other.

'If,' I said a little louder, 'if you will show me to this haunted room of yours, I will relieve you from the task of entertaining me.'

'There's a candle on the slab outside the door,' said the man with the withered arm, looking at my feet as he addressed me. 'But if you go to the red room tonight— '

('This night of all nights!' said the old woman.)

'You go alone.'

'Very well,' I answered. 'And which way do I go?'

'You go along the passage for a bit,' said he, 'until you come to a door, and through that is a spiral staircase, and half-way up that is a landing and another door covered with baize. Go through that and down the long corridor to the end, and the red room is on your left up the steps.'

'Have I got that right?' I said, and repeated his directions. He corrected me in one particular.

'And are you really going?' said the man with the shade, looking at me again for the third time, with that queer, unnatural tilting of the face.

('This night of all nights!' said the old woman.)

'It is what I came for,' I said, and moved towards the door. As I did so, the old man with the shade rose and staggered round the table, so as to be closer to the others and to the fire. At the door I turned and looked at them, and saw they were all close together, dark against the firelight, staring at me over their shoulders, with an intent expression on their ancient faces.

'Goodnight,' I said, setting the door open.

'It's your own choosing,' said the man with the withered arm.

I left the door wide open until the candle was well alight, and then I shut them in and walked down the chilly, echoing passage.

I must confess that the oddness of these three old pensioners in whose charge her ladyship had left the castle, and the deep-toned, old-fashioned furniture of the housekeeper's room in which they forgathered, affected me in spite of my efforts to keep myself at a matter of fact phase. They seemed to belong to another age, an older age, an age when things spiritual were different from this of ours, less certain; an age when omens and witches were credible, and ghosts beyond denying. Their very existence was spectral; the cut of their clothing, fashions born in dead brains. The ornaments and conveniences of the room about them were ghostly – the thoughts of vanished men, which still haunted rather than participated in the world of today. But with an effort I sent such thoughts to the right-about. The long, draughty subterranean passage was chilly and dusty, and my candle flared and made the shadows cower and quiver. The echoes rang up and down the spiral staircase, and a shadow came sweeping up after me, and one fled before me into the darkness overhead. I came to the landing and stopped there for a moment, listening to a rustling that I fancied I heard; then, satisfied of the absolute silence, I pushed open the baize-covered door and stood in the corridor.

The effect was scarcely what I expected, for the moonlight coming in by the great window on the grand staircase picked out everything in vivid black shadow or silvery illumination. Everything was in its place; the house might have been deserted on the yesterday instead of eighteen months ago. There were candles in the sockets of the sconces, and whatever dust had gathered on the carpets or upon the polished flooring was distributed so evenly as to be invisible in the moonlight. I was about to advance, and stopped abruptly. A bronze group stood upon the landing, hidden from me by the corner of the wall, but its shadow fell with marvellous distinctness upon the white panelling and gave me the impression of someone crouching to waylay me. I stood rigid for half a minute perhaps. Then, with my hand in the pocket that held my revolver, I advanced, only to discover a Ganymede and Eagle glistening in the moonlight. That incident for a time restored my nerve, and a porcelain Chinaman on a buhl table, whose head rocked silently as I passed him, scarcely startled me.

The door to the red room and the steps up to it were in a shadowy corner. I moved my candle from side to side, in order to see clearly the nature of the recess in which I stood before opening the door. Here it was, thought I, that my predecessor was found, and the memory of that story gave me a sudden twinge of apprehension. I glanced over my shoulder at the Ganymede in the moonlight, and opened the door of the red room rather hastily, with my face half-turned to the pallid silence of the landing.

I entered, closed the door behind me at once, turned the key I found in the lock within, and stood with the candle held aloft, surveying the scene of my vigil, the great red room of Lorraine Castle, in which the young duke had died. Or, rather, in which he had begun his dying, for he had opened the door and fallen headlong down the steps I had just ascended. That had been the end of his vigil, of his gallant attempt to conquer the ghostly tradition of the place, and never, I thought, had apoplexy better served the ends of superstition. And there were other and older stories that clung to the room, back to the half-credible beginning of it all, the tale of a timid wife and the tragic end that came to her husband's jest of frightening her. And looking around that large sombre room, with its shadowy window bays, its recesses and alcoves, one could well understand the legends that had sprouted in its black corners, its germinating darkness. My candle was a little tongue of light in its vastness, that failed to pierce the opposite end of the room, and left an ocean of mystery and suggestion beyond its island of light.

I resolved to make a systematic examination of the place at once, and dispel the fanciful suggestions of its obscurity before they obtained a hold upon me. After satisfying myself of the fastening of the door, I began to walk about the room, peering round each article of furniture, tucking up the valances of the bed, and opening its curtains wide. I pulled up the blinds and examined the fastenings of the several windows before closing the shutters, leant forward and looked up the blackness of the wide chimney, and tapped the dark oak panelling for any secret opening. There were two big mirrors in the room, each with a pair of sconces bearing candles, and on the mantelshelf, too, were more candles in china candlesticks. All these I lit one after the other. The fire was laid, an unexpected consideration from the old housekeeper – and I lit it, to keep down any disposition to shiver, and when it was burning well, I stood round with my back to it and regarded the room again. I had pulled up a chintz-covered armchair and a table, to form a kind of barricade before me, and on this lay my revolver ready to hand. My precise examination had done me good, but I still found the remoter darkness of the place, and its perfect stillness, too stimulating for the imagination. The echoing of the stir and crackling of the fire was no sort of comfort to me. The shadow in the alcove at the end in particular had that undefinable quality of a presence, that odd suggestion of a lurking, living thing, that comes so easily in silence and solitude. At last, to reassure myself, I walked with a candle into it, and satisfied myself that there was nothing tangible there. I stood that candle upon the floor of the alcove, and left it in that position.

By this time I was in a state of considerable nervous tension, although to my reason there was no adequate cause for the condition. My mind, however, was perfectly clear. I postulated quite unreservedly that nothing supernatural could happen, and to pass the time I began to string some rhymes together, Ingoldsby fashion, of the original legend of the place. A few I spoke aloud, but the echoes were not pleasant. For the same reason I also abandoned, after a time, a conversation with myself upon the impossibility of ghosts and haunting. My mind reverted to the three old and distorted people downstairs, and I tried to keep it upon that topic. The sombre reds and blacks of the room troubled me; even with seven candles the place was merely dim. The one in the alcove flared in a draught, and the fire's flickering kept the shadows and penumbra perpetually shifting and stirring. Casting about for a remedy, I recalled the candles I had seen in the passage, and, with a slight effort, walked out into the moonlight, carrying a candle and leaving the door open, and presently returned with as many as ten. These I put in various knick-knacks of china with which the room was sparsely adorned, lit and placed where the shadows had lain deepest, some on the floor, some in the window recesses, until at last my seventeen candles were so arranged that not an inch of the room but had the direct light of at least one of them. It occurred to me that when the ghost came, I could warn him not to trip over them. The room was now quite brightly illuminated. There was something very cheery and reassuring in these little streaming flames, and snuffing them gave me an occupation, and afforded a helpful sense of the passage of time.

Even with that, however, the brooding expectation of the vigil weighed heavily upon me. It was after midnight that the candle in the alcove suddenly went out, and the black shadow sprang back to its place there. I did not see the candle go out; I simply turned and saw that the darkness was there, as one might start and see the unexpected presence of a stranger. 'By Jove!' said I aloud; 'that draught's a strong one!' and taking the matches from the table, I walked across the room in a leisurely manner to relight the corner again. My first match would not strike, and as I succeeded with the second, something seemed to blink on the wall before me. I turned my head involuntarily, and saw that the two candles on the little table by the fireplace were extinguished. I rose at once to my feet.

'Odd!' I said. 'Did I do that myself in a flash of absent-mindedness?'

I walked back, relit one, and as I did so, I saw the candle in the right sconce of one of the mirrors wink and go right out, and almost immediately its companion followed it. There was no mistake about it. The flame vanished, as if the wicks had been suddenly nipped between a finger and thumb, leaving the wick neither glowing nor smoking, but black. While I stood gaping, the candle at the foot of the bed went out, and the shadows seemed to take another step towards me.

'This won't do!' said I, and first one and then another candle on the mantelshelf followed.

'What's up?' I cried, with a queer high note getting into my voice somehow. At that the candle on the wardrobe went out, and the one I had relit in the alcove followed.

'Steady on!' I said. 'These candles are wanted,' speaking with a half hysterical facetiousness, and scratching away at a match the while for the mantel candlesticks. My hands trembled so much that twice I missed the rough paper of the matchbox. As the mantel emerged from darkness again, two candles in the remoter end of the window were eclipsed. But with the same match I also relit the larger mirror candles, and those on the floor near the doorway, so that for the moment I seemed to gain on the extinctions. But then in a volley there vanished four lights at once in different corners of the room, and I struck another match in quivering haste, and stood hesitating whither to take it.

As I stood undecided, an invisible hand seemed to sweep out the two candles on the table. With a cry of terror, I dashed at the alcove, then into the corner, and then into the window, relighting three, as two more vanished by the fireplace; then, perceiving a better way, I dropped the matches on the iron-bound deedbox in the corner, and caught up the bedroom candlestick. With this I avoided the delay of striking matches; but for all that the steady process of extinction went on, and the shadows I feared and fought against returned, and crept in upon me, first a step gained on this side of me and then on that. It was like a ragged storm cloud sweeping out the stars. Now and then one returned for a minute, and was lost again. I was now almost frantic with the horror of the coming darkness, and my self-possession deserted me. I leaped panting and dishevelled from candle to candle in a vain struggle against that remorseless advance.

I bruised myself on the thigh against the table, I sent a chair headlong, I stumbled and fell and whisked the cloth from the table in my fall. My candle rolled away from me, and I snatched another as I rose. Abruptly this was blown out, as I swung it off the table, by the wind of my sudden movement, and immediately the two remaining candles followed. But there was light still in the room, a red light that staved off the shadows from me. The fire! Of course I could still thrust my candle between the bars and relight it!

I turned to where the flames were still dancing between the glowing coals, and splashing red reflections upon the furniture, made two steps towards the grate, and incontinently the flames dwindled and vanished, the glow vanished, the reflections rushed together and vanished, and as I thrust the candle between the bars darkness closed upon me like the shutting of an eye, wrapped about me in a stifling embrace, sealed my vision, and crushed the last vestiges of reason from my brain. The candle fell from my hand. I flung out my arms in a vain effort to thrust that ponderous blackness away from me, and, lifting up my voice, screamed with all my might – once, twice, thrice. Then I think I must have staggered to my feet. I know I thought suddenly of the moonlit corridor, and, with my head bowed and my arms over my face, made a run for the door.

But I had forgotten the exact position of the door, and struck myself heavily against the corner of the bed. I staggered back, turned, and was either struck or struck myself against some other bulky furniture. I have a vague memory of battering myself thus, to and fro in the darkness, of a cramped struggle, and of my own wild crying as I darted to and fro, of a heavy blow at last upon my forehead, a horrible sensation of falling that lasted an age, of my last frantic effort to keep my footing, and then I remember no more.

I opened my eyes in daylight. My head was roughly bandaged, and the man with the withered arm was watching my face. I looked about me, trying to remember what had happened, and for a space I could not recollect. I rolled my eyes into the corner, and saw the old woman, no longer abstracted, pouring out some drops of medicine from a little blue phial into a glass. 'Where am I?' I asked; 'I seem to remember you, and yet I cannot remember who you are.'

They told me then, and I heard of the haunted red room as one who hears a tale. 'We found you at dawn,' said he, 'and there was blood on your forehead and lips.'

It was very slowly I recovered my memory of my experience. 'You believe now,' said the old man, 'that the room is haunted?' He spoke no longer as one who greets an intruder, but as one who grieves for a broken friend.

'Yes,' said I; 'the room is haunted.'

'And you have seen it. And we, who have lived here all our lives, have never set eyes upon it. Because we have never dared . . . Tell us, is it truly the old earl who– '

'No,' said I; 'it is not.'

'I told you so,' said the old lady, with the glass in her hand. 'It is his poor young countess who was frightened– '

'It is not,' I said. 'There is neither ghost of earl nor ghost of countess in that room, there is no ghost there at all; but worse, far worse– '

'Well?' they said.

'The worst of all the things that haunt poor mortal man,' said I; 'and that is, in all its nakedness – Fear! Fear that will not have light nor sound, that will not bear with reason, that deafens and darkens and overwhelms. It followed me through the corridor, it fought against me in the room– '

I stopped abruptly. There was an interval of silence. My hand went up to my bandages.

Then the man with the shade sighed and spoke. 'That is it,' said he. 'I knew that was it. A power of darkness. To put such a curse upon a woman! It lurks there always. You can feel it even in the daytime, even of a bright summer's day, in the hangings, in the curtains, keeping behind you however you face about. In the dusk it creeps along the corridor and follows you, so that you dare not turn. There is Fear in that room of hers – black Fear, and there will be – so long as this house of sin endures.'

Ancient Sorceries

ALGERNON BLACKWOOD

I

There are, it would appear, certain wholly unremarkable persons, with none of the characteristics that invite adventure, who yet once or twice in the course of their smooth lives undergo an experience so strange that the world catches its breath – and looks the other way! And it was cases of this kind, perhaps, more than any other, that fell into the widespread net of John Silence, the psychic doctor, and, appealing to his deep humanity, to his patience, and to his great qualities of spiritual sympathy, led often to the revelation of problems of the strangest complexity, and of the profoundest possible human interest.

Matters that seemed almost too curious and fantastic for belief he loved to trace to their hidden sources. To unravel a tangle in the very soul of things – and to release a suffering human soul in the process – was with him a veritable passion. And the knots he untied were, indeed, often passing strange.

The world, of course, asks for some plausible basis to which it can attach credence – something it can, at least, pretend to explain. The adventurous type it can understand: such people carry about with them an adequate explanation of their exciting lives, and their characters obviously drive them into the circumstances which produce the adventures. It expects nothing else from them, and is satisfied. But dull, ordinary folk have no right to out-of-the-way experiences, and the world having been led to expect otherwise, is disappointed with them, not to say shocked. Its complacent judgement has been rudely disturbed.

'Such a thing happen to *that* man!' it cries – a commonplace person like that! It is too absurd! There must be something wrong!'

Yet there could be no question that something did actually happen to little Arthur Vezin, something of the curious nature he described to Dr Silence. Outwardly or inwardly, it happened beyond a doubt, and in spite of the jeers of his few friends who heard the tale, and observed wisely that 'such a thing might perhaps have come to Iszard, that crack-brained Iszard, or to that odd fish Minski, but it could never have happened to commonplace little Vezin, who was fore-ordained to live and die according to scale.'

But, whatever his method of death was, Vezin certainly did not 'live according to scale' so far as this particular event in his otherwise uneventful life was concerned; and to hear him recount it, and watch his pale delicate features change, and hear his voice grow softer and more hushed as he proceeded, was to know the conviction that his halting words perhaps failed sometimes to convey. He lived the thing over again each time he told it. His whole personality became muffled in the recital. It subdued him more than ever, so that the tale became a lengthy apology for an experience that he deprecated. He appeared to excuse himself and ask your pardon for having dared to take part in so fantastic an episode. For little Vezin was a timid, gentle, sensitive soul, rarely able to assert himself, tender to man and beast, and almost constitutionally unable to say No, or to claim many things that should rightly have been his. His whole scheme of life seemed utterly remote from anything more exciting than missing a train or losing an umbrella on an omnibus. And when this curious event came upon him he was already more years beyond forty than his friends suspected or he cared to admit.

John Silence, who heard him speak of his experience more than once, said that he sometimes left out certain details and put in others; yet they were all obviously true. The whole scene was unforgettably cinematographed on to his mind. None of the details were imagined or invented. And when he told the story with them all complete, the effect was undeniable. His appealing brown eyes shone, and much of the charming personality, usually so carefully repressed, came forward and revealed itself. His modesty was always there, of course, but in the telling he forgot the present and allowed himself to appear almost vividly as he lived again in the past of his adventure.

He was on the way home when it happened, crossing northern France from some mountain trip or other where he buried himself solitary-wise every summer. He had nothing but an unregistered bag in the rack, and the train was jammed to suffocation, most of the passengers being unredeemed holiday English. He disliked them, not because they were his fellow countrymen, but because they were noisy and obtrusive, obliterating with their big limbs and tweed clothing all the quieter tints of the day that brought him satisfaction and enabled him to melt into insignificance and forget that he was anybody. These English clashed about him like a brass band, making him feel vaguely that he ought to be more self-assertive and obstreperous, and that he did not claim insistently enough all kinds of things that he didn't want and that were really valueless, such as corner seats, windows up or down and so forth.

So that he felt uncomfortable in the train, and wished the journey were over and he was back again living with his unmarried sister in Surbiton.

And when the train stopped for ten panting minutes at the little station in northern France, and he got out to stretch his legs on the platform, and saw to his dismay a further batch of the British Isles debouching from another train it suddenly seemed impossible to him to continue the journey. Even *his* flabby soul revolted, and the idea of staying a night in the little town and going on next day by a slower, emptier train, flashed into his mind. The guard was already shouting '*En voiture*,' and the corridor of his compartment was already packed, when the thought came to him. And, for once, he acted with decision and rushed to snatch his bag.

Finding the corridor and steps impassable, he tapped at the window (for he had a corner seat) and begged the Frenchman who sat opposite to hand his luggage out to him, explaining in his wretched French that he intended to break the journey there. And this elderly Frenchman, he declared, gave him a look, half of warning, half of reproach, that to his dying day he could never forget; handed the bag through the window of the moving train; and at the same time poured into his ears a long sentence, spoken rapidly and low, of which he was able to comprehend only the last few words: '*à cause du sommeil et à cause des chats*.'

In reply to Dr Silence, whose singular psychic acuteness at once seized upon this Frenchman as a vital point in the adventure, Vezin admitted that the man had impressed him favourably from the beginning, though without being able to explain why. They had sat facing one another during the four hours of the journey, and though no conversation had passed between them – Vezin was timid about his stuttering French – he confessed that his eyes were being continually drawn to his face, almost, he felt, to rudeness, and that each, by a dozen nameless little politenesses and attentions, had evinced the desire to be kind. The men liked each other and their personalities did not clash, or would not have clashed had they chanced to come to terms of acquaintance. The Frenchman, indeed, seemed to have exercised a silent protective influence over the insignificant little Englishman, and without words or gestures betrayed that he wished him well and would gladly have been of service to him.

'And this sentence that he hurled at you after the bag?' asked John Silence, smiling that peculiarly sympathetic smile that always melted the prejudices of his patient, 'were you unable to follow it exactly?'

'It was so quick and low and vehement,' explained Vezin, in his small voice, 'that I missed practically the whole of it. I only caught the few words at the very end, because he spoke them so clearly, and his face was bent down out of the carriage window so near to mine.'

' "*A cause du sommeil et à cause des chats*"?' repeated Dr Silence, as though half speaking to himself.

'That's it, exactly,' said Vezin; 'which, I take it, means something like "because of sleep and because of the cats," doesn't it?

'Certainly, that's how I should translate it,' the doctor observed shortly, evidently not wishing to interrupt more than necessary.

'And the rest of the sentence – all the first part I couldn't understand, I mean – was a warning not to do something – not to stop in the town, or at some particular place in the town, perhaps. That was the impression it made on me.'

Then, of course, the train rushed off, and left Vezin standing on the platform alone and rather forlorn.

The little town climbed in straggling fashion up a sharp hill rising out of the plain at the back of the station, and was crowned by the twin towers of the ruined cathedral peeping over the summit. From the station itself it looked uninteresting and modern, but the fact was that the mediaeval position lay out of sight just beyond the crest. And once he reached the top and entered the old streets, he stepped clean out of modern life into a bygone century. The noise and bustle of the crowded train seemed days away. The spirit of this silent hill-town, remote from tourists and motor-cars, dreaming its own quiet life under the autumn sun, rose up and cast its spell upon him. Long before he recognized this spell he acted under it. He walked softly, almost on tiptoe, down the winding narrow streets where the gables all but met over his head, and he entered the doorway of the solitary inn with a deprecating and modest demeanour that was in itself an apology for intruding upon the place and disturbing its dream.

At first, however, Vezin said, he noticed very little of all this. The attempt at analysis came much later. What struck him then was only the delightful contrast of the silence and peace after the dust and noisy rattle of the train. He felt soothed and stroked like a cat.

'Like a cat, you said?' interrupted John Silence, quickly catching him up.

'Yes. At the very start I felt that.' He laughed apologetically. 'I felt as though the warmth and the stillness and the comfort made me purr. It seemed to be the general mood of the whole place – then.'

The inn, a rambling, ancient house, the atmosphere of the old coaching days still about it, apparently did not welcome him too warmly. He felt he was only tolerated, he said. But it was cheap and comfortable, and the delicious cup of afternoon tea he ordered at once made him feel really very pleased with himself for leaving the train in this bold, original way. For to him it had seemed bold and original. He felt something of a dog. His room, too, soothed him with its dark panelling and low, irregular ceiling, and the long, sloping passage that led to it seemed the natural pathway to a real Chamber of Sleep – a little, dim, cubby hole out of the world where noise could not enter. It looked upon the courtyard at the back. It was all very charming, and made him think of himself as dressed in very soft velvet somehow, and the floors seemed padded, the walls provided with cushions. The sounds of the streets could not penetrate there. It was an atmosphere of absolute rest that surrounded him.

On engaging the two-franc room he had interviewed the only person who seemed to be about that sleepy afternoon, an elderly waiter with Dundreary whiskers and a drowsy courtesy, who had ambled lazily towards him across the stone yard; but on coming downstairs again for a little promenade in the town before dinner he encountered the proprietress herself. She was a large woman whose hands, feet, and features seemed to swim towards him out of a sea of person. They merged, so to speak. But she had great, dark, vivacious eyes that counteracted the bulk of her body, and betrayed the fact that in reality she was both vigorous and alert. When he first caught sight of her she was knitting in a low chair against the sunlight of the wall, and something at once made him see her as a great tabby cat, dozing, yet awake, heavily sleepy, and yet at the same time prepared for instantaneous action. A great mouser on the watch occurred to him.

She took him in with a single, comprehensive glance that was polite without being cordial. Her neck, he noticed, was extraordinarily supple in spite of its proportions, for it turned so easily to follow him, and the head it carried bowed so very flexibly.

'But when she looked at me, you know,' said Vezin, with that little, apologetic smile in his brown eyes, and that faintly deprecating gesture of the shoulders that was characteristic of him, 'the odd notion came to me that really she had intended to make quite a different movement, and that with a single bound she could have leaped at me across the width of that stone yard and pounced upon me like some huge cat upon a mouse.'

He laughed a little, soft laugh, and Dr Silence made a note in his book without interrupting, while Vezin proceeded in a tone as though he feared he had already told too much, and more than we could believe.

'Very soft, yet very active she was, for all her size and mass, and I felt she knew what I was doing even after I had passed and was behind her back. She spoke to me, and her voice was smooth and running. She asked if I had my luggage, and was comfortable in my room, and then added that dinner was at seven o'clock, and that they were very early people in this little country town. Clearly, she intended to convey that late hours were not encouraged.'

Evidently, she contrived by voice and manner to give him the impression that here he would be 'managed', that everything would be arranged and planned for him, and that he had nothing to do but fall into the groove and obey. No decided action or sharp personal effort would be looked for from him. It was the very reverse of the train. He walked quietly out into the street, feeling soothed and peaceful. He realized that he was in a milieu that suited him and stroked him the right way. It was so much easier to be obedient. He began to purr again, and to feel that all the town purred with him.

About the streets of that little town he meandered gently, falling deeper and deeper into the spirit of repose that characterized it. With no special aim he wandered up and down, to and fro. The September sunshine fell slantingly over the roofs. Down winding alleyways, fringed with tumbling gables and open casements, he caught fairylike glimpses of the great plain below, and of the meadows and yellow copses lying like a dream-map in the haze. The spell of the past held very potently here, he felt.

The streets were full of picturesquely garbed men and women, all busy enough, going their respective ways; but no one took any notice of him or turned to stare at his obviously English appearance. He was even able to forget that with his tourist appearance he was a false note in a charming picture, and he melted more and more into the scene, feeling delightfully insignificant and unimportant and unselfconscious. It was like becoming part of a softly coloured dream which he did not even realize to be a dream.

On the eastern side the hill fell away more sharply, and the plain below ran off rather suddenly into a sea of gathering shadows in which the little patches of woodland looked like islands and the stubble fields like deep water. Here he strolled along the old ramparts of ancient fortifications that once had been formidable, but now were only vision-like with their charming mingling of broken, grey walls and wayward vine and ivy. From the broad coping on which he sat for a moment, level with the rounded tops of clipped plane trees, he saw the esplanade far below lying in shadow. Here and there a yellow sunbeam crept in and lay upon the fallen yellow leaves, and from the height he looked down and saw the townsfolk were walking to and fro in the cool of the evening. He could just hear the sound of their slow footfalls, and the murmur of their voices floated up to him through the gaps between the trees. The figures looked like shadows as he caught glimpses of their quiet movements far below.

He sat there for some time pondering, bathed in the waves of murmurs and half-lost echoes that rose to his ears, muffled by the leaves of the plane trees. The whole town, and the little hill out of which it grew as naturally as an ancient wood, seemed to him like a being lying there half asleep on the plain and crooning to itself as it dozed.

And, presently, as he sat lazily melting into its dream, a sound of horns and strings and wood instruments rose to his ears, and the town band began to play at the far end of the crowded terrace below to the accompaniment of a very soft deep-throated drum. Vezin was very sensitive to music, knew about it intelligently, and had even ventured, unknown to his friends, upon the composition of quiet melodies with low-running chords which he played to himself with the soft pedal when no one was about. And this music, floating up through the trees, from an invisible and doubtless very picturesque band of the townspeople, wholly charmed him. He recognized nothing that they played, and it sounded as though they were simply improvising without a conductor. No definitely marked time ran through the pieces, which ended and began oddly after the fashion of wind through an Aeolian harp. It was part of the place and scene, just as the dying sunlight and faintly breathing wind were part of the scene and hour, and the mellow notes of old-fashioned, plaintive horns, pierced here and there by the sharper strings, all half smothered by the continuous booming of the deep drum, touched his soul with a curiously potent spell that was almost too engrossing to be quite pleasant.

There was a certain queer sense of bewitchment in it all. The music seemed to him oddly unartificial. It made him think of trees swept by the wind, of night breezes singing among wires and chimney-stacks, or in the rigging of invisible ships; or – and the simile leaped up in his thoughts with a sudden sharpness of suggestion – a chorus of animals, of wild creatures, somewhere in desolate places of the world, crying and singing as animals will, to the moon. He could fancy he heard the wailing, half-human cries of cats upon the tiles at night, rising and falling with weird intervals of sound, and this music, muffled by distance and the trees, made him think of a queer company of these creatures on some roof far away in the sky, uttering their solemn music to one another and the moon in chorus.

It was, he felt at the time, a singular image to occur to him, yet it expressed his sensation pictorially better than anything else. The instruments played such impossibly odd intervals, and the crescendos and diminuendos were so very suggestive of cat-land on the tiles at night, rising swiftly, dropping without warning to deep notes again, and all in such strange confusion of discords and accords. But, at the same time a plaintive sweetness resulted on the whole, and the discords of these half-broken instruments were so singular that they did not distress his musical soul like fiddles out of tune.

He listened a long time, wholly surrendering himself as his character was, and then strolled homewards in the dusk as the air grew chilly.

'There was nothing to alarm?' put in Dr Silence briefly.

'Absolutely nothing,' said Vezin; 'but you know it was all so fantastical and charming that my imagination was profoundly impressed. Perhaps, too,' he continued, gently explanatory, 'it was this stirring of my imagination that caused other impressions; for as I walked back the spell of the place began to steal over me in a dozen ways, though all intelligible ways. But there were other things I could not account for in the least, even then.'

'Incidents, you mean?'

'Hardly incidents, I think. A lot of vivid sensations crowded themselves upon my mind and I could trace them to no causes. It was just after sunset and the tumbled old buildings traced magical outlines against an opalescent sky of gold and red. The dusk was running down the twisted streets. All round the hill the plain pressed in like a dim sea, its level rising with the darkness. The spell of this kind of scene, you know, can be very moving, and it was so that night. Yet I felt that what came to me had nothing directly to do with the mystery and wonder of the scene.'

'Not merely the subtle transformations of the spirit that come with beauty,' put in the doctor, noticing his hesitation.

'Exactly,' Vezin went on, duly encouraged and no longer so fearful of our smiles at his expense. 'The impressions came from somewhere else. For instance, down the busy main street where men and women were bustling home from work, shopping at stalls and barrows, idly gossiping in groups, and all the rest of it, I saw that I aroused no interest and that no one turned to stare at me as a foreigner and stranger. I was utterly ignored, and my presence among them excited no special interest or attention.

'And then, quite suddenly, it dawned upon me with conviction that all the time this indifference and inattention were merely feigned. Everybody, as a matter of fact, was watching me closely. Every movement I made was known and observed. Ignoring me was all a pretence – an elaborate pretence.'

He paused a moment and looked at us to see if we were smiling, and then continued, reassured –

'It is useless to ask me how I noticed this, because I simply cannot explain it. But the discovery gave me something of a shock. Before I got back to the inn, however, another curious thing rose up strongly in my mind and forced my recognition of it as true. And this too, I may as well say at once, was equally inexplicable to me. I mean I can only give you the fact, as fact it was to me.'

The little man left his chair and stood on the mat before the fire. His diffidence lessened from now onwards, as he lost himself again in the magic of the old adventure. His eyes shone a little already as he talked.

'Well,' he went on, his soft voice rising somewhat with his excitement, 'I was in a shop when it came to me first – though the idea must have been at work for a long time subconsciously to appear in so complete a form all at once. I was buying socks, I think,' he laughed, 'and struggling with my dreadful French, when it struck me that the woman in the shop did not care two pins whether I bought anything or not. She was indifferent whether she made a sale or did not make a sale. She was only pretending to sell.

'This sounds a very small and fanciful incident to build upon what follows. But really it was not small. I mean it was the spark that lit the line of powder and ran along to the big blaze in my mind.

'For the whole town, I suddenly realized, was something other than I so far saw it. The real activities and interests of the people were elsewhere and otherwise than appeared. Their true lives lay somewhere out of sight behind the scenes. Their busy-ness was but the outward semblance that masked their actual purposes. They bought and sold, and ate and drank, and walked about the streets, yet all the while the main stream of their existence lay somewhere beyond my ken, underground, in secret places. In the shops and at the stalls they did not care whether I purchased their articles or not; at the inn, they were indifferent to my staying or going; their life lay remote from my own, springing from hidden, mysterious sources, coursing out of sight, unknown. It was all a great, elaborate pretence, assumed possibly for my benefit, or possibly for purposes of their own. But the main current of their energies ran elsewhere. I almost felt as an unwelcome foreign substance might be expected to feel when it has found its way into the human system, and the whole body organizes itself to eject it or to absorb it. The town was doing this very thing to me.

'This bizarre notion presented itself forcibly to my mind as I walked home to the inn, and I began busily to wonder wherein the true life of this town could lie and what were the actual interests and activities of its hidden life.

'And, now that my eyes were partly opened, I noticed other things too that puzzled me, first of which, I think, was the extraordinary silence of the whole place. Positively, the town was muffled. Although the streets were paved with cobbles the people moved about silently, softly, with padded feet, like cats. Nothing made noise. All was hushed, subdued, muted. The very voices were quiet, low-pitched, like purring. Nothing clamorous, vehement, or emphatic seemed able to live in the drowsy atmosphere of soft dreaming that soothed this little hill-town into its sleep. It was like the woman at the inn – an outward repose screening intense inner activity and purpose.

'Yet there was no sign of lethargy or sluggishness anywhere about it. The people were active and alert. Only a magical and uncanny softness lay over them all like a spell.'

Vezin passed his hand across his eyes for a moment as though the memory had become very vivid. His voice had run off into a whisper so that we heard the last part with difficulty. He was telling a true thing obviously, yet something that he both liked and hated telling.

'I went back to the inn,' he continued presently in a louder voice, 'and dined. I felt a new strange world about me. My old world of reality receded. Here, whether I liked it or no, was something new and incomprehensible. I regretted having left the train so impulsively. An adventure was upon me, and I loathed adventures as foreign to my nature. Moreover, this was the beginning apparently of an adventure somewhere deep within me, in a region I could not check or measure, and a feeling of alarm mingled itself with my wonder – alarm for the stability of what I had for forty years recognized as my "personality".

'I went upstairs to bed, my mind teeming with thoughts that were unusual to me, and of rather a haunting description. By way of relief I kept thinking of that nice, prosaic noisy train and all those wholesome, blustering passengers. I almost wished I were with them again. But my dreams took me elsewhere. I dreamed of cats, and soft-moving creatures, and the silence of life in a dim muffled world beyond the senses.'

II

Vezin stayed on from day to day, indefinitely, much longer than he had intended. He felt in a kind of dazed, somnolent condition. He did nothing in particular, but the place fascinated him and he could not decide to leave. Decisions were always very difficult for him and he sometimes wondered how he had ever brought himself to the point of leaving the train. It seemed as though some one else must have arranged it for him, and once or twice his thoughts ran to the swarthy Frenchman who had sat opposite. If only he could have understood that long sentence ending so strangely with '*à cause du sommeil et à cause des chats*'. He wondered what it all meant.

Meanwhile the hushed softness of the town held him prisoner and he sought in his muddling, gentle way to find out where the mystery lay, and what it was all about. But his limited French and his constitutional hatred of active investigation made it hard for him to button-hole anybody and ask questions. He was content to observe, and watch, and remain negative.

The weather held on calm and hazy, and this just suited him. He wandered about the town till he knew every street and alley. The people suffered him to come and go without let or hindrance, though it became clearer to him every day that he was never free himself from observation. The town watched him as a cat watches a mouse. And he got no nearer to finding out what they were all so busy with or where the main stream of their activities lay. This remained hidden. The people were as soft and mysterious as cats.

But that he was continually under observation became more evident from day to day.

For instance, when he strolled to the end of the town and entered a little green public garden beneath the ramparts and seated himself upon one of the empty benches in the sun, he was quite alone – at first. Not another seat was occupied; the little park was empty, the paths deserted. Yet, within ten minutes of his coming, there must have been fully twenty persons scattered about him, some strolling aimlessly along the gravel walks, staring at the flowers, and others seated on wooden benches enjoying the sun like himself. None of them appeared to take any notice of him; yet he understood quite well they had all come there to watch. They kept him under close observation. In the street they had seemed busy enough, hurrying upon various errands; yet these were suddenly all forgotten and they had nothing to do but loll and laze in the sun, their duties unremembered. Five minutes after he left, the garden was again deserted, the seats vacant. But in the crowded street it was the same thing again; he was never alone. He was ever in their thoughts.

By degrees, too, he began to see how it was he was so cleverly watched, yet without the appearance of it. The people did nothing *directly*. They behaved *obliquely*. He laughed in his mind as the thought thus clothed itself in words, but the phrase exactly described it. They looked at him from angles which naturally should have led their sight in another direction altogether. Their movements were oblique, too, so far as these concerned himself. The straight, direct thing was not their way evidently. They did nothing obviously. If he entered a shop to buy, the woman walked instantly away and busied herself with something at the farther end of the counter, though answering at once when he spoke, showing that she knew he was there and that this was her only way of attending to him. It was the fashion of the cat she followed. Even in the dining-room of the inn the be-whiskered and courteous waiter, lithe and silent in all his movements, never seemed able to come straight to his table for an order or a dish. He came by zigzags, indirectly, vaguely, so that he appeared to be going to another table altogether, and only turned suddenly at the last moment, and was there beside him.

Vezin smiled curiously to himself as he described how he began to realize these things. Other tourists there were none in the hostel, but he recalled the figures of one or two old men, inhabitants, who took their *déjeuner* and dinner there and remembered how fantastically they entered the room in similar fashion. First, they paused in the doorway, peering about the room, and then, after a temporary inspection, they came in, as it were, sideways, keeping close to the walls so that he wondered which table they were making for, and at the last minute making almost a little quick run to their particular seats. And again he thought of the ways and methods of cats.

Other small incidents, too, impressed him as all part of this queer, soft town with its muffled, indirect life, for the way some of the people appeared and disappeared with extraordinary swiftness puzzled him exceedingly. It may have been all perfectly natural, he knew, yet he could not make it out how the alleys swallowed them up and shot them forth in a second of time when there were no visible doorways or openings near enough to explain the phenomenon. Once he followed two elderly women who, he felt, had been particularly examining him across the street – quite near the inn this was – and saw them turn the corner a few feet only in front of him. Yet when he sharply followed on their heels he saw nothing but an utterly deserted alley stretching in front of him with no sign of a living thing. And the only opening through which they could have escaped was a porch some fifty yards away, which not the swiftest human runner could have reached in time.

And in just such sudden fashion people appeared when he never expected them. Once when he heard a great noise of fighting going on behind, a low wall, and hurried up to see what was going on, what should he see but a group of girls and women engaged in vociferous conversation which instantly hushed itself to the normal whispering note of the town when his head appeared over the wall. And even then none of them turned to look at him directly, but slunk off with the most unaccountable rapidity into doors and sheds across the yard. And their voices, he thought, had sounded so like, so strangely like, the angry snarling of fighting animals, almost of cats.

The whole spirit of the town, however, continued to evade him as something elusive, protean, screened from the outer world, and at the same time intensely, genuinely vital; and, since he now formed part of its life, this concealment puzzled and irritated him; more – it began rather to frighten him.

Out of the mists that slowly gathered about his ordinary surface thoughts there rose again the idea that the inhabitants were waiting for him to declare himself, to take an attitude, to do this, or to do that; and that when he had done so they in their turn would at length make some direct response, accepting or rejecting him. Yet the vital matter concerning which his decision was awaited came no nearer to him.

Once or twice he purposely followed little processions or groups of the citizens in order to find out, if possible, on what purpose they were bent; but they always discovered him in time and dwindled away, each individual going his or her own way. It was always the same: he never could learn what their main interest was. The cathedral was ever empty, the old church of St Martin, at the other end of the town, deserted. They shopped because they had to, and not because they wished to. The booths stood neglected, the stalls unvisited, the little cafe desolate. Yet the streets were always full, the townsfolk ever on the bustle.

'Can it be,' he thought to himself, yet with a deprecating laugh that he should have dared to think anything so odd, 'can it be that these people are people of the twilight, that they live only at night their real life, and come out honestly only with the dusk? That during the day they make a sham though brave pretence, and after the sun is down their true life begins? Have they the souls of night-things, and is the whole blessed town in the hands of the cats?'

The fancy somehow electrified him with little shocks of shrinking and dismay. Yet, though he affected to laugh, he knew that he was beginning to feel more than uneasy, and that strange forces were tugging with a thousand invisible chords at the very centre of his being. Something utterly remote from his ordinary life, something that had not waked for years, began faintly to stir in his soul, sending feelers abroad into his brain and heart, shaping queer thoughts and penetrating even into certain of his minor actions. Something exceedingly vital to himself, to his soul, hung in the balance.

And, always when he returned to the inn about the hour of sunset, he saw the figures of the townsfolk stealing through the dusk from their shop doors, moving sentry-wise to and fro at the corners of the streets, yet always vanishing silently like shadows at his near approach. And as the inn invariably closed its doors at ten o'clock he had never yet found the opportunity he rather half-heartedly sought to see for himself what account the town could give of itself at night.

''– *à cause du sommeil et à cause des chats'* – the words now rang in his ears more and more often, though still as yet without any definite meaning.

Moreover, something made him sleep like the dead.

III

It was, I think, on the fifth day – though in this detail his story sometimes varied – that he made a definite discovery which increased his alarm and brought him up to a rather sharp climax. Before that he had already noticed that a change was going forward and certain subtle transformations being brought about in his character which modified several of his minor habits. And he had affected to ignore them. Here, however, was something he could no longer ignore; and it startled him.

At the best of times he was never very positive, always negative rather, compliant and acquiescent; yet, when necessity arose he was capable of reasonably vigorous action and could take a strongish decision. The discovery he now made that brought him up with such a sharp turn was that this power had positively dwindled to nothing. He found it impossible to make up his mind. For, on this fifth day, he realized that he had stayed long enough in the town and that for reasons he could only vaguely define to himself it was wiser *and safer* that he should leave.

And he found that he could not leave!

This is difficult to describe in words, and it was more by gesture and the expression of his face that he conveyed to Dr Silence the stage of impotence he had reached. All this spying and watching, he said, had as it were spun a net about his feet so that he was trapped and powerless to escape; be felt like a fly that had blundered into the intricacies of a great web; be was caught, imprisoned, and could not get away. It was a distressing sensation. A numbness had crept over his will till it had become almost incapable of decision. The mere thought of vigorous action – action towards escape – began to terrify him. All the currents of his life had turned inwards upon himself, striving to bring to the surface something that lay buried almost beyond reach, determined to force his recognition of something he had long forgotten – forgotten years upon years, centuries almost ago. It seemed as though a window deep within his being would presently open and reveal an entirely new world, yet somehow a world that was not unfamiliar. Beyond that, again, he fancied a great curtain hung; and when that too rolled up he would see still farther into this region and at last understand something of the secret life of these extraordinary people.

'Is this why they wait and watch?' he asked himself with rather a shaking heart, 'for the time when I shall join them – or refuse to join them? Does the decision rest with me after all, and not with them?'

And it was at this point that the sinister character of the adventure first really declared itself, and he became genuinely alarmed. The stability of his rather fluid little personality was at stake, he felt, and something in his heart turned coward.

Why otherwise should he have suddenly taken to walking stealthily, silently, making as little sound as possible, for ever looking behind him? Why else should he have moved almost on tiptoe about the passages of the practically deserted inn, and when he was abroad have found himself deliberately taking advantage of what cover presented itself? And why, if he was not afraid, should the wisdom of staying indoors after sundown have suddenly occurred to him as eminently desirable? Why, indeed?

And, when John Silence gently pressed him for an explanation of these things, he admitted apologetically that he had none to give.

'It was simply that I feared something might happen to me unless I kept a sharp look-out. I felt afraid. It was instinctive,' was all he could say. 'I got the impression that the whole town was after me – wanted me for something; and that if it got me I should lose myself, or at least the Self I knew, in some unfamiliar state of consciousness. But I am not a psychologist, you know,' he added meekly, 'and I cannot define it better than that.'

It was while lounging in the courtyard half an hour before the evening meal that Vezin made this discovery, and he at once went upstairs to his quiet room at the end of the winding passage to think it over alone. In the yard it was empty enough, true, but there was always the possibility that the big woman whom he dreaded would come out of some door, with her pretence of knitting, to sit and watch him. This had happened several times, and he could not endure the sight of her. He still remembered his original fancy, bizarre though it was, that she would spring upon him the moment his back was turned and land with one single crushing leap upon his neck. Of course it was nonsense, but then it haunted him, and once an idea begins to do that it ceases to be nonsense. It has clothed itself in reality.

He went upstairs accordingly. It was dusk, and the oil lamps had not yet been lit in the passages. He stumbled over the uneven surface of the ancient flooring, passing the dim outlines of doors along the corridor – doors that he had never once seen opened – rooms that seemed never occupied. He moved, as his habit now was, stealthily and on tiptoe.

Half-way down the last passage to his own chamber there was a sharp turn, and it was just here, while groping round the walls with outstretched hands, that his fingers touched something that was not wall – something that moved. It was soft and warm in texture, indescribably fragrant, and about the height of his shoulder; and he immediately thought of a furry, sweet-smelling kitten. The next minute he knew it was something quite different.

Instead of investigating, however, – his nerves must have been too overwrought for that, he said, – he shrank back as closely as possible against the wall on the other side. The thing, whatever it was, slipped past him with a sound of rustling, and retreating with light footsteps down the passage behind him, was gone. A breath of warm, scented air was wafted to his nostrils.

Vezin caught his breath for an instant and paused, stock-still, half leaning against the wall – and then almost ran down the remaining distance and entered his room with a rush, locking the door hurriedly behind him. Yet it was not fear that made him run: it was excitement, pleasurable excitement. His nerves were tingling, and a delicious glow mode itself felt all over his body. In a flash it came to him that this was just what he had felt twenty-five years ago as a boy when he was in love for the first time. Warm currents of life ran all over him and mounted to his brain in a whirl of soft delight. His mood was suddenly become tender, melting, loving.

The room was quite dark, and he collapsed upon the sofa by the window, wondering what had happened to him and what it all meant. But the only thing he understood clearly in that instant was that something in him had swiftly, magically changed: he no longer wished to leave, or to argue with himself about leaving. The encounter in the passageway had changed all that. The strange perfume of it still hung about him, bemusing his heart and mind. For he knew that it was a girl who had passed him, a girl's face that his fingers had brushed in the darkness, and he felt in some extraordinary way as though he had been actually kissed by her, kissed full upon the lips.

Trembling, he sat upon the sofa by the window and struggled to collect his thoughts. He was utterly unable to understand how the mere passing of a girl in the darkness of a narrow passage-way could communicate so electric a thrill to his whole being that he still shook with the sweetness of it. Yet, there it was! And he found it as useless to deny as to attempt analysis. Some ancient fire had entered his veins, and now ran coursing through his blood; and that he was forty-five instead of twenty did not matter one little jot. Out of all the inner turmoil and confusion emerged the one salient fact that the mere atmosphere, the merest casual touch, of this girl, unseen, unknown in the darkness, had been sufficient to stir dormant fires in the centre of his heart, and rouse his whole being from a state of feeble sluggishness to one of tearing and tumultuous excitement.

After a time, however, the number of Vezin's years began to assert their cumulative power; he grew calmer; and when a knock came at length upon his door and he heard the waiter's voice suggesting that dinner was nearly over, he pulled himself together and slowly made his way downstairs into the dining-room.

Every one looked up as he entered, for he was very late, but he took his customary seat in the far corner and began to eat. The trepidation was still in his nerves, but the fact that he had passed through the courtyard and hall without catching sight of a petticoat served to calm him a little. He ate so fast that he had almost caught up with the current stage of the *table d'hote*, when a slight commotion in the room drew his attention.

His chair was so placed that the door and the greater portion of the long *salle à manger* were behind him, yet it was not necessary to turn round to know that the same person he had passed in the dark passage had now come into the room. He felt the presence long before he heard or saw any one. Then he became aware that the old men, the only other guests, were rising one by one in their places, and exchanging greetings with someone who passed among them from table to table. And when at length he turned with his heart beating furiously to ascertain for himself, he saw the form of a young girl, lithe and slim, moving down the centre of the room and making straight for his own table in the corner. She moved wonderfully, with sinuous grace, like a young panther, and her approach filled him with such delicious bewilderment that he was utterly unable to tell at first what her face was like, or discover what it was about the whole presentment of the creature that filled him anew with trepidation and delight.

'Ah, Ma'mselle est de retour!' he heard the old waiter murmur at his side, and he was just able to take in that she was the daughter of the proprietress, when she was upon him, and he heard her voice. She was addressing him. Something of red lips he saw and laughing white teeth, and stray wisps of fine dark hair about the temples; but all the rest was a dream in which his own emotion rose

like a thick cloud before his eyes and prevented his seeing accurately, or knowing exactly what he did. He was aware that she greeted with a charming little bow; that her beautiful large eyes looked searchingly into his own; that the perfume he had noticed in the dark passage again assailed his nostrils, and that she was bending a little towards him and leaning with one hand on the table at his side. She was quite close to him – that was the chief thing he knew – explaining that she had been asking after the comfort of her mother's guests, and was now introducing herself to the latest arrival – himself.

'M'sieur has already been here a few days,' he heard the waiter say; and then her own voice sweet as singing, replied –

'Ah, but M'sieur is not going to leave us just yet, I hope. My mother is too old to look after the comfort of our guests properly, but now I am here I will remedy all that.' She laughed deliciously. 'M'sieur shall be well looked after.'

Vezin, struggling with his emotion and desire to be polite, half rose to acknowledge the pretty speech, and to stammer some sort of reply, but as he did so his hand by chance touched her own that was resting upon the table, and a shock that was for all the world like a shock of electricity, passed from her skin into his body. His soul wavered and shook deep within him. He caught her eyes fixed upon his own with a look of most curious intentness, and the next moment he knew that he had sat down wordless again on his chair, that the girl was already half-way across the room, and that he was trying to eat his salad with a dessert-spoon and a knife.

Longing for her return, and yet dreading it, he gulped down the remainder of his dinner, and then went at once to his bedroom to be alone with his thoughts. This time the passages were lighted, and he suffered no exciting contretemps; yet the winding corridor was dim with shadows, and the last portion, from the bend of the walls onwards, seemed longer than he had ever known it. It ran downhill like the pathway on a mountain side, and as he tiptoed softly down it he felt that by rights it ought to have led him clean out of the house into the heart of a great forest. The world was singing with him. Strange fancies filled his brain, and once in the room, with the door securely locked, he did not light the candles, but sat by the open window thinking long, long thoughts that came unbidden in troops to his mind.

IV

This part of the story he told to Dr Silence, without special coaxing, it is true, yet with much stammering embarrassment. He could not in the least understand, he said, how the girl had managed to affect him so profoundly, and even before he had set eyes upon her. For her mere proximity in the darkness had been sufficient to set him on fire. He knew nothing of enchantments, and for years had been a stranger to anything approaching tender relations with any member of the opposite sex, for he was encased in shyness, and realized his overwhelming defects only too well. Yet this bewitching young creature came to him deliberately. Her manner was unmistakable, and she sought him out on every possible occasion. Chaste and sweet she was undoubtedly, yet frankly inviting; and she won him utterly with the first glance of her shining eyes, even if she had not already done so in the dark merely by the magic of her invisible presence.

'You felt she was altogether wholesome and good?' queried the doctor. 'You had no reaction of any sort – for instance, of alarm?'

Vezin looked up sharply with one of his inimitable little apologetic smiles. It was some time before he replied. The mere memory of the adventure had suffused his shy face with blushes, and his brown eyes sought the floor again before he answered.

'I don't think I can quite say that,' he explained presently. 'I acknowledged certain qualms, sitting up in my room afterwards. A conviction grew upon me that there was something about her – how shall I express it? – well, something unholy. It is not impurity in any sense, physical or mental, that I mean, but something quite indefinable that gave me a vague sensation of the creeps. She drew me, and at the same time repelled me, more than – than— '

He hesitated, blushing furiously, and unable to finish the sentence.

'Nothing like it has ever come to me before or since,' he concluded with lame confusion. 'I suppose it was, as you suggested just now, something of an enchantment. At any rate, it was strong enough to make me feel that I would stay in that awful little haunted town for years if only I could see her every day, hear her voice, watch her wonderful movements, and sometimes, perhaps, touch her hand.'

'Can you explain to me what you felt was the source of her power?' John Silence asked, looking purposely anywhere hut at the narrator.

'I am surprised that *you* should ask me such a question,' answered Vezin, with the nearest approach to dignity he could manage. 'I think no man can describe to another convincingly wherein lies the magic of the woman who ensnares him. I certainly cannot. I can only say this slip of a girl bewitched me, and the mere knowledge that she was living and sleeping in the same house filled me with an extraordinary sense of delight.

'But there's one thing I can tell you,' he went on earnestly, his eyes aglow, 'namely, that she seemed to sum up and synthesize in herself all the strange hidden forces that operated so mysteriously in the town and its inhabitants. She had the silken movements of the panther, going smoothly, silently, to and fro, and the same indirect, oblique methods as the townsfolk, screening, like them, secret purposes of her own – purposes that I was sure had me for their objective She kept me, to my tenor and delight, ceaselessly under observation, yet so carelessly, so consummately, that another man less sensitive, if I may say so' – he made a deprecating gesture – 'or less prepared by what had gone before, would never have noticed it at all. She was always still, always reposeful, yet she seemed to be everywhere at once, so that I never could escape from her. I was continually meeting the stare and laughter of her great eyes, in the corners of the rooms, in the passages, calmly looking at me through the windows, or in the busiest parts of the public streets.'

Their intimacy, it seems, grew very rapidly after this first encounter which had so violently disturbed the little man's equilibrium. He was naturally very prim, and prim folk live mostly in so small a world that anything violently unusual may shake them clean out of it, and they therefore instinctively distrust originality. But Vezin began to forget his primness after a while. The girl was always modestly behaved, and as her mother's representative she naturally had to do with the guests in the hotel. It was not out of the way that a spirit of camaraderie should spring up. Besides, she was young, she was charmingly pretty, she was French, and she obviously liked him.

At the same time, there was something indescribable – a certain indefinable atmosphere of other places, other times – that made him try hard to remain on his guard, and sometimes made him catch his breath with a sudden start. It was all rather like a delirious dream, half delight, half dread, he confided in a whisper to Dr Silence; and more than once he hardly knew quite what he was doing or saying, as though he were driven forward by impulses he scarcely recognized as his own.

And though the thought of leaving presented itself again and again to his mind, it was each time with less insistence, so that he stayed on from day to day, becoming more and more a part of the sleepy life of this dreamy mediaeval town, losing more and more of his recognizable personality. Soon, he felt, the Curtain within would roll up with an awful rush, and he would find himself suddenly admitted into the secret purposes of the hidden life that lay behind it all. Only, by that time, he would have become transformed into an entirely different being.

And, meanwhile, he noticed various little signs of the intention to make his stay attractive to him: flowers in his bedroom, a more comfortable armchair in the corner, and even special little extra dishes on his private table in the dining-room. Conversations, too, with 'Mademoiselle Ilsé' became more and more frequent and pleasant, and although they seldom travelled beyond the weather, or the details of the town, the girl, he noticed, was never in a hurry to bring them to an end, and often contrived to interject little odd sentences that he never properly understood, yet felt to be significant.

And it was these stray remarks, full of a meaning that evaded him, that pointed to some hidden purpose of her own and made him feel uneasy. They all had to do, he felt sure, with reasons for his staying on in the town indefinitely.

'And has M'sieur not even yet come to a decision?' she said softly in his ear, sitting beside him in the sunny yard before *déjeuner*, the acquaintance having progressed with significant rapidity. 'Because, if it's so difficult, we must all try together to help him!'

The question startled him, following upon his own thoughts. It was spoken with a pretty laugh, and a stray bit of hair across one eye, as she turned and peered at him half roguishly. Possibly he did not quite understand the French of it, for her near presence always confused his small knowledge of the language distressingly. Yet the words, and her manner, and something else that lay behind it all in her mind, frightened him. It gave such point to his feeling that the town was waiting for him to make his mind up on some important matter.

At the same time her voice, and the fact that she was there so close beside him in her soft dark dress, thrilled him inexpressibly.

'It is true I find it difficult to leave,' he stammered, losing his way deliciously in the depth of her eyes, 'and especially now that Mademoiselle Ilsé has come.'

He was surprised at the success of his sentence, and quite delighted with the little gallantry of it. But at the same time he could have bitten his tongue off for having said it.

'Then after all you like our little town, or you would not be pleased to stay on,' she said, ignoring the compliment.

'I am enchanted with it, and enchanted with you,' he cried, feeling that his tongue was somehow slipping beyond the control of his brain. And he was on the verge of saying all manner of other things of the wildest description, when the girl sprang lightly up from her chair beside him, and made to go.

'It is *soupe à l'onion* today!' she cried, laughing back at him through the sunlight, 'and I must go and see about it. Otherwise, you know, M'sieur will not enjoy his dinner, and then, perhaps, he will leave us!'

He watched her cross the courtyard, moving with all the grace and lightness of the feline race, and her simple black dress clothed her, he thought, exactly like the fur of the same supple species. She turned once to laugh to him from the porch with the glass door, and then stopped a moment to speak to her mother, who sat knitting as usual in her corner seat just inside the hall-way.

But how was it, then, that the moment his eye fell upon this ungainly woman, the pair of them appeared suddenly as other than they were? Whence came that transforming dignity and sense of power that enveloped them both as by magic? What was it about that massive woman that made her appear instantly regal, and set her on a throne in some dark and dreadful scenery, wielding a sceptre over the red glare of some tempestuous orgy? And why did this slender stripling of a girl, graceful as a willow, lithe as a young leopard, assume suddenly an air of sinister majesty, and move with flame and smoke about her head, and the darkness of night beneath her feet?

Vezin caught his breath and sat there transfixed. Then, almost simultaneously with its appearance, the queer notion vanished again, and the sunlight of day caught them both, and he heard her laughing to her mother about the *soupe à l'onion*, and saw her glancing back at him over her dear little shoulder with a smile that made him think of a dew-kissed rose bending lightly before summer airs.

And, indeed, the onion soup was particularly excellent that day, because he saw another cover laid at his small table, and, with fluttering heart, heard the waiter murmur by way of explanation that 'Ma'mselle Ilsé would honour M'sieur today at *déjeuner*, as her custom sometimes is with her mother's guests.'

So actually she sat by him all through that delirious meal, talking quietly to him in easy French, seeing that he was well looked after, mixing the salad dressing, and even helping him with her own hand. And, later in the afternoon, while he was smoking in the courtyard, longing for a sight of her as soon as her duties were done, she came again to his side, and when he rose to meet her, she stood facing him a moment, full of a perplexing sweet shyness before she spoke –

'My mother thinks you ought to know more of the beauties of our little town, and *I* think so, too! Would M'sieur like me to be his guide, perhaps? I can show him everything, for our family has lived here for many generations.'

She had him by the hand, indeed, before he could find a single word to express his pleasure, and led him, all unresisting, out into the street, yet in such a way that it seemed perfectly natural she should do so, and without the faintest suggestion of boldness or immodesty. Her face glowed with the pleasure and interest of it, and with her short dress and tumbled hair she looked every bit the charming child of seventeen that she was, innocent and playful, proud of her native town, and alive beyond her years to the sense of its ancient beauty.

So they went over the town together, and she showed what she considered its chief interest: the tumble-down old house where her forebears had lived; the sombre, aristocratic-looking mansion where her mother's family dwelt for centuries, and the ancient market-place where several hundred years before the witches had been burnt by the score. She kept up a lively running stream of talk about it all, of which he understood not a fiftieth part as he trudged along by her side, cursing his forty-five years and feeling all the yearnings of his early manhood revive and jeer at him. And, as she talked, England and Surbiton seemed very far away indeed, almost in another age of the world's history. Her voice touched something immeasurably old in him, something that slept deep. It lulled the surface parts of his consciousness to sleep, allowing what was far more ancient to awaken. Like the town, with its elaborate pretence of modern active life, the upper layers of his being became dulled, soothed, muffled, and what lay underneath began to stir in its sleep. That big Curtain swayed a little to and fro. Presently it might lift altogether. . . .

He began to understand a little better at last. The mood of the town was reproducing itself in him. In proportion as his ordinary external self became muffled, that inner secret life, that was far more real and vital, asserted itself. And this girl was surely the high-priestess of it all, the chief instrument of its accomplishment. New thoughts, with new interpretations, flooded his mind, as she walked beside him through the winding streets, while the picturesque old gabled town, softly coloured in the sunset, had never appeared to him so wholly wonderful and seductive.

And only one curious incident came to disturb and puzzle him, slight in itself, but utterly inexplicable, bringing white terror into the child's face and a scream to her laughing lips. He had merely pointed to a column of blue smoke that rose from the burning autumn leaves and made a picture against the red roofs, and had then run to the wall and called her to his side to watch the flames shooting here and there through the heap of rubbish. Yet, at the sight of it, as though taken by surprise, her face had altered dreadfully, and she had turned and run like the wind, calling out wild sentences to him as she ran, of which he had not understood a single word except that the fire apparently frightened her, and she wanted to get quickly away from it, and to get him away, too.

Yet five minutes later she was as calm and happy again as though nothing had happened to alarm or waken troubled thoughts in her, and they had both forgotten the incident.

They were leaning over the ruined ramparts together, listening to the weird music of the band as he had heard it the first day of his arrival. It moved him again profoundly as it had done before, and somehow he managed to find his tongue and his best French. The girl leaned across the stones close beside him. No one was about. Driven by some remorseless engine within he began to stammer something – he hardly knew what – of his strange admiration for her. Almost at the first word she sprang lightly off the wall and came up smiling in front of him, just touching his knees as he sat there. She was hatless as usual, and the sun caught her hair and one side of her cheek and throat.

'Oh, I'm *so* glad!' she cried, clapping her little hands softly in his face, 'so very glad, because that means that if you like me you must also like what I do, and what I belong to.'

Already he regretted bitterly having lost control of himself. Something in the phrasing of her sentence chilled him. He knew the fear of embarking upon an unknown and dangerous sea.

'You will take part in our real life, I mean,' she added softly, with an indescribable coaxing of manner, as though she noticed his shrinking 'You will come back to us.'

Already this slip of a child seemed to dominate him; he felt her power coming over him more and more; something emanated from her that stole over his senses and made him aware that her personality, for all its simple grace, held forces that were stately, imposing, august. He saw her again moving through smoke and flame amid broken and tempestuous scenery alarmingly strong, her terrible mother by her side. Dimly this shone through her smile and appearance of charming innocence.

'You will, I know,' she repeated, holding him with her eyes.

They were quite alone up there on the ramparts, and the sensation that she was overmastering him stirred a wild sensuousness in his blood. The mingled abandon and reserve in her attracted him furiously, and all of him that was man rose up and resisted the creeping influence, at the same time acclaiming it with the full delight of his forgotten youth. An irresistible desire came to him to question her, to summon what still remained to him of his own little personality in an effort to retain the right to his normal self.

The girl had grown quiet again, and was now leaning on the broad wall close beside him, gazing out across the darkening plain, her elbows on the coping, motionless as a figure carved in stone. He took his courage in both hands.

'Tell me, Ilsé,' he said, unconsciously imitating her own purring softness of voice, yet aware that he was utterly in earnest, 'what is the meaning of this town, and what is this real life you speak of? And why is it that the people watch me from morning to night? Tell me what it all means? And tell me,' he added more quickly with passion in his voice, 'what you really are – yourself?'

She turned her head and looked at him through half-closed eyelids, her growing inner excitement betraying itself by the faint colour that ran like a shadow across her face.

'It seems to me,' – he faltered oddly under her gaze – 'that I have some right to know— '

Suddenly she opened her eyes to the full. 'You love me, then?' she asked softly.

'I swear,' he cried impetuously, moved as by the force of a rising tide, 'I never felt before – I have never known any other girl who— '

'Then you *have* the right to know,' she calmly interrupted his confused confession; 'for love shares all secrets.'

She paused, and a thrill like fire ran swiftly through him. Her words lifted him off the earth, and he felt a radiant happiness, followed almost the same instant in horrible contrast by the thought of death. He became aware that she had turned her eyes upon his own and was speaking again.

'The real life I speak of,' she whispered, 'is the old, old life within, the life of long ago, the life to which you, too, once belonged, and to which you still belong.'

A faint wave of memory troubled the deeps of his soul as her low voice sank into him. What she was saying he knew instinctively to be true, even though he could not as yet understand its full purport. His present life seemed slipping from him as he listened, merging his personality in one that was far older and greater. It was this loss of his present self that brought to him the thought of death.

'You came here,' she went on, 'with the purpose of seeking it, and the people felt your presence and are waiting to know what you decide, whether you will leave them without having found it, or whether— '

Her eyes remained fixed upon his own, but her face began to change, growing larger and darker with an expression of age.

'It is their thoughts constantly playing about your soul that make you feel they watch you. They do not watch you with their eyes. The purposes of their inner life are calling to you, seeking to claim you. You were all part of the same life long, long ago, and now they want you back again among them.'

Vezin's timid heart sank with dread as he listened; but the girl's eyes held him with a net of joy so that he had no wish to escape. She fascinated him, as it were, clean out of his normal self.

'Alone, however, the people could never have caught and held you,' she resumed. 'The motive force was not strong enough; it has faded through all these years. But I' – she paused a moment and looked at him with complete confidence in her splendid eyes – 'I possess the spell to conquer you and hold you: the spell of old love. I can win you back again and make you live the old life with me, for the force of the ancient tie between us, if I choose to use it, is irresistible. And I do choose to use it. I still want you. And you, dear soul of my dim past' – she pressed closer to him so that her breath passed across his eyes, and her voice positively sang – 'I mean to have you, for you love me and are utterly at my mercy.'

Vezin heard, and yet did not hear; understood, yet did not understand. He had passed into a condition of exaltation. The world was beneath his feet, made of music and flowers, and he was flying somewhere far above it through the sunshine of pure delight. He was breathless and giddy with the wonder of her words. They intoxicated him. And, still, the tenor of it all, the dreadful thought of death, pressed ever behind her sentences. For flames shot through her voice out of black smoke and licked at his soul.

And they communicated with one another, it seemed to him, by a process of swift telepathy, for his French could never have compassed all he said to her. Yet she understood perfectly, and what she said to him was like the recital of verses long since known. And the mingled pain and sweetness of it as he listened were almost more than his little soul could hold.

'Yet I came here wholly by chance— ' he heard himself saying.

'No,' she cried with passion, 'you came here because I called to you. I have called to you for years, and you came with the whole force of the past behind you. You had to come, for I own you, and I claim you.'

She rose again and moved closer, looking at him with a certain insolence in the face – the insolence of power.

The sun had set behind the towers of the old cathedral and the darkness rose up from the plain and enveloped them. The music of the band had ceased. The leaves of the plane trees hung motionless, but the chill of the autumn evening rose about them and made Vezin shiver. There was no sound but the sound of their voices and the occasional soft rustle of the girl's dress. He could hear the blood rushing in his ears. He scarcely realized where he was or what he was doing. Some terrible magic of the imagination drew him deeply down into the tombs of his own being, telling him in no unfaltering voice that her words shadowed forth the truth. And this simple little French maid, speaking beside him with so strange authority, he saw curiously alter into quite another being. As he stared into her eyes, the picture in his mind grew and lived, dressing itself vividly to his inner vision with a degree of reality he was compelled to acknowledge. As once before, he saw her tall and stately, moving through wild and broken scenery of forests and mountain caverns, the glare of flames behind her head and clouds of shifting smoke about her feet. Dark leaves encircled her hair, flying loosely in the wind, and her limbs shone through the merest rags of clothing. Others were about her, too, and ardent eyes on all sides cast delirious glances upon her, but her own eyes were always for One only, one whom she held by the hand. For she was leading the dance in some tempestuous orgy to the music of chanting voices, and the dance she led circled about a great and awful Figure on a throne, brooding over the scene through lurid vapours, while innumerable other wild faces and forms crowded furiously about her in the dance.

But the one she held by the hand he knew to be himself, and the monstrous shape upon the throne he knew to be her mother.

The vision rose within him, rushing to him down the long years of buried time, crying aloud to him with the voice of memory reawakened. And then the scene faded away, and he saw the clear circle of the girl's eyes gazing steadfastly into his own, and she became once more the pretty little daughter of the inn-keeper, and he found his voice again.

'And you,' he whispered tremblingly – 'you child of visions and enchantment, how is it that you so bewitch me that I loved you even before I saw?'

She drew herself up beside him with an air of rare dignity.

'The call of the Past,' she said; 'and besides,' she added proudly, 'in the real life I am a princess— '

'A princess!' he cried.

'— and my mother is a queen!'

At this, little Vezin utterly lost his head. Delight tore at his heart and swept him into sheer ecstasy. To hear that sweet singing voice, and to see those adorable little lips utter such things, upset his balance beyond all hope of control. He took her in his arms and covered her unresisting face with kisses.

But even while he did so, and while the hot passion swept him, he felt that she was soft and loathsome, and that her answering kisses stained his very soul. . . . And when, presently, she had freed herself and vanished into the darkness, he stood there, leaning against the wall in a state of collapse, creeping with horror from the touch of her yielding body, and inwardly raging at the weakness that he already dimly realized must prove his undoing.

And from the shadows of the old buildings into which she disappeared there rose in the stillness of the night a singular, long-drawn cry, which at first he took for laughter, but which later he was sure he recognized as the almost human wailing of a cat.

V

For a long time Vezin leant there against the wall, alone with his surging thoughts and emotions. He understood at length that he had done the one thing necessary to call down upon him the whole force of this ancient Past. For in those passionate kisses he had acknowledged the tie of olden days, and had revived it. And the memory of that soft impalpable caress in the darkness of the inn corridor come back to him with a shudder. The girl had first mastered him, and then led him to the one act that was necessary for her purpose. He had been waylaid, after the lapse of centuries – caught, and conquered.

Dimly he realized this, and sought to make plans for his escape. But, for the moment at any rate, he was powerless to manage his thoughts or will, for the sweet, fantastic madness of the whole adventure mounted to his brain like a spell, and he gloried in the feeling that he was utterly enchanted and moving in a world so much larger and wilder than the one he had ever been accustomed to.

The moon, pale and enormous, was just rising over the sea-like plain, when at last he rose to go. Her slanting rays drew all the houses into new perspective, so that their roofs, already glistening with dew, seemed to stretch much higher into the sky than usual, and their gables and quaint old towers lay far away in its purple reaches.

The cathedral appeared unreal in a silver mist. He moved softly, keeping to the shadows; but the streets were all deserted and very silent; the doors were closed, the shutters fastened. Not a soul was astir. The hush of night lay over everything; it was like a town of the dead, a churchyard with gigantic and grotesque tombstones.

Wondering where all the busy life of the day had so utterly disappeared, he made his way to a back door that entered the inn by means of the stables, thinking thus to reach his room unobserved. He reached the courtyard safely and crossed it by keeping close to the shadow of the wall. He sidled down it, mincing along on tiptoe, just as the old men did when they entered the *salle à manger*. He was horrified to find himself doing this instinctively. A strange impulse came to him, catching him somehow in the centre of his body – an impulse to drop upon all fours and run swiftly and silently. He glanced upwards and the idea came to him to leap up upon his windowsill overhead instead of going round by the stairs. This occurred to him as the easiest and most natural way. It was like the beginning of some horrible transformation of himself into something else. He was fearfully strung up.

The moon was higher now, and the shadows very dark along the side of the street where he moved. He kept among the deepest of them, and reached the porch with the glass doors.

But here there was light; the inmates, unfortunately, were still about. Hoping to slip across the hall unobserved and reach the stairs, he opened the door carefully and stole in. Then he saw that the hall was not empty. A large dark thing lay against the wall on his left. At first he thought it must be household articles. Then it moved, and he thought it was an immense cat, distorted in some way by the play of light and shadow. Then it rose straight up before him and he saw that it was the proprietress.

What she had been doing in this position he could only venture a dreadful guess, but the moment she stood up and faced him he was aware of some terrible dignity clothing her about that instantly recalled the girl's strange saying that she was a queen. Huge and sinister she stood there under the little oil lamp; alone with him in the empty hall. Awe stirred in his heart, and the roots of some ancient fear. He felt that he must bow to her and make some kind of obeisance. The impulse was fierce and irresistible, as of long habit. He glanced quickly about him. There was no one there. Then he deliberately inclined his head towards her. He bowed.

'Enfin! M'sieur s'est donc décidé. C'est bien alors. J'en suis contente.'

Her words came to him sonorously as through a great open space.

Then the great figure came suddenly across the flagged hall at him and seized his trembling hands.

Some overpowering force moved with her and caught him.

'On pourrait faire un p'tit tour ensemble, n'est ce pas? Nous y allons cette nuit et il faut s'exercer un peu d'avance pour cela. Ilsé, Ilsé, viens donc ici. Viens vite!'

And she whirled him round in the opening steps of some dance that seemed oddly and horribly familiar. They made no sound on the stones, this strangely assorted couple. It was all soft and stealthy. And presently, when the air seemed to thicken like smoke, and a red glare as of flame shot through it, he was aware that someone else had joined them and that his hand the mother had released was now tightly held by the daughter. Ilsé had come in answer to the call, and he saw her with leaves of vervain twined in her dark hair, clothed in tattered vestiges of some curious garment, beautiful as the night, and horribly, odiously, loathsomely seductive.

'To the Sabbath! to the Sabbath!' they cried 'On to the Witches' Sabbath!'

Up and down that narrow hall they danced, the women on each side of him, to the wildest measure he had ever imagined, yet which he dimly, dreadfully remembered, till the lamp on the wall flickered and went out, and they were left in total darkness. And the devil woke in his heart with a thousand vile suggestions and made him afraid.

Suddenly they released his hands and he heard the voice of the mother cry that it was time, and they must go. Which way they went he did not pause to see. He only realized that he was free, and he blundered through the darkness till he found the stairs and then tore up them to his room as though all hell was at his heels.

He flung himself on the sofa, with his face in his hands, and groaned. Swiftly reviewing a dozen ways of immediate escape, all equally impossible, he finally decided that the only thing to do for the moment was to sit quiet and wait. He must see what was going to happen. At least in the privacy of his own bedroom he would be fairly safe. The door was locked. He crossed over and softly opened the window which gave upon the courtyard and also permitted a partial view of the hall through the glass doors.

As he did so the hum and murmur of a great activity reached his ears from the streets beyond – the sound of footsteps and voices muffled by distance. He leaned out cautiously and listened. The moonlight was clear and strong now, but his own window was in shadow, the silver disc being still behind the house. It came to him irresistibly that the inhabitants of the town, who a little while before had all been invisible behind closed doors, were now issuing forth, busy upon some secret and unholy errand. He listened intently.

At first everything about him was silent, but soon he became aware of movements going on in the house itself. Rustlings and creepings came to him across that still, moonlit yard. A concourse of living beings sent the hum of their activity into the night. Things were on the move everywhere. A biting, pungent odour rose through the all, coming he knew not whence. Presently his eyes became glued to the windows of the opposite wall where the moonshine fell in a soft blaze. The roof overhead, and behind him, was reflected clearly in the panes of glass, and he saw the outlines of dark bodies moving with long footsteps over the tiles and along the coping. They passed swiftly and silently, shaped like immense cats, in an endless procession across the pictured glass, and then appeared to leap down to a lower level where he lost sight of them. He just caught the soft thudding of their leaps. Sometimes their shadows fell upon the white wall opposite, and then he could not make out whether they were the shadows of human beings or of cats. They seemed to change swiftly from one to the other. The transformation looked horribly real, for they leaped like human beings, yet changed swiftly in the air immediately afterwards, and dropped like animals.

The yard, too, beneath him, was now alive with the creeping movements of dark forms all stealthily drawing towards the porch with the glass doors. They kept so closely to the wall that he could not determine their actual shape, but when he saw that they passed on to the great congregation that was gathering in the hall, he understood that these were the creatures whose leaping shadows he had first seen reflected in the windowpanes opposite. They were coming from all parts of the town, reaching the appointed meeting-place across the roofs and tiles, and springing from level to level till they came to the yard.

Then a new sound caught his ear, and he saw that the windows all about him were being softly opened, and that to each window came a face. A moment later figures began dropping hurriedly down into the yard. And these figures, as they lowered themselves down from the windows, were human, he saw; but once safely in the yard they fell upon all fours and changed in the swiftest possible second into – cats – huge, silent cats. They ran in streams to join the main body in the hall beyond.

So, after all, the rooms in the house had not been empty and unoccupied.

Moreover, what he saw no longer filled him with amazement. For he remembered it all. It was familiar. It had all happened before just so, hundreds of times, and he himself had taken part in it and known the wild madness of it all. The outline of the old building changed, the yard grew larger, and he seemed to be staring down upon it from a much greater height through smoky vapours. And, as he looked, half remembering, the old pains of long ago, fierce and sweet, furiously assailed him, and the blood stirred horribly as he heard the Call of the Dance again in his heart and tasted the ancient magic of Ilsé whirling by his side.

Suddenly he started back. A great lithe cat had leaped softly up from the shadows below on to the sill close to his face, and was staring fixedly at him with the eyes of a human. 'Come,' it seemed to say, 'come with us to the Dance! Change as of old! Transform yourself swiftly and come!' Only too well he understood the creature's soundless call.

It was gone again in a flash with scarcely a sound of its padded feet on the stones, and then others dropped by the score down the side of the house, past his very eyes, all changing as they fell and darting away rapidly, softly, towards the gathering point. And again he felt the dreadful desire to do likewise; to murmur the old incantation, and then drop upon hands and knees and run swiftly for the great flying leap into the air. Oh, how the passion of it rose within him like a flood, twisting his very entrails, sending his heart's desire flaming forth into the night for the old, old Dance of the Sorcerers at the Witches' Sabbath! The whirl of the stars was about him; once more he met the magic of the moon. The power of the wind, rushing from precipice and forest, leaping from cliff to cliff across the valleys, tore him away. . . . He heard the cries of the dancers and their wild laughter, and with this savage girl in his embrace he danced furiously about the dim throne where sat the Figure with the sceptre of majesty. . . .

Then, suddenly, all became hushed and still, and the fever died a little in his heart. The calm moonlight flooded a courtyard empty and deserted. They had started. The procession was off into the sky. And he was left behind – alone.

Vezin tiptoed softly across the room and unlocked the door. The murmur from the streets, growing momentarily as he advanced, met his ears. He made his way with the utmost caution down the corridor. At the head of the stairs he paused and listened. Below him, the hall where they had gathered was dark and still, but through opened doors and windows on the far side of the building came the sound of a great throng moving farther and farther into the distance.

He made his way down the creaking wooden stair, dreading yet longing to meet some straggler who should point the way, but finding no one; across the dark hall, so lately thronged with living, moving things, and out through the opened front doors into the street. He could not believe that he was really left behind, really forgotten, that he had been purposely permitted to escape. It perplexed him.

Nervously he peered about him, and up and down the street; then, seeing nothing, advanced slowly down the pavement.

The whole town, as he went, showed itself empty and deserted, as though a great wind had blown everything alive out of it. The doors and windows of the houses stood open to the night; nothing stirred; moonlight and silence lay over all. The night lay about him like a cloak. The air, soft and cool, caressed his cheek like the touch of a great furry paw. He gained confidence and began to walk quickly, though still keeping to the shadowed side. Nowhere could he discover the faintest sign of the great unholy exodus he knew had just taken place. The moon sailed high over all in a sky cloudless and serene.

Hardly realizing where he was going, he crossed the open market-place and so came to the ramparts, whence he knew a pathway descended to the high road and along which he could make good his escape to one of the other little towns that lay to the northward, and so to the railway.

But first he paused and gazed out over the scene at his feet where the great plain lay like a silver map of some dream country. The still beauty of it entered his heart, increasing his sense of bewilderment and unreality. No air stirred, the leaves of the plane trees stood motionless, the near details were defined with the sharpness of day against dark shadows and in the distance the fields and woods melted away into haze and shimmering mistiness.

But the breath caught in his throat and he stood stock-still as though transfixed when his gaze passed from the horizon and fell upon the near prospect in the depth of the valley at his feet. The whole lower slopes of the hill, that lay hid from the brightness of the moon, were aglow, and through the glare he saw countless moving forms, shifting thick and fast between the openings of the trees; while overhead, like leaves driven by the wind, he discerned flying shapes that hovered darkly one moment against the sky and then settled down with cries and weird singing through the branches into the region that was aflame.

Spellbound, he stood and stared for a time that he could not measure. And then, moved by one of the terrible impulses that seemed to control the whole adventure, he climbed swiftly upon the top of the broad coping, and balanced a moment where the valley gaped at his feet. But in that very instant, as he stood hovering, a sudden movement among the shadows of the houses caught his eye, and he turned to see the outline of a large animal dart swiftly across the open space behind him, and land with a flying leap upon the top of the wall a little lower down. It ran like the wind to his feet and then rose up beside him upon the ramparts. A shiver seemed to run through the moonlight, and his sight trembled for a second. His heart pulsed fearfully. Ilsé stood beside him, peering into his face.

Some dark substance, he saw, stained the girl's face and skin, shining in the moonlight as she stretched her hands towards him; she was dressed in wretched tattered garments that yet became her mightily; rue and vervain twined about her temples; her eyes glittered with unholy light. He only just controlled the wild impulse to take her in his arms and leap with her from their giddy perch into the valley below.

'See!' she cried, pointing with an arm on which the rags fluttered in the rising wind towards the forest aglow in the distance. 'See where they await us! The woods are alive! Already the Great Ones are there, and the dance will soon begin! The salve is here! Anoint yourself and come!'

Though a moment before the sky was clear and cloudless, yet even while she spoke the face of the moon grew dark and the wind began to toss in the crests of the plane trees at his feet. Stray gusts brought the sounds of hoarse singing and crying from the lower slopes of the hill, and the pungent odour he had already noticed about the courtyard of the inn rose about him in the air.

'Transform, transform!' she cried again, her voice rising like a song. 'Rub well your skin before you fly. Come! Come with me to the Sabbath, to the madness of its furious delight, to the sweet abandonment of its evil worship! See! the Great Ones are there, and the terrible Sacraments prepared. The Throne is occupied. Anoint and come! Anoint and come!'

She grew to the height of a tree beside him, leaping upon the wall with flaming eyes and hair strewn upon the night. He too began to change swiftly. Her hands touched the skin of his face and neck, streaking him with the burning salve that sent the old magic into his blood with the power before which fades all that is good.

A wild roar came up to his ears from the heart of the wood, and the girl, when she heard it, leaped upon the wall in the frenzy of her wicked joy.

'Satan is there!' she screamed, rushing upon him and striving to draw him with her to the edge of the wall. 'Satan has come! The Sacraments call us! Come, with your dear apostate soul, and we will worship and dance till the moon dies and the world is forgotten!'

Just saving himself from the dreadful plunge, Vezin struggled to release himself from her grasp, while the passion tore at his reins and all but mastered him. He shrieked aloud, not knowing what he said, and then he shrieked again. It was the old impulses, the old awful habits instinctively finding voice; for though it seemed to him that he merely shrieked nonsense, the words he uttered really had meaning in them, and were intelligible. It was the ancient call. And it was heard below. It was answered.

The wind whistled at the skirts of his coat as the air round him darkened with many flying forms crowding upwards out of the valley. The crying of hoarse voices smote upon his ears, coming closer. Strokes of wind buffeted him, tearing him this way and that along the crumbling top of the stone wall; and Ilsé clung to him with her long shining arms, smooth and bare, holding him fast about the neck. But not Ilsé alone, for a dozen of them surrounded him, dropping out of the air. The pungent odour of the anointed bodies stifled him, exciting him to the old madness of the Sabbath, the dance of the witches and sorcerers doing honour to the personified Evil of the world.

'Anoint and away! Anoint and away!' they cried in wild chorus about him. 'To the Dance that never dies! To the sweet and fearful fantasy of evil!'

Another moment and he would have yielded and gone, for his will turned soft and the flood of passionate memory all but overwhelmed him, when – so can a small thing alter the whole course of an adventure – he caught his foot upon a loose stone in the edge of the wall, and then fell with a sudden crash on to the ground below. But he fell towards the houses, in the open space of dust and cobble stones, and fortunately not into the gaping depth of the valley on the farther side.

And they, too, came in a tumbling heap about him, like flies upon a piece of food, but as they fell he was released for a moment from the power of their touch, and in that brief instant of freedom there flashed into his mind the sudden intuition that saved him. Before he could regain his feet he saw them scrabbling awkwardly back upon the wall, as though bat-like they could only fly by dropping from a height, and had no hold upon him in the open. Then seeing them perched there in a row like cats upon a roof, all dark and singularly shapeless, their eyes like lamps, the sudden memory came back to him of Ilsé's terror at the sight of fire.

Quick as a flash he found his matches and lit the dead leaves that lay under the wall.

Dry and withered, they caught fire at once, and the wind carried the flame in a long line down the length of the wall, licking upwards as it ran; and with shrieks and wailings, the crowded row of forms upon the top melted away into the air on the other side, and were gone with a great rush and whirring of their bodies down into the heart of the haunted valley, leaving Vezin breathless and shaken in the middle of the deserted ground.

'Ilsé!' he called feebly; 'Ilsé!' for his heart ached to think that she was really gone to the great Dance without him, and that he had lost the opportunity of its fearful joy. Yet at the same time his relief was so great, and he was so dazed and troubled in mind with the whole thing, that he hardly knew what he was saying, and only cried aloud in the fierce storm of his emotion.

The fire under the wall ran its course, and the moonlight came out again, soft and clear, from its temporary eclipse. With one last shuddering look at the ruined ramparts, and a feeling of horrid wonder for the haunted valley beyond, where the shapes still crowded and flew, he turned his face towards the town and slowly made his way in the direction of the hotel.

And as he went, a great wailing of cries, and a sound of howling, followed him from the gleaming forest below, growing fainter and fainter with the bursts of wind as he disappeared between the houses.

VI

'It may seem rather abrupt to you, this sudden tame ending,' said Arthur Vezin, glancing with flushed face and timid eyes at Dr Silence sitting there with his notebook, 'but the fact is – er – from that moment my memory seems to have failed rather. I have no distinct recollection of how I got home or what precisely I did.

'It appears I never went back to the inn at all. I only dimly recollect racing down a long white road in the moonlight, past woods and villages, still and deserted, and then the dawn came up, and I saw the towers of a biggish town and so came to the station.

'But, long before that, I remember pausing somewhere on the road and looking back to where the hill-town of my adventure stood up in the moonlight, and thinking how exactly like a great monstrous cat it lay there upon the plain, its huge front paws lying down the two main streets, and the twin and broken towers of the cathedral marking its torn ears against the sky. That picture stays in my mind with the utmost vividness to this day.

'Another thing remains in my mind from that escape – namely, the sudden sharp reminder that I had not paid my bill, and the decision I made, standing there on the dusty highroad, that the small baggage I had left behind would more than settle for my indebtedness.

'For the rest, I can only tell you that I got coffee and bread at a café on the outskirts of this town I had come to, and soon after found my way to the station and caught a train later in the day. That same evening I reached London.'

'And how long altogether,' asked John Silence quietly, 'do you think you stayed in the town of the adventure?'

Vezin looked up sheepishly.

'I was coming to that,' he resumed, with apologetic wrigglings of his body. 'In London I found that I was a whole week out in my reckoning of time. I had stayed over a week in the town, and it ought to have been September 15th, – instead of which it was only September 10th!'

'So that, in reality, you had only stayed a night or two in the inn?' queried the doctor.

Vezin hesitated before replying. He shuffled upon the mat.

'I must have gained time somewhere,' he said at length – 'somewhere or somehow. I certainly had a week to my credit. I can't explain it. I can only give you the fact.'

'And this happened to you last year, since when you have never been back to the place?'

'Last autumn, yes,' murmured Vezin; 'and I have never dared to go back. I think I never want to.'

'And, tell me,' asked Dr Silence at length, when he saw that the little man had evidently come to the end of his words and had nothing more to say, 'had you ever read up the subject of the old witchcraft practices during the Middle Ages, or been at all interested in the subject?'

'Never!' declared Vezin emphatically. 'I had never given a thought to such matters so far as I know— '

'Or to the question of reincarnation, perhaps?'

'Never – before my adventure; but I have since,' he replied significantly.

There was, however, something still on the man's mind that he wished to relieve himself of by confession, yet could with difficulty bring himself to mention; and it was only after the sympathetic tactfulness of the doctor had provided numerous openings that he at length availed himself of one of them, and stammered that he would like to show him the marks he still had on his neck where, he said, the girl had touched him with her anointed hands.

He took off his collar after infinite fumbling hesitation, and lowered his shirt a little for the doctor to see. And there, on the surface of the skin, lay a faint reddish line across the shoulder and extending a little way down the back towards the spine. It certainly indicated exactly the position an arm might have taken in the act of embracing. And on the other side of the neck, slightly higher up, was a similar mark, though not quite so clearly defined.

'That was where she held me that night on the ramparts,' he whispered, a strange light coming and going in his eyes.

It was some weeks later when I again found occasion to consult John Silence concerning another extraordinary case that had come under my notice, and we fell to discussing Vezin's story. Since hearing it, the doctor had made investigations on his own account, and one of his secretaries had discovered that Vezin's ancestors had actually lived for generations in the very town where the adventure came to him. Two of them, both women, had been tried and convicted as witches, and had been burned alive at the stake. Moreover, it had not been difficult to prove that the very inn where Vezin stayed was built about 1700 upon the spot where the funeral pyres stood and the executions took place. The town was a sort of headquarters for all the sorcerers and witches of the entire region, and after conviction they were burnt there literally by scores.

'It seems strange,' continued the doctor, 'that Vezin should have remained ignorant of all this; but, on the other hand, it was not the kind of history that successive generations would have been anxious to keep alive, or to repeat to their children. Therefore I am inclined to think he still knows nothing about it.

'The whole adventure seems to have been a very vivid revival of the memories of an earlier life, caused by coming directly into contact with the living forces still intense enough to hang about the place, and, by a most singular chance too, with the very souls who had taken part with him in the events of that particular life. For the mother and daughter who impressed him so strangely must have been leading actors, with himself, in the scenes and practices of witchcraft which at that period dominated the imaginations of the whole country.

'One has only to read the histories of the times to know that these witches claimed the power of transforming themselves into various animals, both for the purposes of disguise and also to convey themselves swiftly to the scenes of their imaginary orgies. Lycanthropy, or the power to change themselves into wolves, was everywhere believed in, and the ability to transform themselves into cats by rubbing their bodies with a special salve or ointment provided by Satan himself, found equal credence. The witchcraft trials abound in evidences of such universal beliefs.'

Dr Silence quoted chapter and verse from many writers on the subject, and showed how every detail of Vezin's adventure had a basis in the practices of those dark days.

'But that the entire affair took place subjectively in the man's own consciousness, I have no doubt,' he went on, in reply to my questions; 'for my secretary who has been to the town to investigate, discovered his signature in the visitors' book, and proved by it that he had arrived on September 8th, and left suddenly without paying his bill. He left two days later, and they still were in possession of his dirty brown bag and some tourist clothes. I paid a few francs in settlement of his debt, and have sent his luggage on to him. The daughter was absent from home, but the proprietress, a large woman very much as he described her, told my secretary that he had seemed a very strange, absent-minded kind of gentleman, and after his disappearance she had feared for a long time that he had met with a violent end in the neighbouring forest where he used to roam about alone.

'I should like to have obtained a personal interview with the daughter so as to ascertain how much was subjective and how much actually took place with her as Vezin told it. For her dread of fire and the sight of burning must, of course, have been the intuitive memory of her former painful death at the stake, and have thus explained why he fancied more than once that he saw her through smoke and flame.'

'And that mark on his skin, for instance?' I inquired.

'Merely the marks produced by hysterical brooding,' he replied, 'like the stigmata of the *religieuses*, and the bruises which appear on the bodies of hypnotized subjects who have been told to expect them. This is very common and easily explained. Only it seems curious that these marks should have remained so long in Vezin's case. Usually they disappear quickly.'

'Obviously he is still thinking about it all, brooding, and living it all over again,' I ventured.

'Probably. And this makes me fear that the end of his trouble is not yet. We shall hear of him again. It is a case, alas! I can do little to alleviate.'

Dr Silence spoke gravely and with sadness in his voice.

'And what do you make of the Frenchman in the train?' I asked further – 'the man who warned him against the place, *à cause du sommeil et à cause des chats?* Surely a very singular incident?'

'A *very* singular incident indeed,' he made answer slowly, 'and one I can only explain on the basis of a highly improbable coincidence— '

'Namely?'

'That the man was one who had himself stayed in the town and undergone there a similar experience. I should like to find this man and ask him. But the crystal is useless here, for I have no slightest clue to go upon, and I can only conclude that some singular psychic affinity, some force still active in his being out of the same past life, drew him thus to the personality of Vezin, and enabled him to fear what might happen to him, and thus to warn him as he did.

'Yes,' he presently continued, half talking to himself, 'I suspect in this case that Vezin was swept into the vortex of forces arising out of the intense activities of a past life, and that he lived over again a scene in which he had often played a leading part centuries before. For strong actions set up forces that are so slow to exhaust themselves, they may be said in a sense never to die. In this case they were not vital enough to render the illusion complete, so that the little man found himself caught in a very distressing confusion of the present and the past; yet he was sufficiently sensitive to recognize that it was true, and to fight against the degradation of returning: even in memory, to a former and lower state of development.

'Ah yes!' he continued, crossing the floor to gaze at the darkening sky, and seemingly quite oblivious of my presence, 'subliminal up-rushes of memory like this can be exceedingly painful, and sometimes exceedingly dangerous. I only trust that this gentle soul may soon escape from this obsession of a passionate and tempestuous past. But I doubt it, I doubt it.'

His voice was hushed with sadness as he spoke, and when he turned back into the room again there was an expression of profound yearning upon his face, the yearning of a soul whose desire to help is sometimes greater than his power.

The Interlopers

SAKI

In a forest of mixed growth somewhere on the eastern spurs of the Carpathians, a man stood one winter night watching and listening, as though he waited for some beast of the woods to come within the range of his vision, and, later, of his rifle. But the game for whose presence he kept so keen an outlook was none that figured in the sportsman's calendar as lawful and proper for the chase; Ulrich von Gradwitz patrolled the dark forest in quest of a human enemy.

The forest lands of Gradwitz were of wide extent and well stocked with game; the narrow strip of precipitous woodland that lay on its outskirt was not remarkable for the game it harboured or the shooting it afforded, but it was the most jealously guarded of all its owner's territorial possessions. A famous lawsuit, in the days of his grandfather, had wrested it from the illegal possession of a neighbouring family of petty landowners; the dispossessed party had never acquiesced in the judgment of the Courts, and a long series of poaching affrays and similar scandals had embittered the relationships between the families for three generations. The neighbour feud had grown into a personal one since Ulrich had come to be head of his family; if there was a man in the world whom he detested and wished ill to it was Georg Znaeym, the inheritor of the quarrel and the tireless game-snatcher and raider of the disputed border-forest. The feud might, perhaps, have died down or been compromised if the personal ill-will of the two men had not stood in the way; as boys they had thirsted for one another's blood, as men each prayed that misfortune might fall on the other, and this wind-scourged winter night Ulrich had banded together his foresters to watch the dark forest, not in quest of four-footed quarry, but to keep a look-out for the prowling thieves whom he suspected of being afoot from across the land boundary. The roebuck, which usually kept in the sheltered hollows during a storm-wind, were running like driven things tonight, and there was movement and unrest among the creatures that were wont to sleep through the dark hours. Assuredly there was a disturbing element in the forest, and Ulrich could guess the quarter from whence it came.

He strayed away by himself from the watchers whom he had placed in ambush on the crest of the hill, and wandered far down the steep slopes amid the wild tangle of undergrowth, peering through the tree-trunks and listening through the whistling and skirling of the wind and the restless beating of the branches for sight or sound of the marauders. If only on this wild night, in this dark, lone spot, he might come across Georg Znaeym, man to man, with none to witness – that was the wish that was uppermost in his thoughts. And as he stepped round the trunk of a huge beech he came face to face with the man he sought.

The two enemies stood glaring at one another for a long silent moment. Each had a rifle in his hand, each had hate in his heart and murder uppermost in his mind. The chance had come to give full play to the passions of a lifetime. But a man who has been brought up under the code of a restraining civilization cannot easily nerve himself to shoot down his neighbour in cold blood and without word spoken, except for an offence against his hearth and honour. And before the moment of hesitation had given way to action a deed of Nature's own violence overwhelmed them both. A fierce shriek of the storm had been answered by a splitting crash over their heads, and ere they could leap aside a mass of falling beech tree had thundered down on them. Ulrich von Gradwitz found himself stretched on the ground, one arm numb beneath him and the other held almost as helplessly in a tight tangle of forked branches, while both legs were pinned beneath the fallen mass. His heavy shooting-boots had saved his feet from being crushed to pieces, but if his fractures were not as serious as they might have been, at least it was evident that he could not move from his present position till some one came to release him. The descending twigs had slashed the skin of his face, and he had to wink away some drops of blood from his eyelashes before he could take in a general view of the disaster. At his side, so near that under ordinary circumstances he could almost have touched him, lay Georg Znaeym, alive and struggling, but obviously as helplessly pinioned down as himself. All round them lay a thick-strewn wreckage of splintered branches and broken twigs.

Relief at being alive and exasperation at his captive plight brought a strange medley of pious thank-offerings and sharp curses to Ulrich's lips. Georg, who was nearly blinded with the blood which trickled across his eyes, stopped his struggling for a moment to listen, and then gave a short, snarling laugh.

'So you're not killed, as you ought to be, but you're caught, anyway,' he cried; 'caught fast. Ho, what a jest, Ulrich von Gradwitz snared in his stolen forest. There's real justice for you!'

And he laughed again, mockingly and savagely.

'I'm caught in my own forest-land,' retorted Ulrich. 'When my men come to release us you will wish, perhaps, that you were in a better plight than caught poaching on a neighbour's land, shame on you.'

Georg was silent for a moment; then he answered quietly.

'Are you sure that your men will find much to release? I have men, too, in the forest tonight, close behind me, and they will be here first and do the releasing. When they drag me out from under these damned branches it won't need much clumsiness on their part to roll this mass of trunk right over on the top of you. Your men will find you dead under a fallen beech tree. For form's sake I shall send my condolences to your family.'

'It is a useful hint,' said Ulrich fiercely. 'My men had orders to follow in ten minutes' time, seven of which must have gone by already, and when they get me out – I will remember the hint. Only as you will have met your death poaching on my lands I don't think I can decently send any message of condolence to your family.'

'Good,' snarled Georg, 'good. We fight this quarrel out to the death, you and I and our foresters, with no cursed interlopers to come between us. Death and damnation to you, Ulrich von Gradwitz.'

'The same to you, Georg Znaeym, forest-thief, game-snatcher.'

Both men spoke with the bitterness of possible defeat before them, for each knew that it might be long before his men would seek him out or find him; it was a bare matter of chance which party would arrive first on the scene.

Both had now given up the useless struggle to free themselves from the mass of wood that held them down; Ulrich limited his endeavours to an effort to bring his one partially free arm near enough to his outer coat-pocket to draw out his wine-flask. Even when he had accomplished that operation it was long before he could manage the unscrewing of the stopper or get any of the liquid down his throat. But what a Heaven-sent draught it seemed. It was an open winter, and little snow had fallen as yet, hence the captives suffered less from the cold than might have been the case at that season of the year; nevertheless, the wine was warming and reviving to the bounded man, and he looked across with something like a throb of pity to where his enemy lay, just keeping the groans of pain and weariness from crossing his lips.

'Could you reach this flask if I threw it over to you?' asked Ulrich suddenly; 'there is good wine in it, and one may as well be as comfortable as one can. Let us drink, even if tonight one of us dies.'

'No, I can scarcely see anything; there is so much blood caked round my eyes,' said Georg, 'and in any case I don't drink wine with an enemy.'

Ulrich was silent for a few minutes, and lay listening to the weary screeching of the wind. An idea was slowly forming and growing in his brain, an idea that gained strength every time that he looked across at the man who was fighting so grimly against pain and exhaustion. In the pain and languor that Ulrich himself was feeling the old fierce hatred seemed to be dying down.

'Neighbour,' he said presently,' do as you please if your men come first. It was a fair compact. But as for me, I've changed my mind. If my men are the first to come you shall be the first to be helped, as though you were my guest. We have quarrelled like devils all our lives over this stupid strip of forest, where the trees can't even stand upright in a breath of wind. Lying here tonight, thinking, I've come to think we've been rather fools; there are better things in life than getting the better of a boundary dispute. Neighbour, if you will help me to bury the old quarrel I – I will ask you to be my friend.'

Georg Znaeym was silent for so long that Ulrich thought, perhaps, he had fainted with the pain of his injuries. Then he spoke slowly and in jerks.

'How the whole region would stare and gabble if we rode into the market-square together. No one living can remember seeing a Znaeym and a von Gradwitz talking to one another in friendship. And what peace there would be among the forester folk if we ended our feud tonight. And if we choose to make peace among our people there is none other to interfere, no interlopers from outside. . . . You would come and keep the Sylvester night beneath my roof, and I would come and feast on some high day at your castle. . . . I would never fire a shot on your land, save when you invited me as a guest; and you should come and shoot with me down in the marshes where the wildfowl are. In all the countryside there are none that could hinder if we willed to make peace. I never thought to have wanted to do other than hate you all my life, but I think I have changed my mind about things too, this last half-hour. And you offered me your wine-flask . . . Ulrich von Gradwitz, I will be your friend.'

For a space both men were silent, turning over in their minds the wonderful changes that this dramatic reconciliation would bring about. In the cold, gloomy forest, with the wind tearing in fitful gusts through the naked branches and whistling round the tree-trunks, they lay and waited for the help that would now bring release and succour to both parties. And each prayed a private prayer that his men might be the first to arrive, so that he might be the first to show honourable attention to the enemy that had become a friend.

Presently, as the wind dropped for a moment, Ulrich broke silence.

'Let's shout for help,' he said; 'in this lull our voices may carry a little way.'

'They won't carry far through the trees and undergrowth,' said Georg, 'but we can try. Together, then.'

The two raised their voices in a prolonged hunting call.

'Together again,' said Ulrich a few minutes later, after listening in vain for an answering halloo.

'I heard something that time, I think,' said Ulrich.

'I heard nothing but the pestilential wind,' said Georg hoarsely.

There was silence again for some minutes, and then Ulrich gave a joyful cry.

'I can see figures coming through the wood. They are following in the way I came down the hillside.'

Both men raised their voices in as loud a shout as they could muster.

'They hear us! They've stopped. Now they see us. They're running down the hill towards us,' cried Ulrich.

'How many of them are there?' asked Georg.

'I can't see distinctly,' said Ulrich; 'nine or ten.'

'Then they are yours,' said Georg; 'I had only seven out with me.'

'They are making all the speed they can, brave lads,' said Ulrich gladly.

'Are they your men?' asked Georg. 'Are they your men?' he repeated impatiently as Ulrich did not answer.

'No,' said Ulrich with a laugh, the idiotic chattering laugh of a man unstrung with hideous fear.

'Who are they?' asked Georg quickly, straining his eyes to see what the other would gladly not have seen.

'Wolves.'

The Ghost Ship

RICHARD MIDDLETON

Fairfield is a little village lying near the Portsmouth Road about half-way between London and the sea. Strangers who find it by accident now and then, call it a pretty, old-fashioned place; we who live in it and call it home don't find anything very pretty about it, but we should be sorry to live anywhere else. Our minds have taken the shape of the inn and the church and the green, I suppose. At all events we never feel comfortable out of Fairfield.

Of course the Cockneys, with their vasty houses and noise-ridden streets, can call us rustics if they choose, but for all that Fairfield is a better place to live in than London. Doctor says that when he goes to London his mind is bruised with the weight of the houses, and he was a Cockney born. He had to live there himself when he was a little chap, but he knows better now. You gentlemen may laugh – perhaps some of you come from London way – but it seems to me that a witness like that is worth a gallon of arguments.

Dull? Well, you might find it dull, but I assure you that I've listened to all the London yarns you have spun tonight, and they're absolutely nothing to the things that happen at Fairfield. It's because of our way of thinking and minding our own business. If one of your Londoners were set down on the green of a Saturday night when the ghosts of the lads who died in the war keep tryst with the lasses who lie in the churchyard, he couldn't help being curious and interfering, and then the ghosts would go somewhere where it was quieter. But we just let them come and go and don't make any fuss, and in consequence Fairfield is the ghostiest place in all England. Why, I've seen a headless man sitting on the edge of the well in broad daylight, and the children playing about his feet as if he were their father. Take my word for it, spirits know when they are well off as much as human beings.

Still, I must admit that the thing I'm going to tell you about was queer even for our part of the world, where three packs of ghost-hounds hunt regularly during the season, and blacksmith's great-grandfather is busy all night shoeing the dead gentlemen's horses. Now that's a thing that wouldn't happen in London, because of their interfering ways, but blacksmith he lies up aloft and sleeps as quiet as a lamb. Once when he had a bad head he shouted down to them not to make so much noise, and in the morning he found an old guinea left on the anvil as an apology. He wears it on his watch-chain now. But I must get on with my story; if I start telling you about the queer happenings at Fairfield I'll never stop.

It all came of the great storm in the spring of '97, the year that we had two great storms. This was the first one, and I remember it very well, because I found in the morning that it had lifted the thatch of my pigsty into the widow's garden as clean as a boy's kite. When I looked over the hedge, widow – Tom Lamport's widow that was – was prodding for her nasturtiums with a daisy-grubber. After I had watched her for a little I went down to the Fox and Grapes to tell landlord what she had said to me. Landlord he laughed, being a married man and at ease with the sex. 'Come to that,' he said, 'the tempest has blowed something into my field. A kind of a ship I think it would be.'

I was surprised at that until he explained that it was only a ghost-ship and would do no hurt to the turnips. We argued that it had been blown up from the sea at Portsmouth, and then we talked of something else. There were two slates down at the parsonage and a big tree in Lumley's meadow. It was a rare storm.

I reckon the wind had blown our ghosts all over England. They were coming back for days afterwards with foundered horses and as footsore as possible, and they were so glad to get back to Fairfield that some of them walked up the street crying like little children. Squire said that his great grandfather's great-grandfather hadn't looked so dead-beat since the battle of Naseby, and he's an educated man.

What with one thing and another, I should think it was a week before we got straight again, and then one afternoon I met the landlord on the green and he had a worried face. 'I wish you'd come and have a look at that ship in my field,' he said to me; 'it seems to me it's leaning real hard on the turnips. I can't bear thinking what the missus will say when she sees it.'

I walked down the lane with him, and sure enough there was a ship in the middle of his field, but such a ship as no man had seen on the water for three hundred years, let alone in the middle of a turnip-field. It was all painted black and covered with carvings, and there was a great bay window in the stern for all the world like the Squire's drawing-room. There was a crowd of little black cannon on deck and looking out of her portholes, and she was anchored at each end to the hard ground. I have seen the wonders of the world on picture-postcards, but I have never seen anything to equal that.

'She seems very solid for a ghost-ship,' I said, seeing the landlord was bothered.

'I should say it's a betwixt and between,' he answered, puzzling it over, 'but it's going to spoil a matter of fifty turnips, and missus she'll want it moved.' We went up to her and touched the side, and it was as hard as a real ship. 'Now there's folks in England would call that very curious,' he said.

Now I don't know much about ships, but I should think that that ghost-ship weighed a solid two hundred tons, and it seemed to me that she had come to stay, so that I felt sorry for landlord, who was a married man. 'All the horses in Fairfield won't move her out of my turnips,'he said, frowning at her.

Just then we heard a noise on her deck, and we looked up and saw that a man had come out of her front cabin and was looking down at us very peaceably. He was dressed in a black uniform set out with rusty gold lace, and he had a great cutlass by his side in a brass sheath. 'I'm Captain Bartholomew Roberts,' he said, in a gentleman's voice, 'put in for recruits. I seem to have brought her rather far up the harbour.'

'Harbour!' cried landlord; 'why, you're fifty miles from the sea.'

Captain Roberts didn't turn a hair. 'So much as that, is it?' he said coolly. 'Well, it's of no consequence.'

Landlord was a bit upset at this. 'I don't want to be unneighbourly,' he said, 'but I wish you hadn't brought your ship into my field. You see, my wife sets great store on these turnips.'

The captain took a pinch of snuff out of a fine gold box that he pulled out of his pocket, and dusted his fingers with a silk handkerchief in a very genteel fashion. 'I'm only here for a few months,' he said; 'but if a testimony of my esteem would pacify your good lady I should be content,' and with the words he loosed a great gold brooch from the neck of his coat and tossed it down to landlord.

Landlord blushed as red as a strawberry. 'I'm not denying she's fond of jewellery,' he said, 'but it's too much for half a sackful of turnips.' And indeed it was a handsome brooch.

The captain laughed. 'Tut, man,' he said, 'it's a forced sale, and you deserve a good price. Say no more about it;' and nodding good-day to us, he turned on his heel and went into the cabin. Landlord walked back up the lane like a man with a weight off his mind. 'That tempest has blowed me a bit of luck,' he said; 'the missus will be main pleased with that brooch. It's better than blacksmith's guinea, any day.'

'97 was Jubilee year, the year of the second Jubilee, you remember, and we had great doings at Fairfield, so that we hadn't much time to bother about the ghost-ship, though anyhow it isn't our way to meddle in things that don't concern us. Landlord, he saw his tenant once or twice when he was hoeing his turnips and passed the time of day, and landlord's wife wore her new brooch to church every Sunday. But we didn't mix much with the ghosts at any time, all except an idiot lad there was in the village, and he didn't know the difference between a man and a ghost, poor innocent! On Jubilee Day, however, somebody told Captain Roberts why the church bells were ringing, and he hoisted a flag and fired off his guns like a loyal Englishman.'Tis true the guns were shotted, and one of the round shot knocked a hole in Farmer Johnstone's barn, but nobody thought much of that in such a season of rejoicing.

It wasn't till our celebrations were over that we noticed that anything was wrong in Fairfield.'Twas shoemaker who told me first about it one morning at the Fox and Grapes. 'You know my great great-uncle?' he said to me.

'You mean Joshua, the quiet lad,' I answered knowing him well.

'Quiet!' said shoemaker indignantly. 'Quiet you call him, coming home at three o'clock every morning as drunk as a magistrate and waking up the whole house with his noise.'

'Why, it can't be Joshua!' I said, for I knew him for one of the most respectable young ghosts in the village.

'Joshua it is,' said shoemaker; 'and one of these nights he'll find himself out in the street if he isn't careful.'

This kind of talk shocked me, I can tell you, for I don't like to hear a man abusing his own family, and I could hardly believe that a steady youngster like Joshua had taken to drink. But just then in came butcher Aylwin in such a temper that he could hardly drink his beer. 'The young puppy! the young puppy!' he kept on saying; and it was some time before shoemaker and I found out that he was talking about his ancestor that fell at Senlac.

'Drink?' said shoemaker hopefully, for we all like company in our misfortunes, and butcher nodded grimly.

'The young noodle,' he said, emptying his tankard.

Well, after that I kept my ears open, and it was the same story all over the village. There was hardly a young man among all the ghosts of Fairfield who didn't roll home in the small hours of the morning the worse for liquor. I used to wake up in the night and hear them stumble past my house, singing outrageous songs. The worst of it was that we couldn't keep the scandal to ourselves, and the folk at Greenhill began to talk of 'sodden Fairfield' and taught their children to sing a song about us:

Sodden Fairfield, sodden Fairfield, has no use for
bread-and-butter,
Rum for breakfast, rum for dinner, rum for tea, and
rum for supper!

We are easy-going in our village, but we didn't like that.

Of course we soon found out where the young fellows went to get the drink, and landlord was terribly cut up that his tenant should have turned out so badly, but his wife wouldn't hear of parting with the brooch, so that he couldn't give the Captain notice to quit. But as time went on, things grew from bad to worse, and at all hours of the day you would see those young reprobates sleeping it off on the village green. Nearly every afternoon a ghost-wagon used to jolt down to the ship with a lading of rum, and though the older ghosts seemed inclined to give the Captain's hospitality the go-by, the youngsters were neither to hold nor to bind.

So one afternoon when I was taking my nap I heard a knock at the door, and there was parson looking very serious, like a man with a job before him that he didn't altogether relish. 'I'm going down to talk to the Captain about all this drunkenness in the village, and I want you to come with me,' he said straight out.

I can't say that I fancied the visit much myself, and I tried to hint to parson that as, after all, they were only a lot of ghosts, it didn't very much matter.

'Dead or alive, I'm responsible for their good conduct,' he said, 'and I'm going to do my duty and put a stop to this continued disorder., And you are coming with me, John Simmons.' So I went, parson being a persuasive kind of man.

We went down to the ship, and as we approached her I could see the Captain tasting the air on deck. When he saw parson he took off his hat very politely, and I can tell you that I was relieved to find that he had a proper respect for the cloth. Parson acknowledged his salute and spoke out stoutly enough. 'Sir, I should be glad to have a word with you.'

'Come on board, sir; come on board,'said the Captain, and I could tell by his voice that he knew why we were there. Parson and I climbed up an uneasy kind of ladder, and the Captain took us into the great cabin at the back of the ship, where the bay-window was. It was the most wonderful place you ever saw in your life, all full of gold and silver plate, swords with jewelled scabbards, carved oak chairs, and great chests that look as though they were bursting with guineas. Even parson was surprised, and he did not shake his head very hard when the Captain took down some silver cups and poured us out a drink of rum. I tasted mine, and I don't mind saying that it changed my view of things entirely. There was nothing betwixt and between about that rum, and I felt that it was ridiculous to blame the lads for drinking too much of stuff like that. It seemed to fill my veins with honey and fire.

Parson put the case squarely to the Captain, but I didn't listen much to what he said; I was busy sipping my drink and looking through the window at the fishes swimming to and fro over landlord's turnips. Just then it seemed the most natural thing in the world that they should be there, though afterwards, of course, I could see that that proved it was a ghost-ship.

But even then I thought it was queer when I saw a drowned sailor float by in the thin air with his hair and beard all full of bubbles. It was the first time I had seen anything quite like that at Fairfield.

All the time I was regarding the wonders of the deep parson was telling Captain Roberts how there was no peace or rest in the village owing to the curse of drunkenness, and what a bad example the youngsters were setting to the older ghosts. The Captain listened very attentively, and only put in a word now and then about boys being boys and young men sowing their wild oats. But when parson had finished his speech he filled up our silver cups and said to parson, with a flourish, 'I should be sorry to cause trouble anywhere where I have been made welcome, and you will be glad to hear that I put to sea tomorrow night. And now you must drink me a prosperous voyage.' So we all stood up and drank the toast with honour, and that noble rum was like hot oil in my veins.

After that Captain showed us some of the curiosities he had brought back from foreign parts, and we were greatly amazed, though afterwards I couldn't clearly remember what they were. And then I found myself walking across the turnips with parson, and I was telling him of the glories of the deep that I had seen through the window of the ship. He turned on me severely. 'If I were you, John Simmons,' he said, 'I should go straight home to bed.' He has a way of putting things that wouldn't occur to an ordinary man, has parson, and I did as he told me.

Well, next day it came on to blow, and it blew harder and harder, till about eight o'clock at night I heard a noise and looked out into the garden. I dare say you won't believe me, it seems a bit tall even to me, but the wind had lifted the thatch of my pigsty into the widow's garden a second time. I thought I wouldn't wait to hear what the widow had to say about it, so I went across the green to the Fox and Grapes, and the wind was so strong that I danced along on tiptoe like a girl at the fair. When I got to the inn landlord had to help me shut the door; it seemed as though a dozen goats were pushing against it to come in out of the storm.

'It's a powerful tempest,' he said, drawing the beer. 'I hear there's a chimney down at Dickory End.'

'It's a funny thing how these sailors know about the weather,' I answered. 'When Captain said he was going tonight, I was thinking it would take a capful of wind to carry the ship back to sea, but now here's more than a capful.'

'Ah, yes,' said landlord, 'it's tonight he goes true enough, and, mind you, though he treated me handsome over the rent, I'm not sure it's a loss to the village. I don't hold with gentrice who fetch their drink from London instead of helping local traders to get their living.'

'But you haven't got any rum like his,' I said, to draw him out.

His neck grew red above his collar, and I was afraid I'd gone too far; but after a while he got his breath with a grunt.

'John Simmons,' he said, 'if you've come down here this windy night to talk a lot of fool's talk, you've wasted a journey.'

Well, of course, then I had to smooth him down with praising his rum, and Heaven forgive me for swearing it was better than Captain's. For the like of that rum no living lips have tasted save mine and parson's. But somehow or other I brought landlord round, and presently we must have a glass of his best to prove its quality.

'Beat that if you can!' he cried, and we both raised our glasses to our mouths, only to step half-way and look at each other in amaze. For the wind that had been howling outside like an outrageous dog had all of a sudden turned as melodious as the carol-boys of a Christmas Eve.

'Surely that's not my Martha,' whispered landlord; Martha being his great-aunt that lived in the loft overhead.

We went to the door, and the wind burst it open so that the handle was driven clean into the plaster of the wall. But we didn't think about that at the time; for over our heads, sailing very comfortably through the windy stars, was the ship that had passed the summer in landlord's field. Her portholes and her bay-window were blazing with lights, and there was a noise of singing and fiddling on her decks. 'He's gone,' shouted landlord above the storm, 'and he's taken half the village with him!' I could only nod in answer, not having lungs like bellows of leather.

In the morning we were able to measure the strength of the storm, and over and above my pigsty there was damage enough wrought in the village to keep us busy. True it is that the children had to break down no branches for the firing that autumn, since the wind had strewn the woods with more than they could carry away. Many of our ghosts were scattered abroad, but this time very few came back, all the young men having sailed with Captain; and not only ghosts, for a poor half-witted lad was missing, and we reckoned that he had stowed himself away or perhaps shipped as cabin-boy, not knowing any better.

What with the lamentations of the ghost-girls and the grumblings of families who had lost an ancestor, the village was upset for a while, and the funny thing was that it was the folk who had complained most of the carryings-on of the youngsters, who made most noise now that they were gone. I hadn't any sympathy with shoemaker or butcher, who ran about saying how much they missed their lads, but it made me grieve to hear the poor bereaved girls calling their lovers by name on the village green at nightfall. It didn't seem fair to me that they should have lost their men a second time, after giving up life in order to join them, as like as not. Still, not even a spirit can be sorry for ever, and after a few months we made up our mind that the folk who had sailed in the ship were never coming back, and we didn't talk about it any more.

And then one day, I dare say it would be a couple of years after, when the whole business was quite forgotten, who should come trapesing along the road from Portsmouth but the daft lad who had gone away with the ship, without waiting till he was dead to become a ghost. You never saw such a boy as that in all your life. He had a great rusty cutlass hanging to a string at his waist, and he was tattooed all over in fine colours, so that even his face looked like a girl's sampler. He had a handkerchief in his hand full of foreign shells and old-fashioned pieces of small money, very curious, and he walked up to the well outside his mother's house and drew himself a drink as if he had been nowhere in particular.

The worst of it was that he had come back as soft-headed as he went, and try as we might we couldn't get anything reasonable out of him. He talked a lot of gibberish about keel-hauling and walking the plank and crimson murders – things which a decent sailor should know nothing about, so that it seemed to me that for all his manners Captain had been more of a pirate than a gentleman mariner. But to draw sense out of that boy was as hard as picking cherries off a crab-tree. One silly tale he had that he kept on drifting back to, and to hear him you would have thought that it was the only thing that happened to him in his life. 'We was at anchor,' he would say, 'off an island called the Basket of Flowers, and the sailors had caught a lot of parrots and we were teaching them to swear. Up and down the decks, up and down the decks, and the language they used was dreadful. Then we looked up and saw the masts of the Spanish ship outside the harbour. Outside the harbour they were, so we threw the parrots into the sea and sailed out to fight. And all the parrots were drownded in the sea and the language they used was dreadful.' That's the sort of boy he was, nothing but silly talk of parrots when we asked him about the fighting. And we never had a chance of teaching him better, for two days after he ran away again, and hasn't been seen since.

That's my story, and I assure you that things like that are happening in Fairfield all the time. The ship has never come back, but somehow as people grow older they seem to think that one of these windy nights she'll come sailing in over the hedges with all the lost ghosts on board. Well, when she comes, she'll be welcome. There's one ghost-lass that has never grown tired of waiting for her lad to return. Every night you'll see her out on the green, straining her poor eyes with looking for the mast-lights among the stars. A faithful lass you'd call her, and I'm thinking you'd be right.

Landlord's field wasn't a penny worse for the visit, but they do say that since then the turnips that have been grown in it have tasted of rum.

The Lifting of the Veil

DERMOT O'BYRNE

I think that in the lives of all men there must be fleeting moments invested by the imagination from some intangible cause with a vast and awe-inspiring significance out of all proportion to the actual event. Some simple gesture of the friend with whom we are conversing, the lifting of a hand or drooping of the eyelids, seems for one dusky-vestured and winged instant of higher import than the beacon-flares of the trafficking world and the roar of nations rushing to change or ruin. For in such an instant the veil of enchantment that was woven about our memories in the cave of birth is lifted, only to fall again, alas! before our vision has time to become accustomed to the light that broods upon eternal things. We feel how delicate is the adjustment of external conditions at such a point in time, conscious that another almost exactly similar circumstance would have been empty of any hidden meaning; that because the curled flame of the firelight flickered in just such intensity, hue, and direction, and because that shoulder was turned at precisely that angle and no other, we have become aware of a mystery that would else have slumbered for ever in the mist-hung hollows of that land where time is not. We feel too a certain irritation, mingled with sadness, that such occasions of insight necessarily take us all unready, apprehending that were only a moment of warning and preparation granted to us we should be able easily to wrest the meaning from the lovely or tragic wonder that for a hand's turn hovers in pale radiance on the threshold of the mind.

On very rare occasions it happens, perchance to some men to be able to seize for a fraction of a second the hem of the departing dream, and between the clouds of its twilight hair to catch a half-glimpse of those fateful eyes before they fade again into the folded shadows of the ages.

I have to tell of an experience that occurred to myself a few months ago, an incident of beauty and fear that I shall not forget as long as I live. One autumn. day I wandered with my gun among the hills that surround my Donegal home. All the previous night it had rained and a savage sou'wester had sacked the rocky bastions of the bare glens and plundered fruitlessly among the withered roots of heather and bracken. In the early morning the rain and wind had ceased;

leaving a dull lifeless sky and a sodden earth, veiled in silver and tremulous webs of moisture.

Where I wandered high up in the hills the aspect of the world on that sullen dusky day possessed that strange quality of numbness and stagnation peculiar to certain November mornings in remote places. This atmosphere of unreality lasted all day, heightened later by a light fog that steamed up from the dank earth rendering the fantastic features of inanimate nature, that from hour to hour were almost my only companions, still more illusive. The silence was near to becoming terrifying. All the day scarcely a bird rose and of these I was able to account for very few, for I am a poor shot at the best of times and the shifting blight of which I have spoken rendered the conditions for successful sport very precarious.

In the early evening I began to be oppressed by the sterile desolation and the closeness of the air. Not a feathered thing nor even a rabbit had I sighted for more than an hour and I decided that for this day at least I had had enough of it, and though I was not very certain of my exact whereabouts I set off, as I supposed, in the direction of home.

After plunging downhill through the heavy heather for half an hour or so, sometimes stumbling with a jarring shock into miniature fissures of rock treacherously concealed by the overgrowth of rotting ferns, I became very hot and thirsty, my clothes irritated my skin maddeningly, and I experienced quite painful pricking sensations in my brow and temples. Yet in spite of my urgent need of water this particular hillside, notwithstanding the wet weather, was entirely lacking in any streams or rills.

It was becoming rapidly darker and not knowing my direction very clearly I could not afford to rest. The mist was denser now and filled with a thin dust-like rain, so fine that it seemed scarcely to possess the quality of moisture. To my melancholy mood the pale wall of vapour, ever constant yet ever dissolving above the brown heather immediately before my feet, became invested with a suggestion of sorrowful eternity, and suddenly my imagination became a prey to that strange panic that sometimes comes to young people waking alone in the stillness of night, when the silence echoes nothing to the soul's cry of desire but the beatings of the heart that mark the ebbing of our days. And in the darkness and the loneliness the pulsations of that little time-piece seem so fluttering and feeble and the hours and years that they count so monotonous and grey – a ceaseless pitiful rain of ashes and dust compared with the fiery fantasies we have dreamed, so that within us the desire becomes an agony to live for a single hour with all the might of the imagination, to drown our beings in the proud sunlit tumult of one instant of utter realisation even though it consume us utterly.

At last, just as complete darkness was falling and I was beginning to be seriously alarmed at the prospect of spending the night on the dripping earth without overcoat or covering of any kind, I came upon a solitary cabin, its light breaking through the obscurity startlingly like the eye of some wild animal. I hastened towards it and, picking my way through the evil-smelling morass that surrounded it, knocked at the half-door. Hearing a soft reply that sounded like an invitation to come in, I unhooked the latch and entered the house. It was full of smoke penetrated with the hard glare of a newly-lighted and malodorous lamp. Becoming accustomed to the atmosphere I saw that there were but two occupants of the room. An old woman was crouching forward over the fire, sitting rather precariously upon a rickety kitchen chair and vaguely stretching out her thin speckled and purple-veined hands to the blaze. Her profile was toward me lit dimly by the firelight and I could see that she was very old, the teeth fallen away and the blinking and probably nearly blind eyes embedded in folds of loose skin seamed with a network of wrinkles picked out sharply in the drifted turf-dust of years. The other was a young girl, perhaps the old woman's granddaughter, who was standing in the middle of the uneven mud floor as I entered. The lamplight streamed from immediately behind her, and the only thing about her that I could distinguish clearly was the loose cloud of dark hair which fluttered out from her head and netted the light fantastically. The heavy blue wreaths of smoke swathed her almost tangibly, giving her slight figure a strangely unreal appearance.

'How far am I from Glen?' I inquired, speaking towards the vague shape of the younger woman.

'Four Irish miles,' she replied, as a renewed burst of smoke from the chimney enfolded her in even denser obscurity.

'Is this Meenaveen?' I asked.

'No, but Cúléinean,' said the lips that I could not see, though they were no more than a couple of yards distant from me.

'Can I have a cup of milk?' I said. 'I'm perished with thirst.'

'You can surely. Let you sit up to the fire and rest yourself a wee while.'

She turned towards the dresser, disturbing the sea of smoke in which she seemed to float into a storm that curled up in fantastic tongues and eddies behind her, and then, sucked into the draught between chimney and door, circled for an instant and flowed out in a thin stream into the night.

I laid my gun and bag on the table by the window and sat upon the edge myself, glancing at the old woman whose red-rimmed eyes still blinked over the belching fireplace. She made no motion and indeed seemed wholly unconscious of the presence of a stranger. I addressed some remark to her, but still she did not stir. From the dresser I heard the welcome sound of the milk bubbling into the cup.

'That one's doting,' said the girl, shortly. 'She be's "*deef*," too. She wouldn't heed not if the hill itself would fall in. Here's the milk for yez now.'

She came across to me, approaching from the further end of the table so that the light of the lamp fell directly upon her, her slender form causing a new tumult in the blue billows of smoke.

Then with a sudden catch at my heart I saw that this girl was beautiful, with the proud, sorrowful, maddening loveliness that one associates with dreams of Deirdre or Blanaid or 'the star woman' that haunted the *aisling* of many a half-starved Munster poet of a century or two ago. My hand trembled a little as I took the cup from her so that a few drops spilled on the muddy floor, startling a hen that scuttled from under the table to the opposite corner of the kitchen.

'Sláinte mháith agat,' said the girl unconcernedly, and then suddenly became strangely serious, staring at me with a curious expression of dawning anxiety and embarrassment. I drank the milk at one gulp, looking over the rim of the cup into her eyes, which never left mine though the lids fluttered. Her lips were parted a little and her breathing seemed rather short. She appeared to be afraid of something. I felt her nervous mood intensely.

'What is the matter?' I said, and found that I had not my voice under complete control.

'Arú, nothing,' she murmured, still staring as though hypnotized. 'Sure I don't know. It's quare, so it is— ' She dropped her eyes with a visible effort.

'Will you be taking some more milk?' she added hurriedly and gasping slightly.

I shook my head and handed the cup back to her. I could nowise understand the fancy that gripped me irresistibly – the presentiment that something very frail was being strained to breaking-point, that this desolate day of dimness and mist was about to culminate in a blaze of such light as never was on land or sea.

She put out her right arm, the sleeve of which was turned back above the elbow, and suddenly my whole consciousness – not sight alone, but as it seemed every faculty of my being – became feverishly centred upon that movement. I suppose her gesture was quite rapid in reality, but an instant came when the feeble light of the lamp gleamed along the white curve of her forearm as she stretched it toward me to take the cup. I saw the silky texture of her skin and even the soft down at the sides, and in that flashing moment my thought became a whirling confusion and I seemed to hear a voice within me say with extraordinary distinctness, 'This has happened before!' 'When? How? Where?' my memory cried back in a kind of agony.

Then all at once I remembered that evening – two thousand years ago when I, almost the only survivor of our little army, having fled all through the autumn day from the place where my king had been slain in that terrible and splendid fight in the gap, groped my way half-fainting into our own liss.

I was bleeding from two wounds, one from the blow of an axe in the thigh, which was not very severe, for the black Connaught pig who dealt it had slipped in some blood as he struck at me and there was little weight behind his arm. (Ho ro! I remember the gulp he gave, like a drunken laugh, when I drove the *miodog* between his thick shoulder-blades.) My other hurt was a fearful spear-thrust above the right eye. Also in the midst of the battle the sharp edges of the golden torque, which King Forgael had given me because I had made a great chant in his praise, had been hammered into the hollow above my breast-bone and one of the rays had broken off against the bone so that a fragment remained embedded in the flesh which had swollen up and closed over it. Och! the misery of that fevered wandering through bog and heather, with the blood and sweat oozing into my eyes and the fires that seemed to blaze in my throat and breast and to roar and spit upwards into my brain, and the sick throbbing and ache whenever I turned my head! Towards the end of the day, too, I fancied in my delirium that the heavy war-harp strapped round my shoulders was the moon, with which the gods had burdened me until the end of time. I remembered then how I found myself at last in the grianan of Forgael's daughter, Etain, who was my secret love, and how she had brought me a cup of milk just as she did a moment ago, and how even in my fever my heart had sung and I seeing the light of the smoky rushes gleam golden along the smooth skin of her beautiful fore-arm. But then – that time – she had thrown the cup among the reeds that littered the floor and had caught me in her arms and had caressed my cheeks and eyelids with their marble coolness, and I remembered how the touch of her flesh against my burning face seemed to my bewildered imagination like the sound of the bell-branch shaken in the turmoil of dispute. Afterwards she had kissed me over and over with little soft moaning cries until I swooned away, stifled with the weight of her black hair that fell all about my face and mouth.

Then suddenly there returned to me the remembrance of how in the evening, having arrayed me in my green singing-robe and placed the great war-harp in my hands, they had slain me in order that my king might not go comfortless without music and singing in the land of shadows.

'Etain,' I heard my lips whisper in that memory of tragic death, as though the word were pronounced by another person at an immeasurable distance, and suddenly I felt her hand touch mine as she grasped the cup to take it from me.

We must both have started at the contact, for the cup slipped between our fingers and smashed to atoms on the ground. In its fall the veil of enchantment seemed to be dragged down again, for instantly I discovered that the girl's eyes had left mine and were fixed rather vacantly upon the scattered fragments of crockery on the floor. The exigencies of the present situation called to me, time reasserted itself again, and I suddenly became aware of our social distinctions.

'I am so sorry,' I said. 'It was clumsy of me. You must let me pay for that cup.'

The girl looked up at the sound of my voice. Her eyes were distended and she was very pale, and then I realized that until that moment she had been quite unconscious of the trivial accident which had just occurred.

'You will not then,' she answered with a certain haughtiness, though her voice shook. 'Sure, it was my own fault. I'm all thumbs tonight. Something come on my two eyes. It's quare, I'm thinking.'

She laughed, nervously clasping her hands together. Then she raised her lashes for a moment, but at once dropped them again in confusion.

'What is quare?' said I cruelly, but I could not help myself.

'I don't know, I tell you. I thought a while back – I thought— '

She plucked at her apron for a moment and it seemed to me that I detected the glisten of tears on her dark lashes.

'*Arú*, it's all foolishness,' she said sharply and impatiently, though there was a break in the last word as if it caught in her throat. She glanced up at me and her cheek flushed with sudden anger and bitterness. 'Sure, I've no learning to be telling a high-up fella' the like of yez. Maybe you're thinking you're getting quare gaming, and you tormenting a poor lonely girl.' She turned away as if ashamed at her loss of control, and continued in a softened tone and carefully avoiding my gaze, 'You'll have a right to be stepping out from this now, sir, if you've a mind to be in the Glen before night.'

There was almost a sound of entreaty in her words. She stared at me again helplessly, and her eyes pleaded with me, the mute voices of a soul tormented with nervous excitement and bewildered, utterly uncomprehending emotion. She appeared to be trembling from head to foot and it was evident that I distressed her miserably. Yet her tragic beauty called to me out of the wrecks and sundowns of ancient years.

If only I had some clue as to how much of the truth she had divined and whether she had any clear vision through the whirlwind of the centuries of that sombre and beautiful past that she and I had shared together. But I was inclined to think that it was her very lack of certain knowledge that tortured her, that she was in agonizing dread of the immensity of the burning and haunted darkness that she felt enveloped her soul in that hour, something that had nothing to do with either the heaven or hell of her religious faith.

Pity overwhelmed me and I felt that it would be impossible to trouble her further.

'I will go now,' I said as soothingly as I could, 'but will you tell me your name first?'

She was on the point of answering me when something stirred in the smoky obscurity behind her.

'Mary,' croaked the hoarse and peevish voice of the old woman. 'Come here, will you? Who's yon fella' you're plubbering with? I tell you, you have me bothered entirely with your chat, ever and always, with this one and that. Och! musha! musha! Amn't I the pity of the world, and I left to die for want of a cup of tay?'

The girl gave vent to a gasping sigh of obvious relief. '*Arú*, I'm coming,' she shouted over her shoulder with a kind of cheerful savagery, and then turning to me, a red spot burning in either cheek:

'Mary Cunnigan's my name,' she said swiftly. 'The road's just below now, down the *bothirín* yonder. Let you keep on over the old bridge at Stradearg crossroads. Safe home now. You'd best be moving or it'll fail you to make Glen before the clouds of night are on ye.'

She turned to the old woman, and gathering up my things abstractedly I stumbled out into the dripping darkness.

I never saw her again, for, as I heard later; her grandmother died a few days after my visit and the girl emigrated the following week to America.

The Tarn

HUGH WAPOLE

I

As Foster moved unconsciously across the room, bent towards the book-case, and stood leaning forward a little, choosing now one book, now another, with his eyes, his host, seeing the muscles of the back of his thin, scraggy neck stand out above his low flannel collar, thought of the ease with which he could squeeze that throat, and the pleasure, the triumphant, lustful pleasure, that such an action would give him.

The low, white-walled, white-ceilinged room was flooded the mellow, kindly Lakeland sun. October is a wonderful month in the English Lakes, golden, rich, and perfumed, slow suns moving through apricot-tinted skies to ruby evening glories; the shadows lie then thick about that beautiful country, in dark purple patches, in long web-like patterns of silver gauze in thick splotches of amber and grey. The clouds pass in galleons across the mountains, now veiling, now revealing, now descending with ghost-like armies to the very breast of the plains, suddenly rising to the softest of blue skies and lying thin in lazy languorous colour.

Fenwick's cottage looked across to Low Fells; on his right, seen through side windows, sprawled the hills above Ullswater.

Fenwick looked at Foster's back and felt suddenly sick, so that he sat down, veiling his eyes for a moment with his hand. Foster had come up there, come all the way from London, to explain. It was so like Foster to want to explain, to want to put things right. For how many years had he known Foster? Why, for twenty at least, and during all those years Foster had been for ever determined to put things right with everybody. He could never bear to be disliked; he hated that anyone should think ill of him; he wanted everyone to be his friends. That was one reason, perhaps, why Foster had got on so well, had prospered so in his career; one reason, too, why Fenwick had not.

For Fenwick was the opposite of Foster in this. He did not want friends, he certainly did not care that people should like him – that is people for whom, for one reason or another, he had contempt – and he had contempt for quite a number of people.

Fenwick looked at that long, thin, bending back and felt his knees tremble. Soon Foster would turn round and that high, reedy voice would pipe out something about the books. 'What jolly books you have, Fenwick!' How many, many times in the long watches of the night, when Fenwick could not sleep, had he heard that pipe sounding close there – yes, in the very shadows of his bed! And how many times had Fenwick replied to it: 'I hate you! You are the cause of my failure in life! You have been in my way always. Always, always, always! Patronising and pretending, and in truth showing others what a poor thing you thought me, how great a failure, how conceited a fool! I know. You can hide nothing from me! I can hear you!'

For twenty years now Foster had been persistently in Fenwick's way. There had been that affair, so long ago now, when Robins had wanted a sub-editor for his wonderful review, the *Parthenon*, and Fenwick had gone to see him and they had had a splendid talk. How magnificently Fenwick had talked that day; with what enthusiasm he had shown Robins (who was blinded by his own conceit, anyway) the kind of paper the *Parthenon* might be; how Robins had caught his own enthusiasm, how he had pushed his fat body about the room, crying: 'Yes, yes, Fenwick – that's fine! That's fine indeed!' – and then how, after all, Foster had got that job.

The paper had only lived for a year or so, it is true, but the connection with it had brought Foster into prominence just as it might have brought Fenwick!

Then, five years later, there was Fenwick's novel, *The Bitter Aloe* – the novel upon which he had spent three years of blood-and-tears endeavour and then, in the very same week of publication, Foster brings out *The Circus*, the novel that made his name; although, Heaven knows, the thing was poor enough sentimental trash. You may say that one novel cannot kill another – but can it not? Had not *The Circus* appeared would not that group of London know-alls – that conceited, limited, ignorant, self-satisfied crowd, who nevertheless can do, by their talk, so much to affect a book's good or evil fortunes – have talked about *The Bitter Aloe* and so forced it into prominence? As it was, the book was stillborn and *The Circus* went on its prancing, triumphant way.

After that there had been many occasions – some small, some big and always in one way or another that thin, scraggy body of Foster's was interfering with Fenwick's happiness.

The thing had become, of course, an obsession with Fenwick. Hiding up there in the heart of the Lakes, with no friends, almost no company, and very little money, he was given too much to brooding over his failure. He *was* a failure and it was not his own fault. How could it be his own fault with his talent and his brilliance? It was the fault of modern life and its lack of culture, the fault of the stupid material mess that made up the intelligence of human beings – and the fault of Foster.

Always Fenwick hoped that Foster would keep away from him. He did not know what he would not do did he see the man. And then one day, to his amazement, he received a telegram:

> *Passing through this way. May I stop with you Monday and Tuesday ? – Giles Foster.*

Fenwick could scarcely believe his eyes, and then – from curiosity, from cynical contempt, from some deeper, more mysterious motive that he dared not analyse – he had telegraphed – *Come.*

And here the man was. And he had come – would you believe it? – to 'put things right.' He had heard from Hamlin Eddis that Fenwick was hurt with him, had some kind of grievance.

'I didn't like to feel that, old man, and so I thought I'd just stop by and have it out with you, see what the matter was, and put it right.'

Last night after supper Foster had tried to put it right. Eagerly, his eyes like a good dog's who is asking for a bone that he knows he thoroughly deserves, he had held out his hand and asked Fenwick to 'say what was up.'

Fenwick simply had said that nothing was up; Hamlin Eddis was a damned fool.

'Oh, I'm glad to hear that!' Foster had cried, springing up out of his chair and putting his hand on Fenwick's shoulder. 'I'm glad of that, old man. I couldn't bear for us not to be friends. We've been friends so long.'

Lord! How Fenwick hated him at that moment!

II

'What a jolly lot of books you have!' Foster turned round and looked at Fenwick with eager, gratified eyes. 'Every book here is interesting! I like your arrangement of them, too, and those open bookshelves – it always seems to me a shame to shut up books behind glass!'

Foster came forward and sat down quite close to his host. He even reached forward and laid his hand on his host's knee. 'Look here! I'm mentioning it for the last time – positively! But I do want to make quite certain. There is nothing wrong between us, is there, old man? I know you assured me last night, but I just want. . . .'

Fenwick looked at him and, surveying him, felt suddenly an exquisite pleasure of hatred. He liked the touch of the man's hand on his knee; he himself bent forward a little and, thinking how agreeable it would be to push Foster's eyes in, deep, deep into his head, crunching them, smashing them to purple, leaving the empty, staring bloody sockets, said:

'Why, no. Of course not. I told you last night. What could there be?'

The hand gripped the knee a little more tightly.

'I am so glad! That's splendid! Splendid! I hope you won't think me ridiculous, but I've always had an affection for you ever since I can remember. I've always wanted to know you better. I've admired your talent so greatly. That novel of yours – the – the – the one about the aloe – '

'The Bitter Aloe?'

'Ah, yes, that was it. That was a splendid book. Pessimistic, of course, but still fine. It ought to have done better. I re member thinking so at the time.'

'Yes, it ought to have done better.'

'Your time will come, though. What I say is that good work always tells in the end.'

'Yes, my time will come.'

The thin, piping voice went on:

'Now, I've had more success than I deserved. Oh, yes, I have. You can't deny it. I'm not falsely modest. I mean it I've got some talent, of course, but not so much as people say. And you! Why, you've got so *much* more than they acknowledge. You have, old man. You have indeed. Only – I do hope you'll forgive my saying this – perhaps you haven't advanced quite as you might have done. Living up here, shut away here, closed in by all these mountains, in this wet climate – always raining – why, you're out of things! You don't see people, don't talk and discover what's really going on. Why, look at me!'

Fenwick turned round and looked at him.

'Now, I have half the year in London, where one gets the best of everything, best talk, best music, best plays; and then I'm three months abroad, Italy or Greece or somewhere, and then three months in the country. Now, that's an ideal arrangement. You have everything that way.'

Italy or Greece or somewhere!

Something turned in Fenwick's breast, grinding grinding, grinding. How he had longed, oh, how passionately, for just one week in Greece, two days in Sicily! Sometimes he had thought that he might run to it, but when it had come to the actual counting of the pennies. . . . And how this fool, this fat-head, this self-satisfied, conceited, patronising. . . .

He got up, looking out at the golden sun.

'What do you say to a walk?' he suggested. 'The sun will last for a good hour yet.'

III

As soon as the words were out of his lips he felt as though some one else had said them for him. He even turned half-round to see whether any one else were there. Ever since Foster's arrival on the evening before he had been conscious of this sensation. A walk? Why should he take Foster for a walk, show him his beloved country, point out those curves and lines and hollows, the broad silver shield of Ullswater, the cloudy purple hills hunched like blankets about the knees of some recumbent giant? Why? It was as though be had turned round to some one behind him, and had said 'You have some further design in this.'

They started out. The road sank abruptly to the lake, then the path ran between trees at the water's edge. Across the lake tones of bright yellow light, crocus-hued, rode upon the blue. The hills were dark.

The very way that Foster walked bespoke the man. He was always a little ahead of you, pushing his long, thin body along with little eager jerks, as though, did he not hurry, he would miss something that would be immensely to his advantage. He talked, throwing words over his shoulder to Fenwick as you throw crumbs of bread to a robin.

'Of course I was pleased. Who would not be? After all, it's a new prize. They've only been awarding it for a year or two, but it's gratifying – really gratifying – to secure it. When I opened the envelope and found the cheque there – well, you could have knocked me down with a feather. You could, indeed. Of course, a hundred pounds isn't much. But it's the honour. . . .'

Whither were they going? Their destiny was as certain as though they had no free will. Free will? There is no free will. All is Fate. Fenwick suddenly laughed aloud.

Foster stopped.

'Why, what is it?'

'What's what?'

'You laughed.'

'Something amused me.'

Foster slipped his arm through Fenwick's.

'It *is* jolly to be walking along together like this, arm in arm, friends. I'm a sentimental man. I won't deny it. What I say is that life is short and one must love one's fellow-beings, or where is one? You live too much alone, old man.' He squeezed Fenwick's arm. 'That's the truth of it.'

It was torture, exquisite, heavenly torture. It was wonderful to feel that thin, bony arm pressing against his. Almost you could hear the beating of that other heart. Wonderful to feel that arm and the temptation to take it in your hands and to bend it and twist it and then to hear the bones crack . . . crack . . . crack. . . . Wonderful to feel that temptation rise through one's body like boiling water and yet not to yield to it. For a moment Fenwick's hand touched Foster's. Then he drew himself apart.

'We're at the village. This is the hotel where they all come in the summer. We turn off at the right here. I'll show you my tarn.'

IV

'Your tarn?' asked Foster. 'Forgive my ignorance, but what *is* a tarn exactly?'

'A tarn is a miniature lake, a pool of water lying in the lap of the hill. Very quiet, lovely, silent. Some of them are immensely deep.'

'I should like to see that.'

'It is some little distance – up a rough road. Do you mind?'

'Not a bit. I have long legs.'

'Some of them are immensely deep – unfathomable – nobody touched the bottom – but quiet, like glass, with shadows only— '

'Do you know, Fenwick, I have always been afraid of water – I've never learnt to swim. I'm afraid to go out of my depth. Isn't that ridiculous? But it is all because at my private school, years ago, when I was a small boy, some big fellows took me and held me with my head under the water and nearly drowned me. They did indeed. They went farther than they meant to. I can see their faces.'

Fenwick considered this. The picture leapt to his mind. He could see the boys – large, strong fellows, probably – and this skinny thing like a frog, their thick hands about his throat, his legs like grey sticks kicking out of the water, their laughter, their sudden sense that something was wrong, the skinny body all flaccid and still. . . .

He drew a deep breath.

Foster was walking beside him now, not ahead of him, as though he were a little afraid and needed reassurance. Indeed, the scene had changed. Before and behind them stretched the uphill path, loose with shale and stones. On their right, on a ridge at the foot of the hill, were some quarries, almost deserted, but the more melancholy in the fading afternoon because a little work still continued there; faint sounds came from the gaunt listening chimneys, a stream of water ran and tumbled angrily into a pool below, once and again a black silhouette, like a question-mark, appeared against the darkening hill.

It was a little steep here, and Foster puffed and blew.

Fenwick hated him the more for that. So thin and spare and still he could not keep in condition! They stumbled, keeping below the quarry, on the edge of the running water, now green, now a dirty white-grey, pushing their way along the side of the hill.

Their faces were set now towards Helvellyn. It rounded the cup of hills, closing in the base and then sprawling to the right.

'There's the tarn!' Fenwick exclaimed; and then added, 'The sun's not lasting as long as I had expected. It's growing dark already.'

Foster stumbled and caught Fenwick's arm.

'This twilight makes the hills look strange-like living men. I can scarcely see my way.'

'We're alone here,' Fenwick answered. 'Don't you feel the stillness? The men will have left the quarry now and gone home. There is no one in all this place but ourselves. If you watch you will see a strange green light steal down over the hills. It lasts for but a moment and then it is dark.

'Ah, here is my tarn. Do you know how I love this place, Foster? It seems to belong especially to me, just as much as all your work and your glory and fame and success seem to belong to you. I have this and you have that. Perhaps in the end we are even, after all. Yes. . . .

'But I feel as though that piece of water belonged to me and I to it, and as though we should never be separated – yes . . . Isn't it black?

'It is one of the deep ones. No one has ever sounded it. Only Helvellyn knows, and one day I fancy that it will take me, too, into its confidence, will whisper its secrets— '

Foster sneezed.

'Very nice. Very beautiful, Fenwick. I like your tarn. Charming. And now let's turn back. That is a difficult walk beneath the quarry. It's chilly, too.'

'Do you see that little jetty there?' Fenwick led Foster by the arm. 'Someone built that out into the water. He had a boat there, I suppose. Come and look down. From the end of the little jetty it looks so deep and the mountains seem to close round.'

Fenwick took Foster's arm and led him to the end of the jetty. Indeed, the water looked deep here. Deep and very black. Foster peered down, then he looked up at the hills that did indeed seem to have gathered close around him. He sneezed again.

'I've caught a cold, I am afraid. Let's turn homewards, Fenwick, or we shall never find our way.'

'Home, then,' said Fenwick, and his hands closed about the thin, scraggy neck. For the instant the head half-turned, and two startled, strangely childish eyes stared; then, with a push that was ludicrously simple, the body was impelled forward, there was a sharp cry, a splash, a stir of something white against the swiftly gathering dusk, again and then again, then far-spreading ripples, then silence.

V

The silence extended. Having enwrapped the tarn, it spread as though with finger on lip to the already quiescent hills. Fenwick shared in the silence. He luxuriated in it. He did not move at all. He stood there looking upon the inky water of the tarn, his arms folded, a man lost in intensest thought. But he was not thinking. He was only conscious of a warm, luxurious relief, a sensuous feeling that was not thought at all.

Foster was gone – that tiresome, prating, conceited, self-satisfied fool! Gone, never to return. The tarn assured him of that. It stared back into Fenwick's face approvingly as though it said: 'You have done well – a clean and necessary job. We have done it together, you and I. I am proud of you.'

He was proud of himself. At last he had done something definite with his life. Thought, eager, active thought, was beginning now to flood his brain. For all these years he had hung around in this place doing nothing but cherish grievances, weak, backboneless – now at last there was action. He drew himself up and looked at the hills. He was proud – and he was cold. He was shivering. He turned up the collar of his coat. Yes, there was that faint green light that always lingered in the shadows of the hills for a brief moment before darkness came. It was growing late. He had better return.

Shivering now so that his teeth chattered, he started off down the path, and then was aware that he did not wish to leave the tam. The tarn was friendly – the only friend he had in all the world. As he stumbled along in the dark this sense of loneliness grew. He was going home to an empty house. There had been a guest in it last night. Who was it? Why, Foster, of course – Foster with his silly laugh and amiable, mediocre eyes. Well, Foster would not be there now. No, he never would be there again.

And suddenly Fenwick started to run. He did not know why, except that, now that he had left the tarn, he was lonely. He wished that he could have stayed there all night, but because it was cold he could not, and so now he was running so that be might be at home with the lights and the familiar furniture – and all the things that he knew to reassure him.

As he ran the shale and stones scattered beneath his feet they made a tittattering noise under him, and someone else seemed to be running too. He stopped, and the other runner also stopped. He breathed in the silence. He was hot now. The perspiration was trickling down his cheeks. He could feel a dribble of it down his back inside his shirt. His knees were pounding. His heart was thumping. And all around him the hills were so amazingly silent, now like india-rubber clouds that you could push in or pull out as you do those india-rubber faces, grey against the night sky of a crystal purple, upon whose surface, like the twinkling eyes of boats at sea, stars were now appearing.

His knees steadied, his heart beat less fiercely, and he began to run again. Suddenly he had turned the corner and was out at the hotel. Its lamps were kindly and reassuring. He walked then quietly along the lakeside path, and had it not been for the certainty that some one was treading behind him he would have been comfortable and at his ease. He stopped once or twice and looked back, and once he stopped and called out, 'Who's there?' Only the rustling trees answered.

He had the strangest fancy, but his brain was throbbing so fiercely that he could not think, that it was the tarn that was following him, the tarn slipping, sliding along the road, being with him so that he should not be lonely. He could almost hear the tarn whisper in his ear: 'We did that together, and so I do not wish you to bear all the responsibility yourself. I will stay with you, so that you are not lonely.'

He climbed down the road towards home, and there were the lights of his house. He heard the gate click behind him as though it were shutting him in. He went into the sitting-room, lighted and ready. There were the books that Foster had admired.

The old woman who looked after him appeared.

'Will you be having some tea, sir?'

'No, thank you, Annie.'

'Will the other gentleman be wanting any?'

'No; the other gentleman is away for the night.'

'Then there will be only one for supper?'

'Yes, only one for supper.'

He sat in the corner of the sofa and fell instantly into a deep slumber.

VI

He woke when the old woman tapped him on the shoulder and told him that supper was served. The room was dark save for the jumping light of two uncertain candles. Those two red candlesticks – how he hated them up there on the mantelpiece! He had always hated them, and now they seemed to him to have something of the quality of Foster's voice – that thin, reedy, piping tone.

He was expecting at every moment that Foster would enter, and yet he knew that he would not. He continued to turn his head towards the door, but it was so dark there that you could not see. The whole room was dark except just there by the fireplace, where the two candlesticks went whining with their miserable twinkling plaint.

He went into the dining-room and sat down to his meal. But he could not eat anything. It was odd – that place by the table where Foster's chair should be. Odd, naked, and made a man feel lonely.

He got up once from the table and went to the window, opened it and looked out. He listened for something. A trickle as of running water, a stir, through the silence, as though some deep pool were filling to the brim. A rustle in the trees, perhaps. An owl hooted. Sharply, as though someone had spoken to him unexpectedly behind his shoulder, he closed the window and looked back, peering under his dark eyebrows into the room.

Later on he went up to bed.

VII

Had he been sleeping, or had he been lying lazily, as one does, half-dozing, half-luxuriously not thinking? He was wide awake now, utterly awake, and his heart was beating with apprehension. It was as though someone had called him by name. He slept always with his window a little open and the blind up. To-night the moonlight shadowed in sickly fashion the objects in his room. It was not a flood of light nor yet a sharp splash, silvering a square, a circle, throwing the rest into ebony darkness. The light was dim, a little green, perhaps, like the shadow that comes over the hills just before dark.

He stared at the window, and it seemed to him that something moved there. Within, or rather against the green-grey light, something silver-tinted glistened. Fenwick stared. It had the look, exactly, of slipping water.

Slipping water! He listened, his head up, and it seemed to him that from beyond the window he caught the stir of water, not running, but rather welling up and up, gurgling with satisfaction as it filled and filled.

He sat up higher in bed, and then saw that down the wallpaper, beneath the window, water was undoubtedly trickling. He could see it lurch to the projecting wood of the sill, pause, and then slip, slither down the incline. The odd thing was that it fell so silently.

Beyond the window there was that odd gurgle, but in the room itself absolute silence. Whence could it come? He saw the line of silver rise and fall as the stream on the window-ledge ebbed and flowed.

He must get up and close the window. He drew his legs above the sheets and blankets and looked down.

He shrieked. The floor was covered with a shining film of water. It was rising. As he looked it had covered half the short stumpy legs of the bed. It rose without a wink, a bubble, a break! Over the sill it poured now in a steady flow, but soundless. Fenwick sat up in the bed, the clothes gathered up to his chin, his eyes blinking, the Adam's apple throbbing like a throttle in his throat.

But he must do something, he must stop this. The water was now level with the seats of the chairs, but still was soundless. Could he but reach the door!

He put down his naked foot, then cried again. The water was icy cold. Suddenly, leaning, staring at its dark unbroken sheen, something seemed to push him forward. He fell. His head, his face was under the icy liquid; it seemed adhesive and, in the heart of its ice, hot like melting wax. He struggled to his feet. The water was breast-high. He screamed again and again. He could see the looking-glass, the row of books, the picture of Dürer's 'Horse,' aloof, impervious. He beat at the water, and flakes of it seemed to cling to him like scales of fish, clammy to his touch. He struggled, ploughing his way towards the door.

The water now was at his neck. Then something had caught him by the ankle.

Something held him. He struggled, crying: 'Let me go! Let me go! I tell you to let me go! I hate you! I hate you! I will not come down to you! I will not— '

The water covered his mouth. He felt that someone pushed in his eyeballs with bare knuckles. A cold hand reached up and caught his naked thigh.

VIII

In the morning the little maid knocked and, receiving no answer, came in, as was her wont, with his shaving-water. What she saw made her scream. She ran for the gardener.

They took the body with its staring, protruding eyes, its tongue sticking out between the clenched teeth, and laid it on the bed.

The only sign of disorder was an overturned water-jug. A small pool of water stained the carpet.

It was a lovely morning. A twig of ivy idly, in the little breeze, tapped the pane.

A Place Of No Return

HUGH B. CAVE

As professor Leslie Carter understood it, there were two kinds of zombies in the Republic of Haiti, and he didn't believe in either.

Accepted even by some of the educated elite was a theory that zombies could be produced through the use of poison. Formula: admister one of several potions known to be capable of inducing a physical condition resembling death. Remove the body from its grave immediately after burial. Revive it. And you had a living creature with a damaged mind who could be trained as a canefield labourer, a household servant, et cetera.

The barefoot peasant believed in zombies of another kind, however, in dead persons brought back to life by a kind of sorcery practised by *bocors*, whose services were always for sale if one had sufficient money.

'So what I want you to do for me, Dieudonne,' said Carter to the old black man standing before him on the pension veranda, 'is take me to where I can see some zombies and talk to them. Do you understand?'

The old man hesitated.

'I am a learned man,' Carter continued patiently. 'I teach anthropology, the science of man and his beliefs, in a renowned American university. And though I am here in your country on a vacation, I look upon my visit as an opportunity to determine once and for all whether zombies really exist.' Smilingly he repeated his favourite phrase: 'Do you understand?'

Dieudonne Malfam solemnly nodded. Having worked for years for a Catholic priest in the village of his birth, he understood Carter's words. All but the hard ones, anyway. He was not sure, however, that he understood what was meant by them.

'Do you have time enough, *m'sieu*, to go with me into the mountains?'

'How much time will it require?'

'Well, if we leave now, we can be in Furcy by mid-afternoon. There we must leave the jeep and walk awhile. You are not against walking?'

Carter had to smile. He was at least twenty years younger than the man who seemed to be questioning his fitness, and at the Ivy League university where he taught he had been jogging at least five miles a day for the past two years. 'I can walk.'

'These will be difficult mountain trails, *m'sieu*.'

'No more so for me than for you. Where will we be sleeping?'

'I will arrange a bed for you. Have no fear.'

'All right,' Carter said. 'Just give me a few minutes to make ready.' And, striding boldly through the pension's drawing room to show the old peasant how well he could walk, he leaped up the stairs two at a time to go to his room.

In the upper hall he encountered the pension's Haitian proprietor, round little Claude Jeannot, and Jeannot said, beaming, 'Ah, Professor Carter. Will the man I obtained for you be satisfactory, do you think?'

'It was not simple, you know,' the proprietor said. 'With you speaking no Creole, you had to have someone who spoke English well enough to understand you. Also someone with a vehicle, for you said you did not wish the expense of a separate car and driver, remember.'

'Dieudonne came in a jeep.'

'He owns it.'

'How could such a man afford to buy a jeep, Jeannot?'

'He has ways of acquiring things, it seems. At any rate, he makes a living with it.'

'How?'

'Well, you are paying him for his services, are you not?'

'We've agreed on two hundred dollars.'

'A thousand *gourdes*, eh? For that he should certainly find you some zombies, *m'sieu*.'

'He'd better,' Carter said darkly. 'Will he, do you think?'

'Do you doubt it?'

'It's just that he seems – well, not too bright.' But then, Carter thought no one he had yet encountered in this Caribbean land of voodoo, sorcery and zombies had seemed really bright. Perhaps he was expecting too much.

In his room Carter tossed into a small overnight bag the few items he thought he might need, added his camera, then counted the money in his billfold. He had a little more than the two hundred American dollars required for Dieudonne. The rest of his money, in traveler's cheques, was locked in the pension safe.

Returning to the ground floor, he found his guide waiting outside in the jeep. The vehicle had seen better days, he observed as he climbed into it. Still, it was probably as clean as some small boy with a rag and a bucket of water had been able to make it. Depositing his bag in the back, he said, 'Aren't you taking anything, Dieudonne?'

'I need nothing, *m'sieu*.'

'These people know you? The ones we're going to?'

'They know me.'

'Well, then,' Carter said loudly, unable to suppress his excitement, 'lets get going, man!'

From the sweltering August heat of Port-au-Prince they first climbed the steep, curving road to Petionville, then the even steeper one to the mountain village of Kenscoff. On the unpaved, almost vertical ladder from there to Furcy, Carter found himself fiercely clinging to various parts of the vehicle as though he were riding a bucking horse.

He had not been to Furcy before. After the shock of the road, which left him nearly breathless, came the awesome view from the height his guide told him was called La Decouverte – The Discovery. *'Deye morne ge morne,'* the old man murmured, quoting an old Haitian proverb. 'Beyond the mountains are mountains.' These, in range after misty range, filled a wilderness extending all the way to the Caribbean Sea.

Now began the walking.

It was not, after all, quite the same as jogging through an Ivy League campus. True, the sea-level heat of Port-au-Prince was gone now, but the trail they followed was demanding. It descended so steeply at times that Carter had to cling to anything his fingers could reach. Then it invariably reversed itself to climb so steeply that he had to crawl.

The old man plodded on without comment, but looked back occasionally to make sure he was being followed. After an hour or so he indicated they should rest.

'You are all right, *m'sieu?*'

'Of course. I'm not used to this kind of hiking, that's all. How much farther have we to go?'

'Two three hours.'

'Well, don't worry about me. I can do anything you can.'

When they stopped again, Carter prolonged the resting time by probing a little into his companion's background. 'How,' he asked, 'did you happen to be given that odd name Dieudonne? It means God-given, doesn't it?'

The old fellow nodded. 'My mother had wanted a child for many years. When it finally happened, she called me that to show her gratitude.'

'Where do you live?'

'Oh, here and there in these mountains. Or in the capital. Or elsewhere, when it suits me.'

'You have no real home, you mean?'

'My home, *m'sieu,* is where I happen to be at the moment.'

Feeling the mountain stillness like a spell, Carter looked about him and said, frowning, 'Doesn't anyone live in these hills?'

'A few, *m'sieu*. Not many.'

'We haven't seen a single village.'

'There are none. Only – well, you will see. Very few visitors come here, of course.'

That must be true, Carter thought with satisfaction. No mere tourist would ever do what he was doing. It would be something for him to talk about when he returned to the States. He must instruct his wife to organize an evening for him to tell about it. His colleagues, her friends among the faculty wives. He would show his color slides. With luck he would have some pictures of 'zombies' – to prove they were not zombies at all.

He spoke about them to this guide when they stopped again to rest – a badly needed halt this time for Carter who was nearing exhaustion. 'Tell me, Dieudonne – what does a zombie look like?'

The old man sat on a fallen pine tree and picked his nose. 'Like you and me, *m'sieu*.'

'Are they dead?'

'Dead but alive.'

'If they look like living persons, how can you know they're zombies?'

'There are signs, *m'sieu*. A lostness in the eyes. A foul smell about them. The way they walk and talk.'

'They can talk.'

'In their own way. Not our way.'

From the boulder onto which he had gratefully lowered his aching body Carter said, 'I think you're putting me on, old man.'

'Pardon, *m'sieu*?'

'There is no such thing as a zombie. We both know it.'

'Would you also say, *m'sieu*, there is no such thing as a *bocor*?'

'Oh, there are sorcerers. I believe that. But their powers are vastly exaggerated. They can't make zombies.'

'Should we turn back, then, *m'sieu*?' Dieudonne asked softly.

'No, no. We've come this far; we'll see it through.'

Half-an-hour later they arrived.

As the old man had warned, it was not a village. The trail wriggled down to a patch of almost level mountainside about two acres in extent, and on the level stood a dozen widely separated huts with wattle-and daub walls and thatch roofs. Most of the ground not given up to the huts was used for growing vegetables. 'These people carry produce to the Iron Market in Port-au-Prince,' Dieudonne explained. 'Beyond the houses, where the land is less level, the gardens are larger.'

'And that is where the zombies are employed?'

'I see that you know more about my people than you have led me to believe, *m'sieu*.'

'I warned you I was a man of learning,' Carter retorted as they trudged side by side toward the largest hut.

'Ah, yes, so you did.'

'And let me warn you now not to try deceiving me about these zombies, friend. If they are not the real thing, you won't be paid, I promise you.'

The old Haitian shot him a sidelong glance out of eyes resembling black opals, but offered no retort.

Outside the hut Dieudonne halted. The door was open but he rapped on it with his bony black knuckles. *'Honneur, compere,'* he called out. 'It is Dieudonne.'

A tall, muscular man of middle age appeared in the doorway, blending with the gloom behind him because the hut had no windows. *'Respect, compere,'* he murmured, then offered Carter a smile of hospitality and spoke in Creole.

Dieudonne answered in the same peasant tongue and, turning to Carter, explained in English, 'Ti-Jean asked who you are, and I have told him you are a man of great learning from America. I said you are here to talk to his zombies and take some photographs.'

'Good. Is he the one who owns the zombies?'

'He is the leader here.'

'Where does he find them? I want to know that, too.'

The old man's shoulders eloquently rose and fell. 'Such a question is not to be asked *m'sieu*.'

'From some local *bocor*, I suppose,' Carter persisted with a smile that was half smirk.

'Perhaps. But let me talk to him now about a place for you to sleep tonight.' Again Dieudonne addressed the muscular man in Creole.

The reply came without hesitation, and the old man was obviously pleased. 'There is an empty house you may use,' he said. 'The man and woman who live there went to the capital with produce yesterday and will not return till Monday. Come, please.'

The hut in question was smaller than Ti-Jean's and had for furniture only a table, two chairs and a bed, all crudely handmade of the Carribbean pine that grew in these mountains. Carter examined the bed and was not happy with its grass-filled mattress and soiled blanket, but was at this point too tired to reject it. 'I believe I'll just rest a little before we do anything else, Dieudonne.'

'Of course, *m'sieu*.'

'Don't let me sleep too long, now, I want to see those zombies at work!'

'I doubt they are working this late, *m'sieu*.'

'What do you mean, late? They work all the time, I've read.'

'Perhaps on moonlit nights, *m'sieu*. But there will be no moon tonight, and the day is already dying.'

Seated on the bed, Carter paused in the act of removing his shoes to look out the open door. Seen through tall pines on a western ridge, the setting sun was a fiery crimson ball that bloodied all in its reach. The day *was* nearly over, he realized. They had walked for an eternity to get here. No wonder he felt an irresistible yearning to sleep.

He lay back and closed his eyes, and knew no more until a sound of drumming awoke him.

The glowing hands of the watch on his wrist said midnight.

Having fallen asleep fully dressed except for his shoes, he had only to put the shoes back on before angrily jerking the hut door open to look for the source of the drumming. He hadn't far to look. In an open space among the peasant houses, glowing lanterns hung from the horizontal branches of a solitary mapou – a tree supposed to possess magical powers, he knew from his extensive reading. Among the mapou's buttressed roots, on a low stool, sat the drummer.

It was the man who, according to Dieudonne, owned the zombies.

In the space lit by the lanterns some twenty persons were dancing, if one could properly call it dancing. They moved in procession very slowly with their knees bent and their shoulders undulating. A voodoo thing? He had read about certain voodoo dances – the *yanvalou*, for instance – but had no way of knowing what this was. At any rate, it was damned inconsiderate of them to be holding such a noisy affair at midnight when they had an important guest so badly in need of sleep.

As Dieudonne had predicted, there was no moon in the black-velvet sky. He was not noticed as he left his doorway and strode toward the dancers. Only when he marched into the lanternlight were they aware of his intrusion.

The drumming dribbled away to silence. The dancing slowed and stopped. Carter went straight to the drummer, in such a way that some of the performers had to stumble out of his path.

'Do you *have* to do this tonight?' he demanded. The fellow spoke no English, of course, but perhaps the anger in his voice. . . .

Suddenly old Dieudonne appeared at his side. 'Something is wrong, *m'sieu*?'

'Of course something is wrong! If I'm to pay these people for a night's sleep here, I want to *sleep*! Tell him that!'

'M'sieu,' the old man gently protested, 'this is a thing they do at times to insure that the crops – '

'I know that, I know it! At least, I can guess. But let them do it after I'm gone!'

Dieudonne gazed at him in silence for a few seconds, perhaps attempting to decide just how resolute he might be. Then, with a shrug, he turned to the man at the drum. Squatting, which made him no taller than the drum itself, he spoke almost inaudibly into Ti-Jean's ear.

Ti-Jean, too, regarded Carter in silence. Then he rose, swung the drum up under an arm, and with a command in Creole to the dancers, walked off toward his hut.

The dancers drifted away in to the darkness.

Carter, satisfied, returned to his hut and slept undisturbed until daybreak.

At dawn he washed his face in a basin of water that had been placed on the table while he slept. It would be a nice day for what he had to do, he observed. The sky was clear, the mountain air crisp and clean. Opening his overnight bag, he took out his camera and checked it. Now if Dieudonne could produce some zombies. . . .

But, of course, they would not be zombies. He already knew what they would be, in a remote clan community such as this. Even his students at the university could be expected to know.

Dieudonne came with some breakfast for him – a white enamelled dish containing what appeared to be roasted yams and boiled green plantains; a cup of some sort of bush tea.

'Thanks,' Carter said, 'but if you don't mind, I'd like to get on with what we came here for. I'm not hungry.' Nor was he – for a breakfast such as that.

'You wish to visit the zombies now, *m'sieu*?'

'That's the idea.'

'Very well. Come.' And Dieudonne led him through the settlement to the mountain-slope fields beyond.

Carter was surprised at the extent of these. In carefully constructed terraces they descended for what seemed a good half mile: fields of cabbages, turnips, carrots, sweet potatoes, scallions, yam vines climbing forests of slender poles. Far down near the bottom a dozen or so figures could be seen at work, spread out in a line. The bright early sunlight flashed on tools of some sort that rose and fell in unison.

'This path will take us down to them,' Dieudonne said. 'Come.'

Bare feet had worn the path almost as smooth and hard as troweled concrete, Carter observed as he descended through the switchbacks. Years of labor must have gone into these fields. But, of course, when the produce was headed down to the capital it must bring in a handsome return. Don't underestimate these people, he told himself, even though they seem to live in a world apart.

Suddenly he became aware of the smell.

It was like . . . well, what was it like? The first thing that came to mind was the acrid stench of bat guano in a wild Kentucky cave he had once explored. Next, the stink of a pig farm near his sister's rural home in Vermont. A distressing odor, it rode the light breeze here like a chemical cloud, assailing not only his nostrils but his mind.

Halting, he said to his guide, 'My God, man, don't they ever wash?'

'They see no need to.'

'Oh, come on. You know as well as I do they're not dead men!'

'If you wish to go closer, *m'sieu*, the smell must be endured.'

Negotiating the last switchback, they reached the level on which the men were working. Still in a row, the toilers in unison lifted huge, heavy hoes above their heads and brought them down to send the reddish earth flying in clods. All were barechested. The sole garment of each was a pair of black trousers, earth-stained and worn.

And that awful stench!

'How do they stand one another?' he demanded. 'Where do they sleep at night?'

'There,' the old man said, pointing to a long, thatch-roofed shelter where the cleared part of the mountainside became forest. It had no walls.

'Don't they feel the cold? It must be really cold up here at times.'

'They have few feelings.' Dieudonne seemed a trifle impatient.

'Perhaps you can take your pictures now, *m'sieu*?'

'No! I must go closer.'

'As you wish.'

Carter would not let the smell stop him. Not until he stood within three feet of the nearest worker did he halt. About twenty years old, with a face that was not black but oddly grey and wore an expression of eternal sadness, the creature paid him absolutely no attention.

Carter studied him and then, trying not to inhale too much of that abominable odor, moved on down the line to scrutinize the others. He took pictures, changed the film, took more. Old Dieudonne resignedly waited for him. Then in silence they toiled back up the mountainside.

In the clearing some of the inhabitants of that lost-world community stood in their doorways watching. Wondering, Carter decided, how he would react to having been made a fool of. Well . . . he would show them.

Inside the hut in which he had spent the night he angrily confronted his guide. 'All right, Dieudonne. I was stupid to come here – all this way for nothing. But you were even more stupid to bring me, if you expect to be paid!'

Dieudonne eyed him in apparent surprise. *'M'sieu?'*

'Zombies, ha! I'm an anthropologist, not a gullible tourist! Those men in the fields aren't dead; they're just a result of the inbreeding that's been going on in this place. They're idiots, morons, imbeciles, without any intelligence. What's needed here is some new *blood*.'

'M'sieu,' Dieudonne said, his dark eyes seeming to smoulder, 'I say those men are zombies, and I brought you here in good faith.'

'You're a liar.'

'I am a truthful man, *m'sieu*.'

'Oh, all right, I'll pay you something for your trouble. Not the two hundred we agreed on, but something.'

'Thank you, *m'sieu*.'

'I'll give you twenty.'

'What, *m'sieu*?'

'You ought to be grateful! You know damned well you've played me for a dupe!'

'Very well,' Dieudonne said, turning away. 'I will get us something to eat, and then we can start back.' At the door he paused to fix his gaze on the American's face for a moment. 'I am sorry you think me dishonest, *m'sieu*. In time you will believe otherwise.'

He disappeared, but in fifteen minutes was back with food and drink on a wooden tray. Transferring the dishes to the table, he motioned Carter to begin. The food this time was chicken and sweet potatoes. The drink was again some kind of tea.

'What's in this?' Carter demanded, tapping his cup with a fingernail. 'We make it from leaves of the corossol tree, *m'sieu*. The soursop. It is good.' To show how good it was, the old man drank some of his own.

'I dislike bush teas,' Carter said. And at the moment also distrust them, he added mentally. Rejecting the sweet potatoes too, he attacked the chicken, discovering he was ravenous.

Finished, he rose and looked about the room to make certain he had forgotten nothing. Opened his overnight bag on the bed to be sure it contained his camera. Glancing at the old man, who was still leisurely eating, he said irritably, 'Well, are you ready?' He was not looking forward to the long walk back to the jeep.

'Yes, m'*sieu*, I am ready,' Dieudonne said, pushing away his plate with his portion of the chicken untouched.

'Let's get out of here, then,' Carter grumbled, and turned to the door. Something happened to the doorway as he went toward it. Its outlines blurred. From a rectangle of brilliant sunlight it became one of swirling mist, then of total darkness. He felt himself falling but had no sensation of reaching the floor. The fall simply continued, as into a bottomless black pit.

Time passed – unmeasurable – and he was on the bed. The room was the same but blurred, as though seen through thick green glass. He was naked. There was no feeling in his hands, his feet – none, really, in his entire body. Near by stood the old man on whom a grateful mother had bestowed the name Dieudonne, holding in his hands a pair of trousers and lifting from them a billfold. 'Thief!' Carter silently screamed. Now the old man was removing money from the billfold and counting it. And again, 'Thief!' Carter shouted, but knew he was only thinking the word, not voicing it.

Into the hut came the man they had first spoken with in this terrible place. He and Dieudonne conversed but their talk was in Creole and Carter could not understand it, was not even sure he was hearing it. A wad of paper money was thrust into old Dieudonne's hand – Haitian money this time, not American – and the old man stuffed it into his pocket along with what he had removed from the billfold. '*Merci*, Ti-Jean,' he said, and then, '*Adieu*.' The two solemnly shook hands.

Turning then, Dieudonne came to the bed and looked down at Carter, who saw him only through veiled eyes. 'And *adieu* to you also, *m'sieu*,' he said. 'You believe there is no such creature as a zombie, eh? And that your belief makes it right for you to cheat a poor old *bocor*. Oh, but I forget – the powers of a sorcerer are greatly exaggerated, you said. And, of course, you know because you are a man of learning.'

With a nod to the man who had paid him, he walked out of the hut. The other stepped to the doorway after him but halted there and spoke to someone outside.

The two men who shuffled into the hut then were naked except for black, earth-stained trousers, and they stank. They lifted Carter from the bed and set him on his feet. With a muttered command that sounded like '*Vini!*' they walked him to the door, then across the compound, then down the hard, red-earth path he had traveled earlier with Dieudonne to take pictures of them and their companions.

Holding him between them, they escorted him to the thatched shelter in which, according to Dieudonne, the workers were housed at night. The floor was a bed of dried grass. They pushed him and he sprawled face first onto it and once more felt himself falling, falling, falling into a pit of blackness that had no bottom.

When he awoke this time, or drifted into what passed for wakefulness, dawn was breaking over the mountains.

Full of despair, he sat up and looked about him and saw he was not alone. More than a dozen others shared the shelter with him. The muscular peasant leader called Ti-Jean stood there making pistolshot sounds with a bullwhip and snarling commands. Some of the men who had been dancing last night flanked him.

With the other workers Carter staggered to his feet. Someone had handed him a wooden bowl filled with grey, watery gruel from a black iron pot. Taking his cue from his companions, he lifted it to his mouth with both hands and drained it. The gruel had no taste.

Those being fed with him did not have that hellish odor now, either. Perhaps he had become used to it?

Discarding the empty bowls, they formed a line. The man with the whip pushed Carter into it and someone thrust a hoe at him. He was no longer naked, he realized vaguely. He wore ill-fitting black trousers that seemed strangely funeral on his dead-white body. The whip cracked and the line trudged out of the shelter, along a path to the fields.

As it halted at the work site Carter looked about him, aware that his mind was slowly becoming incapable of thought. He was receiving only impressions, and even those were now fragile and fleeting. In the golden dawn light the mountains all around him were part of a terrifying world in which he was a prisoner or slave. *Deye morne ge morne*. He was uncountable miles away from the home he would never see again.

By tomorrow would he even remember it?

Yours truly, Jack the Ripper

ROBERT BLOCH

I looked at the stage Englishman. He looked at me.

'Sir Guy Hollis?' I asked.

'Indeed. Have I the pleasure of addressing John Carmody, the psychiatrist?'

I nodded. My eyes swept over the figure of my distinguished visitor. Tall, lean, sandy-haired – with the traditional tufted moustache. And the tweeds. I suspected a monocle concealed in a vest pocket, and wondered if he'd left his umbrella in the outer office.

But more than that, I wondered what the devil had impelled Sir Guy Hollis of the British Embassy to seek out a total stranger here in Chicago.

Sir Guy didn't help matters any as he sat down. He cleared his throat, glanced around nervously, tapped his pipe against the side of the desk. Then he opened his mouth.

'What do you think of London?' he said.

'Why – '

'I'd like to discuss London with you, Mr Carmody.'

I meet all kinds. So I merely smiled, sat back, and gave him his head.

'Have you ever noticed anything strange about that city?' he asked.

'Well, the fog is famous.'

'Yes, the fog. That's important. It usually provides the perfect setting.'

'Setting for what?'

Sir Guy Hollis gave me an enigmatic grin.

'Murder,' he murmured.

'Murder?'

'Yes. Hasn't it struck you that London, of all cities, has a peculiar affinity for those who contemplate homicide?'

They don't talk that way, except in books. Still, it was an interesting thought. London as an ideal spot for a murder!

'As you mentioned,' said Sir Guy, 'there is a natural reason for this. The fog is an ideal background. And then too the British have a peculiar attitude in such matters. You might call it their sporting instinct. They regard murder as sort of a game.'

I sat up straight. Here was a theory.

'Yes, I needn't bore you with homicide statistics. The record is there. Aesthetically, temperamentally, the Englishman is interested in crimes of violence.

'A man commits murder. Then the excitement begins. The game starts. Will the criminal outwit the police? You can read between the lines in their newspaper stories. Everybody is waiting to see who will score.

'British law regards a prisoner as guilty until proven innocent. That's *their* advantage. But first they must catch their prisoner. And London bobbies are not allowed to carry fire-arms. That's a point for the fugitive. You see? All part of the rules of the game.'

I wondered what Sir Guy was driving at. Either a point or a strait jacket. But I kept my mouth shut and let him continue.

'The logical result of this British attitude towards murder is – Sherlock Holmes,' he said.

'Have you ever noticed how popular the theme of murder is in British fiction and drama?'

I smiled. I was back on familiar ground.

'*Angel Street*,' I suggested.

'*Ladies in Retirement*,' he continued. '*Night Must Fall*.'

'*Payment Deferred*,' I added. '*Laburnum Grove, Kind Lady. Love from a Stranger. Portrait of a Man with Red Hair. Black Limelight*.'

He nodded. 'Think of the motion pictures of Alfred Hitchcock and Emlyn Williams. The actors – Wilfred Lawson and Leslie Bank.'

'Charles Laughton,' I continued for him. 'Edmund Gwenn. Basil Rathbone. Raymond Massey. Sir Cedric Hardwicke.'

'You're quite an expert on this sort of thing yourself,' he told me.

'Not at all.' I smiled. 'I'm a psychiatrist.'

Then I leaned forward. I didn't change my tone of voice. 'All I want to know,' I said sweetly, 'is why you come up to my office and discuss murder melodramas with me.'

It stung him. He sat back and blinked a little.

'That isn't my intention,' he murmured. 'No. Not at all. I was just advancing a theory – '

'Stalling,' I said. 'Stalling. Come on, Sir Guy – spit it out.'

Talking like a gangster is all part of the applied psychiatric technique. At least, it worked for me.

It worked this time.

Sir Guy stopped bleating. His eyes narrowed. When he leaned forward again he meant business.

'Mr Carmody,' he said, 'have you ever heard of – Jack the Ripper?'

'The murderer?' I asked.

'Exactly. The greatest monster of them all. Worse than Spring-heel Jack or Crippen. Jack the Ripper. Red Jack.'

'I've heard of him,' I said.

'Do you know his history?'

I got tough again. 'Listen, Sir Guy,' I muttered. 'I don't think we'll get any place swapping old wives' tales about famous crimes of history.'

Another bull's-eye. He took a deep breath.

'This is no old wives' tale. It's a matter of life or death.'

He was so wrapped up in his obsession he even talked that way. Well – I was willing to listen. We psychiatrists get paid for listening.

'Go ahead,' I told him. 'Let's have the story.'

Sir Guy lit a cigarette and began to talk.

'London, 1888,' he began. 'Late summer and early fall. That was the time. Out of nowhere came the shadowy figure of Jack the Ripper – a stalking shadow with a knife, prowling through London's East End. Haunting the squalid dives of Whitechapel, Spitalfields. Where he came from no one knew. But he brought death. Death in a knife.

'Six times that knife descended to slash the throats and bodies of London's women. Drabs and alley sluts. August 7th was the date of the first butchery. They found her body lying there with thirty-nine stab wounds. A ghastly murder. On August 31st, another victim. The press became interested. The slum inhabitants were more deeply interested still.

'Who was this unknown killer who prowled in their midst and struck at will in the deserted alleyways of night-town? And what was more important – when would he strike again?

'September 8th was the date. Scotland Yard assigned special deputies. Rumors ran rampant. The atrocious nature of the slayings was the subject for shocking speculation.

'The killer used a knife – expertly. He cut throats. He chose victims and settings with a fiendish deliberation. No one saw him or heard him. But watchmen making their grey rounds in the dawn would stumble across the hacked and horrid thing that was the Ripper's handiwork.

'Who was he? What was he? A mad surgeon? A butcher? An insane scientist? A pathological degenerate escaped from an asylum? A deranged nobleman? A member of the London police?

'Then the poem appeared in the newspapers. The anonymous poem, designed to put a stop to speculations – but which only aroused public interest to a further frenzy. A mocking little stanza:

I'm not a butcher, I'm not a kid
Nor yet a foreign skipper,
But I'm your own true loving friend,
Yours truly – Jack the Ripper.

'And on September 30th, two more throats were slashed open.'

I interrupted Sir Guy for a moment.

'Very interesting,' I commented. I'm afraid a faint hint of sarcasm crept into my voice.

He winced, but didn't falter in his narrative.

'There was silence, then, in London for a time. Silence, and a nameless fear. When would Red Jack strike again? They waited through October. Every figment of fog concealed his phantom presence. Concealed it well – for nothing was learned of the Ripper's identity, or his purpose. The drabs of London shivered in the raw wind of early November. Shivered, and were thankful for the coming of each morning's sun.

'November 9th. They found her in her room. She lay there very quietly, limbs neatly arranged. And beside her, with equal neatness, were laid her head and heart. The Ripper had outdone himself in execution.

'Then, panic. But needless panic. For though press, police and populace alike awaited in sick dread, Jack the Ripper did not strike again.

'Months passed. A year. The immediate interest died, but not the memory. They said Jack had skipped to America. That he had committed suicide. They said – and they wrote. They've written ever since. Theories, hypotheses, arguments, treatises. But to this day no one knows who Jack the Ripper was. Or why he killed. Or why he stopped killing.'

Sir Guy was silent. Obviously he expected some comment from me.

'You tell the story well,' I remarked. 'Though with a slight emotional bias.'

'I've got all the documents,' said Sir Guy Hollis. 'I've made a collection of existing data and studied it.'

I stood up. 'Well,' I yawned, in mock fatigue, 'I've enjoyed your little bedtime story a great deal, Sir Guy. It was kind of you to abandon your duties at the British Embassy to drop in on a poor psychiatrist and regale him with your anecdotes.'

Goading him always did the trick.

'I suppose you want to know why I'm interested?' he snapped.

'Yes. That's exactly what I'd like to know. Why are you interested?'

'Because,' said Sir Guy Hollis, 'I am on the trail of Jack the Ripper now. I think he's here – in Chicago!'

I sat down again. This time I did the blinking act.

'Say that again,' I stuttered.

'Jack the Ripper is alive, in Chicago, and I'm out to find him.'

'Wait a minute,' I said. 'Wait – a – minute!'

He wasn't smiling. It wasn't a joke.

'See here,' I said. 'What was the date of these murders?'

'August to November 1888.'

'1888? But if Jack the Ripper was an able-bodied man in 1888, he'd surely be dead today! Why look, man – if he were merely born in that year, he'd be fifty-five years old today!'

'Would he?' smiled Sir Guy Hollis. 'Or should I say, "Would she?" Because Jack the Ripper may have been a woman. Or any number of things.'

'Sir Guy,' I said. 'You came to the right person when you looked me up. You definitely need the services of a psychiatrist.'

'Perhaps. Tell me, Mr Carmody, do you think I'm crazy?'

I looked at him and shrugged. But I had to give him a truthful answer.

'Frankly – no.'

'Then you might listen to the reasons I believe Jack the Ripper is alive today.'

'I might.'

'I've studied these cases for thirty years. Been over the actual ground. Talked to officials. Talked to friends and acquaintances of the poor drabs who were killed. Visited with men and women in the neighborhood. Collected an entire library of material touching on Jack the Ripper. Studied all the wild theories or crazy notions.

'I learned a little. Not much, but a little. I won't bore you with my conclusions. But there was another branch of inquiry that yielded more fruitful returns. I have studied unsolved crimes. Murders.

'I could show you clippings from the papers of half the world's great cities, San Francisco, Shanghai, Calcutta, Omsk, Paris, Berlin, Pretoria, Cairo, Milan, Adelaide.

'The trail is there, the pattern. Unsolved crimes. Slashed throats of women. With the peculiar disfigurations and removals. Yes, I've followed a trail of blood. From New York westward across the continent. Then to the Pacific. From there to Africa. During the World War of 1914 – 18 it was Europe. After that, South America. And since 1930, the United States again. Eighty-seven such murders – and to the trained criminologist, all bear the stigma of the Ripper's handiwork.

'Recently there were the so-called Cleveland torso slayings. Remember? A shocking series. And finally, two recent deaths in Chicago. Within the past six months. One out on South Dearborn. The other somewhere up on Halsted. Same type of crime, same technique. I tell you, there are unmistakable indications in all these affairs – indications of the work of Jack the Ripper!'

I smiled.

'A very tight theory,' I said. 'I'll not question your evidence at all, or the deductions you draw. You're the criminologist, and I'll take your word for it. Just one thing remains to be explained. A minor point, perhaps, but worth mentioning.'

'And what is that?' asked Sir Guy.

'Just how could a man of, let us say, eighty-five years commit these crimes? For if Jack the Ripper was around thirty in 1888 and lived, he'd be eighty-five today.'

Sir Guy Hollis was silent. I had him there. But –

'*Suppose he didn't get any older*?' whispered Sir Guy.

'What's that?'

'Suppose Jack the Ripper didn't grow old? Suppose he is still a young man today?'

'All right,' I said. 'I'll suppose for a moment. Then I'll stop supposing and call for my nurse to restrain you.'

'I'm serious,' said Sir Guy.

'They all are,' I told him. 'That's the pity of it all, isn't it? They *know* they hear voices and see demons. But we lock them up just the same.'

It was cruel, but it got results. He rose and faced me.

'It's a crazy theory, I grant you,' he said. 'All the theories about the Ripper are crazy. The idea that he was a doctor. Or a maniac. Or a woman. The reasons advanced for such beliefs are flimsy enough. There's nothing to go by. So why should my notion be any worse?'

'Because people grow older,' I reasoned with him. 'Doctors, maniacs and women alike.'

'What about – *sorcerers*?'

'Sorcerers?'

'Necromancers. Wizards. Practisers of Black Magic?'

'What's the point?'

'I studied,' said Sir Guy. 'I studied everything. After a while I began to study the dates of the murders. The pattern those dates formed. The rhythm. The solar, lunar, stellar rhythm. The sidereal aspect. The astrological significance.'

He *was* crazy. But I still listened.

'Suppose Jack the Ripper didn't murder for murder's sake alone? Suppose he wanted to make – a sacrifice?'

'What kind of a sacrifice?'

Sir Guy shrugged. 'It is said that if you offer blood to the dark gods they grant boons. Yes, if a blood offering is made at the proper time – when the moon and the stars are right – and with the proper ceremonies – they grant boons. Boons of youth. Eternal youth.'

'But that's nonsense!'

'No. That's Jack the Ripper.'

I stood up. 'A most interesting theory,' I told him. 'But Sir Guy – there's just one thing I'm interested in. Why do you come here and tell it to me? I'm not an authority on witchcraft. I'm not a police official or criminologist. I'm a practicing psychiatrist. What's the connection?'

Sir Guy smiled.

'You are interested, then?'

'Well, yes. There must be some point.'

'There is. But I wished to be assured of your interest first. Now I can tell you my plan.'

'And just what is that plan?'

Sir Guy gave me a long look. Then he spoke.

'John Carmody,' he said, 'you and I are going to capture Jack the Ripper.'

That's the way it happened. I've given the gist of that first interview in all its intricate and somewhat boring detail, because I think it's important. It helps to throw some light on Sir Guy's character and attitude. And in view of what happened after that –

But I'm coming to those matters.

Sir Guy's thought was simple. It wasn't even a thought. Just a hunch.

'You know the people here,' be told me. 'I've inquired. That's why I came to you as the ideal man for my purpose. You number among your acquaintances many writers, painters, poets. The so-called intelligentsia. The Bohemians. The lunatic fringe from the near north side.

'For certain reasons – never mind what they are – my clues lead me to infer that Jack the Ripper is a member of that element. He chooses to pose as an eccentric. I've a feeling that with you to take me around and introduce me to your set, I might hit upon the right person.'

'It's all right with me,' I said. 'But just how are you going to look for him? As you say, be might be anybody, anywhere. And you have no idea what he looks like. He might be young or old. Jack the Ripper – a Jack of all trades? Rich man, poor man, beggar man, thief, doctor, lawyer – how will you know?'

'We shall see.' Sir Guy sighed heavily. 'But I must find him. At once.'

'Why the hurry?'

Sir Guy sighed again. 'Because in two days he will kill again.'

'Are you sure?'

'Sure as the stars. I've plotted his chart, you see. All eighty-seven of the murders correspond to certain astrological rhythm patterns. If, as I suspect, he makes a blood sacrifice to renew his youth, he must murder within two days. Notice the pattern of his first crimes in London. August 7th. Then August 31st. September 8th. September 30th. November 9th. Intervals of 24 days, 9 days, 22 days – he killed two this time – and then 40 days. Of course there were crimes in between. There had to be. But they weren't discovered and pinned on him.

'At any rate, I've worked out a pattern for him, based on all my data. And I say that within the next two days he kills. So I must seek him out, somehow, before then.'

'And I'm still asking you what you want me to do.'

'Take me out,' said Sir Guy. 'Introduce me to your friends. Take me to parties.'

'But where do I begin? As far as I know, my artistic friends, despite their eccentricities, are all normal people.'

'So is the Ripper. Perfectly normal. Except on certain nights.' Again that faraway look in Sir Guy's eyes. 'Then he becomes an ageless pathological monster, crouching to kill, on evenings when the stars blaze down in the blazing patterns of death.'

'All right,' I said. 'All right. I'll take you to parties, Sir Guy. I want to go myself, anyway. I need the drinks they'll serve there, after listening to your kind of talk.'

We made our plans. And that evening I took him over to Lester Baston's studio.

As we ascended to the penthouse roof in the elevator I took the opportunity to warn Sir Guy.

'Baston's a real screwball,' I cautioned him. 'So are his guests. Be prepared for anything and everything.'

'I am.' Sir Guy Hollis was perfectly serious. He put his hand in his trousers pocket and pulled out a gun.

'What the – ' I began.

'If I see him I'll be ready,' Sir Guy said. He didn't smile, either.

'But you can't go running around at a parry with a loaded revolver in your pocket, man!'

'Don't worry, I won't behave foolishly.'

I wondered. Sir Guy Hollis was not, to my way of thinking, a normal man.

We stepped out of the elevator, went towards Baston's apartment door.

'By the way,' I murmured, 'just how do you wish to be introduced? Shall I tell them who you are and what you are looking for?'

'I don't care. Perhaps it would be best to be frank.'

'But don't you think that the Ripper – if by some miracle he or she is present – will immediately get the wind up and take cover?'

'I think the shock of the announcement that I am hunting the Ripper would provoke some kind of betraying gesture on his part,' said Sir Guy.

'You'd make a pretty good psychiatrist yourself,' I conceded. 'It's a fine theory. But I warn you, you're going to be in for a lot of ribbing. This is a wild bunch.'

Sir Guy smiled.

'I'm ready,' he announced. 'I have a little plan of my own. Don't be shocked by anything I do,' he warned me.

I nodded and knocked on the door.

Baston opened it and poured out into the hall. He teetered back and forth regarding us very gravely. He squinted at my square-cut homburg hat and Sir Guy's moustache.

'Aha,' he intoned. 'The Walrus and the Carpenter.'

I introduced Sir Guy.

'Welcome,' said Baston, gesturing us inside with over-elaborate courtesy. He stumbled after us into the garish parlor.

I stared at the crowd that moved restlessly through the fog of cigarette smoke.

It was the shank of the evening for this mob. Every hand held a drink. Every face held a slightly hectic flush. Over in one corner the piano was going full blast.

Sir Guy got a monocle-full right away. He saw Laverne Gonnister, the poetess, hit Hymie Kralik in the eye. He saw Hymie sit down on the floor and cry until Dick Pool accidentally stepped on his stomach as he walked through to the dining-room for a drink.

He heard Nadia Vilinoff the commercial artist tell Johnny Odcutt that she thought his tattooing was in dreadful taste.

His zoological observations might have continued indefinitely if Lester Baston hadn't stepped to the center of the room and called for silence by dropping a vase on the floor.

'We have distinguished visitors in our midst,' bawled Lester, waving his empty glass in our direction. 'None other than the Walrus and the Carpenter. The Walrus is Sir Guy Hollis, a something-or-other from the British Embassy. The Carpenter. as you all know, is our own John Carmody, the prominent dispenser of libido-liniment.'

He turned and grabbed Sir Guy by the arm, dragging him to the middle of the carpet. For a moment I thought Hollis might object, but a quick wink reassured me. He was prepared for this.

'It is our custom, Sir Guy,' said Baston, loudly, 'to subject our new fiends to a little cross-examination. Just a little formality at these very formal gatherings, you understand. Are you prepared to answer questions?'

Sir Guy nodded and grinned.

'Very well,' Baston muttered. 'Friends – I give you this bundle from Britain. Your witness.'

Then the ribbing started. I meant to listen, but at that moment Lydia Dare saw me and dragged me off into the vestibule for one of those Darling-I-waited-for-your-call-all-day routines.

By the time I got rid of her and went back, the impromptu quiz session was in full swing. From the attitude of the crowd, I gathered that Sir Guy was doing all right for himself.

Then Baston himself interjected a question that upset the applecart.

'And what, may I ask, brings you to our midst tonight? What is your mission, oh Walrus?'

'I'm looking for Jack the Ripper.'

Nobody laughed.

Perhaps it struck them all the way it did me. I glanced at my neighbors and began to *wonder*.

Laverne Gonnister. Hymie Kralik. Harmless. Dick Pool. Nadia Vilinoff. Johnny Odcutt and his wife. Barclay Melton. Lydia Dare. All harmless.

But what a forced smile on Dick Pool's face! And that sly, self-conscious smirk that Barclay Melton wore!

Oh, it was absurd, I grant you. But for the first time I saw these people in a new light. I wondered about their lives – their secret lives beyond the scenes of parties.

How many of them were playing a part concealing something?

Who here would worship Hecate and grant that horrid goddess the dark boon of blood?

Even Lester Baston might be masquerading.

The mood was upon us all, for a moment. I saw questions flicker in the circle of eyes around the room.

Sir Guy stood there, and I could swear he was fully conscious of the situation he'd created, and enjoyed it.

I wondered idly just what was *really* wrong with him. Why he had this odd fixation concerning Jack the Ripper. Maybe he was hiding secrets, too. . . .

Baston, as usual, broke the mood. He burlesqued it.

'The Walrus isn't kidding, friends,' he said. He slapped Sir Guy on the back and put his arm around him as he orated. 'Our English cousin is really on the trail of the fabulous Jack the Ripper. You all remember Jack the Ripper, I presume? Quite a cutup in the old days; as I recall. Really had some ripping good times when he went out on a tear.

'The Walrus has some idea that the Ripper is still alive, probably prowling around Chicago with a Boy Scout knife. In fact' – Baston paused impressively and shot it out in a rasping stage-whisper – 'in fact, he has reason to believe that Jack the Ripper might even be right here in our midst tonight.'

There was the expected reaction of giggles and grins. Baston eyed Lydia Dare reprovingly. 'You girls needn't laugh,' he smirked. 'Jack the Ripper might be a woman, too, you know. Sort of a Jill the Ripper.'

'You mean you actually suspect one of us?' shrieked Laverne Gonnister, simpering up to Sir Guy. 'But that Jack the Ripper person disappeared ages ago, didn't he? In 1888?'

'Aha!' interrupted Baston. 'How do you know so much about it, young lady? Sounds suspicious! Watch her, Sir Guy – she may not be as young as she appears. These lady poets have dark pasts.'

The tension was gone, the mood was shattered, and the whole thing was beginning to degenerate into a trivial party joke.

Then Baston caught it.

'Guess what?' he yelled. 'The Walrus has a gun.'

His embracing arm had slipped and encountered the hard outline of the gun in Sir Guy's pocket. He snatched it out before Hollis had the opportunity to protest.

I stared hard at Sir Guy, wondering if this thing had carried far enough. But he flicked a wink my way and I remembered he had told me not to be alarmed.

So I waited as Baston broached a drunken inspiration.

'Let's play fair with our friend the Walrus,' he cried. 'He came all the way from England to our party on this mission. If none of you is willing to confess, I suggest we give him a chance to find out – the hard way.'

'What's up?' asked Johnny Odcutt.

'I'll turn out the lights for one minute. Sir Guy can stand here with his gun. If anyone in this room is the Ripper he can either run for it or take the opportunity to – well, eradicate his pursuer. Fair enough?'

It was even sillier than it sounds, but it caught the popular fancy. Sir Guy's protests went unheard in the ensuing babble. And before I could stride over and put in my two cents' worth, Lester Baston had reached the light switch.

'Don't anybody move,' he announced, with fake solemnity. 'For one minute we will remain in darkness – perhaps at the mercy of a killer. At the end of that time, I'll turn up the lights again and look for bodies. Choose your partners, ladies and gentlemen.'

The lights went out.

Somebody giggled.

I heard footsteps in the darkness. Mutterings.

A hand brushed my face.

The watch on my wrist ticked violently. But even louder, rising above it, I heard another thumping. The beating of my heart.

Absurd. Standing in the dark with a group of tipsy fools. And yet there was real terror lurking here, rustling through the velvet blackness.

Jack the Ripper prowled in darkness like this. And Jack the Ripper had a knife. Jack the Ripper had a madman's brain and a madman's purpose.

But Jack the Ripper was dead, dead and dust these many years – by every human law.

Only there are no human laws when you feel yourself in the darkness, when the darkness hides and protects and the outer mask slips off your face and you feel something welling up within you, a brooding shapeless purpose that is brother to the blackness.

Sir Guy Hollis shrieked.

There was a grisly thud.

Baston had the lights on.

Everybody screamed.

Sir Guy Hollis lay sprawled on the floor in the center of the room. The gun was still clutched in his hand.

I glanced at the faces, marveling at the variety of expressions human beings can assume when confronting horror.

All the faces were present in the circle. Nobody had fled. And yet Sir Guy Hollis lay. . . .

Laverne Gonnister was wailing and hiding her face.

'All right.'

Sir Guy rolled over and jumped to his feet. He was smiling.

'Just an experiment, eh? If Jack the Ripper *were* among those present, and thought I had been murdered, he would have betrayed himself in some way when the lights went on and he saw me lying there.

'I am convinced of your individual and collective innocence. Just a gentle spoof, my friends.'

Hollis stared at the goggling Baston and the rest of them crowding in behind him.

'Shall we leave, John?' he called to me. 'It's getting late, I think.'

Turning, he headed for the closet. I followed him. Nobody said a word.

It was a pretty dull party after that.

I met Sir Guy the following evening as we agreed, on the corner of 29th and South Halsted.

After what had happened the night before, I was prepared for almost anything. But Sir Guy seemed matter-of-fact enough as he stood huddled against a grimy doorway and waited for me to appear.

'Boo!' I said, jumping out suddenly. He smiled. Only the betraying gesture of his left hand indicated that he'd instinctively reached for his gun when I startled him.

'All ready for our wild goose chase?' I asked.

'Yes.' He nodded. 'I'm glad that you agreed to meet me without asking questions,' he told me. 'It shows you trust my judgment.' He took my arm and edged me along the street slowly.

'It's foggy tonight, John,' said Sir Guy Hollis. 'Like London.'

I nodded.

'Cold, too, for November.'

I nodded again and half-shivered my agreement.

'Curious,' mused Sir Guy. 'London fog and November. The place and the time of the Ripper murders.'

I grinned through darkness. 'Let me remind you, Sir Guy, that this isn't London, but Chicago. And it isn't November 1888. It's over fifty years later.'

Sir Guy returned my grin, but without mirth. 'I'm not so sure, at that,' he murmured. 'Look about you. These tangled alleys and twisted streets. They're like the East End. Mitre Square. And surely they are as ancient as fifty years, at least.'

'You're in the poor neighborhood off South Clark Street,' I said, shortly. 'And why you dragged me down here I still don't know.'

'It's a hunch,' Sir Guy admitted. 'Just a hunch on my part, John. I want to wander around down here. There's the same geographical conformation in these streets as in those courts where the Ripper roamed and slew. That's where we'll find him, John. Not in the bright lights of the Bohemian neighborhood, but down here in the darkness. The darkness where he waits and crouches.'

'Is that why you brought a gun?' I asked. I was unable to keep a trace of sarcastic nervousness from my voice. All of this talk, this incessant obsession with Jack the Ripper, got on my nerves more than I cared to admit.

'We may need the gun,' said Sir Guy, gravely. 'After all, tonight is the appointed night.'

I sighed. We wandered on through the foggy, deserted streets. Here and there a dim light burned above a doorway. Otherwise, all was darkness and shadow. Deep, gaping alley-ways loomed as we proceeded down a slanting side street.

We crawled through that fog, alone and silent, like two tiny maggots floundering within a shroud.

When that thought hit me, I winced. The atmosphere was beginning to get *me,* too. If I didn't watch my step I'd go as loony as Sir Guy.

'Can't you see there's not a soul around these streets?' I said, tugging at his coat impatiently.

'He's bound to come,' said Sir Guy. 'He'll be drawn here. This is what I've been looking for. A *genius loci*. An evil spot that attracts evil. Always, when he slays, it's in the slums.

'You see, that must be one of his weaknesses. He has a fascination for squalor. Besides, the women he needs for sacrifice are more easily found in the dives and stewpots of a great city.'

I smiled. 'Well, let's go into one of the dives or stewpots,' I suggested. 'I'm cold. Need a drink. This fog gets into your bones. You Britishers can stand it, but I like warmth and dry heat.'

We emerged from our side street and stood upon the threshold of an alley.

Through the white clouds of mist ahead, I discerned a dim blue light, a naked bulb dangling from a beer sign above an alley tavern.

'Let's take a chance,' I said. 'I'm beginning to shiver.'

'Lead the way,' said Sir Guy. I led him down the alley passage. We halted before the door of the dive.

'What are you waiting for?' he asked.

'Just looking in,' I told him. 'This is a tough neighborhood, Sir Guy. Never know what you're liable to run into. And I'd prefer we didn't get into the wrong company.'

'Good idea, John.'

I finished my inspection through the doorway. 'Looks deserted,' I murmured. 'Let's try it.'

We entered a dingy bar. A feeble light flickered above the counter and railing, but failed to penetrate the farther gloom of the back booths.

A gigantic Negro lolled across the bar. He scarcely stirred as we came in, but his eyes flickered open quite suddenly and I knew he noted our presence and was judging us.

'Evening,' I said.

He took his time before replying. Still sizing us up. Then he grinned.

'Evening, gents. What's your pleasure?'

'Gin,' I said. 'Two gins. It's a cold night.'

'That's right, gents.'

He poured, I paid, and took the glasses over to one of the booths. We wasted no time in emptying them. The fiery liquor warmed.

I went over to the bar and got the bottle. Sir Guy and I poured ourselves another drink. The big Negro went back into his doze, with one wary eye half-open against any sudden activity.

The clock over the bar ticked on. The wind was rising outside, tearing the shroud of fog to ragged shreds. Sir Guy and I sat in the warm booth and drank our gin.

He began to talk, and the shadows crept up about us to listen.

He rambled a great deal. He went over everything he'd said in the office when I met him, just as though I hadn't heard it before. The poor devils with obsessions are like that.

I listened very patiently. I poured Sir Guy another drink. And another.

But the liquor only made him more talkative. How he did run on! About ritual killings and prolonging life unnaturally – the whole fantastic tale came out again. And, of course, he maintained his unyielding conviction that the Ripper was abroad tonight.

I suppose I was guilty of goading him.

'Very well,' I said, unable to keep the impatience from my voice. 'Let us say that your theory is correct – even though we must overlook every natural law and swallow a lot of superstition to give it any credence.

'But let us say, for the sake of argument, that you are right. Jack the Ripper was a man who discovered how to prolong his own life through making human sacrifices. He did travel around the world as you believe. He is in Chicago now and he is planning to kill. In other words, let us suppose that everything you claim is gospel truth. So what?'

'What do you mean, "so what"?' said Sir Guy.

'I mean – so what?' I answered. 'If all this is true, it still doesn't prove that by sitting down in a dingy gin-mill on the South Side, Jack the Ripper is going to walk in here and let you kill him, or turn him over to the police. And come to think of it, I don't even know now just what you intend to *do* with him if you ever did find him.'

Sir Guy gulped his gin. 'I'd capture the bloody swine,' he said. 'Capture him and turn him over to the government, together with all the papers and documentary evidence I've collected against him over a period of many years. I've spent a fortune investigating this affair, I tell you, a fortune! His capture will mean the solution of hundreds of unsolved crimes, of that I am convinced.

'I tell you, a mad beast is loose on this world! An ageless, eternal beast, sacrificing to Hecate and the dark gods!'

In vino veritas. Or was all this babbling the result of too much gin? It didn't matter. Sir Guy Hollis had another. I sat there and wondered what to do with him. The man was rapidly working up to a climax of hysterical drunkenness.

'One other point.' I said, more for the sake of conversation than in any hopes of obtaining information. 'You still don't explain how it is that you hope to just blunder into the Ripper.'

'He'll be around,' said Sir Guy. 'I'm psychic. I know.'

Sir Guy wasn't psychic. He was maudlin.

The whole business was beginning to infuriate me. We'd been sitting here an hour, and during all this time I'd been forced to play nursemaid and audience to a babbling idiot. After all, he wasn't a regular patient of mine.

'That's enough,' I said, putting out my hand as Sir Guy reached for the half-emptied bottle again. 'You've had plenty. Now I've got a suggestion to make. Let's call a cab and get out of here. It's getting late and it doesn't look as though your elusive friend is going to put in his appearance. Tomorrow, if I were you, I'd plan to turn all those papers and documents over to the F.B.I. If you're so convinced of the truth of your wild theory, they are competent to make a very thorough investigation and find your man.'

'No.' Sir Guy was drunkenly obstinate. 'No cab.'

'But let's get out of here anyway,' I said, glancing at my watch. 'It's past midnight.'

He sighed, shrugged, and rose unsteadily. As he started for the door, he tugged the gun free from his pocket.

'Here, give me that!' I whispered. 'You can't walk around the street brandishing that thing.'

I took the gun and slipped it inside my coat. Then I got hold of his right arm and steered him out of the door. The Negro didn't look up as we departed.

We stood shivering in the alleyway. The fog had increased. I couldn't see either end of the alley from where we stood. It was cold. Damp. Dark. Fog or no fog, a little wind was whispering secrets to the shadows at our backs.

The fresh air hit Sir Guy just as I had expected it would. Fog and gin fumes don't mingle very well. He lurched as I guided him slowly through the mist.

Sir Guy, despite his incapacity, still stared apprehensively at the alley, as though he expected to see a figure approaching.

Disgust got the better of me.

'Childish foolishness,' I snorted. 'Jack the Ripper, indeed! I call this carrying a hobby too far.'

'Hobby?' He faced me. Through the fog I could see his distorted face. 'You call this a hobby?'

'Well, what is it?' I grumbled. 'Just why else are you so interested in tracking down this mythical killer?'

My arm held him. But his stare held me.

'In London,' he whispered. 'In 1888 . . . one of those women the Ripper slew . . . was my mother.'

'What?'

'My father and I swore to give our lives to find the Ripper. My father was the first to search. He died in Hollywood in 1926 – on the trail of the Ripper. They said he was stabbed by an unknown assailant in a brawl. But I know who that assailant was.

'So I've taken up his work, do you see, John? I've carried on. And I will carry on until I do find him and kill him with my own hands.

'He took my mother's life and the lives of hundreds to keep his own hellish being alive. Like a vampire, he battens on blood. Like a ghoul, he is nourished by death. Like a fiend, he stalks the world to kill. He is cunning, devilishly cunning. But I'll never rest until I find him, never!'

I believed him then. He wouldn't give up. He wasn't just a drunken babbler any more. He was as fanatical, as determined, as relentless as the Ripper himself.

Tomorrow he'd be sober. He'd continue the search. Perhaps he'd turn those papers over to the F.B.I. Sooner or later, with such persistence – and with his motive – he'd be successful. I'd always known he had a motive.

'Let's go,' I said, steering him down the alley.

'Wait a minute,' said Sir Guy. 'Give me back my gun.' He lurched a little. 'I'd feel better with the gun on me.'

He pressed me into the dark shadows of a little recess.

I tried to shrug him off, but he was insistent.

'Let me carry the gun now, John,' he mumbled.

'All right,' I said.

I reached into my coat, brought my hand out.

'But that's not a gun,' he protested. 'That's a knife.'

'I know.'

I bore down on him swiftly.

'John!' he screamed.

'Never mind the "John",' I whispered, raising the knife. 'Just call me . . . Jack.'

Peter and the Wolf

ANGELA CARTER

At length the grandeur of the mountains becomes monotonous; with familiarity, the landscape ceases to provoke awe and wonder and the traveller sees the alps with the indifferent eye of those who always live there. Above a certain line, no trees grow. Shadows of clouds move across the bare alps as freely as the clouds themselves move across the sky.

A girl from a village on the lower slopes left her widowed mother to marry a man who lived up in the empty places. Soon she was pregnant. In October, there was a severe storm. The old woman knew her daughter was near her time and waited for a message but none arrived. After the storm passed, the old woman went up to see for herself, taking her grown son with her because she was afraid.

From a long way off, they saw no smoke rising from the chimney. Solitude yawned round them. The open door banged backwards and forwards on its hinges. Solitude engulfed them. There were traces of wolf-dung on the floor so they knew wolves had been in the house but left the corpse of the young mother alone although of her baby nothing was left except some mess that showed it had been born. Nor was there a trace of the son-in-law but a gnawed foot in a boot.

They wrapped the dead in a quilt and took it home with them. Now it was late. The howling of the wolves mutilated the approaching silence of the night.

Winter came with icy blasts, when everyone stays indoors and stokes the fire. The old woman's son married the blacksmith's daughter and she moved in with them. The snow melted and it was spring. By the next Christmas, there was a bouncing grandson. Time passed. More children came.

When the eldest grandson, Peter, reached his seventh summer, he was old enough to go up the mountain with his father, as the men did every year, to let the goats feed on the young grass. There Peter sat in the new sunlight, plaiting the straw for baskets, until he saw the thing he had been taught most to fear advancing silently along the lea of an outcrop of rock. Then another wolf, following the first one.

If they had not been the first wolves he had ever seen, the boy would not have inspected them so closely, their plush, grey pelts, of which the hairs are tipped with white, giving them a ghostly look, as if they were on the point of dissolving at the edges; their sprightly, plumey tails; their acute, inquisitive masks.

Then Peter saw that the third wolf was a prodigy, a marvel, a naked one, going on all fours, as they did, but hairless as regards the body although hair grew around its head.

The sight of this bald wolf so fascinated him that he would have lost his flock, perhaps himself been eaten and certainly been beaten to the bone for negligence had not the goats themselves raised their heads, snuffed danger and run off, bleating and whinnying, so that the men came, firing guns, making hullabaloo, scaring the wolves away.

His father was too angry to listen to what Peter said. He cuffed Peter round the head and sent him home. His mother was feeding this year's baby. His grandmother sat at the table, shelling peas into a pot.

'There was a little girl with the wolves, granny,' said Peter. Why was he so sure it had been a little girl? Perhaps because her hair was so long, so long and lively. 'A little girl about my age, from her size,' he said.

His grandmother threw a flat pod out of the door so the chickens could peck it up.

'I saw a little girl with the wolves,' he said.

His grandmother tipped water into the pot, got up from the table and hung the pot of peas on the hook over the fire. There wasn't time that night, but, next morning, very early, she herself took the boy back up the mountain.

'Tell your father what you told me.'

They went to look at the wolves' tracks. On a bit of dampish ground they found a print, not like that of a dog's pad, much less like that of a child's footprint, yet Peter worried and puzzled over it until he made sense of it.

'She was running on all fours with her arse stuck up in the air . . . therefore . . . she'd put all her weight on the ball of her foot, wouldn't she? And splay out her toes, see . . . like that.'

He went barefoot in summer, like all the village children; he inserted the ball of his own foot in the print, to show his father what kind of mark he would have made if he, too, always ran on all fours.

'No use for a heel, if you run that way. So she doesn't have a heel-print: Stands to reason.'

At last his father made a slow acknowledgement of Peter's powers of deduction, giving the child a veiled glance of disquiet. It was a clever child.

They soon found her. She was asleep. Her spine had grown so supple she could curl into a perfect C. She woke up when she heard them and ran, but somebody caught her with a sliding noose at the end of a rope; the noose over her head jerked tight and she fell to the ground with her eyes popping and rolling. A big, grey, angry bitch appeared out of nowhere but Peter's father blasted it to bits with his shotgun. The girl would have choked if the old woman hadn't taken her head on her lap and pulled the knot loose. The girl bit the grandmother's hand.

The girl scratched and fought until the men tied her wrists and ankles together with twine and slung her from a pole to carry her back to the village. Then she went limp. She didn't scream or shout, she didn't seem to be able to, she made only a few dull, guttural sounds in the back of her throat, and, though she did not seem to know how to cry, water trickled out of the corners of her eyes.

How burned she was by the weather! Bright brown all over; and how filthy she was! Caked with mud and dirt. And every inch of her chestnut hide was scored and scabbed with dozens of scars of sharp abrasions of rock and thorn. Her hair dragged on the ground as they carried her along; it was stuck with burrs and it was so dirty you could not see what colour it might be. She was dreadfully verminous. She stank. She was so thin that all her ribs stuck out. The fine, plump, potato-fed boy was far bigger than she, although she was a year or so older.

Solemn with curiosity, he trotted behind her. Granny stumped alongside with her bitten hand wrapped up in her apron. Once the girl was dumped on the earth floor of her grandmother's house, the boy secretly poked at her left buttock with his forefinger, out of curiosity, to see what she felt like. She felt warm but hard. She did not so much as twitch when he touched her. She had given up the struggle; she lay trussed on the floor and pretended to be dead.

Granny's house had the one large room which, in winter, they shared with the goats. As soon as it caught a whiff of her, the big tabby mouser hissed like a pricked balloon and bounded up the ladder that went to the hayloft above. Soup smoked on the fire and the table was laid. It was now about supper-time but still quite light; night comes late on the summer mountain.

'Untie her,' said the grandmother.

Her son wasn't willing at first but the old woman would not be denied, so he got the breadknife and cut the rope round the girl's ankles. All she did was kick, but when he cut the rope round her wrists, it was as if he had let a fiend loose. The onlookers ran out of the door, the rest of the family ran for the ladder to the hayloft but Granny and Peter both ran to the door, to shoot the bolt, so she could not get out.

The trapped one knocked round the room. Bang – over went the table. Crash, tinkle – the supper dishes smashed. Bang, crash, tinkle – the dresser fell forward upon the hard white shale of crockery it shed in falling. Over went the meal barrel and she coughed, she sneezed like a child sneezes, no different, and then she bounced around on fear-stiffened legs in a white cloud until the flour settled on everything like a magic powder that made everything strange. Her first frenzy over, she squatted a moment, questing with her long nose and then began to make little rushing sorties, now here, now there, snapping and yelping and tossing her bewildered head.

She never rose up on two legs; she crouched, all the time, on her hands and tiptoes, yet it was not quite like crouching, for you could see how all fours came naturally to her as though she had made a different pact with gravity than we have, and you could see, too, how strong the muscles in her thighs had grown on the mountain, how taut the twanging arches of her feet, and that indeed, she only used her heels when she sat back on her haunches. She growled; now and then she coughed out those intolerable, thick grunts of distress. All you could see of her rolling eyes were the whites, which were the bluish, glaring white of snow.

Several times, her bowels opened, apparently involuntarily. The kitchen smelled like a privy yet even her excrement was different to ours, the refuse of raw, strange, unguessable, wicked feeding, shit of a wolf.

Oh, horror!

She bumped into the hearth, knocked over the pan hanging from the hook and the spilled contents put out the fire. Hot soup scalded her forelegs. Shock of pain. Squatting on her hindquarters, holding the hurt paw dangling piteously from its wrist before her, she howled, in high, sobbing arcs.

Even the old woman, who had contracted with herself to love the child of her dead daughter, was frightened when she heard the girl howl.

Peter's heart gave a hop, a skip, so that he had a sensation of falling; he was not conscious of his own fear because he could not take his eyes off the sight of the crevice of her girl-child's sex, that was perfectly visible to him as she sat there square on the base of her spine. The night was now as dark as, at this season, it would go – which is to say, not very dark; a white thread of moon hung in the blond sky at the top of the chimney so that it was neither dark nor light indoors yet the boy could see her intimacy clearly, as if by its own phosphorescence. It exercised an absolute fascination upon him.

Her lips opened up as she howled so that she offered him, without her own intention or volition, a view of a set of Chinese boxes of whorled flesh that seemed to open one upon another into herself, drawing him into an inner, secret place in which destination perpetually receded before him, his first, devastating, vertiginous intimation of infinity.

She howled.

And went on howling until, from the mountain, first singly, then in a complex polyphony, answered at last voices in the same language.

She continued to howl, though now with a less tragic resonance.

Soon it was impossible for the occupants of the house to deny to themselves that the wolves were descending on the village in a pack.

Then she was consoled, sank down, laid her head on her forepaws so that her hair trailed in the cooling soup and so closed up her forbidden book without the least notion she had ever opened it or that it was banned. Her heavy eyelids closed on her brown, bloodshot eyes. The household gun hung on a nail over the fireplace where Peter's father had put it when he came in but when the man set his foot on the top rung of the ladder in order to come down for his weapon, the girl jumped up, snarling and showing her long yellow canines.

The howling outside was now mixed with the agitated dismay of the domestic beasts. All the other villagers were well locked up at home.

The wolves were at the door.

The boy took hold of his grandmother's uninjured hand. First the old woman would not budge but he gave her a good tug and she came to herself. The girl raised her head suspiciously but let them by. The boy pushed his grandmother up the ladder in front of him and drew it up behind them. He was full of nervous dread. He would have given anything to turn time back, so that he might have run, shouting a warning, when he first caught sight of the wolves, and never seen her.

The door shook as the wolves outside jumped up at it and the screws that held the socket of the bolt to the frame cracked, squeaked and started to give. The girl jumped up, at that, and began to make excited little sallies back and forth in front of the door. The screws tore out of the frame quite soon. The pack tumbled over one another to get inside.

Dissonance. Terror. The clamour within the house was that of all the winds of winter trapped in a box. That which they feared most, outside, was now indoors with them. The baby in the hayloft whimpered and its mother crushed it to her breast as if the wolves might snatch this one away, too; but the rescue party had arrived only in order to collect their fosterling.

They left behind a riotous stench in the house, and white tracks of flour everywhere. The broken door creaked backwards and forwards on its hinges. Black sticks of dead wood from the extinguished fire were scattered on the floor.

Peter thought the old woman would cry, now, but she seemed unmoved. When all was safe, they came down the ladder one by one and, as if released from a spell of silence, burst into excited speech except for the mute old woman and the distraught boy. Although it was well past midnight, the daughter-in-law went to the well for water to scrub the wild smell out of the house. The broken things were cleared up and thrown away. Peter's father nailed the table and the dresser back together. The neighbours came out of their houses, full of amazement; the wolves had not taken so much as a chicken from the hen-coops, not snatched even a single egg.

People brought beer into the starlight, and schnapps made from potatoes, and snacks, because the excitement had made them hungry. That terrible night ended up in one big party but the grandmother would eat or drink nothing and went to bed as soon as her house was clean.

Next day, she went to the graveyard and sat for a while beside her daughter's grave but she did not pray. Then she came home and started chopping cabbage for the evening meal but had to leave off because her bitten hand was festering.

That winter, during the leisure imposed by the snow, after his grandmother's death, Peter asked the village priest to teach him to read the Bible. The priest gladly complied; Peter was the first of his flock who had ever expressed any interest in learning to read.

The boy became very pious, so much so that his family were startled and impressed. The younger children teased him and called him 'Saint Peter' but that did not stop him sneaking off to church to pray whenever he had a spare moment. In Lent, he fasted to the bone. On Good Friday, he lashed himself. It was as if he blamed himself for the death of the old lady, as if he believed he had brought into the house the fatal infection that had taken her out of it. He was consumed by an imperious passion for atonement. Each night, he pored over his book by the flimsy candlelight, looking for a clue to grace, until his mother shooed him off to sleep.

But, as if to spite the four evangelists he nightly invoked to protect his bed, the nightmare regularly disordered his sleeps. He tossed and turned on the rustling straw pallet he shared with two little ones.

Delighted with Peter's precocious intelligence, the priest started to teach him Latin. Peter visited the priest as his duties with the herd permitted. When he was fourteen, the priest told his parents that Peter should now go to the seminary in the town in the valley where the boy would learn to become a priest himself. Rich in sons, they spared one to God, since his books and his praying made him a stranger to them. After the goats came down from the high pasture for the winter, Peter set off. It was October.

At the end of his first day's travel, he reached a river that ran from the mountain into the valley. The nights were already chilly; he lit himself a fire, prayed, ate bread and cheese his mother had packed for him and slept as well as he could. In spite of his eagerness to plunge into the white world of penance and devotion that awaited him, he was anxious and troubled for reasons he could not explain to himself.

In the first light, the light that no more than clarifies darkness like egg shells dropped in cloudy liquid, he went down to the river to drink and to wash his face. It was so still he could have been the one thing living.

Her forearms, her loins and her legs were thick with hair and the hair on her head hung round her face in such a way that you could hardly make out her features. She crouched on the other side of the river. She was lapping up water so full of mauve light that it looked as if she were drinking up the dawn as fast as it appeared yet all the same the air grew pale while he was looking at her.

Solitude and silence; all still.

She could never have acknowledged that the reflection beneath her in the river was that of herself. She did not know she had a face; she had never known she had a face and so her face itself was the mirror of a different kind of consciousness than ours is, just as her nakedness, without innocence or display, was that of our first parents, before the Fall. She was hairy as Magdalen in the wilderness and yet repentance was not within her comprehension.

Language crumbled into dust under the weight of her speechlessness.

A pair of cubs rolled out of the bushes, cuffing one another. She did not pay them any heed.

The boy began to tremble and shake. His skin prickled. He felt he had been made of snow and now might melt. He mumbled something, or sobbed.

She cocked her head at the vague, river-washed sound and the cubs heard it, too, left off tumbling and ran to burrow their scared heads in her side. But she decided, after a moment, there was no danger and lowered her muzzle, again, to the surface of the water that took hold of her hair and spread it out around her head.

When she finished her drink, she backed a few paces, shaking her wet pelt. The little cubs fastened their mouths on her dangling breasts.

Peter could not help it, he burst out crying. He had not cried since his grandmother's funeral. Tears rolled down his face and splashed on the grass. He blundered forward a few steps into the river with his arms held open, intending to cross over to the other side to join her in her marvellous and private grace, impelled by the access of an almost visionary ecstasy. But his cousin took fright at the sudden movement, wrenched her teats away from the cubs and ran off. The squeaking cubs scampered behind. She ran on hands and feet as if that were the only way to run towards the high ground, into the bright maze of the uncompleted dawn.

When the boy recovered himself, he dried his tears on his sleeve, took off his soaked boots and dried his feet and legs on the tail of his shirt. Then he ate something from his pack, he scarcely knew what, and continued on the way to the town; but what would he do at the seminary, now? For now he knew there was nothing to be afraid of.

He experienced the vertigo of freedom.

He carried his boots slung over his shoulder by the laces. They were a great burden. He debated with himself whether or not to throw them away but, when he came to a paved road, he had to put them on, although they were still damp.

The birds woke up and sang. The cool, rational sun surprised him; morning had broken on his exhilaration and the mountain now lay behind him. He looked over his shoulder and saw, how, with distance, the mountain began to acquire a flat, two-dimensional look. It was already turning into a picture of itself, into the postcard hastily bought as a souvenir of childhood at a railway station or a border post, the newspaper cutting, the snapshot he would show in strange towns, strange cities, other countries he could not, at this moment, imagine, whose names he did not yet know, places where he would say, in strange languages, 'That was where I spent my childhood. Imagine!'

He turned and stared at the mountain for a long time. He had lived in it for fourteen years but he had never seen it before as it might look to someone who had not known it as almost a part of the self, so, for the first time, he saw the primitive, vast, magnificent, barren, unkind, simplicity of the mountain. As he said goodbye to it, he saw it turn into so much scenery, into the wonderful backcloth for an old country tale, tale of a child suckled by wolves, perhaps, or of wolves nursed by a woman.

Then he determinedly set his face towards the town and tramped onwards, into a different story.

'If I look back again,' he thought with a last gasp of superstitious terror, 'I shall turn into a pillar of salt.'

Interview with the Vampire (extract)

ANNE RICE

'I see . . .' said the vampire thoughtfully, and slowly he walked across the room towards the window. For a long time he stood there against the dim light from Divisadero Street and the passing beams of traffic. The boy could see the furnishings of the room more clearly now, the round oak table, the chairs. A wash basin hung on one wall with a mirror. He set his brief case on the table and waited.

'But how much tape do you have with you?' asked the vampire, turning now so the boy could see his profile. 'Enough for the story of a life?'

'Sure, if it's a good life. Sometimes I interview as many as three or four people a night if I'm lucky. But it has to be a good story. That's only fair, isn't it?'

'Admirably fair,' the vampire answered. 'I would like to tell you the story of my life, then. I would like to do that very much.'

'Great,' said the boy. And quickly he removed the small tape recorder from his brief case, making a check of the cassette and the batteries. 'I'm really anxious to hear why you believe this, why you . . .'

'No,' said the vampire abruptly. 'We can't begin that way. Is your equipment ready?'

'Yes,' said the boy.

'Then sit down. I'm going to turn on the overhead light.'

'But I thought vampires didn't like light,' said the boy. 'If you think the dark adds to the atmosphere . . .' But then he stopped. The vampire was watching him with his back to the window. The boy could make out nothing of his face now, and something about the still figure there distracted him. He started to say something again but he said nothing. And then he sighed with relief when the vampire moved towards the table and reached for the overhead cord.

At once the room was flooded with a harsh yellow light. And the boy, staring up at the vampire, could not repress a gasp. His fingers danced backwards on the table to grasp the edge. 'Dear God!' he whispered, and then he gazed, speechless, at the vampire.

The vampire was utterly white and smooth, as if he were sculpted from bleached bone, and his face was as seemingly inanimate as a statue, except for two brilliant green eyes that looked down at the boy intently like flames in a skull. But then the vampire smiled almost wistfully, and the smooth white substance of his face moved with the infinitely flexible but minimal lines of a cartoon. 'Do you see?' he asked softly.

The boy shuddered, lifting his hand as if to shield himself from a powerful light. His eyes moved slowly over the finely tailored black coat he'd only glimpsed in the bar, the long folds of the cape, the black silk tie knotted at the throat, and the gleam of the white collar that was as white as the vampire's flesh. He stared at the vampire's full black hair, the waves that were combed back over the tips of the ears, the curls that barely touched the edge of the white collar.

'Now, do you still want the interview?' the vampire asked.

The boy's mouth was open before the sound came out. He was nodding. Then he said, 'Yes.'

The vampire sat down slowly opposite him and, leaning forward, said gently, confidentially, 'Don't be afraid. Just start the tape.'

And then he reached out over the length of the table. The boy recoiled, sweat running down the sides of his face. The vampire clamped a hand on the boy's shoulder and said, 'Believe me, I won't hurt you. I want this opportunity. It's more important to me than you can realize now. I want you to begin.' And he withdrew his hand and sat collected, waiting.

It took a moment for the boy to wipe his forehead and his lips with a handkerchief, to stammer that the microphone was in the machine, to press the button, to say that the machine was on.

'You weren't always a vampire, were you?' he began.

'No,' answered the vampire. 'I was a twenty-five-year-old man when I became a vampire, and the year was 1791.'

The boy was startled by the preciseness of the date and he repeated it before he asked, 'How did it come about?'

'There's a simple answer to that. I don't believe I want to give simple answers,' said the vampire. 'I think I want to tell the real story. . . .'

'Yes,' the boy said quickly. He was folding his handkerchief over and over and wiping his lips now with it again.

'There was a tragedy . . .' the vampire started. 'It was my younger brother. . . . He died.' And then he stopped, so that the boy cleared his throat and wiped at his face again before stuffing the handkerchief almost impatiently into his pocket.

'It's not painful, is it?' he asked timidly.

'Does it seem so?' asked the vampire. 'No.' He shook his head. 'It's simply that I've only told this story to one other person. And that was so long ago. No, it's not painful. . . .'

'We were living in Louisiana then. We'd received a land grant and settled two indigo plantations on the Mississippi very near New Orleans . . .'

'Ah, that's the accent . . .' the boy said softly.

For a moment the vampire stared blankly. 'I have an accent?' He began to laugh.

And the boy, flustered, answered quickly. 'I noticed it in the bar when I asked you what you did for a living. It's just a slight sharpness to the consonants, that's all. I never guessed it was French.'

'It's all right,' the vampire assured him. 'I'm not as shocked as I pretend to be. It's only that I forget it from time to time. But let me go on. . . .'

'Please . . .' said the boy.

'I was talking about the plantations. They had a great deal to do with it, really, my becoming a vampire. But I'll come to that. Our life there was both luxurious and primitive. And we ourselves found it extremely attractive. You see, we lived far better there than we could have ever lived in France. Perhaps the sheer wilderness of Louisiana only made it seem so, but seeming so, it was. I remember the imported furniture that cluttered the house.' The vampire smiled. 'And the harpsichord; that was lovely. My sister used to play it. On summer evenings, she would sit at the keys with her back to the open french windows. And I can still remember that thin, rapid music and the vision of the swamp rising beyond her, the moss-hung cypresses floating against the sky. And there were the sounds of the swamp, a chorus of creatures, the cry of the birds. I think we loved it. It made the rosewood furniture all the more precious, the music more delicate and desirable. Even when the wisteria tore the shutters off the attic windows and worked its tendrils right into the whitewashed brick in less than a year. . . . Yes, we loved it. All except my brother. I don't think I ever heard him complain of anything, but I knew how he felt. My father was dead then, and I was head of the family and I had to defend him constantly from my mother and sister. They wanted to take him visiting, and to New Orleans for parties, but he hated these things. I think he stopped going altogether before he was twelve. Prayer was what mattered to him, prayer and his leather-bound lives of the saints.

'Finally I built him an oratory removed from the house, and he began to spend most of every day there and often the early evening. It was ironic, really. He was so different from us, so different from everyone, and I was so regular! There was nothing extraordinary about me whatsoever.' The vampire smiled.

'Sometimes in the evening I would go out to him and find him in the garden near the oratory, sitting absolutely composed on a stone bench there, and I'd tell him my troubles, the difficulties I had with the slaves, how I distrusted the overseer or the weather or my brokers . . . all the problems that made up the length and breadth of my existence. And he would listen, making only a few comments, always sympathetic, so that when I left him I had the distinct impression he had solved everything for me. I didn't think I could deny him anything, and I vowed that no matter how it would break my heart to lose him, he could enter the priesthood when the time came. Of course, I was wrong.' The vampire stopped.

For a moment the boy only gazed at him and then he started as if awakened from deep thought, and he floundered, as if he could not find the right words. 'Ah . . . he didn't want to be a priest?' the boy asked. The vampire studied him as if trying to discern the meaning of his expression. Then he said:

'I meant that I was wrong about myself, about my not denying him anything.' His eyes moved over the far wall and fixed on the panes of the window. 'He began to see visions.'

'Real visions?' the boy asked, but again there was hesitation, as if he were thinking of something else.

'I didn't think so,' the vampire answered. 'It happened when he was fifteen. He was very handsome then. He had the smoothest skin and the largest blue eyes. He was robust, not thin as I am now and was then . . . but his eyes . . . it was as if when I looked into his eyes I was standing alone on the edge of the world . . . on a windswept ocean beach. There was nothing but the soft roar of the waves. Well,' he said, his eyes still fixed on the window panes, 'he began to see visions. He only hinted at this at first, and he stopped taking his meals altogether. He lived in the oratory. At any hour of day or night, I could find him on the bare flagstones kneeling before the altar. And the oratory itself was neglected. He stopped tending the candles or changing the altar cloths or even sweeping out the leaves. One night I became really alarmed when I stood in the rose arbor watching him for one solid hour, during which he never moved from his knees and never once lowered his arms, which he held outstretched in the form of a cross. The slaves all thought he was mad.' The vampire raised his eyebrows in wonder. 'I was convinced that he was only . . . overzealous. That in his love for God, he had perhaps gone too far. Then he told me about the visions. Both St Dominic and the Blessed Virgin Mary had come to him in the oratory. They had told him he was to sell all our property in Louisiana, everything we owned, and use the money to do God's work in France. My brother was to be a great religious leader, to return the country to its former fervor, to turn the tide against atheism and the Revolution. Of course, he had no money of his own. I was to sell the plantations and our town houses in New Orleans and give the money to him.'

Again the vampire stopped. And the boy sat motionless regarding him, astonished. 'Ah . . . excuse me,' he whispered. 'What did you say? Did you sell the plantations?'

'No,' said the vampire, his face calm as it had been from the start. 'I laughed at him. And he . . . he became incensed. He insisted his command came from the Virgin herself. Who was I to disregard it? Who indeed?' he asked softly, as if he were thinking of this again. 'Who indeed? And the more he tried to convince me, the more I laughed. It was nonsense, I told him, the product of an immature and even morbid mind. The oratory was a mistake, I said to him; I would have it torn down at once. He would go to school in New Orleans and get such inane notions out of his head. I don't remember all that I said. But I remember the feeling. Behind all this contemptuous dismissal on my part was a smoldering anger and a disappointment. I was bitterly disappointed. I didn't believe him at all.'

'But that's understandable,' said the boy quickly when the vampire paused, his expression of astonishment softening. 'I mean, would anyone have believed him?'

'Is it so understandable?' The vampire looked at the boy. 'I think perhaps it was vicious egotism. Let me explain. I loved my brother, as I told you, and at times I believed him to be a living saint. I encouraged him in his prayer and meditations, as I said, and I was willing to give him up to the priesthood. And if someone had told me of a saint in Arles or Lourdes who saw visions, I would have believed it. I was a Catholic; I believed in saints. I lit tapers before their marble statues in churches; I knew their pictures, their symbols, their names. But I didn't, couldn't believe my brother. Not only did I not believe he saw visions, I couldn't entertain the notion for a moment. Now, why? Because he was my brother. Holy he might be, peculiar most definitely; but Francis of Assisi, no. Not my brother. No brother of mine could be such. That is egotism. Do you see?'

The boy thought about it before he answered and then he nodded and said that yes, he thought that he did.

'Perhaps he saw the visions,' said the vampire.

'Then you . . . you don't claim to know . . . now . . . whether he did or not?'

'No, but I do know that he never wavered in his conviction for a second. That I know now and knew then the night he left my room crazed and grieved. He never wavered for an instant. And within minutes, he was dead.'

'How?' the boy asked.

'He simply walked out of the french doors onto the gallery and stood for a moment at the head of the brick stairs. And then he fell. He was dead when I reached the bottom, his neck broken.' The vampire shook his head in consternation, but his face was still serene.

'Did you see him fall?' asked the boy. 'Did he lose his footing?'

'No, but two of the servants saw it happen. They said that he had looked up as if he had just seen something in the air. Then his entire body moved forward as if being swept by a wind. One of them said he was about to say something when he fell. I thought that he was about to say something too, but it was at that moment I turned away from the window. My back was turned when I heard the noise.' He glanced at the tape recorder. 'I could not forgive myself. I felt responsible for his death,' he said. 'And everyone else seemed to think I was responsible also.'

'But how could they? You said they saw him fall.'

'It wasn't a direct accusation. They simply knew that something had passed between us that was unpleasant. That we had argued minutes before the fall. The servants had heard us, my mother had heard us. My mother would not stop asking me what had happened and why my brother, who was so quiet, had been shouting. Then my sister joined in, and of course I refused to say. I was so bitterly shocked and miserable that I had no patience with anyone, only the vague determination they would not know about his "visions". They would not know that he had become, finally, not a saint, but only a . . . fanatic. My sister went to bed rather than face the funeral, and my mother told everyone in the parish that something horrible had happened in my room which I would not reveal; and even the police questioned me, on the word of my own mother. Finally the priest came to see me and demanded to know what had gone on. I told no one. It was only a discussion, I said. I was not on the gallery when he fell, I protested, and they all stared at me as if I'd killed him. And I felt that I'd killed him. I sat in the parlor beside his coffin for two days thinking, I have killed him. I stared at his face until spots appeared before my eyes and I nearly fainted. The back of his skull had been shattered on the pavement, and his head had the wrong shape on the pillow. I forced myself to stare at it, to study it simply because I could hardly endure the pain and the smell of decay, and I was tempted over and over to try to open his eyes. All these were mad thoughts, mad impulses. The main thought was this: I had laughed at him; I had not believed him; I had not been kind to him. He had fallen because of me.'

'This really happened, didn't it?' the boy whispered. 'You're telling me something . . . that's true.'

'Yes,' said the vampire, looking at him without surprise. 'I want to go on telling you.' But as his eyes passed over the boy and returned to the window, he showed only faint interest in the boy, who seemed engaged in some silent inner struggle.

'But you said you didn't know about the visions, that you, a vampire . . . didn't know for certain whether . . .'

'I want to take things in order,' said the vampire, 'I want to go on telling you things as they happened. No, I don't know about the visions. To this day.' And again he waited until the boy said:

'Yes, please, please go on.'

'Well, I wanted to sell the plantations. I never wanted to see the house or the oratory again. I leased them finally to an agency which would work them for me and manage things so I need never go there, and I moved my mother and sister to one of the town houses in New Orleans. Of course, I did not escape my brother for a moment. I could think of nothing but his body rotting in the ground. He was buried in the St Louis cemetery in New Orleans, and I did everything to avoid passing those gates; but still I thought of him constantly. Drunk or sober, I saw his body rotting in the coffin, and I couldn't bear it. Over and over I dreamed that he was at the head of the steps and I was holding his arm, talking kindly to him, urging him back into the bedroom, telling him gently that I did believe him, that he must pray for me to have faith. Meantime, the slaves on Pointe du Lac (that was my plantation) had begun to talk of seeing his ghost on the gallery, and the overseer couldn't keep order. People in society asked my sister offensive questions about the whole incident, and she became an hysteric. She wasn't really an hysteric. She simply thought she ought to react that way, so she did. I drank all the time and was at home as little as possible. I lived like a man who wanted to die but who had no courage to do it himself. I walked black streets and alleys alone; I passed out in cabarets. I backed out of two duels more from apathy than cowardice and truly wished to be murdered. And then I was attacked. It might have been anyone – and my invitation was open to sailors, thieves, maniacs, anyone. But it was a vampire. He caught me just a few steps from my door one night and left me for dead, or so I thought.'

'You mean . . . he sucked your blood?' the boy asked.

'Yes,' the vampire laughed. 'He sucked my blood. That is the way it's done.'

'But you lived,' said the young man. 'You said he left you for dead.'

'Well, he drained me almost to the point of death, which was for him sufficient. I was put to bed as soon as I was found, confused and really unaware of what had happened to me. I suppose I thought that drink had finally caused a stroke. I expected to die now and had no interest in eating or drinking or talking to the doctor. My mother sent for the priest. I was feverish by then and I told the priest everything, all about my brother's visions and what I had done. I remember I clung to his arm, making him swear over and over he would tell no one. "I know I didn't kill him," I said to the priest finally. "It's that I cannot live now that he's dead. Not after the way I treated him."

' "That's ridiculous," he answered me. "Of course you can live. There's nothing wrong with you but self-indulgence. Your mother needs you, not to mention your sister. And as for this brother of yours, he was possessed of the devil." I was so stunned when he said this I couldn't protest. The devil made the visions, he went on to explain. The devil was rampant. The entire country of France was under the influence of the devil, and the Revolution had been his greatest triumph. Nothing would have saved my brother but exorcism, prayer, and fasting, men to hold him down while the devil raged in his body and tried to throw him about. "The devil threw him down the steps; it's perfectly obvious," he declared. "You weren't talking to your brother in that room, you were talking to the devil." Well, this enraged me. I believed before that I had been pushed to my limits, but I had not. He went on talking about the devil, about voodoo amongst the slaves and cases of possession in other parts of the world. And I went wild. I wrecked the room in the process of nearly killing him.'

'But your strength . . . the vampire . . . ?' asked the boy.

'I was out of my mind,' the vampire explained. 'I did things I could not have done in perfect health. The scene is confused, pale, fantastical now. But I do remember that I drove him out of the back doors of the house, across the courtyard, and against the brick wall of the kitchen, where I pounded his head until I nearly killed him. When I was subdued finally, and exhausted then almost to the point of death, they bled me. The fools. But I was going to say something else. It was then that I conceived of my own egotism. Perhaps I'd seen it reflected in the priest. His contemptuous attitude towards my brother reflected my own; his immediate and shallow carping about the devil; his refusal to even entertain the idea that sanctity had passed so close.'

'But he did believe in possession by the devil.'

'That is a much more mundane idea,' said the vampire immediately. 'People who cease to believe in God or goodness altogether still believe in the devil. I don't know why. No, I do indeed know why. Evil is always possible. And goodness is eternally difficult. But you must understand, possession is really another way of saying someone is mad. I felt it was, for the priest. I'm sure he'd seen madness. Perhaps he had stood right over raving madness and pronounced it possession. You don't have to see Satan when he is exorcised. But to stand in the presence of a saint . . . To believe that the saint has seen a vision. No, it's egotism, our refusal to believe it could occur in our midst.'

'I never thought of it in that way,' said the boy. 'But what happened to you? You said they bled you to cure you, and that must have nearly killed you.'

The vampire laughed. 'Yes. It certainly did. But the vampire came back that night. You see, he wanted Pointe du Lac, my plantation.

'It was very late, after my sister had fallen asleep. I can remember it as if it were yesterday. He came in from the courtyard, opening the french doors without a sound, a tall fair-skinned man with a mass of blond hair and a graceful, almost feline quality to his movements. And gently, he draped a shawl over my sister's eyes and lowered the wick of the lamp. She dozed there beside the basin and the cloth with which she'd bathed my forehead, and she never once stirred under that shawl until morning. But by that time I was greatly changed.'

'What was this change?' asked the boy.

The vampire sighed. He leaned back against the chair and looked at the walls. 'At first I thought he was another doctor, or someone summoned by the family to try to reason with me. But this suspicion was removed at once. He stepped close to my bed and leaned down so that his face was in the lamplight, and I saw that he was no ordinary man at all. His gray eyes burned with an incandescence, and the long white hands which hung by his sides were not those of a human being. I think I knew everything in that instant, and all that he told me was only aftermath. What I mean is, the moment I saw him, saw his extraordinary aura and knew him to be no creature I'd ever known, I was reduced to nothing. That ego which could not accept the presence of an extraordinary human being in its midst was crushed. All my conceptions, even my guilt and wish to die, seemed utterly unimportant. I completely forgot myself!' he said, now silently touching his breast with his fist. 'I forgot myself totally. And in the same instant knew totally the meaning of possibility. From then on I experienced only increasing wonder. As he talked to me and told me of what I might become, of what his life had been and stood to be, my past shrank to embers. I saw my life as if I stood apart from it, the vanity, the self-serving, the constant fleeing from one petty annoyance after another, the lip service to God and the Virgin and a host of saints whose names filled my prayer books, none of whom made the slightest difference in a narrow, materialistic, and selfish existence. I saw my real gods . . . the gods of most men. Food, drink, and security in conformity. Cinders.'

The boy's face was tense with a mixture of confusion and amazement. 'And so you decided to become a vampire?' he asked. The vampire was silent for a moment.

'Decided. It doesn't seem the right word. Yet I cannot say it was inevitable from the moment that he stepped into that room. No, indeed, it was not inevitable. Yet I can't say I decided. Let me say that when he'd finished speaking, no other decision was possible for me, and I pursued my course without a backward glance. Except for one.'

'Except for one? What?'

'My last sunrise,' said the vampire. 'That morning, I was not yet a vampire. And I saw my last sunrise.

'I remember it completely; yet I do not think I remember any other sunrise before it. I remember the light came first to the tops of the french windows, a paling behind the lace curtains, and then a gleam growing brighter and brighter in patches among the leaves of the trees. Finally the sun came through the windows themselves and the lace lay in shadows on the stone floor, and all over the form of my sister, who was still sleeping, shadows of lace on the shawl over her shoulders and head. As soon as she was warm, she pushed the shawl away without awakening, and then the sun shone full on her eyes and she tightened her eyelids. Then it was gleaming on the table where she rested her head on her arms, and gleaming, blazing, in the water in the pitcher. And I could feel it on my hands on the counterpane and then on my face. I lay in the bed thinking about all the things the vampire had told me, and then it was that I said goodbye to the sunrise and went out to become a vampire. It was . . . the last sunrise.'

The vampire was looking out the window again. And when he stopped, the silence was so sudden the boy seemed to hear it. Then he could hear the noises from the street. The sound of a truck was deafening. The light cord stirred with the vibration. Then the truck was gone.

'Do you miss it?' he asked then in a small voice.

'Not really,' said the vampire. 'There are so many other things. But where were we? You want to know how it happened, how I became a vampire.'

'Yes,' said the boy. 'How did you change, exactly?'

'I can't tell you exactly,' said the vampire. 'I can tell you about it, enclose it with words that will make the value of it to me evident to you. But I can't tell you exactly, any more than I could tell you exactly what is the experience of sex if you have never had it.'

The young man seemed struck suddenly with still another question, but before he could speak the vampire went on. 'As I told you, this vampire Lestat, wanted the plantation. A mundane reason, surely, for granting me a life which will last until the end of the world; but he was not a very discriminating person. He didn't consider the world's small population of vampires as being a select club, I should say. He had human problems, a blind father who did not know his son was a vampire and must not find out. Living in New Orleans had become too difficult for him, considering his needs and the necessity to care for his father, and he wanted Pointe du Lac.

'We went at once to the plantation the next evening, ensconced the blind father in the master bedroom, and I proceeded to make the change. I cannot say that it consisted in any one step really – though one, of course, was the step beyond which I could make no return. But there were several acts involved, and the first was the death of the overseer. Lestat took him in his sleep. I was to watch and to approve; that is, to witness the taking of a human life as proof of my commitment and part of my change. This proved without doubt the most difficult part for me. I've told you I had no fear regarding my own death, only a squeamishness about taking my life myself. But I had a most high regard for the life of others, and a horror of death most recently developed because of my brother. I had to watch the overseer awake with a start, try to throw off Lestat with both hands, fail, then lie there struggling under Lestat's grasp, and finally go limp, drained of blood. And die. He did not die at once. We stood in his narrow bedroom for the better part of an hour watching him die. Part of my change, as I said. Lestat would never have stayed otherwise. Then it was necessary to get rid of the overseer's body. I was almost sick from this. Weak and feverish already, I had little reserve; and handling the dead body with such a purpose caused me nausea. Lestat was laughing, telling me callously that I would feel so different once I was a vampire that I would laugh, too. He was wrong about that. I never laugh at death, no matter how often and regularly I am the cause of it.

'But let me take things in order. We had to drive up the river road until we came to open fields and leave the overseer there. We tore his coat, stole his money, and saw to it his lips were stained with liquor. I knew his wife, who lived in New Orleans, and knew the state of desperation she would suffer when the body was discovered. But more than sorrow for her, I felt pain that she would never know what had happened, that her husband had not been found drunk on the road by robbers. As we beat the body, bruising the face and the shoulders, I became more and more aroused. Of course, you must realize that all this time the vampire Lestat was extraordinary. He was no more human to me than a biblical angel. But under this pressure, my enchantment with him was strained. I had seen my becoming a vampire in two lights: The first light was simply enchantment; Lestat had overwhelmed me on my deathbed. But the other light was my wish for self-destruction. My desire to be thoroughly damned. This was the open door through which Lestat had come on both the first and second occasion. Now I was not destroying myself but someone else. The overseer, his wife, his family. I recoiled and might have fled from Lestat, my sanity thoroughly shattered, had not he sensed with an infallible instinct what was happening. Infallible instinct. . . .' The vampire mused. 'Let me say the powerful instinct of a vampire to whom even the slightest change in a human's facial expression is as apparent as a gesture. Lestat had preternatural timing. He rushed me into the carriage and whipped the horses home. "I want to die," I began to murmur. This is unbearable. I want to die. You have it in your power to kill me. Let me die." I refused to look at him, to be spellbound by the sheer beauty of his appearance. He spoke my name to me softly, laughing. As I said, he was determined to have the plantation.'

'But would he have let you go?' asked the boy. 'Under any circumstances?'

'I don't know. Knowing Lestat as I do now, I would say he would have killed me rather than let me go. But this was what I wanted, you see. It didn't matter. No, this was what I thought I wanted. As soon as we reached the house, I jumped down out of the carriage and walked, a zombie, to the brick stairs where my brother had fallen. The house had been unoccupied for months now, the overseer having his own cottage, and the Louisiana heat and damp were already picking apart the steps. Every crevice was sprouting grass and even small wildflowers. I remember feeling the moisture which in the night was cool as I sat down on the lower steps and even rested my head against the brick and felt the little wax-stemmed wildflowers with my hands. I pulled a clump of them out of the easy dirt in one hand. "I want to die; kill me. Kill me," I said to the vampire. "Now I am guilty of murder. I can't live." He sneered with the impatience of people listening to the obvious lies of others. And then in a flash he fastened on me just as he had on my man. I thrashed against him wildly. I dug my boot into his chest and kicked him as fiercely as I could, his teeth stinging my throat, the fever pounding in my temples. And with a movement of his entire body, much too fast for me to see, he was suddenly standing disdainfully at the foot of the steps. "I thought you wanted to die, Louis," he said.'

The boy made a soft, abrupt sound when the vampire said his name which the vampire acknowledged with the quick statement, 'Yes, that is my name,' and went on.

'Well, I lay there helpless in the face of my own cowardice and fatuousness again,' he said. 'Perhaps so directly confronted with it, I might in time have gained the courage to truly take my life, not to whine and beg for others to take it. I saw myself turning on a knife then, languishing in a day-to-day suffering which I found as necessary as penance from the confessional, truly hoping death would find me unawares and render me fit for eternal pardon. And also I saw myself as if in a vision standing at the head of the stairs, just where my brother had stood, and then hurtling my body down on the bricks.

'But there was no time for courage. Or shall I say, there was no time in Lestat's plan for anything but his plan. "Now listen to me, Louis," he said, and he lay down beside me now on the steps, his movement so graceful and so personal that at once it made me think of a lover. I recoiled. But he put his right arm around me and pulled me close to his chest. Never had I been this close to him before, and in the dim light I could see the magnificent radiance of his eye and the unnatural mask of his skin. As I tried to move, he pressed his right fingers against my lips and said, "Be still. I am going to drain you now to the very threshold of death, and I want you to be quiet, so quiet that you can almost hear the flow of blood through your veins, so quiet that you can hear the flow of that same blood through mine. It is your consciousness, your will, which must keep you alive." I wanted to struggle, but he pressed so hard with his fingers that he held my entire prone body in check; and as soon as I stopped my abortive attempt at rebellion, he sank his teeth into my neck.'

The boy's eyes grew huge. He had drawn farther and farther back in his chair as the vampire spoke, and now his face was tense, his eyes narrow, as if he were preparing to weather a blow.

'Have you ever lost a great amount of blood?' asked the vampire. 'Do you know the feeling?'

The boy's lips shaped the word *no,* but no sound came out. He cleared his throat. 'No,' he said.

'Candles burned in the upstairs parlor, where we had planned the death of the overseer. An oil lantern swayed in the breeze on the gallery. All of this light coalesced and began to shimmer, as though a golden presence hovered above me, suspended in the stairwell, softly entangled with the railings, curling and contracting like smoke. "Listen, keep your eyes wide," Lestat whispered to me, his lips moving against my neck. I remember that the movement of his lips raised the hair all over my body, sent a shock of sensation through my body that was not unlike the pleasure of passion. . . .'

He mused, his right fingers slightly curled beneath his chin, the first finger appearing to lightly stroke it. 'The result was that within minutes I was weak to paralysis. Panic-stricken, I discovered I could not even will myself to speak. Lestat still held me, of course, and his arm was like the weight of an iron bar. I felt his teeth withdraw with such a keenness that the two puncture wounds seemed enormous, lined with pain. And now he bent over my helpless head and, taking his right hand off me, bit his own wrist. The blood flowed down upon my shirt and coat, and he watched it with a narrow, gleaming eye. It seemed an eternity that he watched it, and that shimmer of light now hung behind his head like the backdrop of an apparition. I think that I knew what he meant to do even before he did it, and I was waiting in my helplessness as if I'd been waiting for years. He pressed his bleeding wrist to my mouth, said firmly, a little impatiently, "Louis, drink". And I did. "Steady, Louis," and "Hurry," he whispered to me a number of times. I drank, sucking the blood out of the holes, experiencing for the first time since infancy the special pleasure of sucking nourishment, the body focused with the mind upon one vital source. Then something happened.' The vampire sat back, a slight frown on his face.

'How pathetic it is to describe these things which can't truly be described,' he said, his voice low almost to a whisper. The boy sat as if frozen.

'I saw nothing but that light then as I drew blood. And then this next thing, this next thing was . . . sound. A dull roar at first and then a pounding like the pounding of a drum, growing louder and louder, as if some enormous creature were coming up on one slowly through a dark and alien forest, pounding as he came, a huge drum. And then there came the pounding of another drum, as if another giant were coming yards behind him, and each giant, intent on his own drum, gave no notice to the rhythm of the other. The sound grew louder and louder until it seemed to fill not just my hearing but all my senses, to be throbbing in my lips and fingers, in the flesh of my temples, in my veins. Above all, in my veins, drum and then the other drum; and then Lestat pulled his wrist free suddenly, and I opened my eyes and checked myself in a moment of reaching for his wrist, grabbing it, forcing it back to my mouth at all costs; I checked myself because I realized that the drum was my heart, and the second drum had been his.' The vampire sighed. 'Do you understand?'

The boy began to speak, and then he shook his head. 'No . . . I mean, I do,' he said. 'I mean, I . . .'

'Of course,' said the vampire, looking away.

'Wait, wait!' said the boy in a welter of excitement. 'The tape is almost gone. I have to turn it over.' The vampire watched patiently as he changed it.

'What happened then?' the boy asked. His face was moist, and he wiped it hurriedly with his handkerchief.

'I saw as a vampire,' said the vampire, his voice now slightly detached. It seemed almost distracted. Then he drew himself up. 'Lestat was standing again at the foot of the stairs, and I saw him as I could not possibly have seen him before. He had seemed white to me before, starkly white, so that in the night he was almost luminous; and now I saw him filled with his own life and own blood: he was radiant, not luminous. And then I saw that not only Lestat had changed, but all things had changed.

'It was as if I had only just been able to see colors and shapes for the first time. I was so enthralled with the buttons on Lestat's black coat that I looked at nothing else for a long time. Then Lestat began to laugh, and I heard his laughter as I had never heard anything before. His heart I still heard like the beating of a drum, and now came this metallic laughter. It was confusing, each sound running into the next sound, like the mingling reverberations of bells, until I learned to separate the sounds, and then they overlapped, each soft but distinct, increasing but discrete, peals of laughter.' The vampire smiled with delight. 'Peals of bells.

' "Stop looking at my buttons," Lestat said. "Go out there into the trees. Rid yourself of all the human waste in your body, and don't fall so madly in love with the night that you lose your way!"

'That, of course, was a wise command. When I saw the moon on the flagstones,

I became so enamored with it that I must have spent an hour there. I passed my brother's oratory without so much as a thought of him, and standing among the cottonwood and oaks, I heard the night as if it were a chorus of whispering women, all beckoning me to their breasts. As for my body, it was not yet totally converted, and as soon as I became the least accustomed to the sounds and sights, it began to ache. All my human fluids were being forced out of me. I was dying as a human, yet completely alive as a vampire; and with my awakened senses, I had to preside over the death of my body with a certain discomfort and then, finally, fear. I ran back up the steps to the parlor, where Lestat was already at work on the plantation papers, going over the expenses and profits for the last year. "You're a rich man," he said to me when I came in. "Something's happening to me," I shouted.

' "You're dying, that's all; don't be a fool. Don't you have any oil lamps? All this money and you can't afford whale oil except for that lantern. Bring me that lantern."

' "Dying!" I shouted. "Dying!"

' "It happens to everyone," he persisted, refusing to help me. As I look back on this, I still despise him for it. Not because I was afraid, but because he might have drawn my attention to these changes with reverence. He might have calmed me and told me I might watch my death with the same fascination with which I had watched and felt the night. But he didn't. Lestat was never the vampire I am. Not at all.' The vampire did not say this boastfully. He said it as if he would truly have had it otherwise.

'*Alors,*' he sighed. 'I was dying fast, which meant that my capacity for fear was diminishing as rapidly. I simply regret I was not more attentive to the process. Lestat was being a perfect idiot. "Oh, for the love of hell!" he began shouting. "Do you realize I've made no provision for you? What a fool I am." I was tempted to say, "Yes, you are," but I didn't. "You'll have to bed down with me this morning. I haven't prepared you a coffin."'

The vampire laughed. 'The coffin struck such a chord of terror in me I think it absorbed all the capacity for terror I had left. Then came only my mild alarm at having to share a coffin with Lestat. He was in his father's bedroom meantime, telling the old man goodbye, that he would return in the morning. "But where do you go, why must you live by such a schedule!" the old man demanded, and Lestat became impatient. Before this, he'd been gracious to the old man, almost to the point of sickening one, but now he became a bully. "I take care of you, don't I? I've put a better roof over your head than you ever put over mine! If I want to sleep all day and drink all night, I'll do it, damn you!" The old man started to whine. Only my peculiar state of emotions and most unusual feeling of exhaustion kept me from disapproving. I was watching the scene through the open door, enthralled with the colors of the counterpane and the positive riot of color in the old man's face. His blue veins pulsed beneath his pink and grayish flesh. I found even the yellow of his teeth appealing to me, and I became almost hypnotized by the quivering of his lip. "Such a son, such a son," he said, never suspecting, of course, the true nature of his son. "All right, then, go. I know you keep a woman somewhere; you go to see her as soon as her husband leaves in the morning. Give me my rosary. What's happened to my rosary?" Lestat said something blasphemous and gave him the rosary. . . .'

'But . . .' the boy started.

'Yes?' said the vampire. 'I'm afraid I don't allow you to ask enough questions.'

'I was going to ask, rosaries have crosses on them, don't they?'

'Oh, the rumor about crosses!' the vampire laughed. 'You refer to our being afraid of crosses?'

'Unable to look on them, I thought,' said the boy.

'Nonsense, my friend, sheer nonsense. I can look on anything I like. And I rather like looking on crucifixes in particular.'

'And what about the rumor about keyholes? That you can . . . become steam and go through them.'

'I wish I could,' laughed the vampire. 'How positively delightful. I should like to pass through all manner of different keyholes and feel the tickle of their peculiar shapes. No.' He shook his head. 'That is, how would you say today . . . bullshit?'

The boy laughed despite himself. Then his face grew serious.

'You mustn't be so shy with me,' the vampire said. 'What is it?'

'The story about stakes through the heart,' said the boy, his cheeks coloring slightly.

'The same,' said the vampire. 'Bull-shit,' he said, carefully articulating both syllables, so that the boy smiled. 'No magical power whatsoever. Why don't you smoke one of your cigarettes? I see you have them in your shirt pocket.'

'Oh, thank you,' the boy said, as if it were a marvellous suggestion. But once he had the cigarette to his lips, his hands were trembling so badly that he mangled the first fragile book match.

'Allow me,' said the vampire. And, taking the book, he quickly put a lighted match to the boy's cigarette. The boy inhaled, his eyes on the vampire's fingers. Now the vampire withdrew across the table with a soft rustling of garments. 'There's an ashtray on the basin,' he said, and the boy moved nervously to get it. He stared at the few butts in it for a moment, and then; seeing the small waste basket beneath, he emptied the ashtray and quickly set it on the table. His fingers left damp marks on the cigarette when he put it down. 'Is this your room?' he asked.

'No,' answered the vampire. 'Just a room.'

'What happened then?' the boy asked. The vampire appeared to be watching the smoke gather beneath the overhead bulb.

'Ah . . . we went back to New Orleans posthaste,' he said. 'Lestat had his coffin in a miserable room near the ramparts.'

'And you did get into the coffin?'

'I had no choice. I begged Lestat to let me stay in the closet, but he laughed, astonished. ''Don't you know what you are?'' he asked. ''But is it magical? Must it have this shape?'' I pleaded. Only to hear him laugh again. I couldn't bear the idea; but as we argued, I realized I had no real fear. It was a strange realization. All my life I'd feared closed places. Born and bred in French houses with lofty ceilings and floor-length windows, I had a dread of being enclosed. I felt uncomfortable even in the confessional in church. It was a normal enough fear. And now I realized as I protested to Lestat, I did not actually feel this anymore. I was simply remembering it. Hanging on to it from habit, from a deficiency of ability to recognize my present and exhilarating freedom. ''You're carrying on badly,'' Lestat said finally. ''And it's almost dawn. I should let you die. You will die, you know. The sun will destroy the blood I've given you, in every tissue, every vein. But you shouldn't be feeling this fear at all. I think you're like a man who loses an arm or a leg and keeps insisting that he can feel pain where the arm or leg used to be.'' Well, that was positively the most intelligent and useful thing Lestat ever said in my presence, and it brought me around at once. ''Now, I'm getting into the coffin,'' he finally said to me in his most disdainful tone, ''and you will get in on top of me if you know what's good for you.'' And I did. I lay face-down on him, utterly confused by my absence of dread and filled with a distaste for being so close to him, handsome and intriguing though he was. And he shut the lid. Then I asked him if I was completely dead. My body was tingling and itching all over. ''No, you're not then,'' he said. ''When you are, you'll only hear and see it changing and feel nothing. You should be dead by tonight. Go to sleep.'''

'Was he right? Were you . . . dead when you woke up?'

'Yes, changed, I should say. As obviously I am alive. My body was dead. It was some time before it became absolutely cleansed of the fluids and matter it no longer needed, but it was dead. And with the realization of it came another stage in my divorce from human emotions. The first thing which became apparent to me, even while Lestat and I were loading the coffin into a hearse and stealing another coffin from a mortuary, was that I did not like Lestat at all. I was far from being his equal yet, but I was infinitely closer to him than I had been before the death of my body. I can't really make this clear to you for the obvious reason that you are now as I was before my body died. You cannot understand. But before I died, Lestat was absolutely the most overwhelming *experience* I'd ever had. Your cigarette has become one long cylindrical ash.'

'Oh!' The boy quickly ground the filter into the glass. 'You mean that when the gap was closed between you, he lost his . . . spell?' he asked, his eyes quickly fixed on the vampire, his hands now producing a cigarette and match much more easily than before.

'Yes, that's correct,' said the vampire with obvious pleasure. 'The trip back to Pointe du Lac was thrilling. And the constant chatter of Lestat was positively the most boring and disheartening thing I experienced. Of course as I said, I was far from being his equal. I had my dead limbs to contend with . . . to use his comparison. And I learned that on that very night, when I had to make my first kill.'

The vampire reached across the table now and gently brushed an ash from the boy's lapel, and the boy stared at his withdrawing hand in alarm. 'Excuse me,' said the vampire. 'I didn't mean to frighten you.'

'Excuse me,' said the boy. 'I just got the impression suddenly that your arm was . . . abnormally long. You reached so far without moving!'

'No,' said the vampire, resting his hands again on his crossed knees. 'I moved forward much too fast for you to see. It was an illusion.'

'You moved forward? But you didn't. You were sitting just as you are now, with your back against the chair.'

'No,' repeated the vampire firmly. 'I moved forward as I told you. Here, I'll do it again.' And he did it again, and the boy stared with the same mixture of confusion and fear. 'You still didn't see it,' said the vampire. 'But, you see, if you look at my outstretched arm now, it's really not remarkably long at all.' And he raised his arm, first finger pointing heavenward as if he were an angel about to give the Word of the Lord. 'You have experienced a fundamental difference between the way you see and I see. My gesture appeared slow and somewhat languid to me. And the sound of my finger brushing your coat was quite audible. Well, I didn't mean to frighten you, I confess. But perhaps you can see from this that my return to Pointe du Lac was a feast of new experiences, the mere swaying of a tree branch in the wind a delight.'

'Yes,' said the boy; but he was still visibly shaken. The vampire eyed him for a moment, and then he said, 'I was telling you . . .'

'About your first kill,' said the boy.